Four to Dorsai!

Other books in the *Dorsai* series

Lost Dorsai: The New Dorsai Companion
The Spirit of Dorsai
Young Bleys
The Final Encyclopedia (rev. ed.)
The Chantry Guild

Four to Dorsai!

**Necromancer
Tactics of Mistake
Dorsai!
Soldier, Ask Not**

GORDON R. DICKSON

**SCIENCE
FICTION**

Published by arrangement with:
Tor Books
Published by Tom Doherty Associates, Inc.
175 Fifth Avenue
New York, NY 10010

Tor® is a registered trademark of Tom Doherty Associates, Inc.

Visit our website at www.sfbc.com

ISBN: 0-7394-2454-8

PRINTED IN THE UNITED STATES OF AMERICA

CONTENTS

NECROMANCER   1

TACTICS OF MISTAKE   157

DORSAI!   379

SOLDIER, ASK NOT   555

NECROMANCER

CONTENTS

BOOK ONE: ISOLATE   7

BOOK TWO: SET   67

BOOK THREE: PATTERN   119

"But now the path divides. I see
Inchoate, dark reality
Twin-struck from ancient Unity
—And I, my Brother's enemy!..."

—*The Enchanted Tower*
by Hal Mayne

Book One: **ISOLATE**

And now, through double glass, I see
My brother's image, darklingly.
Now, aid us, Thor, who prisoners be.
Come—hammer, Lord! And set us free.

THE ENCHANTED TOWER

Chapter 1

The mine, generally speaking, was automatic. It consisted of some hundred and eighty million dollars' worth of equipment, spread out through three and a half cubic miles of gold-ore-bearing rock—granite and quartz—all controlled by the single console where the shift engineer on duty sat.

Like some ponderous, many-purposed organism, the mine walked in the layered rock. On various levels it gnawed out the gold-bearing ore, ground it up to pebble-sized chunks, and sent it by the carload up six hundred feet or more to the open air and the equipment above. As the mine machinery moved, it created and abandoned surface shafts, elevator tubes, new exploratory levels and stopes; and extended the vast central cavern through which the heavier machinery and its controlling console slid with the work in progress, laying down rails before and taking them up behind.

The single engineer on shift at the time controlled all this. And a touch of megalomania did him no harm on the job. He was seated before the control panels of the console like the identity before the brain. His job was the job of ultimate control. Logical decision, and the facts on which to base decision were supplied by the computer element in the equipment. The logically optimum answer was available at the touch of a button. But it had been discovered that, like the process of living itself, there was more to modern mining than logic.

The best engineers had *feel*. It was a sensitivity born of experience, of talent, and even of something like love, with which they commanded, not only the mountains, but the machine they rode and directed.

Now this too was added to the list of man's endeavors for which some special talent was needed. Less than ten per cent of the young mining engineers graduating every year turned out to have the necessary extra ability to become one with the titan they directed. Even in the twenty-first century's overcrowded employment marts, mines were continually on the hunt for more shift engineers. Even four hours at a time, and even for the talented ten per cent, was a long time to be the faultless god in the machine. And the machinery never rested.

Six hundred feet overhead of the man at the console, Paul Formain, on his first morning at Malabar Mine, stepped from his small individual quarters of white bubble plastic, and saw the mountains.

And suddenly, there it was again, as it had been time and again since his boating accident of five years before, and had been more recently, lately.

But it was not now the open sea that he saw. Or even the dreamlike image of a strange, shadowy figure in some sort of cape and a high-peaked hat, who had seemed to bring him back to life after he had died in the boat, and returned him to the boat to be finally found and rescued by the coast guard.

This time, it was the mountains.

Suddenly, turning from the white, plastic door, he stopped and saw them. Around him was a steep slope with the other white buildings of the Malabar Mine. Above him the fragile blue of a spring sky spoke to the dark blue of the deep lake below, which filled this cleft in the mountain rock. About him in every direction were the Canadian Rockies, stretching thirty miles in one direction to the British Columbia city of Kamloops, in the other to the Coast Range and the stony beaches touching the salt Pacific Ocean surf. Unexpectedly, he felt them.

Like kings they stood up around him, the mountains. The surf sounded in his blood, and abruptly he was growing, striding to meet them. He was mountain-size with the mountains. With them, he felt the eternal movement of the earth. For a moment he was naked but unshaken to the winds of understanding. And they blew to him one word:

Fear.

Do not go down into the mine.

". . . You will get over this, this sort of thing," the psychiatrist in San Diego had assured him, five years before, after the accident. "Now that you've worked it out for yourself and understand it."

"Yes," said Paul.

It had made sense then, the way he had explained it to himself under the psychiatrist's guidance. He was an orphan, since the time of his parents' simultaneous deaths in a transportation accident, when he was nine. He had been assigned to good foster parents, but they were not the same. He had always been solitary.

He had lacked what the San Diego psychiatrist called "protective selfishness." He had the knack of understanding people without the usual small urge to turn this understanding to his own advantage. It had embarrassed those who might have been his friends, once they understood this capability in him. They had an instinctive urge to put a protective distance between himself and them. Underneath, they feared his knowledge and did not trust his restraint. As a boy he felt their withdrawal without understanding the reasons behind it. And this, said the psychiatrist, gave him a false picture of his own situation.

". . . After all," said the psychiatrist, "this lack of a desire to take advantage of a capability, amounted to a disability. But no worse than any other disability, such as blindness or loss of a limb. There was no need to feel that you could not live with it."

But that was the way, it seemed, that unconsciously he had felt. And that feeling had culminated in an unconscious attempt at suicide.

". . . There's no doubt," said the psychiatrist, "that you got the bad-weather, small-craft warning put out by the coast guard. Or that you knew you were dangerously far offshore for any weather, in such a light sailboat."

So the storm had driven him out to sea and lost him. He had been adrift, and in the still days following, death had come like some heavy gray bird to sit perched on the idle mast, waiting.

". . . You were in a condition for hallucination," said the psychiatrist. "It was natural to imagine you had already died. Then, when afterward you were rescued, you automatically searched for some justification of the fact that you were still alive. Your unconscious provided this fantasy of having been brought back to life by a father-like figure, tall and mysterious, and wrapped in the garments that denote magical ability. But when you had fully recovered, your conscious mind could not help finding this story somewhat thin."

No, thought Paul, it couldn't help thinking so. He remembered, in the San Diego hospital, lying there and doubting the whole memory.

"So to bolster it, you produced these moments of extreme, almost painful sensitivity. Which filled two needs. They provided support for your delirium fantasy of having been raised from the dead, and they acted as an excuse for what had caused the death-wish in the first place. Unconsciously you were telling yourself that you were not crippled, but 'different.' "

"Yes," Paul had said at that point. "I see."

"Now that you've dug out the true situation for yourself, the need for justification should diminish. The fantasy should fade and the sensitivity moments grow less frequent, until they disappear."

"That's good to hear," said Paul.

Only, in the past five years the moments had not dwindled and disappeared. They had stayed with him, as the original dream had stuck stubbornly in the back of his mind. He thought of seeing another psychiatrist, but then the thought would come that the first had done him no good at all. So what was there to expect from a second?

Instead, in order to live with his problem, he had anchored himself to something that he had discovered in himself since the accident. Deep within him now, something invincible stood four-square to the frequent gusts from the winds of feeling. Somehow he thought of it as being connected to, but independent of, the dream magician in the tall hat. So when, as now, the winds blew warnings, he felt them without being driven by them.

Fear: said the mountains. *Do not go down into the mine.*

That's foolish, said Paul's conscious mind. It reminded him that he was at last hired for the work to which all his education had pointed him. To a job that in the present overcrowded world was the dream of many and the achievement of few. He reached for that which stood unconquerable in the back of his mind.

Fear, it replied, is merely one more in the multitude of factors to be taken into account in moving from point *A* to point *B*.

Paul shook himself free from the winds of feeling, back to the ordinary existence of the world. The buildings of the Malabar Mine were all around him. A little distance down the slope from where he stood the wife of the company auditor came out on her back step and called something across a small white fence to the wife of the surface engineer in the yard adjoining. It was Paul's first day on the job and already he was close to being overdue on the job underground. He turned his gaze from the mountains and the buildings, to the near concrete walk leading to the main shaft head of the mine. And headed toward it, and the waiting skip.

Chapter 2

The skip slid Paul down some six hundred steeply slanting feet through mountain stone. For all the romanticism of its old-fashioned name, it was nothing more in fact than a magnetic tube elevator. Through the transparent walls of the tube, granite and rose quartz flickered at him as he descended. They spoke to him as the mountains had, but in smaller voices, fine, thin, crystalline voices with no yield, no kindness to them, and no mercy. Between them and himself, Paul's own faint image in the tube wall kept pace with his descent—it was the image of a square-shouldered young man of twenty-three, already past any look of boyishness or youth.

He was large-boned and tall, strong-featured, round-headed, and athletic-looking. A football-player type, but not one of the game's commoner varieties. He was not bulky enough for a lineman, not tense enough for the backfield. End—that was the sort of position he fitted. And, strongly calm, with long-fingered capable hands to catch the ball, he remembered playing it well. That had been on the first team at Colorado Institute of Mines, where he had taken his undergraduate work.

His eyes were curiously deep, and a warm, gray color. His mouth was thin-lipped, but a little wide and altogether friendly. His light, straight brown hair was already receding at the temples. He wore it clipped short, and he would be nearly bald before his thirties were out, but since he was not the sort of man to whom good looks are necessary, this would make little difference.

He looked instinctively in command of things. Strongly male, intelligent, physically large and strong, with a knack for doing things right the first time around. And he was all these things. It was only when people got to know him intimately that they saw past to the more complex inner part of him, the part where his own very different image of himself was kept. There were moments like this, as he suddenly caught sight of his outer self mirrored somewhere, when Paul was as startled as if he had come face to face with some stranger.

The skip stopped at Dig Level.

Paul stepped out into a bright, huge cavern filled to its lofty ceiling with the bright metal of equipment mounted ponderously on rails. The acid-damp air of below-ground struck coolly into his lungs, and the atmosphere of the mine seemed to flow into and through him as he walked down alongside the crusher to the small cleared space that surrounded the console. There, seated upon the rails, was the console itself. And at it—at the keys and stops that resembled nothing so much as the keyboard of some huge electronic organ, with the exception of the several small viewing tanks in the console's very center—a small, round-bodied, black-haired man in his forties sat winding up the duties of the shift he was just ending.

Paul came up to the edge of the platform on which the console and its operator sat.

"Hi," he said.

The other man glanced down.

"I'm the new man—Paul Formain," said Paul. "Ready for relief?"

The departing engineer made several quick motions about the console, his short thick fingers active. He leaned back in the control seat, then stretched. He stood up to turn a tough, friendly face toward Paul.

"Paul?" he asked. "What was the last name?"

"Formain. Paul Formain."

"Right. Pat Teasely." He held out a small, square hand with a good deal of strength in its grip.

They shook. Teasely's accent was Australian—that particular accent which Australians are continually infuriated to have called cockney by inexperienced North Americans. He gave forth a personality that was as plain and straightforward as common earth. It touched soothingly against Paul, after the violence of the mountains.

"Looks like a nice clear dig for your first shift," Teasely said. "Judging by the cores."

"Sounds good," replied Paul.

"Right. No large faults in sight and the vein drift's less than eight degrees off the vertical. Watch for crowding on the ore trains going up Number One surface shaft, though."

"Oh?" said Paul. "Bug in the works?"

"Not really. They've been jackknifing and getting jammed just above Number Eight hatch, about sixty feet short of exit. The shaft's cut a little small; but no point in widening it when we'll be driving a new one in about a hundred and fifty hours. I've been up twice this last shift, though, to kick a car back on the tracks."

"All right," said Paul. "Thanks." He stepped past Teasely and sat down at the console. He looked up at the smaller man. "See you topside at the bar this evening, perhaps?"

"Might." Teasely lingered. His blunt face looked down, uncompromising, individualistic, and congenial. "You out of one of the American colleges?"

"Colorado."

"Wife and family along?"

Paul shook his head. His fingers were already moving about, becoming acquainted with the console.

"No," he said. "I'm a bachelor—and an orphan."

"Come have dinner at our place then, sometime," said Teasely. "I've got the sort of wife likes to cook for guests."

"Thanks," said Paul. "I'll do that."

"See you."

Paul heard Teasely's footsteps crunch away in the loose rubble of the cavern floor. He went back to the controls, and ran through his take over check list. It took him about six minutes. When that was done he knew the position of every piece of equipment and how it was behaving. Then he turned to the programming section and ran a four-hour estimate and forecast.

It checked with Teasely's estimate. A routine, easy shift. For a moment he laid his fingers on the gross control tabs of the computer override and sought for the individual qualities of the machine through the little working vibrations that reached him through his finger tips. A sensation of blind, purposeful, and irresistible force at work was returned to him; like, but not identical with, the feel of all other mine controls he had touched before. He took his hands away.

For the moment, he had nothing to do. He leaned back in his bucket seat at the console and thought about leaving things here for a look at the surface shaft where Teasely had reported the ore cars had occasionally been getting stuck. He decided against it. It was best to stick close to the console until he had built up a familiarity with this new mine.

The little lights and gauges and small viewing screens showed their flickers of color and movement normally before him. He reached over and switched a Vancouver news broadcast onto the screen of his central viewing tank.

Abruptly, he looked down as if from a window onto the plaza entrance to the Koh-i-Nor Hotel, at Chicago Complex. He recognized the location—it was a hotel he had stayed at once or twice himself when he was in the Chicago area. As he looked down on it now, he saw a small knot of people carrying the cameras and equipment of reporters, gathered around three people. The view zoomed in for a shot from an apparent distance of only a few feet and Paul had a second's close-up glimpse of two of the three who were standing a little back from the third. The two were a flat-bodied, crop-haired man of middle age, and a tall, slim girl of Paul's age, whose appearance jerked suddenly at Paul's attention before the camera moved away from her, and left him frowning over what could have seemed so remarkable about her. He had never seen either her or the flat-bodied man before.

But then he forgot about her. For the third member of the group was filling the screen. And there was something about him that would have held any viewer's attention.

He was a gaunt giant of an old man in the formal black-and-white of evening clothes. Very stark and somber in these, he bent his head a little to avoid the low edge of a candy-striped beach umbrella overhead. And, although straight enough for the years he seemed to own, he leaned heavily on the carved handle of a thick cane in his right hand. The motion spread his wide shoulders, so that he seemed to stoop above the crowd of reporters. Dark glasses obscured the expression around his eyes—but even without these, his face was an enigma. Though it stood clear and sharp on the screen before him, Paul could not seem to grasp its image as a whole. It was a collection of features, but there was no totality to it. Paul found himself staring at the straight lips and the deep parentheses of creases around the corners of the mouth as the man spoke.

". . . robes?" one of the newspeople was just finishing asking.

The lips smiled.

"You wouldn't expect a mechanic to go out to dinner in his working clothes, now would you?" The voice from the lips was deep and pleasantly sardonic. "If you people want to see me in my official robes, you'll have to make an appointment to meet me during my office hours."

"Do they have office hours in the Chantry Guild, Mr. Guildmaster?" asked another reporter. There was laughter, but not disrespectful laughter. The lips smiled with them.

"Come and find out," said the lips. Paul frowned. A small closed pocket in his memory had opened up. He had heard of the Chantry Guild—or Société Chanterie. Come to think of it, he had heard of them now and again—quite often, in fact. They were a cult group—devil-worshipers, or some such. He had always dismissed them as a group of crackpots. But this man—this Guildmaster—was nothing so simple as a crackpot. He was . . .

Frustrated, Paul put his fingers instinctively out to the image of the man before him. But the cold glassy surface of the screen baffled his finger tips. The reporters were still asking questions.

"What about Operation Springboard, Mr. Guildmaster?"

The lips quirked.

"What about it?"

"Is the Guild against an attempt to reach the nearer stars?"

"Well now, ladies and gentlemen . . ." The lips smiled. "What did the Sumerian and Semite say in the days of the older gods? I believe they called the planets *'sheep that are far away.'* Did they not? Shamash and Adad were the deities responsible for that statement, as you can find by checking your ancient histories. And if habitable worlds are like sheep, then surely there must be a great many strayed around farther stars which we can find again."

And the smile stayed on the lips.

"Then the Guild is in favor of the station on Mercury? You don't object to work on methods for interstellar travel?"

"Such," said the lips, and the smile vanished, "is not my concern, or the concern of the Guild. Man may play with the technical toys and sciences as he has in the past; he may play with space and the stars. But it will only sicken him further, as it has already sickened him almost to his end. There is only one thing that concerns us of the Guild and that's the destruction that will save Man from himself."

"Mr. Guildmaster," said a voice, "you can't mean total——"

"Total and absolute!" The deep voice strengthened in the speaker. "Complete. Destruction. The destruction of Man and all his works." The voice grew, sonorously near to chanting, on a note that sent a sudden wild surge of feeling through Paul, like a powerful shock from a vein-injected stimulant. "There have been forces at work for eight hundred years that would save Man from his destruction. Woe to Man when that day comes, that he is safe and saved. Woe to Woman and children unborn, when the last strength to destroy himself is finally stolen from him. For by his own eternal life will he be doomed, and only by his destruction may he survive."

The buzzing of an alarm signaled the sudden jackknifing and jamming of an ore train in surface tube *A*. Paul's hand went out automatically and slapped a fifteen-minute break on shaft power.

"And so I charge you"—the voice rolled like drums below a guillotine from the screen before him—"that you look to the welfare of man and not to yourselves. That you turn your backs on the false promise of life and face the reality of death. That you charge yourselves with a duty. And that duty is complete—is utter—is total destruction. Destruction. Destruction! *Destruction....*"

Paul blinked and sat up.

The mine was all around him. The console was before him and in its center screen the group on the plaza of the Koh-i-Nor was breaking up. The newspeople were dispersing. The old man and the girl and man with him were following a fourth man—a thin young man with black hair and a tense, driving walk—into the hotel. Paul stared. He felt that only a minute had gone by, but even that was startling. For one of the peculiar facts about him was that he was completely unresponsive to hypnosis. It was a trait that had complicated matters for the psychiatrist who had worked with him following the boating accident. How, then, could he have lost even a minute?

Sudden memory of the jackknifed cars in the surface tube broke him away from his personal puzzle. A more general power shutoff of equipment would be required unless he could solve that problem shortly. He left the console and took the chain lift alongside surface shaft Number One. The telltale on the console had spotted the jam-up at a hundred and forty-three feet below the shaft mouth. He reached Number Eight trouble hatch, turned on the lights in the shaft, and crawled through into the shaft himself. He saw the trouble, almost directly before him.

The Number One surface shaft, like the skip tube, approached the surface from the mine below at an angle of roughly sixty degrees. A single powered rail ran up the bottom center of the shaft, and the fat-bodied, open-topped ore cars, filled with pebble-sized rock from below, rolled their cogwheels up the cleated rail. The cleats themselves served Paul now as hand and footholds as he climbed up to where one of the cars sat off the rail, angled against the stony wall.

Still wondering about the familiar-looking girl and the extraordinary cultist who called himself the Guildmaster, Paul braced himself against the sharp-pointed wall of the shaft and the last car. He kicked at the hitch between the two cars. On the third kick, the hitch suddenly unbound the kink it had acquired when the car had jackknifed. With a snap and a grunt from the stored power in the motorized base of each car, the train suddenly straightened out.

As it did, the lights in the shaft dimmed, then flashed up again without warning as all the motors in all the cars hummed steadily to life. The train jerked and moved up the shaft, and without thinking, instinctively, Paul leaped and clung to the final car of the train.

It burst on him then, brilliantly as mountains seen suddenly against a high spring sky, that in his preoccupation with the news broadcast he had only put a temporary fifteen-minute hold on power to the shaft. And afterward, following his little blackout, he had omitted to set the power controls for the shaft on manual.

Now he was being carried up the shaft by the last car in the train. A few inches below him, the powered rail promised instant electrocution if he touched it. And the high-sided cars, all but filling the shaft, would block any try he could make to open the emergency hatches yet between him and the surface, as the train passed them.

The walls and the roof were close.

The roof in particular pressed down near to him. Rough-chewed from the granite and quartz, it rose and dipped unevenly. At points along the shaft, Paul knew, it would all but scrape the tops of the ore cars. If he could keep low, he might be able to ride the car he was holding to, to the surface. But, clinging to the back of it as he was, he felt his grip weakening.

He pulled himself upward, flat onto the bed of ore in the car. The roof under which he was passing scraped harshly against the back of his head as the ore train, leaving the lighted section where he had put it back on the track, plunged upward into darkness. His hands pawing at the small sharp rock in the car, Paul dug furiously, burrowing himself in. Swaying and rumbling, the train climbed on. In the blackness Paul did not even see ahead the low point of the roof that was approaching. . . .

Out in the clear mountain morning the surface engineer on duty had been drawn to the mouth of the Number One shaft by the blinking of a white trouble light on his own console, and a later automatic signal that power to that shaft had been cut. He had come to the shaft mouth, only to be joined a few minutes later by the managing engineer, who had been keeping his eye on the telltales in his office, this day with a new man underground for the first time.

"There it goes," said the surface engineer, a slight man named Diego and as young as Paul, as the hum of motors echoed once more up the natural speaking tube of the shaft. "He got it fixed."

"A little slow," said the Malabar mine manager. He frowned. "Let's wait a minute here and see what the trouble was."

They waited. The humming and the clank of the cogwheels approached. The first car poked its front out into the sunlight and leveled off on the flat.

"What's that?" asked the mine manager, suddenly. There was a shadowy outline visible in the gloom around the approaching final car.

The train trundled automatically on. The last car emerged into the sunlight and the bright illumination fell full on the shape of a man, half-buried and unmoving in the load of ore.

"My God!" said the mine manager. "Stop those cars and help me get him off there!"

But the young surface engineer was already being sick, turned away and leaning against the millhouse wall, in the early shadow of the mountains.

Chapter 3

The clerk working the afternoon division, day shift, on the room desk of the Koh-i-Nor Hotel in the downtown area of the Chicago Complex, was conscious of the fact that his aptitude tests had determined that he should find work in a particular class of job. The class was that of ornament—actually unnecessary from the point of view of modern hotel equipment. Accordingly he worked conscientiously at the primary virtue of a good ornament—being as hard to overlook as possible.

He did not look up when he heard footsteps approach his desk and stop before it. He continued to write in elegant longhand at the list of currently newsworthy guests he was making on a bulletin sheet laid down beside the guest register.

"I have a reservation," said a man's voice. "Paul Formain."

"Very good," said the clerk, adding another name to his list without looking up. He paused to admire the smooth, flowing loops in the *p*'s and *l*'s of his penmanship.

Abruptly he felt his hand caught and held by a fist considerably larger than his own. It checked his pen's movement. The strange grasp held his hand like an imprisoned fly—not crushingly, but with a hint of unyielding power in reserve. Startled, a little scared, the clerk looked up.

He found himself facing a tall young-old man with only one arm, the hand of which was holding him with such casual power.

"Sir?" said the clerk. His voice pitched itself a little higher than he would have preferred.

"I said," said the tall man, patiently, "I have a reservation. Paul Formain."

"Yes sir. Of course." Once more the clerk made an effort to free his trapped hand. As if by an afterthought, the tall man let go. The clerk turned hurriedly to his desk register and punched out the name. The register lighted up with information. "Yes sir. Here it is. An outside single. What décor?"

"Modern."

"Of course, Mr. Formain. Room 1412. Elevators around the corner to your left. I'll see your luggage is delivered to you immediately it arrives. Thank you. . . ."

But the tall, one-armed man had already gone off toward the elevators. The clerk looked after him, and then down at his own right hand. He moved the fingers of it experimentally. It had never before occurred to him what wonderfully engineered things those fingers were.

Up in room 1412 Paul stripped and showered. By the time he stepped out of the shower, his single suitcase had emerged from the luggage-delivery chute in the wall of the room. Half-dressed, he caught sight of himself in the mirror, which gave back his lean, flat-muscled image wearing the gray-green disposable slacks he had pressed for from the room dispenser after the shower. Above the waistband of the slacks, his chest and shoulders showed a healthy tan. The fine scars left by the plastic surgery had now faded almost to the point of invisibility. It was eight months since the accident in the mine, early in a new spring, with gray skies and a March wind blowing chilly off Lake Michigan.

The stub of his left arm looked shrunken. Not so much, it seemed, because it no longer had the rest of the limb to support, but in contrast to the right arm that remained to him.

The compensation development of the right arm had proceeded with unusual speed and to extremes, according to Paul's physicians. It hung now, reflected in the mirror's surface, like a great, living club of bone and muscle. The deltoid humped up like a rock over the point where clavicle toed into shoulder frame; and from the lower part of the deltoid, triceps and biceps humped like whale-backs down to the smaller, knot-like muscles above the elbow. Below the elbow, the flexors and the brachioradialis rose like low hills. The thenar group was a hard lump at the base of his thumb.

And it was as a club that he sometimes thought of it. No—nothing so clumsy as a club. Like some irresistible, battering-ram force made manifest in flesh and skeleton. In the three-quarters of a year since the mine accident, through the long process of hospitalization, operation, and recuperation, that invincible part of him which sat in the back of his mind seemed to have chosen the arm for itself. The arm was *that* part of Paul, the part that doubted nothing, and least of all itself. Nor had time to waste on the posing of a hotel clerk.

Obscurely, it bothered Paul. Like a man testing a sore tooth continually with a tongue, he found himself frequently trying the arm's strength on things, and being disturbed anew each time by the result. Now, standing before the mirror, he reached out and closed his hand around the single ornament in the starkly modern hotel room—a tulip-shaped pewter vase about nine inches high, with a single red rose in it, that had been sitting on the dresser top. The vase fitted easily into his grasp, and he lifted it, slowly tightening the grip of his fingers.

For a moment it almost seemed that the thick metal walls would resist. Then slowly the vase crumpled inward, until the rose, pinched halfway up its stem, toppled to one side, and water, brimming up over the rim of the vase, ran down onto Paul's contracting hand. Paul relaxed his grasp, opened his hand, and looked down at the squeezed shape of the vase lying in it for a second. Then he tossed the ruin— vase, flower and all—into the waste-basket by the dresser and flexed his fingers. They were not even cramped. With that much strength the arm should already be becoming muscle-bound and useless. It was not.

He finished dressing and went down to the subway entrance in the basement of the hotel. There was a two-seater among the empty cars waiting on the hotel switchback. He got in and dialed the standard 4441, which was the directory address in all cities, centers, and Complexes over the fifty-thousand population figure. The little car moved out into the subway traffic and fifteen minutes after deposited him forty miles away at the Directory terminal.

He registered his credit card with Chicago Complex bookkeeping, and a routing service directed him to a booth on the ninth level. He stepped onto the disk of a large elevator tube along with several other people and found his eye caught by a book a girl was carrying.

The book was in a small, hand-sized portable viewer, and the book's cover looked out at him from the viewer's screen. It gazed at him with the dark glasses and clever old mouth of the face he had been watching that day in the mine. It was the same face. Only, below the chin instead of the formal white collar and knotted scarf, here was the red and gold of some ceremonial robe.

Against this red and gold were stamped the black block letters of the book's title. DESTRUCT.

Glancing up from the book, for the first time he looked at the girl carrying it. She was staring at him with an expression of shock, and at the sight of her face he felt a boundless impact within himself. He found himself looking directly into the features of the girl who had stood beside and a little behind the Guildmaster in the viewing tank of the console at the mine.

"Excuse me," she said. "Excuse me."

She had turned, and pushing blindly past the other people on the disk stepped quickly off onto the level above that level on which Paul had entered.

Reflexively, he followed her. But she was already lost in the crowd. He found himself standing in the heart of the musical section of the Directory library. He stood, brushed against by passers-by, gazing vainly out over the heads of the crowd for the sight of her. He was only half a pace from a row of booths, and from the partly open door of one of these came the thin thread of melody that was a woman's soprano singing to a chimed accompaniment in a slow, minor key. . . .

In apple comfort, long I waited thee

The music ran through him like a wind blowing from far off, and the pushing people about him became distant and unimportant as shadows. It was the voice of the girl in the elevator just now. He knew it, though he had only heard those few words from her. The music swelled and encompassed him, and one of his moments of feeling moved in on him, on wings too strong for love and too wide for sadness.

And long I thee in apple comfort waited.

She was the music, and the music was a wind blowing across an endless snow field to a cavern where ice crystals chimed to the tendrils of the wind. . . .

In lonely autumn and uncertain springtime
My apple longing for thee was not sated. . . .

Abruptly he wrenched himself free.

Something had been happening to him. He stared about him, once more conscious of the moving crowd. The music from the booth was once more only a thread under the shuffle of feet and the distant sea-roar of conversations.

He turned around and saw nothing on every side but the prosaic music section of a library floor in the directory. The magic was gone.

But so was the girl.

Paul went on up to the ninth level and found an open booth. He sat down, closed the door, and punched for a list of local psychiatrists, giving his now-registered credit number. As an afterthought, he added a stipulation that the list be restricted to those psychiatrists who had been interested or concerned with the problems of amputees in the past. The board before him flashed an acknowledgment of the request, and a statement that the answer would require about a ten-to-fifteen-minute wait.

Paul sat back. On impulse he coded the title of the book the girl had been carrying with a purchase request, and a second later a copy in a commercial viewer was delivered to the desk in front of him from the delivery chute.

He picked it up. The face on the book's cover seemed to be staring at him with a sardonic expression, as if it amused itself with some secret it was keeping from him. The imaged face was not as he had seen it in the viewing tank at the mine, when the features had seemed to refuse to join in a clearly observed face. Now Paul saw the whole face, but something else was wrong. It was not so much a face but a wax mask. Something lifeless and without meaning. Paul punched the trip that would change the cover picture to the first page within.

On the white expanse of paper shown, the title leaped at him once again.

DESTRUCT, by *Walter Blunt*

Paul turned the page. He found himself looking at the first page of an introduction written by someone whose name he did not recognize. Paul skimmed through its half-dozen pages.

Walter Blunt, he read, was the son of rich parents. His family had owned a controlling interest in one of the great schools of bluefin tuna that followed the circle migratory route between North and South America and Japan. Blunt had grown up brilliant but undisciplined. He had lived the life of the wealthy who have nothing important to do, until one day when with thousands of other hunters he had been caught in an uncontrolled freak early-winter blizzard, while out stalking deer in the Lake Superior Range.

Four others in Blunt's party had died of exposure. Blunt, equally city-bred and unprepared, had in a wry moment conceived of the Alternate Forces of existence, and offered to trade them his life's service for the protection of his life itself. Following this, he had walked unerringly out of the woods to safety and arrived warm and unexhausted at shelter, in spite of the sleeting wind, the dropping temperature, and the fact that he was wearing only the lightest of hunting clothes.

Following this experience, he had dedicated himself to the Alternate Forces. Over a lifetime he had created and organized the Chantry Guild, or Société Chanterie, composed of students of, and graduate workers with, the Alternate Forces. The aim of the Chantry Guild was universal acceptance of the positive principle of destruction. Only by destruction could mankind signify its adherence to the Alternate Laws, and only the Alternate Laws remained strong enough to save mankind from the technical civilization that was now on the verge of trapping mankind like a fly in amber.

The delicate chime of a response counter drew Paul's attention to the screen before him. He looked at a double list of names, addresses, and call numbers. He turned his attention to the typewriter-like keyboard below the screen and tapped out a message to all the names on the list.

My left arm was amputated slightly over seven months ago. My body has to date rejected three attempts to graft on a replacement. No reason for the intolerance can be discovered in the ordinary physiological processes. My physicians have recommended that I explore the possibility of a psychological factor being involved in the causes of the intolerance, and have suggested that I try my case among psychiatrists of this area, where a large amount of work with amputees has been done. Would you be interested in accepting me as a patient? Paul Allen Formain. File No. 432 36 47865 2551 OG3 K122b, Room 1412, Koh-i-Nor Hotel, Chicago Complex.

Paul got up, took the book he had just purchased, and headed back toward the hotel. On the way back and after he had returned to his room, he read on into Blunt's writing. Sprawled out on his hotel-room bed he read a collection of wild nonsense mixed with sober fact, and an urgent appeal to the reader to enlist himself as a student under the instruction of some graduate Chantry Guild member. The reward promised for successfully completing the course of instruction was apparently to be a power encompassing all wild dreams of magical ability that had ever been conceived.

It was too ridiculous to be taken seriously.

Paul frowned.

He found himself holding the book gingerly. It did not stir in a physical sense, but a vibration came from it that seemed to quiver deep in the marrow of Paul's bones. A singing silence began to swell in the room. One of his moments was coming on him. He held himself still as a wolf come suddenly upon a trap. About him the walls of the room breathed in and out. The silence sang louder. The place and moment spoke to him:

DANGER.

Put the book down.

Louder sang the silence, blinding the ears of his sensing . . .

Danger, said the invincible part of him, is a word invented by children, and is essentially meaningless to the adult.

He pressed the button to turn the page. A new chapter heading looked up at him.

ALTERNATE FORCES AND REGROWTH. THE REPLACE-
MENT OF MISSING LIMBS, OR EVEN OF THE BODY ENTIRE.

The reparative regeneration of parts of the human body by epimorphosis, or regrowth beginning from a regeneration bud or blastema formed at the wound surface, is a property capable of stimulation by the Alternate Forces. It has its justification and instigation in the intended action of self-destruct. Like all use and manipulation of the Alternate Forces, the mechanism is simple once the underlying principles are grasped. In this case, they are the Non-Evolutionary (blocking to the Natural Forces) and the Regressive (actively in reversal of the Natural Forces). These principles are not merely statically negative, but dynamically negative, so that from the fact of their dynamism derives the energy necessary for the process of regeneration. . . .

The call note on Paul's room telephone chimed, breaking the spell. The room fled back to naturalness and the book sagged in his hand. From the bed he saw the screen of the phone light up.

"A Directory report on your query, sir," said a canned voice from the lighted screen.

The screen dissolved into a list of names with medical and mental science degrees after them. One by one the names winked out until only one was left. Paul read it from the bed.

DR. ELIZABETH WILLIAMS

A moment later the word *accept* was printed beside it. Paul put the book aside where it could be picked up later.

Chapter 4

"How do you feel?"

It was a woman's voice. Paul opened his eyes. Dr. Elizabeth Williams was standing over the chair in which he sat. She put the hypodermic spray gun down on the desk beside him, and walked around to take her seat behind the desk.

"Did I say anything?" Paul sat up straighter in his chair.

"If you mean, did you reply to my questions? No." Dr. Williams looked across the desk at him. She was a small, square-shouldered woman with brown hair and an unremarkable face. "How long have you known about this strong resistance of yours to hypnosis?"

"Is it resistance?" asked Paul. "I'm trying to co-operate."

"How long have you known about it?"

"Since the sailing accident. Five years." Paul looked at her. "What *did* I say?"

Dr. Williams looked at him.

"You told me I was a foolish woman," she said.

Paul blinked at her.

"Is that all?" he asked. "I didn't say anything but that."

"That's all." She looked at him across the desk. He felt curiosity and a sort of loneliness emanating from her.

"Paul, can you think of anything in particular that you're afraid of?"

"Afraid?" he asked, and frowned. "Afraid . . . ? Not really. No."

"Worried?"

He thought for a long moment.

"No—not worried, actually," he said. "There's nothing you could say was actually worrying me."

"Unhappy?"

He smiled. Then frowned, suddenly.

"No," he said, and hesitated. "That is, I don't think so."

"Then why did you come to see me?"

He looked at her in some surprise.

"Why, about my arm," he said.

"Not about the fact that you were orphaned at an early age? Not that you've always led a solitary life, with no close friends? Not that you tried to kill yourself in a sailboat five years ago, and tried again in a mine, less than a year ago?"

"Wait a minute!" said Paul. She looked at him politely, inquiringly. "Do you think I arranged those accidents to try and kill myself?"

"Shouldn't I think so?" ·

"Why, no," said Paul.

"Why not?"

"Because . . ." A sudden perfect moment of understanding broke through to Paul. He saw her sitting there in complete blindness. He stared at her, and before his eyes, looking back at him, she seemed to grow shrunken and a little older. He got to his feet. "It doesn't matter," he said.

"You should think about it, Paul."

"I will. I want to think over this whole business."

"Good," she said. She had not moved out of her chair, and in spite of the assurance of her tone, she did not seem quite herself since he had looked at her. "My receptionist will set up your next time in."

"Thanks," he said. "Good-by."

"Good afternoon, Paul."

He went out. In the outer office the receptionist looked up from a filing machine as he passed.

"Mr. Formain?" She leaned forward over the machine. "Don't you want to make your next appointment now?"

"No," said Paul. "I don't think so." He went out.

He went down a number of levels from Dr. Williams' office to the terminal in the base of the building. There were public communications booths nearby. He stepped into one and closed the door. He felt both naked and relieved. He dialed for a listing of the Chantry Guild members in the area. The screen lighted up.

Walter Blunt, *Guildmaster* (no listed phone number)
Jason Warren, *Necromancer*, Chantry Guild Secretary, phone
    number 66 433 35246

Kantele Maki (no listed phone number)
Morton Brown, 66 433 67420
Warra, *Mage*, 64 256 89235
(*The above list contains only the names of those requesting
    listing under the Chantry Guild heading.*)

Paul punched 66 433 35246. The screen lighted up whitely, but it
was half a minute before it cleared to show the face of one of the
people Paul remembered from the television broadcast in the mine a
year before, the face of a thin, black-haired young man with deep-set,
unmoving eyes.

"My name is Paul Formain," said Paul. "I'd like to talk to Jason
Warren."

"I'm Jason Warren. What about?"

"I've just read a book by Walter Blunt that says the Alternate
Forces can grow back limbs that are missing." Paul moved so that the
stub of his left arm was visible to the other.

"I see." Warren looked at him with the movelessness of his dark
eyes. "What about it?"

"I'd like to talk to you about it."

"I suppose that can be arranged. When would you like to talk to
me?"

"Now," said Paul.

The black eyebrows in the screen went up a fraction.

"Now?"

"I was planning on it," said Paul.

"Oh, you were?"

Paul waited.

"All right, come ahead." Abruptly the screen went blank, but leaving Paul's vision filled with the after-image of the dark face that had
been in it looking at him with a curious interest and intent. He rose,
breathing out a little with relief. He had moved without thinking from
the second of perception that had come to him in Elizabeth Williams'
office. Suddenly he had realized that her education and training had
made her blind to understanding in his case. She had not understood.
That much had been explosively obvious. She had been trying to rec-
oncile the speed of light with the clumsy mechanism of the stop watch
she believed in. And if she had made that error, then the psychiatrist
at San Diego, after the boating accident, had been wrong in the same
way, as well.

Paul had reacted without thinking, but, strongly now, his instinct told him he was right. He had labored under the handicap of a belief in stop watches. Somewhere, he told himself now, there was a deeper understanding. It was a relief to go searching for it at last with an unfettered mind—a mind awake.

Chapter 5

As Paul entered through the automatically opening front door of Jason Warren's apartment, he saw three people already in the room—a sort of combination office-lounge—he found himself stepping into.

Two of the three were just going out through a rear door. Paul got only a glimpse of them—one, a girl who with a start Paul recognized as the girl with the book he had encountered earlier at Chicago Directory. The other was a flat-bodied man in middle age with an air of quiet competence about him. He, too, had been with the girl and Blunt on the broadcast Paul had witnessed in the mine a year before. Paul wondered briefly if Blunt, also, was nearby. Then the thought passed from his mind. He found himself looking down, slightly, into the dark, mercurial face of Jason Warren.

"Paul Formain," said Paul. "I phoned—"

"Sit down." Warren waved Paul into a chair and took a facing one himself. He looked at Paul with something of the direct, uninhibited stare of a child. "What can I do for you?"

Paul considered him. Warren sat loosely, almost sprawled, but with his thin body held in the balance of a dancer or a highly trained athlete, so that a single movement might have brought him back to his feet.

"I want to grow a new arm," said Paul.

"Yes," said Warren. He flicked a forefinger toward the phone. "I punched information for your public file after you called," he said. "You're an engineer."

"I was," said Paul, and was a little surprised to hear himself say it, now, with such a small amount of bitterness.

"You believe in the Alternate Laws?"

"No," said Paul. "Truthfully—no."

"But you think they might give you an arm back?"

"It's a chance."

"Yes," said Warren. "An engineer. Hardheaded, practical—doesn't care what makes it work as long as it works."

"Not exactly," said Paul.

"Why bother with the Alternate Laws? Why not just have a new arm out of the culture banks grafted on?"

"I've tried that," said Paul. "It doesn't take."

Warren sat perfectly still for a couple of seconds. There was no change in his face or attitude, but Paul got an impression as if something like a delicately sensitive instrument in the other man had suddenly gone *click* and begun to register.

"Tell me," said Warren, slowly and carefully, "the whole story."

Paul told it. As he talked, Warren sat still and listened. During the fifteen minutes or so it took for Paul to tell it all, the other man did not move or react. And with no warning, even as Paul was talking, it came to Paul where he had seen that same sort of concentration before. It was in a bird dog he had seen once, holding its point, one paw lifted, nose straight and tail in line with the body, as still as painted Death.

When Paul stopped, Warren did not speak at once. Instead, without moving a muscle otherwise, he lifted his right hand into the air between them and extended his forefinger toward Paul. The movement had all the remote inevitability of a movement by a machine, or the slow leaning of the top of a chopped tree as it begins its fall.

"Look," Warren said slowly, "at my finger. Look at the tip of my finger. Look closely. Right there at the end of the nail, under the nail, you can see a spot of red. It's a drop of blood coming out from under the nail. See it swelling there. It's getting larger. In a moment it'll drop off. But it's getting larger, larger—"

"No," said Paul. "There's no drop of blood there at all. You're wasting your time—and mine."

Warren dropped his hand.

"Interesting," he said. "Interesting."

"Is it?" asked Paul.

"Graduate members of the Chantry Guild," said Warren, "can't be hypnotized, either. But you say you don't believe in the Alternate Laws."

"I seem to be a sort of free-lance, then," said Paul.

Warren rose suddenly from his chair with the single motion Paul had expected. He walked lightly and easily across the room, turned, and came back.

"In order to resist hypnosis," he said, standing over Paul, "you must make use of the Alternate Laws, whether you recognize them as such or not. The keystone of the use of the Alternate Laws is complete independence of the individual—independence from any force, physical or otherwise."

"And vice versa?" asked Paul, smiling.

"And vice versa." Warren did not smile. He stood looking down at Paul. "I'll ask you again," he said. "What do you expect me to do for you?"

"I want an arm," said Paul.

"I can't give you an arm," said Warren. "I can't do anything for you. The use of the Alternate Laws is for those who would do things for themselves."

"Show me how, then."

Warren sighed slightly. It was a sigh that sounded to Paul not only weary, but a little angry.

"You don't know what the hell you're asking," said Warren. "To train whatever aptitude you have for use of the Alternate Laws, I'd have to take you on as my apprentice in necromancy."

"Blunt's book gave me to understand the Guild was eager for people."

"Why, we are," said Warren. "We have an urgent need right now for someone comparable to Leonardo da Vinci. We'd be very glad to get someone with the qualifications of Milton or Einstein. Of course, what we really need is someone with a talent no one has conceived of yet—a sort of X-Genius. So we advertise."

"Then you don't want people."

"I didn't say that," said Warren. He turned and paced the room and came back. "You're serious about joining the Guild?"

"If it'll get me my arm."

"It won't get you your arm. I tell you, no one can put that arm back but you. There's a relation between the Alternate Laws and the work of the Guild, but it isn't what you think."

"Perhaps I'd better be enlightened," said Paul.

"All right," said Warren. He put his hands in his pockets and stood with shoulders hunched slightly, looking down at Paul. "Try this on for size. This is an ill world we live in, Formain. A world sick from a surfeit of too many technical luxuries. An overburdened world, swarming with people close to the end of their ropes." His deep-set eyes were steady on Paul. "People today are like a man who thought that if he made his success in the world, everything else that makes life good would come automatically. Now they've made their success—the perfection of a technological civilization in which no one lacks anything in the way of a physical comfort—and they find themselves in a false paradise. Like an electric motor without a load upon it, the human spirit without the weight of the need to achieve and progress is beginning to rev up toward dissolution. Faster and faster, until they'll fly apart and destroy this world they've made."

He stopped.

"What do you say to that?" he asked.

"It might be the case," said Paul. "I don't really believe that's the situation we're in, myself, but it might be the case."

"All right," said Warren. "Now try this: In a climate of confusion, one of the surest ways of confounding the enemy is to tell him the plain truth. And the Guildmaster has stated the plain truth plainly in his book. The Chantry Guild is not interested in propagating the use of the Alternate Laws. It only wants to train and make use of those who can already use the Laws, to its own end. And that end's to hurry the end that is inevitably coming, to bring about the destruction of present civilization."

Warren stopped. He seemed to wait for Paul to say something. But Paul also waited.

"We," said Warren, "are a small but powerful revolutionary body with the aim of driving this sick world into complete insanity and collapse. The Alternate Laws are real, but most of our structure is completely fake. If you come in as my apprentice, you'll be committed to the job of destroying the world."

"And that's my only way to a use of the Alternate Forces?" asked Paul.

"For you to accept the Guild's philosophy and aim, yes," said Warren. "Otherwise, no."

"I don't believe that," said Paul. "If your Alternate Forces exist, they'll work for me as well as all the Chantry Guild put together."

Warren dropped into a chair and stared at Paul for a long moment.

"Arrogant," he said. "Completely arrogant. Let's see. . . ." He rose lightly to his feet, crossed the room, and touched a spot on one of the walls.

The wall slid back, revealing an area which seemed half modern laboratory and half alchemist's den. On the table in its center were earthenware containers, some metal jars, and a large flask full of dark-red liquid.

Warren opened a drawer in the table, and took out something which his body hid from Paul's view. He closed the drawer, turned, and came back carrying a rather decrepit-looking conch shell, brown-stained and polished by handling and age.

He put the shell down on an occasional table a few feet from Paul's chair.

"What does that do?" Paul asked, looking at it curiously.

"For me," said Warren, "it does a lot of things. Which is no advantage to you except that we might say it's been sensitized to the action of the Alternate Laws. Let's see if this arrogance of yours can do anything with it."

Paul frowned. He stared at the shell. For a second the situation was merely ridiculous. And then it was as if a thread of brightness ran through him. There was a sudden weird sensation, as if a great, deep gong sounded, somewhere deep inside him. And then a rushing, back in the depths of his mind, as if a host of memories long forgotten ran and beat upon a locked door held shut to them since he could not exactly remember when.

The conch shell stirred. It rolled to a point of balance and hung there. The bright daylight lanced through a far window of the room and a faint wisp of some light music sounded from the apartment next door. A thin, reedy voice spoke faintly but clearly from the shell.

"From greater dark into the little light. And then once more to greater dark he goes."

The beating on the locked door in Paul's mind dwindled away into silence. The shell lost its balance and fell over, still, on one side. Across from Paul, Warren drew a deep breath and picked up the shell.

"You may be a natural," he said.

"A natural?" Paul looked up at him.

"There are certain abilities in the province of the Alternate Powers which can be possessed by those who know nothing of the true nature of the Alternate Powers. Mind reading, for example. Or artistic inspiration."

"Oh?" said Paul. "How do you tell the difference between people with that, and your Alternate Power people?"

"Very simply," answered Warren. But the tone of his voice and the way he held the shell and continued to watch Paul did not imply simpleness. "For such people their abilities work spasmodically and unreliably. For us, they always work."

"For example, mind reading?"

"I'm a Necromancer," said Warren, shortly, "not a seer. Besides, I used the common, recognizable term. I'm told minds aren't so much *read* as experienced."

"When you go into someone else's mind, you lose your own point of view?"

"Yes," said Warren, "you must be a natural." He took the conch shell back across to the cabinet and put it away. He turned around and spoke from where he was.

"You've got something," he said. "It may be a valuable aptitude, and it may not. But I'm willing to take you on as a probationary apprentice. If I think you have promise after a while, you'll be taken fully into the Guild on an apprenticeship basis. If that happens, you'll be required to assign everything you own and all future personal income to the Guild. But if it reaches that point, you needn't worry about material things." Warren's lips twisted slightly. "The Guild will take care of you. Study and learn, and you'll be able to grow your arm back one day."

Paul stood up.

"You guarantee me an arm?" he said.

"Of course," said Warren. He did not move from where he stood, watching Paul across the widths of laboratory and apartment room with unmoving gaze.

Chapter 6

Shuttling through the many-leveled maze of the Chicago Complex's streets and buildings in a one-man subway car, Paul leaned his head back against the cushions of the seat and closed his eyes.

He was exhausted, and exhaustion, he now suspected, had its roots in something besides the physical efforts he had been put to today. Something almost physical had taken place in him following his recognition of the ridiculousness of the psychiatric approach to his situation. And the business with the shell had also drained him.

But the exhaustion was something that rest could cure. More important were two other things. The first of these was a clear recognition that too many things were happening around him and to him for them all to be accidents. And accidents, once the notion that he was subconsciously bent on self-destruction had been discarded, had been the obvious alternative answer.

The second was the fact that the Necromancer, Warren, had called him arrogant.

Disturbed by this, Paul for the first time faced the fact that such disturbance was unusual with him. Now that he stopped to consider the fact, in spite of all that had happened to him it had never before occurred to him that he might be at the mercy of any other force than that of his own will. Perhaps, he thought, this was arrogance, but the idea did not ring true. Above all else, he trusted his own feelings, and he did not feel arrogant. All that came to him when he reached back into himself for reasons was a calm feeling of certainty. It was that invincible element in him which took all things calmly.

For, thought Paul, leaning back with his eyes closed, above all he must not be arrogant. He was like a man peering through the glass-clearness of still water into the secret life of a tide pool on an ocean beach. Wonderful things were happening just a little before him, and would continue to happen as long as the pool was not disturbed. But a touch of wind or a dabbled finger, a ripple across the water's surface, and the life going on under his nose would no longer be isolated, pure, and complete. Gentleness was the watchword. Gentleness and extreme care. Already he had begun to separate and identify elements: by a hint of movement, a change of color, an emerging shape. . . .

Leaning back with his eyes closed, Paul lost himself in a half-doze and a dream of things half-seen.

Sudden deceleration of his small car pulled him upright in his seat. The car jerked to a stop. He opened his eyes and looked out through the unopaqued bubble of the car's top.

He was at a mid-level intersection of streets. Above and below him were residential and business layers of the great three-dimensional community that was Chicago Complex. On his own level his car had halted part-way out into an intersection the four corners of which were occupied by small shops and offices, beyond which was a large rec-reation area, parklike with trees. But no people were visible. The shops were empty. The park was empty. The streets were clear and still.

Paul once more leaned forward and pressed for the terminal at the Koh-i-Nor Hotel. The car did not move. He punched for the transpor-tation control center, malfunction division.

The communications tank above the car's dashboard lighted up.

"Sir?" said a woman's canned voice. "Can I help you?"

"I'm in a one-man car that won't move," said Paul. "It's stopped at the intersection of "—he glanced at a street-corner sign—"N Level 2432 and AANB."

"Checking," said the canned voice. There was a moment's wait and the voice spoke again. "Sir? Are you certain of your location. The area you report yourself in has been closed to traffic. Your car could not have entered in the last half hour."

"It seems to have anyway." Paul broke off suddenly. He seemed to have heard something odd. He got out of the car and stood up alongside it. The sound came thinly but more clearly to his ears. It was the noise of people chanting, and the noise was approaching.

"The area you report yourself in," the tank in the car as saying, "has been cleared to allow for a public demonstration. Would you please check your location again? If is the location you have already reported, please leave your car at once and ascend one level immedi-ately to find another. Repeat, leave your car *immediately*."

Paul swung away from the car. Across the street from him was an escalator spiral ramp. He reached it and let himself be borne upward. It swung up and out over the street he had just left. The chanting now came clearly to his ears. It was not words, but sounds without meaning.

"Hey, hey! Hey, hey! Hey, hey! . . ."

Puzzled, he stepped off the upward-moving surface of the ramp and looked out over the chest-high siding. Down round a curve of the cross street to the one on which his car had stalled he saw people pouring toward him in a sort of orderly mob, twenty abreast, and filling the street solidly from curb to curb.

They came quickly. They were at jog trot. Young men and women for the most part wearing blue slacks, white shirts, and green-colored, odd, cocked hats. They ran with arms interlinked, in step with the rhythm of their chanting.

Abruptly, Paul identified them. They represented, evidently, one of the so-called marching societies. Such groups gathered together for no other purpose than to run through the streets perhaps once or twice a month. It was a sort of controlled and channeled hysteria, or so Paul remembered reading. Such exercises blew off a lot of emotional steam safely, said the societies' advocates. For unless the group ran directly into some obstacle, they did no harm and were not harmed.

They came on now and Paul could see their eyes, which were all fixed straight ahead. But their gazes were not glassy, as of people drunk or drugged. Rather, they were clear, but fixed, as with people undergoing a moment of exaltation or frenzy. They were almost below Paul, now. Almost to the intersection.

Suddenly, Paul realized that his one-man car, stalled where it was, would be in their way. They were practically upon it now. The cadenced slapping of their river of feet was shaking the ramp on which he stood. It was making, it seemed, the whole structure of the city Complex, level on level, vibrate to a high, almost supersonic singing. A wave of heat struck up to him from their onrushing bodies, and the louder, ever-louder yelping of their chant rocked on his ears like the unnatural amplification of sounds heard in a fever. Whirlpooled about by noise and heat, Paul saw their first ranks run into his empty car and, without halting, like a stampede of mindless cattle, tumble it, rolling, over and over until it bounced at last to a railing overhanging the level below. Paul watched it mount the railing and drop from sight, the ultimate noise of its impact below lost in the encompassing noise of the running crowd.

He looked back along the road, in the direction from which they had come. The river of people was unended, still passing out of sight around the curve. But now, as he watched, the final ranks began to thin and quieten, and over the other sounds he heard the thin wail of ambulance sirens following slowly after.

Paul went on up to the level above, found a two-man car that was empty on a siding, and returned to the hotel.

When he got to his room, the door was open. A small gray man in a business suit rose smoothly from a chair as Paul entered, and offered an opened wallet cardcase for Paul's inspection.

"Hotel security, Mr. Formain," said the small man. "My name's James Butler."

"Yes?" said Paul. He felt his tiredness like a cloak around him.

"A routine matter, Mr. Formain. Maintenance discovered a vase in your room that had been rather bent out of shape."

"Put it on my bill," said Paul. "Now, if you don't mind——"

"The vase isn't important, Mr. Formain. But we understand you have been seeing a psychiatrist?"

"A Dr. Elizabeth Williams. Today. Why?"

"As a routine matter, this hotel asks for and is notified if any of its guests are currently under psychiatric care. The Chicago Complex Public Health Unit permits us to refuse occupancy to guests who might disturb the hotel. Of course, no such refusal is anticipated in your case, Mr. Formain."

"I'm checking out in the morning," said Paul.

"Oh? I'm sorry to hear that," said James Butler evenly. "I assure you there was no intention to offend you. It's just one of the management rules that we inform our guests that we have been notified about them."

"I was leaving anyway," said Paul. He looked at the man's unchanging face and motionless body, and James Butler's personality came clearly through to him. Butler was a dangerous little man. An efficient little machine of suspicion and control. Underneath, though, was something repressed, something guarded by an inner fear. "Right now, I want to turn in. So if you don't mind . . ."

Butler inclined his head slightly.

"Unless, of course," he said, "there's something more."

"Nothing."

"Thank you." Butler turned and walked smoothly to the door. "Feel free to call on hotel services at any time," he said, and went out, closing the door behind him.

Paul frowned. But weariness was like a great load on him. He undressed and dropped into the bed. And sleep closed down about him like great, gray wings, enfolding.

He dreamed that he walked a cobbled road, in darkness under the stars, alone. And the cobbles grew as he went until they were great boulders to be climbed. And then that dream vanished and he dreamed that he was paralyzed, drifting upright through the nighttime streets of the Chicago Complex. He drifted along without touching the ground and after a while he came on an arc light on its pole that had been changed into a monstrous candy cane. And just beyond it a store front had been turned from plastic to ice, and was melting.

In the morning he woke feeling as if he had slept fourteen years, rather than fourteen hours, packed, and went down to the main lobby to pay his bill.

He cut through one of the hotel bars on his way down to the basement terminal. At this early hour it was all but deserted except for a plump middle-aged man who sat alone at a table with a small tulip-shaped glass of some purplish liquid before him. For a moment, passing, Paul thought that the man was drunk. And then he caught the scent of cinnamon from the glass and saw the man's eyes had pinpoint pupils. And looking behind this, he caught sight of Butler, seated in the darkness of a corner, watching. Paul went over to the hotel security man.

"Are you notified about drug addicts, too?" Paul asked.

"Our bars stock the non-habit-forming synthetics," said Butler. "It's quite legal."

"You didn't answer my question," said Paul.

"The hotel," said Butler, "feels a certain responsibility to certain guests." He glanced up at Paul. "That's legal, too. And any extra charges are quite reasonable. If you hadn't already planned to leave, Mr. Formain, I could have told you what services we had available."

Paul turned and went on. He found a one-man car at the terminal, and, getting in, punched for Warren's apartment. The first demand the Necromancer had made of his probationary apprentice was that Paul should move into the apartment, where Warren could have him under constant observation.

He found Warren waiting for him. The Necromancer turned over one of the bedrooms in the apartment to him, and then to all intents and purposes left Paul to his own devices. For the rest of the week Paul hardly saw the intense young man.

It was five days later that Paul, thoroughly bored with the apartment by this time, happened to be going through the music Warren had listed in his apartment player. Abruptly, he came across a title which caught his attention.

IN APPLE COMFORT . . . vocal. Sung by *Kantele*

Kantele. Suddenly the mental connection was made. It had been there in the list of local members of the Chantry Guild. *Kantele Maki.* And he remembered now, there was a girl who sang professionally under the single name *Kantele.* She was the girl with the book that he had first seen on the news broadcast, and after that at the Directory. He pressed the small black button alongside the initial letter of the song title.

There was the barest second of a pause, and then the chimed music rose softly ringing from the player, interspersed by the cool, shifting silver of the voice he recognized.

> *In apple comfort, long I waited thee*
> *And long I thee in apple comfort waited.*
> *In lonely autumn and uncertain——*

A sudden gasp from behind him made Paul shut off the player abruptly and turn about. He found himself facing the girl herself.

She stood a little to one side of a bookcase of old-fashioned volumes. But the bookcase, to Paul's surprise, was swung out from its usual place, revealing not a wall behind it, but an entrance to a small room furnished and equipped like an office. Seeing his gaze go to it, Kantele broke suddenly out of the rigidity that had been holding her, and, putting out a hand, pushed the bookcase back into position, closing the entrance. They stood, looking across the room at each other.

"I didn't know . . ." she said. "I forgot you were living here now."

He watched her, curiously. She was noticeably pale.

"Did you think I was someone else?" he asked.

"Yes. I mean"—she said—"I thought you were Jase."

She was one of the kind who lie defiantly. He felt her untruthfulness across all the distance separating them.

"You've got a fine voice," he said. "I was playing that song of yours——"

"Yes. I heard you," she interrupted. "I—I'd rather you wouldn't play it, if you don't mind."

"Would you?" asked Paul.

"It has associations for me. If you don't mind . . ."

"I won't play it if you don't want me to, of course," said Paul. He walked toward her and then stopped suddenly, seeing her reflexively take the one step back from him that the wall behind her allowed.

"Jase . . ." she said. "Jase will be here at any minute."

Paul watched her, frowning a bit. He felt puzzled and a little exasperated by her, but also oddly touched, as he might be by anyone or anything defenseless that did not realize he meant it no harm. And that was odd too, because Kantele did not give the impression generally of defenselessness, but of wire-like courage. Paul was reaching to approach this problem in words when the sound of the opening front door of the apartment brought both their heads around in its direction.

Warren and the flat-bodied, crop-haired man Paul had seen in the news broadcast, and again leaving the apartment with Kantele the first time he had come to see Warren, had just come in. They headed straight for Paul and Kantele.

Chapter 7

"You didn't answer the door," said Warren, stopping before them and looking at Kantele.

"You didn't ring," said Paul.

"He means me—my apartment, next door," said Kantele, but without looking away from Warren to Paul. "I forgot he was here, Jase. I heard noise and I knew you were out. I stepped in from the office."

"Yes," said Warren. His thin, dark, bright face looked from her to Paul without smiling. "Well, you'd have met anyway. You know each other now? This is Paul Formain, Kantele. Paul, Kantele Maki."

"How do you do?" said Paul to her, and smiled. She gave a little spasm of a smile back.

"And this is Burton McLeod."

"McCloud?" echoed Paul, shaking hands with the flat-bodied man.

"Spelled McLeod, pronounced McCloud," said McLeod. His voice was mild and a little husky. His hand-grip was dry and firm. His brown eyes were the lonely, sad, and savage eyes of a hawk on leash and perch. A week before, the hotel security man, Butler, had impressed Paul as dangerous. McLeod radiated dangerousness of a different order. If Butler was like a stiletto, needle-pointed and polished, then this man was scarred and heavy as some ancient broadsword.

While Paul and McLeod had been shaking hands, Warren and Kantele had held each other's eyes for a long second. Now, suddenly, Warren turned away from her with a quickness that was almost like a shrug and took a small box from his pocket. He opened it in front of Paul.

Paul saw neat rows of white gelatin capsules within. Warren took one out and handing the box aside to McLeod, broke it and poured a white powder from it into his palm.

"Taste," said Warren. Paul frowned.

"It's quite harmless," said Warren. He dipped a finger in the powder himself, and put it to his tongue. Paul hesitated a second and then followed suit. He tasted sweetness.

"Sugar?" said Paul, looking at Warren.

"That's right." The Necromancer dusted off his hands over a nearby ash tray. "But to the man you'll be giving it to it'll be cocaine. I said"—Warren stared at Paul tightly—"it'll *be* cocaine. The minute you let the box into anyone's hands but your own. I mention this so that you'll realize you're legally in the clear in delivering it, as long as you keep it in your pocket until the last moment."

"You want me to deliver it?" asked Paul. "Who to?"

"You know how the Koh-i-Nor's laid out. I want you to take this box to suite 2309. Don't ask directions from the desk clerk or anyone else. Give it to the man you find there. If you run into any trouble . . ." Warren hesitated and glanced for a second at Kantele. "I don't expect you will. But if you do, there's a chess tournament going on on the sixtieth level in the banquet rooms there. Go up there and look for Kantele. She'll get you out."

He stopped talking. There was a moment of silence in the room.

"If it was cocaine," said Paul, "of course I wouldn't take it."

"You'll be carrying sugar," said Warren. His thin face seemed to flash for a second like a drawn blade in the brightness of the sunlight coming through the far windows of the room. "It'll be transmuted into the drug only after you deliver it. You can believe or not believe, go or part company with me, just as you like."

"I'll take it," said Paul. He held out his hand. McLeod gave him the box. "Twenty-three-o-nine?"

"Twenty-three-o-nine," said Warren. The eyes of all three followed him, Paul could feel in the muscles of his back, as he took the box and left the apartment.

The desk clerk he passed at the Koh-i-Nor was a stranger and did not look up as Paul went by. Paul took the elevator tube to the twenty-third level.

It turned out to be a level of modern-décor, semi-VIP suites. The type of establishments that would require income in excess of forty thousand a year to be supported without strain by their occupants. Paul walked down the wide, tiled hallway, coolly lighted by the high, blue-curtained windows at each end of it, until he came to a door marked with the numerals 2309. Below it in small letters were the two words *service entrance.*

Paul touched the door. It was not only unlocked but ajar. It swung noiselessly back into its wall recess at his touch. He stepped into the kitchen of the suite.

Voices broke on his ear from elsewhere in the suite. He stopped dead, and with a faint noise the door slid closed again behind him. One of the voices was an incisive, middle-aged tenor, sharp with emotion. The other was thick and deeper in tone, stumbling, sullen.

". . . pull yourself together!" the tenor voice was saying. The deeper voice muttered something unintelligible.

"You know better than that!" said the tenor. "You don't want to be cured, that's what it is. The substitutes were bad enough. But your monkeying around with real drugs makes you a danger to the whole Department, if not the whole Division. Why didn't you take psychiatric leave when I offered it to you last March?"

The heavy voice muttered something, it seemed to Paul, about the soup, or super.

"Get that out of your head!" said the tenor. "You've let the statistics on mental health get you to seeing ghosts in the woodwork. Electronic equipment is electronic equipment. No more. No less. Don't you think that if there was anything more there, I'd know it?"

"Unless . . ." muttered the heavy voice, "got you already."

"For your own sake"—the tenor was disgusted—"see your physician. Get yourself committed. I won't investigate your Department for the next four days. That'll give you time to get safely into a hospital room where you can decently refuse to answer questions. That's it, now. It's up to you." There was the sound of footsteps walking across hard flooring and a door button snapped to unlatch. "Four days. I won't give you an hour more."

A wind of sudden suspicion blew coolly through Paul, chilling him. He turned quickly himself, stepped silently back through the door he had just entered, and out into the hall. There was a small alcove in the wall about six feet to his left. He stepped to it and pressed himself, back to its wall, deep in its shadow, looking along the hall to 2309's main entrance.

It opened immediately. A small, sparely erect man with thin gray hair came out, closed the door behind him, and went away from Paul toward the far set of elevator tubes at the other end of the hall. For a second as he turned to the elevators, Paul saw a sparrow-like profile against the blue illumination from the curtain windows, and recognized the man. In the suite the tenor voice had sounded vaguely familiar, and Paul had thought it might be the security man, Butler, speaking. But he saw now that there was another reason he had half-recognized the voice.

The man by the elevators was Kirk Tyne, World Complex Engineer. He was the executive head of the theoretical machinery that correlated the activities of the interlocking Complexes of technological devices that made modern life possible about the planet. In theory he and his Division of Engineers performed the functions of a sort of super-computing element, since sooner or later mechanical decisions had to find their ultimate authority and review in human ones. He reached out his hand now to open the elevator tube.

He had not quite touched it when a fair portion of the blue illumination from the window was suddenly occulted by the dark, wide-shouldered body of a tall man who stepped off the downshaft alongside the one toward which Tyne was reaching.

"Well, Kirk," said the tall man. "Didn't expect to see you here."

His voice struck and reverberated on Paul's listening ear like the little echoes chasing each other, on and on, from the sound of a gong struck in some deep and stony cave. It was the voice of Walter Blunt. Almost involuntarily, Paul stepped forward to the edge of his recess to get a better look at this head of the Chantry Guild. But Blunt was standing just so slightly turned that his face was shadowed and averted from Paul.

"Got off here by mistake," replied Tyne, sharply and smoothly. "I was headed for the chess matches upstairs. How about you, Walt?"

"Why," Blunt leaned on his heavy cane, and his voice had a humorous note in it, "I saw you and stepped out to say hello. Headed for the lobby myself for a moment, to meet someone. You look good, Kirk." He laid aside his cane, leaning it against the wall of a tube, and offered his hand. Tyne shook it.

"Thank you Walter," said Tyne, shaking hands. He added, drily, "I imagine we'll both live a while, yet."

"Why, no, Kirk," said Blunt. "The instrument of Armageddon is already at work. I intend to survive the conflict when it comes, but I don't expect you will."

Tyne shook his head.

"You amaze me, Walt," he said. "You know very well I'm the one man who knows all about your little sect—right down to the fact that it numbers only a little more than sixty thousand members, scattered all over the globe. Yet you keep on insisting to my face that you're about to take over the world. And what would you do with it, once you'd taken it over? You can't run things without the very Complex technologies you claim you intend to destroy."

"Well, now," said Blunt, "there're a lot of different versions of this world of ours, Kirk. You've got one, with your Complexes of equipment—a nice steady-ticking world. The only pity is, it won't stop growing and complicating itself. Then, there's the world of the fanatics, the people who go in for dangerous sports, wild cults, and marching societies. And then again, there's a vague, gauzy world of the spiritually inclined, and the world of the asymbolic pioneers, artist and scientist. There's the world of those to whom tradition and an anchored existence are the only worthwhile basis for life. There's even the world of the psychotics, the neurotically crippled."

"You talk," said Tyne, "as if these other . . . attitudes, had an equal value with normal civilized society."

"But they have, Kirk, they have," said Blunt, looming over the smaller man. "Ask anyone who belongs to one of them. Don't look at me, man. This is your world—the world you boys made out of the industrial revolution three hundred years ago. To put it somewhat crudely, if this here's heaven, how come we still got stomachaches?"

"We got stomachaches," said Tyne, stepping a little aside toward his elevator tubes. "But we also got doctors to physic 'em. Which we didn't always have before. If you'll excuse me, Walt, I want to get upstairs to the chess matches. Are you coming back up?"

"Right away," said Blunt. Tyne stepped onto a disk floating up the tube beside him, with one foot. The disk checked itself. "And how's Mrs. Tyne been?" asked Blunt.

"Excellent," said Tyne. He stepped completely onto the disk and was borne upward out of sight.

Blunt turned, stepped through the open door of the down tube onto a descending disk, and disappeared himself.

Paul came out from the shadow, still looking toward the elevators where the two men had stood. They were gone now, but Blunt's stick was still leaning where he had placed it before shaking hands with Tyne. Paul remembered abruptly how Blunt had stood, half-turned away from the alcove. It came to Paul that he had never got a square look at the head of the Chantry Guild. Before, this had been only a minor omission in the back of his mind. But suddenly it moved to the forefront.

Paul was suddenly conscious of something that most of the time he merely took for granted. That for him to meet someone was automatically to gain a great deal of insight into them. And Blunt was an enigma. But an enigma with whom Paul's life had become considerably entangled. With Blunt, as with the Guild itself, there seemed to be considerably more going on than met the eye. Deciding, Paul strode out from his alcove, down to the elevators, and picked up the stick. Blunt could hardly avoid facing the man who returned his walking stick to him in person.

Paul came back to suite 2309, the main entrance this time, the one through which he had seen Tyne leave. He pressed the door button. It was unlocked and opened at his touch. He stepped inside, closing the door behind him, and found himself in the sitting room of the suite, and facing the man he had seen drugged and under watch by Butler in the hotel bar, the morning of his leaving.

The sound of the closing door brought the man's head around. He had been half-turned away, blowing his nose on a tissue. At the click of the door's latching, he jerked about to face Paul. And then he went backward across the room, mouthing and stumbling like a creature scared out of all common, ordinary sense, until the high, wide window of the room stopped him.

He stood, trapped and staring, blinking, shivering, pushing against the window as if he could shove himself through it into the twenty-three levels of unblocked air that separated him from the ground level before the hotel.

Paul checked instinctively. And the wave of sick fear emanating from the man crested and broke over Paul like solid ocean surf. Paul stood, momentarily and in spite of himself, stunned. He had never thought a thinking being could go so bad.

The man's eyes flicked and bored into Paul. The eyes themselves were watering, and the nose sniffled uncontrollably. The man's face was gray and rigid. Something mangled whimpered within him.

"It's all right," said Paul. "All right . . ." He came gently toward the man, Blunt's stick tucked under his right arm and the box of capsules in his single hand out-stretched. "Here . . . I'm just bringing you these. . . ."

The man continued to stare and sniffle spasmodically. Paul, now within arm's length of him, laid the box down on a table. As an afterthought, he opened it with two fingers and took out one of the white capsules.

"See?" he said. "Here . . ." He held it out to the man, but the other, either jerkily reaching for it, or jerkily pushing it away, knocked it from Paul's fingers. Automatically, Paul bent to pick it up.

His head was still down when warning rang loud within him. He straightened up suddenly to see the drug addict facing him now, a small handgun black and deadly in one trembling hand. The pinhole of its muzzle wavered at Paul's chest.

"Easy," said Paul. "Easy . . ."

His voice seemed not even to reach the ears of the other man. The drug addict stepped forward and Paul automatically stepped back.

"It sent you," said the man, hoarsely. "It sent you."

"Nothing sent me," said Paul. "I came to bring you that box on the table. There it is." He nodded toward it.

The man did not look at it. Moving out into the room, he began to circle Paul, while keeping gun and eyes aimed at Paul.

"I'm going to kill you," he said. "You think I won't kill you, but I will."

"Why?" asked Paul. And that monosyllable, he thought, should at least have made the other pause, but again it seemed the drug addict did not even hear him.

"It sent you to kill me," said the man. "It can't kill. It isn't built to allow itself to kill. But it can fix things so some other factor does the dirty work."

"I don't want to hurt you," said Paul.

"It's no use," said the man. Paul could sense the will to pull the trigger accumulating in the mind opposite him. The man's back began to straighten with something like pride. "I understand, you see. I know all about it."

The man was almost between Paul and the room's entrance, now. He was at a distance of about eight feet, out of arm's reach. Paul made a move to step toward him and the tiny muzzle of the gun came up sharply.

"No, no!" said the man. "*No!*"

Paul stopped. He became conscious suddenly of the hard roundness of Blunt's walking stick under his arm. It was a good three feet in length. Paul began to let the stick slip down into his hand.

"Just a little," said the man. "Just a moment more . . . It thought you'd find me alone here. It didn't know I had a gun. When you steal something, there's no way for it to know. No record—*what're you doing?*"

The last three words came out in a scream, as the man noticed the end of the walking stick slide into Paul's hand. The pinhole muzzle leaped up and forward. Paul jumped aside and forward. There was no time to throw the stick as he had planned. He saw the man swinging to bring the gun's aim upon him. The other was close.

"*Now!*" screamed the man. The walking stick leaped in Paul's grasp and he felt it connect solidly. The man fell away from him.

The man fell and rolled over on his back on the carpet. The small gun tumbled foolishly out of his hand. He lay, looking in terrified accusation at the ceiling.

Still holding the walking stick, Paul stepped forward. He stared down at the drug addict. The man lay still. His bloodshot eyes did not focus upon Paul. Paul lifted the stick in his hand and stared at it. The dark wood was dented and splintered a little but in no way broken or weakened. Paul looked back down at the man on the floor, letting the heavy weight of his unnaturally muscled right arm, holding the stick, drop limply at his side.

Among the sparse black hair on the man's skull, the blood was beginning to flow, slowly and darkly. Paul felt emptiness inside him, as if he had deeply inhaled on nothingness. The broken skull looked as if it had been stricken almost in two by some heavy sword.

Chapter 8

The man's dead, thought Paul. He took a deep, shuddering breath, but the emptiness inside him did not go away. *Why don't I feel anything more than this?*

Once he would have expected an answer from the unconquerable element back in the depths of his mind. But with the overgrowth of his right arm, and the decision in the psychiatrist's office, that part of him seemed to have melted into the rest of his consciousness. He was all of one piece now. Still, he could almost imagine he heard the ghost of a whisper replying to his thought.

Death, it whispered, *is a factor also.*

The stick was still poised in his hand. Paul opened his hand about it and a small object fell onto the carpet. He bent and picked it up. It was the capsule he had offered the dead man, flattened and bent now from being between his palm and the walking stick. He put it in his pocket. Swiftly he turned and went out of the suite.

He closed the door behind him and was halfway to the same elevator tubes which Tyne and Blunt had taken, when his mind started working sensibly again. He stopped dead.

Why should he run, he asked himself? He had only acted in self-defense on being attacked by what amounted to an insane man waving a gun. Paul went back into 2309 and used the phone there to call the hotel's security office.

The office answered without lighting up the vision tank. A voice spoke to him from out of blank grayness.

"Who is calling, please?"

"Suite 2309. But I'm not a guest of the hotel. I want to report——"

"One minute, please."

There was a moment of silence. The tank still did not light up. Then suddenly it cleared and Paul found himself looking into the neat, expressionless features of James Butler.

"Mr. Formain," said Butler. "I was informed twenty-eight minutes ago that you had entered the hotel by the plaza entrance."

"I was bringing something——"

"So we assumed," said Butler. "As a matter of routine, our hall monitor cameras are lighted to follow nonguests under conditions when we haven't been notified of their visit in advance. Is the occupant of suite 2309 with you now, Mr. Formain?"

"Yes," said Paul. "But I'm afraid there's been an accident here."

"Accident?" Butler's voice and expression stayed invariable.

"The man I met here threatened me with a gun." Paul hesitated. "He's dead."

"Dead?" asked Butler. For a second he merely looked at Paul. "You must be mistaken about the gun, Mr. Formain. We have a complete file and check on the occupant of 2309. He did not own a gun."

"No. He told me he stole it."

"I don't mean to argue with you, Mr. Formain. But I must inform you that in accordance with police regulations this conversation is being irreversibly recorded."

"Recorded!" Paul stared into the tank.

"Yes, Mr. Formain. You see, we happen to know that it would have been impossible for the resident in 2309 to steal any kind of weapon. He has been under constant surveillance by our staff."

"Well, your staff slipped up!"

"I'm afraid that's impossible, too. The only way a gun could have entered the suite where you are now would have been if you had carried it in yourself."

"Just a minute." Paul leaned down toward the tank. "Mr. Kirk Tyne, the World Complex Engineer, was here just before I came."

"Mr. Tyne," said Butler, "left the North Tower lobby at 14:09 by up tube on the elevators and arrived at the chess tournament on the sixtieth level at 14:10. Our hall monitors show no one entering 2309 in the past six hours but you. Accordingly . . ."

The barest flicker of Butler's eyes to the side woke Paul suddenly to the nearness of the trap into which he was sliding. The hotel security agent was no mean hypnotist himself. The dead monotony of his voice, the expressionless face that classed all things with the dull unimportance of a lost hotel key or misdirected luggage, would have been lethal against anyone who lacked Paul's inherent immunity.

Without waiting even to shut off the phone Paul moved, letting his reflexes take over. He was at the door and through it into the hall before Butler had time to stop talking. The hall outside was empty.

Moving swiftly, Paul turned from the elevators and raced down the hall to a heavy fire door. He pulled it open and passed through into the concrete shaft of a stairway. He found himself on a small landing with steps leading up from one end and down from another. The edge of another fire door recessed in its slot in the wall stood level with the first step of the down flight of steps.

Paul ran down the stairs. He was quiet about it, but the stair shaft itself was as silent as something that had been sealed for eternity. He made four floors without a hint of danger. Then, when he reached the landing of the fifth level below where he had started, he saw the staircase fire door closed, barring further progress.

He turned to the door leading out into the hallway of that level and went through it, onto soft carpeting.

"Mr. Formain?" asked a polite voice in his ear. "If you'll just come . . ."

A security agent, a young man by his voice, had been standing back by the side of the door where the latch was, his back to the wall alongside and waiting for Paul to come out. As Paul stepped through, the agent spoke and stepped forward to take hold of him. Paul felt the left hand of the other man expertly seeking the twin nerves just above his elbow and the man's right reaching out to catch his thumb and bend it back wrist-ward in that unobtrusive hold long familiar to police people, known as the "comealong."

The searching hands of the security man failed of their mark, for no fault of the man himself, but for two reasons he could not have expected. The first was that his pinching left hand missed its mark completely, the seeking thumb and middle finger not finding the nervepoints they sought since they were hidden under the greatly overdeveloped muscles of Paul's arm, just above the elbow. The second was that Paul was no longer thinking his reactions out in conscious terms, but in this emergency abandoning himself to that invulnerable part of him that had earlier claimed his overdeveloped arm as its own. So, what actually happened was that even as the security man reached out to take him prisoner, even as he felt the man's hands upon him, Paul was already in movement.

At the other's touch, all in a split second, he checked, balanced, moved a fraction of an inch to the right, and drove the point of his elbow backward with all the natural strength of his arm.

It was a move executed with a hesitationless smoothness and accuracy that would have made it lethal against a trained fighter. It was aimed to be lethal. The elbow-point was fired with impossible accuracy into the unprotected area just below the man's breastbone, and driving upward. It would have torn lungs, crushed arteries, and possibly burst the heart. The only reason it did not do so, and did not kill, was that at the last split second Paul realized what was about to happen and managed to slightly deflect the aim.

Still, it lifted the man and slammed him back against the hallway wall, from which he fell forward and lay on his side, eyes half showing under fallen lids, legs a little drawn up and twitching with little spasmodic movements. Even as it was, he had been severely damaged.

And so almost, it seemed, had Paul.

It was nearly as if the blow he had just struck had recoiled on him with most of its original force. He doubled up as if he had been the target. A washback of emotion shuddered through his whole body, and he staggered blindly down the hall, dizzy, nauseated, half-blinded, and bent over. Still moving, however, he got himself under control. Somehow he sought for and found the control in him that was necessary, and it was like pushing a button. So swiftly that it almost seemed he had never felt it, the reaction vanished from him and he straightened up.

He found himself now at the end of the hall, by more tall, curtained windows. The elevator tubes were close and there was no place else to go. He remembered that in case of trouble he was to seek out Kantele on the sixtieth level, and he stepped onto a disk floating up the up tube.

It carried him up with it. Over his head the bottom of the immediately superior disk closed him off into a little tube-shaped enclosure of which the bottom was his own disk, with him filling the tube. For the moment he was safe. Looking out through the transparent wall of the tube, he saw the various levels dropping past him, but though he saw occasional figures in the halls and standing by the tubes, none of them seemed to pay any special attention to him.

If the hotel security men were waiting for him anywhere, he thought, it would be at the roof-garden top of the hotel where the small-craft landing pad was. But that was thirty levels above the floor where he intended to get off.

He was at the fifty-eighth level now. He moved forward to the edge of the disk, and as the sixtieth level approached, he stepped off.

He stepped almost immediately into a hallway crowd of people coming and going, and standing around in small, talkative groups. He pushed his way through them and stepped into the first entrance to a banquet room he found. Within were tables at which chess matches were going on, here and there with a few watchers clustered around some special pair of players. Kantele was not in view. He left the room and went on.

In the third room he visited he found Kantele. She was with several other people who were watching an individual match across the room from the entrance, and not too far from the French windows which indicated an outside balcony or terrace beyond the banquet room. She was standing behind the chair of a man who, with a sudden quickening of his pulse, Paul recognized to be Blunt. Blunt sat leaning forward, absorbed in the condition of the board he was observing, and Kantele stood with one hand on his wide shoulder.

It occurred to Paul that he was going to have the chance of facing Blunt sooner than he had expected. He started toward the table where Blunt and Kantele watched, and abruptly stopped.

He no longer had the walking stick.

Paul stood still, and for a second the hum and movement of the room faded almost out of his consciousness. His hand was empty. But he could not remember either dropping the stick or laying it aside. All that occurred to him was that he must have let go of it in the reaction that followed his elbow-jabbing of the security man. Well, if that was the case, Blunt might have something to explain to the police—and then he might not. It might be that, as in the case of Tyne's visit to 2309, hotel security would, on finding the stick, politely cover up for him.

At any rate, Paul intended to face the Chantry Guild head *now*. Paul went forward again.

But he was already too late. Kantele, he found, had already looked up and seen him. Her face unnaturally expressionless, she shook her head at his advance and then gestured with a nod at the French windows. Paul hesitated for a second, then turned and obeyed.

He passed the tables and stepped through one of the French windows, closing it behind him. He found himself, as he had expected, on a long and fairly narrow terrace with a waist-high parapet of ornamental stone around it. Beyond the parapet he could see the rooftops of lower surrounding buildings, and beyond them the farther levels of Chicago Complex. The afternoon had turned out to be almost cloudless, and the bright sun lanced warmly across the white, round tables and translucent, single-legged chairs on the terrace. He walked to the parapet and looked over.

Below him the side of the Koh-i-Nor's North Tower fell sheer in an unbroken pattern of alternate window glass and marbled tile to the top level of commuter traffic, sixty stories below. Postage-stamp-size directly underneath him was the main concourse in front of the tower, and, a narrow two hundred yards away across it, some sort of office building with a single aircar on its landing pad, and the highly-polished surface of the building's construction tile reflecting the utter blue of the sky.

He turned back from the parapet. On the white table top nearly beside him was a brightly-illustrated throw-away magazine left by some earlier visitor to the terrace. The breeze across the terrace ruffled and tried to turn its pages. He glanced at the titles in colorful type on its cover. The lead one jumped at him.

WAS GANDHI'S WAY RIGHT?

And under this, in slightly less bold print:

The Psychotics of Our Overcrowded Cities

The author of this later article, he noticed with interest, was the same Dr. Elizabeth Williams, psychiatrist, he had encountered only the week before.

He reached for the magazine to turn to the article.

"Formain," said a voice. He looked up and turned.

Facing him from about fifteen feet away, his hand on the half-open French door through which he must just have stepped out onto the terrace, was Butler. The small hotel security man stood with one hand thrust into the right pocket of his barrel-cut jacket. His face was as polite as ever.

"You better come along quietly with me, Formain," he said.

Paul let go of the magazine. The fingers of his single hand flexed reflexively. He took a casual step in Butler's direction.

"Stop there," said Butler. He took his hand out of his pocket, revealing a small finger gun. Paul stopped.

"Don't be foolish," said Paul.

Butler looked at him with the closet approach to a flicker of emotion in his face that Paul had yet seen.

"I think that's my line," Butler said. "Don't be foolish, Formain. Come along quietly."

Paul looked across the short distance separating them. His first impulse, as it had been with the agent in the hallway, had been to go into action. He had checked that. And now a part of him waited critically to see what the other part of him might do. He looked at Butler, trying to narrow down his mental field of vision. Trying to see the man as something individual, unique, limited by the forces that tied him into his environment, by the very elements that made him dangerous.

Anyone can be understood, Paul told himself. Anyone.

For a second, Butler's image seemed to swim in Paul's retina with the effort Paul was making, like a figure seen through the bottom of a drinking glass. Then the image cleared.

"I don't intend to be foolish," said Paul. He sat down on the edge of the table beside him. "I'm not going with you."

"Yes," said Butler. He held the finger gun steady.

"No," said Paul. "If you take me in, I'll tell the police that you were the source of supply for the drugs of the man in 2309. I'll tell them you used to be a drug addict yourself."

Butler gave a small, tired sigh.

"Come along, Formain," he said.

"No," said Paul. "To take me, you'll have to shoot me first. If you kill me, there's bound to be the kind of investigation you don't want. If you do less than kill me, I'll tell them what I just told you I'd say."

There was a moment's silence on the terrace. While it lasted, they could both hear the leaves of the magazine rustling in the breeze.

"I am not a drug addict," said Butler.

"No," said Paul. "But you were until some fanaticism, some particular blind faith gave you the strength to kick the habit. You're not afraid of the fact being found out so much as the fact that an investigation into the fact would cause you to be cut off from this source of strength. If I mention it, the police will have to investigate the matter. So, you're going to let me go."

Butler regarded him. The security man's expression was as unreadable as ever, but the finger gun jerked for a second as his hand trembled momentarily. He hid the hand back in the pocket of his jacket.

"Who told you?" he asked.

"You did," said Paul. "Being the sort of man you are, the rest had to follow."

Butler watched him for a second more, then turned toward the French door behind him.

"Someday I'll make you tell me who told you," he said, and went back into the banquet rooms where the chessmen were at war.

The French door had barely closed behind him when one of the other doors opened and Kantele stepped through, quickly closing the door behind her. She came quickly over to Paul, her fine-cut features pale and her lips a little compressed above the square blue shoulders of her tailored jacket and the tooled-leather strap of the heavy handbag cutting into one of them.

"How did you—no, don't tell me," she corrected herself as she met him. "There isn't time. There are a dozen more hotel men going through the banquet rooms. Here . . ."

She lifted her large handbag onto one of the tables and pressed it at certain points. It opened out like a slow-motion jack-in-the-box. It was a one-man parachute copter, of the emergency type used by aircraft and fire departments. She unbuckled the straps that would fit around his shoulders and helped him into it.

"As long as the air-traffic police don't spot you, you'll be all right," she said, tightening the straps upon him. "Head for the rooftop of that building opposite."

The sound of one of the French doors opening made them both turn. It flew open, smashing against one of the tables, and two men catapulted onto the terrace, drawing guns from their jackets.

Paul did not hesitate. With one sweep of his powerful arm he snatched up the table alongside and threw it, as if it had been a balsawood mock-up of itself, at the two charging men.

They dodged, but not quickly enough. They went down before it. And Paul, sweeping Kantele up in his grasp, took one long step to the top of the parapet, and another off into sixty levels of emptiness.

Chapter 9

They fell like a stone, while Paul's hand, restricted by the fact that his arm must keep its hold on Kantele, fumbled with the controls of the parachute copter. He located them finally and switched them on, and suddenly it was like a heavy brake being applied against the force of gravity as the spinning blades blurred into action to break their fall.

"I'm sorry," he said to Kantele. "But they'd seen you with me. I couldn't leave you behind to face the music."

She did not answer. Her head lay back and sideways against his shoulder and her eyes were closed. Her face was like the face of someone who has surrendered completely to some superior force.

Paul turned his attention to guiding the copter toward the building across the concourse from the hotel. He was only partially successful. The copter, powerful enough to handle a two-hundred-and-fifty-pound individual, was fighting a losing battle in trying to uphold the combined weights of a man and woman both well above the average in size. They were drifting off and down at a long slant, the way the winged seed of a maple tree flutters to earth in fall winds.

"The rooftop, you said?" asked Paul. Her eyes remained closed. He joggled her a little. "Kantele!"

She opened her eyes, slowly.

"Yes," she said. "What's that noise?"

There were faint, piping noises around them. Looking back over his shoulder, Paul saw the two men he had bowled over with the table, leaning on the parapet with their forearms, almost casually. But the fists of both held dark objects. They were shooting at Paul and Kantele.

The anesthetic slivers of metal which were the missiles of their weapons could not be too accurate at the present and steadily increasing range. Air police were the greater danger. Paul fingered the controls and they rotated slowly through a hundred-and-eighty-degree angle.

To the north of them and about five hundred feet up, were two specks approaching rapidly. Kantele saw them as Paul did, but she said nothing.

"And after we land on the roof, what?" asked Paul. He looked down into her face. She had closed her eyes again.

"Jase is waiting, on the floor below." She answered almost dreamily, and her head was back against his shoulder again.

"The floor below?" Paul was puzzled and nearly provoked by her. She seemed to have given the matter completely over into his hands. "We haven't time for the roof. I'll try for a window."

"If he has it open," she said dreamily, without opening her eyes.

He understood what she meant. They were falling swiftly, even though at a slant. If Jason Warren did not see them coming and get the window open in time, they would most certainly smash themselves against the unbreakable glass, bending their copter blades and ending on an unchecked drop to the traffic level thirty or forty stories below. There would be no hope for them.

"He'll have it open," said Paul. She did not disagree.

The police cars were swelling in size visibly with the swiftness of their approach. But the building before them was close now, too. Looking down, Paul suddenly saw one of the top level's larger windows slide back.

He angled the copter toward it.

For a moment he thought that he would be falling too rapidly to make it over the open sill. Then it leaped up before him. He jammed the controls on to full braking power, ready to burn the copter's small motor out now that it had served its purpose.

The last burst of effort from the device saved them. The copter shot them through the window, checked itself in the midst of its own suddenly enclosed hurricane, and froze its bearings with an ear-splitting screech. Paul and Kantele dropped less than three inches to land on their feet, upright upon an office floor.

The hurricane with its floating documents and light objects blew itself suddenly out, and the Necromancer came toward the two of them from a far corner of the room. Kantele opened her eyes and looked about her; then, suddenly stiffening, pushed herself almost violently away from Paul and, turning her back, walked several steps from him until a desk blocked her path. Paul looked after her, frowning.

"Get that copter off," said Warren. But Paul was already shrugging out of the straps. The piece of ruined equipment fell heavily to the floor.

"Well, Jase?" asked Paul. The minute he had said it the name sounded oddly on his tongue. For the first time he realized that he had always thought of the Necromancer in terms of his last name. That he had called him by the name everybody else who knew him used, was like cracking a barrier. He saw the other man glance at him for a moment, oddly.

"We're located, now," said the man called Jase. "We're probably surrounded already. We'll have to take another way out with you."

"Why bother?" asked Paul. Jase looked at him again, oddly.

"We take care of our own people, of course," Jase said.

"Am I one?" asked Paul.

The Necromancer stopped dead and looked at him.

"Don't you want to be?" he asked. He nodded toward the door of the office. He added, dryly, "If you want to walk out there, I won't stop you."

"No," said Paul, and to his own surprise found himself smiling a little sadly, "no, I'm one of you, all right."

"Good." Jase turned briskly to a desk and swept it clean of papers, desk pad, and office instruments. "Shut the window," he said, and Kantele went across the room to it. As the window closed, Jase lifted a brief case from below the table and opened it.

He took from the brief case a large, hooded, black cloak which, when he put it on and pulled the hood over his head, covered him almost completely. In the shadow of the hood his face lost something of its identity. Kantele had come back to the table. He took also from the brief case what looked like three good-sized cones of incense, and lighted them. They immediately began to pour forth a dense, heavy smoke which quickly started to obscure the room. The smoke, to Paul's senses, had a sweet, almost cloying smell and evidently something narcotic about it, for he felt himself getting light-headed with the first few inhalations.

They were all standing close around the desk. The room was a fog of dark smoke now, in which Paul's drugged senses were already having difficulty focusing on nearby objects. Across the desk from him the Necromancer's voice came suddenly, deeper-toned than ordinary, measured, chanting. . . .

"This ae nighte, this ae nighte, everie night and alle . . ."

Kantele's voice, from another quarter of the table, chimed in. And what had been pure doggerel recital from Jase's lips acquired a touch of music with the addition of her voice.

"Fire and sleete and candlelight, destruction take thee alle,"

The Necromancer produced one more item and put it on the desk. At the sight of it Paul's mind went suddenly white with an awareness of danger. He would have been a poor sort of mining engineer not to have recognized it. What Jase had just put on the table was a cotton block of blasting jelly two inches on a side, enough to reduce the office and everyone within it to uncollectable fragments. It was topped with no more than a ninety-second fuse, and as Paul peered through the gathering smoke, the Necromancer pinched the fuse and started it burning.

Jase chanted alone:

"If from hence away thou'rt past"

And Kantele's voice joined him in chorus:

"Everie nighte and alle . . ."

"To Whinny-muir thou comest at last," Jase chanted alone.

"Destruction take thee alle," Kantele joined again.

He should not have recognized what they were chanting, but it happened that Paul did. From where or how it came to him, he could not in that smoke-fogged moment remember. But it was a somewhat changed version of one of the old north-of-England corpse chants, sung at wakes with the corpse under the table and a dish of salt on its breast. It was a ritual with its roots going back beyond Christianity to the ancient Celts, to a time when small dark men crept together in the forests to sing their dead kinsman on his road of shadows, in the first nights after his departure. And the version Paul heard now had none of the solemn music of its seventeenth-century shape, but was nearly back to the harsh atonal chant of the original primitive, cold as winter stones and unsparing as the wind across them. On it went, with Jase speaking alone and then Kantele joining in the chorus. It was a "lyke-wake dirge":

> "If ever thou gavest roof and flame,
>   *Everie nighte and alle . . .*
>   Pass thee by the standing stane,
>   *Destruction take thee alle.*

> "The standing stane, when thou art past,
>   *Everie nighte and alle . . .*
>   To empty airt thou comest fast,
>   *Destruction take thee alle.*

> "If ever thou feddest fish or fowl,
>   *Everie nighte and . . ."*

Distantly, through the chanting and the swirling smoke, came the sound of a loud-speaker from beyond the closed window.

"Formain! Paul Formain! This is the police. We have you completely surrounded. If you do not come out within two minutes, and those with you, we will force an entrance." There was a momentary pause, and then the speaker once more rattled the window. "Formain! Paul Formain. This is the police. We have you. . . ."

Meanwhile, in the office the smoke was now so thick that even the cotton block of blasting jelly and its rapidly diminishing fuse was hidden from Paul's eyes. He seemed to hear the chanting of Jase and Kantele mounting in volume:

> "From empty airt when thou'rt past
> *Everie nighte and alle . . .*
> To Alleman's Ende thou comest at last,
> *Destruction take thee alle.*"

Something was happening now. The fuse was shortening fast. A pressure was building up about the three of them and the desk between them. Paul felt a sudden deep-moving urge to join with Kantele in the chorus of the chant. He heard the fuse fizzing. A part of him shouted that in seconds he would be blown to pieces. But another part watched, detached and curious, and checked the chant in him before it reached his lips.

> "And if thou holdest to any thinge
> *Everie nighte and alle . . .*
> The Ende thou canst not enter in,
> *Destruction take thee alle.*"

Jase's and Kantele's voices were all around Paul now, like a loop of rope holding them all together and drawing tighter. The fuse must be all burned down now.

> "But if thou guardest nae thing at all,
> *Everie nighte and alle . . .*
> To Alleman's Ende thou'lt passe and falle
> *And Destruction'll take thee alle!*"

Suddenly, Jase and Kantele were gone, and almost in the same fraction of a second the world lighted up around Paul and he felt the sudden slam of enormous pressure against him, as if he were a fly clapped between two giant hands. He was aware, for one tiny moment of perception, of the office flying to pieces around him as the blasting jelly exploded, and then he himself seemed to fly off into nothingness.

Book Two: **SET**

By stony staircase, hall, and pier,
Those shadows mazed around me there,
Wove doubt on doubt, and—fools!—broke out
That part in me that feared no doubt.

THE ENCHANTED TOWER

Chapter 10

With the situation fully and correctly understood, it becomes entirely reasonable that the very small fraction of a second preceding a violent death could be a trigger to speculative thought.

Ninety-three years after Paul was caught by the explosion of the block of blasting jelly, the phenomenon of *no-time*—that is, of a state of existence in which time is lacking—was finally and fully explained. It had been made use of, of course, even by people preceding the Chantry Guild. On a hit-and-miss basis. But with the development of the phase-shift form of transportation that permitted the interstellar expansion of the human race, it became necessary to understand the a-time state which was basic to the phase shift. Briefly and crudely, the explanation was that there is a reciprocal relationship between time and position. And if time becomes nonexistent (perhaps *nonoperative* would be a better word) then the choice of position becomes infinite.

There are, of course, practical difficulties limiting the use of this, which arise when the problem of exactly calculating the desired position arises. But that has been explained in a different place.* Once more, in the future and again in a different place, the problem of no-time will be entered into once again when the philosophical aspects of it become relevant. But for now, to return once more to the historical moment of the exploding blasting-jelly cube, the important thing is that for vulgar practical purposes, no-time can be taken merely to mean sufficient, uncounted time.

No one—literally, *no one*—is immune to error. It had been an error for Paul to linger behind Jase and Kantele in their departure and

*Dorsai!—Commander-in-Chief II

be caught by the first edge of the explosion. Having been caught, there was only one way out. He went instinctively into no-time to escape being destroyed, as lesser individuals have done before him. Nearly everyone has heard of the authenticated instance of the man who walked around the horses of his coach into nonexistence, and there are many others.

In no-time he remained conscious, and was triggered into a sudden awareness that since the original boating accident, at no time had he ever been without some element of awareness. Even his sleep had been given over either to periods of asymbolic thought on the subconscious level or to dreams. And his dreams, in fact, seemed a fine mill in the complex of his mental machinery. A mill which took the results of the crude data that had been mined from the solid substances of his day-time surroundings by the tools of his senses, then rough-crushed by the intellectual upper processes of his intelligence, and now were ground to fine powders and begun on the obscurer process that would separate out the pure valuable elements of comprehension.

Other than this he did not approach any letting go of his awareness. It had occurred to him that this might be the basic cause of his un-yielding refusal to accept hypnosis. But this explanation failed to com-pletely satisfy him in that area of his perception in which he was most sensitive—it did not *feel* like the complete answer. If the recognizable processes by which he attempted to understand and control his envi-ronment could be compared to the mechanical, this last could be best compared to something chemical. And this was so powerful and ef-fective a tool in its own way that for practical purposes it blinded him to the common channels of reasoning. It was extremely difficult for him to add two and two and get four. It was exceedingly simple and natural for him to contemplate two by itself, as an isolated element, and find four as an implied, characteristic possibility of it.

He looked out on all existence through a window that revealed only unique elements. He approached everything in terms of isolates. Isolates and their implied possibilities of characteristics. All time, for example, was implied in any single moment that he might choose to examine. But the moment itself was unique and unalterably separated from any other moment, even though the other moment also implied all of time.

It followed that it was almost impossible for him to be tricked or lied to. Any falsity palmed off on him almost immediately collapsed like fraudulently understrength construction under the natural weight of its own proliferating possibilities. It also followed, and this was not always an advantage, that he was almost impossible to surprise. Any turn of events, being implied in the moment preceding its taking place, seemed perfectly natural to him. As a result he did not question a great many things that he might normally have been expected to question.

He had not, therefore, questioned the abilities the Chantry members seemed to claim for themselves. It had seemed—to this part of him, at least—quite reasonable that Jase and Kantele should attempt to make their escape with him by means of narcotic smoke, archaic corpse chant, and a block of blasting jelly with a short fuse. He had, however, allowed himself to get so interested in what was going on that he found himself left behind and caught in the first microsecond of the explosion.

He was driven out to the very edges of his consciousness, but no farther. He was aware of himself moving very swiftly and at the same time being driven by the explosion away down into the impossibly tiny end of something like an enormous funnel. He flew through this into all but complete unconsciousness, fighting for survival. He was an infinity of fathoms deep in darkness, but somewhere above him was light and life.

He came up, fighting.

His mind was quicker to react to full consciousness again than his body. He woke to find himself plunging clear across some sort of small, bare room with a circular, raised stage in the center of it, and carrying four men along with him as they attempted to restrain him. He was headed for the door to the room.

He checked, understanding. And, after a second, the men holding on to him let go. As they cleared away from in front of him, Paul caught sight of himself in the mirror surface of a far wall. His clothes were torn, apparently by the explosion, and his nose was bleeding slightly. He got a handkerchief tissue from his pocket and wiped the blood away from his upper lip. The nose stopped bleeding. Jase and Kantele watched him from across the room.

"I don't understand this," said one of the men who had been holding him, a small, brisk-looking man with a shock of brown hair over a sharp-featured face. He looked at Paul almost challengingly. "How did you get here? If Jase brought you, why didn't you come with Jase?"

Paul frowned.

"I seem to have been a little slow," he said.

"Never mind," spoke up Jase from across the room. "If you're all right now, Paul, come on."

He led the way out of the room, Kantele following with a momentary, troubled glance in Paul's direction. Paul went after them.

He caught up with them in a hall outside the room. It was a blank wall without windows, and it led them up an incline until they stepped suddenly around a corner and emerged into open air. Paul looked curiously around himself. They had emerged onto a vast field spotted with the raised white concrete pads from which space-going vehicles fitted with their great collars of lifting equipment took off. Beyond were the snow-topped peaks of a mountain range Paul did not recognize.

It was no commercial field. The uniformity of the constructions about the field and the khaki coveralls of the personnel about spoke clearly to the effect that this was a government installation.

"Where are we?" asked Paul. But Jase was already striding away with Kantele to a pad occupied by the squat, almost bulbous shape of an outer-space vessel looking like an ancient artillery shell many times enlarged, and fitted with its spreading soup-plate collar of atmosphere engines, ducted fans in the outer ring, ram-jets in toward the center. Paul caught up with Jase and Kantele.

"Where are we?" he asked again.

"Tell you after we're aboard," said Jase economically. They walked along together, Jase staring straight ahead toward the ship, his face like a knife edge, Kantele with her wordless gaze down and ahead, so that she looked at the treated gravel surface of the field on which no green grew, just before her as she walked. Paul felt a sudden small rush of sorrow that human beings should be so locked away and separate in their body and mind, so bound to different wheels. And, with a sudden soundless shock, it occurred to him that out of all the real universe the one class of isolates who strove and threatened to burst the bounds of their separateness was people.

This realization, simple as it appeared in bald statement, exploded in Paul like a pan of flash powder set off before a man in a vast and complex city, standing lightless under the stars. It blinded, rather than illuminated, but its light left an afterimage printed on the retinas of the explorer in the dark, and would be permanently remembered. With his mind washed clean of other matters for the moment, Paul walked automatically into the base tunnel of the take-off pad, rode the elevator up through pad and collar, and paid little attention to anything until the whine of the outer ring of fans began to impinge on his consciousness. He came back to present awareness to see that he was seated in a convertible acceleration couch-chair, in a passenger compartment of the ship. In front of him he could see the black top of Jase's head just showing above the top cushion of the next couch-chair, and across the aisle from Jase, up against the rounded wall enclosing the elevator-tunnel running up the center of the ship, he saw the profile of Kantele.

The ship lifted. After a little the sound of the fans was drowned out in the beginning thunder of the jets, which mounted the ladder of volume into silence. A little after that, the viewing tank in the wall beside Paul lighted up, and, looking into this illusion of a window, he saw the lifting collar of atmosphere engines, their earth-bound clumsiness all left behind, fall away gracefully like some enormous soaring bird toward the cloud-laced earth far below.

"Couchback, all passengers," announced a speaker system somewhere above Paul's head. "All passengers, couchback now."

The chairs tilted and leveled into horizontal position. Deep cushioning buffers moved in about his body. There was a moment of silence and then the space engines fired, and their mighty thrust threw the blunt body of the ship, with Kantele, and Jase, and Paul, and all within it, out between the stars.

Mercury, Paul discovered, was a five-day run. The ship had four cross levels between the pilot room in the nose and the engines in the rear. The passengers were restricted to two of them. Evidently because it was government procedure, they were required to take mild sedatives during the actual flight. These made Kantele and three other passengers whom Paul did not know sleepy. They spent most of their time dozing with their couch-chairs in a reclining position. Jase had disappeared early up into the crew's section and Paul had not seen him after that for the first four days of the run. Since Kantele seemed to reinforce the effect of her sedatives with an obvious disinclination to have anything to do with Paul, once more that left Paul solitary.

To Paul's unusual set of mental and physical reactions, the sedatives brought a bodily lethargy, but an increase in mental speculation and introspection. Jase had escaped early before Paul could question him again, but a tall, stiff-backed man, in the seat behind Paul and across the aisle which with the two rows of seats circled the central elevator shaft, had replied to Paul's question.

"Operation Springboard," he had said sharply. He stared almost fiercely at Paul out of middle-aged eyes above a neat white mustache that contrasted with the brown tan of his face. "You know about the project to reach the Arcturian planets, don't you? Apprentice, are you?"

"Yes," said Paul.

"Ask your master, boy! He'll answer you. Who is he? Necromancer Warren?"

Secretly a little amused to be addressed as "boy," a term he had not had used to him since he was fourteen, Paul nodded.

"That's right," he said. "Do you happen to be a Necromancer, too?"

"No, no," said the man. "Sociologist—what they call 'untitled.' Don't have the patience for the rigmarole. But it's fine work for a younger man like yourself to get into." He grew fiercer, suddenly. The white mustache seemed to bristle. "A good work!"

"Necromancy?" asked Paul.

"All of it. All of it. Think of our children . . . and their children."

A man of about the same age as the white-mustached speaker leaned out of a couch-chair farther back on Paul's side of the circular aisle.

"Heber," he said.

"Yes, yes," said the white-mustached man, sinking back into his seat. "You're right, Tom. Don't ask me questions, boy; ask your master. I've got to take my medication now, anyway." He reached into the little compartment in one arm of his chair, and Paul, giving up that avenue of information, turned and sat back in his own place.

He had plenty to occupy his mind. He let his attention go free among it.

It was a type of mental activity having its own element of actual built-in pleasure reward, a pleasure to which, he had lately come to realize, it would be quite possible to become addicted, if it were not for the fact that the basic drive to accomplish forbade too much loitering on the pathway from means to end. It was the sheer pleasure of turning the questioning spirit loose in the great dark city of all personal knowledge. For those who panicked easily in the dark, it was no occupation. But for those without fear and the true night-sight of understanding, there was no pleasure like that of wandering some strange and intricate part of that city, until out of shadow rose shapes, and out of shapes, plan, and out of plan—original purpose. Only then, at last with original purpose encompassed and understood, came—perhaps— the greater occupation of putting that knowledge to work in new building.

So for five days Paul all but lost himself in a new part of his city of knowledge. It was only shortly before landing on Mercury that he was abruptly called back from it, and the one who called him back was Kantele.

"I wasn't going to ask you why," she said. He awoke to the fact that she was standing in the aisle before his seat, looking down at him. "But I just can't. . . . Why did you do it? Why did you have to kill Malorn?"

"Kill who?" asked Paul. For a second she and her question was still mixed in with the shapes of his thoughts. Then the shapes faded and he became aware that they were, at least as far as he could see on this side of the elevator shaft, alone on the level among the couch-chairs.

"Kevin Malorn—the man at the hotel."

"Kevin Malorn," echoed Paul. For a part of a second the only thing that was in his mind was a feeling of unutterable sadness that he should have been the instrument of the man's death and never until now known the name under which other people had known him alive.

"You won't tell me," said Kantele, when he did not answer immediately. He looked up at her pale, set face.

"Yes," he said. "But you probably won't believe me. I didn't kill him. I don't know why he died."

She stared at him for a moment longer, then whirled about and walked off around the elevator tube. Following a little later, he discovered all the other passengers one level up in the lounge, watching in the large tank there the ascent of the landing collar, with chemical engines fueled by native Mercury products, that would carry them safely down to that planet's surface.

Chapter 11

It was a strange tumbled landscape through which they all walked the half mile from the ship to the reception dome of Station Springboard. The sky was white to the right and dark to the left, and cloudless. There was enough of an atmosphere here on the surface of Mercury's twilight zone to scatter the light in this direction. The resulting illumination seen through the face windows of Paul's protective suit was like the yellow glare before a thunderstorm back under the kinder sky of Earth. In this all-pervasive, unchanging light, the terrain appeared to be peopled with the split and damaged fragments of fantastic sculptures. It would be the temperature changes of alternating dark-side and light-side storms that had caused this, and the volcanic action along the line of weakness in Mercury's crust that the Twilight Zone represented. But still it looked like a country out of a dream of unreality, a garden out of a nightmare, set up and despoiled by witches.

They entered the dome and stepped through a lock into an elevator which sank for a quite noticeable distance. Paul guessed that he might now be in the neighborhood of forty to sixty levels underground, for the elevator had been a large mechanical, rather than magnetic, one, and the descent had been uncomfortably swift. As the elevator halted, a further door opened and they passed into a desuiting room.

From the desuiting room they were herded into separate cubicles for what Jase informed Paul were purposes of decontamination. Paul found himself instructed by a wall speaker to strip, pass through a shower area, and a further door where new clothes for him would be waiting.

He did so and came out into another cubicle, this one not much more than an area hacked out of the solid granitic rock. On a concrete bench there a pile of clothing was waiting for him.

He set about putting them on and found them to be of a peculiar style. There were soft leather shoes, pointed at the toe, fawn-colored; what seemed to be long green stockings; shorts; a green smock with a loose belt to cinch it up, and a sort of half-sleeved leather jacket.

It seemed likely to Paul that the Chantry Guild was given to dressing for dinner, so to speak, here on Mercury. He put the clothes on— the left arm of smock and jacket had been designed sleeveless and all the clothes were in his size—and stepped through the further door of the second cubicle.

He checked instinctively.

He had emerged into a single, low-ceilinged room, crudely hollowed out of the rock and lighted by two flaring torches in heavy wall brackets of some metal-like blackened iron. The floor itself was rough-hewed of rock and pressed hard against the soles of his feet through the soft leather of his shoes. Beyond the torches was darkness and he could see no far wall.

He turned quickly, back the way he had come. And stopped. There was no door behind him, through where he had stepped a minute before. He faced more of the hewn-rock wall, only that. He reached out and touched it with his hand. It felt as solid as judgment day.

He turned back to the light of the torches. Between them now, he saw standing the man called Heber, the torchlight sparkling on his white mustache. Unlike Paul, he was clothed in a single scarlet robe and hood. The hood threw a shadow across his forehead and the long sleeves of the robe fell together from his hands, which were joined together before him.

"Come here," said Heber. His lips trembled a second after the last word, as if he could just barely restrain himself from adding "boy!" Paul walked up to him and stopped. Heber was looking past him, the older man's shadowed eyes seeming fantastically deep-socketed in the shadow of the hood.

"I am here to sponsor this apprentice," announced Heber, "to his initiation into the Société Chanterie. It is required that there be two sponsors, one visible and one invisible. Is the other sponsor here?"

"I am," said the voice of Jason Warren, startlingly at Paul's right ear. He turned and saw nothing but the walls of the room. But he could now feel the presence of Jase beside him.

Paul turned back to Heber. The white-mustached man, he saw, was now holding in one arm a heavy, leather-bound, archaic-looking book.

In the other hand he held by the middle a snake about four feet in length, which twisted and writhed.

"To the jurisdiction of the Alternate Laws you have come," said Heber. "To the jurisdiction of the Alternate Laws are you now committed and sealed. And to the jurisdiction of the Alternate Laws will you be bound, for all time past or present, and beyond time until the Alternate Laws cease their effect."

"I witness this," said the voice of Jason, at Paul's shoulder.

"Take then your spear," said Heber. He held out the snake toward Paul's single hand. Paul reached for it, but at the first touch of his fingers around it, it ceased suddenly to move and live. He found himself holding, in fact, a tall wooden spear with a dully gleaming metal point.

"Take then your shield," said Heber, stepping forward with the book. But it was a kite-shaped metal shield, with leather grips riveted to a wooden frame, that he hung from Paul's armless left shoulder by a wide leather strap.

"Now follow me," said Heber. He strode off into the darkness beyond the torches. And Paul, following after, found himself proceeding down slanted tunnels and around corners in the rock until he came finally to a small, square, carved-out room where two more torches burned on either side of what looked like a stone altar, more long than wide. Along the top of the altar were laid out, from left to right, a small toy sailboat with the tiny figure of the toy sailor within it spilled out as the boat lay over on one side, a toy model of the console of a mine, a stained and weathered conch shell, and a three-dimensional snapshot of the head of Malorn, the dead drug addict, showing the broken skull.

Heber and Paul stopped before the altar.

"Let the other sponsor now instruct the apprentice," he said. Jase's voice spoke from Paul's other side. He looked at empty air.

"The apprentice is an apprentice in the art of Necromancy," his voice said. "Therefore we have brought him to the root of the tree. Let the apprentice look."

Paul turned his attention back to the altar. A massive tree root now emerged from the rock and arched out over the objects on the altar, down to his feet and Heber's.

"This," said the voice of Jase, "is the well Hvergelmer, in the realm of death. The root is the first root of the ash, Yggdrasil, which is the tree of life, knowledge, fate, time, and space. During the period of his vigil here, it is the duty of the apprentice to defend it, and the parts of his life which are on the altar. It may be that the apprentice will not be attacked during his time of vigil. But it may be that the dragon Nidhug and his brood will come to gnaw at the root of the tree. If the tree and the parts of his life are attacked, the apprentice may call on the Alternate Forces or not, as he chooses; but if he does not conquer Nidhug, Nidhug will devour him."

Jase ceased speaking. Heber spoke, and Paul turned his head to the white-mustached man.

"The tree," said Heber solemnly, "is an illusion. Life is an illusion. Nidhug and his brood are an illusion, as is all the universe, eternity, and time. Only the Alternate Forces exist, and time, space, and all things within them are merely toys of the Alternate Forces. Know this and know yourself unconquerable."

"You shall keep vigil," put in the sound of the Necromancer's voice, "until the third sounding of the gong. With the third sounding of the gong, you will be freed from the realm of death, back to the world of light and life once more. Now I leave you, until the third ringing of the gong."

Paul felt a void suddenly beside him. He turned instinctively toward Heber. The white-mustached man was still standing beside him.

"I leave now, too," said Heber. "Until the gong rings for the third time." He stepped past Paul, back toward the entrance to the room; and as he did, Paul caught the ghost of a wink from the man's near eye, and a *sotto voce* mutter, "Rigmarole."

Then Heber was gone.

Silence held the room.

It was the silence of the rock where the rock is igneous in nature and far below ground. Here there was no water dripping, only the still cold. Even the torches flared in silence. Paul's breath went out in a frosty plume in that red, dancing light, and vanished with each fresh inhalation.

But he began to become aware.

About him was stone, the mineral flesh of Mercury, in all directions. The rough, cut stone underfoot pressed sharply against his feet, the cold wrapped him like a chilly cloak. The minutes passed in solemn procession, all but identical one with the other. Time piled up in the quiet of the room, the strap of the shield cut into his shoulder and his fingers grew a little cramped around the wooden shaft of the spear. He held it with its butt on the floor, its point elevated, angled a little out from him like a Roman sentry. An hour went by, and then another. And then, perhaps, another. . . .

The solemn, brassy note of a deep gong struck once, reverberated through the entrance to the room, and beat about his ears. It rang away into silence, leaving a memory behind it in the noiselessness of the room until that, too, was buried and smoothed over by the marching minutes.

Paul's mind drifted out to an unconscionable distance. He leaned on his spear, now, and the shield had swung forward with its own weight. He thought of mountains whose stony sides and slopes were constructed of empty space, and of the twinkling illuminations of distant habitations upon the mountain peaks, which were the lights of the farther stars, stars not seen from Earth. A bittersweet emotion of sorrow and desire stirred in him like faint smoke from burning incense. Love and hunger pulled against each other within him. . . .

And then suddenly, distant in the back of his mind, came a chime of warning.

He came back to the stony room. It was as it had been before. The torches still flared upward and his breath smoked peacefully on the still air. But now there was something more. While he had daydreamed, the deep waters of some unseen danger had welled up to the very entrance of the room. It lapped now in the darkness just beyond the reach of his sight. And in those deep waters, there was something stirring.

It was Nidhug and his scaly brood.

They were not real. They were an illusion, as was the deep mass of waters making a beleaguered island of this room. Paul recognized this with a sure and certain swiftness. Those minds among the Chantry Guild who were capable of such tricks were flooding the solid (but to these productions of their minds, transparent) rock with the emanations of fear, pictured as heavy, secret waters. And through the fear, in the guise of a monstrous, scaly worm and its litter, they were now lifting the image of self-doubt. These things were fantasies, but nonetheless dangerous. Fear can be a deadly danger to the mind, and self-doubt can cause an organism to destroy itself, as Paul knew. Knowledge could be a shield and wisdom a weapon, but it took something uniquely human to use them.

He braced himself. The rising tide of fear was already flooding into the room. If he allowed his senses to yield to the fantasy, he could see it, like a gray, quicksilver tide, pushing its sullen rivulets into this and that small indentation in the rough floor. Nidhug and his children were very close.

The gong rang for a second time.

The waters crested suddenly, swirling into the room. They mounted up to his knees, surged to his waist, and in seconds eddied about his throat. They swelled over his head. And touched the ceiling. The room was drowned.

One massive body length below the unblocked opening of the room, Nidhug gave his final surge of approach. He lifted like a demon out of darkness, and a second later his hideous mask blocked the entrance to the room.

Leveling his spear, hunching his shoulder behind the shield, Paul went to meet him. As in a nightmare, the heavy waters of fear slowed his thrust to a dreamlike slowness. The point of his spear slid deliberately through the impending medium and glanced off the tortured dragon-face.

But the overdeveloped muscles of Paul's arm, like what they represented in Paul himself, were something more than ordinary strength. The spear point, glancing off, dug a deep furrow from the twisted jaw to the staring eyes, and a flood of deep, luminescent, reddish blood stained and clouded the atmosphere of the room.

In this murk the battle became obscure. It became drearily a matter of Paul's thrusting back what came at him again and again. Gradually there broke on him the understanding that this was a contest that he perpetuated by the very act of fighting in it. The way to victory here was to deny the enemy. He laughed.

He threw away both shield and spear.

Like an express train, Nidhug leaped upon him. Paul stood still. And the gaping jaws, monstrous before him, closed as if on the invisible substance of an inch-thick wall between them. And the creature vanished.

The waters began to slowly ebb from the room. Far away the first shivering sounds of the third striking of the gong reached out to Paul's ears.

And in that moment, that tiny piece of a second, with the dragon vanished and the waters failing, something real and deadly reached through and struck.

It came from a distance to which the distance to the farthest stars was like a step to a long day's journey. It came with a speed beside which the speed even of thought was too slow to be measurable. It came along the dark and cobbled road of which Paul had dreamed on returning to the hotel after he had first seen Jase. It was blind and young and not yet fully formed, but it recognized its still-unarmored foe by sure instinct. And it struck.

It brought Paul to his knees as a giant might strike down a baby with a sword of steel—but it clashed like steel on steel against his invincible self behind. For a moment the forces hung together, and then the crest wave of the sounding gong finished closing the door through which the unknown had reached for a micro-second, for almost no time at all. And Paul knelt, free, but numb and blinded on the hard rock floor.

Paul's sight returned to show him the white ceiling of a room above the cot on which he lay. He was vaguely aware that they had carried him here.

Jase's face loomed over him. It was as keenly honed as ever, but there was a touch of friendliness there Paul had not seen before. Beside him was the white-mustached face of Heber showing concern.

"Quite a reaction you had there," said Jase, "after it was all over. We didn't expect to see you go down like that."

Paul focused on the Necromancer.

"You didn't?" he said. He frowned. "You certainly didn't expect me to stay on my feet?"

It was Jase's turn to frown, slightly.

"Why not?" he said. "If you'd stood up to things while it was going on, why collapse after it's all over?"

Paul faced it then. Jase and the other watchers had remained unaware. He closed his eyes wearily and a little bitterly, for he felt the beginnings of some sort of understanding seep into him at last; and understanding, he was discovering, like money, does not always bring happiness.

"Of course. Why not?" he agreed. "You must be right. I'm still suffering from the reaction."

Chapter 12

Dressed in ordinary jacket and slacks, one week later Paul sat with three other journeymen Chantry Guild members in a conference room of the orthodox part of Station Springboard. Talking to them was a brisk athletic young man with a short haircut and no older than Paul. Younger, in fact, than two of the journeymen, who looked disconcertingly like overfed salesmen in their thirties, except that one, who smelled strongly of after-shaving lotion, was twice as tall as the other.

"You can't *teach* the Alternate Laws," the instructor had begun by saying, as he half-perched on the edge of a table, facing the low, comfortable chairs in which the four sat. "Any more than you can *teach* the essential ability to create art, or the essential conviction of a religious belief. Does that make sense to you?"

"Ah, teaching!" said the fourth member of the journeymen group, a pleasant-faced, brown-headed young man, in an entirely unexpected, bell-toned bass. "What crimes have been committed in thy name!"

Since he had not spoken previously, the rest—even including the instructor—appeared somewhat startled, not only by his pronouncement, but by the volume and timbre of it. The young man smiled at them.

"True enough," said the instructor, after a slight pause. "And very true to the Alternate Laws. Let's simplify the Laws to a ridiculous extreme and say that the point they express is that as a rule of thumb, if it works best one way for everybody else, chances are that way won't be the best for you. In other words, if you want to get to the top of a mountain and you see a broad, well-marked, much-traveled road headed straight for it, the last route you should choose to the top of the mountain would be up that road."

He stopped talking. They all looked at him expectantly.

"No," he said, "I'm not going to tell you why. That would be teaching. Teaching is good only for learners, not for discoverers. Right now is the one and only time in the Chantry Guild that you're going to encounter anything like a question-and-answer period." He looked them over. "You're at liberty to try and tell *me* why, if you want to."

"Ah," said the large salesman sort with the shaving-lotion smell. He got the interjection out hurriedly, and it was at once noticeable to all his audience that his voice, though loud and determined, was neither bass nor bell-toned. "I—ah—understand that the Alternate Laws are parapsychological in nature. Can it be that involvement with the ordinary, that is to say—ah—scientific, laws has an inhibiting effect upon the person's—I mean the different sort of person who is able to take advantage of the powers of the Alternate Forces?" He drew a quick breath and added quickly, "I mean, his essential difference, so to speak?"

"No," said the instructor, kindly.

"No? Oh," said the other. He sat back, cleared his throat, crossed his legs, got out a handkerchief, and blew his nose loudly.

"The area of parapsychology," said the instructor, "is only a small part of the universe of time and space. The Alternate Laws cover all this and more."

"They mean what they say, don't they?" asked the smaller salesman-type unexpectedly. "Alternate Laws—other laws. And the only way to find the other ways is by deliberately avoiding the established way."

"That's right," said the instructor.

"Creative," rang the young man with the bass voice.

"And that's very right," said the instructor. He ran his glance from right to left over them. "None of you here would have got this far if you hadn't each demonstrated some capability in the area of the Alternate Laws. That capability may be parapsychological—say, teleportation. Or it might be an ability to write truly creative poetry, say. It might even be a particular sensitivity to the needs of growing plants. Not that I mean to give you the impression that creativity is all of the Alternate Laws, or even the key to them."

"Ah," said the large salesman, uncrossing his legs determinedly, "you certainly don't expect us just to write poetry or grow plants, or even teleport."

"No," said the instructor.

"Then—ah—can it be that you mean," said the large salesman, perspiration beginning to stand out on his brow, "that these things—

whatever they may be—are a part, only a part, of the Alternate Laws? And it's the rest we have to go after? We have to try? We have to get?"

"Yes," said the instructor. "That's very good. It's not a full answer by any means—"

"No, no, of course not," said the large salesman, flushing and smiling, and pulling out his handkerchief. He blew his nose again as if it were a soldier's bugle.

"—a full answer by any means," said the instructor. "In fact, if there is a full answer, I don't know it. Everyone, in this, is on his own. And now," he said, standing up, "I think you've already had enough discussion about an inherently undiscussable subject to last you a lifetime. If indeed we haven't already done the damage of setting up some artificial concepts. Remember"—his whole voice and manner changed abruptly; it was almost as if he had reached out and wrapped some invisible cloak about him—"life is an illusion. Time and space and all things are an illusion. There is nothing, nothing but the Alternate Laws."

He ceased speaking suddenly. The journeymen got up automatically and began to file out. As Paul walked past, however, he felt his arm touched by the instructor.

"Just a minute," the instructor said. Paul turned. The other waited until the three other journeymen were out of the room. "You didn't say anything at all."

"Yes," said Paul. "That's right. I didn't."

"Mind if I ask why?"

"If I remember rightly," Paul said, "the key word of Walter Blunt's book is *destruct*."

"Yes, it is."

"And we," said Paul, looking down at the instructor from his own greater height, "were talking about creativity."

"Mmm," said the instructor, nodding his head thoughtfully, "I see. You think somebody's lying?"

"No," said Paul. He felt a sudden weariness that was not physical at all. "It's just that there was nothing to say."

The instructor stared at him.

"Now you're the one who's baffling me," the instructor said. "I don't understand you."

"I mean," said Paul patiently, "that it's no use saying anything."

The instructor shook his head again.

"I still don't understand you," he said. "But that's all right." He smiled. "In the Guild it's: To thine own self be true, thou needst not then explain to any man."

He patted Paul on the shoulder.

"Go, man!" he said, and on that note they parted.

Returning to his room, as Jase had warned him to do when not otherwise occupied, Paul passed along the catwalk above the relay room in the orthodox part of the Station. He had only a vague notion of what went on in the three-step accelerator that stretched through nearly a quarter mile of the vast cavern five levels high, with thirty- and forty-foot banks of equipment surrounding its tube shape. From news and magazine accounts he had acquired the general knowledge that its function was a matter of shuttling a point of higher-level energy back and forth along a line of constantly lower energy until the point's speed was just under the speed of light. At which time it "broke" (i.e., disappeared) and became instead a point of no-time, if perfectly synchronized with a point of no-time back in the laboratory building of World Engineer's Headquarters Complex, created a path for instantaneous, timeless transmission between the two points.

Since the point of no-time had universal dimension, it could, by a complicated technical process, be used to transport objects of any size from the primary station on the Earth to the secondary station here on Mercury Station. For some reason there had to be a critical minimum distance between stations—Mars and Venus were too close to Earth. Stations there had been tried and had failed. But theoretically at least, by this method Springboard could have been directly supplied from World Engineer's Complex, with anything it needed. It was not, in practice, because its function on Mercury was to tinker and experiment with its end of the transmission path. Instead, most of the Station's solid needs were met by resolution of materials from Mercury's crust.

It was also not only theoretically possible, but practically possible, to send living creatures including humans by the same route. However, those who tried it flirted with insanity or death from psychic shock, and even if they missed both these eventualities, could never be induced to try it again. Apparently what was experienced by the transmittee was a timeless moment of complete consciousness in which he felt himself spread out to infinite proportions and then recondensed at the receiving end. It did no good to use present known sedatives or anesthetics—these merely seemed to insure a fatal level of shock. Medicine was reported working on a number of drugs that showed some promise, but no immediate hope of discovering a specific was in sight.

Meanwhile drone ships had been started off at sublight velocities for some of the nearer stars known to have surrounding systems. The ships bore automatic equipment capable of setting up secondary receiving stations on their arrival on some safe planetary base. If and when medicine came through, the transportation setup would be already established.

All of this touched Paul only slightly. He recognized it and passed on, noting only that in passing by and over the equipment, as he was doing now, he received from it an emanation of mild, pleasurable excitement. Like the so-called "electric" feeling in the air before a thunderstorm, which comes not only from an excess of ions, but from the sudden startling contrast of dark and light, from the black thunderheads piling up in one quarter of a clear sky, the mutter and leap of sheet lightning and thunder along the cloud flanks, and the sudden breath and pause of cooler air in little gusts of wind.

He passed on and entered the area of smaller corridors and enclosures. He passed by the double airlock doors of the transparent enclosure that held the swimming pool. With the relative preciousness of water, this had been set up as a closed system independent of the rest of the station and supplied with a certain amount of artificial gravitation for Earth-normal swimming and diving. Kantele was all alone in the pool. As he passed, he saw her go gracefully off the low board. He paused to watch her swim, not seeing him, to the side of the pool just beyond the glass where he stood. She did not look so slim in a bathing suit, and for a moment a deep sensation of loneliness moved him.

He went on, before she could climb out of the pool and see him. When he got to his room there was a notice attached to the door: "Orientation. Room eight, eighteenth level, following lunch, 1330 hours."

Orientation took place in another conference room. The man in charge was in his sixties and looked and acted as if he had been on an academic roster for some time. He sat on a small raised stage and looked down at Paul, the three men who had been with him for the meeting with the instructor on the subject of Alternate Laws, and six other people, of whom one was a young woman just out of her teens, not pretty, but with an amazingly quick and cheerful expression. The man in charge, who introduced himself as Leland Minault, did not begin with a lecture. Instead he invited them to ask him questions.

There was the usual initial pause at this. Then one of the five men Paul had not met before spoke up.

"I don't understand the Chantry Guild's connection with Project

Springboard and the Station, here," he said. Leland Minault peered down at the speaker as if through invisible spectacles.

"That," said Minault, "is a statement, not a question."

"All right," said the speaker. "Is the Chantry Guild responsible for Station Springboard, or the work on a means of getting out between the stars?"

"No," said Minault.

"Well then," asked the other, "just what are we doing here, anyway?"

"We are here," said Minault deliberately, folding both hands over a slight potbelly, "because a machine is not a man—beg pardon"—he nodded at the one woman in the group—"human being. A human being, if you bring him, or her, say, to some place like Mercury, to an establishment that seems to be completely at odds with his purpose in being there, will sooner or later get around to asking what the connection is."

He beamed at the man who had spoken.

"Then," Minault went on, "when you give him the answer, it's liable to sink in and promote further thought, instead of merely being filed as a completed explanation. Which is what is likely to happen to it if you just volunteer the information."

There was a general round of smiles.

"All right," said the one who had asked, "any one of us could have been the patsy. And you still haven't answered me."

"Quite right," said Minault. "Well, the point is that human beings react this way because they have an innate curiosity. A machine—call it a technological monster—may have everything else, but it'll be bound to lack innate curiosity. That is a talent reserved for living beings."

He paused again. Nobody said anything.

"Now our world," Minault said, "is at the present time firmly in the grip of a mechanical monster, whose head—if you want to call it that—is the World Engineer's Complex. That monster is opposed to us and can keep all too good a tab on us through every purchase we make with our credit numbers, every time we use the public transportation or eat a meal or rent a place to live—that is, it can as long as we stay on Earth. The Complex of sustaining equipment at Springboard here is officially a part of the Complex-Major back on Earth. But actually there's no connection beyond the bridge of transportation and communication between these two planets." He smiled at the group.

"So," he went on, "we hide here, under the cloak of Springboard. Actually, we control Springboard. But its work is not our work—it merely serves us as a cover. Of course, we're an open secret to those Springboard workers who aren't Chantry Guild members as well. But a machine, as I say, doesn't react as a human being would. If it doesn't see anything, it simply assumes nothing is there—it doesn't poke and pry into dark corners, because it *might* find enemies."

A hand was up. Turning his head slightly, Paul saw it was the cheerful-looking young woman.

"Yes?" said Minault.

"That doesn't make sense," she said. "The World Engineer's Complex is run by men, not machines."

"Ah," said Minault. "But you're making the assumption that the World Engineer and his staff are in control. They aren't. They are controlled by the physics of the society of our time, which in turn is controlled by the Earth Complex—to give it a convenient name—without which that society couldn't exist."

She frowned.

"You mean"—she wavered a moment on the verge of plunging into the cold waters of the wild statement—"the Complex-Major has *intelligence?*"

"Oh, I'm pretty sure we can say that," replied Minault cheerfully. "Fantastic amounts of knowledge, of course; but a sort of definite rudimentary intelligence as well. But I don't think that's what you meant to ask. What you meant to ask was whether the Complex-Major— Super-Complex, I understand a lot of people have begun calling it lately—has an ego, a conscious identity and personality of its own."

"Well . . . yes," she said.

"I thought so. Well, the answer to that, lady and gentlemen, is astoundingly enough, Yes, it has."

The group in the room, which had settled back to listen to a Socratic dialogue between the young woman and Minault, woke up suddenly and muttered disbelief.

"Oh, not in the human sense, not in the human sense," said Minault, waving them back to calmness. "I don't mean to insult your credulity. But surely you all realize that sooner or later a point of complication had to be reached where a certain amount of elementary reasoning power was necessary to the machine. In fact, why not? It's a very handy thing to have a machine that can reason, and consequently protect itself from falling into its own errors."

"Ah," said Paul's large salesman-type companion from the earlier gathering. "In that case I fail to see—that is, the implied problem was one of control, which we wished to avoid. Wasn't it?"

"I was," said Minault, peering at the large man, "explaining the personality of the Complex-Major."

"Ah, I see," said the large man, sitting back. He blew his nose.

"Your question was a good one," said Minault, "but slightly premature. For the moment, you must understand what I mean by a machine ego. Think of the growing Complexes of computer-directed equipment back on Earth as if they were an animal whose purpose is to take over more and more of the work of keeping mankind alive and well. It grows until it is *the* means by which mankind is kept alive and well; it grows until a certain amount of independent reasoning ability must be built into it, so that it doesn't provide fine weather for California when that action will later on cause hailstorms on the Canadian wheat crop. Given this much of a thinking creature, what's the next evolutionary step?"

"An instinct for self-preservation?" asked the girl quickly, while the large man was clearing his throat preparatory to another "ah."

"Quite right."

"Ah, I should think it would regard human actions not in line with its reasoning—ah—like grit in a smooth-running motor, so to speak?"

"Would it have that much power of imagination?" asked the girl. She and the large man were both looking at Minault, who sat relaxed, peering at them.

"I did not mean actual imagination. Ah—it was an illustration."

"A rather good one," said Minault, as the girl opened her mouth again. "The Complex-Major is a sort of benevolent monster whose only desire is to choke us with a surfeit of service and protection. It has a sort of mechanical intelligence with no specific locus, but an instinct to protect itself and its ability to go on taking over control of human caretaking. And it does regard not only us in the Chantry Guild, but all those whose independence manifests itself in the taking of drugs, joining of cult societies, or any non-machine-planned action, as a sort of grit in its smooth-running motor. A grit that one day must be neatly cleaned out."

He glanced toward the back of his group of auditors.

"Yes?" he asked.

Paul, turning, saw a young, swarthy-skinned man in the back putting his hand back down.

"It seems," said this man, "almost silly to be going to all this trouble just to oppose a pile of equipment, no matter how complicated."

"My dear young friend," said Minault, "we in the Chantry Guild are not opposing a pile of equipment. We're opposing an idea—an idea that has been growing for some hundreds of years—that happiness for the human race consists of wrapping it tighter and tighter in the swaddling bands of a technological civilization." He stood up. "I think that should be enough to chew on for the moment. I suggest you all think the situation over."

He got down from the platform and headed toward the door of the room. His audience rose and also began to move out, and the orderly manner of the room dissolved into a babble of conversation and people slowly swarming out the exit. As Paul pushed his way out the door behind Minault, he caught sight of the girl, who had just buttonholed the large man.

"I think you're quite wrong about the power of imagination you implied to the Complex-Major," she was saying, severely.

Chapter 13

"You've handled explosives before?" asked the lean instructor with the sun-leathered face above the open collar. He was holding a package of plastic, adhesive blasting jelly with a three-minute pinch fuse.

"Yes," said Paul.

Paul stood on one cliff-edge of a remarkably realistic simulation of a mountain gorge some five hundred feet wide, across which had been thrown the thin long web of a temporary snap-to arch bridge of magnesium-alloy sections. The bridge-end by which Paul and the instructor stood, just the two of them, had been anchored in a local timber cradle, or box, filled with loose rock. And the cradle extended its wooden underarms in support about fifteen feet out from the lip of the cliff.

"This amount of jelly," said the instructor, hefting it, "can be carried inconspicuously in a brief case and still leave room for enough other material to make it look as if the brief case is full. It's powerful enough to cut two or three of those timbers or one or two of the metal members you see there. How would you go about completely knocking out this bridge with it?"

Paul looked again at the bridge. In the past nine days since his first class he had been put through a number of *sessions*—that was the only word to describe them. They appeared to be classes, on a strange variety of subjects, some of which appeared to bear no relation to the Chantry Guild. The longest of them had lasted not much more than twenty minutes, and the information imparted by each of them had been obscure. In fact, it had not been quite clear whether the intent of the sessions had been to inform or to test the journeyman audience, which seemed to consist of different individuals from session to ses-

sion. Paul was privately of the opinion that the intent had been both
to inform and test—and probably, as well, to stimulate and confuse.
Some of the journeymen, he was sure, were ringers. Some of the sessions had been nonsense.

And this session—himself alone with the instructor, the explosive,
and the simulated bridge in the mountains on Earth. Was it instruction,
test, nonsense—or something else?

The simulation was a magnificent job. For the scene it pretended
to show was clearly an impossibility, here deep under the surface of
Mercury's rocky hide. What Paul's eyes saw was a gorge at least eight
hundred feet in depth, up from which came the distant sound of a
narrow mountain river in its gallop to lower levels. The air was the
thin, dry air of high altitudes. The sky was cloudless.

The question was, How much was real and how much false? For
if the blasting-jelly block was real, and it was to be set off in the reality
of a small underground room of the size Paul had had his sessions in
lately, then it would take Alternate Laws indeed to show cause why
Paul and the instructor should survive the explosion. Paul laid his hand
on the timber cradle and looked over the cliff edge. His gaze plunged
away into spray-misted depths. There was distance down there, by any
test of his feelings. Just how much, he could not be sure. But it *felt*
deep below the cliff. On the other hand, under his hand the materials
of the bridge felt solid but deceitful.

"Well," said Paul, "I'm no expert on bridges. But I imagine the
trick would be to break this end loose, so that it falls. If this end goes
down, it'll tear the other end loose and it'll all drop into the gorge."

"Good enough," said the instructor. "How'd you go about breaking
this end loose?"

"I think," said Paul, pointing to where the end of the cradle met a
magnesium I-beam, fifteen feet out above the gorge's depth, "if we
blew it loose just there, cutting that stringer, or whatever the proper
term is, that runs along the left side of the travel-surface of the bridge,
the weight of the rest of it would cause it to sag and twist, and tear
the other stringer loose. Then this whole end would drop."

"All right." The instructor handed the block of jelly to Paul. "Let's
see you do it."

Paul looked at the bridge again. Then he stuffed the block of jelly
inside the waistband of his slacks and began to climb out along the
timbers of the cradle. The lack of a second arm hampered him but not
so much as Paul thought it might have seemed to the instructor. The
strength of his remaining arm was such as to lift the weight of his
body from angles clearly impossible to an ordinary climber. When he

got to the end of the stone enclosing the timbers, Paul paused, ostensibly to rest, but actually to reach some sort of conclusion.

The bridge still felt deceitful. He quietly loosed a splinter from the timber on which he rested, and dropped it. It floated down until he lost sight of it some thirty or forty feet below. So, that much of distance under him at least was real. He looked once more at the spot where he would stick the explosive.

It was at a point just above the single final timber of the supporting cradle. He would have to stand on that timber and place the jelly above the upright at the timber's end, where that upright met the magnesium I-beam. He began to move again. He climbed on up to the I-beam and out onto it until he was above the timber. Hanging to the I-beam, he cautiously let his feet down until they rested on the timber.

Then, as unobtrusively as possible, he increased his hold on the I-beam and pressed down with both feet on the timber.

There was a sudden screech of tearing wood. The timber ripped away from beneath him, and he dropped suddenly to the length of his arm, and hung there sustained only by his grip on the I-beam. Below him he saw the falling timber on which he would have stood tumbling and shrinking until it vanished suddenly fifty or sixty feet below him. Still hanging, he looked across to the point where the underfoot timber had been joined to the upright by a metal collar held by four thick magnesium rivets.

There were no rivet-hole marks or broken rivet ends in the wood of the upright at all. What was visible was the snapped end of a quarter-inch-diameter wooden dowel rod.

Paul pulled himself easily back up on the I-beam. The bridge stood firm and secure—it had been balanced, evidently, somewhat differently than it appeared to be, on its supports. He climbed back to the instructor, on solid ground, and handed the jelly block back to the man.

"Now what?" Paul said.

"Well," said the instructor, "we'll go up to the front offices. I don't know what your master will say, and of course it's up to him. But as far as I'm concerned, I'd say you've graduated."

They left the simulated scene in the mountains and went out into the Station proper, and took an elevator up a good number of levels. Paul had the impression that they were almost to, if not right at, the surface. And this impression was justified a second or two later when they entered a large lounge-office with, not a vision tank, but an actual window looking out on the yellow twilight and the witches' garden of Mercury's surface around the Station.

Jase was there, along with Heber, the white-mustached unlisted member, and a couple of men Paul did not recognize. The instructor had Paul wait while he went over and talked to the three for a few minutes in a voice too low for Paul to hear. Then Jase came over alone, and the instructor, with the other two men, went over to one of the desks at the other end of the room and began going over what, judging from their quite audible conversation, were the files of journeymen currently undergoing tests.

"Come on over to the window," said Jase. Paul followed him. The slim, dark young man was as relaxed as Paul had ever seen him, though he still walked with the prowling balance of a cat. "Sit down."

Paul sat, in a low, comfortably overstuffed chair. Jase took one opposite.

"To all intents and purposes," said Jase, and his deep-set, clear brown eyes watched Paul closely, "you're a Chantry Guild member now. Before you first came to me, you'd gotten the psychiatric viewpoint on yourself and your missing arm. Now, I'll tell you the true situation from the point of someone like myself who is acquainted with the Alternate Laws."

He stopped.

"—You were going to say something," he said.

"No," said Paul.

"All right," said Jase, "here it is, then. You have an ability under the Alternate Laws which is probably parapsychological in nature. I told you when I first met you—and I've an ability myself where it comes to judging character—something to the effect that your arrogance was astounding."

Paul frowned. He had all but put aside the memory of the Necromancer calling him arrogant. It was the one thing he could not accept about himself.

"I understand now better why you should be so arrogant," Jase was saying. "I've no idea, none of us have in the regular membership, about the possibilities or limitations of your ability. But we've no doubt about its essential nature. Your ability is to make use of the Alternate Laws for purposes of almost total defense. We've done everything but try to kill you outright and without reservation. You've come through beautifully. Tell me, do you think you could explain to me in words just how you came to suspect that bridge timber just a little while ago? I'm not asking you to explain, I'm asking you if you think you *could* explain it to me."

"No," said Paul, slowly. "No, I don't think so."

"We thought as much. Well, what you want to do with your ability

from here on out is up to you. I myself think that the reason a grafted
arm won't take on your left side there, is because this defensive ability
of yours sees some danger to you in an arm graft. If you find what
that danger is, maybe you can discover another counter to it, and the
next arm you have attached to you will live instead of dying. But, as
I say, that's up to you. However, there's something else."

He stopped. There seemed to be almost a touch of indecision in
his manner, for the first time since Paul had met him.

"As I say," said Jase, not quite as quickly as he usually spoke, "in
all but name now, you're a member. We haven't only been active with
you up here, but we've been active for you back down on Earth. If
you go back, you'll have to stand police investigation in connection
with the death of Kevin Malorn, that man in the Koh-i-Nor you took
the drug to."

"I was wondering about that," said Paul.

"You needn't wonder any longer," said Jase. "The purchase desk
in the music section of the library at Chicago Complex Directory now
has among its records one showing that you purchased a song tape
there at the same time that Malorn was being killed. You will simply
have to show up and add your testimony to the evidence of the record.
Since the records are machine-made and regarded as untamperable,
you'll be clear of any connection with Malorn's death an hour or so
after arriving back in Chicago."

"I see." Paul nodded. "The song tape—it isn't one of Kantele singing something about *'in apple comfort time,'* is it?"

Jase frowned.

"Yes," he said. "As a matter of fact it is. Why?"

"Nothing," said Paul. "I've heard it, but not all the way through."

"It's a natural choice," said Jase. "The record shows my credit
number—you were buying it at my request. That's reasonable enough,
since Kantele and I are old friends and the song was written for her
by Blunt."

"Blunt?"

"Why yes." Jase smiled a little at him. "You didn't know the
Guildmaster wrote music?"

"No."

"He does a great many things," said Jase, a little dryly. "However,
the point is you can go back to Earth as free as you ever were. Except
that as a Guild member you'll be required to take orders from the
masters, like myself."

"I see," said Paul, a little grimly.

"Do you?" replied Jase. He sighed. "I don't think you do. Not by a damn sight. Would you listen with an open mind for about five minutes?"

"Of course," said Paul.

"All right," said Jase. "Modern man got his motor to turning over with the Renaissance. At that time two things were initiated. One was the attitude of enlightened inquiry that began people on the road to a technological society and civilization. The road that sought to build a man a home and keep him well fed and happy within it by use of the machine."

"Which was bad?" said Paul.

"No, no," said Jase. "There's nothing wrong with a prosthetic appliance if nothing else is available. But you'd rather have a flesh-and-blood arm just like your own grafted on, wouldn't you?"

"Go on," said Paul.

"However, the original role of the machine started to get perverted around the time of the industrial revolution. It came to be regarded not as a means to a desired end, but as part of the end in itself. The process accelerated in the nineteenth century, and exploded in the twentieth. Man kept demanding more in the way of service from his technology, and the technology kept giving it—but always at the price of a little more of man's individual self-contained powers. In the end—in our time—our technology has become second thing to a religion. Now we're trapped in it. And we're so enfeebled by our entrapment that we tell ourselves it's the only possible way to live. That no other way exists."

"I—" began Paul, and checked himself.

"Yes, 'I,' " said Jase. "The arrogant 'I,' with the built-in survival qualities. But other people aren't like you."

"That wasn't what I was going to say," observed Paul.

"It doesn't matter," said Jase. "The point isn't you, but the world, which is at the mercy of an ever-growing technological system."

"Which the Chantry Guild wishes to attack."

"Attack?" said Jase. "The Chantry Guild was formed by Walt Blunt to protect its members against the attack of the technological system."

"What you're saying," Paul said, "is that your members grew up out of something other than the technological system."

"That's quite right," said Jase calmly. "They did. And so did you."

Paul looked searchingly at the Necromancer, but the dark face was as full of honesty as Paul had ever seen it.

"I said, two things were initiated at the time of the Renaissance," said Jase. "One was the roots of the single system that has given us

our technological civilization, that says there is only one way for Man
to live, and that's swaddled by the machine. And the other was all
other systems—the principle of freedom which lies at the base of the
Alternate Laws. The first would make Man an inferior, the second
acknowledges his superiority."

He looked at Paul as if expecting a protest.

"I'm not in disagreement with the idea of superiority," said Paul.

"Side by side, but not noticed except by a few," said Jase, "while
everybody and his Uncle Charlie was engaged in making a god out of
the machine, a few talented people were proving that Man had already
reached that level of deity and wasn't even started yet. Genius was at
work in every generation—and genius works with the Alternate Laws.
Only, after a while the machine got enough muscles so that it started
crowding genius—and that brings it down to our time, Paul."

"We do seem to end there, all the time," said Paul, and could not
stop himself from smiling a little.

"I thought you promised me an open mind," said Jase.

"I'm sorry."

"All right, then," said Jase. "Answer me something. Suppose
you're a person in any generation up to about fifty years ago whose
abilities and inclinations make him inclined to have something more
or something different than what's available to the mass of people in
his time. What happens?"

"I'm listening," said Paul, "with an open mind."

"He can go under to the general attitude and be essentially destroyed by denying his own possibilities. Or he can rise above the
general attitude and keep afloat by sheer dint of extra ability-muscle.
Agreed?"

Paul nodded.

"In other words, he can lose or win his own personal battle with
the mass-opinion of his time. In either case he's resolved his problem."
Jase looked at Paul. Paul nodded again.

"But in our time," said Jase, "such a person isn't up against the
opinions and attitudes of his fellows. He's up against an attitude
brought to life and resolved into a mechanical monster that can't be
reasoned with, and can't be adjusted to. He can't win for the same
reason he can't outwrestle a bulldozer with his bare hands. And he
can't submit because the bulldozer doesn't understand submission. It
only understands a complete job."

Jase leaned forward with his hands on both of his knees. The
emotion in the man came at Paul as sharp as an arrow.

"Don't you understand?" asked the Necromancer. "The Chantry

Guild was established because the technological system of our own time was trying to kill these people who belong to the Guild—each and every one of them, and any more like them—kill them off." His eyes blazed at Paul. "Just as it's been trying to kill you!"

Paul looked back at him for a long moment.

"Me?" he asked, at last.

"The weather warning you didn't get when you were out sailing," said Jase. "The temporal disorientation that caused you to be caught by the starting ore cars in the shaft of the mine. The misdirection of the subway car that stranded you in the middle of a street cleared for use by a marching society. Yes," he added, as Paul's eyebrows raised slightly, "we had a tracer on you from the time you first left my place. That's usual." He looked a little thin-lipped for a moment. "It's part of the war between us and it."

"I see," said Paul, his mind running back over a number of things.

"You're in it, on the side of the Guild, whether you like it or not. We'd like your active, working co-operation. If your ability under the Alternate Laws is what it seems to be, you'll be more valuable to your fellow Guild members than anyone else could be."

"Why?" asked Paul.

Jase shrugged a little angrily.

"I won't tell you that—*now*, of course," he said. "How could I? You've got to commit yourself to the Guild—that is, try for the rank of Necromancer, a master in the Guild. We'll put you to the test. If you come through all right, then some time in the future you'll learn what you can do for the Guild. You'll hear it from the only man who can give you commands once you're a master—the Guildmaster himself, Walt Blunt."

"Blunt!"

Paul felt the name slide into place with the events here on Mercury at Springboard. He felt a rage of passion remembered, and a lonely sorrow, and then the hard, driving core of his determination to bring this man Blunt face to face.

"Of course," Jase was saying. "Who else could there be to give orders to the master rank? Blunt's our general."

"I'm committed," said Paul, quietly. "What do I do?"

"Well," said Jase, taking his hands off his knees and sitting up straight, "I told you it's this ability of yours we want to determine. I said we'd done everything but try to kill you outright and without reservation. We'd like to take that last step now—make a serious effort with the resources of the Guild behind it and no safety hatch—and see if you survive."

Chapter 14

Master and Necromancer in name only, and under the shadow of a sometime attempt to be made upon his life, Paul returned to Earth and the Chicago Complex—ostensibly from a canoe trip up in the Quetico-Superior wilderness park area along the Canadian border near Lake Superior. He was picked up at the Complex Outer Terminal, taken to Complex Police Headquarters, and gave his statement concerning his whereabouts at the time of Malorn's murder by person or persons unknown. A police-beat reporter for one of the newssheets questioned him perfunctorily as he was leaving after his release by the police.

"How does it feel?" asked the reporter, matching strides with Paul as Paul walked toward the waiting cars at the Police terminal, "not to be facing a possible sentence of death?"

"You tell me," said Paul, as he got in a two-man car and went off. The reporter considered a moment and erased the reply from his hand recorder. It had been too flippant, he thought.

" 'I am relieved, of course,' " dictated the reporter into the recorder. " 'However, knowing modern police methods and equipment I never had any real doubt they would find out I hadn't done it.' " He put the recorder back in his pocket and returned to the booking desk inside.

Paul, reporting to Jase, who also had returned, was told to rent himself an apartment not too far from Suntden Place and amuse himself for the present. Paul did so. There followed several weeks of idleness in which Paul slept late, wandered around the Complex soaking up the feel of it and its crowds, and generally waited for his personal ax to fall.

It did not fall. Paul seemed almost forgotten—pensioned off and

put aside by the Chantry Guild. Yet Jase, when Paul checked in with
the Necromancer, and Kantele, on the one or two brief glimpses Paul
had of her, seemed caught up in a smoothly constant, high-temperature
state of activity. On one of his visits Paul had attempted to find out
how he might get in touch with Blunt. Jase had told him quite bluntly
that when Paul needed to know such information, it would be given
to him. Blunt, Paul gathered, had no fixed address. His location at any
time was a matter for his own immediate decision, and known only to
those like Jase and Kantele, who were close to him.

The first week in May, on a Monday, found Paul up around the
Wisconsin Dells, ostensibly squirrel-hunting. He had largely given over
any conscious watch for the attack he had been promised by Jase, but
that anterior part of his mind which took care of such things had not
forgotten. Midday found him seated with his back to the trunk of a
silver maple, half drowsy with the warmth of the strong spring sun out
of a blue sky, and lost in a collection of newspapers and periodicals.
However, his gun was across his knees, a steep fifty-foot cliff of loose
gravel fell away behind the maple, and before him he could see clear
down through a small grove of maple, pine, and poplar to a wide field
of black earth faintly dusted with the new green of coming corn plants.
It was an automatically perfect defensive position.

There were gray squirrels in the trees down the slope. They had
taken care not to get too close when Paul had first settled himself
against the trunk of the maple, but, *Sciurus carolinensis* not being
known for any lack of curiosity, they had been allowing themselves to
work and play closer to where he sat in motionlessness. Now, after
about two hours of Paul's sitting and reading, one slim youngster had
grown so swashbuckling as to slip out from behind a narrow poplar
trunk not fifteen feet from the human and sit up boldly to stare.

Paul was aware of these small attentions, but he felt a certain
definite pleasure in letting them go on uninterrupted. The last thing
from his mind was the desire to kill. He had more than a moral conviction against it, he was discovering. He almost regarded it as a sort
of self-performed amputation. Particularly at this moment when he had
allowed himself to go deep into the life and stir of the small section
of the world at the moment around him. He let himself float in the
sensation of the warming earth, the light and movement surrounding,
and gave the full attention of his thinking processes to the reading
material he had brought with him.

The material was merely a chance selection among the many
publications currently on sale or merely available for the picking up.
But they struck hard upon him. He found himself wondering how, with

such a universal voice of unhappiness sounding in the world, he had
failed to be overwhelmed by it before.

The publications were full of the statistics of distress. Testing of
grade-school children revealed that seven per cent of those under the
age of eight were headed for major mental illnesses. The world crime
rate had been climbing steadily for fifty years and this last year had
jumped twenty-three per cent again. And this in a world in which
nobody needed to lack for the necessities, and even most of the luxuries, of life. The world suicide rate was climbing sharply. Cultism
was commonplace. Hysteria such as the marching societies exemplified
was growing steadily. The birth rate was down.

Article after article either explored the situation, or offered some
self-help method of individual adjustment to it. And yet—Paul went
back through the pages before him again—there was enough of other
topics, of sports, news, humor, art, and science, so that someone like
himself who had not suffered individually could ignore the notes of
trouble in the general symphony of modern achievement otherwise.

And still—Paul frowned a little. He did not believe what he read,
or what people told him. He believed only what he himself could check
against the touchstone of his feelings, and it occurred to him now that
he seemed to sense something about the catalogue of unhappiness. A
faint tone as of something whining. Or was he being unfair?

He pushed the newssheets and periodicals aside, and half-closed
his eyes to the sunlight coming through the young leaves. He was
conscious of the weight of the gun across his legs as well as the peaceful rustlings of the woods. The adventurous squirrel had been followed
into the open by two of his fellows, but the first one, the one with guts,
was still in the lead. As Paul watched without stirring, the adventurous
one made a sudden dash right up to the toe of Paul's left hiking boot,
and examined it with a quivering black nose.

The other two followed after. Man, thought Paul slowly, proceeds
by dashes like the squirrel, and each new discovery is the one which
is going to turn the world upside down. Each new setback seems to
threaten eternal night. He looked at the squirrels. All three were now
examining the rifle stock of the gun where it projected out into the air
beyond his right knee on a level with their small, black, fascinated
eyes. He tried to feel what it was like to be one with them, and for a
second his point of view flooded into a fantastic, pillared world of
attack and defense, sleep, hunger, and the unknown.

Another squirrel raced suddenly toward him from the cover of the
nearest tree. Suddenly there was concerted movement. As the newcomer reached the two followers, all three with unnaturally perfect

teamwork threw their squirrel-weights suddenly against and on top of the projecting rifle stock. The gun tilted and swung, the muzzle of the barrel coming up thump against the left side of Paul's chest.

And at the same moment the adventurous squirrel leaped fair and true for the trigger button of the gun.

All in one explosive instant, it happened. And all in one movement of coldly swift and certain reaction, Paul's arm had galvanized into movement with the first rush of the fourth squirrel across the dappled earth. His long fingers met the leaping squirrel in mid-air, caught him, and broke his neck.

There was a scuttling rush away in all directions. Then silence. Paul found himself standing on his feet with the spilled gun, the scattered throwaway publications at his feet, and no other living creature in sight. He held the dead squirrel still in his hand.

Paul's heart thumped once, savagely, in his chest. He looked down at the dead squirrel. The small, black, animal eyes were squeezed tightly shut, as they might have been in any living being forced into risking all, in one wild tourney with the unknown.

The wound of an amputation bled somewhere in the depths of Paul. His eyes dimmed. The sun had lost its way momentarily behind a cloud, and the forest floor was all one color. Paul laid the small gray body gently down at the foot of the silver maple and smoothed its rumpled fur. He picked up his gun by the cold, slickly-machined metal of its barrel, and went off through the trees.

When he got back to his apartment in the Chicago Complex, Jase was already inside it and waiting for him as he entered.

"Congratulations," said Jase, "—Necromancer."

Paul looked at him. Involuntarily, Jase stepped back.

Chapter 15

Paul was, he learned in the next few days, now a part of the more or less "Cabinet" group in the Guild, which operated directly with and under Blunt himself. The other Cabinet members consisted of Jase, Kantele, Burton McLeod—the heavy broadsword of a man Paul had met earlier in Jase's apartment—and an elusive gray wafer of a little man whose name was Eaton White. White, it seemed, was posted high on the personal staff of Kirk Tyne, and the first thing he did was take Paul in to see Tyne about a job in the World Engineer's office.

"I suppose," asked Tyne, when he had shaken hands with Paul in the clear morning sunlight coming through the high windows of a luxurious office lounge two hundred levels above the Chicago traffic, "you wonder why I seem so little hesitant to have a member of the Guild on my personal staff? Sit down, sit down. You, too, Eat."

Paul and Eaton White took comfortable chairs. Tyne also sat down, stretching his slim legs before him. He looked as fit as a well-kept bowstring, and as unfrayed by the demands of his work. His eyes, glancing directly into Paul's under neat brown eyebrows, were startlingly perceptive.

"I was a little surprised, yes," said Paul.

"Well, there's a number of reasons," said Tyne. "Did you ever consider the difficulties of changing the present?"

"Changing the present?"

"It's impossible," said Tyne, almost merrily. "Though very few people stop to think about it and realize the fact. When you pick up an inch of the present to move it, you also pick up several thousand miles of history."

"I see," said Paul. "You mean, to change the present you'd have to first change the past."

"Exactly," replied Tyne. "And that's what reformers invariably forget. They talk about changing the future. As if doing so was some new and great feat. Nonsense. Our main business as living human beings is changing the future. In fact, that's all we can change. The present is the result of the past; and even if we could monkey with the past, who'd dare to? Change one tiny factor and the result in the present might well be the whole human race blown apart. So your reformers, your great changers, are kidding themselves. They talk about changing the future, when what they really mean is that they want to change the present, the present they're living in right at the moment. They don't realize they're trying to move furniture that's already nailed down."

"So you think the Chantry Guild is made up of furniture movers?" asked Paul.

"Essentially—essentially," said Tyne. He sat forward in his chair. "Oh, I want you to know I have a high opinion of the Guild, and the Guild members. And I have something more than a high opinion of Walt Blunt. Walt awes me, and I don't mind admitting it. But that doesn't alter the fact that he's barking up the wrong tree."

"Apparently," said Paul, "he thinks the same of you."

"Of course!" said Tyne. "He'd be bound to. He's a natural revolutionist. I'm a real revolutionist. I know the present can't be changed, so I concentrate on changing the future. Really changing it—by hard work, discovery, and progress; the way it actually gets changed."

Paul looked at him interestedly.

"What's your idea of the future?" asked Paul.

"Utopia," said Tyne. "A practical utopia that we've all adjusted to. That's all that's really wrong with the present, you know. We've achieved, through our science and technology, a practical utopia. Our only trouble is that we aren't adjusted to it yet. We keep feeling there must be a catch somewhere, something to be fought against and licked. That's Walt's trouble, incidentally. He can't help feeling he ought to be revolting against something intolerable. And since he can't find anything intolerable, he's gone to a great deal of trouble to work up a revolt against what's not only tolerable, but infinitely desirable—the very things we've been working for for centuries. Comfort, freedom, and wealth."

"I take it," said Paul, and frowned for a second as the ghost of a small gray squirrel scampered for a moment unbidden across his thoughts, "you don't worry too much about the increases in crime, suicides, mental disorders, and so forth?"

"I consider them. I don't *worry* about them," said Tyne, leaning forward with argumentative relish. "In the Super-Complex—I mean by that, the reconciling units here in the Headquarters building—we've got the greatest tool ever forged by Man for solving all Man's problems. It'll take a few generations, no doubt, but eventually we'll iron out the essentially emotional reaction that's causing these things you talk about."

"Emotional reaction?" asked Paul.

"Of course! For the first time in the history of Man, for the first time since he first stuck his nose out of a nice safe hole in the ground, people have absolutely nothing to be afraid of, nothing to worry about. Is it any wonder that all their little individual quirks and idiosyncrasies sprout wings and fly off with them?"

"I can't believe," said Paul slowly, "that the causes for what I read about in the newssheets and periodicals now are caused just by idiosyncrasies in the individual."

"Well, of course, it isn't that simple." Tyne sat back in his chair. "There are strong group elements in the human character. Religion, for one—that's at the root of all these sects and cults. The tendency toward hysteria and mob action that's been the cause of the marching societies. We're getting a social fragmentation. But just because Utopia's new, and there's no reason not to run hog wild. As I say, a generation or two will see us settling back down."

He stopped talking.

"Well," said Paul, when it seemed to be up to him, "this is all very interesting. I take it you're trying to convert me."

"Exactly right," said Tyne. "As I say, I don't agree with Walt, but he recruits some of the best material in the world. Eaton here's an example. And poor Malorn was a Guild member."

"Malorn!" said Paul, looking closely at the World Engineer.

"Yes—in a way you might say I owe you something for having been unfairly accused in connection with his death. It was a breakdown misfunction in the police machinery, and I'm responsible for the smooth working of all machinery."

"But that isn't why you'd give me a job?"

"Not by itself, of course. No. But Eat here speaks highly of you and says you don't seem to be completely blinkered and blinded by all those theories of Walt's. I'm willing to take a chance on talking you over to my point of view, if you're willing to take the chance of being talked. And of course, Walt will be tickled to have you on the inside, here. You see, he thinks he's outsmarting me by being completely open and aboveboard about planting his people on me."

"And you," said Paul, "think you're outsmarting him."

"I know I am," said Tyne, smiling. "I have an intelligent friend who tells me so."

"It seems to be settled, then," said Paul. He stood up. Tyne and Eaton rose with him. "I'd like to meet your intelligent friend, some-time."

"Some day, you might do that," said Tyne. They shook hands. "In fact, I imagine you will. It was this friend's recommendation that rather clinched this matter of taking you on here."

Paul looked at the World Engineer sharply. With his last words something had come and gone so swiftly in the other man that it was impossible now to say what it might have been. It was as if a metal edge had shown itself for a moment.

"I'll look forward to it, then," said Paul. And Eaton led him out.

Outside the World Engineer Complex Headquarters they parted. Eaton went back in to work. Paul went on to Jase's.

As he stepped through the entrance to Jase's apartment and put his key back in his pocket, he heard voices. One was Jase's. But the other—he stopped at the sound of it—was the deep, resonant, and sardonic voice of Blunt.

"I realize, Jase," the voice of Blunt was saying, "that you find me a little too much of a playboy at times. It's something you'll just have to bear with, however."

"I don't mean that at all, Walt!" The younger man's voice was charged and grim. "Who's going to lay down rules for *you*, of all people? It's just that if I find myself having to take over, I want to know what you had in mind."

"If you take over, it's your own mind you'll follow, and that's the way it should be," said Blunt. "Let's cross such bridges when we come to them. You may not have to take over. Who just came in?"

The last words coincided with Paul's stepping around the corner from the entrance hall into the main lounge of Jase's apartment. The wall entrance to the office in Kantele's apartment next door was open, and through it Paul now saw the wide shoulders and back of Blunt, with the dark, startled visage of Jase beyond.

"Me. Formain," answered Paul, and he walked toward the office. But Jase stepped swiftly past Blunt and came down into his own lounge, closing the office entrance behind him.

"What is it?" asked Jase.

"It seems I'm now on the immediate staff of the World Engineer," said Paul. He looked past Jase at the closed wall. "That's Walter Blunt in there, isn't it? I'd like to speak to him."

He stepped around Jase, went to the wall, and opened it. Within, the office was empty. He turned back to Jase.

"Where did he go?"

"I imagine," said Jase, dryly, "if he'd wanted to stay and talk to you, he'd have stayed."

Paul turned again and went on into the office. He went through it into the farther reaches of Kantele's apartment. It was a feminine dwelling, but empty. Paul paused by its front door, but there was no clue about it to signal whether Walter Blunt had walked out through it in the last few minutes.

He went back to the office, and through it. Jase was no longer in his own lounge. He seemed to have left the apartment. Paul was about to leave, too, in a mood of puzzled disturbance, when the entrance to Jase's apartment clicked open—he heard it—and someone came in.

Expecting Jase, Blunt, or both, he was turning toward the entrance hall when Kantele came out of it, carrying some sort of package, and stopped.

"Paul!" she said.

It was not a happy, or even pleased, sounding of his name. Rather, it was on a note of dismay that she said it.

"Yes," he said, a little sadly.

"Where's"—she hesitated—"Jase?"

"And Walter Blunt," he said. "I'd like to know where they disappeared to, and why, myself."

"They probably had to go someplace." She was ill-at-ease. It showed in the way she held the package to her.

"I hadn't realized," he said, reaching for a neutral topic, "that Blunt wrote that 'apple comfort' song of yours. Jase told me."

She looked abruptly a little sharply at him. Almost challengingly.

"That surprised you, did it?" she asked.

"Why—" he said. "No."

"It didn't?"

"I don't know," he said, "exactly whether to call it 'surprise.' I didn't know the Guildmaster wrote songs, that was all. And—" He stopped, feeling her bristle.

"And what?"

"Nothing," he said, as peaceably as he could, "I only heard the first verse before you came in that day, and the one time I heard it before. But it seemed to me more a young man's song."

She strode angrily past him. He got the impression that she was rather pleased then otherwise to find something to get angry about. She punched buttons on Jase's music player and swung about with her back to it.

"Then it's time you heard the second verse, isn't it?" she asked. A second later her own voice swelled from the player behind her.

> *In apple comfort, long I waited thee*
> *And long I thee in apple comfort waited.*

"Young man's song," she said bitingly.

> *In lonely autumn and uncertain springtime*
> *My apple longing for thee was not sated.*

The clear, mountain rivulet of her recorded voice paused, and then went on into the second verse. She looked across at him with her eyes fixed and her lips together.

> *Now come thee near anigh my autumn winding.*
> *In cider-stouted jugs, my memories*
> *Shall guard thee by the fireside of my passion,*
> *And at my life's end keep thy gentle lees.*

The music shut off. He saw that she was profoundly moved by it and deeply unhappy. He went to her.

"I'm sorry," he said, standing before her. "You mustn't let what I think disturb you. Forget I had any opinion at all."

She tried to take a step back from him and found the wall behind her. She leaned her head back against the wall, and he put out his long hand to the wall beside her, half-convinced for a moment that she was about to fall. But she stood with her shoulders against the wall and closed her eyes, turning her face away to one side. Tears squeezed from under her closed eyelids and ran down her cheeks.

"Oh," she whispered, "why won't you leave me alone?" She pressed her face against the wall. "Please, just leave me alone!"

Torn by her unhappiness, he turned and left, leaving her still standing there, pressed in sorrow against the wall.

Chapter 16

In the days that followed, Paul did not see her again. It was more than obvious that she was avoiding him, and she must at least have spoken to Jase about him, for the Necromancer made it a point one day to speak about her.

"You're wasting your time, there," Jase said bluntly. "She's Walt's."

"I know that," said Paul. He glanced across the table at Jase. The other man had met him for lunch near World Engineering Headquarters, bringing him a long and curious list of cults and societies with which, as Jase put it, the Guild had some "influence." Paul was supposed to learn the names and habits of these groups against some future date when the Guild might want to cultivate them. Paul accepted the list without protest. In spite of the fact that he was theoretically supposed to take orders only from the Guildmaster, he had yet to meet Blunt. Jase brought him all his instructions. Paul had decided not to make an issue of this for the moment. There was too much to be learned even as things were.

There were about sixty thousand members in the Chantry Guild. Of these, perhaps fifteen hundred had dramatic parapsychological talents. Even in a world which accepted such things—even though mostly as interesting parlor tricks or talents on a par with wiggling one's ears—fifteen hundred people represented a pretty remarkable pool of potential ability. Paul was supposed to learn all about each one of the fifteen hundred odd: who could do what, and when, and, most important, who was improving his powers by exploring them in the curious, mystical, long-way-around light of the Alternate Laws.

In addition, there were other aspects of the Guild for Paul to learn, like the list Jase had just brought over on Paul's lunch hour. And all the work connected with the World Engineering Complex, where Tyne had Paul studying procedure like any executive trainee. Weather all over the world had been freakishly bad. In the southern hemisphere the winter had been stormy and cold. Here, the summer days were muggy and sweltering, but no rain fell. The Weather Control Complex found itself in the position of having to rob Peter to pay Paul—moisture diverted to one needy section of the Earth left other sections either twice as arid or drowned in torrential, flooding rains that caused widespread damage. It was no crisis, but it was annoyingly uncomfortable. The internal climate of the great city Complexes held the outside weather at arms length, but the emotional impact of the season's aberrancies came through even into air-conditioned interiors like this one where Paul and Jase sat at lunch.

"It's just as well you realize she does belong to Walt," said Jase. For perhaps the first time since Paul had met him, there was a gentleness in Jase's voice. "She's Finnish, you know—you know where her name comes from?"

"No," said Paul. "No, I don't."

"The Kalevala—the Finnish national epic. Longfellow wrote his Hiawatha poem from it."

"No," said Paul, "I didn't know."

"Kaleva—Finland," said Jase.

(Wind across snow fields. Tinkling among the icicles of a cavern— I knew it the first time, thought Paul.)

"Kaleva had three sons. Handsome Lemminkainen, the art-smith, Ilmarinen, and the ancient Väinämöinen." Paul watched Jase with interest; for the first time the drive and rush of the man was gone. He spoke the names of the old legend with the lingering love of a scholar in his voice. "Väinämöinen invented the sacred harp—Kantele. And she is a harp, our Kantele. A harp for the hand of gods or heroes. That's why Walt holds her, old as he is, unyielding as he is to anything but his own way of doing things." Jase shook his head across the table. "You may be arrogant, Paul. But even you have to face the fact that Walt's something more than us ordinary men."

Paul smiled a little, Jase, watching him, laughed shortly. Abruptly the Necromancer was his own hard, glittering self again.

"Because you don't think you can be killed," said Jase, "you think you can't be defeated, either!"

Paul shook his head.

"I'm quite sure I can be killed," he answered. "It's the defeat I doubt."

"Why?" asked Jase, leaning forward. Paul was a little surprised to see that the man was seriously asking.

"I don't know. I—feel it," said Paul, hesitantly.

Jase let the breath out through his nose with a faint, impatient sound. He stood up.

"Learn that list," he said. "Burt said to tell you he'd pick you up tonight after you're through at your office, if you weren't otherwise tied up. You might give him a call."

"I will," said Paul, and watched the other man leave, moving lithely and swiftly among the tables of the restaurant.

Burton McLeod, two-handed broadsword with human brain and soul, had become the nearest thing to a close friend Paul could ever remember having in his life. And this just in the past few weeks and months.

McLeod was in his early forties. Occasionally he looked immeasurably older. Sometimes he looked almost boyish. There was a deep, unvarying sadness in him, which was there as a result of the violence he had done, but not as a result of the ordinary reactions.

He did not regret the killing he had done. His conscience saw no reason why an enemy should not die. But deep within him, it saddened him that battle was not sanctified. Surely there had been something right and holy at one time about a flat field, a fair fight, and a fair death? He would never have thought to ask quarter for himself, and it embarrassed him that the world in which he lived insisted upon the concept of unvarying quarter for all, even for those he regarded as needing killing. He was a kind and gentle man, a little shy with those of the human race he considered worthwhile, in which class, along with Blunt, Kantele, and Jase, Paul was pleased and embarrassed in turn to find himself numbered. His mind was brilliant and he was an instinctive bookworm, and his essential moral code was so innate that there seemed to be a wall between him and any possibility of dishonesty.

Like Paul, his life had been solitary. That might have been part of what drew them together. But a mutual honesty and a lack of ordinary fear played a part, also. It began with Paul being sent for some rudimentary tutoring in unarmed self-defense, as part of his Guild teachings, and went on from there with Paul's and McLeod's mutual discovery that Paul's overdeveloped arm was not amenable to ordinary training, or susceptible to ordinary attack and disablement.

"It's speed that does it," McLeod had said, one evening in a gym, after several unsuccessful attempts on his part to lock and hold Paul's arm. "Given speed and leverage, you don't need much in the way of muscle. But you've got the muscle, too." He examined Paul's arm with interest. "I don't understand it. You ought to be slow as a truck. But you're as fast or faster than I am."

"A freak," said Paul, opening and closing his fist to watch the muscles in his forearm bulge and retreat.

"That's it," agreed McLeod, without any overtone of comment. "That isn't just an overdeveloped arm. It's just a properly developed, trained arm for somebody six inches bigger than you. Someone rather lean, but in top shape, and about six-seven or so. Was your other arm as long as this one?"

Paul dropped his arm down by his side. To his intense and sudden interest, he saw that the tips of his fingers hung down almost to his kneecap.

"No," he said. "This one wasn't, either."

"Well," said McLeod, shrugging. He began to put on the shirt he had taken off to instruct Paul. "We didn't really work up a sweat. I'll wait until I get home to shower. Buy you a drink?"

"If I can buy the second," said Paul. And that was the beginning of their friendship.

It was late July of the summer that Jase made his call, left the list of the cults and societies for Paul to learn, and the word about McLeod seeing Paul after working hours that evening.

Paul called up the other man from back at the office and agreed to meet McLeod in the bar of the same restaurant where he had had lunch with Jase. He spent the rest of the afternoon *running the charts*, as the office phrase was, down in the heart of the huge two-hundred-level building that was the core of the world's machinery, actually in the Super-Complex, itself.

This duty was one which everyone on Tyne's staff, including Tyne, had to perform for himself about once a month. The equipment of the Super-Complex was semi-self-adapting. Changes were constantly being made in it to keep it in line with changes being made in the ultimate mechanisms out in the world with which it was in contact and control. Also, within certain limits, it was capable—and exercised that capability—of making changes in itself. Accordingly, everyone on Tyne's staff had the obligation of keeping up their own portfolio of charts and information about the Super-Complex. You started out with a thick sheaf of notices of alteration, and went down among the working levels, checking the actual changes and seeing they were entered in your portfolio. Without these, there might have been a number of shifts in responsibility from one recording, computing, or controlling element to another, and the human staff might have found itself trying to initiate changes through automatic channels that had already been closed.

It was simply the homework connected with the job of being on the World Engineer's staff, the necessary duty of keeping up-to-date in your own field of endeavor.

Nonetheless, in Paul's case he found it to be much more than the routine duty it was supposed to be. Moving about through chance corridors allowed by the mobile units of the Super-Complex itself, surrounded level by level by the impossible intricacies of softly humming and clicking equipment, Paul could now understand why someone like the weak, drug-fogged Malorn could have been pushed over the unstable border of his mind by moving around here. There was life, all right, in this steadily operating maze of understanding and control; Paul felt it certainly and surely. But it was not life in the human sense of the living, and it did not face him directly. Rather, it slid behind the massed equipment, hid in a corridor closed a second before by a unit moving to block a path that had once been open.

The two previous times he had been down to bring his portfolio up-to-date he had not seemed to notice so much purposefulness to the feeling of mechanical life about him. He wondered if he was becoming sensitized, perhaps in the same way that Malorn had.

The idea was ridiculous. The moment he held Malorn's broken personality up alongside his own for purposes of comparison, that much became immediately plain. Malorn had been afraid.

Paul stood still for a moment on the sixty-seventh level, looking about him. Far down the open corridor in which he was standing, a tall gleaming bank of units slid across the opening, blocking it, and a new path opened up, angling off to the right. It was like being down in among the moving parts of some engine. An engine equipped to be careful of crushing any small creature climbing about within it as it moved to break old connections between its parts, and make new connections.

Paul turned back to his portfolio with a suddenly inquiring eye. It had not occurred to him before to consider areas within the levels of equipment. He, like all other staff members, simply went to the point where it was necessary to check on a change, checked on it, then took the most direct route to the next closest change point. But the portfolio was simply a history of changes running back to the general chart put out at the beginning of each year. He glanced through it.

The forty-ninth to the fifty-second level, he saw, showed no changes whatsoever since the beginning of the year. In this area the chart showed the Earth terminal of the no-time connection with Station

Springboard on Mercury, and the equipment dealing with the relationship of this project to Earthside economy, social factors, and science.
Paul frowned over the immediate chart of that area. It seemed incred-
ible that an area dealing with research and discovery should have failed
to show a multitude of changes in seven months, let alone showing
none.

It occurred to Paul, abruptly, that information about the changes
in that area might be restricted to certain qualified people. Perhaps to
Tyne himself. The World Engineer had, not once but a number of times
in the past weeks, recommended that Paul ask about anything that
puzzled him. Paul lifted his wrist phone and buzzed the office on the
two hundredth level.

"Nancy," he said to the receptionist, "this is Paul. Do you know
anything about any area down here I'm not supposed to go into or
know about?"

"Why, no," said the girl. In the small tank of Paul's wrist phone,
her face was slim, cheerful, but puzzled. "Staff members from this
office can go anywhere in the Supe."

"I see," said Paul. "Could I talk to Mr. Tyne?"

"Oh, he just went down into the Supe himself, about five minutes
ago."

"Portfolio?"

"That's right."

"He's wearing a phone, isn't he?"

"Just a minute." She glanced at her board. "I guess he must have
left it on his desk here. You know he doesn't like wearing one." She
grinned at Paul. "It's just the rest of us have to follow rules."

"Well," said Paul, "I'll catch him later after he's back."

"I'll tell him you called, Paul. 'By."

" 'By, Nancy." Paul clicked off his phone. He thought for a second
and then headed himself for the unchanged area between the forty-
ninth and fifty-second levels.

He found it no different on the forty-ninth level than on other
levels in the Supe, until he came suddenly upon the long, looming
roundness of the three-step accelerator tube. He passed around the end
of this and found himself crossing the small open area that was a
counterpart of the contact point he had seen at Springboard. This was
one end of the no-time pathway that abolished the distance between
terminals.

As his first step came down on the highly polished surface of the
area, the alarm of a sudden warning rang loudly in his inner sensitivity.

He almost checked himself. But just at that moment something attracted his attention otherwise.

The sound of a conversation came to his ears. Both voices used the deeper, male register of tones, and one was the voice of Kirk Tyne. The other voice was unnatural.

They reached Paul's ears down an angled corridor between high units of equipment. Paul went quickly and, he did not think why, quietly up the corridor toward them.

He turned the angle of the corridor. And stopped, finding himself shielded behind the angle of a projecting unit some eighteen or twenty feet high. Just beyond this angle he looked out into a fairly good-sized open space, almost a square, surrounded by units a good two levels in height. Their lower levels were lighted for the benefit of those living people who might need to work among them, as all units were lighted. But their upper part projected up into the dusk where lights were not. All around the square of open space they loomed like finely machined and polished idols in a temple. Tiny below them, facing one wall of these great shapes, stood Tyne.

"There's no doubt about it," Tyne was saying, "the weather—all this rioting and upset. The world situation is abnormal."

"It has been recorded." The voice came from somewhere in the wall of units facing the World Engineer. "It has been symbolized and integrated with the base situation. No apparent need for extraordinary measures is now indicated."

"There's an atmosphere of unrest. I can feel it myself."

"No concrete indications have been signalized or recorded."

"I don't know," said Tyne, almost to himself. He raised his voice slightly. "I think I may override you on this."

"Override," said the voice, "would introduce an uncalculable factor rising to a peak unit influence of twelve per cent and extending over an eighteen-month period."

"I can't simply ignore the situation."

"No situation is ignored. Ordinarily measures are in process to correct the aberrancies."

"And you think they'll prove sufficient?"

"They will correct."

"By which you mean, you think they'll correct," said Tyne, a little harshly. "Sometime I'm going to take a summer off and design an honest element of self-doubt for you."

The other voice did not answer.

"What should I do?" asked Tyne, finally.

"Continue normal routine."

"I guess," said Tyne. He turned suddenly and strode off toward an opposite side of the square. Before him, a corridor opened up. He went away down it, and it closed behind him.

Paul was left watching in silence.

Quietly, he came out into the square and looked about him. The units he looked at were in appearance no different than the larger computer elements on other levels. He walked over to the side where Tyne had stood. But he could not even discern a loud-speaker element in the faces of the units he was observing.

A slight sound behind him made him glance over his shoulder. He turned completely around. The corridor by which he had come to this spot was now closed. The units stood looming, side by side, unbroken around him.

"Paul Formain," said the voice that had spoken to Tyne. Paul turned back to the units he had just been looking over.

"Your presence at this point in space and time is unjustified within the symbolic structure of human society. Accordingly, your removal may now justifiably be effected."

Book Three: **PATTERN**

Emerging on that final plain,
Once more the watch-bell tolled again.
—Twice! Thor's soul and mine were one,
And a dragon shape had crossed the sun.

THE ENCHANTED TOWER

Chapter 17

"Set!" said Paul.

The word went out and was lost in the shadowy stillness above and behind the metallic shapes of the huge units standing over and around Paul. There was a slight noise behind him. He glanced toward it and saw a corridor opening once more in the general direction from which he had reached this area on the forty-ninth level. In the opposite direction a single unit slid out to fill most of the open space, and turned toward Paul. It rolled slowly toward him. He backed up and saw he was being forced into the newly opened corridor.

"So you can do violence to people," said Paul.

"No," said the voice that had spoken to Tyne. Now it seemed to come from the unit that was crowding Paul backward.

"You're doing violence to me right now."

"I am correcting a misplacement," said the voice. "Your value is external and false. It is perverting the symbological matrix of society at this moment."

"Nonetheless," said Paul, "you have a responsibility to me, as well as to society."

"More latitude," said the unit, forcing him back along the corridor, "is possible with those not sane, who are not responsible."

"I'm not sane?"

"No," said the machine, "you are not."

"I'd like," said Paul, "to hear your definition of sanity."

"Sanity," replied the voice, "in the human being is a response to natural instincts. It is sane to sleep, to eat, to seek to feed oneself, to fight if attacked, to sleep if no occupation is at hand."

Paul's shoulder blades came up against something hard. Turning

around, he saw he had reached a turn in the corridor down which he
was backing. The unit rolling toward him on invisible smooth-turning
cylinders had not paused. He changed direction and backed away
again.

"How about thinking? Is that sane?"

"Thought is a perfectly sane process, as long as it follows sane
paths in the human brain."

"Such as those concerned with feeding and sleeping?"

"Yes."

"But not," said Paul, "those concerned with painting a picture or
discovering a new method of interstellar travel?"

"Such thinking," said the unit, "is a response to abnormal irrita-
tions in the environment of the human concerned. Perfectly sane human
beings have no need to do more than live and propagate, all under the
conditions of greatest comfort."

"By those standards," said Paul, still backing up, "most of the
human race is insane."

"You are quite wrong," said the voice, "roughly eighty-five per
cent of the human race has had no real desire outside the framework
I mentioned. Of the remaining fifteen, only about five in any generation
have made any real effort to put their insanities into practice. Perhaps
two per cent have some effect on future generations and one-tenth of
one per cent are later admired even by the sane."

"I won't argue your figures," said Paul, feeling his left shoulder
brush a unit, unyielding as the brick wall against which a man stands
before a firing squad. "Even though I could. But don't you think the
fact that your final category is admired even by the sane, as you put
it, is some kind of an indication that maybe others had something
besides insanity at work for them?"

"No," said the voice.

"Forgive me," said Paul. "I think I overestimated you. Let me say
that again in terms you might be able to handle. Once you achieve an
ideal existence for the human race, what's going to become of the arts,
scientific research of all kinds, and the exploration of the natural universe?"

"They will be abandoned by the sane," said the machine.

Paul, backing up, saw the flanking units on either side of his corridor suddenly give way to open space. At the same time, the unit
which had been herding him forward rolled level with the mouth of
the corridor and stopped, so that Paul now found himself facing a final
wall. He turned and looked about him. He stood, completely hemmed
in by a wall of units, upon the contact area at the end of the three-step

accelerator. The end of the tube, the terminal that could tear him from this spot off into the universal ubiquity of no-time, loomed high above his head like a cannon mouth over the head of a sparrow which, in its muzzle, had taken refuge from a hawk.

"And the insane, at that time?" asked Paul.

"There will be no more insane," said the voice. "They will have destroyed themselves."

Paul saw nothing to give him any impression, and heard nothing; but deep within his flesh and bones he felt the accelerator warming to life. Even now, back and forth over flashing yards of distance, the point of no-time to be, was warming to life. Paul thought of Springboard, and of the emptiness of space.

"You tried to get me to destroy myself, didn't you?" said Paul, remembering what Jase had said. "In the mine; in front of the marching society that day."

"Always," said the voice, "the way has been open for you to destroy yourself. It is what works best with the insane. The sane are easy to kill. The insane fight very hard against being killed, but are more susceptible where it comes to the opportunities of self-destruction."

"Do you realize," asked Paul, feeling the accelerator warming to life over him, "your definition of sane and insane is completely artificial and wrong?"

"No," said the machine, "I cannot be anything but correct. It is impossible for me to be incorrect."

"You ought to see," said Paul, "that one false assumption used as a basis for later decisions could cause all your conclusions to be in error."

"I know this. I also know I contain no false assumptions," answered the voice. Above the looming curve of the accelerator the dusk of the dark higher up seemed to be pressing down on Paul. Almost, the voice seemed to descend also, becoming confidential. "My assumptions must stand the test of whether the structures built upon them guarantee a safe and continued life to mankind. This they do. I am humanity's guardian. You, in contrast, are its destroyer."

"I—?" asked Paul, staring up into the darkness.

"I know you. You are the destroyer of mankind. You are the warrior who will not fight and cannot be conquered. You are proud," said the machine. "I know you, Necromancer. Already you have done incalculable damage, and created the first blind living form of the inconceivable enemy."

A barrier went down in Paul's mind. What was beyond it, he could not at this moment see; but it brought him relief and strength. It was as if a soldier, after long waiting, had at last received definite orders commanding him upon a long and desperate journey.

"I see," said Paul quietly, as much to himself as to the machine.

"To see is not enough," said the voice. "It is not enough excuse. I am the living wish of mankind expressed in solidity. I have the right to direct people. You have not. They are not yours. They are mine." The tones of the voice did not vary, but Paul got an impression of total effort being directed against him. "I will not let you lead mankind blindfold through a dark maze to an end they cannot conceive of, and final destruction. I cannot destroy you, or I would. But I can put you aside."

The voice paused slightly.

Paul was suddenly aware of a slight humming from the great cylinder head beside and above him. The acceleration was nearing the point of break into no-time which, like a sudden spark jumping, would contact and remove him from the point where he stood. He had just time to remember that he had been through no-time before, on the heels of Jase and Kantele when they escaped the police in the office across the concourse from the Koh-i-Nor. But that had been like running down a flight of stairs, while this would be like being thrown down them. He had just time to brace his awareness.

"*Now*," said the machine.

And Paul was ripped from the position he held in time and space and spread out to the uttermost reaches of the universe.

Chapter 18

Paul was not immediately delivered at the destination to which the machine had sent him.

From the psychic point of view the action of the accelerator upon him was like that of hurling him down an endless flight of infinitely stretching stairs. But even as he tumbled that invincible part of him, like the reflexes of a superbly conditioned athlete, was instinctively gathering his feet under him, regaining his balance, and stopping his fall. It checked him, got him upright; but the conscious part of him was for the moment stunned and dazed, out of action. Instinctively in action, like a half-knocked-out fighter too well trained to stay down, he fought clear of the push of the accelerator and wandered, as it were, off sideways along one of the stair surfaces.

The situation was entirely different from when he had gone through no-time on the heels of Jase and Kantele, when he and they had been escaping the air police across from the Koh-i-Nor Hotel. The way by which they had entered no-time then, had been by a much more bearable emotional route. The accelerator method (lacking the medication that was yet to be discovered) was simply and plainly brutal.

It achieved its desired end by sheer savagery of action. It was this that had caused effects ranging from severe nervous breakdown to death in early Springboard volunteers transmitted to the terminal from which Paul had left. In essence, under the accelerator method, the individual's identity fled the immediate level of no-time to escape the suddenly intolerable conditions under which it had been forced to experience real time and space. Inanimate objects, of course, had no such difficulties. But the human psyche could not have retained its orientation under a full experiencing of conscious dispersal to universal dimensions and later reassembly. In instinctive self-protection it made the great step upward into the subjective universe.

Now, experiencing this, Paul suddenly understood the operation of the Alternate Laws, which were naturally entirely subjective in nature. However, at the moment this understanding could make no contact with the operative areas of his mind, which were still stunned. These wandered the subjective dimension of that line of endeavor to which the greater part of his being was dedicated.

There was no shape or dimension to the subjective universe in which he now wandered. It was, however, subject to the reality imposed on it by the symbolic processes of Paul's deeper self. Consequently, to him now, it took on the appearance of a vast, pebbled plain, with the pebbles growing in size in the distance. It was the plain of which he had dreamed on returning to the hotel after his first meeting with Jase.

Before, he had toiled over it as if walking. Now he skimmed rapidly just above its surface. Gray, black, rubbled, and bleak, the plain stretched off about him in all directions, not to any horizons, but to a great but finite distance. An emptiness of spirit, a sense of desolation, made up the atmosphere around him. He chilled in it, even while the unstunned part of him struggled to remind him that it was all subjective, all interpretative of the job he had, at a great distance in time and space, once dedicated himself to do.

"Arrogant," murmured a wind across the larger pebbles with the voice of Jase.

"These are my people, not yours," whispered a metallic breeze from another direction. And then, from a little farther off, and fainter even: *"I know you, Necromancer...."*

He went quickly from the voices. The pebbles grew to boulders, to huge and mammoth shapes, to vast mountains with darkness between them. Then, at last, over the farthest and largest of these, he came to the final edge of the plain.

He went swiftly to it. From a point above the last and most mountainous boulder shapes he hung and looked down, out, and up at the same time upon a shifting infinity of darkness.

It was a gulf beyond which he felt there was light. But he could not see it, for the closer darkness. And in the darkness, something stirred.

It was barely living yet. It was an embryo, an amoeba, with only so much of consciousness as had allowed it to sense his existence when he had been under initiation, deep in the rock of Mercury. And only so much of reaction as had allowed it to make that one reactive, whip-lash attack in his direction. Its growing was all yet before it.

And it was all in the way of evil that the Super-Complex had said it was. And Paul had created it. Without him it would never have been, but now it lived, and grew in power and understanding.

A terrible desire came over him then, to attack it now and settle the matter once and for all. But when he moved to go beyond the edge of his plain, he found something invisible there that would not let him pass. It was the barrier of the laws under which he had created what stirred out there. The laws that protected it from him as much as he from it, until the time when both he and it should be strong enough to break all barriers. And suddenly his dazed mind cleared, and he realized that if he should meet and conquer it now, nothing would be proved. Nothing accomplished. There would have been no point in its creation in the first place.

Abruptly, his mind was clear again. He retreated swiftly from the edge of the plain. He returned to the area where the boulders were again down to the size of pebbles. And here, close to where he had wandered astray, he found something like a cairn, or stony pile, new-built. It was about three times his own height, and the chance crevices between its stones gave an errie impression of tiny arrowslits or win-dows, though he felt instinctively that there was nothing alive about it as yet, nothing within. Standing beside it, he looked once more about the plain, and saw now that here and there at the farthest limits, this subjective landscape of his seemed to have elevated itself slightly, as if in the beginnings of hills, in a circle, surrounding him.

With that, he gave in to the original impulse that had brought him here and went forward to his destination.

He came to ordinary consciousness again in what looked like a small apartment. He had one brief glimpse of it before his legs—he had come through standing in the same position in which he had faced the Supe—crumpled under him and the full shock of what had been done to him took its price from his physical body. He pitched to the floor.

Here again, as always, he did not go completely under into un-consciousness. By all ordinary standards he should have gone com-pletely out, but in actuality he only passed into a foggy, uncertain state which was the physical equivalent of his dazed condition while he had been wandering the subjective universe. During the succeeding several days in which this state gradually wore itself out, he was vaguely conscious of the fact that he had dragged himself from the floor to a nearby couch, and that he had once or twice drunk from a water dispenser that was nearby. Otherwise, he had not eaten or slept, or even fallen into the half-active dream-filled state that was his ordinary slumber.

He did not suffer in a physical sense. He had in no meaning of the term suffered any physical damage as a result of being transmitted to this spot. What had been torn about and attacked in him was his essential, immaterial identity. And the effect was similar to that of an attack of profound depression. He was perfectly capable physically of getting up and examining his surroundings. The act of will required to do so, however, was like that of lifting his own body's weight to a man drained of blood almost to the point of death.

Gradually, however, he recovered.

He became aware first that the apartment was shaped like a section of a cylinder, its bottom curve having a floor built across it. It was fitted with the compact luxury of an ocean-going submersible liner. Between the curved walls were couch and easy chairs, tape cabinets, music player, bar, kitchen—even some finger-sculptures, and a couple of interesting stochastic paintings, one in oils, the other in red, black and yellow clays.

There was also the cleared area, floored in polished black, which had been the terminal point of his arrival.

It was sometime on the third day that he found himself staring at the paintings, as he had for some hours now, like a man stupefied. His feeble but certain perception made the connection immediately, and he laughed weakly. He had suddenly realized the existence of a plasma that could in part replace the psychic blood of which he had been drained.

He struggled wearily up from the couch and went clumsily on hands and knees across the room to the music player. From there he went to the tape cabinets, and to some adjoining shelves where he found a reference printer.

Twenty minutes later found him back on the couch. The fine, golden threads of *Il Trovatore* were spinning themselves out of the speakers of the music player, the rich canvas of Rubens' "Adoration of the Magi" was displayed in the tank of the tape cabinets, and the solemn heartbreak of Milton's sonnet on his blindness tolled like a slow and shadowed bell from a printer sheet in Paul's hand:

> *When I consider how my light is spent*
> *Ere half my days in this dark world and wide . . .*

Paul lay there, changing art, music, and poetry for mathematics, philosophy, medicine, and all the fields of man's endeavor. And slowly the life of those who had had something to give to life seeped back into his own drained being, and his strength came back to him.

By the fourth day after his arrival he was back to normal. He got himself a large meal out of the kitchen, and then set about exploring the limits of this prison to which he had been sentenced.

It was about thirty feet in length, and about that same height and width at its greatest points of those two dimensions. Either end of it was a great circle flattened off at the bottom by the chord-line of the floor. One circle overlooked the terminal area of his arrival. The other merely filled up the far end of the living space.

It was this second circle that Paul looked over with interest. The first, overhanging the terminal point of his arrival, presumably simply hid the business end of an accelerator. The second might, however, be blocking the way to an escape route. When he looked closely, he discovered that the second in fact did appear to be something in the nature of a removable cover, held in place by a simple magnetic lock.

He unlocked the cover and the lower half of it swung away from him like half of a huge Dutch door. He walked through it and found himself in a farther extension of the cylinder, three times as big as the living quarters and filled with crated equipment and tools. He let his gaze settle over the tools and crates, and the answer he was looking for became easily apparent to him. This was the material with which the accelerator terminal here could be fitted to transmit as well as receive. He paused to glance at the tickets attached to some of the crates, but they were punch cards notated in a technician's shorthand that he did not know. He went on to the still farther circular wall that ended this division of the cylinder.

This had been sealed with a running bead of plastic weld all around its rim. It was evidently intended to be easily removed, but only by someone who knew how to do so, and why he was doing it.

Paul turned back and searched the second room once more, but there was no message or instruction list in sight.

He went back into the living quarters, and proceeded to make a methodical search of that area. He excavated drawers and investigated files and cabinets. There was no instruction sheet or manual. Evidently, whoever this place had been designed for had been expected to have that sort of information in his head. Paul was standing in the middle of the living-area floor and looking about for some hiding place he might have overlooked, when there was a sound from behind him, from the direction of the terminal area.

He looked. There on the bare and polished surface he saw a newssheet lying, still slightly curled from the printer. He went to it and picked it up.

For a moment he could not imagine what reason had caused the Supe to send it through to him. The headings of the various stories on the front page screamed of riots, panics, and earthquakes. Then, sliding his eye up one column and down the next in automatic speed-reading, Paul saw a small item: WORLD ENGINEER GIVEN EXTRAORDINARY POWERS.

By an unprecedented world-wide register vote, the World Engineer yesterday was awarded authority to freeze the credit numbers and deny all Complex services to rioters and those suspected of disturbing the peace. The Complex-Major tabulated an almost inconceivable 82 per cent of the total voting population, with 97.54 per cent of those voting registering in favor of awarding the additional authority to the World Engineer.

A tiny item. But Paul frowned. Highly important it was, but that did not seem to him sufficient cause for the Supe to send him the newssheet. Nor—he glanced back at the other stories upon the front page—was the news of widespread emotional disturbances and rioting sufficient. The machine was not equipped to gloat, and surely with Paul imprisoned here as he was, there could be no other reason for informing him about events he was powerless to have an effect upon.

Still puzzling, Paul opened the newssheet to its second and third pages. Then he saw it.

By some apparent freak mishap, the printer had failed to bring out the printing on these two pages otherwise than as an unreadable blur, except for one item as small as the front-page item Paul had just frowned over. That one stood out as if framed.

DRONE LOST

The Complex-Major today noted the information that one of its Springboard drones, carrying automatic terminal receiving equipment to the planet known as New Earth, fourth world of the star Sirius, has suffered a malfunction of the directing system and been lost in space. This drone, which three days ago was noted as being in position to land shortly on New Earth, apparently missed its landing and has fallen beyond that planet under conditions of movement which will carry it out

*of the Sirian system. There can be no hope of reestablishing
contact, notes the Complex-Major, or of recovery of the drone.*

Paul dropped the newssheet and, spinning about, strode swiftly
back into the farther room. Seizing a tool like a chisel, he attacked the
plastic weld around the rim of the circular end wall. The plastic peeled
up under his gouging and a thin edge of the metal was revealed. He
forced the chisel edge in under the edge of the revealed metal. For a
moment there was resistance, and then the chisel plunged through.
There was a sudden whistling insuck of air past Paul's hand, the plastic
weld cracked loose halfway around the rim, and the lower half spanged
sharply on a deep bass note. Before Paul's eyes a horizontal crack ran
across the metal, and the lower half of it broke clean from the top and
fell into the room.

Paul caught it. It was a thin sheet of light magnesium alloy. He
bent it inward and laid it flat on the floor. Then he stepped one step
forward and looked out, through heavy glass.

Before him was a rolling landscape under a slightly yellowish sky,
an atmosphere hazed with fine dust. Something like tiny, close-packed
fern leaves covered the ground and grew thickly and a little larger
about an occasional boulder or outcropping of granitic rock. Farther
back were low, broad trees whose trunks and limbs looked as if they
had been shaped out of dark, twisted cable. The brilliant white points
of two Ao-type stars, so close they seemed at the moment to be swimming into each other, peered burningly through the dust haze and made
the illumination for the day outside.

From the sight of these and the landscape they lighted—a landscape rich in promise for the yet infant science of terraforming—Paul
had no difficulty making the connection between his present location
and one of the worlds described in popular articles as destinations for
the Springboard drones.

The double star in the sky out there could only be Sirius and its
close companion. Which meant that this was New Earth, and the message of the newssheet the Supe had sent him was clear. Paul, and this
drone in which he found himself imprisoned, had been deliberately and
officially "lost" from the records.

For a moment Paul leaned his forehead wearily against the cool
pane of the glass. The long palm and fingers of his single hand pressed
uselessly against the glass' thick surface. Out there beyond its protection was, according to all official reports, an atmosphere suffocating
with hydrogen sulphide. Behind him was crated equipment he had not
the education and training to assemble.

Suddenly he stiffened. His hand slipped down from the glass and he raised his head to look sharply out through the transparency.

Leaning against a boulder on this alien world a little more than a dozen feet from the drone and incongruous against the small, carpeting ferns, was a heavy cane of dark wood; Walter Blunt's cane, one end of which was cracked and splintered as it would have been from being used to smash a human skull.

Chapter 19

"I see," said Paul quietly to the empty room and the landscape beyond the glass. "Of course."

It was like driving through a strange city at night and being convinced that north lay on your right hand. Then, suddenly, a chance-glimpsed street sign, some small but undeniable scrap of information, brings suddenly the undeniable orientation that places north on the left. Abruptly, silently, without real physical movement, the universe swaps ends and you realize that all this time you have been heading west, not east.

Suddenly the pattern about Paul had become clear and correct, down to the last detail.

It was Blunt, of course. As he had instinctively felt all along, it was Blunt—this man who would not turn and show his face openly and clearly—who was the demon. Paul spoke out loud again, but not to Blunt.

"Get me out of here," he said.

No, came an answer from deep inside him, from the invincible part in the back of his mind.

"You mean," asked Paul, "we end here, you and me? The two of us?"

No.

"Then—?"

There's only one of us.

"I see," said Paul again, quietly. "I should have known that."

I can do anything you want. But if I do it, what's the use? We won't have found any way other than force. Our work will all have been wasted, as the living darkness we created beyond the boulders

*would have been wasted if you had killed it then, or if you kill it now,
while it's ungrown. It's up to you now to find the different way.*

"Not the machine's way," said Paul. "Not the way you moved me
out of that office just behind Jase and Kantele that time? A different
way than either of those?"

Yes.

"I don't know where to start."

Perceive. Recapitulate. Feel.

"All right," said Paul. He looked out at the cable trunks and limbs
of the trees beyond the window, and at the cane. "There is only one
thing common to both the objective and subjective universe. This is
identity."

Yes. Go on.

"The objective universe can be expressed in its lowest common
denominators as an accumulation of identity isolates, both living and
nonliving."

That's right.

"The isolates, however, in order to live—that is, to have function
along the single dimension of the time line—must pass in and out of
combinations which can be called sets."

Continue, Brother.

"The sets, in order to create the illusion of reality in objective time
and space, must at all times arrange themselves into a single pattern.
The pattern may vary, but it can't be abandoned or destroyed without
also destroying or abandoning the illusion of reality."

*Entirely correct. And very good for a partial identity that is re-
stricted to reasoning by use of emotion and response. We can be proud
of you. Go on. The next step?*

Paul frowned.

"Next step?" he asked. "That's all."

Application.

"Application? Ah!" said Paul, suddenly. "Of course. The so-called
Alternate Laws"—he glanced once more at the cane against the boulder beyond the window—"and the talents deriving from them are
merely methods of altering the pattern so that the illusion of reality
temporarily permits actions ordinarily not permitted." He thought for
a second. "Blunt doesn't understand this," he said.

Are you certain of that?

Paul smiled a little in the empty silence of the room.

"That's my department, isn't it? Understanding."

I submit myself. Go on.

Paul hesitated.

"Is there more?" he asked.

You wanted to get out of here. You have perceived and recapitulated. From here on you leave me for your own territory. Feel.

Paul closed his eyes. Standing with the yellow light from outside showing faintly through his lids, he tried for a total contact with all that surrounded him—room, drone, planet, suns, space. It was like attempting to make some delicate last connection with blind fingers at arm's length, out of sight inside a piece of complicated equipment. Only, Paul's effort was completely nonphysical. He was reaching out to feel fully and correctly the great pattern of the objective universe, so that he could fit his own identity perfectly into pivot position within its structure.

For a moment he made no progress. For a fraction of a second he felt the completely stripped feeling of total awareness, but lacking even a single point of contact as he floated free, swinging into position. Then, suddenly, it was like the moment of orientation that had followed his seeing the cane beyond the glass, but much greater. And mixed with it the sensation of melting together, like but greater than that which had come to him to finish his interview with the psychiatrist Elizabeth Williams.

In one sudden moment of no-time, Paul and the invincible part of him fused irreversibly together.

It was as if he had stood on a narrow stage and suddenly, on all sides, great curtains had been raised, so that he found himself looking away in all directions to enormous distances. But now—alone.

"Ave atque vale," he said, and smiled a little sadly. "Hail and farewell." He turned back to the glass of the window. "Destruct," he said. "Of course. Blunt planted that for me, and in his own limited way, he was right."

Paul turned back to the tools behind him. He chose a heavy sledge hammer and took it to the window. His first blow bent the metal handle of the sledge but merely starred the glass. But his next blow sent the sledge crashing through and the whole wall of glass fell out in ruins.

He took three rapid steps toward the boulder where the cane leaned, as the acid, choking atmosphere numbed his sense of smell with the assault of its odor and filled his lungs. He reached the cane and seized it even as his eyesight began to sear and blur with tears. Almost, he could hear Blunt chanting, as he had chanted in the vision tank back there underground at Malabar Mine while Paul watched.

"Destruct! The ultimate destruct! The creative destruct that will rescue Man from being saved forever . . ."

Then Paul felt his knees strike the ground as he fell. And with that

his identity quit his body forever and left it there, fallen and dying in
the suffocation of the yet-untamed atmosphere of the world which
would be called New Earth, with a splintered walking stick clutched
in its single fist.

Chapter 20

*Full twenty-fathoms times five, thy body lies. Of its bones is ocean
debris made . . .*

Thirty miles due west of La Jolla, California, which is a few miles
up the coast line from San Diego, on a sandy underwater plateau six-
hundred-odd feet below the surface of the ever-moving blue Pacific,
Paul's bodiless identity hovered above a skeleton of a man wrapped
and weighted with half-inch chain. This place had not been his original
intended destination, but he had detoured here to settle a purely emotional point in his own mind. Now, hovering above the chain-wrapped
skeleton, he sensed with relief that the body it once supported had died
a natural death. It was not that he doubted that Blunt had been willing
to murder to gain the results he wanted. It was just that he wished the
ledger sheet on which he and Blunt were totaled up together and
against each other to be as clean as possible.

He left the white bones in the peace of their eternal darkness, and
went his way.

His way—the way Blunt's cane on New Earth had been designed
to send him—led him to an awakening in something like a coffin. He
lay, legs together, arms at his sides, on his back, and tightly enclosed
in a metal container. His eyes were open but they saw nothing but
blackness. His pattern-linked perception, however, recognized that he
was in a sort of cold-storage vault—something very like the slide-out
six-and-a-half-foot drawers for unclaimed bodies in a public morgue.
The body he now inhabited was identical with the one he was used to,
except that it had two good arms. However, it seemed completely paralyzed.

It was paralyzed, he recognized with a sudden grim humor, because it was frozen stiff. The container in which he lay was surrounded with refrigerator coils and his body's temperature was a little more than twenty degrees below zero, Fahrenheit. The body would first have to be thawed before any life could be brought to it.

Paul surveyed the surrounding pattern. It would be surprising if Blunt, who had made so many arrangements where Paul was concerned, had not also made some here. Sure enough, the container lay on tilted tracks and was held inside the freezing unit by the bare hooking of a catch. Paul made the necessary slight alterations in the pattern and the catch failed. He slid out into the light of a brightly illuminated room without windows.

As he emerged into the room, the temperature rose sharply and suddenly from close to freezing to seventy-six degrees Fahrenheit. Lying at a tilted angle that put his feet close to the floor below the container and his head several inches higher, Paul saw it was a small room with a single door and no furniture, tilted in white.

The single item of interest in it was a message neatly printed in large letters on the wall opposite Paul. It read:

Paul: As soon as you find yourself able,
come and join us in suite 1243, at the Koh-i-Nor.
—Walt Blunt

Paul's container had gone into action on its own now. It was beaming deep, gentle heat into the very center of his frozen bones and tissues. It would take—what? Half an hour, perhaps longer, to bring him up to a living temperature so that his identity could take over command of his new body in the ordinary sense. Of course, almost undoubtedly Blunt had planned that Paul would help and hurry the process along. In any case it was rather fine scheduling, and showed an attitude toward other people and the universe that was far from modest. For the first time—in such small unexpected ways, thought Paul, do past things of minor importance explain themselves—Paul received a sudden extra insight into Jase's repeated accusation of arrogance. Over the years Jase must have become well acquainted with arrogance, in the person of Blunt.

Yes, thought Paul, he would hurry things along. But in a way in which Blunt, with his less complete awareness of the pattern, could not expect. Blunt would not expect that the message on the wall would be a clear warning to Paul that the Chantry Guild had already made its move. Outside this room the world would be trapped in a war—a strange, weird war such as it had never known before. And Blunt, general of the attacking forces, would have timed the entrance of Paul upon the battlefield for the most effective moment from Blunt's point of view.

Only Paul would come early.

He reached into the pattern and to the invincible knowledge that had become a part of him with his own individual ability. He cut certain lines of causal relationship, and established new ones. The pattern altered, in the immediate identity area of the body. And the body itself floated upright out of its container.

It floated toward the door. The door opened. Skimming just above the steps, it mounted a flight of stairs and passed through a farther door into a small hallway. Beyond, was a third door, a transparent door to the traffic level, on a street Paul recognized as being less than a dozen blocks from the Koh-i-Nor. It was night beyond this last door, and for some reason the Complex without seemed darker than it should be.

Paul's body floated to the last door. It opened and he floated out into the hot July night. The Complex Internal Weather Control seemed to have failed in its functioning, for the temperature outside here was in the high nineties at the very least and humidity must be close to a hundred per cent. The still air of the Complex seemed to hang heavily in the unusual shadows between structures, and its heat wrapped itself steamily around Paul's icy body.

No vehicles were in motion. And here, at least, the streets seemed deserted. Paul swung about and skimmed off along the concrete walk in the direction which he knew would take him to the Koh-i-Nor.

The streets were as empty as if the people in the Complex had locked and barred their doors against some plague or roaming madness. In the first half block the only sound Paul heard was the insane, insect-like buzzing of a defective street light. He looked up at its pulsating, uncertain glow, and saw at least part of the reason it did not do well. Its pole had become a monstrous cane of red-and-white striped candy.

Paul floated on. At the next corner he passed a closed door. From the crack beneath it, however, a flood of red fluid remarkably like blood in its color and viscosity was flowing. One block farther on, Paul turned down into a new street and saw his first living person of the night.

This was a man with his shirt half torn off, who was sitting in a doorway and turning a kitchen knife over and over in his hands. He looked up as Paul came toward him.

"Are you a psychiatrist?" he said. "I need—" His lifted eyes caught sight of Paul's feet and the space between them and the pavement. "Oh," he said. He looked down at his hands and went back to playing with his knife again.

Paul paused. And then he realized that his body could not speak. He went on, and as he did so he reached once more into the pattern. It was possible, as he had suspected Blunt had intended, to hurry things up. Living cells could not be thawed quite as crudely as dead meat, but borrowing heat uniformly from the general surroundings was even more efficient than the deep-heating mechanism of the storage container had been. Slowly, but at the same time much more rapidly than might have been expected, a living warmth came to Paul's body as he proceeded on toward the Koh-i-Nor.

He passed other things of the night which bore little relation to normality. A monument in the center of one street crossing was slowly melting down as he passed, like wax in a warm oven. The stone head of a lion, at the corner of a heavy balcony running around one large building, dipped its heavy muzzle and roared down at him as he passed below. In the center of one street he passed a circle of blackness—a hole of nothingness that showed, not the level below, but a spatial distortion on which the human eye was not equipped to focus. No cars were running—Complex Transportation must have been as inactive or powerless as Internal Weather—but occasionally Paul saw other people, alone, on foot, and at some distance. None of them stayed to talk when they saw him coming, but hurried off rapidly.

Life was rapidly taking over Paul's body. He had started the heart early. By the time he reached the concourse his temperature was at ninety-six and a fraction of a degree, pulse and respiration almost normal. He could have walked it, but he waited until he actually reached the entrance to the North Tower of the hotel before he put his feet to the ground.

He walked into a dim-lit lobby illuminated only by emergency lighting, and empty of guests. A white face stared at him from well back of the desk counter. It was the clerk with the elegant longhand. Paul paid him no attention, but walked on around the corner to the elevators.

These, being a balanced system running on stored power, had been unaffected by the obvious curtailment of services otherwise. Silently, gently, efficiently, as if the human race were already dead and only a mechanical duty remained, the disks floated one after another in regular, spaced intervals, up and down the transparent tubes of their shafts. Paul stepped onto a disk ascending the up shaft.

He slid smoothly up, past a succession of empty hallways, barely lighted by the red emergency light above the door to the stairs on each level. Only once did he see someone. That was in passing the ninth level. It was a woman—a young woman, almost a girl. At the sight of him passing up the elevator tube, she turned hastily and ducked into a doorway.

He went on up.

The twelfth level of the hotel, in contrast to the rest of the world Paul had seen that night, was fully lighted. Its illumination seemed almost garish in contrast to the surrounding dark. But no one stirred about its corridor, either. More than this, Paul received from the closed doors he passed an impression of darkness and emptiness beyond, as if suite 1243 toward which he walked was the only space with life within it on this bright level.

When he turned a last corner of the corridor and approached 1243, he saw its door was ajar. It stood three-quarters of the way rolled back into its wall socket, and the sound of a voice came audibly through the opening.

The voice was that of Kirk Tyne.

". . . your blind spot," he was saying. "That's what I can't understand, Walt. A man of your intelligence who thinks the present can be changed *in* the present, without going back and altering the predisposing factors of the past. And so you let loose this madness on the world."

Paul stopped just short of the entrance. He had heard this argument from Tyne before, at the time when Tyne had taken him onto the World Engineer's personal staff. Now it struck Paul as interesting to know what Blunt's answer to it would be.

"You've sold your birthright for a mess of circuits," answered Blunt's voice. "You don't think, Kirk. You parrot what the Supe tells you. If the past can't be changed, the present must. For the future's sake."

"Will you use a little logic?" asked Tyne. "I tell you the present *cannot* be changed without changing the past. Even the Supe, with all its stored knowledge, wouldn't be able to calculate the ultimate possibilities of a single insect's life pattern being altered in the past. And that's the easier way. What you're trying here, now, tonight, is the harder."

"Kirk," said Blunt's voice. "You're a fool. The predisposing factors leading up to this hour have been laid and set up for centuries now. All that's necessary for us is to recognize them and use them."

"I tell you that's not true!"

"Because your Supe . . ." Blunt was beginning, with hard irony forming a cutting edge to his resonant voice, when Paul stirred himself again. He stepped forward, entered the doorway, and walked into the main lounge of what was probably one of the best suites the Koh-i-Nor had to offer its guests.

Around this large room seven people stood in tableau. Close and on Paul's left was Kantele. Just beyond her, half turned away from the entrance, was Blunt, an odd tall hat on his head and a heavy black cape with purple lacings rippling down from his wide shoulders. Beyond Blunt stood Burton McLeod, who of all seven showed the least concern, and Jase, also in cape and hat. His back to the blue curtains closed across the wide, far window wall of the room opposite the door, stood Eaton White, like a small, colorless silhouette. To White's left, on the opposite side of the room, stood the Koh-i-Nor Hotel's security agent, James Butler. But the bizarre touch was upon him, too. He wore the all-black jumper and slacks of one of the better-known marching societies, an outfit that left only face and hands whitely exposed; and in one of those white hands, he held a slim, lethal police handgun which had had its front sight removed. In place of the sight gleamed a small, blue metal cross.

He and McLeod stood across from each other with perhaps a dozen feet of carpet between them. The police handgun casually covered the chest of McLeod, and both men stood untensely, but as if aware of no others in the room besides themselves.

Closest of all, on Paul's right, stood Tyne. He faced the half-turned-away Blunt, and so was, like the colorless and motionless Eaton White, the first to see Paul as he entered. The sudden widening of his eyes made Blunt check his speech. The rest all turned, even Butler and McLeod. And Kantele gasped. They, all except Blunt, stood like people who witness a basic violation of the natural laws by which they have lived all their lives.

But Blunt leaned upon the straight silver knob of a new walking stick and smiled. As perhaps the Athenian pole-march Callimachus smiled on that day in late September, twenty-five hundred and forty years previous, on seeing in the cool bright sunlight between clouds, the dust of his reinforced Greek wings close in on the Persian horde on the plain of Marathon.

"You're a little early, not too much," he said, looking at Paul. "Kirk here hasn't quite been softened up enough yet. But come on in— myself."

And Paul, walking into the suite, seeing Blunt full and clearly face on for the first time, saw indeed—himself.

Chapter 21

Paul strode into the suite. The eyes of all of them were fixed on him, but none showed more shattering from the blow than the blue eyes of Kantele. For, of course, she alone of them all had felt it from the beginning, even though she would not admit it to herself. It was the reason she had been so drawn to Paul, and had denied being drawn so fiercely. Paul had not blamed her then; and understanding as he did now, he blamed her less. Even for him, as he stopped, facing Blunt from the distance of a few feet, the experience had its unnatural elements.

To those standing watching, he knew, it must be worse. For it was not a physical resemblance that he shared with Walter Blunt. They were both tall, wide-shouldered, long-boned, with strong facial features. But there the similarity of the flesh ceased. Their common identity was all the more jolting to the emotions because it was a matter of nonphysical duplications. They should not have looked alike. But they did.

It was weirdly as if the same man wore two different costumes and disguises. The surface appearances were totally different, but identically the same way of standing, the same balance of movement, the same mannerisms and attitudes, glowed through the outer shells like the same candle-flame through two differently ornamented lanterns.

"You understand," said Blunt conversationally to Paul, "why I've dodged you all this time?"

"Of course," said Paul.

At that, Kirk Tyne finally found his voice again. And a note that rang clearly in it witnessed to the fact that for the first time the World Engineer was seriously shaken in his convictions.

"What kind of unnatural devil-thing is this, Walt?" he burst out.

"It's a long story," said Blunt. He still leaned on his cane, examining Paul almost the way a connoisseur might examine a particularly valued work of art. "But that's what I brought you here to hear, Kirk."

Kirk glanced from Paul to Blunt and back, as if magnetically attracted against his will.

"I don't believe it," he said.

"Neither the world nor I," answered Blunt, without shifting his gaze off Paul, "will care what you think after tonight, Kirk."

"Satan!" said a voice. Those in the room, including Paul and Blunt, all looked. It was James Butler, the hotel agent, and he was lifting the gun in his hand. The blue cross on the end of its barrel centered on Paul, wavered, and swung over to point at Blunt. "Denier of God."

Something black flickered through the air of the room. There was the sound of a soft impact, and Butler staggered and dropped the gun from his suddenly limp grasp. The polished haft of a leaf-shaped, hiltless knife stood out from the muscles of the agent's shoulder. McLeod came walking calmly across the room. He bent to scoop up the gun and tucked it into his waistband, and then taking hold of Butler's shoulder with his left hand, he pulled out the knife with his right. He pulled a self-adjusting pressure bandage from his pocket, put it around Butler's shoulder to cover the wound, and lifted the crippled arm across Butler's chest into the grasp of Butler's other arm.

"Hold that," he said. Butler looked at him. The agent had not made a sound. McLeod went back to his position beyond Blunt.

"Now," asked Kirk, out of a white face, "you sick your hoods on me, and decent people?"

"You call that fanatic decent?" asked Blunt, nodding at the black-clad Butler. "How decent would he have been if he'd shot me, or Paul? As he would have, if Burt hadn't stopped him."

"It makes no difference," said Kirk. Before their eyes, with a remarkable effort of will, they saw the man pull himself together. He repeated himself more calmly. "It makes no difference. None of this makes any difference. There are still only sixty thousand of you. That's not enough to wreck the world."

"Kirk," said Blunt, "you know I enjoy arguing with you. You make such a fine straight man."

"The credit goes to you as the comic," said Kirk, dryly.

"Now, that's more like it," said Blunt, nodding his head thoughtfully. "You see, Kirk, I want to break you. If I can get you nicely broken, I can enlist you in tearing this civilization up by the roots and get it done twice as fast. Otherwise, I wouldn't waste time talking with you like this."

"I assure you," said Kirk, "I don't feel the least bit broken."

"You aren't supposed to—yet," said Blunt.

"All I see so far," said Kirk, "is a series of adult-scale Halloween tricks."

"For example?" asked Blunt. "Paul, here?"

Kirk glanced at Paul and for a moment hesitated.

"I don't believe in the supernatural," he said.

"Nor do I," said Blunt. "I believe in the Alternate Laws. Under their power, I created Paul. Didn't I, Paul?"

"No," said Paul. "Creation isn't that easy."

"I beg your pardon," said Blunt. "Let me put it this way then—I built you. I brought you to life. How much do you remember?"

"I remember dying," said Paul. "I remember a tall figure wearing the cape and hat you're wearing now, who brought me back to life."

"Not brought you back," said Blunt. "The real Paul Formain is dead—you knew that?"

"I know it now," said Paul. "I investigated."

"I had tracers on a number of youngsters like him for over fifteen years," said Blunt, "waiting for an opportunity. Odds were with me. Sooner or later one was bound to die under convenient conditions."

"You could have rescued him from that sailboat while he was still alive," said Paul.

"I could have," said Blunt. He looked squarely at Paul. "I think you know why I wouldn't do such a thing. I got to him in time for the moment of his death. I got several cells from his body, living cells. Under the powers of the Alternate Laws, I regrew from each of those cells a living body."

"More?" ejaculated Kirk, staring in something like horror at Paul. Blunt shook his head.

"Living," he said, "but not alive, any more than the dying body I took them from was alive in the true sense. The conscious personality of a living human being is something more than an arithmetical total of the consciousness of its parts." He gazed at Paul for a second without speaking, then said slowly, "Under the Alternate Laws I sparked his life with a portion of my own."

There was a silence in the room, so complete that it seemed that for a moment everyone there had ceased breathing.

"I made another *me*," said Blunt. "His body, his memories, his skills were those that belonged to the boy who had just died. But in essence, he was me."

"In one essence," corrected Paul, "I was you."

"The most important essence, then," said Blunt. "That was why your body wouldn't take an arm graft. Your body's cells had used up their ability to make large adjustments and repairs in forming you."

"He has two arms now," said Kirk.

"This isn't the original body I started him in," said Blunt. "I assume he had to leave the first one on New Earth?" He looked inquiringly at Paul.

"By your cane," said Paul.

"Yes," said Blunt. "That cane."

"What cane?" asked Kirk.

"The cane that killed Malorn," said Paul. He gazed with a still face at Blunt. "The cane with which *he* killed Malorn."

"No," said McLeod, from behind Blunt. "I did it. It took someone who knew how to handle it like a single-stick. Walt just twisted the Alternate Laws to let me do it."

"But why?" cried Kirk. "Murder, canes, New Earth! I don't understand." He stared. "To educate Paul in—" He broke off.

"You're breaking very nicely, Kirk," said Blunt, turning his head briefly toward the World Engineer and then coming back as always to look at Paul. "You see how little you know? Even your Supe didn't inform you that it had used the accelerator down in its guts to ship Paul off to a planet circling Sirius and its companion star. I'll tell you the rest now and we'll see how you stand up to it." He nodded at the curtained window. "Open that," he said to Eaton White.

The colorless little man hesitated.

"Go ahead," said Kirk, harshly.

White reached in among the folds of the curtains, and down. They drew back revealing a wall-wide window above a low ledge about two feet high.

"All the way," said Blunt.

White reached and pressed again. The whole window slid down into and through the ledge. The hot air of the steamy night outside welled into the conditioned coolness of the room.

"Look!" said Blunt. "Listen out there." He pointed with his stick at the bulking darkness of the Complex outside, lighted here and there dimly. On the hot still air came the sound of chanting, the "*Hey-ha! Hey-ha!*" of a marching society. And from closer by, out of sight somewhere twelve stories below the window ledge, came a long drawn-out howl from something human that had gone a long ways back toward the animal.

"Look," said Blunt. Turning, he threw his cane out the window.

Wheeling, spinning about the axis of its center point, the two rotating ends blurred themselves into scalloped, raking wings. The center acquired a rodent body, and a bat-shape instead of what had been a stick beat upward blackly against the dim glow of the Complex, turned and swooped back, gliding into the room to end up a stick in Blunt's hand again.

"Sixty thousand, you said," said Blunt to Kirk. "The unstable groups, organizations, and elements in this world of ours total nearly one-fifth the world population. For forty years the Chantry Guild has primed them for this moment of final breakdown. One-fifth of the world is out of its senses tonight, Kirk."

"No," said Kirk. "I don't believe it. No, Walt."

"Yes, Kirk." Blunt leaned on his cane again. His dark eyes under the eaves of his aging eyebrows bored in on the other man. "For centuries now you and your kind kept the hound of Unreason chained and locked away from the world. Now we've set him loose again—loose for good. From now on, there'll always be the possibility that the invariable laws won't work. Reason and past experience and the order of the community will fail as guides, and the individual will be left with nothing to anchor to, only himself."

"It won't work," said Kirk. "Those streets out there are mostly empty. We moved too fast for you, my staff and the Super-Complex. Lack of light, lack of comfort, lack of services—people are hiding in their rooms now, because we forced them there. They can only hide so long; then the basic needs—hunger, reaction against boredom—will take over. They'll come out in the daylight and see how little your Halloween tricks have changed the essential structure of their lives. They'll adjust and learn to live with the necessarily small percentage of your magic in the same way they live with the small possibilities of other freak accidents or being struck by lightning."

"*You* moved too fast!" said Blunt. "You only reacted with all the fine obedience of one of your machines. The streets are dark because I wanted them that way. The heat is driving people to huddle apart from each other alone with their fears, each in his own room, because these are the best breeding grounds for Unreason. Tonight is not something to which people can become accustomed, it's only the first battle in a war that will go on and on, waged with new weapons, fought in different ways, waged on altering battlefields, until you and your kind are destroyed."

Blunt's hard old jaw lifted.

"Until the final moment of destruct!" His voice rang through the room and out into the night. "Until Man is forced to stand without his crutches. Until his leg irons are struck off him and the bars he has built around him are torn down and thrown away! Until he stands upright and alone, free—*free* in all his questioning, wandering spirit, with the knowledge that in all existence there are only two things: himself, and the malleable universe!"

Blunt's heavy shoulders swayed forward over the cane on which he leaned, almost as if he was about to leap on Kirk Tyne where he stood. The World Engineer did not retreat before Blunt's words, or that movement, but he seemed to have shrunk slightly and his voice was a trifle hoarse when he answered.

"I'm not going to give in to you, Walt," he said. "I'll fight you to the bitter end. Until one of us is dead."

"Then you've lost already," said Blunt, and his voice was almost wild. "Because I'm going on forever." He pointed aside at Paul. "Let me introduce you, Kirk, to a younger, stronger, greater man than yourself, and the continuing head of the Chantry Guild."

He stopped speaking, and as the sound of his voice ceased, a sudden violent silence like summer sheet lightning flashed across the room. On the heels of it came an abrupt, instinctive, inarticulate cry from Jase.

"No," said Paul, "it's all right, Jase. The Guild will go to you. My job is something different."

They stared at him.

"Something different?" asked Blunt, dryly. "What is it *you* think you're going to do?"

Paul smiled at him and at the others a little sadly.

"Something brutal and unfair to you all," he said. "I'm going to do nothing."

Chapter 22

For a moment they merely looked back at him. But in that moment
something inevitable, and not at all unique, happened. It has taken
place before at gatherings that those present arrange themselves in a
social pattern oriented around the strong point of one individual present. Then, something is said or something takes place. And suddenly,
though none present have made an actual movement, the strong point
is displaced to a different individual. The pattern reorients itself, and
though nothing physical has happened, the emotional effect of the reorientation is felt by everyone in the room.

So with Paul, at that moment. He had reached out and touched the
pattern, and like one drop melting into another, abruptly he was the
focus for the emotional relationships in the room, where Blunt had
been, a moment before.

He met Blunt's eyes across the little distance that separated them.
And Blunt looked back, without expression, and without speaking. He
leaned still on his cane, as if nothing had taken place. But Paul felt
the sudden massive alertness of Blunt's genius swinging to bear completely on him, in the beginnings of a recognition of what Paul was.

"Nothing?" asked Jase, breaking the silence. Sudden alarm for the
Chantry Guild, in this breakdown of whatever Blunt had planned for
it, was obvious upon Jase, obvious even to others in the room besides
Paul.

"Because," said Paul, "if I do nothing, you'll all go your separate
ways. The Chantry Guild will continue and grow. The technical elements in civilization will continue and grow. So will the marching
societies and the cult groups. So"—Paul's eyes, ranging backward in

the room, met for a moment with Burton McLeod's—"will other elements."

"You want that to happen?" challenged Tyne. *"You?"*

"I think it's necessary," said Paul, turning to the World Engineer. "The time has come when mankind must fragment so that his various facets may develop fully and unaffected by other facets nearby. As you yourself know, the process has already started." Paul looked over at Blunt. "A single strong leader," said Paul, "could halt this process temporarily—only temporarily, because there would be no one of his stature to replace him when he was dead—but even in temporarily halting it, he could do permanent damage to later development of fragments he didn't favor."

Paul looked back at Kirk. There was something like horror on Kirk's face.

"But you're saying you're *against* Walt!" stammered Kirk. "You've been against him all along."

"Perhaps," said Paul, a little unhappily, "in a sense. It'd be kinder to say that I haven't been *for* anyone, including Walt."

Kirk stared at him for a moment, still with an expression varying from shock almost to repugnance.

"But *why?"* Kirk burst out finally. *"Why?"*

"That," said Paul, "is a little hard to explain, I'm afraid. Perhaps you might understand it if I used hypnosis as an example. After Walt first brought that last body of mine to consciousness, I had quite a period in which I didn't really know who I was. But a number of things used to puzzle me. Among them the fact that I couldn't be hypnotized."

"The Alternate Laws—" began Jase, from back in the room.

"No," said Paul. "I think someday you Chantry people are going to discover something to which your Alternate Laws bear the same relation alchemy does to modern chemistry. I couldn't be hypnotized because the lightest form of hypnosis requires the giving up of a certain portion of the identity, just as does really complete unconsciousness, and this is impossible to me." He looked around at all of them. "Because, having experienced a shared identity with Walt, it was inevitable that I should come to the capability of sharing the identity of any other human with whom I came in contact."

They all looked back at him. With the exception of Blunt, he saw, they had not fully understood.

"I'm talking about understanding," he said, patiently. "I've been able to share identities with all of you, and what I've found is that each one of you projects a valid form of the future of human society. But a form in which the others would emerge as stunted personalities if they managed to live in it at all. I can't further any one of these futures, because they'll all be coming into existence."

"All?" asked Kirk, just as, at the same moment, Jase also asked, "All?"

"You, yourself, were aware of the situation, Kirk," said Paul. "As you told me yourself, society is going through a necessary stage of fragmentation. It's only a matter of time, now, until a medication is devised that makes Springboard's work into the basis of a practical transportation system. As people spread out to the stars, the fragmentation will be carried further."

He stopped speaking to let that point sink in.

"None of you," said Paul, "should be wasting time fighting each other. You should be busy hunting up your own kind of people and working with them toward your own separate future."

He paused, to give them a chance, this time, to answer. No one seemed disposed to do so. And then, from perhaps the most unexpected quarter, came the protest.

"There's no reason to believe any of this," said Eaton White, in his thick, dry voice from beside the open window.

"Of course not," said Paul reasonably. "If you disbelieve me, you only have to have the courage of your convictions and ignore what I've said." He looked around at them all. "Certainly you don't believe I'm trying to talk you into anything? All I want to do is step out of the picture and go my own way, and I should think the rest of you would want to do likewise."

He turned back to meet Blunt's eyes.

"After all," he said, "this has been a transition period in history, as Kirk has, no doubt, often told other people besides myself. It's been a time of stress and strain, and in such times things tend to become dramatic. Actually, each generation likes to think of itself as at the pivot point in history, that in its time the great decision is made which puts man either on the true road or the false. But things aren't really that serious. Truthfully, the way of mankind is too massive to be kinked, suddenly; it only changes direction in a long and gradual bend over many generations."

Paul turned to the World Engineer.

"Kirk," he said, "as I say, I'm not trying to convince anyone. But certainly *you* can see I'm talking sense?"

Kirk Tyne's head came up with decision.

"Yes," he said sharply, "I can." He looked at Blunt and back to Paul. "Everything you say makes sense. Everybody has one person who can put the Indian sign on them. With me it's always been Walt."

He turned to Blunt. "Because I always admired you, Walt. I wanted to believe in you. And as a result you were able to con me into thinking that the world was upside down and just about to be inside out. It took someone with his feet on the ground, like Paul here, to bring me back to Earth. Of course, our centuries-old technical civilization wasn't the sort of thing that could be hoodooed out of existence by black magic overnight. But you almost had me thinking it could."

He stepped up to Paul and held out his hand. Paul took it.

"Everybody owes you a lot," said Kirk, shaking Paul's hand. "But I, most of all. I want you to know I haven't any doubts where you're concerned. I'll get the services back in action immediately. Come on, Eat." He turned to Blunt, hesitated, shook his head, and turning away again, walked toward the door. Blunt smiled grimly after him.

Eaton White came forward from his position at the window. As he passed by Paul, he hesitated, turned to Paul, and opened his mouth as if to speak. Then he turned and went on out, after Kirk. Jase followed.

"Jim," said Paul gently, looking across at the black-clad hotel agent, still holding his helpless arm across his chest with his other hand, "you probably have responsibilities calling."

Butler snapped his head around at the sound of his first name like a man coming out of a dream. His eyes were like gun-muzzles trained on Paul.

"Yes," he interrupted. "Responsibilities. But not the sort you think. You've been the instrument of a revelation to me—the revelation of the New Jerusalem. The future may hold more than many think."

He turned and walked upright away, still holding his arm, until he passed through the door, and turning, vanished.

"Good-by, Walt," said a voice. Paul and Kantele turned to see that McLeod had come up and put his hand on Blunt's shoulder. Blunt, still leaning on his cane, turned his face sideways toward that hand.

"You, too?" he asked a little huskily.

"You'll be all right, Walt," said McLeod. "Truth is, I've been thinking of it for some time."

"For the last six weeks—I know," said Blunt with a wolf's grin. "No, no, go on, Burt. There's nothing to stay here for now, anyway."

Burt squeezed the caped shoulder, looked across it compassionately at Paul, and went toward the door. The three who were left watched him out in silence.

When Burt had gone, Blunt swung about a little on his cane and looked sardonically at Paul.

"Do I have to love you, too?" he asked.

"No," said Paul. "No, of course not! I wouldn't ask that."

"Then, damn you," said Blunt. "Damn you and may you rot in hell until judgment day!"

Paul smiled sadly.

"You won't tell me why?" asked Blunt.

"If I could," said Paul, "I would. But it's a matter of language. I don't have words for you." He hesitated. "You could take it on faith."

"Yes," said Blunt, suddenly and heavily as if the strength had gone out of him. "I could take it on faith, if I were bigger." He straightened up suddenly and looked with a deep, penetrating curiosity at Paul.

"*Empath*," he said. "I should have suspected it sooner. But where did the talent come from?"

"From your plans for me," said Paul. "I told the truth. It's a high wall that separates the inner parts of one identity from the inner being of another. From having the experience of no wall between you and me, I could learn to tear down the walls between myself and all others."

"But why?" said Blunt. "Why would you want to?"

Paul smiled again.

"Partly," he said, "because unlimited power or strength is a little like credit. In the beginning it seems that enough of it would do anything. But, when you achieve it, you find that it, too, is limited. There are areas in which it's helpless, like other things. Can you hammer out a roughness in a delicate piece of carved jade?"

Blunt shook his head.

"I don't see how it applies," he said.

"It's just that I have some things in common," said Paul. "And Kirk was very nearly right. It's not possible to change the future except by changing the present. And the only way to change the present is to return to the past and change that."

"Return?" asked Blunt. "Change?" Blunt's eyes had lost their earlier hardness. They were now fully alive. He leaned on his cane and looked directly at Paul. "Who could change the past?"

"Perhaps," said Paul, "someone with intuition."

"Intuition?"

"Yes. Someone," Paul said, "who could see a tree in a garden. And who knew that if that tree were to be cut down, then some years in time and some light-years in distance away, another man's life would be changed. A man, say, who has conscious intuitive process and can immediately realize all the end possibilities of an action the moment he considers it. Someone like that could step back into time, perhaps, and make changes without risk of error."

Blunt's face was perfectly still.

"You aren't me, at all," Blunt said. "You never were me. I think it was you who animated Paul Formain's body, not me at all. Who are you?"

"Once," said Paul, "I was a professional soldier."

"And an Intuit?" asked Blunt. "And now an Empath as well?" His voice was a little harsh. "What next?"

"An identity," said Paul slowly, "needs to be a dynamic, not a static, quantity. If it is static, it becomes helpless within the pattern of its existence. This is a lesson man eventually will have to learn. But if it is dynamic, it may direct its existence as a mining machine is directed, through the otherwise impassable fusion of rocky elements known as reality. From being dominated and imprisoned by them, it can pass to dominating and making use of them, and with its existence plow through, pulverize, and handle reality until it separates out those uniquely real and valuable parts of it which the identity wishes to make its own."

Blunt nodded, slowly, like an old man. It was not clear whether he had understood and was agreeing, or whether he had given up the attempt to understand and was merely being agreeable.

"They all would have their futures," he said. "That's what you told them, wasn't it?" He stopped nodding and looked at Paul for the first time with eyes that were a little faded. "But not me."

"Of course, you," said Paul. "Yours was the greatest vision, and simply the one furthest from realization, that was all."

Blunt nodded again.

"Not," he said, "in my lifetime. No."

"I'm sorry," said Paul. "No."

"Yes," said Blunt. He took a deep breath and straightened up. "I had plans for you," he said. "Plans rooted in ignorance. I had everything set up for you." He glanced at Kantele. "It was almost like having a—" He checked himself, threw back his head, and took a firmer grip on his cane. "I planned to retire after tonight, anyway."

He started to turn away. As he turned, he stooped a little. He hesitated and looked back at Kantele. "I don't suppose. . . . No," he said, interrupting himself. He straightened up once again, so straight the cane merely brushed the surface of the rug underfoot. He threw back his shoulders and for a moment towered in the room, as if he were young again.

"It's been an education," he said, and saluted Paul with the cane. Turning, he strode out. Behind his back, Kantele made a little gesture after him with her hands, and then let her hands and gaze drop. She stood, her head bent, her eyes on the carpet at her feet, like a maiden, captive to the stranger's bow and spear.

Paul looked at her.

"You love him," he said.

"Always. Very much," she said, almost inaudibly, not looking up.

"Then you're a fool to stay," he said.

She did not answer that. But after a moment she spoke again, uncertainly, her gaze still on the carpet.

"You could be mistaken," she said.

"No," said Paul; and she did not see the centuries-old pain that came into his eyes as he said it. "I never make mistakes."

TACTICS OF MISTAKE

Trouble rather the tiger in his lair than the sage amongst his books. For to you Kingdoms and their armies are things mighty and enduring, but to him they are but toys of the moment, to be overturned by the flicking of a finger. . . .

LESSONS: *Anonymous*

Chapter 1

The young lieutenant-colonel was drunk, apparently, and determined to rush upon disaster.

He came limping into the spaceship's dining lounge the first night out from Denver on the flight to Kultis, a row of bright service ribbons on the jacket of his green dress uniform, and looked about. He was a tall, lean officer, youthful to hold the rank he wore in the Expeditionary Forces of Earth's Western Alliance; and at first glance his open-featured face looked cheerful to the point of harmlessness.

He gazed around the room for a few seconds, while the steward tried unsuccessfully to steer him off to a booth nearby, set for a single diner. Then, ignoring the steward, he turned and headed directly for the table of Dow deCastries.

The white-faced, waspish little man called Pater Ten, who was always at deCastries' elbow, slipped away from his chair as the officer approached, and went toward the steward, still staring blank-faced with dismay after the lieutenant-colonel. As Pater Ten approached, the steward frowned and bent forward to talk. The two of them spoke for a moment in low voices, glancing back at the lieutenant-colonel, and then went quickly out of the lounge together.

The lieutenant-colonel reached the table, pulled up an empty float seat from the adjoining table without waiting for an invitation and seated himself across from the tawny-haired, beautiful young girl at deCastries' left.

"Privilege of first night out, they tell me," he said pleasantly to all of them at the table. "We sit where we like at dinner and meet our fellow passengers. How do you do?"

For a second no one spoke. DeCastries only smiled, the thin edge of a smile that barely curved the lips in his handsome face, framed by the touches of gray in the black hair at his temples. For five years, now, Secretary of Outworlds Affairs for Earth's Coalition of Eastern Nations, he was known for success with women; and his dark eyes had concentrated on the tawny-haired girl ever since he had invited her— with her mercenary soldier father and the Exotic Outbond who made up the third in their party—to join his table, earlier. There was no obvious threat in that smile of his; but reflexively at the sight of it, the girl frowned slightly and put a hand on the arm of her father, who had leaned forward to speak.

"Colonel . . ." The mercenary wore the pocket patch of an officer from the Dorsai World, under contract to the Bakhallan Exotics, and he was a full colonel. His darkly tanned face with its stiffly waxed mustache might have looked ridiculous if it had not been as expressionlessly hard as the butt-plate of a cone rifle. He broke off, feeling the hand on his sleeve, and turned to look at his daughter; but her attention was all on the interloper.

"Colonel," she said to him in her turn—and her young voice sounded annoyed and concerned at once, after the flat, clipped tones of her father, "don't you think you ought to lie down for a while?"

"No," said the lieutenant-colonel, looking at her. She caught her breath, finding herself seized, suddenly like a bird on the hand of a giant, by the strange and powerful attention of his gray eyes—entirely at odds with the harmless appearance he had given on entering the room. Those eyes held her momentarily helpless, so that without warning she was conscious of being at the exact focus of his vision, naked under the spotlight of his judgment. ". . . I don't," she heard him say.

She sat back, shrugging her tanned shoulders above her green dinner gown, and managed to pull her gaze from its direct link with his. Out of the corner of her eye she saw him look about the table, from the blue-robed Exotic at its far end, back past her father and herself to the dark, faintly smiling deCastries.

"I know you, of course, Mr. Secretary," he went on to deCastries. "In fact, I picked this particular flight to Kultis just so I could meet you. I'm Cletus Grahame—head of the Tactics Department at the Western Alliance Military Academy until last month. Then I put in for transfer to Kultis—to Bakhalla, on Kultis."

He looked over at the Exotic. "The purser tells me you're Mondar, Outbound from Kultis to the Enclave in St. Louis," he said. "Bakhalla's your home town, then."

"The capital of Bakhalla Colony," said the Exotic, "not just a town, nowdays, Colonel. You know, I'm sure we're all pleased to meet you,

Cletus. But do you think it's good judgment for an officer in the armed forces of the Alliance to try to mix with Coalition people?"

"Why not—on shipboard?" said Cletus Grahame, smiling unconcernedly at him. "You're mixing with the secretary, and it's the Coalition who's supplying Neuland with arms and material. Besides, as I say, it's the first night out."

Mondar shook his head. "Bakhalla and the Coalition aren't at war," he said. "The fact the Coalition's given some aid to Neuland Colony is beside the point."

"The Alliance and the Coalition aren't at war," said Cletus, "and the fact that they're backing different sides in the brush war between you and Neuland's beside the point."

"It's hardly beside the point—" began Mondar. But then he was interrupted.

There was a sudden hush in the buzz of conversation about the lounge. While they had been talking, the steward and Pater Ten had returned, behind an impressively large, uniformed man wearing the stripes of a spaceliner's first officer, who now reached the table and dropped a big hand heavily on Cletus' shoulder.

"Colonel," said the shipman, loudly, "this is a Swiss ship of neutral registry. We carry Alliance and Coalition people, both, but we don't like political incidents on shipboard. This table belongs to the Coalition Secretary of Outworlds Affairs, Dow deCastries. Your place is back there across the room . . ."

But from the first word, Cletus paid him no attention. Instead, he looked back to the girl—at her alone—and smiled and raised his eyebrows as if leaving it up to her. He made no move to rise from the table.

The girl glared back at him but still he did not move. For a long second her glare held; then it wavered and broke. She turned to deCastries.

"Dow . . ." she said, interrupting the ship's officer, who had begun to repeat his words.

DeCastries' thin smile widened slightly. He, too, raised his eyebrows, but with a different expression than Cletus. He let her gaze appealingly at him for a long second before he turned to the shipman.

"It's all right," he said, his deep, musical voice stilling the voice of the other, instantly. "The colonel's just making use of his first-night privileges to sit where he wants."

The shipman's face reddened. His hand dropped slowly from Cletus' shoulder. Suddenly his size made him seem no longer large and impressive, but clumsy and conspicuous.

"Yes, Mr. Secretary," he said stiffly, "I see. Sorry to have bothered you all . . ."

He darted a glance of pure hatred at Pater Ten, which affected the little man no more than the shadow of a rain cloud affects the glowing radiance of a white-hot iron ingot; and, carefully avoiding the eyes of the other passengers, he turned and walked from the lounge. The steward had already evaporated, at deCastries' first words. Pater Ten slid into the seat he had vacated earlier, scowling at Cletus.

"About the Exotic Enclave at St. Louis," Cletus said to Mondar— he did not seem to be disturbed by what had just happened—"they've been very good about lending me library materials for research."

"Oh?" Mondar's face was politely interested. "You're a writer, Colonel?"

"A scholar," said Cletus. His gray eyes fastened now on the Exotic. "I'm writing volume four right now, of a twenty-volume work I started three years ago—on tactics and strategical considerations. But never mind that now. May I meet the rest of the people here?"

Mondar nodded. "I'm Mondar, as you say."

"Colonel Eachan Khan," he said, turning to the Dorsai at his right, "may I introduce Lieutenant-Colonel Cletus Grahame of the Alliance forces?"

"Honored, Colonel," said Eachan Khan, in a clipped, old-fashioned British accent.

"Honored to meet you, sir," said Cletus.

"And Colonel Khan's daughter, Melissa Khan," went on Mondar.

"Hello." Cletus smiled again at her.

"How do you do?" she said, coldly.

"Our host, Secretary Dow deCastries, you've already recognized," Mondar said. "Mr. Secretary—Colonel Cletus Grahame."

"I'm afraid it's a little late to invite you to dinner, Colonel," said deCastries deeply. "The rest of us have eaten." He beckoned the steward. "We can offer you some wine."

"And, finally, the gentleman on the secretary's right," said Mondar. "Mr. Pater Ten. Mr. Ten's got an eidetic memory, Colonel. You'll find he's got an encyclopedic fund of knowledge on just about everything."

"Pleased to meet you, Mr. Ten," said Cletus. "Maybe I ought to arrange to borrow you, instead of library materials, for my next research."

"Don't bother!" said Pater Ten, unexpectedly. He had a creaky, high-pitched, but surprisingly carrying, voice. "I looked at your first three volumes—wild theories, backed up by warmed-over military history. They must've been going to kick you out of the Academy if you hadn't requested a transfer first. Anyway, you're out. Now, who'll read you? You'll never finish a fourth book."

"I told you," said Mondar in the conversational pause that followed this small verbal explosion. Cletus was gazing at the small man with a faint smile not unlike that of deCastries, earlier. "Mr. Ten has an encyclopedic fund of knowledge."

"I see what you mean," said Cletus. "But knowledge and conclusions are two different things. That's why I'll be finishing all sixteen of the other volumes in spite of Mr. Ten's doubts. In fact that's why I'm headed for Kultis, now, to make sure I get them written."

"That's right—haul victory out of defeat there," creaked Pater Ten. "Win the war at Bakhalla in six weeks and become an Alliance hero."

"Yes, not such a bad idea," said Cletus, as the lounge steward deftly slid a clean wineglass in front of him and filled it from the bottle of canary-yellow liquid on the table. "Only it isn't either the Alliance or the Coalition that's going to win in the long run."

"That's a strong statement, Colonel," said deCastries. "Also, a little close to treason, isn't it? That part about the Alliance, spoken by an Alliance officer?"

"You think so?" Cletus said, and smiled. "Is someone here thinking of reporting me?"

"Possibly." There was abruptly a note of something chilling in deCastries' deep voice. "Meanwhile, it's interesting to hear you talk. What makes you think it won't be either the Alliance or the Coalition that'll end up having the strongest voice among the colonies on Kultis?"

"The laws of historical development," said Cletus, "are working to that end."

"Laws," said Melissa Khan, angrily. The tension she had been feeling beneath the calm talk had become too much to bear. "Why does everybody think"—she glanced a moment, almost bitterly at her father—"that there's some impractical set of principles or theories or codes that everybody ought to live by? It's practical people who make things happen! You have to be practical, nowdays, or you might as well be dead."

"Melissa," said deCastries, smiling at her, "honors the practical man. I'm afraid I have to agree with her. Practical experience works."

"As opposed to theories, Colonel," flung in Pater Ten, gibingly, "as opposed to bookish theories. Wait'll you get out among practical field officers in the Neuland-Bakhalla jungle in a practical fire-fight, and discover what war's really like! Wait'll you hear your first energy weapon sending its sizzle overhead, and you'll find out—"

"He's wearing the Alliance Medal of Honor, Mr. Ten."

The sudden, flat, clipped tones of Eachan Khan chopped across the small man's tirade like an ax. In the new silence Eachan pointed a steady, brown forefinger at the red, white and gold bar at the far right of the row of ribbons decorating Cletus' jacket.

Chapter 2

The silence continued a moment at the table.

"Colonel," said Eachan, "what's the trouble with your leg?"

Cletus grinned wryly. "It's part prosthetic about the knee, now," he said. "Perfectly comfortable, but you can notice it when I walk." He looked back at Pater Ten. "Actually, Mr. Ten's pretty close to being right about my practical military experience. I only had three months of active duty after being commissioned, during the last Alliance—Coalition brush war on Earth seven years ago."

"But you ended up those three months with the Medal of Honor," said Melissa. The expression with which she had watched him before had now changed completely. She swung about to Pater Ten. "I suppose that's one of the few things you don't know anything about, though?"

Pater Ten stared hatingly back at her.

"Do you, Pater?" murmured deCastries.

"There was a Lieutenant Grahame decorated seven years ago by the Alliance," spat out Pater Ten. "His division had made an attack drop and landing on a Pacific island held by our garrisons. The division was routed and cut up, but Lieutenant Grahame managed to put together a guerrilla force that was successful in bottling our people up in their strong fortified areas until Alliance reinforcements came a month later. He ran into a traveling mine the day before he would have been relieved. They stuck him in their Academy because he couldn't qualify physically for field duty after that."

There was another, but shorter, moment of silence at the table.

"So," said deCastries, in an oddly thoughtful tone, turning in his fingers the half-filled wineglass on the tablecloth before him, "it seems the scholar was a hero, Colonel."

"No, Lord no," said Cletus. "The lieutenant was a rash soldier, that's all. If I'd understood things then as well as I do now, I'd never have run into that mine."

"But here you are—headed back to where the fighting is!" said Melissa.

"That's true," said Cletus, "but as I said, I'm a wiser man now. I don't want any more medals."

"What *do* you want, Cletus?" asked Mondar, from the end of the table. The Outbond had been watching Cletus with an un-Exotic-like intensity for some few minutes now.

"He wants to write sixteen more volumes," sneered Pater Ten.

"As a matter of fact, Mr. Ten's right," said Cletus quietly to Mondar. "What I really want to do is finish my work on tactics. Only I've found out first I'm going to have to create the conditions they'll apply to."

"Win the war on Neuland in sixty days!" said Pater Ten. "Just as I said."

"Less time than that, I think," said Cletus, and he gazed calmly about at the sudden changes of expression on the faces of all but Mondar and Pater Ten.

"You must believe in yourself as a military expert, Colonel," said deCastries. Like Mondar's, his gaze upon Cletus had grown interested.

"But I'm not an expert," said Cletus. "I'm a scholar. There's a difference. An expert's a man who knows a great deal about his subject. A scholar's someone who knows all there is that's available to be known about it."

"It's still only theories," said Melissa. She looked at him puzzledly.

"Yes," he said to her, "but the effective theorist's got an advantage over the practician."

She shook her head, but said nothing—sinking back against the cushion of her seat, gazing at him with her lower lip caught between her teeth.

"I'm afraid I'd have to agree with Melissa again," said deCastries. For a moment his gaze was hooded, as if he looked inward rather than outward at them all. "I've seen too many men with nothing but theory get trampled on when they ventured out into the real world."

"Men are real," said Cletus. "So are weapons. . . . But strategies? Political consequences? They're no more real than theories. And a sound theorist, used to dealing with unreal things, is a better manipulator of them than the man used to dealing only with the real tools that are actually only end products. . . . Do you know anything about fencing?"

DeCastries shook his head.

"I do," said Eachan.

"Then maybe you'll recognize the tactic in fencing I use as an example for some I call the *tactics of mistake*. It's in the volume I'm writing now." Cletus turned to him. "The fencing tactic is to launch a series of attacks, each inviting ripostes, so that there's a pattern of engages and disengages of your blade with your opponent's. Your purpose, however, isn't to strike home with any of these preliminary attacks, but to carry your opponent's blade a little more out of line with each disengage so gradually he doesn't notice you're doing it. Then, following the final engage, when his blade has been drawn completely out of line, you thrust home against an essentially unguarded man."

"Take a damn good fencer," said Eachan, flatly.

"There's that, of course," said Cletus.

"Yes," said deCastries, slowly, and waited for Cletus to look back at him. "Also, it seems a tactic pretty well restricted to the fencing floor, where everything's done according to set rules."

"Oh, but it can be applied to almost any situation," said Cletus. There were coffee cups, as yet unfilled, spaced about the table. He reached out and captured three of these and lined them up, upside down between himself and deCastries. Then he reached into a bowl of sugar cubes standing on the table and brought his fist back to drop a cube onto the tablecloth by the central cup.

He covered the sugar cube with the central cup and moved all the cups about, interchanging their positions rapidly. Then he stopped.

"You've heard of the old shell game," he said to deCastries. "Which one of those cups would you say the sugar cube's under?"

DeCastries looked at the cups but made no attempt to reach out to them. "None of them," he said.

"Just for purposes of illustration—will you pick one, anyway?" asked Cletus.

DeCastries smiled. "Why not?" he said.

He reached out and lifted the middle cup. His smile vanished for a second and then returned again. In plain view sat a sugar cube, white against white on the tablecloth.

"At least," said deCastries, "you're an honest shell-game operator."

Cletus took up the middle cup, which deCastries had set down, and covered the sugar cube. Once again he rapidly switched around the positions of the overturned cups.

"Try it again?" he asked deCastries.

"If you want." This time deCastries chose to lift the cup at the right end of the row as it faced him. Another sugar cube was exposed.

"Once more?" said Cletus. Again he covered the cube and mixed the cups. DeCastries picked up the cup now in the center and put it down with some force when he saw the sugar cube he had exposed.

"What's this?" he said. His smile was definitely gone now. "What's the point of all this?"

"It seems you can't lose, Mr. Secretary, when I control the game," said Cletus.

DeCastries looked penetratingly at him for a second, then covered the cube and sat back, glancing at Pater Ten.

"You move the cups this time, Pater," he said.

Smiling maliciously at Cletus, Pater Ten rose and switched the cups about—but so slowly that everyone at the table easily kept track of the cup deCastries had last handled. That particular cup ended up once more in the middle. DeCastries looked at Cletus and reached for the cup to the right of the one that plainly contained the cube. His hand hesitated, hovered over it for a moment, and then drew back. His smile returned.

"Of course," he said, looking at Cletus, "I don't know how you do it, but I do know that if I lift that cup there'll be a sugar cube under it." His hand moved to the cup at the opposite end of the line. "And if I choose this one, it'll probably be there?"

Cletus said nothing. He only smiled back.

DeCastries nodded. The customary easiness of his manner had returned to him. "In fact," he said, "the only cup I can be sure doesn't have a sugar cube under it is the one that we all know must have a cube—the one in the middle. Am I right?"

Cletus still only smiled.

"I am right," said deCastries. He extended his hand out over the central cup for a second, watching Cletus' eyes, then withdrew the hand. "And that was what you were after, in this demonstration with the cups and sugar cubes, wasn't it, Colonel? Your aim was to make me figure out the situation just the way I have—but also to make me so unsure of myself after being wrong three times in a row, that I'd still have to turn the center cup over to prove to myself it really was empty. Your real purpose was to strike at my confidence in my own judgment according to these *tactics of mistake* of yours, wasn't it?"

He reached out and snapped the central cup with his fingernail so that it rang with a sound like that of a small, flat-toned bell.

"But I'm not going to turn it over," he went on, looking at Cletus.

"You see, having reasoned it out, I've gone one step further and worked out your purpose in trying to make me do it. You wanted to impress me. Well, I am impressed—but only a little. And in token of just how little, suppose we leave the cup sitting there, unturned? What do you say?"

"I say your reasoning's excellent, Mr. Secretary." Cletus reached out and gathered in the other two cups upside down, covering the mouth of each briefly with his hand before turning them right-side-up to expose their empty, open mouths to the lounge ceiling. "What else can I say?"

"Thank you, Colonel," said deCastries, softly. He had leaned back in his chair and his eyes had narrowed down to slits. He reached out now with his right hand to take the stem of his wineglass and rotate it once more between thumb and forefinger with precise quarter turns, as if screwing it delicately down into the white tablecloth. "Now, you said something earlier about taking this flight to Kultis only because you knew I'd be on it. Don't tell me you went to all that trouble just to show me your tactical shell game?"

"Only partly," said Cletus. The tension in the atmosphere around the table had suddenly increased, although the voices of both Cletus and deCastries remained pleasant and relaxed. "I wanted to meet you, Mr. Secretary, because I'm going to need you to arrange things so I can finish my work on tactics."

"Oh?" said deCastries, "And just how did you expect me to help?"

"Opportunities ought to present themselves to both of us, Mr. Secretary"—Cletus pushed back his chair and stood up—"now that you've met me and know what I'm after. With that much done it's probably time for me to apologize for intruding on your dinner party and leave—"

"Just a moment, Colonel . . ." purred deCastries.

A small sound of breaking glass interrupted them. Melissa's wineglass lay spilled and shattered against a saucer before her, and she was pushing herself unsteadily to her feet, one hand holding her forehead.

Chapter 3

"No, no—it's all right!" she said to her father. "I'm just a little dizzy, suddenly, that's all. I'll go lie down. . . . No, Dad, you stay here! Colonel Grahame, you can help me to my cabin, can't you—as long as you are leaving anyway."

"Of course," said Cletus.

He came quickly around the table and she took hold of his arm. She was tall, and she leaned the not inconsiderable weight of her healthy young body heavily against him. Almost irritably, she waved her father and deCastries back into their seats.

"Really!" she said. Her voice sharpened. "I'm all right. I just want to lie down for a bit. Will you please not make a fuss about it? Colonel . . ."

"Right here," said Cletus. They moved off together slowly, she still leaning against him as they crossed the lounge and went out into the corridor turning left.

She continued to lean on him until they had made a turn in the corridor that hid them from the lounge entrance, then she stopped abruptly, straightened up and pulled away turning to face him.

"I'm all right," she said. "I just had to do something to get you out of there. You aren't drunk at all!"

"No," said Cletus, good-humoredly. "And not a very good actor either, evidently."

"You couldn't have fooled me, if you were! I can feel . . ." She half-raised her hand, fingers spread out as if to touch him on the chest; and then dropped the hand abruptly as he looked curiously at it. "I can see right through people like you. Never mind that. It would have been bad enough if you *were* drunk. Trying to play games with a man like Dow deCastries!"

"I wasn't exactly playing games," said Cletus, soberly.

"Oh, don't tell me!" she said. "Don't you think I know what kind of idiots professional soldiers can make of themselves when they try to deal with people outside their own special military world? But a Medal of Honor means something to me, even if most civilians don't know what it is!" Her eyes had slipped into line with his again. She almost wrenched her gaze away. "And that's why I helped get you away from him just now. The only reason! . . . And I'm not going to do it again!"

"I see," said Cletus.

"So you get back to your cabin now, and stay there! Stay away from Dow deCastries from now on. From Dad and me, too. . . . Are you listening?"

"Of course," said Cletus. "But I'll see you the rest of the way to your cabin, at least."

"No thanks. I can get there by myself."

"What if someone sees you doing just that and the word gets back to the Secretary that your dizziness cleared up this quickly, once you were out of the lounge?"

She glared at him, turned and stalked off down the corridor. Cletus caught up with her in two long strides and fell into step.

"About professional soldiers," he said, mildly. "One isn't just like another . . ."

She stopped and faced him abruptly, forcing him to stop also. "I suppose," she said, grimly, "you think my father never was anything but a mercenary."

"Of course not," Cletus said. "A lieutenant-general in the Royal Army of Afghanistan, wasn't he, up until ten years or so ago?"

She stared at him. "How did you know?" Her tone was accusing.

"Military history—even recent military history—is part of my field," he said. "The University Revolution at Kabul twelve years ago, which ended up by taking over the government at Kabul, is part of it. The Afghanistani Army wouldn't have had more than one General Eachan Khan. He must have emigrated from Earth not more than a couple of years after the takeover."

"He didn't have to leave!" she said. "They still wanted him in the Army, even after Afghanistan gave up its independence to become a sector area of the Coalition. But there were other things . . ." She broke off.

"Other things?" asked Cletus.

"You wouldn't understand!" She turned and began walking once more down the corridor. But, after a few steps, the words came from her as if she could not keep them in. "My mother had died . . . and . . . *Salaam Badshahi Daulat Afghanistan*—when they began enforcing the death penalty for anyone singing the old Afghanistani anthem, he resigned. So he emigrated—to the Dorsai."

"It's a new world full of soldiers there, I understand," said Cletus. "It shouldn't have been too—"

"They found him work as a captain—a *captain* in a mercenary battalion!" she flashed at him. "And since then, in ten years, he's managed to work his way just back up to colonel—and there he'll stay. Because the Dorsai mercenaries can't find employment for anything larger than a short regiment—and after his expenses are paid we don't have enough left over from what he makes to visit Earth, let alone live there again, unless the Exotics or someone pay our way there on official business."

Cletus nodded. "I see," he said. "But it's a mistake for you to try to mend things through deCastries. He's not capable of being influenced the way you hope."

"Mend things . . ." She turned her head and stared at him, meeting his eyes this time in unthinking shock, her face suddenly pale.

"Of course," said Cletus. "I'd been wondering what you were doing at his table. You'd have been underage at the time your father emigrated to the Dorsai, so you must have dual Coalition-Dorsai citizenship. You have the right to go back and live on Earth any time you want to take up your Coalition citizenship. But your father can't be repatriated except by special political dispensation, which is almost impossible to get. Either you or he must think you can get deCastries to help you with that—"

"Dad's got nothing to do with it!" Her voice was fierce. "What kind of a man do you think he is?"

He looked at her. "No. You're right of course," he said. "It must have been your idea. He's not the type. I grew up in a military family back on Earth, and he reminds me of some of the generals I'm related to. In fact, if I hadn't wanted to be a painter—"

"A painter?" She blinked at the sudden change of topic.

"Yes," said Cletus, smiling a little wryly. "I was just starting to make a living at it when my draft number came up, and I decided to go into the Alliance Military Academy after all, the way my family had wanted me to from the beginning. Then I got wounded, of course, and discovered I liked the theory of military art. So painting got left behind."

While he was talking she had come to a halt automatically before one of the stateroom doors lining the long, narrow corridor. But she made no attempt to open it. Instead she stood, staring at him.

"Why did you ever leave teaching at the Academy, then?" she asked.

"Someone," he said, humorously, "has to make the worlds safe for scholars like myself."

"By making a personal enemy out of Dow deCastries?" she said, incredulously. "Didn't it teach you anything when he saw through your game with the teacups and the sugar cubes?"

"But he didn't," said Cletus. "Oh, I ought to admit he did a very good job of covering up the fact he hadn't."

"*He* covered up?"

"Certainly," Cletus answered. "He lifted the first cup out of over-confidence, feeling sure he could handle whatever came of my shell game. When he turned up the first cube he thought I had blundered, not he. With the second cube, he revised his ideas, but was still over-confident enough to try again. When he turned up the third cube he finally woke to the fact that the game was completely under my control. So he had to find an excuse for stopping it and refusing to choose a fourth time."

She shook her head. "This is all the wrong way around," she said, unbelievingly. "You're twisting what happened to make it look the way you want it."

"No," said Cletus. "DeCastries was the one who twisted it, with his actually very clever explanation of why he wouldn't lift a cup a fourth time. The only trouble was, it was a false explanation. He knew he'd find a sugar cube under any cup he lifted."

"How could he?"

"Because I had cubes under all three cups, of course," said Cletus. "When I lifted one cube from the bowl, I palmed two others. By the time he got around to the fourth choice, deCastries had probably figured that out. The fact that the game turned out to be the avoiding of finding a cube, instead of trying to find one, misled him at first. But pointing it out by then would have been too late to keep him from looking foolish at having played the game three times already. People like deCastries can't afford to look foolish."

"But why did you do it?" Melissa almost cried. "Why do you want to make an enemy like that?"

"I need to get him involved with me," said Cletus, "so I can make use of him. Unless I can make him annoyed enough to thrust, I can't parry. And only by successfully continuing to parry every attempt he makes can I finally get his whole attention. . . . Now you see," he went on, a little more gently, "why you ought to be worrying about your own involvement with Dow deCastries instead of mine. I can handle him. On the other hand, you—"

"*You . . .*" Suddenly blazing with anger, she turned and jerked open the door. "You absolute—go mix yourself up with Dow. Get yourself chewed up to mincemeat. I hope you do. But stay away from me. . . . And from Dad! Do you hear me?"

He looked at her, and a slight shadow of something like pain passed through him. "Of course," he said, stepping back. "If that's what you want."

She went in, slamming the door behind her. He stood for a second, looking at its blank surface. For a moment with her there, the self-imposed barrier of isolation he had set up around himself many years ago, when he found others did not understand him, had almost melted. But it was back now.

He drew a short, deep breath that was almost a sigh. Turning, he went off down the corridor in the direction of his own stateroom.

Chapter 4

For the next four days Cletus punctually avoided Melissa and her father—and was ignored in turn by deCastries and Pater Ten. Mondar, on the other hand, grew to be almost a close acquaintance, a circumstance Cletus found not only pleasant, but interesting.

The fifth day out from Earth, the spaceliner went into parking orbit around Kultis. Like its sister planet Mara, Kultis was a green, warm world with transient icecaps and only two major continental masses, north and south, as it had been true with Earth during the Gondwana-land period of the home planet's geological past. The shuttleboats from the chief cities of the various Kultan colonies began to come up to take off passengers.

On a hunch, Cletus tried to phone down to Alliance Headquarters in Bakhalla for reporting and billeting information. But the space-to-surface circuits were all tied up by the party for Neuland, in the forward evacuation lounge. Which meant, Cletus discovered with a little quiet inquiry, Pater Ten speaking for Dow deCastries. This, of course, was blatant favoritism on the part of a vessel of supposedly neutral registry. Cletus' hunch flowered into suspicion. One of those calls could well be concerned with him.

Glancing around as he turned from the phone, Cletus caught sight of the blue robe of Mondar, who was standing by the closed hatch of the midship lounge, only a few steps from Melissa and Eachan Khan. Cletus limped briskly over to the Exotic.

"Phones tied up," Cletus said. "Thought I'd ask Alliance Forces HQ for instructions. Tell me, is there much activity in close to Bakhalla by Neuland guerrillas these days?"

"Right up to our front doors," answered Mondar. He looked at

Cletus shrewdly. "What's the matter? Just now remembering how you impressed Dow at dinner, that first day on board here?"

"That?" Cletus lifted an eyebrow. "You mean deCastries goes to the trouble of making special guerrilla targets out of every light colonel he meets?"

"Not every one, of course," said Mondar, and smiled. "But in any case there's no cause for alarm. You'll be riding into Bakhalla with Melissa, Eachan and myself in a command car."

"That's reassuring," said Cletus. But his thoughts were already halfway elsewhere. Clearly, whatever effect he had achieved with Dow deCastries had been at least partly transparent to Mondar. Which was all right, he thought. The trail he had laid out toward his announced goal was baited along its length for just the sort of subtle mind that could envision purposes at work invisible to less perceptive men. It was that sort of mind deCastries possessed, and Mondar's was complex and deep enough in its own way to prove a useful control subject.

A gong rang through the lounge, cutting through the sounds of conversation.

"Shuttleboat for Bakhalla, now docking," droned the first officer's voice from a wall speaker. *"Now docking, midships lounge hatch, the shuttleboat for Bakhalla. All passengers for Bakhalla should be ready to board . . ."*

Cletus found himself swept forward as the hatch opened, revealing the bright metal connecting tunnel to the shuttleboat. He and Mondar were separated by the crowd.

The shuttleboat was little more than a cramped, uncomfortable, space- and atmosphere-going bus. It roared, dropped, plunged, jerked and finally skidded them all to a halt on a circle of scarred brown concrete surrounded by broad-leaved jungle—a green backdrop laced with what seemed to be threads of scarlet and bright yellow.

Shuffling out of the shuttleboat door into the bright sunlight, Cletus stepped a little aside from the throng to get his bearings. Other than a small terminal building some fifty yards off, there was no obvious sign of man except the shuttleboat and the concrete pad. The jungle growth towered over a hundred feet high in its surrounding circle. An ordinary, rather pleasant tropical day, Cletus thought. He looked about for Mondar—and was abruptly jolted by something like a soundless, emotional thunderclap.

Even as it jarred him, he recognized it from its reputation. It was "reorientation shock"—the abrupt impact of a whole spectrum of differences from the familiar experienced all at once. His absentmindedness as he had stepped out into this almost Earth-like scene had heightened its effect upon him.

Now, as the shock passed, he recognized all at once that the sky was not blue so much as bluish-green. The sun was larger and a deeper golden yellow than the sun of Earth. The red and yellow threads in the foliage were not produced by flowers or vines, but by actual veins of color running through the leaves. And the air was heavily humid, filled with odors that intermingled to produce a scent something like that of a mixture of grated nutmeg and crushed grass stems. Also, it was vibrant with a low-level but steady chorus of insect or animal cries ranging from the sounds like the high tones of a toy tin flute to the mellow booming of an empty wooden barrel being thumped—but all with a creakiness foreign to the voices of Earth.

Altogether the total impact of light, color, odor and sound, even now that the first shock was passed, caught Cletus up in a momentary immobility, out of which he recovered to find Mondar's hand on his elbow.

"Here comes the command car," Mondar was saying, leading him forward. The vehicle he mentioned was just emerging from behind the terminal building with the wide shape of a passenger float-bus behind it. "Unless you'd rather ride the bus with the luggage, the wives and the ordinary civilians?"

"Thanks, no. I'll join you," said Cletus.

"This way, then," said Mondar.

Cletus went with him as the two vehicles came up and halted. The command car was a military, plasma-powered, air-cushion transport, with half-treads it could lower for unusually rough cross-country going. Over all, it was like an armored version of the sports cars used for big game hunting. Eachan Khan and Melissa were already inside, occupying one of the facing pair of passenger seats. Up front on the open seat sat a round-faced young Army Spec 9 at the controls, with a dally gun beside him.

Cletus glanced at the clumsy hand weapon with interest as he climbed aboard the car over the right-side treads. It was the first dally gun he had seen in use in the field—although he had handled and even fired one back at the Academy. It was a crossbreed—no, it was an out-and-out mongrel of a weapon—designed originally as a riot-control gun and all but useless in the field, where a speck of dirt could paralyze some necessary part of its complex mechanism inside the first half hour of combat.

Its name was a derivative from its original, unofficial designation of "dial-a-gun," which name proved that even ordnance men were capable of humor. With proper adjustment it could deliver anything from a single .29 caliber pellet slug to an eight-ounce, seeker-type canister shell. It was just the sort of impractical weapon that set Cletus' tactical imagination perking over possible unorthodox employments of it in unexpected situations.

But he and Mondar were in the car now. With a hiss from its compressor, the command car's heavy body rose ten inches from the concrete and glided off on its supporting cushion of air. An opening in the jungle wall loomed before them; and a moment later they were sliding down a narrow winding road of bonded earth, with two deep, weed-choked ditches on each side unsuccessfully striving to hold back the wall of jungle that towered up on either side to arch thinly together, at last, over their heads.

"I'm surprised you don't burn back or spray-kill a cleared area on each side of the road," said Cletus to Mondar.

"On the important military routes, we do," said the Exotic. "But we're short-handed these days and the local flora grows back fast. We're trying to variform an Earth grain or grass to drive out the native forms, and plant it alongside our roads—but we're short-handed in the laboratories, too."

"Difficult—the services and supply situation," jerked out Eachan Khan, touching the right tip of his waxed gray mustache protectively as the command car came unexpectedly upon a giant creeper that had broken through the bonded earth of the roadway from below, and was forced to put down its treads to climb across.

"What do you think of the dally gun?" Cletus asked the Dorsai mercenary, his own words jolted from his lips by the lurching of the command car.

"Wrong sort of direction for small arms to go . . ." The creeper left behind, the car rose smoothly onto its supporting air cushion again. "Nagle sticks—dally guns—ultrasonics to set off, jam or destroy the components in your enemy's weapons—it's all getting too complicated. And the more complicated, more difficult the supply situation, the tougher to keep your striking forces really mobile."

"What's your idea, then?" Cletus asked. "Back to crossbows, knives and short swords?"

"Why not?" said Eachan Khan, surprisingly, his flat, clipped voice colored with a new note of enthusiasm. "Man with a crossbow in the proper position at the proper time's worth a corps of heavy artillery half an hour late and ten miles down the road from where it should be. What's that business about '. . . *for want of a nail a horseshoe was lost . . .'?*"

" 'For want of a horseshoe a horse was lost. For want of a horse a rider was lost...' " Cletus quoted it through to the end; and the two men looked at each other with a strange, wordless but mutual, respect.

"You must have some training problems," said Cletus, thoughtfully. "On the Dorsai, I mean. You must be getting men with all sorts of backgrounds, and you'd want to turn out a soldier trained for use in as many different military situations as possible."

"We concentrate on basics," said Eachan. "Aside from that, it's our program to develop small, mobile, quick-striking units, and then get employers to use them as trained." He nodded at Mondar. "Only real success in use so far's been with the Exotics, here. Most employers want to fit our professionals into their classical tables of organization. Works, but it's not an efficient use of the men, or the units. That's one reason we've had some arguments with the regular military. Your commanding officer here, General Traynor—" Eachan broke off. "Well, not for me to say."

He dropped the subject abruptly, sat up and peered out through the open window spaces in the metal sides of the command car at the jungle. Then he turned and called up to the driver on the outside seat.

"Any sign of anything odd out there?" he asked. "Don't like the feel of it, right along in here."

"No sir, Colonel!" called the driver back down. "Quiet as Sunday din—"

A thunderclap of sound burst suddenly all around them. The command car lurched in the same moment and Cletus felt it going over, as the air around them filled with flying earth. He had just a glimpse of the driver, still holding the dally gun but now all but headless, pitching into the right-hand ditch. And then the car went all the way over on its side and there was a blurred moment in which nothing made sense.

Things cleared again, suddenly. The command car was lying on its right side, with only its armored base and its left and rear window spaces exposing them to the outside. Mondar was already tugging the magnesium shutter across the rear window and Eachan Khan was pulling the left window-space shutter closed overhead. They were left in a dim metal box with only a few narrow, sunlit apertures toward the front and around the armored section behind the driver's seat.

"You armed, Colonel?" asked Eachan Khan, producing a flat, little, dart-thrower sidearm from under his tunic and beginning to screw a long sniper's barrel onto it. Solid pellets from sporting guns—theoretically civilian weapons, but deadly enough at jungle ranges—were already beginning to whang and yowl off the armor plating of the car surrounding them.

"No," said Cletus, grimly. The air was already close in the car and the smell of crushed grass and nutmeg was overwhelming.

"Pity," said Eachan Khan. He finished screwing on the sniper barrel, poked its muzzle through one of the aperture cracks and squinted into the daylight. He fired—and a big, blond-bearded man in a camouflage suit came crashing out of the jungle wall on the far side of the road, to lie still.

"The bus will hear the firing as it comes up behind us," said Mondar out of the dimness behind Cletus. "They'll stop and phone ahead for help. A relief squad can get here by air in about fifteen minutes after Bakhalla hears about us."

"Yes," said Eachan Khan, calmly, and fired again. Another body, invisible this time, could be heard crashing down out of a tree to the ground below. "They might get here in time. Odd these guerrillas didn't let us pass and wait for the bus in the first place. Bigger package, less protection, and more prizes inside. . . . I'd keep my head down, Colonel."

This last sentence was directed at Cletus, who was heaving and wrenching in a fury at the shutter on the down side of the car. Half-propped off the road surface as the car was by the bulge of that same surface under it, opening the shutter gradually produced a space facing on the ditch into which the dead driver had pitched—a space large enough for Cletus to crawl out.

The jungle-hidden riflemen became aware of what he was up to, and a fusillade of shots rang against the armored underside of the car—though, because of the narrow angle it made with the ground, none came through the opening Cletus had produced. Melissa, suddenly recognizing what was in his mind, caught at his arm as he started through the opening.

"No," she said. "It's no use! You can't help the driver. He was killed when the mine went off—"

"The hell . . . with that . . ." panted Cletus, for a fire-fight did not encourage the best in manners. "The dally gun went with him when he fell."

Wrenching himself free of her grasp, he wriggled out from under the armored car, jumped to his feet and made a dash for the ditch where the body of the driver lay unseen. An explosion of shots from the surrounding jungle rang out, and he stumbled as he reached the ditch edge, tripped, spun about and plunged out of sight. Melissa gasped, for there was the sound of thrashing from the ditch, and then an arm was flung up into sight to quiver for a second and then hang there in plain view, reaching up like a last and desperate beckoning for help.

In response, a single shot sounded from the jungle and a slug blew away half the hand and wrist. Blood spattered from it, but the hand was not withdrawn; and almost immediately the bleeding dwindled, with none of the steady spurt and flow that would have signaled a still-pumping, living heart behind it.

Melissa shuddered, staring at the arm, and a shivering breath came from her. Glancing about for a minute, her father put his free hand for a moment on her shoulder.

"Easy, girl," he said. He squeezed her shoulder for a second and then was forced back to his loophole as a new burst of shots rang against the body of the car. "They'll rush us—any minute now," he muttered.

Sitting cross-legged in the dimness like a figure meditating and remote, Mondar reached out and took one of the staring girl's hands in his own. Her gaze did not move from the arm in the ditch, but her own grip tightened, tightened, on Mondar's hand with a strength that was unbelievable. She did not make a sound, but her gaze never moved and her face was as white and still as a mask.

The shots from the jungle stopped suddenly. Mondar turned to look at Eachan.

The Dorsai looked back over his own shoulder and their eyes met.

"Any second now," said Eachan, in businesslike tones. "You're a fool if you let them take you alive, Outbond."

"When there is no more point in living, I can always die," answered Mondar, serenely. "No man commands this body but myself."

Eachan fired again.

"The bus," said Mondar, calmly, "ought to have gotten close enough to hear the firing and phoned, by this time."

"No doubt," said the Dorsai. "But help'd have to be on top of us right now to do any good. Any second, as I said, they'll give up sniping at us and make a rush. And one pistol won't hold off a dozen or more. . . . Here they come now!"

Through the aperture, over the soldier's shoulder strap, Mondar could see the two waves of camouflaged-overalled figures that erupted suddenly from both sides of the jungle trail and came pouring down upon the car. The little handgun in Eachan's hand was speaking steadily, and, magically—for its voice was almost lost in the general din and uproar—figures in the front of the rush were going down.

But there was only a matter of fifteen meters or so for the attackers to cover; and then the jungle and the little patch of sunlight Mondar could see were blotted out by camouflaged overalls.

The gun in Eachan's hand clicked empty—and in that second, just as the shape of the first guerrilla darkened the opening through which Cletus had gotten out, the wild yammer of a dally gun roared from behind the attackers, and they melted like sand figures under the blow of a heavy surf.

The dally gun yammered on for a second longer, and then stopped. Stillness flowed in over the scene like water back into a hole made in a mountain lake by a falling stone. Eachan pushed past the frozen figures of Mondar and Melissa and crawled out from the car. Numbly, they followed him.

Limping on his artificial left knee joint, Cletus was climbing out of the ditch, dragging the shape of the dally gun behind him. He got to his feet on the roadway just as Eachan came up to him.

"Very well done," said the Dorsai, with a rare note of warmth back in his usually stiff voice. "Thank you, Colonel."

"Not at all, Colonel," said Cletus, a little shakily. Now that the excitement was over, his one knee that was still flesh and blood was trembling with reaction, invisibly but perceptibly under his uniform trouser leg.

"Very well done, indeed," said Mondar, as quietly as ever, joining them. Melissa had halted and was staring down into the ditch where the dead driver lay. It was his arm that had been upflung, obviously with intention by Cletus, as he lay thrashing about like a deeply wounded man, unseen in the ditch. Melissa shivered and turned away to face the rest of them.

She stared at Cletus out of her white face, in which a strange mixture of emotions were now intermingled. Mondar spoke:

"Here come our relief forces," commented the Exotic, gazing skyward. A couple of battle aircars, with a squad of infantry aboard each, were dropping down to the roadway. A hiss of a braking airjet sounded behind them and they turned to see the bus slide into view around a turn in the road. "As well as our signal section," he added, smiling a little.

Chapter 5

The command car, its compressor damaged by guerrilla fire, was left behind. One of the battle aircars carried its four surviving passengers the rest of the way into the port-city of Bakhalla. The aircar dropped the four of them off at the transport section of Alliance Headquarters in Bakhalla. Eachan Khan and Melissa said goodbye and left by autocab for their own residence in the city. Mondar opened the door of another autocab and motioned Cletus inside.

"You'll need to go to Alliance HQ for your assignment and billeting, and that's on my way. I'll drop you off."

Cletus got in; Mondar reached to punch out a destination on the control board of the autocab. The cab rose on its air cushion and slid smoothly off between the rows of white-painted military buildings.

"Thanks," said Cletus.

"Not at all," said Mondar. "You saved all our lives back in the jungle just now. I want to do more than just thank you. I take it you might like to talk to Dow deCastries again?"

Cletus looked at the Outbond curiously. All his life he had enjoyed watching people of strong aims at work to achieve them; and in the five days since he had met Mondar he had become aware of a purposefulness in the Exotic that might well be as dedicated as his own.

"I thought deCastries went down to Capital Neuland."

"He did," said Mondar, as the autocab made a right turn into a somewhat broader boulevard and began to approach a large building of white concrete with the Alliance flag flying on top of it. "But Neuland's only twenty-five minutes from here by air. The Coalition hasn't any direct diplomatic relations with our Exotic government here on Kultis, and neither our people nor Dow want to pass up a chance to talk. After all, it's really the Coalition we're fighting—Neuland couldn't last six weeks without them. So I'm giving an unofficial little party at my home this evening—with a buffet supper and general conversation. Eachan and Melissa will be there. I'd appreciate having you, too."

"Be happy to come," said Cletus. "May I bring my aide?"

"Aide?"

"A second lieutenant named Arvid Johnson, if I'm lucky enough to find him still unassigned," Cletus said. "One of my former students at the Academy. He came to visit me when he was home from here on leave a couple of months ago. It was what he told me that got me interested in Bakhalla."

"Was it? Well, bring him by all means." The autocab slid to a halt before the walkway leading up to the entrance of the large white building. Mondar pressed a button and the autocab door next to Cletus swung open. "Bring anyone you think might enjoy it. About eight o'clock."

"We'll be there," said Cletus. He turned and let the walkway carry him up into the Headquarters building.

"Colonel Cletus Grahame?" echoed the narrow-faced, young second lieutenant at the cluttered desk behind the glass door of the billeting and assignments office, when Cletus confronted him. "You're to report to General Traynor immediately—*immediately* when you arrive."

He had a high tenor voice and he grinned unpleasantly as he spoke. Cletus smiled agreeably, asked directions to the general's office and left.

The glass door he finally found marked *Brigadier General John Houston Traynor* led him first into an outer office where a square-set, half-bald colonel in his early fifties stood, evidently just completing the giving of some directions to an overweight, thirtyish captain behind the room's single desk. Finishing, the colonel turned around and eyed Cletus.

"You're Grahame?" he asked abruptly.

"That's right, Colonel," said Cletus pleasantly, "and you . . . ?"

"Dupleine," said the other, ungraciously. "I'm chief of staff to General Traynor. You're not going into the officers pool, then?"

"I'm on special assignment from Geneva, Colonel," said Cletus.

Dupleine grunted, whirled around and went out the door Cletus had just entered. Cletus looked back at the fat captain behind the desk.

"Sir," said the captain. His voice held the hint of a note of sympathy. His face was not unkind, and even intelligent, in spite of the heavy dewlap of the double chin supporting it from beneath. "If you'll just sit down a moment, I'll tell General Traynor you're here."

Cletus sat down and the captain leaned forward to speak into the intercom grille of his desk. The reply he received was inaudible to Cletus, but the captain looked up and nodded.

"You can go right in, Colonel," he said, nodding to another door behind his desk.

Cletus rose and obeyed. . . . As he stepped through the door into the farther office, he found himself directly facing a much larger desk, behind which sat a bull-like man in his mid-forties with a heavy-boned face decorated by a startling pair of thick, black eyebrows. "Bat" Traynor, the general had been nicknamed, Cletus recalled, because of those brows. Bat Traynor stared now, the brows pulled ominously together as Cletus walked forward toward his desk.

"Colonel Cletus Grahame reporting, sir," Cletus said, laying his travel orders on the desk. Bat shoved them aside with one big-knuckled hand.

"All right, Colonel," he said. His voice was a rough-edged bass. He pointed to a chair facing him at the left side of his desk. "Sit down."

Cletus limped gratefully around to the chair and dropped into it. He was beginning to feel the fact that he had strained one or more of the few remaining ligaments in his bad knee during the episode in the ditch outside of town. He looked up to see Bat still staring point-blank at him.

"I've got your dossier here, Colonel," Bat said after a moment. He flipped open the gray plastic folder that lay on the desk before him and looked down at it. "You come from an Academy family, it says here. Your uncle was General Chief of Staff at Geneva Alliance HQ just before he retired eight years ago. That right?"

"Yes, sir," said Cletus.

"And you"—Bat flipped papers with a thick forefinger, scowling a little down at them—"got that bad knee in the Three-Month War on Java seven years ago? . . . Medal of Honor, too?"

"Yes," said Cletus.

"Since then"—Bat flipped the folder shut and raised his eyes to stare unwaveringly once more across it at Cletus' face—"you've been on the Academy staff. Except for three months of active duty, in short, you've done nothing in the Army but pound tactics into the heads of cadets."

"I've also," said Cletus, carefully, "been writing a comprehensive 'Theory of Tactics and Strategical Considerations.' "

"Yes," said Bat, grimly. "That's in there, too. Three months in the field and you're going to write twenty volumes."

"Sir?" said Cletus.

Bat threw himself back heavily in his chair.

"All right," he said. "You're supposed to be here on special assignment to act as my tactical adviser." The black eyebrows drew together in a scowl and rippled like battle flags in the wind. "I don't suppose I've got you because you heard some rumor they were going to clean out all the dead wood at the Academy and you pulled strings to be sent to some nice soft job where there's nothing for you to do?"

"No, sir," said Cletus, quietly. "I may have pulled a string or two to get sent here. But, with the General's permission, it wasn't because I thought this a soft job. I've got to do a great deal out here."

"I hope not, Colonel. I hope not," said Bat. "It just happens I put in a request for a dozen jungle-breaker tanks three months ago. . . . You're what I got instead. Now, I don't give a damn what the Academy wants to do with its Tactics Department. The kids just have to come out here into the field and relearn it all over again under practical conditions, anyway. But I needed those tanks. I still need them."

"Possibly," said Cletus, "I can come up with some means to help the General get along without them."

"I don't think so," said Bat, grimly. "What I think is that you're going to hang around here for a couple of months or so and turn out not to be particularly useful. Then I'm going to mention that fact to Alliance HQ back on Earth and ask for my jungle-breakers again. I'll get them, and you'll be transferred back to Earth—if with no commendations, at least without any black marks on your record. . . . That's if everything goes smoothly, Colonel. And"—Bat reached across to a corner of his desk and pulled a single sheet of paper toward him—"speaking of the way things go, I've got a report here that you got drunk your first night out, on the ship headed here, and made a fool of yourself in front of the Outworld's Secretary for the Coalition, who was aboard."

"That's fast reporting," said Cletus, "considering that, when our party for Bakhalla left the ship, the phones aboard were all still tied up by Coalition people. I take it this report to the General comes from one of them?"

"It's none of your business who made the report!" rumbled Bat. "As a matter of fact, it comes from the captain of the spaceship."

Cletus laughed.

"What's the joke, Colonel?" Bat's voice rose.

"The idea, sir," said Cletus, "of a civilian ship commander reporting on the fitness of an Alliance officer."

"You won't find it all that funny if I have the information entered in your record, Colonel," said Bat. He stared at Cletus, at first grimly, and then a trifle disconcertedly, when Cletus did not seem greatly sobered by this threat. "But, never mind the Coalition or any civilian shipmaster. I'm your commanding officer, and *I'm* asking for an explanation of your drunkenness."

"There isn't any explanation . . ." began Cletus.

"Oh?" said Bat.

"No explanation, I was going to say," continued Cletus, "because no explanation's necessary. I've never been drunk in my life. I'm afraid the ship's captain was wrongly advised—or drew the wrong conclusion."

"Just made a mistake, eh?" said Bat, ironically.

"As it happens," said Cletus, "I think I've got a witness who'll testify I wasn't drunk. He was at the table. Mondar, the former Outbond from here to St. Louis Enclave."

Bat's mouth, opened to retort before Cletus was half done, closed instead. The general sat silent for several seconds. Then his eyebrows quivered and the frown line between his eyes smoothed somewhat.

"Then why this report?" he asked in a more neutral voice.

"The ship's people, from what I saw," said Cletus, "seemed partial to the Coalition people aboard."

"Well, then, damn it!" exploded Bat, "if you saw them jumping to the wrong conclusion, why didn't you set them straight?"

"As a matter of elementary strategy," said Cletus, "I thought it wouldn't do any harm to let the Coalition people pick up as low an opinion of me as possible—of me, and my usefulness to you, as a tactical expert."

Bat looked balefully at him. "Their opinion couldn't be any lower than mine, anyway," he said. "You're no use to me, Colonel. This is a dirty, little, hole-in-the-wall war, with no room for strategical mysteries. This Exotic colony's got brains, money, technical developments and a seacoast. The Neulanders've got no seacoast, no industry and too much population for their back-country farms to support—because of this multiple-wife religious cult of theirs. But that same excess population's just fine for supplying guerrillas. So, the Neulanders want what the Exotics've got and the Coalition's trying to help them get it. We're here to see they don't. That's the whole situation. What the Neuland guerrillas try to do, and what we do to stop them from doing it, is just plain obvious. I need a book-strategy and tactics expert like

I need a hundred-piece symphony orchestra. And I'm sure deCastries and the other Coalition people on that ship knew it as well as I do."

"Maybe I won't be quite as useless as the General thinks," said Cletus, unperturbed. "Of course, I'll have to survey and study the situation, starting by setting up a plan for trapping those guerrillas they'll be infiltrating through Etter's Pass, up country, in the next few days."

Bat's eyebrows shot up into flag position again. "New guerrillas? Who told you anything about Etter's Pass?" he snapped. "What kind of a rabbit is this you're trying to pull out of your hat?"

"No rabbit," said Cletus, "not even a professional judgment, I'm afraid. Just common sense. With Dow deCastries here, the Neulanders have to try to put on some sort of spectacular during his visit. . . . Have you got a map handy?"

Bat jabbed a button on the surface of his desk, and the wall of the room to Cletus' left lit up suddenly with the projection of a large map showing the long, narrow coastline country of the Exotic colony, and the interior range of mountains that divided it from the Neuland colony inland. Cletus stepped over to the projection, looked it over and reached up to tap with his left forefinger at a point in the middle of the mountain range running down the left side of the map.

"Here's Etter's Pass," he said to Bat. "A good, broad cut through the mountains, leading from Neuland down to Bakhalla—but according to reports, not much used by the Neulanders, simply because there's nothing much worth raiding on the Exotic side for over a hundred miles in any direction. On the other hand, it's a fairly easy pass to get through. There's nothing but the small town of Two Rivers down below it, here. Of course, from a practical standpoint, the Neulanders are better off sending their guerrillas into the country through passes closer to the larger population centers. But if they aren't after profit so much as spectacle, it'd pay them to infiltrate a fairly good-sized force through here in the next few days, so that a week from now they can hit one of the smaller coastal towns in force—maybe even capture and hold it for a few days."

Cletus turned, limped back to his chair and sat down. Bat was frowning at the map.

"At any rate," Cletus said, "it shouldn't be too difficult to set up a net to sweep most of them in, as they try to pass Two Rivers. In fact, I could do it myself. If you'd let me have a battalion of jump troops—"

"Battalion! *Jump troops!*" Bat started suddenly out of his near-trance and turned a glare on Cletus. "What do you think this is? A classroom, where you can dream up whatever force you need for a job? There're no jump troops on Kultis. And as for giving you a battalion of any kind of troops—even if your guess has something going for it . . ." Bat snorted.

"The guerrillas are coming, all right. I'd bet my reputation on it," said Cletus, undisturbed. "In fact, you might say I've already bet it, come to think of it. I remember talking to some of my fellow staff members at the Academy, and a friend or two down in Washington, and forecasting that infiltration, just as soon as Dow deCastries reached Neuland."

"You forecast . . ." Bat's tone became thoughtful—almost cunning—suddenly. He sat behind his desk, pondering Cletus with knitted brows. Then his dark eyes sharpened. "So you bet your reputation on this, did you, Colonel? But spare troops are something I haven't got, and in any case, you're here as a technical adviser. . . . Tell you what. I'll pull a company off Rest and Retraining and send them out with a field officer in charge. He'll be junior to you, of course, but you can go along if you want to. Officially, as an observer only, but I'll tell the officer commanding that he's to keep your advice in mind. . . . Good enough?"

The last two words were barked sharply at Cletus, in a put-up-or-shut-up tone of voice.

"Certainly," said Cletus. "If the General wishes."

"All right!" Bat beamed suddenly, showing his teeth in a hearty, wolfish grin. "You can go on and see about your quarters, then, Colonel. But stay on call."

Cletus rose to his feet. "Thank you, sir," he said, and took his leave.

"Not at all, Colonel. Not at all," he heard Bat's voice saying, with almost a chuckle in it, as Cletus closed the door of the office behind him.

Cletus left the Headquarters building and went to see about establishing himself. Once set up in the Bachelor Officers' Quarters, he strolled over to the Officers' Pool HQ with a copy of his orders and checked to see if that Second Lieutenant Arvid Johnson, of whom he had spoken to Mondar, was still unattached. Informed that he was, Cletus filed a request for the lieutenant to be assigned to him as a research staff member and requested that he get in touch with him at the BOQ immediately.

He returned to the BOQ. Less than fifteen minutes later, the signal outside his room buzzed to announce a visitor. Cletus rose from his chair and opened the door.

"Arvid!" he said, letting the visitor in and closing the door behind him. Arvid Johnson stepped inside, turned and smiled happily down at Cletus as they shook hands. Cletus was tall, but Arvid was a tower, from the soles of his black dress boots to the tips of his short-cropped, whitish-blond hair.

"You came after all, sir," Arvid said, smiling. "I know you said you'd come, but I couldn't believe you'd really leave the Academy for this."

"This is where things are going on," said Cletus.

"Sir?" Arvid looked incredulous. "Away out here on Kultis?"

"It's not the locality so much," said Cletus, "as the people in it that makes things happen. Right now we've got a man among us named Dow deCastries and the first thing I want from you is to go with me to a party for him tonight."

"Dow deCastries?" Arvid said, and shook his head. "I don't think I know—"

"Secretary to the Outworlds for the Coalition," said Cletus. "He came in on the same ship from Earth as I did. . . . A gamesman."

Arvid nodded. "Oh, one of the Coalition bosses," he said. "No wonder you say things might start to happen around here. . . . What did you mean by gamesman, sir? You mean he likes sports?"

"Not in the usual sense," said Cletus. He quoted, " 'Whose game was empires and whose stakes were thrones. Whose table, earth— whose dice were human bones . . .' "

"Shakespeare?" asked Arvid, curiously.

"Byron," said Cletus, "in his 'The Age of Bronze,' referring to Napoleon."

"Sir," said Arvid, "you don't really mean this deCastries is another Napoleon?"

"No more," answered Cletus, "than Napoleon was an earlier deCastries. But they've got points in common."

Arvid waited for a moment longer, but Cletus said nothing more. The big young man nodded again.

"Yes, sir," he said. "What time are we supposed to go to this party, Colonel?"

Chapter 6

Thunder, deeper toned than Earth's, muttered beyond the ridge of hills
inland from Bakhalla like a grumbling of giants, as Cletus and Arvid
arrived at the residence of Mondar. But above the city the sky was
clear. Out over the rooftops of the buildings leading down the harbor,
the yellow sun of Kultis was filling the sky and sea alike with pinkish
gold.

Mondar's home, surrounded by trees and flowering shrubs, both
native and Earth variform, sat alone on a small hill in the eastern
suburbs of the city. The building itself was made up of an assortment
of basic building units put together originally with an eye more toward
utility than appearance. However, utility no longer controlled any but
the basic forms of the house. In everything else an artistic and gentle
influence had been at work.

The hard white blocks of the building units, now tinted by the
sunset, did not end abruptly at the green lawn, but were extended into
arbors, patios and half-rooms walled with vine-covered trellises. Once
Cletus and Arvid had left their car and passed into the first of these
outer structures of the house, it became hard for them to tell at any
time whether they were completely indoors or not.

Mondar met them in a large, airy half-room with solid walls on
three sides only, and an openwork of vines on the fourth. He led them
deeper into the house, to a long, wide, low-ceilinged room deeply
carpeted and scattered with comfortably overstuffed chairs and
couches. A number of people were already there, including Melissa
and Eachan Khan.

"DeCastries?" Cletus asked Mondar.

"He's here," said Mondar. "He and Pater Ten are just finishing their talk with some of my fellow Exotics." As he spoke he was leading the two of them toward the small bar in one corner of the room. "Punch for whatever you'd like to drink. I've got to see some people right now—but I'd like to talk to you later, Cletus. Is that all right? I'll look you up just as soon as I'm free."

"By all means," said Cletus. He turned toward the bar as Mondar went off. Arvid was already picking up the glass of beer for which he had punched.

"Sir?" asked Arvid. "Can I get you . . ."

"Nothing right now, thanks," said Cletus. He was glancing around again and his eye lit upon Eachan Khan, standing alone with a glass in his hand next to a wide window screen. "Stay around here, will you, Arvid? So I can find you easily when I want you?"

"Yes, sir," said Arvid.

Cletus went toward Eachan Khan. The older man glanced around, with a stony face, as though to discourage conversation, as he came up. Then, seeing who it was, Eachan's face relaxed—insofar as it could ever be said to be relaxed.

"Evening," Eachan said. "I understand you've met your commanding officer."

"News travels fast," said Cletus.

"We're a military post, after all," said Eachan. His gaze went past Cletus for a moment, and then returned. "Also, I hear you suggested something about a new infiltration of Neulander guerrillas through Etter's Pass?"

"That's right," said Cletus. "You don't think it's likely?"

"Very likely—now you've pointed it out," said Eachan. "By the way—I got hold of those three volumes on tactics you've already published. The Exotic library here had copies. I've only had time to glance through them, so far"—his eyes suddenly locked with Cletus'—"but it looks like sound stuff. Very sound. . . . I'm still not sure I follow your tactics of mistake, though. As deCastries said, combat's no fencing match."

"No," said Cletus, "but the principle's applicable, all the same. For example, suppose a simple tactical trap you lay for an enemy consists of enticing his forces to strike at what seems to be a weak section of your line. But when they do, your line pulls back and draws them into a pocket, where you surround them and pinch them off with hidden, superior forces of your own."

"Nothing new about that," said Eachan.

"No," Cletus said, "but apply the tactics of mistake to essentially the same situation. Only this time, in a succession of contacts with the enemy, you entice him into picking up a series of what seem to be small, easy victories. Meanwhile, however, you're getting him to engage a larger amount of his available forces with each contact. Then, when he finally commits the greatest part of his strength for what he conceives as one more easy win—you convert that contact into a trap and he discovers that you've gradually drawn him into a field position where he's outflanked and completely at your mercy."

"Tricky," Eachan frowned. "Too tricky, perhaps . . ."

"Not necessarily," said Cletus. "Imperial China and Russia both used a crude version of this, drawing invaders deeper into their territories, until the invader suddenly realized he was too far from his supply and support based and completely surrounded by the native enemy. . . . Napoleon and the retreat from Moscow."

"Still—" Eachan broke off suddenly. His gaze had gone past Cletus; and Cletus, turning, saw that Dow deCastries was now in the room. The tall, dark and elegant Secretary to the Outworlds for the Coalition was now standing in conversation with Melissa, by the opposite wall.

Glancing from the two figures back to Eachan, Cletus saw that the older man's face had become as cold and still as the first sheet of ice on the surface of a deep pond on a windless winter day.

"You've known deCastries awhile now?" Cletus asked. "You and Melissa?"

"The women all like him." Eachan's voice was grim. His gaze was still on Melissa and Dow.

"Yes," said Cletus. "By the way—" He broke off, and waited. With reluctance, Eachan removed his gaze from the pair across the room and looked back at him.

"I was going to say," said Cletus, "that General Traynor came up with something strange when I was talking to him. He said he didn't have any jump troops here in Bakhalla. That surprised me. I did some reading up on you Dorsais before I came out here, and I thought a jump course was part of the training you gave your mercenaries?"

"We do," replied Eachan, dryly. "But General Traynor's like a lot of your Alliance and Coalition commanders. He doesn't think our training's good enough to qualify the men for jump-troop work—or a lot of other combat field duties."

"Hmm," said Cletus. "Jealousy? Or do you suppose they look on you mercenaries as competitors of a sort?"

"I don't say that," said Eachan, frostily. "You draw your own conclusions, of course." His eyes showed a desire once more to wander back across the room to Melissa and Dow.

"Oh, and something else I was going to ask you," said Cletus.

"The assignment sheets for Bakhalla that I looked at back on Earth listed some Navy officers, on detached duty as marine engineers—something about river-and-harbors work. But I haven't seen any Navy people around."

"Commander Wefer Linet," said Eachan, promptly, "wearing civies, down at the end of the couch across the room there. Come along. I'll introduce you."

Cletus followed Eachan at a long slant across the room, which brought them to a couch and several chairs where half a dozen men sat talking. Here, they were less than a quarter of the distance they had been before from Dow and Melissa—but still too distant to catch the conversation going on between the two.

"Commander," said Eachan, as they reached the couch, and a short, square-faced man in his middle thirties got up promptly from the end of the couch, a drink still in his hand, "I'd like you to meet Colonel Cletus Grahame, just out from Earth, to be attached to General Traynor's staff—tactical expert."

"Happy to meet you, Colonel," said Wefer Linet, shaking Cletus' hand with a hard, friendly grip. "Dream something up for us to do besides dredging river mouths and canals and my men'll love you."

"I'll do that," said Cletus, smiling. "It's a promise."

"Good!" said Wefer energetically.

"You've got those large, underwater bulldozers, haven't you?" asked Cletus. "I read about them in the Alliance Forces Journal, seven months back, I think."

"The Mark V, yes," Linet's face lit up. "Six of them here. Care for a ride in one someday? They're beautiful pieces of machinery. Bat Traynor wanted to take them out of the water and use them knocking down jungles for him. Do it better than anything you Army people have, of course. But they're not designed for land work. I couldn't tell the general no, myself, but I insisted on direct orders from Earth and kept my fingers crossed. Luckily, they turned him down back there."

"I'll take you up on that ride," said Cletus. Eachan was once more watching Melissa and Dow with a stony concentration. Cletus glanced about the room and discovered Mondar, standing talking to a pair of women who looked like the wives of diplomatic personnel.

As if Cletus' gaze had an actual physical touch to it, the Exotic turned toward him just then, smiled and nodded. Cletus nodded back and turned once more to Wefer, who had launched into an explanation of how his Mark V's worked, at depths down to a thousand feet or in the teeth of thirty-knot currents and tides.

"It looks as if I may be tied up for the next few days, out of the city," Cletus said. "But after that, if for some reason I shouldn't leave town . . ."

"Give me a ring, anytime," Wefer said. "We're working on the main harbor here at Bakhalla right now. I can have you off the docks and down inside my command unit in ten minutes, if you'll just phone me half an hour or so ahead of time to make arrangements. . . . Hello, Outbond. The Colonel here's going to take a ride with me one of these days in a Mark V."

Mondar had come up while Wefer had been speaking.

"Good," said the Exotic, smiling. "He'll find that interesting." His gaze shifted to Cletus. "But I believe you wanted to talk to Dow deCastries, Cletus? His business with my people's over for the evening. You can see him, right across the room there, with Melissa."

"Yes . . . I see," said Cletus. He looked around at Wefer and Eachan. "I was just going over there. If you gentlemen will excuse me?"

He left Wefer with a promise to phone him at the earliest opportunity. As he turned away, he saw Mondar touch Eachan lightly on the arm and draw him off to one side in conversation.

Cletus limped over to where Dow and Melissa were still standing together. As Cletus came up they both turned to look at him, Melissa with a sudden, slight frown line between her darkened eyebrows. But Dow smiled genially.

"Well, Colonel," he said. "I hear all of you had a close call coming in from the spaceport earlier today."

"Only the sort of thing to be expected here on Bakhalla, I suppose," said Cletus.

They both laughed easily, and the slight frown line between Melissa's eyes faded.

"Excuse me," she said to Dow. "Dad's got something to say to me, I guess. He's beckoning me over. I'll be right back."

She left. The gazes of the two men met and locked.

"So," said Dow, "you came off with flying honors—defeating a guerrilla band single-handed."

"Not exactly. There was Eachan and his pistol." Cletus watched the other man. "Melissa might have been killed, though."

"So she might," said Dow, "and that would have been a pity."

"I think so," said Cletus. "She deserves better than that."

"People usually get what they deserve," said deCastries. "Even Melissas. But I didn't think scholars concerned themselves with individuals?"

"With everything," said Cletus.

"I see," said deCastries. "Certainly with sleight-of-hand. You know, I found a sugar cube under that middle cup after all? I mentioned it to Melissa and she said you'd told her you'd had cubes under all three cups."

"I'm afraid so," Cletus said.

They looked at each other.

"It's a good trick," said deCastries. "But not one that'd work a second time."

"No," said Cletus. "It always has to be different, a second time."

DeCastries smiled, an animal smile.

"You don't sound much like a man in an ivory tower, Colonel," he said. "I can't help thinking you like theory less, and action more, than you admit. Tell me"—his eyes hooded themselves amusedly under his straight brows—"if it comes down to a simple choice, aren't you tempted to practice rather than preach?"

"No doubt about it," said Cletus. "But one drawback to being a scholar is you're likely to be an idealist, too. And in the long run, when these new worlds are free to work out their own destinies without Earth's influence, one man's theories could have a longer and more useful effect than one man's practice."

"You mentioned that, back aboard ship," deCastries said. "You talked about Alliance and Coalition influence being removed from worlds like Kultis. Do you still feel as safe talking like that here, with your Alliance superiors all around the place?"

"Safe enough," said Cletus. "None of them would believe it—any more than you do."

"Yes. I'm afraid I don't." DeCastries picked up a wineglass from the small table beside which he was standing and held it briefly up to the light, twisting it slowly between thumb and forefinger. He lowered the glass and looked back at Cletus. "But I'd be interested in hearing how you think it's going to happen."

"I'm planning to help the change along a little," said Cletus.

"Are you?" said deCastries. "But you don't seem to have anything to speak of in the way of funds, armies or political influence to help with. Now, for example, I've got those things, myself, which puts me in a much stronger position. If I thought a major change could be accomplished—to my benefit, of course—I'd be interested in altering the shape of things to come."

"Well," said Cletus, "we can both try."

"Fair enough." DeCastries held the wineglass, looking over it at Cletus. "But you haven't told me how you'd do it. I told you what my tools are—money, armed troops, political power. What have you got? Only theories?"

"Theories are enough, sometimes," said Cletus.

DeCastries slowly shook his head. He put the wineglass back down on the small table and lightly dusted against one another fingertips of the hand that had held the glass, as if to get rid of some stickiness.

"Colonel," he said, quietly, "you're either some new kind of agent the Alliance is trying to fasten on me—in which case I'll find out about you as soon as I can get word back from Earth—or you're a sort of interesting madman. In which case, events will take care of you in not much more time than it takes to establish the fact you're an agent."

He watched Cletus for a second. Cletus met his eye expressionlessly.

"I'm sorry to say," deCastries went on, "you're beginning to sound more and more like a madman. It's too bad. If you'd been an agent, I was going to offer you a better job than the one you have with the Alliance. But I don't want to hire a madman—he'd be too unpredictable. I'm sorry."

"But," said Cletus, "if I turned out to be a successful madman . . . ?"

"Then, of course, it'd be different. But that's too much to hope for. So all I can say is, I'm sorry. I'd hoped you wouldn't disappoint me."

"I seem to have a habit of disappointing people," said Cletus.

"As when you first decided to paint instead of going on to the Academy and then gave up painting for a military life, after all?" murmured deCastries. "I've been a little disappointing to people in my life that way. I've got a large number of uncles and cousins about the Coalition world—all very successful managers, business chiefs, just as my father was. But I picked politics—" He broke off, as Melissa rejoined them.

"It wasn't anything. . . . Oh, Cletus," she said, "Mondar said if you wanted to find him he'd be in his study. It's a separate building, out behind the house."

"Which way do I go?" asked Cletus.

She pointed through an arched entrance in a farther wall of the room. "Just go straight through there and turn left," she said. "The corridor you'll be in leads to a door that opens on the garden. His study building's just beyond it."

"Thank you," said Cletus.

He found the corridor, as Melissa had said, and followed it out into the garden, a small, terraced area with paths running to a line of trees, the tops of which tossed sharply in a hot, wet wind against a sky full of moonlight and torn cloud ends. There was no sign of any building.

At that moment, however, just as Cletus hesitated, he caught sight of light glimmering through the trees ahead of him. He went out across the garden and through the trees. Past their narrow belt he came into the open before a low-roofed, garage-like structure so comfortably fitted in among the vegetation surrounding it that it gave the impression of being comfortably half-sunk in the earth. Low, heavily curtained windows let out the small amount of light he had seen just now. There was a door before him; and as he approached, it slid noiselessly open. He stepped inside and it closed behind him. He stopped, instinctively.

He had walked into a softly but clearly lit room, more library than study in appearance, although it had something of both about it. Its air tasted strangely thin and dry and clean like air on some high mountain peak. Bookshelves inset in all four of the walls held a surprisingly large collection of old-fashioned, printed volumes. A study console and a library retrieval system each occupied a corner of the room. But Mondar, the only other person in the room besides Cletus, was seated apart from these devices on a sort of wide-surfaced and armless chair, his legs up and crossed before him, so that he sat like a Buddha in the lotus position.

There was nothing except this to mark the moment and place as anything out of the ordinary—but as Cletus stepped through the door, a deep, instinctive warning shouted loudly at him, checking him just inside the threshold. He sensed an impalpable living tension that held the very air of the room—a feeling as of a massive, invisible force in delicate, temporary balance. For a second his mind recoiled.

Then it cleared. For one fleeting but timeless moment he saw that which was in the room—and that which was not.

What his eyes registered were like two versions of the same scene, superimposed on each other, but at the same time distinct and separate. One was the ordinary room, with Mondar seated on his chair, and all things ordinary.

The other was the same room, but filled with a difference. Here, Mondar did not sit on his chair but floated, in lotus position, a few inches above its seat cushion. Stretching out before and behind him was a succession of duplicating images, semitransparent, but each clearly identifiable—and while those closest to him, before and behind him, were duplicates of himself, those farther from him wore different faces—faces still Exotic, but of different men, different Outbonds. Before and behind him, these stretched away until they were lost to sight.

Cletus, too, he became aware, had his images in line with him. He could see those before and he was somehow conscious of those behind him. Before him was a Cletus with two good knees, but beyond this and two more Cletuses were different men, bigger men. But a common thread ran through them, tying the pulses of their lives to his, and continuing back through him to a man with no left arm, on and on, through the lives of all those others behind him until it ended, at last, with a powerful old man in half-armor sitting on a white horse with a baton in hand.

Nor was this all. The room was full of forces and currents of living pressures coming from vast distances to this focal point, like threads of golden light they wove back and forth, tying each other together, connecting some of Cletus' images with Mondar's, and even Cletus, himself, with Mondar, himself. They two, their forerunners and their followers, hung webbed in a tapestry of this interconnecting pattern of light during that single moment in which Cletus' vision registered the double scene.

Then, abruptly, Mondar turned his gaze on Cletus, and both tapestry and images were gone. Only the normal room remained.

But Mondar's eyes glowed at Cletus like twin sapphires illuminated from within by a light identical in color and texture to the threads that had seemed to fill the air of the room between both men.

"Yes," said Mondar. "I knew . . . almost from the moment I first saw you in the spaceship dining lounge. I knew you had potential. If it'd only been part of our philosophy to proselytize or recruit in the ordinary way, I'd have tried to recruit you from that minute on. Did you talk to Dow?"

Cletus considered the unlined face, the blue eyes, of the other, and slowly nodded.

"With your help," he said. "Was it actually necessary to get Melissa away, too? DeCastries and I could have talked over her head."

"I wanted him to have every advantage," Mondar said, his eyes glowing. "I wanted no doubt left in your mind that he'd been able to bid as high for you as he wanted to go. . . . He did offer you a job with him, didn't he?"

"He told me," said Cletus, "that he couldn't—to an interesting madman. From which I gathered he was extremely eager to hire one."

"Of course he is," said Mondar. "But he wants you only for what you can do for him. He's not interested in what you could make of yourself. . . . Cletus, do you know how we Exotics came about?"

"Yes," said Cletus. "I looked you up before I put in my request for transfer to here. The Association for the Investigation and Development of Exotic Sciences—my sources say you developed out of a

black-magic cult of the early twenty-first century called the Chantry
Guild."

"That's right," Mondar said. "The Chantry Guild was the brain-
child of a man named Walter Blunt. He was a brilliant man, Cletus,
but like most of the people of his time, he was reacting against the
fact that his environment had suddenly been enlarged from the surface
of one world to the surfaces of any number of worlds spread out
through light-years of interstellar space. You probably know the history
of that period as well as I do—how that first, instinctive, racial fear of
space beyond the solar system built up and erupted in a series of bloody
social eruptions. It spawned any number of societies and cults for people attempting to adjust psychologically to feelings of vulnerability and
insignificance, deep down on the unconscious level. Blunt was a
fighter, an anarchist. His answer was revolution—"

"Revolution?" asked Cletus.

"Yes. Literally—revolution," Mondar answered. "Blunt wanted to
destroy part of actual, objective physical reality as well—by using
primitive psychic leverage. He called what he wanted to do 'creative
destruction.' He called on people to *'Destruct!'* But he couldn't quite
push even the intense neurotics of his time all the way over the emotional brink. And then he was deposed as head of the Guild by a young
mining engineer who'd lost an arm in a mine accident—"

"Lost an arm?" said Cletus sharply. "Which arm?"

"The left—yes, I think it was the left that was gone," said Mondar.
"Why?"

"Nothing," said Cletus. "Go on."

"His name was Paul Formain—"

"Fort-Mayne?" Cletus interrupted a second time.

"No *t*," answered Mondar, "F-o-r-m-a-i-n." He spelled it out looking curiously at Cletus. "Something about this interests you particularly, Cletus?"

"Only the coincidences," said Cletus. "You said he had only one
arm, so the right arm he had left would have been overmuscled from
compensation development. And his name sounds almost like *fort-
mayne*, which are the words used by the Norman French to describe
their policy to the conquered English after they took over England in
the eleventh century. *Fort-mayne*—literally, 'strong-hand.' It described
a policy of using whatever force was necessary to keep the native
English under control. And you say he took over the Chantry Guild,
deposing this Blunt?"

"Yes." Mondar frowned. "I see the coincidences, Cletus, but I
don't see why they're important."

"Maybe they aren't," said Cletus. "Go on. Formain took over the Chantry Guild and started your Exotic Association?"

"He almost had to wreck the Chantry Guild to do it," said Mondar. "But he did. He changed its aim from revolution to evolution. The evolution of man, Cletus."

"Evolution." Cletus repeated the word thoughtfully. "So, you don't think the human race is through evolving? What comes next, then?"

"We don't know, of course," said Mondar, folding his hands in his lap. "Can an ape imagine a man? But we're convinced the seeds of further evolution are alive in man, still—even if they aren't already germinating. We Exotics are dedicated to searching for those seeds, and protecting them once we've found them, so that they can flourish and grow until evolved man is part of our community."

"Sorry." Cletus shook his head. "I'd make a poor Exotic, Mondar. I've got my own job to do."

"But this is part of your job—and your job is part of it!" Mondar leaned forward, and his hands slid apart. "There's no compulsion on our members. Each one searches and works for the future the way he thinks best. All we ask is that when the skills of anyone are needed by the community, he makes them available to it. In return the community offers him its skills to improve *him*, physically and mentally, so he can be that much more effective in his own work. You know what you can do now, Cletus. Think what you might be able to do if you could make use of all we can teach you!"

Cletus shook his head again.

"If you turn us down," said Mondar, "it signals a danger to you, Cletus. It signals an unconscious desire on your part to go the de-Castries way—to let yourself be caught up by the excitement of directly manipulating people and situations instead of dealing with what's much more valuable, but less emotionally stimulating—the struggle with ideas to find principles that'll lift people eventually above and beyond manipulation."

Cletus laughed, a little grimly. "Tell me," he said, "isn't it true that you Exotics won't carry or use weapons yourself, even in self-defense? And that's why you hire mercenaries like the Dorsai, or make agreements with political groups like the Alliance to defend yourselves?"

"Yes—but not for the reason most people think, Cletus," said Mondar, swiftly. "We haven't any moral objection to fighting. It's just that the emotions involved interfere with clear thinking, so people like myself prefer not to touch weapons. But there's no compulsion on our people on this. If you want to write your work on military tactics, or even keep and carry guns—"

"I don't think you follow me," said Cletus. "Eachan Khan told me something. You remember when you were in the command car after it overturned, earlier today, and he suggested you not let yourself be taken alive by the Neulander guerrillas—for obvious reasons? You answered that you could always die. *'No man,'* you said, *'commands this body but myself.'* "

"And you think suicide is a form of violence—"

"No," said Cletus. "I'm trying to explain to you why I'd never make an Exotic. In your calmness in the face of possible torture and the need to kill yourself, you were showing a particular form of ruthlessness. It was ruthlessness toward yourself—but that's only the back side of the coin. You Exotics are essentially ruthless toward all men, because you're philosophers, and by and large, philosophers are ruthless people."

"Cletus!" Mondar shook his head. "Do you realize what you're saying?"

"Of course," said Cletus, quietly. "And you realize it as well as I do. The immediate teaching of philosophers may be gentle, but the theory behind their teaching is without compunction—and that's why so much bloodshed and misery has always attended the paths of their followers, who claim to live by those teachings. More blood's been spilled by the militant adherents of prophets of change than by any other group of people down through the history of man."

"No Exotic spills blood," said Mondar, softly.

"Not directly, no," said Cletus. "But to achieve the future you dream of means the obliteration of the present as we know it now. You may say your aim's changed from revolution to evolution, but your goal is still the destruction of what we have now to make room for something different. You work to destroy what presently is—and that takes a ruthlessness that's not my way—that I don't agree with."

He stopped speaking. Mondar met his eyes for a long moment.

"Cletus," said Mondar at last, "can you be that sure of yourself?"

"Yes," said Cletus. "I'm afraid I can." He turned toward the door. As he reached the door and put his hand on its button, he turned back.

"Thanks all the same, Mondar," he said. "You and your Exotics may end up going my way. But I won't go yours. Good night."

He opened the door.

"Cletus," said Mondar, behind him, "if you refuse us now, you do it at your own risk. There are larger forces at work in what you want to do than I think you understand."

Cletus shook his head. "Good night," he said again, and went out.

Back in the room where he had left Arvid, he found the young lieutenant and told him they were leaving. As they reached the parking area together and Cletus opened the door of their aircar, the sky split open above them in a wild explosion of lightning and thunder, with raindrops coming down like hailstones.

They bolted for the interior of the car. The rain was icy and the few seconds of being exposed to it had left their jackets soaked and clinging to their shoulders. Arvid put power on the vehicle and lifted it out of the lot.

"All hell's broke loose tonight," he murmured, as they swung back across the city. Then, startled, he looked at Cletus, sitting beside him.

"Now, why did I say that?" he asked. Cletus did not answer and after a second Arvid answered himself.

"All the same," he said, half to himself, "it has."

Chapter 7

Cletus woke to the sensation that his left knee was being slowly crushed in a heavy vise. The dull, unyielding pain of it had roused him from his sleep, and for a moment he was its captive—the sensation of pain filling the whole universe of his consciousness.

Then, practically, he took action to control the crippling sensation. Rolling over on his back, he stared up at the white ceiling seven feet above him. One by one, starting with his thigh muscles, he commanded the large muscles of his arms and legs to lose their tensions and relax. He moved on to the neck and face muscles, the belly muscles, and finally into a feeling of relaxation pervading him completely.

His body was heavy and limp now. His eyes were drooping, half-closed. He lay, indifferent to the faint noises that filtered to him from other parts of the BOQ. He drifted, sliding gently away, like a man lax upon the surface of some warm ocean.

The state of relaxation he had induced had already muffled the dull-jawed, relentless grip of the pain upon his knee. Slowly, so as not to reawaken an alertness that would allow tension to form in him once more, he propped the pillow behind and pulled himself up in the bed. Half-sitting, he folded the covers back from his left leg and looked at it.

The knee was puffed and swollen to stiffness. There was no darkness or bruise-shade of discoloration about it, but it was swollen to the point of immobility. He fastened his gaze steadily on the swollen knee, and set about the larger job of bringing it back down to normal size and movement.

Still drifting, still in that more primitive state of mind known as regression, he connected the pain response in his knee with the pain message in his mind, and began to convert the message to a mental equivalent of that same physical relaxation and peace which held his body. Drifting with it, he felt the pain message lose its color. It faded, like an instruction written in evaporating ink, until it was finally invisible.

He felt what he had earlier recognized as pain, still present in his knee. It was a sensation only, however, neither pain nor pressure, but co-equal with both. Now that he had identified this former pain as a separate sensation-entity, he began to concentrate upon the actual physical feeling of pressure within the blood and limb, the vessels now swollen to the point of immobilizing his leg.

He formed a mental image of the vessels as they were. Then, slowly, he began to visualize them as relaxing, shrinking, returning their fluid contents to those pipe systems of the leg to which they were severally connected.

For perhaps as much as ten minutes there was no visible response from the knee area. Then gradually he began to be aware of a yielding of the pressure and a sensation of faint warmth within the knee itself. Within another five minutes it was possible to see that the swelling was actually going down. Ten minutes later, he had a knee that was still swollen, but which he could bend at a good sixty-degree angle. It was good enough. He swung good leg and bad out of bed together, got up and began to dress.

He was just buckling on a weapons belt over his jungle suit, when there was a knock at his door. Cletus glanced over at the clock beside his bed. It showed eight minutes before 5 A.M.

"Come on in," he said.

Arvid stepped into the room.

"You're up early, Arv," Cletus said, snapping the weapons belt shut and reaching for his sidearm on top of the chest of drawers beside him. He slid the weapon into its holster, hanging from the belt. "Did you get the things I wanted?"

"Yes, sir," said Arvid, "the loudspeaker horn and the singleton mines are tucked away out of sight in duffle packs. I couldn't get the rifle into a pack, but it's with the packs, clipped onto the electric horse you asked for."

"And the horse, itself?"

"I've got it in the back of a courier car, outside . . ." Arvid hesitated. "I asked to go with you, sir, but the orders just called for you and the field officer in charge of the company. I want to tell you about him. They've given you a first lieutenant named Bill Athyer."

"And this Bill Athyer is no good, is that it?" asked Cletus, cheerfully, picking up his communications helmet and leading the way out of the room.

"How did you know?" Arvid stared down at Cletus, following him as they went out down the long center aisle of the BOQ.

Cletus smiled back at him, limping along, but delayed his answer until they had stepped out the front door into the misty, predawn darkness where the courier car waited for Cletus. They got in, Arvid behind the controls. As the big young lieutenant sent the vehicle sliding off on its air cushion, Cletus went on:

"I rather thought the general'd be giving me someone like that. Don't worry about it, Arv. You're going to have your hands full enough today, as it is. I want you to find office space for me and line me up a staff—a warrant officer, if you can get one for office manager, a couple of clerical tech fives and a file clerk tech two with a research specialty. Can you get right to work on that?"

"Yes, sir," answered Arvid. "But I didn't know we had authority for something like that—"

"We don't, yet," said Cletus. "But I'll get it for you. You just find the premises and the people, so we know where to lay hands on them as soon as we have authorization."

"Yes, sir," said Arvid.

Having arrived at the transport area, Cletus found his company, under the command of First Lieutenant William Athyer, standing at ease in ranks, equipped, armed and apparently ready to take off. Cletus assumed that the men had had breakfast—not being the field officer in command of them, it was not up to him to see that they had; and asking Athyer about it would be impolitic, not to say insulting. Cletus descended a little stiffly from the courier car and watched as Arvid unloaded the electric horse, with its equipment.

"Colonel Grahame?" a voice said behind him. "I'm Lieutenant Athyer, in command of this company. We're ready to take off . . ."

Cletus turned. Athyer was a short, dark, fairly slim man, in his mid-thirties, with a beak-like nose. A vaguely sour expression sat on his features, as if habit had made it permanent there. His speech was abrupt, even aggressive, but the words at the end of each speech tended to thin out into a whine.

"Now that you're finally here, sir," he added.

The extra, unnecessary statement verged on impertinence. But Cletus ignored it, looking past Athyer's shoulder at the men behind the lieutenant. Their tanned skin and the mixture of old and new equipment and clothing about them suggested experience. But they were more silent than they should be; and Cletus had little doubt about the reason for this. To be put back under weapons and flown off into combat in the middle of Rest and Retraining was not likely to make soldiers happy. He looked back at Athyer.

"I imagine we'll start loading right away, then. Won't we, Lieutenant?" he said pleasantly. "Let me know where you want me."

"We're taking two atmosphere support ships for transport," growled Athyer. "I've got my top sergeant in the second. You'd better ride with me in the first, Colonel—"

He broke off to stare at the electric horse, as its overhead vanes whined into movement. Arvid had just switched its satchel turbine on, and the single-person vehicle had lifted into the air so that it could be moved easily under its own power to the support ship. Evidently, Athyer had not connected the horse with Cletus until this moment. In truth, it was an unlikely little contraption for such an outing—designed for spaceport inspection work, mainly, and looking like a wheel-less bicycle frame suspended fore and aft from metal rods leading down from a side-by-side pair of counter-rotating ducted vanes driven by a nuclear-pack, satchel turbine just below them. Cletus' cone rifle and duffle bags were hung before its saddle on the crossbar.

It was not pretty, but that was no reason for Athyer to scowl at it as he was doing.

"What's this?" he demanded.

"It's for me, Lieutenant," said Cletus, cheerfully. "My left knee's half-prosthetic, you know. I didn't want to hold you and your men up if it came to moving someplace along the ground in a hurry."

"Oh? Well . . ." Athyer went on scowling. But the fact that the sentence he had begun trailed off was evidence enough that his imagination was failing him in its search for a valid excuse to forbid taking the electric horse. Cletus was, after all, a lieutenant-colonel. Athyer turned, snapping at Arvid. "Get it on board, then! Quick, Lieutenant!"

He turned away to the business of getting the company of perhaps eighty men into the two atmosphere support ships waiting on the transport area pad some fifty feet distant.

The boarding of the ships went smoothly and easily. Within twenty minutes they were skimming northward over the tops of the jungle trees toward Etter's Pass—and the sky beyond the distant mountain range was beginning to grow pale with the dawn.

"What're your plans, Lieutenant?" began Cletus, as he and Athyer sat facing each other in the small, forward passengers' compartment of the ship.

"I'll get the map," said Athyer, ducking away resentfully from Cletus' gaze. He dug into the metal command case on the floor between his boots and came up with a terrain map of the Exotic side of the mountains around Etter's Pass. He spread the map out on the combined knees of himself and Cletus.

"I'll set up a picket line like this," Athyer said, his finger tracing an arc through the jungle on the mountain slopes below the pass, "about three hundred yards down. Also, place a couple of reserve groups high up, behind the picket line on either side of the pass mouth. When the Neulanders get through the pass and far enough down the trail to hit the lower curve of the picket line, the reserve groups can move in behind them and we'll have them surrounded. . . . That is, if any guerrillas do come through the pass."

Cletus ignored the concluding statement of the lieutenant's explanation. "What if the guerrillas don't come straight down the trail?" Cletus asked. "What if they turn either right or left directly into the jungle the minute that they're on this side of the mountains?"

Athyer stared at Cletus at first blankly, and then resentfully, like a student who has been asked an exam question he considers unfair.

"My support groups can fall back ahead of them," he said at last, ungraciously, "alerting the rest of the picket line as they go. The other men can still close in behind them. Anyway, we've got them enclosed."

"What's visibility in the jungle around there, Lieutenant?" asked Cletus.

"Fifteen—twenty meters," Athyer answered.

"Then the rest of your picket line is going to have some trouble keeping position and moving upslope at an angle to enclose guerrillas who're probably already beginning to split up into groups of two and three and spread out for their trek to the coast. Don't you think?"

"We'll just have to do the best we can," said Athyer, sullenly.

"But there're other possibilities," said Cletus. He pointed to the map. "The guerrillas have the Whey River to their right as they come out of the pass, and the Blue River to their left, and both those rivers meet down at Two Rivers Town, below. Which means that any way the Neulanders turn, they've got to cross water. Look at the map. There're only three good crossing spots above the town on the Blue River, and only two on the Whey—unless they'd want to go right through the town itself, which they wouldn't. So, any or all of those five crossings could be used."

Cletus paused, waiting for the junior officer to pick up on the unspoken suggestion. But Athyer was obviously one of those men who need their opportunities spelled out for them.

"The point is, Lieutenant," Cletus said, "why try to catch these guerrillas in the jungle up around the pass, where they've got all sorts of opportunities to slip past you, when you could simply be waiting for them at these crossings, and catch them between you and the river?"

Athyer frowned reluctantly, but then bent over the map to search out the five indicated crossing points that Cletus had mentioned.

"The two Whey River crossings," Cletus went on, "are closest to the pass. Also they're on the most direct route to the coast. Any guerrillas taking the passes on the Blue River are going to have to circle wide to get safely around the town below. The Neulanders know you know this. So I think it's a fairly safe bet that they'll count on your trying to stop them—if they count on anyone trying to stop them at all—at those two passes. So they'll probably merely feint in that direction and make their real crossing at these three other fords over on the Blue River."

Athyer stared at Cletus' finger as it moved around from point to point on the map in time with his words. The lieutenant's face tensed.

"No, no, Colonel," he said, when Cletus had finished. "You don't know these Neulanders the way I do. In the first place, why should they expect us to be waiting for them, anyway? In the second place, they're just not that smart. They'll come through the pass, break up into twos and threes going through the jungle and join up again at one, maybe two, of the Whey River crossings."

"I wouldn't think so—" Cletus was beginning. But this time, Athyer literally cut him short.

"Take my word for it, Colonel!" he said. "It's those two points on the Whey River they'll be crossing at."

He rubbed his hands together. "And that's where I'll snap them up!" he went on. "I'll take the lower crossing with half the men, and my top sergeant can take the upper crossing with most of the rest. Put a few men behind them to cut off their retreat, and I'll bag myself a nice catch of guerrillas."

"You're the field officer in command," said Cletus, "so I don't want to argue with you. Still, General Traynor did say that I was to offer you my advice, and I'd think you'd want to play safe, over on the Blue. If it was up to me . . ."

Cletus let his voice trail off. The lieutenant's hands, with the map already half-folded, slowed and ceased their movement. Cletus, looking at the other's lowered head, could almost see the gears turning over inside it. By this time Athyer had left all doubts behind about his own military judgment. Still, situations involving generals and colonels were always touchy for a lieutenant to be involved in, no matter who seemed to be holding all the high cards.

"I couldn't spare more than a squad, under a corporal," muttered

Athyer to the map, at last. He hesitated, plainly thinking. Then he lifted his head and there was a craftiness in his eyes. "It's your suggestion, Colonel. Maybe if you'd like to take the responsibility for diverting part of my force over to the Blue. . . . ?"

"Why, I'd be perfectly willing to, of course," said Cletus. "But as you pointed out, I'm not a field officer, and I can't very well take command of troops under combat conditions . . ."

Athyer grinned. "Oh, that!" he said. "We don't stick right with every line in the book out here, Colonel. I'll simply give orders to the corporal in charge of the squad that he's to do what you say."

"What I say? You mean—*exactly* what I say?" asked Cletus.

"Exactly," said Athyer. "There's an authority for that sort of thing in emergencies, you know. As commanding officer of an isolated unit I can make emergency use of any and all military personnel in whatever manner I feel is necessary. I'll tell the corporal I've temporarily allowed you status as a field officer, and of course your rank applies."

"But if the guerrillas do come through the Blue River crossings," said Cletus, "I'll have only a squad."

"They won't, Colonel," said Athyer, finishing his folding of the map with a flourish. "They won't. But if a few stray Neulanders *should* show up—why, use your best judgment. An expert on tactics like yourself, sir, ought to be able to handle any little situation like that, that's liable to turn up."

Leaving the barely concealed sneer to linger in the air behind him, he rose and went back with the map into the rear passenger compartment where the soldiers of half his command were riding.

The support ship in which they were traveling set Cletus down with his squad at the uppermost of the three crossing points on the Blue River, and took off into the dawn shadows, which still obscured this western slope of the mountain range dividing Bakhalla from Neuland Athyer had sorted out a weedy, nineteen-year-old corporal named Ed Jarnki and six men to be the force Cletus would command. The moment they were deshipped, the seven dropped automatically to earth, propping their backs comfortably against nearby tree trunks and rocks that protruded from the unbroken, green ferny carpet of the jungle floor. They were in a little clearing surrounded by tall trees that verged on a four-foot bank over the near edge of the river; and they gazed with some curiosity at Cletus as he turned about to face them.

He said nothing. He only gazed back. After a second, Jarnki, the corporal, scrambled to his feet. One after the other the rest of the men rose also, until they all stood facing Cletus, in a ragged line, half at attention.

Cletus smiled. He seemed a different man entirely, now, from the officer the seven had glimpsed earlier as they were boarding and descending from the support ship. The good humor had not gone from his face. But in addition, now, there was something powerful, something steady and intense, about the way he looked at them, so that a sort of human electricity flowed from him to them and set all their nerves on edge, in spite of themselves.

"That's better," said Cletus. Even his voice had changed. "All right, you're the men who're going to win the day for everyone, up here at Etter's Pass. And if you follow orders properly, you'll do it without so much as skinning your knuckles or working up a sweat."

Chapter 8

They stared at him.

"Sir?" said Jarnki, after a moment.

"Yes, Corporal?" said Cletus.

"Sir . . . I don't understand what you mean." Jarnki got it out, after a second's struggle.

"I mean you're going to capture a lot of Neulanders," said Cletus, "and without getting yourselves hurt in the process." He waited while Jarnki opened his mouth a second time, and then slowly closed it again.

"Well? That answer your question, Corporal?"

"Yes sir."

Jarnki subsided. But his eyes, and the eyes of the rest of the men, rested on Cletus with a suspicion amounting to fear.

"Then we'll get busy," said Cletus.

He proceeded to post the men—one across the shallow ford of the river, which here swung in a lazy curve past the clearing, two men down below the bank on each side of the clearing, and the four remaining in treetop positions strung out away from the river and upslope of the direction from which any guerrillas crossing the ford would come.

The last man he posted was Jarnki.

"Don't worry, Corporal," he said, hovering on the electric horse in midair a few feet from where Jarnki swayed in the treetop, clutching his cone rifle. "You'll find the Neulanders won't keep you waiting long. When you see them, give them a few cones from here, and then get down on the ground where you won't get hit. You've been shot at before, haven't you?"

Jarnki nodded. His face was a little pale, and his position in a crotch of the smooth-barked, variform Earth oak he perched in was somewhat too cramped to be comfortable.

"Yes, sir," he said. His tone left a great deal more unsaid.

"But it was under sensible conditions, with the rest of the men in your platoon or company all around you, wasn't it?" said Cletus.

"Don't let the difference shake you, Corporal. It won't matter once the firing starts. I'm going to check the two lower crossings. I'll be back before long."

He swung the electric horse away from the tree and headed down-river. . . . The vehicle he rode was almost silent in its operation, producing nothing much more than the kind of hum a room exhaust fan makes. Under conditions of normal quiet it could be heard for perhaps fifteen meters. But this upland Kultan jungle was busy with the sounds of birds and animals. Among these was a cry like the sound of an ax striking wood, which sounded at intervals; and another sound that resembled heavy snoring, which would go on for several seconds, only to break off, pause, and then begin again. But most of the woodlife noises were simply screams of different pitches and volumes and musical character.

Altogether these made an unpredictable pattern of sound, among which the low hum of the electric horse could easily be lost to ears not specifically listening for it—such as the ears of a guerrilla from Neuland who was probably both unfamiliar with the noise and not expecting it in any case.

Cletus flew downriver and checked both the lower crossings, finding them empty of all human movement. He turned from the lowest crossing to move through midair into the jungle from the river, upslope, in the direction of the pass. With luck, he thought, since they had the longest distance to cover if several crossings were being used. Undoubtedly a rendezvous point and time would have been set up for all groups on the far side of the river.

He drifted forward just under treetop level, some forty to sixty meters above the ground, at a speed of not more than six kilometers per hour. Below him, the upland jungle flora showed less of the yellow veining than there had been in the greenery near the shuttleboat landing pad; but the threads of scarlet ran everywhere, even through the outsize leaves of the variform Earth trees—oak, maple and ash—with which Kultis had been seeded twenty years back.

The Earth flora had taken more strongly in these higher altitudes. But there was still a majority of the native plants and trees, from fern-like clumps reaching ten meters into the air, to a sprawling tree-type with purple fruits that were perfectly edible but exhaled a faint but sickening scent through their furry skins as they ripened.

Cletus was about eight hundred meters away from the river crossing before he spotted his first sign of movement, a waving of fern tops below him. He checked his forward movement and drifted downward.

A second later the foreshortened figure of a man in a brown- and green-splashed jungle suit moved into sight from under the fern.

The infiltrator was unequipped except for the pack on his back, a soft camouflage-cloth cap on his head and the pellet-gun sporting firearm he carried by its strap over his right shoulder. This was to be expected where the guerrillas were concerned. The convention that had grown up on the newer worlds in fifty years of intercolony disputes was that, unless a man carried military weaponry or equipment, he was subject only to civil law—and civil law had to prove damage to property, life or limb before any action could be taken against an armed man, even from another colony. A guerrilla caught with nothing but a sporting gun was usually only deported or interned. One with any kind of military equipment, however—even as little as a military-issue nail file—could be taken by the military courts, which usually adjudged him a saboteur and condemned him to prison or death. If this man below him was typical of the infiltrators in his group, then Jarnki and his men with their cone rifles would have a massive advantage in weapons to make up for their scarcity of numbers, which was a relief.

Cletus continued to watch the man for several minutes. He was making his way through the jungle with no real regard for silence or cover. As soon as Cletus had a line of march estimated for this individual, he turned off to one side to locate the other members of the same guerrilla force.

The rapidly rising sun, burning through the sparse leaves at treetop level, heated the back of Cletus' neck. He was sweating from his armpits, all across his chest and back under his jungle suit, and his knee was threatening to revive its ache once more. He took a moment out to force his muscles to relax and push the knee discomfort from him. There was not time for that—not yet. He went back to searching the jungle for more guerrillas.

Almost immediately he found the second man, moving along parallel to and perhaps thirty meters from the infiltrator Cletus had spotted first. Cletus continued looking, and within the next twenty minutes he ranged out to both ends of the skirmish line that was pushing through the jungle below him and counted twenty men moving abreast over a front perhaps three hundred meters in width. If the Neulanders had split their forces equally between the three crossings, which would be only elementary military precaution, that would mean an infiltration force of sixty men. Sixty men, assuming they lost something like 20 percent of their group's strength in getting through the jungle from here to the coast, would leave about forty-eight men available for whatever assault the Neulanders planned to celebrate deCastries' visit.

Forty-eight men could do a lot in the way of taking over and holding the small coastal fishing village. But a good deal more could be done with double that number. Perhaps there was a second skirmish line behind the first.

Cletus turned the electric horse in midair and drifted it back under the treetops behind the man he had just spotted advancing. Sure enough, about eighty meters back, he discovered a second skirmish line—this time with fifteen men in it, including at least a couple who looked like officers, in that they carried more in the way of communication and other equipment and wore sidearms rather than rifles. Cletus turned the electric horse about, slid quietly through the air just below the treetops and back toward the outside lower end of the approaching skirmish line. He located it, and saw that—as he had expected—the guerrillas were already beginning to close up so as to come into the crossing point together. Having estimated the line along which their lower edge would be drawing in, he went ahead on the electric horse, stopping to plant singleton personnel mines against the trunks of trees not more that four inches thick at intervals of about twenty meters. He planted the last of these right at the water's edge, about twenty meters below the crossing. Then he swooped back to make contact with the end of the second skirmish line.

He found the end of the line just coming level with the first mine he had planted, the end man some ten meters away from it in the jungle. Cletus swooped out and around to come up behind the center of the line. Careful not to approach any closer than twenty meters, he halted the electric horse, unlimbered his rifle and sprayed a long burst up and down the line through about a sixty-degree angle.

The sound of a cone rifle firing was not the sort of noise that went unnoticed. The tiny, self-propelled cones, leaving the muzzle of the rifle at relatively low velocity but accelerating as they went, whistled piercingly through the air until their passage was concluded by the dull, abrupt thud of the impact explosion that ended their career. A man not in body armor, as these guerrillas were not, could be torn in half by one of those explosions—so that it was no wonder that, for a second after the sound of his firing had ceased, there was utter silence in the jungle. Even the birds and beasts were still. Then, somewhat

laggardly, but bravely enough, from immediately in front of Cletus and
all up and down the invisible skirmish line of the infiltrators, pellet
guns began to snap back, like a chorus of sprung mousetraps.

The firing was blind. The pellets, zipping through the leaves of the
trees about Cletus like so many hailstones, went wide. But there was
an uncomfortable amount of them. Cletus had already flung the electric
horse about and was putting distance between himself and those who
were shooting. Fifty meters back, he turned once more around the
downriver end of the line and reached for the remote trigger that set
off the first of his singleton personnel mines.

Up ahead of him and to his left, there was a single loud explosion.
A tree—the tree to which the land mine had been stuck—leaned like
a sick giant among its fellows, and slowly at first, then faster, came
toppling down among the underbrush.

By now, the jungle was alive with sound. The guerrillas were apparently firing in every direction, because the wildlife were screaming
at the tops of their lungs. Cletus moved in at an angle to the end of
the line, fired another long burst from his weapon and quickly moved
up level with his second mine.

The heavy vegetation of the jungle hid the actions of the individual
guerrillas. But they were shouting to each other now; and this, as well
as the wild life sounds, gave Cletus a rough idea of what was going
on. Clearly, they were doing the instinctive, if not exactly the militarily
wise, thing. They were beginning to draw together for mutual support.
Cletus gave them five minutes in which to get well clumped, so that
what had been two spread-out skirmish lines was now a single group
of thirty-five individuals within a circle of jungle no more than fifty
meters in diameter.

Then he swung around to the rear of this once more, set off his
second singleton mine ahead of them and once more commenced firing
into them from behind.

This time he evoked a veritable cricket chorus of answering pellet-
gun fire—what sounded like all thirty-five weapons snapping at him
at once, in every direction. The nearby Kultan wild life burst out in a
cacophony of protest; and the toppling of a tree cut down by a third
singleton mine added its crash to the general uproar just as the firing
began to slack off. By this time, Cletus was once more around behind
his line of remaining unfired mines, downriver from the guerrillas. . . .
He waited.

After a few minutes commands were shouted and the guerrilla
firing ceased. Cletus did not have to see into the center of the hundred-
meter-wide area to know that the officers among the infiltrators were

talking over the situation they had encountered. The question in their minds would be whether the explosions and cone-rifle firing they had heard had been evoked from some small patrol that just happened to be in this area, or whether they had—against all normal expectations and reason—run head-on into a large enemy force set here directly to bar their route to the coast. Cletus let them talk it over.

The obvious move by a group such as these guerrillas in a situation such as this was to sit tight and send out scouts. The infiltrators were by this time less than eight hundred meters from the river's edge clearing of the crossing point and scouts would easily discover that the point was actually undefended, which would not be good. Cletus set off a couple more of his mines and commenced firing upon the down-river side of the guerrilla area. Immediately the guerrillas answered.

But then this fire, too, began to dwindle and become more sporadic, until there was only a single gun snapping from moment to moment. When it, at last, fell silent, Cletus took the electric horse up and swung wide, away from the river into a position about five hundred meters upriver. Here he hovered, and waited.

Sure enough, within a very few minùtes, he was able to make out movement in the jungle. Men were coming toward him, cautiously, and once more spread out in a skirmish line. The Neulander guerrillas, having encountered renewed evidence of what they thought was at least a sizable force at the lowest crossing, had chosen discretion over valor. They were withdrawing to the next higher crossing, where either their passage would not be barred or they would have the comfort of joining forces with that other group of their force which had been sent to cross at the middle ford.

Cletus swung wide once more, circled in, away from the river, and headed upstream toward the second crossing. As he approached this general area, he slowed the electric horse, to minimize the noise of its ducted fans, and crept along, high up, just under treetop level.

Shortly, he made contact with a second group of the guerrilla force, also in two skirmish lines, but a good nine hundred meters yet from the middle of the three river crossings. He paused long enough to plant another row of singleton personnel mines on trees in a line just down-river from the crossing, then slipped upriver again.

When he reached the area inland of the ford, highest up on the Blue River, where Jarnki and the others waited, he found that the third group of guerrillas, approaching this highest crossing, were not on schedule with the two other groups below. This upper group was already almost upon the crossing—less than 150 meters from it.

There was no time here for a careful reconnaissance before acting.

Cletus swept across thirty meters in front of their first skirmish line, firing one long whistling burst from his cone rifle when he judged he was opposite the line's center.

Safely beyond the farther end of it, he waited until the snapping of answering fire from the guerrillas had died down, and then slipped back across their front once more, this time pausing to plant four singleton mines in their path. Once he was back beyond the downriver end of their lines, he set off a couple of these mines and began firing again.

The results were gratifying. The guerrillas opened up all along their front. Not only that, but, fortunately, the men he had left at the crossing, spooked by the guerrilla firing, began instinctively returning it with their cone rifles. The result, as far as the ear could tell, was a very good impression of two fair-sized groups in a fire-fight.

There was only one thing wrong with these additional sound effects Cletus was getting from his own men. One of the heavily whistling guns belonged to Jarnki; and evidently, from the sounds of it, the corporal was on the ground within fifteen meters of the front guerrilla lines—up where the exchange of shots could well prove lethal to him.

Cletus was tempted to swear, but stifled the urge. He pulsed a sharp message over his throat mike communicator to Jarnki to fall back. There was no response, and Jarnki's weapon went on speaking. This time Cletus did swear. Dropping his electric horse to just above the ground, he threaded the vehicle through the jungle cover up to right behind the corporal's position, led to it easily by the sound of Jarnki's firing.

The young soldier was lying in the prone position, legs spread out, his rifle barrel resting upon a rotting tree trunk, firing steadily. His face was as pale as the face of a man who has already lost half the blood in his body, but there was not a mark on him. Cletus had to dismount from the horse and shake the narrow shoulder above the whistling rifle before Jarnki would wake to the fact that anyone was beside him.

When he did become conscious of Cletus' presence, the convulsive reaction sent him scrambling to get to his feet like a startled cat. Cletus held him down against the ground with one hand and jerked the thumb of the other toward the crossing behind them.

"Fall back!" whispered Cletus harshly.

Jarnki stared, nodded, turned about and began to scramble on hands and legs toward the crossing. Cletus remounted the electric horse. Swinging wide again, he approached the guerrillas from their opposite side to ascertain their reaction to these unexpected sounds of opposition.

He was forced, in the end, to dismount from the electric horse and wriggle forward on his stomach after all, for perhaps ten meters, to get close enough to understand some of what was being said. Happily, what he heard was what he had hoped to hear. This group, like the group farthest downriver, had decided to stop and talk over these sounds of an unexpected opposition.

Painfully, Cletus wriggled back to the electric horse, mounted it and flew a wide curve once more back to the crossing itself. He reached it just as Jarnki, by this time back on his feet, also reached it. Jarnki had recovered some of his color, but he looked at Cletus apprehensively, as if expecting a tongue-lashing. Instead, Cletus grinned at him.

"You're a brave man, Corporal," Cletus said. "You just have to remember that we like to keep our brave men alive, if possible. They're more useful that way."

Jarnki blinked. He grinned uncertainly.

Cletus turned back to the electric horse and took one of his boxes of singleton mines. He handed it to Jarnki.

"Plant these between fifty and eighty meters out," Cletus said. "Just be sure you don't take any chances on getting shot while you're doing it. Then hang back in front of those Neulanders as they advance, and keep them busy, both with the mines and with your weapon. Your job is to slow those Neulanders down until I can get back up here to help you. At a guess, that's going to be anywhere from another forty-five minutes to an hour and a half. Do you think you can do it?"

"We'll do it," said Jarnki.

"I'll leave it to you, then," said Cletus.

He mounted the electric horse, swung out over the river and headed down to make contact with the group of guerrillas moving toward the middle ford.

They were doing just that when he found them. The Neulanders were by this time fairly close to the middle crossing, and right in among his mines. There was no time like the present—Cletus set them off, and compounded the situation by cruising the Neulander rear and firing a number of bursts at random into them.

They returned his fire immediately; but, shortly after that, their return shooting became sporadic and ceased. The silence that followed lengthened and lengthened. When there had been no shots for five minutes, Cletus circled downriver with the electric horse and came up behind where the middle-crossing group had been when it was firing back at him.

They were not there, and, following cautiously just under treetop level, he soon caught up with them. They were headed upriver, and their numbers seemed to have doubled. Clearly, the group from the lower crossing had joined up with them and with common consent both groups were now headed for the highest crossing and a reunion with the group scheduled to cross there.

It was as he had expected. These infiltrators were saboteurs rather than soldiers. They would have been strictly ordered to avoid military action along the way to their destination if it was at all possible to avoid it. He followed them carefully until they were almost in contact with the group of their fellows pinned down at the highest crossing, and then swung out over the river to reconnoiter the situation at that crossing.

He came in from above and cautiously explored the situation of the upper guerrilla group. They were strung out in a ragged semicircle the ends of which did not quite reach the riverbanks some sixty meters above and thirty meters below the crossing. They were laying down fire but making no real effort to fight their way across the river—as he listened, the sound of their firing dwindled and there was a good deal of shouting back and forth as the two groups from downriver joined them.

Hovering above ground level, Cletus produced a snooper mike from the equipment bar of the horse and slipped its earphone to his right ear. He swung the snooper barrel, scanning the undergrowth, but the only conversations he could pick up were by ordinary members of the guerrilla force, none by officers discussing the action they would take next. This was unfortunate. If he had been up to crawling fifty meters or so to make a personal reconnaissance—but he was not, and there was no point considering it. Reconnaissance on the electric horse would by now be too risky. There remained the business of putting himself in the shoes of the guerrilla force commander and trying to second-guess the man's thoughts. Cletus half-closed his eyes, relaxing in the same fashion as he had relaxed that morning in order to conquer the pain of his knee. Eyelids drooping, slumping bonelessly in the saddle of the horse, he let his mind go free.

For a long moment there was nothing but a random sequence of thoughts flowing across the surface of his consciousness. Then his imagination steadied down, and a concept began to form. He felt as though he was no longer sitting on the seat of the electric horse, but standing on the soft, spongy surface of the jungle floor, his camouflaged suit glued to his body by sweat as he squinted up at the sun, which was already past its zenith, moving into afternoon. An irritation of combined frustration and apprehension filled his mind. He looked back down at the circle of guerrilla under-officers gathered about him and realized that he had to make an immediate decision. Two-thirds of his force had already failed to get across the Blue River at the time and places they were supposed to cross. Now, already behind schedule, he was faced with the last opportunity for a crossing—but also with the opposition of enemy forces, in what strength he did not know.

Clearly, at least one thing was true. The infiltration of this group he commanded had turned out to be not the secret from the Exotics that it had been expected it would be. To that extent, his mission was already a failure. If the Exotics had a force here to oppose him, what kind of opposition could he expect on the way to the coast?

Clearly, the mission now stood little or no chance of success. Sensibly, it should be abandoned. But could he turn back through the pass now without some excuse to give his superiors so that he would not be accused of abandoning the mission for insufficient reason?

Clearly, he could not. He would have to make an attempt to fight his way across the river, and just hope that the Exotic forces would oppose him hard enough so that he would have an excuse to retreat. . . .

Cletus returned to himself, opened his eyes and straightened up in the saddle once more. Lifting the electric horse up just under treetop level once more, he tossed three singleton mines at different angles toward the guerrilla position, and then set them off in quick succession.

Immediately, also, he opened up with both his rifle and sidearm, holding the rifle tucked against his side and firing it with his right hand while firing his sidearm with the left.

From the crossing, and from the two other sides of the guerrilla position, came the sound of the gunfire of his soldiers upon the Neulanders.

Within seconds the guerrilla force was laying down answering fire. The racket was the worst to disturb the jungle so far this day. Cletus waited until it began to die down slightly, so that he could be heard. Then he took the loudspeaker horn from the crossbar of the electric horse. He lifted the horn to his lips and turned it on. His amplified voice thundered through the jungle:

"CEASE FIRING! CEASE FIRING! ALL ALLIANCE FORCES CEASE FIRING!"

The cone rifles of the men under Cletus' command fell silent about the guerrilla area. Gradually, the answering voice of the guerrilla weapons also dwindled and silence filled the jungle again. Cletus spoke once more through the loudspeaker horn:

"ATTENTION NEULANDERS! ATTENTION NEULANDERS! YOU ARE

COMPLETELY SURROUNDED BY THE ALLIANCE EXPEDITIONARY FORCE
TO BAKHALLA. FURTHER RESISTANCE CAN ONLY END IN YOUR BEING
WIPED OUT. THOSE WHO WISH TO SURRENDER WILL BE GIVEN HONOR-
ABLE TREATMENT IN ACCORDANCE WITH THE ESTABLISHED RULES GOV-
ERNING THE CARE OF PRISONERS OF WAR. THIS IS THE COMMANDER OF
THE ALLIANCE FORCE SPEAKING. MY MEN WILL HOLD THEIR FIRE FOR
THREE MINUTES, DURING WHICH YOU WILL BE GIVEN A CHANCE TO
SURRENDER. THOSE WISHING TO SURRENDER MUST DIVEST THEMSELVES
OF ALL WEAPONS AND WALK INTO THE CLEARING AT THE CROSSING IN
PLAIN SIGHT WITH THEIR HANDS CLASPED ON TOP OF THEIR HEAD. I
REPEAT, THOSE WISHING TO SURRENDER MUST DIVEST THEMSELVES OF
ALL WEAPONS AND WALK INTO PLAIN SIGHT IN THE CLEARING AT THE
CROSSING WITH THEIR HANDS CLASPED ON TOP OF THEIR HEAD. YOU
HAVE THREE MINUTES TO SURRENDER IN THIS FASHION STARTING FROM
WHEN I SAY NOW."

Cletus paused for a moment, then added:

"ANY MEMBERS OF THE INVADING FORCE WHO HAVE NOT SURREN-
DERED BY THE TIME THREE MINUTES IS UP WILL BE CONSIDERED AS
INTENDING TO CONTINUE RESISTANCE, AND MEMBERS OF THE ALLIANCE
FORCE ARE INSTRUCTED TO OPEN FIRE UPON SUCH INDIVIDUALS ON
SIGHT. THE THREE MINUTES IN WHICH TO SURRENDER WILL NOW BEGIN.
NOW!"

He clicked off the loudspeaker horn, replaced it on the horse and
quickly swung toward the river, out and around to where he had a view
of the clearing without being visible himself. For a long moment nothing happened. Then there was a rustle of leaves, and a man in a Neulander camouflage suit, his hands clasped over his head and some
jungle grass still stuck in his bushy beard, stepped into the clearing.
Even from where Cletus watched, the whites of the guerrilla's eyes
were visible and he looked about him apprehensively. He came forward
hesitantly until he was roughly in the center of the clearing, then
stopped, looking about him, his hands still clasped on top of his head.

A moment later another guerrilla appeared in the clearing; and
suddenly they were coming from every direction.

Cletus sat watching and counting for a couple of minutes. By the
end of the time, forty-three men had entered the clearing to surrender.
Cletus nodded, thoughtfully. Forty-three men out of a total of three
groups of thirty guerrillas—or ninety—all told. It was as he had expected.

He glanced down along the riverbank to the place, less than ten
meters from him, where Jarnki crouched with the two other men who

had been left here to defend this crossing and were now covering the growing mass of prisoners.

"Ed," Cletus transmit-pulsed at the young corporal. "Ed, look to your right."

Jarnki looked sharply to his right, and jerked a little in startlement at seeing Cletus so close. Cletus beckoned to him. Cautiously, still crouching low to keep under the ridge of the riverbank, Jarnki ran up to where Cletus hovered on the electric horse a few feet off the ground.

As Jarnki came up, Cletus set the vehicle down on the ground and, safely screened from the clearing by the jungle bushes before him, stepped stiffly off the horse and stretched himself gratefully.

"Sir?" said Jarnki, inquiringly.

"I want you to hear this," said Cletus. He turned to the horse again and set its communications unit for the channel number of Lieutenant Athyer, over on the Blue River.

"Lieutenant," he pulse-messaged, "this is Colonel Grahame."

There was a short pause, and then the reply came, crackling not only in the earphones plug in Cletus' ear but over the small speaker built into the electric horse, which Cletus had just turned on.

"Colonel?" said Athyer. "What is it?"

"It seems the Neulander guerrillas attempted to infiltrate across the Blue River crossings here, after all," Cletus said. "We were lucky and managed to capture about half of them—"

"Guerrillas? Captured? Half . . ." Athyer's voice faltered in the earphones and over the speaker.

"But that isn't why I messaged," Cletus went on. "The other half got away from us. They'll be headed back toward the pass, to escape back into Neuland. But you're closer to the pass than they are. If you get there with even half your men, you ought to be able to round up the rest of them without any trouble."

"Trouble? Look . . . I . . . how do I know the situation's the way you say it is? I . . ."

"Lieutenant," said Cletus, and for the first time he put a slight emphasis on the word, "I just told you. We've captured half their force, here at the upper crossing on the Blue."

"Well . . . yes . . . Colonel. I understand that. But—"

Cletus cut him short. "Then get going, Lieutenant," he said. "If you don't move fast, you may miss them."

"Yes, sir. Of course. I'll message you again, shortly, Colonel. . . . Maybe you'd better hold your prisoners there, until they can be picked up by support ship. . . . Uh, some of them might get away if you try to move them through the jungle with only your six men." Athyer's voice was strengthening as he got control of himself. But there was a bitter note in it. Clearly, the implications of the capture of a large group of enemy infiltrators by a desk-bound theoretician, when Athyer himself was the sole field officer in command of the capturing force, was beginning to register on him. There was little hope that General Traynor would overlook this kind of a failure on his part.

His voice was grim as he went on.

"Do you need a medic?" he asked. "I can spare you one of the two I've got here and send him right over by one of the support ships, now that secrecy's out and the Neulanders know we're here."

"Thanks, Lieutenant. Yes, we could use a medic," said Cletus. "Good luck with the rest of them."

"Thanks," said Athyer, coldly. "Out, sir."

"Out," replied Cletus.

He cut transmission, stepped away from the electric horse and lowered himself stiffly to the ground into a sitting position, with his back to a nearby boulder.

"Sir?" said Jarnki. "What do we need a medic for? None of the men got hurt. You don't mean you, sir . . . ?"

"Me," said Cletus.

He extended his left leg, reached down and took his combat knife from its boot sheath. With its blade he ripped open his left pants leg, from above the knee to the top of his boot. The knee he revealed was extremely swollen and not pretty to look at. He reached for the first-aid kit at his belt and took out a spray hypo. He put the blunt nose of the spray against his wrist and pulled the trigger. The cool shock of the spray being driven through his skin directly into his bloodstream was like the touch of a finger of peace.

"Christ, sir," said Jarnki, white-faced, staring at the knee.

Cletus leaned back gratefully against the boulder, and let the soft waves of the narcotic begin to fold him into unconsciousness.

"I agree with you," he said. Then darkness claimed him.

Chapter 9

Lying on his back in the hospital bed, Cletus gazed thoughtfully at the stiff, sunlit form of his left leg, upheld in traction above the surface of the bed.

"So," the duty medical officer, a brisk, round-faced, fortyish major had said with a fiendish chuckle when Cletus had been brought in, "you're the type who hates to take time out to give your body a chance to heal, are you, Colonel?" The next thing Cletus had known he was in the bed with his leg balanced immovably in a float cast anchored to the ceiling.

"But it's been three days now," Cletus remarked to Arvid, who had just arrived, bringing, as per orders, a local almanac, "and he promised that the third day he'd turn me loose. Take another look out in the corridor and see if he's been in any of the other rooms along here."

Arvid obeyed. He returned in a minute or two, shaking his head.

"No luck," he said. "But General Traynor's on his way over, sir. The nurse on the desk said his office just phoned to see if you were still here."

"Oh?" said Cletus. "That is right. He'd be coming, of course." He reached out and pressed the button that tilted the bed to lift him up into a sitting position. "Tell you what, Arv. Take a look up and down the other rooms for me and see if you can scrounge me some spacepost covers."

"Spacepost covers?" replied Arvid, calmly unquestioningly. "Right, I'll be back in a minute."

He went out. It took him more like three minutes than one; but when he returned he had five of the flimsy yellow envelopes in which mail sent by spaceship was ordinarily carried. The Earth Terminal post-mark was square and black on the back of each. Cletus stacked them loosely together and laid them in a face-down pile on the table surface of his bedside console. Arvid watched him.

"Did you find what you wanted in the almanac, sir?" he asked.

"Yes," said Cletus. Seeing Arvid still gazing at him curiously, he added, "There's a new moon tonight."

"Oh," said Arvid.

"Yes. Now, when the general comes, Arv," Cletus said, "stay out in the corridor and keep your eyes open. I don't want that doctor slipping past me just because a general's talking to me, and leaving me hung up here for another day. What time was that appointment of mine with the officer from the Security Echelon?"

"Eleven hundred hours," said Arvid.

"And it's nine-thirty, already," said Cletus, looking at his watch. "Arv, if you'll step into the bathroom there, its window should give you a view of the drive in front of the hospital. If the general's coming by ground car, you ought to be able to see him pulling up about now. Take a look for me, will you?"

Arvid obediently disappeared into the small bath cubicle attached to Cletus' hospital room.

"No sign, sir," his voice came back.

"Keep watching," Cletus said.

Cletus relaxed against the upright slope of the bed behind him, half-closing his eyes. He had been expecting the general—in fact, Bat would be merely the last in a long line of visitors that had included Mondar, Eachan Khan, Melissa, Wefer Linet—and even Ed Jarnki. The gangling young noncommissioned officer had come in to show Cletus the new sergeant's stripes on his sleeve and give Cletus the credit for the fact they were there.

"Lieutenant Athyer's report tried to take all the credit for himself," Jarnki said. "We heard about it from the company clerk. But the rest of the squad and me—we spread the real story around. Maybe over at the Officers' Club they don't know how it was, but they do back in the barracks."

"Thank you," said Cletus.

"Hell . . ." said Jarnki, and paused, apparently at somewhat of a loss to further express his feelings. He changed the subject. "You wouldn't be able to use me yourself, would you, Colonel? I haven't been to clerks' school, but I mean—you couldn't use a driver or anything?"

Cletus smiled. "I'd like to have you, Ed," he said, "but I don't think they'd give you up. After all, you're a line soldier."

"I guess not, then," said Jarnki, disappointed. He went off, but not before he extracted from Cletus a promise to take him on if he should ever become available.

Jarnki had been wrong, however, in believing that Athyer's report would be accepted at face value among the commissioned ranks. Clearly, the lieutenant was known to his fellow officers for the kind of field commander he was—just as it had been fairly obvious that Bat had not by chance chosen an officer like him to test Cletus' prophecy of guerrilla infiltration. As Arvid had reported to him, after that night at Mondar's party, the word was that Bat Traynor was out to get Cletus. In itself this information had originally meant merely that Cletus would be a good person for his fellow officers to avoid. But now, since he had pulled his chestnut out of the fire up on the Blue River without burning his fingers, there was plainly a good deal of covert sympathy for him among all but Bat's closest supporters. Eachan Khan had dryly hinted as much. Wefer Linet, from his safe perch inside the Navy chain of command, had blandly alluded to it. Bat could hardly be unaware of this reaction among the officers and men he commanded. Moreover, he was a conscientious commanding officer in the formal sense. If anything, it was surprising that he had not come to pay a visit to Cletus at the hospital before this.

Cletus relaxed, pushing back the tension in his body that threatened to possess it in impatience at being anchored here on the bed when so many things were yet to be done. What would be, would be. . . .

The sound of the door opening brought his eyes open as well. He raised his head and looked to his right and saw Bat Traynor entering the hospital room. There had been no warning from Arvid, still in the bathroom. Fleetingly, Cletus permitted himself the hope that the young lieutenant would have the sense to stay out of sight now that his chance discreetly to leave the hospital room was barred.

Bat strode up to the edge of the bed and stared down at Cletus, his expressive eyebrows drawing together in a faint scowl.

"Well, Colonel," he said, as he pulled a nearby chair close to the bed and sat down so that he stared into Cletus' face. He smiled, in hard, genial fashion. "Still got you tied up, I see."

"I'm supposed to be turned loose today," Cletus answered. "Thank you for dropping by, sir."

"I usually drop by to see one of my officers who's in the hospital," said Bat. "Nothing special in your case—though you did do a good job with those six men up on the Blue River, Colonel."

"The guerrillas weren't very eager to make a fight of it, sir," said Cletus. "And then I was lucky enough to have them do just what I'd guessed they'd do. The General knows how unusual it is when everything works out in the field just the way it's planned."

"I do. Believe me, I do," answered Bat. Under the heavy brows, his eyes were hard but wary upon Cletus. "But that doesn't alter the fact you were right in your guess about where they'd come through and what they'd do once they were through."

"Yes, I'm happy about that," said Cletus. He smiled. "As I told the General, I pretty much bet my reputation on it to my friends back on Earth just before I left."

He glanced, as if unthinkingly, at the loose pile of facedown spaceship covers. Bat's eyes, following the direction of Cletus' gaze, narrowed slightly at sight of the yellow envelopes.

"You've been getting congratulations, have you?" Bat asked.

"There've been a few pats on the back," Cletus said. He did not add that these had been only from such local people as Eachan, Mondar and newly made Sergeant Ed Jarnki. "Of course, the operation wasn't a total success. I heard the rest of the guerrillas managed to get back through the pass before Lieutenant Athyer could contain them."

Bat's eyebrows jerked together into a solid angry line of black. "Don't push me, Colonel," he rumbled. "Athyer's report said he got word from you too late to take his men up into position to bar the pass."

"Was that it, sir?" said Cletus. "I'd guess it was my fault, then. After all, Athyer's an experienced field officer and I'm just a desk-jockey theoretician. I'm sure everybody realizes it was just luck that the contact my squad had with the enemy was successful and the contact the lieutenant and the rest of his company had wasn't."

For a moment their eyes locked.

"Of course," said Bat, grimly. "And if they don't understand it, I do. And that's what's important—isn't it, Colonel?"

"Yes, sir," said Cletus.

Bat sat back in his chair, and his brows relaxed. "Anyway," he said, "I didn't come here just to congratulate you. A suggestion by you came through to my office that you set up a staff to make regular weekly forecasts of enemy activity. There was also your request for personnel and office space to facilitate your making such forecasts. . . . Understand, Colonel, as far as I'm concerned, I still need you like I need a fifty-man string ensemble. But your success with the guerrillas has got us some good publicity back at Alliance HQ, and I don't see how you can do any harm to the rest of the war effort here on Kultis by setting up this forecast staff. So, I'm going to approve it." He paused, then shot the words at Cletus. "That make you happy?"

"Yes, sir," said Cletus. "Thank you, General."

"Don't bother," said Bat, grimly. "As for Athyer—he had his chance, and he fell on his face. He'll be coming up for a Board of Inquiry into his fitness as an Alliance officer. Now—anything else you want?"

"No," said Cletus.

Bat stood up abruptly. "Good," he said. "I don't like having my arm twisted. I prefer handing out favors before they're asked. Also, I still need those tanks, and you're still going back to Earth at the first opportunity, Colonel. Tuck that fact into your prognostications and don't forget it!"

He turned on his heel and went toward the door.

"General," said Cletus. "There is a favor you could do me . . ."

Bat checked and swung about. His face darkened. "After all?" His voice was hard. "What is it, Colonel?"

"The Exotics have quite a library here in Bakhalla," said Cletus. "With a good deal of military text and information in it."

"What about it?"

"If the General will pardon me," said Cletus, slowly, "Lieutenant Athyer's main problems are too much imagination coupled with not enough confidence in himself. If he could get away and season himself for a while—say, as Information Officer for the Expeditionary Forces, to that Exotic library—he might turn out highly useful, after all."

Bat stared at Cletus. "Now why," said Bat softly, "would you want something like that for Athyer instead of a Board of Inquiry?"

"I don't like to see a valuable man wasted," said Cletus.

Bat grunted. He turned on his heel and went out without a further word. Looking a little sheepish, Arvid emerged from the bathroom.

"I'm sorry, sir," he said to Cletus. "The General must've come by air and landed on the roof."

"Think nothing of it, Arv," said Cletus, happily. "Just get out in that corridor and find me that doctor. I've got to get out of here."

Twenty minutes later, Arvid having finally located and produced the medical officer, Cletus was finally out of his cast and on his way to the office space Arvid had located for him. It was one of a set of three office suites, each consisting of three rooms and a bath, that had originally been erected by the Exotics for housing VIP guests. The other two suites were empty, so that, in essence, they had the building to themselves—a point Cletus had stipulated earlier when he had sent Arvid out to search. When they reached the office, Cletus found it furnished only with some camp chairs and a temporary field desk. A lean major in his early forties, with a white scar across his chin, was examining these in disparaging fashion.

"Major Wilson?" asked Cletus, as the officer turned to face them. "I'm Colonel Grahame."

They shook hands.

"Security sent me over," Wilson said. "You said you were expecting some special problem here, Colonel?"

"I'm hoping for one," replied Cletus. "We're going to be handling a good deal of material here, from the classified category on up. I'm going to be making weekly forecasts of enemy activity for General Traynor. Sooner or later the Neulanders are bound to hear of this and take an interest in this office. I'd like to set it up as a trap for anyone they send to investigate."

"Trap, sir?" echoed Wilson, puzzled.

"That's right," said Cletus, cheerfully. "I want to make it possible for them to get in, but, once in, impossible for them to get back out."

He turned to indicate the walls around them.

"For example," he said, pointing, "heavy steel mesh on the inside of the windows, but anchored so that it can't be pried loose or cut through with ordinary tools. An obvious lock on the outer door that can be easily picked—but a hidden lock that fastens the door securely once the open lock has been picked and the door opened and shut once. Metal framing and center panel for the door frame and door itself, so that they can't break out once the hidden lock has closed the door. . . . Possibly a wiring system to electrify the doors, windows and ventilator system just to discourage any attempt to break loose."

Wilson nodded slowly, but doubtfully. "That's going to add up to a good bit in the way of work-time and materials," he said. "I suppose you have authorization for this, Colonel . . . ?"

"It'll be forthcoming," said Cletus. "But the thing is for your division to get to work on this right away. The general was just talking to me less than an hour ago in the hospital about getting this office set up."

"The general—oh!" said Wilson, becoming brisk. "Of course, sir."

"Good, then," said Cletus. "That's settled."

After discussion of a few details, and after Wilson had taken a few measurements, the security officer left. Cletus set Arvid to getting Eachan Khan on the field telephone, which, with the table and chairs, was the office's only equipment. The Dorsai colonel was finally located out in the training area set aside for his mercenary troops.

"Mind if I come out?" asked Cletus.

"Not at all." In the small vision screen of the field phone, Eachan's face looked faintly curious. "You're welcome anytime, Colonel. Come along."

"Right," said Cletus. "I'll be there in half an hour."

He broke the connection. Leaving Arvid to see about getting the office supplied with furniture and staff, Cletus went out and took the staff car in which Arvid had driven him here to the training area of the Dorsai troops.

He found Eachan Khan standing at the edge of a field with a ten-meter metal tower in its center, from which what looked like a company of the tanned Dorsai professionals were practicing jump-belt landings. The line of those waiting their turn stretched out behind the tower, from the top of which mercenaries were going off, one by one, the shoulder jets of the jump belts roaring briefly and kicking up a cloud of whitish-brown dust as each one fell earthward. For men not trained exclusively as jump troops, Cletus noted with satisfaction as he limped up to the watching Eachan Khan, there were a great many more soft, upright landings than might have been expected.

"There you are," said Eachan, without turning his head, as Cletus came up behind him. The Dorsai colonel was standing with his legs slightly spread, his hands clasped behind him as he watched. "What do you think of our level of jump training, now you see it?"

"I'm impressed," answered Cletus. "What do you know about guerrilla traffic on the Bakhalla River?"

"Fair amount. Bound to be, of course, with the river running right through the city into the harbor here." Eachan Khan stared at him curiously. "Not so much infiltrators as sabotage materials, I understand, though. Why?"

"There's a new moon tonight," explained Cletus.

"Eh?" Eachan stared at him.

"And according to the local tide tables," said Cletus, "we're having an unusually high tide—all the tributaries and canals will be running deeper than usual as much as twenty miles inland. A good time for the Neulanders to smuggle in either large amounts of supplies or unusually heavy equipment."

"Hm . . ." Eachan fondled the right tip of his mustache. "Still . . . if you don't mind a word of advice?"

"Go right ahead," said Cletus.

"I don't think there'd be anything you could do about it," said Eachan. "River security is maintained by a half-dozen Army amphibs with half a dozen soldiers and light weapons on each one. That's not enough to do any good at all, and everybody knows it. But your General Traynor opts for dryfoot war equipment. About six months back he got five armored personnel carriers by swearing to your Alliance HQ that his river defenses were perfectly adequate and that, instead of sending him a couple of patrol boats, they could give him the personnel carriers instead. So if you go pointing out probable trouble on the river, you're not going to be making Traynor very happy. My advice would be to let any Neulander activity there go by on your blind side."

"Maybe you're right," said Cletus. "How about lunch?"

They left the training ground and drove in to the Officers' Club for lunch, where Melissa joined them in response to a telephone call from her father at Cletus' suggestion. She was somewhat reserved, and did not often meet Cletus' eye. She had come with her father for one brief visit to Cletus in the hospital, during which she stood back and let Eachan do most of the talking. She seemed inclined to let him do most of the talking now, although she glanced at Cletus from time to time when his attention was on her father. Cletus, however, ignored her reactions and kept up a steady, cheerful flow of conversation.

"Wefer Linet's been after me," Cletus said to her when they were having coffee and dessert, "to take one of his underwater tours in one of the Mark V submarine dozers. How about joining us this evening, and we can come back into Bakhalla afterward for a late supper?"

Melissa hesitated, but Eachan broke in, almost hastily. "Good idea, girl," he said, almost gruffly. "Why don't you do that? Do you good to get out for a change."

The tone of Eachan's voice made his words sound like a command. But the naked voice of appeal could be heard beneath the brusqueness of the words. Melissa surrendered.

"Thank you," she said, raising her eyes to meet those of Cletus, "that sounds like fun."

Chapter 10

Stars were beginning to fill the Bakhallan sky as Cletus and Melissa
reached the gates to the Navy Yard and were met by an ensign attached
to Wefer Linet's staff. The ensign conducted them inside to the ramp
where the massive, black, two-story-tall shape of a Mark V squatted
on its treads just above the golden-tinged waters of the Bakhallan harbor. Cletus had phoned Wefer immediately on parting from Eachan
and Melissa to set up the evening's excursion.

Wefer had been enthusiastic. Navy regulations, he gleefully informed Cletus, absolutely forbade his allowing a civilian such as Melissa aboard a duty Navy vehicle like the Mark V. But, personally, he
did not give a damn. For the record, he had caught only the words
"Dorsai" and "Khan" when Cletus had phoned him earlier—and to
whom, of course, could those words apply but to a mercenary colonel
of his acquaintance, who was certainly no civilian? So he would be
waiting for Colonel Grahame and Colonel Khan aboard the Mark V at
7 P.M.

Awaiting them he was. Moreover, he seemed to have shared the
joke of his little deception of Navy regulations with his under-officers
and crew. The ensign meeting Cletus and Melissa at the Navy Yard
gate had gravely addressed Melissa as "Colonel"; and they were hardly
aboard the Mark V before three of the seamen, grinning broadly, had
found occasion to do the same.

This small and ridiculous joke, however, turned out to be just the
straw needed to break the back of Melissa's stiffness and reserve. On
the fourth occasion of being addressed as "Colonel," she laughed out
loud—and began from then on to take an honest interest in the outing.

"Any place in particular you'd like to see?" asked Wefer, as the

Mark V put itself into motion and rumbled slowly down its ramp into the bay.

"Up the river," said Cletus.

"Make it so, Ensign."

"Aye, sir," said the ensign who had met them at the gate. "Balance all tanks fore and aft, there!"

He was standing at the con, a little to the left of Wefer, Cletus and Melissa, who were placed before the large, curved shape of the hemispherical screen, which looked through the muddy water ahead and about them as though it were clear as glass, to pick up the shapes of ships' undersides and other solid objects below water level in the harbor.

There was a faint hissing and rumbling noise all around them. The vibration and sound of the heavy treads on the ramp suddenly ceased, and the water line shown on the hemispherical screen moved up above the horizon mark as the huge vehicle balanced out its ballast, replacing water with compressed air where necessary, and vice versa, so that the submarine dozer—its hundreds of tons of land weight now brought into near balance with an equal volume of water—floated as lightly as a leaf in air down to the muddy bottom of the harbor, sixty feet below.

"All forward, right thirty degrees horizontal," ordered the ensign; and they began their underwater tour upriver from Bakhalla.

"You'll notice," said Wefer in the fond tone of a father pointing out the talents of his first newborn, "our treads aren't touching the bottom here. There's nearly ten feet of loose silt and muck underneath us before we hit anything solid enough for the Mark V to walk on. Of course, we could settle down into it and do just that, if we wanted to. But why bother? We're as much at home and a lot more mobile to staying up in the water itself and simply swimming with the treads. . . . Now look there . . ."

He pointed to the screen, where, some two hundred yards ahead of them, the bottom dipped abruptly below their level of sight for a space of perhaps fifty yards before it rose again.

"That's the main channel—the main current line to the sea," Wefer said. "We clean that out daily—not because there're any ships here with draft enough to need a hundred and ten feet of water under them, but because that trench provides a channel for the current that helps keep the harbor from silting up. Half of our work's understanding and using existing patterns of water movement. By keeping that channel deep, we cut our normal silt-removal work in half. Not that we need to. It's just the Navy way to do it as efficiently as possible."

"You mean you've got enough Mark V's and crews to keep the harbor clear even if the channel wasn't there?" Cletus asked.

Wefer snorted good-humoredly. "Got enough..." he echoed. "You don't know what these Mark V's can do. Why I could keep the harbor clean, even without the current channel, with this one machine alone!... Let me show you around here."

He took Cletus and Melissa on a tour of the Mark V's interior, from the diver's escape chamber down between the massive treads to the arms turret at the top of the vehicle, which could be uncovered to allow the Mark V to fire either its two heavy energy rifles or the underwater laser with which it was provided.

"You see why Traynor wanted these Mark V's for use in the jungles," concluded Wefer, as they ended their tour back in the control room before the hemispherical screen. "It hasn't got the fire power of the Army's jungle-breaker tanks, but in every other respect, except land speed, it's so far superior that there's no comparison—"

"Sir," interrupted the ensign behind him, "deep-draft surface vessel coming down the channel. We're going to have to get down and walk."

"Right. Make it so, Ensign," answered Wefer. He turned to the screen and pointed at the V-shaped object cutting the line of the river surface some two hundred yards ahead of them. "See that, Cletus?... Melissa? It's a boat drawing nine or ten feet of water. The channel here's less than fifty feet deep and we're going to have to get right down on the bottom to make sure that boat goes over with a good couple of fathoms of clearance."

He squinted at the V shape growing on the screen. Suddenly, he laughed. "Thought so!" he said. "That's one of your river patrol boats, Cletus. Want to have a look at its topside?"

"You mean, with a sensor float?" asked Cletus, quietly.

Wefer's jaw dropped. "How'd you know about that?" he demanded, staring.

"There was an article about it in the *Navy-Marine Journal* a little less than two years ago," answered Cletus. "It struck me as the sort of device a sensible navy would put aboard a vehicle like this."

Wefer still stared at him, almost accusingly. "Is that so?" he said. "What else about the Mark V do you know that I don't know you know?"

"I know that with a bit of luck you might be able to capture a boatload of Neulander saboteurs and supplies bound for Bakhalla tonight, if you want to try for it. Have you got a map of the river?"

"A map?" Wefer lit up. He leaned forward and punched buttons below the hemispherical screen. The image on it vanished, to be replaced by a map showing the main river channel with its tributaries from the harbor mouth at Bakhalla to some thirty miles upstream. A barely moving red dot in the shape of a Mark V seen from above was crawling up the main channel in representation of the vehicle enclosing them. "What guerrillas? Where?"

"About six kilometers upstream from here," Cletus answered. He reached out to point with his forefinger to a spot ahead of the small, red, moving shape of the Mark V, where a tributary almost as large as the main river joined it at that spot. Up beyond the point of joining, the tributary spread itself out into a number of small streams and then marshland.

"There's an unusually high tide tonight, as you know," Cletus said. "So from this point on down there will be at least an extra eight feet of water in the main channel. Enough extra depth so that any small upriver motor launch could make it down into Bakhalla harbor towing a good load of supplies, and even personnel, behind it, safely under-water in a drogue pod. It's just a guess on my part, of course, but it hardly seems to me that the guerrillas would let a chance like this slip by without making an effort to get men and supplies to their people in the city."

Wefer stared at the map and slapped his leg in delight. "You're right!" he exploded. "Ensign, we're headed for that confluence Colonel Grahame just pointed out. Button up for noise, and get the weapons turret uncovered topside."

"Aye, sir," answered the ensign.

They reached the juncture point between the tributary point and the mainstream, which Cletus had pointed out. The Mark V crept out of the channel into the relatively shallow water near the riverbank opposite the mouth of the tributary and stopped there, its turrets less than five feet below the river surface. The sensor float was released from the upper hull of the vehicle and popped to the surface—a small, buoyant square of material with the thin metal whisker of a sensor rod rising one meter from it into the air, the two connected by a fine wire to the communications equipment of the Mark V. The sensor rod had to view the scene around it by available light only; but its resolving power was remarkable. The image of the scene it sent down to the hemispherical screen in the command room of the Mark V below was very nearly as clear as if broad daylight, rather than a fingernail paring of a moon, was illuminating the conjunction of the two streams.

"Not a hull in sight," muttered Wefer, rotating the view in the hemispherical screen to take in the full 180 degrees scanned by the sensor rod. "I suppose we'll just have to sit here and wait for them."

"You could be taking a few precautions, meanwhile," suggested Cletus.

Wefer glanced aside at him. "What precautions?"

"Against their getting away downstream if by some chance they manage to slip by you," said Cletus. "Is there anything to stop you now from moving enough material into the channel downriver so that, if they do come by, they'll run aground just below us?"

Wefer stared at him in astonishment, which slowly changed to delight. "Of course!" he exploded. "Ensign! Take her downstream!"

The Mark V moved roughly a hundred yards downstream; and, extending its massive dozer blade crosswise in front of it, began to shovel sand and silt from beneath the water near the river's edges into the main channel. Fifteen minutes work filled the channel for some fifty yards to a level even with the rest of the river bottom. Wefer was inclined to stop at that point, but Cletus suggested he further refine it into a barrier consisting of a wide, sloping ramp rising gradually to within half a dozen feet of the surface. Then, also at Cletus' suggestion, the Mark V returned, not merely upstream, but up into the tributary some fifty yards behind the point where it met with the waters of the main river.

Here the water was so shallow that the Mark V sat with its turret out in the air. But a few moments work with the dozer blade sufficed to dig a shallow depression so that they could lie in wait completely underwater.

Then the wait began. It was three hours—nearly midnight—before the sensor rod on its float, invisible against the shadow of the foliage lining the tributary's bank, picked up the image of a motor launch sliding down the main channel of the tributary, its motor turning at a speed barely sufficient to keep the drogue pod, towed behind it, underwater.

They waited, holding their breaths, until ship and drogue had passed. Then Wefer jumped for the command phone, from which he had, some hours since, displaced the ensign.

"Wait," said Cletus.

Wefer hesitated, staring at Cletus. "Wait?" he said. "What for?"

"You know that launch isn't going to be able to get past the barrier you built downstream," answered Cletus. "So why not sit here a little longer and see if another boat comes along?"

Wefer hesitated. Then he stepped back from the command phone. "You really think another one might come along?" he asked, thoughtfully.

"I wouldn't be surprised," said Cletus, cheerfully.

The answer was hardly out of his mouth before the sensor picked up another approaching motor launch with pod in tow. By the time this was well passed and out into the main river, still another launch had appeared. As Wefer stood staring with incredulous delight into the hemispherical screen, twenty boats towing pods passed within thirty yards of the submerged Mark V.

When a couple of minutes had gone by following the passage of the twenty boats and pods, Cletus suggested that probably it was time they were checking up on what had happened downstream. Wefer put the Mark V in motion. It surged up out of its shallow hole and plunged under the surface again down into the main channel of the tributary.

They reached the central channel of the main river, and turned downstream. Their infrared searchlights underwater, as well as the sensor rod being towed on its float above them, gave them a picture of wild confusion just ahead of them. Of the twenty launches that had passed them, fully half were firmly aground in the sloping ramp of river bottom that the Mark V had built. The rest, still afloat but with their drogue pods bobbing helplessly on the surface behind them, were valiantly trying to tow the stranded vessels free.

Wefer commanded the Mark V to a halt. He stared into the screen with mingled elation and dismay.

"Now what?" he muttered to Cletus. "If I charge on down there, the ones that aren't stuck are just going to turn around and beat it upriver and get away. Of course I've got the weapons in the turret. But still, a lot of them are going to get past me."

"As a suggestion," said Cletus, "how's this Mark V of yours at making a wave?"

Wefer stared at him. "A wave?" he said—and then repeated, joyously. "A *wave*!"

He barked orders into the command phone. The Mark V backed up a hundred yards along the channel of the main river and stopped. The two wings of its dozer blade, which had been folded back against its body to reduce drag while traveling, folded forward again and extended themselves to right and left until the blades' full area of twenty yards of width and ten feet of height were exposed. Delicately, Wefer tilted the front of the Mark V upward until the top half of the blade poked through the surface of the river and the treads were swimming freely in the water. Then he threw the engines into full speed, forward.

The Mark V rushed down the river in a roar of water, checked itself and sank itself to the bottom of the channel just fifty yards short of the still-floating launches. For a moment a wall of water hid the scene ahead; and then this passed, speeding like an ever-diminishing ripple farther downstream.

Left behind was a scene of wreckage and confusion.

Those launches that had already been aground had had their decks swept by the wave that the Mark V had created. In some cases they had been flipped on their sides by the wave or even turned completely upside down. But the greatest effect was to be seen upon those launches that had still had water under their keels and had been trying to tow the grounded ones loose.

Without exception these free-floating boats had been driven aground as well. In many cases they had been literally hammered into the soft soil of the piled-up river bed. One launch was standing on its nose, its prow driven half a dozen feet into the sand and silt below.

"I think they're ready for you now," Cletus said to Wefer.

If anything more was needed to complete the demoralization of the guerrillas aboard the launches it was the sight of the black shape of the Mark V roaring up into view out of the river depths, the two heavy energy rifles in its turret sweeping ominously back and forth. Almost without exception those who had managed to cling to their battered crafts dove overboard at the sight and began to swim frantically for the banks of the river.

"Turret—" began Wefer excitedly. But Cletus put his hand over the phone.

"Let them go," Cletus said: "The important men'll still be sealed inside the pods. Let's see about collecting them before they get too worried by all that's happened and start breaking out."

The advice was good. The Neulanders inside the pods had reached the limits of their endurance with the tossing about they had taken in the wave generated by the Mark V. Already more than one of the pods bobbing helplessly on the surface of the water, still tethered to their grounded launches, was beginning to split along the top, as those within activated their emergency exits. Wefer wheeled the Mark V into the midst of the wreckage and sent his ensign with three seamen out the Mark V's top hatch with hand weapons to cover the Neulanders as they emerged. They were ordered to swim to the Mark V, where they were searched, put in wrist restraints and herded down the hatch to be locked up in the Mark V's forward hold. Cletus and Melissa stayed discreetly out of sight.

Its forward hold crammed with prisoners, and the cargo pods filled with supplies in tow, the Mark V returned to its base at the Bakhalla Navy Yard. After disposing of their prisoners and their spoils, Cletus, Melissa and Wefer at last got into the city for that late—now early morning—supper they had planned. It was after four in the morning when Cletus took a tired but happy Melissa back to her father's residence. However, as they approached their destination, Melissa sobered and fell silent; and when they pulled up in front of the door of the house that the Exotics had put at the disposal of Melissa and Eachan, she did not offer to get out of the car right away.

"You know," she said, turning to Cletus, "you're pretty remarkable, after all. First those guerrillas on our way into Bakhalla, then the ones you captured up at Etter's Pass. And now, tonight."

"Thanks," he said, "but all I did was anticipate the optimum moves for deCastries to make, and arrange to be on the scene when they were made."

"Why do you keep talking about Dow as if he was having some sort of personal duel with you?"

"He is," said Cletus.

"The Outworlds Secretary for the Coalition—against some unknown lieutenant-colonel in an Alliance Expeditionary Force? Does that make sense?"

"Why not?" Cletus said. "He has a great deal more to lose than an unknown lieutenant-colonel in an Alliance Expeditionary Force."

"But you're just imagining it all. You have to be!"

"No," said Cletus. "Remember I pushed him into an error of judgment with the sugar cubes in the dining lounge of the ship? The Outworlds Secretary for the Coalition can't afford to be made a fool of by an unknown Alliance lieutenant-colonel—as you describe me. It's true nobody but you knows—and only because I told you—that he did make a mistake, then—"

"Was that why you told me what you'd done?" Melissa interrupted quickly. "Just so I'd tell Dow?"

"Partly," said Cletus. She drew in her breath sharply in the darkness. "But only incidentally. Because it really didn't matter whether you told him or not. He knew I knew. And it simply wasn't good policy to let someone like me walk around thinking that I could beat him, at anything."

"Oh!" Melissa's voice trembled on the verge of anger. "You're making all this up. There's no proof, not a shred of proof for any of it."

"There is, though," said Cletus. "You remember the guerrillas on the way into Bakhalla attacked the command car, in which I was riding, instead of—as your father pointed out—the bus, which would have been a much more natural target for them. And this after Pater Ten had been burning up the ship-to-planet phone lines to Neuland before we left the ship."

"That's coincidence—stretched coincidence, at that," she retorted.

"No," said Cletus, quietly. "No more than the infiltration through Etter's Pass, which, while it was also made to provide a coup for the Neulanders, would have had the effect of discrediting me as a tactical expert before I had a chance to get my feet on the ground here and learn about the local military situation."

"I don't believe it," Melissa said vehemently. "It has to be all in your head!"

"If that's so, then deCastries shares the delusion," answered Cletus. "When I slipped out of the first trap, he was impressed enough to offer me a job with him—a job, however, which obviously would have put me in a subordinate position with regard to him. . . . That happened at Mondar's party, when you stepped over to talk to Eachan, and de-Castries and I had a few moments together."

She stared at him through the night shadow of the car, as if trying to search out the expression on his face in the little light that reached them from the lamp beside the doorway of the house and the dawn-pale sky above the aircar.

"You turned him down?" she said, after a long moment.

"I just have. Tonight," said Cletus, "after the guerrillas on landing and Etter's Pass, he couldn't delude himself that I wouldn't expect that the next obvious move for the Neulanders would be to take advantage of the high tide on the river to run in supplies and saboteurs to Bak-halla. If I'd let that infiltration take place without saying or doing anything, he'd have known that I'd become, to all intents and purposes, his hired man."

Again, she stared at him. "But you—" She broke off. "What can you expect to get out of all this, this . . . chain of things happening?"

"Just what I told you on the ship," said Cletus. "To trap deCastries into a personal fencing match with me, so that I can gradually lead him into larger and larger conflicts—until he commits himself completely in a final encounter where I can use his cumulative errors of judgment to destroy him."

Slowly, in the shadow, she shook her head. "You must be insane," she said.

"Or perhaps a little more sane than most," he answered. "Who knows?"

"But . . ." She hesitated, as though she was searching for an argument that would get through to him. "Anyway, no matter what's happened here, Dow's going to be leaving now. Then what about all these plans of yours about him? Now he can just go back to Earth and forget you—and he will."

"Not until I've caught him in an error of judgment too public for him to walk away from or hide," said Cletus. "And that's what I have to do next."

"One more—what if I tell him you're going to do that?" she demanded. "Just suppose the whole wild thing's true, and I go to Capital Neuland tomorrow and tell him what you're planning? Won't that ruin everything for you?"

"Not necessarily," said Cletus. "Anyway, I don't think you'll do that."

"Why not?" she challenged. "I told you on the ship, that first night, that I wanted help from Dow for Dad and myself. Why shouldn't I tell him anything that might make him more likely to help me?"

"Because you're more your father's daughter than you think," said Cletus. "Besides, your telling him would be a waste of effort. I'm not going to let you throw yourself away on deCastries for something that'd be the wrong thing for Eachan and you anyway."

She stared at him, saying nothing, for one breathless minute. Then she exploded.

"*You* aren't going to let me!" she blazed. "*You're* going to order my life and my father's, are you? Where'd you get that kind of conceit, to think you could know what's best for people and what isn't best for them—let alone thinking you could get what you think best for them, or take it away from them if they want it? Who made you . . . king of everything . . ."

She had been fumbling furiously with the latch of the door on her side of the aircar as the words tumbled out of her. Now her fingers found it, the door swung open and she jumped out, turning to slam the door behind her.

"Go back to your BOQ—or wherever you're supposed to go!" she cried at him through the open window. "I knew there was no point going out with you tonight, but Dad asked me. I should have known better. *Good night!*"

She turned and ran up the steps into the house. The door slammed behind her. Cletus was left to silence and the empty, growing light of the pale dawn sky, unreachable overhead.

Chapter 11

"Well, Colonel," said Bat, grimly, "what am I supposed to do with you?"

"The General could put me to use," said Cletus.

"Put you to use!" They were standing facing each other in Bat's private office. Bat turned in exasperation, took two quick steps away, wheeled and stepped back to glare up at Cletus once more. "First you make a grandstand play up by Etter's Pass, and it pays off so that you collect about five times as many prisoners as you had men to collect them with. Now you go out for a midnight picnic with the Navy and come back loaded with guerrillas and supplies bound for Bakhalla. Not only that, but you take a civilian along with you on this Navy spree!"

"Civilian, sir?" said Cletus.

"Oh yes, I know the official story!" Bat interrupted him, harshly. "And as long as it's a Navy matter, I'm letting it ride. But I *know* who you had with you out there, Colonel! Just as I know that wooden-headed young character, Linet, couldn't have dreamed up the idea of capturing those motor launches full of guerrillas. It was your show, Colonel, just like it was your show up at Etter's Pass! . . . And I repeat, what am I going to do with you?"

"In all seriousness, General," said Cletus, in a tone of voice that matched his words, "I mean what I say. I think you ought to put me to use."

"How?" Bat shot at him.

"As what I'm equipped to be—a tactician," said Cletus. He met the glare from under the general's expressive brows without yielding, and his voice remained calm and reasonable. "The present moment's one in which I could be particularly useful, considering the circumstances."

"What circumstances?" Bat demanded.

"Why, the circumstances that've more or less combined to trap the Military Secretary of the Coalition here on Kultis," Cletus replied. "I imagine there's little doubt, in the ordinary way of things, that Dow deCastries would be planning on leaving this planet in the next day or two."

"Oh, he would, would he?" said Bat. "And what makes you so sure that you know what a Coalition high executive like deCastries would be doing—under any circumstances?"

"The situation's easily open to deduction," answered Cletus. "The Neulander guerrillas aren't in any different situation than our Alliance forces here when it comes to the matter of getting supplies out from Earth. Both they and we could use a great many things that the supply depots back on Earth are slow to send us. You want tanks, sir. It's a safe bet the Neulander guerrillas have wants of their own, which the Coalition isn't eager to satisfy."

"And how do you make that out?" Bat snapped.

"I read it as a conclusion from the obvious fact that the Coalition's fighting a cheaper war here on Kultis than we are," said Cletus, reasonably. "It's typical of Alliance-Coalition confrontations for the past century. We tend to supply our allies actual fighting forces and the equipment to support them. The Coalition tends merely to arm and advise the opposition forces. This fits well with their ultimate aim, which isn't so much to win all these minor conflicts they oppose us in but to bleed dry the Alliance nations back on Earth, so that eventually the Coalition can take over, back there where they believe all the important real estate is."

Cletus stopped speaking. Bat stared at him. After a second, the general shook his head like a man coming out of a daze.

"I ought to have my head examined," Bat said. "Why do I stand here and listen to this?"

"Because you're a good general officer, sir," said Cletus, "and because you can't help noticing I'm making sense."

"Part of the time you're making sense . . ." muttered Bat, his eyes abstracted. Then his gaze sharpened and he fastened it once more on Cletus' face. "All right, the Neulanders want equipment from the Coalition that the Coalition doesn't want to give them. You say that's why deCastries came out here?"

"Of course," said Cletus. "You know yourself the Coalition does this often. They refuse material help to one of their puppet allies, but then, to take the sting out of the refusal, they send a highly placed dignitary out to visit the puppets. The visit creates a great deal of stir, both in the puppet country and elsewhere. It gives the puppets the impression that their welfare is very close to the Coalition's heart—and it costs nearly nothing. Only, in this one instance, the situation's backfired somewhat."

"Backfired?" said Bat.

"The two new guerrilla thrusts that were supposed to celebrate deCastries' visit—that business up at Etter's Pass, and now last night's unsuccessful attempt to infiltrate a good number of men and supplies into the city of Bakhalla—have blown up in the Neulanders' faces," Cletus said. "Of course, officially, Dow's got nothing to do with either of those two missions. Naturally we know that he undoubtedly did know about them, and maybe even had a hand in planning them. But as I say, officially, there's no connection between him and them, and theoretically he could leave the planet as scheduled without looking backward once. Only I don't think he's likely to do that now."

"Why not?"

"Because, General," said Cletus, "his purpose in coming here was to give the Neulanders a morale boost—a shot in the arm. Instead, his visits have coincided with a couple of bad, if small, defeats for them. If he leaves now, his trip is going to be wasted. A man like deCastries is bound to put off leaving until he can leave on a note of success. That gives us a situation we can turn to our own advantage."

"Oh? Turn to our advantage, is it?" said Bat. "More of your fun and games, Colonel?"

"Sir," answered Cletus, "I might remind the General that I was right about the infiltration attempt through Etter's Pass, and I was right in my guess last night that the guerrillas would try to move men and supplies down the river and into the city—"

"All right! Never mind that!" snapped Bat. "If I wasn't taking those things into consideration I wouldn't be listening to you now. Go ahead. Tell me what you were going to tell me."

"I'd prefer to show you," answered Cletus. "If you wouldn't mind flying up to Etter's Pass—"

"Etter's Pass? Again?" said Bat. "Why? Tell me what map you want, and show me here."

"It's a short trip by air, sir," said Cletus, calmly. "The explanation's going to make a lot more sense if we have the actual terrain below us."

Bat grunted. He turned about, stalked to his desk and punched open his phone circuit.

"Send over Recon One to the roof here," he said. "We'll be right up."

Five minutes later, Cletus and Bat were en route by air toward the Etter's Pass area. The general's recon craft was a small but fast passenger vehicle, with antigrav vanes below its midsection and a plasmathrust engine in the rear. Arvid, who had been waiting for Cletus in the general's outer office, was seated up front in the co-pilot's seat, with the pilot and the vessel's one crewman. Twenty feet behind them, in the open cabin space, Bat and Cletus conversed in the privacy provided by their distance and lowered voices. The recon craft approached the Etter's Pass area and, at Cletus' request, dropped down from its cruising altitude of eighty thousand feet to a mere six hundred. It began slowly to circle the area encompassing Etter's Pass, the village of Two Rivers and the two river valleys that came together just below the town.

Bat stared sourly at the pass and the town below it, nestled in the bottom of the V that was the conjunction of the two river valleys.

"All right, Colonel," he said. "I've taken an hour out of my day to make this trip. What you've got to tell me had better be worth it."

"I think it is," answered Cletus. He pointed at Etter's Pass and swung his fingertip from it down to the town below. "If you'll look closely there, sir, you'll see Two Rivers is an ideal jump-off spot for launching an attack through the pass by our forces, as the first step in an invasion of Neuland."

Bat's head jerked around. He stared at Cletus. "*Invade Neuland . . .*" He lowered his voice hastily, for the heads of all three men up front had turned abruptly at the sound of his first words. "Have you gone completely out of your skull, Grahame? Or do you think I have, that I'd even consider such a thing? Invading Neuland's a decision that's not even for the General Staff back on Earth to make. It'd be the political boys in Geneva who'd have to decide that!"

"Of course," said Cletus, unruffled. "But the fact is, an invasion launched from Two Rivers could very easily be successful. If the General will just let me explain—"

"No!" snarled Bat, keeping his voice low. "I told you I don't even want to hear about it. If you got me all the way up here just to suggest that—"

"Not to suggest it as an actuality, sir," said Cletus. "Only to point out the benefits of the appearance of it. It's not necessary actually to invade Neuland. It's only necessary to cause the Neulanders, and deCastries, to realize such an invasion could be successful, if launched. Once they realize the possibility, they'll be under extreme pressure to take some counteraction to prevent it. Then, if after they've taken such action, we move to show that invasion was never our intention, Dow deCastries will have been involved in a local blunder from which it'll be impossible for him to detach his responsibility. The Coalition's only way of saving face for him and itself will be to cast all blame on the Neulanders and penalize them as evidence that the blame-casting isn't just rhetoric. The only form that penalizing can take is a lessening of Coalition help to Neuland. . . . Naturally, any reduction in Coalition aid to the Neulanders puts the Alliance contribution to the Exotics in that much stronger position."

Cletus stopped talking. Bat sat for a long second, gazing at him with an unusual expression—something almost like awe—below the heavy, expressive eyebrows.

"By God!" Bat said, at last, "you don't think in simple terms, do you, Grahame?"

"The complexity's more apparent than real," answered Cletus. "Everyone's more or less the prisoner of his current situation. Manipulate the situation and the individual often hasn't much choice but to let himself be manipulated as well."

Bat shook his head, slowly. "All right," he said, drawing a deep breath, "just how do you plan to signal this fake invasion attempt?"

"In the orthodox manner," answered Cletus. "By maneuvering of a couple of battalions of troops in this area below the pass—"

"Hold on. Whoa—" broke in Bat. "I told you once before I didn't have spare battalions of troops lying around waiting to be played with. Besides, if I order troops up here on anything like maneuvers, how am I going to claim later that there never was any intention to provoke Neuland in this area?"

"I realize you haven't any regular troops to spare, General," said Cletus. "The answer, of course, is not to use regular troops. Nor should you order them up here. However, the Dorsai regiment under Colonel Khan is engaged in jump-belt training right now. You could agree to a suggestion which Colonel Khan might make to the Exotics—and which the Exotics will certainly check out with you—that he bring his Dorsais up here for a week of live training jumps in this ideal terrain, which combines river valleys, jungle and hill country."

Bat opened his mouth as if to retort—then closed it sharply. His brows drew together in a thoughtful frown.

"Hmm," he said. "The Dorsais . . ."

"The Dorsais," Cletus reminded him, "don't operate out of your budget. They're financed separately by the Exotics."

Bat nodded, slowly.

"A full two battalions of men in this area," went on Cletus, "are too many for deCastries and the Neulanders to ignore. The fact that they're Dorsais rather than your own troops makes it seem all the more likely you're trying to pretend innocence, when in fact you've got some thrust into Neulander territory in mind. Add one more small factor, and you'll make suspicion of such a thrust a certainty, to deCastries at least. He knows I've been concerned with the two recent incidents when the Neulanders were frustrated. Appoint me your deputy general commander of this Dorsai unit, with authority to move them wherever I want, and nobody on the other side of the mountains will have any doubt left that the jump training's only a cover for an attack on Neuland territory."

Bat jerked his head up and stared at Cletus suspiciously. Cletus returned his gaze with the calm innocence of a man whose conscience has nothing to hide.

"But you *won't* be moving those Dorsais anywhere, except between Bakhalla and this area, will you, Colonel?" he demanded softly.

"I give you my word, sir," said Cletus. "They'll go nowhere else."

For a long moment Bat continued to stare, hard, at Cletus. But then, once again, slowly he nodded.

They returned to Bat's office in Bakhalla. As Cletus was leaving, headed for his staff car in the parking lot, a flyer settled into one of the marked spaces and Mondar got out, followed by the small, waspish shape of Pater Ten.

"There he is," said Pater Ten in a brittle voice, as he spotted Cletus. "Why don't you go ahead into the Headquarters building, Outbond? I'll stop a minute with Colonel Grahame. Dow wanted me to extend his congratulations on Grahame's success last week—and last night."

Mondar hesitated briefly, then smiled. "As you like," he said, turned and went on toward the Headquarters building.

Pater Ten walked over to face Cletus.

"Congratulate me?" asked Cletus.

"The Military Secretary," said Pater Ten, almost viciously, "is a very fair-minded man—"

In mid-sentence he broke off. For a second some inner change seemed to wipe his face clean of expression, and then it shaped itself again into a different kind of expression—an expression like that of an excellent stage mimic who has decided to impersonate the character and mannerisms of Dow deCastries. Except that Pater Ten's eyes were fixed and remote, like a man under hypnosis.

When he spoke, it was in an eerie echo of Dow's ordinary speech:

"Evidently," said those silkily urbane tones, "you're still trying to raise the ante, Grahame. Take my advice. Be warned. It's an occupation that's fraught with danger."

As abruptly as it had come, the unnatural resemblance to Dow smoothed itself from the little man's features and his gaze became normal again. He looked sharply up at Cletus.

"Very fair-minded," Pater said. "You underestimate him. I promise you, you've underestimated him—" The little man broke off, abruptly. "What're you looking at me like that for?" he snapped, acidly. "You don't believe me, is that it?"

Cletus shook his head, sadly. "I believe you," he said.

"It's just that I see I did underestimate him. It seems he's not just a dealer in other people's minds. He buys souls as well."

He turned and walked off to his car, leaving Pater Ten staring after him uncomprehendingly but with the automatic rage on his face with which the violent little man viewed nearly all things in the universe.

Chapter 12

They met in Eachan Khan's office a week later—Cletus, Eachan and the four other top officers among the Dorsais. There was Eachan's second-in-command, Lieutenant-Colonel Marcus Dodds, a tall, quiet, narrow-boned man. There were also a major with a shaved head and expressionless features in a hard, round, blue-black face, with the single name of Swahili, a Major David Ap Morgan, who was thin and slightly buck-toothed and as fair-skinned as Swahili was dark; and, last, there was Captain Este Chotai, short, heavy-fleshed and handsome, with narrow eyes in a slightly mongoloid face. They sat around the long conference table in Eachan's wide office, with Eachan at the head of the table and Cletus seated at his right.

"And so, gentlemen," said Eachan Khan, winding up his explanation of Cletus' presence in their midst, "we have a new commanding officer from the Alliance Forces. I'll let Colonel Grahame speak for himself from this point on."

Eachan got up from his chair at the head of the table and stepped aside. Cletus rose, and Eachan took Cletus' former place at the table. Cletus moved over behind the chair Eachan had occupied, but he did not sit down immediately.

Instead, he turned about to look at the large map of Etter's Pass—Two Rivers area projected on the wall behind him. He looked at it and something deep, powerful and unyielding moved without warning through him. He drew in a slow deep breath and the silence of the room behind him seemed to ring suddenly in his ears. The features of the map before him seemed to leap out at him as if he saw, not the projected representation, but the actual features of jungle, hill and river that they represented.

He turned about and faced the Dorsai officers. Under his gaze they stiffened and their eyes narrowed as though something massive and unknown had stepped suddenly among them. Even Eachan stared at Cletus as though he had never seen him before.

"You're all professional soldiers," said Cletus. His voice was completely flat, without inflection or emphasis, but it rang in the room with a finality that left no room for doubt or argument in its listeners. "Your future depends on what you'll be doing in the next two weeks. Therefore I'm going to tell you what no one else on this planet yet knows, and I'm going to trust you to keep that information locked inside you."

He paused. They sat staring at him like men in a trance.

"You're going to fight a battle. My aim isn't going to be to kill the enemy in this battle, but to force him to surrender in large numbers, so if all goes according to plan you ought to win with little or no casualties. . . . I don't guarantee that. I only say that it ought to be that way. But, in any case, you'll have fought a battle."

He paused for a second, looking into their faces one by one. Then he went on.

"Behind me here," he said, "you see the upland area into which you're going to move at the end of this week for further jump-training and jungle practice. This practice isn't just to fill time. The better shape your men are in at the end of the training period, and the better they know the area, the better chance they'll have to survive in the fight, later. Colonel Khan will give you your specific orders. That's all I'll tell you now. As I say, I don't want you to tell anyone, not even the men you command, that any sort of real action's in prospect. If you're the kind of officers I think you are, and they're the kind of men I think they are, they'll absorb the feeling that something is going to happen without your having to tell them. . . . That's all."

He sat down abruptly and turned to Eachan.

"Take over, Colonel," he said to Eachan.

Eachan, unmoving, continued to gaze at him for just a fraction of a second longer before he rose, cleared his throat and began to describe the patterns of movement of the various units from Bakhalla into the Two Rivers area.

Four days later support ships of the type that had flown Cletus with Lieutenant Athyer and his troops up to Etter's Pass began ferrying the mercenary soldiers to Two Rivers. Cletus went up on one of the early flights and toured the area with Eachan Khan. Cletus' first concern was for the town or village—it was really more village than town—of Two Rivers itself.

The settlement was actually a tight little V-shaped clump of condominiums and individual homes surrounding a warehouse and business section and filling the triangular end-point of flatland where the valleys of the Blue and Whey rivers came together. This patch of flatland extended itself, with a few scattered streets and buildings, up the valley of each river for perhaps a quarter of a mile before the riverbanks became too high and steep for much building to be practical. The town was a community supported essentially by the wild-farming of a majority of its inhabitants, wild-farming being the planting, in the surrounding jungle areas, of native or mutated trees and plants bearing a cash crop without first dividing up or clearing the land. A wild-farmer owned no territory. What he owned was a number of trees or plants that he tended and from which he harvested the crops on a regular basis. Around Two Rivers a sort of native wild cherry and mutated rubber plants introduced by the Exotics four years ago were the staple wild-farm crops.

The local people took the invasion by the Dorsais in good spirits. The mercenaries were much quieter and better-mannered in their off-duty hours than were regular troops. Besides, they would be spending money in the town. The locals, in general, paid little attention to Cletus, as, with Eachan Kahn, he marked out positions for strong points with dug-in weapons on the near banks of the two rivers just above the town and down within the open land of the community itself. When Cletus had finished, he had laid out two V-shaped lines of strong points, one inside the other, covering the upriver approaches to the town and the river junction itself.

"Now," said Cletus to Eachan, when this was done, "let's go take a look up beyond the pass."

They took one of the support ships that had just discharged its cargo of Dorsai soldiers and was about to return to Bakhalla for another load. With it they flew up and over the area of Etter's Pass and made a shallow sweep over the some ten miles of mountainous territory beyond it to where the ground sloped away into the farther jungle that was Neuland territory.

"I expect the Neulanders will be coming around to see what we're doing," he said to Eachan, "as soon as their people in Bakhalla tell them the Dorsais have moved up here for training. I want this side of the mountains kept under observation by men who won't be spotted. I assume you've got people like that?"

"Of course!" said Eachan. "I'll have a watch on up here all twenty-six hours of the day. How soon do you want it to start?"

"Right away," answered Cletus.

"I'll have men started out in half an hour," Eachan answered. "Anything else?"

"Yes," Cletus said. "I want those defensive strong points, in and above the town, dug in, with an earth wall inside and sandbags outside so that it's at least six feet thick at the base and seven feet above the level of the ground outside."

Eachan frowned slightly. But his reply was laconic. "Yes, Colonel," he said.

"That's it, then," said Cletus. "I'm headed back to Bakhalla. I'll have the ship drop you back down at Two Rivers first. Are you planning on coming back to town later?"

"This evening," he answered, "as soon as I've got all the men moved in here and set up. I'm planning on commuting. Here, days—Bakhalla, nights."

"I'll see you back at the city then," said Cletus. He turned to the pilots of the support ship. "Take us back to Two Rivers."

He dropped off Eachan and went back to Bakhalla. There he found his work waiting for him—in two stacks, for, in accepting a role as Bat's deputy commanding officer of the Dorsais, he had in essence taken on another full job. The Dorsais operated with a small to non-existent Headquarters staff, as they did in all areas requiring noncombatant personnel. In the field, each Dorsai was his own cook, launderer and bottle washer, and each officer was responsible for all paper work involving his command. Away from the field, in barracks so to speak, men were hired from the regular fighting units, at a small addition to their ordinary wages, to work as clerks, cooks, vehicle drivers and the rest, but in the field there was none of this.

Those Dorsais, therefore, who ordinarily would have lightened Cletus' paper workload concerning the mercenary soldiers were now in battle gear up at Two Rivers. It was this fact that also required Eachan to commute back to Bakhalla every night to take care of his own paper work.

Cletus, of course, had the use of the staff Arvid had collected to help in making his forecasts of enemy activity. But members of the staff, including Arvid himself, were fully occupied with their regular jobs, at least during normal working hours. Cletus had set them to functioning as a research service. They were collecting information on both Neuland and the Exotic colony, plus all the physical facts about Kultis—weather, climate, flora and fauna—that pertained to the two opposed peoples. This information was condensed and fed to Cletus as soon as it was available; at least half his working day was taken up in absorbing and digesting it.

So it was that the first five days after the Dorsais had been moved up to Two Rivers, Cletus spent at his office between the hours of seven in the morning and midnight, with very few breaks in between. About seven o'clock of the fifth evening, after the rest of the staff had already left for the day, Wefer Linet showed up unexpectedly.

"Let's go catch some more Neulander guerrillas," Wefer suggested.

Cletus laughed, leaned back in his chair and stretched wearily. "I don't know where there are any, right now," Cletus said.

"Let's go have dinner then and talk about it," said Wefer craftily. "Maybe between the two of us we can figure out how to find some."

Cletus laughed again, started to shake his head, and then let himself be persuaded. After the dinner, however, he insisted on returning to his desk. Wefer came back with him, and only reluctantly took his leave when Cletus insisted that the work yet undone required his immediate attention.

"But don't forget," Wefer said on his way out, "you'll call me if anything comes up. I've got five Mark V's, and four of them are yours on half an hour's notice. It's not just me, it's my men. Everyone who was with us there on the river has been spreading the story around until I haven't got anyone in my command who wouldn't want to go with you if another chance comes up. . . . You'll find something for us to do?"

"It's a promise," said Cletus. "I'll turn up something for you shortly."

Wefer at last allowed himself to be ushered out. Cletus went back to his desk. By eleven o'clock he had finished the extensive and detailed orders he had been drafting to cover the actions and contingencies of the next two days. He made up a package of the orders, which were to be passed on to Eachan Khan for application to the Dorsai troops, and, going out, drove himself in a staff aircar to the Headquarters building in the Dorsai area.

He parked in front of it. There were two other cars waiting there; the one window of Eachan's office that faced him was alight. The rest of the building—a temporary structure of native wood painted a military light green that looked almost white in the pale light of the now-waxing new moon overhead—was dark, as were all the surrounding office and barracks buildings. It was like being in a ghost town where only one man lived.

Cletus got out of the car and went up the steps into the front hall of the building. Passing through the swinging gate, which barred visitors from the clerks normally at work in the outer office, he went down the corridor beyond the outer office to where the half-open door of Eachan's private office was marked by an escaping swathe of yellow light that lay across the corridor floor. Coming quietly up on that patch of light, Cletus checked, suddenly, at the sound of voices within the room.

The voices were those of Eachan and Melissa—and their conversation was no public one.

Cletus might have coughed, then, or made some other noise to warn that he had come upon them. But at that moment he heard his own name mentioned—and instantly guessed at least half of the conversation that had gone before. He neither turned and retreated nor made a sound. Instead he stood, listening.

"I thought you liked young Grahame," Eachan had just finished saying.

"Of course I like him!" Melissa's voice was tortured. "That's got nothing to do with it. Can't you understand, Dad?"

"No." Eachan's voice was stark.

Cletus took one long step forward, so that he could just see around the corner of the half-open door into the lighted room. The illumination there came from a single lamp, floating a foot and a half above the surface of Eachan's desk. On opposite sides of the desk, Eachan and Melissa stood facing each other. Their heads were above the level of the lamp, and their faces were hidden in shadow, while the lower parts of their bodies were clearly illuminated.

"No, of course you can't!" said Melissa. "Because you won't try! You can't tell me you like this better—this hand-to-mouth mercenary soldiering—than our home in Jalalabad! And with Dow's help you can go back. You'll be a general officer again, with your old rank back. That's *home*, Dad! Home on Earth, for both of us!"

"Not any more," said Eachan deeply. "I'm a soldier, Melly. Don't you understand? A *soldier!* Not just a uniform with a man walking around inside it—and that's all I'd be if I went back to Jalalabad. As a Dorsai, at least I'm still a soldier!" His voice became ragged, suddenly. "I know it's not fair to you—"

"I'm not doing it for me!" said Melissa. "Do you think I care? I was just a girl when we left Earth—it wouldn't be the same place at all for me, if we went back. But Mother told me to take care of you. And I am, even if you haven't got the sense to take care of yourself."

"Melly . . ." Eachan's voice was no longer ragged, but it was deep with pain. "You're so sure of yourself . . ."

"Yes, I am!" she said. "One of us has to be. I phoned him, Dad. Yesterday."

"Phoned deCastries?"

"Yes," Melissa said. "I called him in Capital Neuland. I said we'd come anytime he sent for us from Earth. *We'd* come, I said, Dad. But I warn you, if you won't go, I'll go alone."

There was a moment's silence in the darkness hiding the upper part of Eachan's stiff figure.

"There's nothing there for you, girl," he said, hoarsely. "You said so yourself."

"But I'll go!" she said. "Because that's the only way to get you to go back, to say I'll go alone if I have to—and mean it. Right now, I promise you, Dad . . ."

Cletus did not wait to hear the end of that promise. He turned abruptly and walked silently back to the front door of the building. He opened and closed the door, banging the heel of his hand against it noisily. He walked in, kicked open the gate in the fence about the outer office area and walked soundingly down the hall toward the light of the partly opened door.

When he entered the office room, the overhead lights had been turned on. In their bright glare, Melissa and Eachan still stood a little apart from each other, with the desk in between.

"Hello, Melissa!" Cletus said. "Good to see you. I was just bringing in some orders for Eachan. Why don't you wait a few minutes and we can all go have a cup of coffee or something?"

"No, I . . ." Melissa stumbled a little in her speech. Under the overhead lights her face looked pale and drawn. "I've got a headache. I think I'll go right home to bed." She turned to her father. "I'll see you later, Dad?"

"I'll be home before long," Eachan answered.

She turned and went out. Both men watched her go.

When the echo of her footsteps had been brought to an end by the sound of the outer door of the office building closing, Cletus turned back to face Eachan and threw the package of papers he was carrying onto Eachan's desk.

"What's the latest word from the scouts watching the Neulander side of the mountains?" Cletus asked, watching the older man's face and dropping into a chair on his side of the desk. Eachan sat down more slowly in his own chair.

"The Neulanders've evidently stopped moving men into the area," Eachan said. "But the scouts estimate they've got thirty-six hundred men there now—nearly double the number of our Dorsai troops. And they're regular Neulander soldiery, not guerrillas, with some light tanks and mobile artillery. My guess is that's better than 60 percent of their fully equipped, regular armed forces."

"Good," said Cletus. "Pull all but a couple of companies back into Bakhalla."

Eachan's gaze jerked up from the packet of orders to stare at Cletus' face. "Pull back?" he echoed. "What was the point in going up there, then?"

"The point in going up there," said Cletus, "was to cause Neuland to do exactly what they've done—assemble troops on their side of the mountain border. Now we pull back most of our men, so that it looks as though we've lost our nerve. Either that, or never intended to be a threat after all."

"And was that what we intended?" Eachan looked narrowly at Cletus.

Cletus laughed cheerfully. "Our intent, just as I say," he answered, "was to make them assemble a large force on their side of the pass through the mountains. Now we can pack up and go home—but can they? No doubt you've heard the army rumor—and by this time the Neulanders will have heard it too—that General Traynor and myself were overheard discussing an invasion of Neuland, and that we made a special trip up to Etter's Pass to survey it with that in mind."

"You mean," said Eachan, "that deCastries and the Neulanders will be sure that we really meant to invade them?"

"I mean just the opposite," said Cletus. "There's a great deal of truth to the fact that a liar is always going to suspect you of lying and a thief'll always suspect your honesty. DeCastries is a subtle man, and the weakness of subtle men is to suspect any straightforward action of being a screen for some kind of trick. He'll be sure to have concluded the rumor was leaked specifically for the purpose of causing him— and Neuland—to move a lot of troops into position on a false invasion scare, which would evaporate then and leave them looking foolish. Consequently, being the man he is, he'll have resolved to play along with our game and take advantage of us at the very moment we plan to be chuckling over his embarrassment."

Eachan frowned. "I don't believe I follow you," he said.

Cletus nodded at the package of papers. "It's all in the orders, there," he said. "You'll start withdrawing men from the Two Rivers area early tomorrow, a shipload at half hour intervals. As each shipload gets back here and gets sorted out, turn them loose on three-day passes."

Eachan stared at him, grimly. "And that's it?" Eachan said, at last.

"That's it—until I give you further orders," said Cletus, getting to his feet. He turned about and headed toward the door.

"Good night," said Eachan behind him. As Cletus went out the door and turned left to go off down the corridor, he caught a glimpse of Eachan, still standing behind the desk, looking after him.

Cletus went back to his quarters and to bed. The next morning he allowed himself the unusual luxury of sleeping late. It was 10 A.M. by the time he drifted into the Officers' Club for a late breakfast and just short of noon when he finally arrived at his office. Arvid and the staff Arvid had accumulated there were all diligently at work. Cletus smiled at them like an indulgent father and called them all together.

"I'm flying up to Two Rivers this afternoon," he said, "to supervise the windup of the Dorsai exercises up there. So there's not much point in your feeding me with a lot of information material that'll go stale between now and Monday morning anyway. I've been working you all above and beyond the call of duty. So take the rest of the day off— all of you, that is, except Arvid"—he smiled at the big young officer— "and I'll see you again at the beginning of next week."

The staff evaporated like a scattering of raindrops on hot pavement after a tropical shower. Once they were gone, Cletus went carefully around the office, making sure all its security systems were in working order and ready to be put in operation. Then he came back, sat down opposite Arvid's desk and reached over to pick up Arvid's phone. He dialed the number of the Navy base.

"This is Colonel Cletus Grahame," he told the duty petty officer at the far end. "Would you try to locate Commander Linet for me, and have him call me back? I'm at my office."

He put the phone back on Arvid's desk and waited. Arvid was watching him curiously. Cletus got up and walked over to his own desk. He picked up his own phone there and brought it back to exchange it for the phone in front of Arvid. Arvid's phone he took back to his own desk.

He punched out the first two digits of the five-digit number that would connect him with Bat Traynor's office. Then, with the phone activated, but the call incompleted, he pushed the phone from him and looked over at Arvid.

"Arv," he said, "some time in the next few hours Eachan Khan's going to be calling me. If anyone but Colonel Eachan calls, I've just stepped out and you don't know when I'll be back. But if Colonel Eachan calls, tell him that I'm on the phone to General Traynor at the moment—and I will be. Ask him if you can take a message, or say I'll call him back in a few minutes."

Arvid frowned in slight puzzlement—but the frown evaporated almost immediately into his usual agreeable expression.

"Yes, sir," he said. . . . "And now?" he asked, after Cletus had made the call.

"Now, we wait."

Wait, they did—for nearly two hours, during which perhaps a dozen unimportant phone calls came in and were neatly fielded by Arvid. Then the phone Cletus had moved from his desk to that of the lieutenant buzzed abruptly and Arvid lifted the receiver.

"Colonel Grahame's office, Lieutenant Johnson speaking—" Arvid broke off, glancing over at Cletus. "Colonel Khan? Yes, sir . . ."

Cletus had already picked up Arvid's phone and was completing the punching of the proper sequence of numbers for contact with Bat's office. In the background he heard Arvid saying that he could take a message. Bat's office answered.

"This is Colonel Grahame," Cletus said into the phone.

"I'd like to talk to General Traynor right away—in fact, immediately. It's red emergency."

He waited. There was a fractional delay at the other end of the line. Arvid, meanwhile, had hung up. There was silence in the office. Cletus could see out of the corner of his eye how Arvid was standing, watching him.

"Grahame?" Bat's voice exploded suddenly against Cletus' ear. "What's all this?"

"Sir," said Cletus, "I discovered something, and I think I ought to talk to you about it right away—privately. I can't tell you over the phone. It's got to do with the Coalition and it involves not only us, here on Kultis, but the whole Alliance. I'm at my office. I've given my staff the rest of the day off. Could you make some excuse to leave your office and come over here so that we could talk privately?"

"Talk? What is all this—" Bat broke off. Cletus heard the other's voice, suddenly withdrawn from the mouthpiece of the phone, speaking distantly to someone else. "Joe, go get me that file on . . . the plans for the new military district south of town."

There were a few more seconds of pause, and then Bat's voice came back close to the phone but muted and cold in tone.

"*Now* you can tell me," he said.

"I'm sorry, sir," said Cletus.

"Sorry? You mean you don't even trust the phone circuits to my office?"

"I didn't say that, sir," answered Cletus evenly. "I only suggested that you make some excuse to get out of your office and meet me privately over here at mine."

His voice was almost wooden in its lack of expression. There was a long pause at the other end of the phone circuit. Then Cletus heard Bat's indrawn breath hiss sharply.

"All right, Grahame," said Bat, "but this better be as serious as you're making it sound."

"Sir," said Cletus seriously, "without exaggeration, it concerns not only the highest Coalition personnel presently on the planet, but members of our own Alliance command here in Bakhalla as well."

"See you in fifteen minutes," said Bat. The phone circuit clicked in Cletus' ear, and then went dead.

Cletus put the phone down and turned to look at Arvid, who was staring at him.

"Eachan's message?" Cletus prompted gently. With a start, Arvid came out of his trance.

"Sir, the Neulanders are attacking Two Rivers!" he burst out. "Colonel Khan says they're coming in both by air and through the pass— and there's less than three companies of Dorsais left in Two Rivers, not counting a few scouts still out in the jungle who'll have been captured or bypassed by the Neulander troops by this time."

Cletus picked up the phone and punched for Lieutenant-Colonel Marcus Dodds at the landing field by the Dorsai military area.

"Colonel Dodds—sir?" said the lean, quiet face of Eachan's second-in-command, appearing in the small phone screen.

"Have you heard about the Neulander attack at Two Rivers?" Cletus asked.

"Yes, sir," Dodds answered. "Colonel Khan just messaged us to stop all release of men. We're starting to get them turned around now."

"Good," said Cletus. "I'll join you shortly."

He broke the circuit, put the phone down and crossed the room to an arms cabinet. Unlocking it, he took out a pistol belt and sidearm. He turned and tossed these to Arvid. Arvid put out one hand automatically and caught them.

"Sir?" he said, puzzled, "the Neulanders aren't attacking in the city, here, are they?"

Cletus laughed, reclosing and locking the arms cabinet. "No, Arv," he said, turning back to the tall lieutenant, "but the Neulanders have started to move up at Two Rivers, and Dow deCastries is the kind of man to want to take out insurance, even when he has a sure thing. I'd look a little strange wearing a sidearm, but you can wear it for me."

He turned back to his desk phone and punched for the Navy base.

"This is Colonel Grahame," he said. "A little while ago I put in an important call for Commander Linet . . ."

"Yes, sir," said the voice of the ensign who had answered the phone. "The commander's been trying to get you sir, but your circuits were busy just now. Just a minute, sir . . ."

Wefer's voice broke in on the line. "Cletus! What's up?"

"You offered me the use of four of your Mark V's," Cletus said. "I need only three of them. But they have to move upriver between here and the town of Two Rivers, at the confluence of the Blue and the Whey. That's nearly two hundred and thirty miles of river travel. Do you think they could make it between now and, say, an hour before dawn tomorrow?"

"Two hundred and thirty miles? Between now and an hour to dawn? Nothing to it!" shouted Wefer over the phone circuit. "What's up?"

"The Neulanders have moved regular troops across the border at Etter's Pass," said Cletus, in a level voice. "They'll be attacking Two Rivers shortly after sunup tomorrow. I'll give you the details of what I want you for later. But can you move your Mark V's to within a mile downstream of where the two rivers come together and hold them there without being seen?"

"You know I can!" said Wefer. "But you'll be in touch?"

"I'll be contacting you before dawn tomorrow," said Cletus.

"Right! We're on our way!" The phone clicked dead at Wefer's end.

"Go ahead, Arv," said Cletus. "Wait for me outside at the car. I'll be along in a minute."

Arv stared. "We're leaving?" he said. "But, sir, isn't the general due . . ."

His voice ran down into silence as Cletus stood patiently waiting. "Yes, sir," he said.

He went out.

Cletus put the phone in his hand back down on the desk, by which he was standing. He glanced at his watch. Some eight minutes had gone by since he had spoken to Bat, and Bat had said he would be here in fifteen minutes. Cletus made a last tour of the office to make sure all the security devices were in order. Then he let himself out the front door, pulling the door to, but leaving it slightly unlatched, with the trap spring activated. The next person to walk through that door would find it closing automatically behind him, locking him into an area from which escape was not easily possible.

Cletus turned and went out to his staff car, where Arvid waited. They drove off toward the BOQ.

Chapter 13

As Cletus' command car tilted on its air cushion and slid around the corner into the short street leading toward the BOQ, Cletus saw the parking lot before the BOQ half filled with parked cars, clustered before the main entrance of the building in two rows with a narrow aisle in between.

Both ends of the parking lot were empty; the building itself, with those other buildings of the officers' compound beyond it, seemed to slumber emptily under the afternoon sun. The BOQ's occupants for the most part would now be either at work, having a late lunch, or asleep within. As the staff car slid on its air cushion toward the entrance to the parking lot, Cletus raised his eyes and caught the glint of sunlight on something metallic just below the ridge of the roof over the BOQ's main entrance.

Cletus looked at the empty-windowed double row of cars sitting flat on the cement of the parking lot, with their air cushions turned off. His lips thinned. At that moment, as they turned into the aisle between the two rows of cars, there were sizzling sounds like the noise of enormous slices of bacon frying above them, followed by several licking dragons' breaths of superheated air, as energy weapons sliced into the metal sides and roof of his command car like the flames of acetylene torches into thin tinfoil. Arvid fell heavily against Cletus, his uniform jacket black and smoking on the upper right side, and the staff car careened out of control, to its right, into two empty parking spaces between cars, where it wedged itself, still on its air cushion between the grounded vehicles.

A bleak fury exploded inside Cletus. He turned, jerked the sidearm from its holster at Arvid's side, ducked down and punched open the door on his side of the staff car. He dove through it into the space between his car and the grounded one on the right. He rolled back under his own floating car and crawled rapidly to the back end of the grounded car on his left. Lying flat, he peered around its end. There was a man on his feet, energy rifle in hand, coming toward him between the two rows of parked vehicles at a run. Cletus snapped a shot from the sidearm and the man went tumbling, head over heels. Cletus ducked around the car to his right and into the next space between it and the car farther on.

The charge weapons now were silent. From memory of the sound and damage to the command car, Cletus guessed no more than three gunmen were involved. That left two to deal with. Glancing out, Cletus could see the man he had shot sprawled, lying still on the pavement, his energy weapon rolled out of his grasp, its transparent, rifle-like barrel reflecting the sunlight. Cletus backed up, opened the near door of the car on his right and crawled in. Lying flat on its floorboards, he raised it on its air cushion and set it backing out in reverse.

As it reached the center space between the two rows of parked cars, he dived out the opposite door, just as two beams cut into the other side and the roof of the car behind him. He snatched up the fallen charge weapon and, carrying it, scuttled behind the screen of the still-moving car until it slammed into the opposite row of cars. Then he ducked into the closest available space there, turned about and looked back around the nearest car end.

The other two gunmen were visible, standing out in the open now, back to back, by the car Cletus had last sent smashing into the ones opposite. One was facing Cletus' direction, the other in the opposite direction, both with their charge weapons up and scanning the spaces between the vehicles for any sign of movement.

Cletus pulled back, cradled the charge weapon in his left elbow and lobbed his sidearm in a high arc over the heads of the two standing men to fall with a clatter by Cletus' own cut-up command car.

Both of the gunmen spun about to face in the direction of the noise. Cletus, standing up and stepping out from between his two parked cars, cut them down with the energy weapon he still held in his hands.

Breathing heavily, Cletus leaned for a second against the back of the car by which he had emerged. Then, throwing aside the energy weapon, he limped hastily back toward the staff car in which Arvid still lay.

The lieutenant was conscious when Cletus arrived. He had taken a bad burn through the upper part of his chest and shoulder on the right side, but energy-weapon wounds were self-cauterizing; the wound was ugly, but there was no bleeding. Cletus eased him down onto the grass and went into the BOQ to call for medical aid from an astounded military hospital unit.

"Guerrillas!" Cletus said briefly, in answer to their questions. "There're three of them—all dead. But my aide's wounded. Get over here as soon as you can."

He cut the connection and went back out to see how Arvid was doing.

"How . . ." whispered Arvid, when Cletus bent over him.

"I told you deCastries would like insurance," said Cletus. "Lie still now, and don't talk."

The ambulance unit from the military hospital swooped down then, its shadow falling across them like the shadow of some hawk from the skies just before it landed softly on the grass beside them. White-uniformed medics personnel tumbled out, and Cletus got to his feet.

"This is Lieutenant Johnson, my aide," said Cletus. "Take good care of him. The three guerrillas out in the parking lot are all dead. I'll write up a full report on this later—but right now I've got to get going. You can handle things?"

"Yes, sir," said the medic in charge. He was a senior, with the gold and black bars of a warrant officer on his collar. "We'll take care of him."

"Good," said Cletus.

Without stopping to say anything further to Arvid, he turned and went up into the BOQ and down the hall to his own quarters. Swiftly, he changed into combat overalls and the straps for battle gear. When he came out, Arvid had already been taken away to the hospital and the three dead gunmen had been brought up and laid on the grass. Their clothes were the ordinary sort of civilian outfits normally seen on the streets of Bakhalla, but the lower part of the faces of each was pale in contrast to the tan of their foreheads, showing where heavy Neulander beards had been shaved off recently.

Cletus tried his command car, found it operable, and slid off in the direction of the Dorsai area.

When he arrived there, he found most of the returned Dorsai troops already marshaled by units on the exercise ground—armed, equipped and ready to be enshipped back to Two Rivers. Cletus went directly to the temporary Headquarters unit set up at one side of the field and found Lieutenant-Colonel Marcus Dodds there.

"You haven't sent any shiploads back up yet, have you?" Cletus demanded the moment Dodds saw him.

"No, Colonel," answered the tall, lean man. "But we should probably be thinking about moving men back up soon. If we try to have troops jump into Two Rivers after dark, three out of four of them are going to land in the rivers. And by daylight tomorrow, those Neulander troops will probably be in position in both river valleys above the town. They'd have a field day picking off our jump troops if we send men in then."

"Don't worry about it," Cletus said brusquely. "We aren't going to jump into the town in any case."

Marc Dodds' eyebrows raised in his narrow, brown face. "You're not going to support—"

"We'll support. But not that way," said Cletus. "How many of the men that were sent back and turned loose on pass are still out?"

"Not more than half a company, probably, all told. They've been hearing about this and coming back on their own," said Marc. "No Dorsai's going to let other Dorsais be surrounded and cut up when he can help—"

He was interrupted by the phone ringing on the field desk before him. He picked it up and listened for a moment without comment.

"Just a minute," he said, and lowered the phone, pushing in on the muffle button. "It's for you. Colonel Ivor Dupleine—General Traynor's chief of staff."

Cletus reached out his hand and Marc passed the phone into it.

"This is Colonel Grahame," Cletus said into the mouthpiece. Dupleine's choleric face, tiny in the phone screen by Cletus' thumb, glared up at him.

"Grahame!" Dupleine's voice barked in his ear. "This is Colonel Dupleine. The Neulanders've moved troops over the border at Etter's Pass and seem to be setting up around Two Rivers. Have you still got any Dorsai troops up there?"

"A couple of companies in the town itself," said Cletus.

"Only a couple? That's not so bad then!" said Dupleine. "All right, listen now. Apparently those Dorsais over there with you are getting all stirred up. You're not to make any attempt against those Neulander troops without direct orders. *That's* a direct order—from General Traynor himself. You understand? You just sit tight there until you hear from me or the general."

"No," said Cletus.

For a moment there was a dead silence at the other end of the circuit. Dupleine's face stared out at Cletus from the phone screen.

"What? What did you say?" snapped Dupleine, at last.

"I ought to remind you, Colonel," said Cletus, quietly, "that the general put me in complete command of these Dorsais with responsibility only to him."

"You . . . but I'm giving you the general's orders, Grahame! Didn't you hear me?" Dupleine's voice choked on the last word.

"I've got no proof of that, Colonel," said Cletus, in the same unvarying tone of voice. "I'll take my orders from the general, himself. If you'll have the general tell me what you've just told me, I'll be happy to obey."

"You're insane!" For a long moment, he once more stared at Cletus. When he spoke again, his voice was lower, more controlled, and dangerous. "I think you know what refusing to obey an order like that means, Colonel. I'm going to sign off here and give you five minutes to think it over. If I haven't heard from you within five minutes, I'll have to go to the general with your answer just the way you gave it. Think about it."

The little screen in the phone went dark, and the click of the disconnected circuit sounded in the earphone. Cletus put the phone back on the desk.

"Where's your map projector?" he asked Marc.

"Right over here," he answered, leading the way across the room to a horizontal table-screen, with the black shape of a projector bolted beneath it. A map of the Etter's Pass area showed on the screen. As they both reached the edge of the table-screen, Cletus put his finger on the marked position of Two Rivers town where the streams of the Whey and the Blue came together.

"By dawn tomorrow," he said to Marc, "whoever's commanding those Neulanders will want to be in a position to start his attack on our troops in the town. That means"—Cletus' finger traced horseshoe-shaped curves, their open ends facing downstream, about the valleys of both the Whey and the Blue rivers just above the town—"our men from here should be able to go in as jump troops—since they're fresh from training for it—just upriver of both those positions with comparative safety—since the Neulander forces should all be looking downriver. Now, I understand that the Neulanders don't have any real artillery, any more than we do. Is that right?"

"That's right, sir," Marc said. "Kultis is one of the worlds where we've had an unspoken agreement with the Coalition not to supply our allies, or our troops stationed with those allies, with anything more than portable weapons. So far as we know, they've kept to their part of the bargain as far as Neuland's concerned. Actually, they haven't needed anything more than hand weapons, just as we haven't, since up till now all their fighting's been done with native guerrillas. We can expect their troops to have light body armor, energy weapons, rocket and fire bomb launchers . . ."

Together they plotted the probable future positions of the Neulander troops, particularly those carrying the launchers and other special weapons. While they worked, a ceaseless stream of orders came in and out of the field HQ, frequently interrupting their talk.

The sun had set several hours before one of the junior officers tapped Cletus deferentially on the elbow and offered him the phone.

"Colonel Dupleine again, sir," the officer said.

Cletus took the phone and looked at the image of Dupleine. The face of the Alliance colonel looked haggard.

"Well, Colonel?" asked Cletus.

"Grahame—" began Dupleine, hoarsely, and then broke off. "Is anyone there with you?"

"Colonel Dodds of the Dorsais," answered Cletus.

"Could I . . . talk to you privately?" said Dupleine, his eyes searching around the periphery of the screen as though to discover Marc, who was standing back to one side out of line of sight from the phone. Marc raised his eyebrows and started to turn away. Cletus reached out a hand to stop him.

"Just a minute," he said. He turned and spoke directly into the phone. "I've asked Colonel Dodds to stay. I'm afraid I'd prefer having a witness to whatever you say to me, Colonel."

Dupleine's lips sagged. "All right," he said. "The word's probably spreading already. Grahame . . . General Traynor can't be located."

Cletus waited a second before answering. "Yes?" he said.

"Don't you understand?" Dupleine's voice started to rise. He stopped, visibly fought with himself and got his tones down to a reasonable level again. "Here the Neulanders have moved not just guerrillas, but regular troops, into the country. They're attacking Two Rivers—and now the general's dis . . . not available. This is an emergency, Grahame! You have to see the point in canceling any orders to move the Dorsai troops you have there, and coming over to talk with me, here."

"I'm afraid I don't," answered Cletus. "It's Friday evening. General Traynor may simply have gone somewhere for the weekend and forgotten to mention he'd be gone. My responsibility's to his original orders, and those leave me no alternative but to go ahead with the Dorsais in any way I think best."

"You can't believe he'd do a thing like that—" Dupleine interrupted himself, fury breaking through the self-control he had struggled to maintain up until this point. "You nearly got gunned down by guerrillas yourself, today, according to the reports on my desk! Didn't it mean anything to you that they were carrying energy weapons instead of sport rifles? You know the Neulander guerrillas always carry civilian-level weapons and tools so they can't be shot as saboteurs if they're captured! Doesn't the fact that three men with energy weapons tried to cut you down mean anything to you?"

"Only that whoever's giving the orders on the Neuland side," said Cletus, "would like to have me removed as commander of the Dorsai troops. Clearly, if they don't want me commanding, the best thing I can do for our side is to command."

Dupleine glared at him wearily from the phone screen. "I warn you, Grahame!" he said. "If anything's happened to Traynor, or if we don't find him in the next few hours, I'll take emergency command of the Alliance Forces here myself. And the first thing I'm going to do is to revoke Bat's order to you and put you under arrest!"

The tiny screen in the phone went dark, the voice connection went dead. A little wearily, Cletus put the phone down on the table-screen and rubbed his eyes. He turned to Marcus Dodds.

"All right, Marc," he said. "We won't delay any longer. Let's start moving our men back up to Two Rivers."

Chapter 14

Cletus went in with the first wave of six transport craft, which circled eight miles upstream from Two Rivers and dropped their jump troops on both sides of the two river valleys. A reconnaissance aircraft, swinging low over the jungle in the darkness following moon-set, two hours before, had picked up the heat images of two large bodies of Neulander troops waiting for dawn in both the river valleys, five miles above the town. Another, smaller, reserve force was camped just below the mouth of Etter's Pass—but its numbers were slight enough so that the Dorsais could disregard any counterattack from that direction. Cletus watched the flares of the jets from the jump belts of the descending men, and then ordered the pilot of his transport ship to fly low above the river, heading downstream from the town.

A quarter mile below the town, the river curved to the right, and it was just around this curve that the response came from the MV's. The transport ship came down and hovered above the water, and the turret of one of the huge submarine dozers rose blackly from the dark waters.

Cletus went down an elevator sling to the turret, and the hatch in it opened. Wefer stepped out. Together they stood on the slight slope of the wet metal casing below the tower.

"Here we are, then," Wefer said. "Three of us, just like the doctor ordered." Under his black hair, his friendly, pugnacious face was excited in the dim light. "What do you want us to do?"

"The Neulander troops—and their regular troops," said Cletus, "are concentrated in the two river valleys a few miles above the town. They'll be pushing down those valleys and into the town along the flatland below the river bluffs. But I don't think they'll be trying to come at the town from this downriver side. So you ought to be able to work without being seen."

"Sure, sure," said Wefer, sniffing the chilly dawn air like a hunting dog. "But what do you want us to do?"

"Can you plow up the bottom of the river just below the town, to raise the water level in and above the town?"

"In this little trickle of a river?" answered Wefer. "No trouble at all. We'll simply raise an underwater ridge at some point where the river bluffs on either side come straight down to the water's edge. The water has to rise to get over it. How high a dam? How much do you want to raise the water level?"

"I want the water six feet deep, a mile above the town," Cletus said.

For the first time, Wefer frowned. "Six feet? A full fathom? You'll flood the town itself. That flat spot between the rivers that the town's built on can't be more than six or eight feet above water level on both sides. You'll have another four to six feet of running water in the streets. Do you want that?"

"That's exactly what I want," said Cletus.

"Well . . . of course there's plenty of solid buildings there in the warehouse district for people to climb into," said Wefer. "I just don't want to get the Navy billed for flood damage—"

"It won't be," said Cletus. "I'm still under General Traynor's direct orders as commander here. I'll take the responsibility."

Wefer peered at Cletus in the growing light, shook his head and whistled admiringly. "We'll get right at it then," he said. You ought to have your fathom of water up above the city there in about four hours."

"Good," said Cletus. He stepped into the elevator sling and waved to the transport ship to pull him back in. "Good luck."

"Good luck to you and your Dorsais!" Wefer replied. "You'll need it more than we do. We're just going to be doing our daily jobs."

Once back inside the transport, Cletus ordered it to swing back up to within line of sight of Two Rivers itself. The sky was lightening rapidly now, and the individual buildings in Two Rivers were easily picked out. Cletus had a coherent light beam trained on the curved reception mirror on the roof of the warehouse building that the Dorsais had taken over as their Two River HQ during the week of jump practice. He sent a call down the light beam and got an immediate answer from Eachan.

"Colonel?" Eachan's voice was distant, clipped and unruffled. "Been expecting to hear from you. I haven't had any reports from my scouts out in the jungle for better than three hours now. They're all either captured or lying low. But I gather the Neulanders are clustered in both river valleys above town. I've got all strong points here manned and ready."

"Fine, Colonel," said Cletus. "I just wanted to tell you to expect to get your feet wet. You might also warn the civilians in town to gather in the higher buildings of the warehouse district above the second floor."

"Oh? Thunderstorm coming?"

"We're not that lucky, I'm afraid," said Cletus. A good heavy rainstorm would have been all to the advantage of the well-trained Dorsai, both the jump troops and those in fixed positions in the city. "The weather forecast is for hot and clear. But the river's going to rise. I'm told you'll have four to six feet of water in the streets there."

"I see. I'll take care of it—with the troops and civilians too—" Eachan broke off. "Are we getting reinforcements here in the town?"

"I'm afraid I can't spare you any," Cletus said. "But with luck, it'll be over one way or the other before the Neulanders are really on top of you. Do the best you can with the men you have."

"Understood," said Eachan. "That's all from this end then, Colonel."

"That's all from my end for the moment, too, Colonel," replied Cletus. "Good luck."

He broke the light-beam contact and ordered the transport ship back to Bakhalla for a new load of jump troops. Now that it was open daylight over Two Rivers and there was no more secrecy to be gained by operating at low altitudes in the shadows below the peaks above the town, Cletus accompanied the next wave of jump troops riding in a courier craft, which he set to circling above the reach of hand-weapon fire from the ground.

The second wave of Dorsai troops to go down on their jump belts were harassed, but ineffectively so, by angled fire from the Neulander troops downriver.

"Good enough," commented Marc Dodds, who had accompanied Cletus in the courier ship, leaving Major David Ap Morgan to take charge of getting off the last two remaining waves and accompanying the last as its commanding officer. "They'll have aircraft hitting our next wave, though. I don't know why they haven't had Neulander ships in the air over here before now."

"Another instance of the too imaginative mind," said Cletus. Marc glanced at him inquiringly, and Cletus went on to explain. "I was telling Eachan last night that too much subtlety would lead to mistakes.

The Neulanders know that the Alliance has supplied the Exotics with many more and better air-combat craft than the Coalition supplied them. So automatically they've drawn the wrong conclusion. They think our lack of air cover is only apparent—bait to trap them into putting their own ships up so our superior air power can knock them down. Also, they know that only the Dorsais were jump-training, and they'll be suspecting that the Dorsais are the only ones who're being sent against them for that reason. They know they outnumber us two or three to one on the ground, which would tend to make them complacent."

The third wave came in and jumped to the jungle below. True to Cletus' assessment of the situation, there was no appearance of Neuland aircraft to oppose the jump. Nor was there with the fourth and final wave. With all four waves of Dorsai jump troops now down on the ground, the pattern of Cletus' battle plan began to make itself felt. He had set his Dorsais down in the jungle on the top of the bluffs on either side of both rivers upstream from the concentration of Neulander troops. Now, spread out in skirmish lines, the Dorsais began to open up on the rear of the Neulander troops. The Neulanders fought back, but withdrew steadily, as their force began to move down into the river valleys toward the town. They showed no tendency to turn and fight and no panic at being caught by small-arms fire from their rear. Up in their circling aircraft, Cletus and Marc kept in touch with their units on the ground by line-of-sight light-beam voice transmission.

"We aren't even slowing them down," said Marc, his mouth a straight line as he observed the scene below in the multiple reconnaissance screens set up before them.

"They'll be slowed up later," replied Cletus.

He was very busy plotting the movements of the running battle below on the reconnaissance screen, even as he issued a steady stream of orders to individual small units of the Dorsai troops.

Marc fell silent and turned back to examining the situation on the reconnaissance screens as it was developing under the impetus of Cletus' orders. Before him the two main elements of the Neulander forces were like large fat caterpillars crawling down the inner edge of the valley troughs of the two rivers, converging as the rivers converged toward the single point that was the town of Two Rivers. Behind, and inland from the rivers, the Dorsai troops, like thin lines of tiny ants, assailed these two caterpillars from the rear and the inland sides. Not that all this was visible to the naked eye below the thick screen of jungle cover. But the instruments and Cletus' plotting on the chart revealed it clearly. Under attack the caterpillars humped their rearward ends closer toward their front, bunching up under the attacks of the ants, but otherwise were undisturbed in their progress.

Meanwhile, Cletus was extending his pursuing Dorsai troops forward along the inland side of each enemy force until the farthest extended units were almost level with the foremost troops of the enemy units they harassed. Occasionally they dented the Neulander lines they faced. But in case of trouble the Neulanders merely withdrew over the edge of the steeply sloping bluff and fought the Dorsai back over, what was in effect, a natural parapet. Not merely that, but more and more their forward-moving units were dropping below the edge of the bluff with a skirmish line along its edge to protect their march—so that fully 80 percent of the enemy force was beyond the reach of the Dorsai weapons in any case.

Cletus broke off abruptly from his work on the screens and turned to Marc.

"They're less than two miles from the upper edge of the town," he said. "I want you to take over here and keep those Neulander forces contained all along their lines. Make them get down below the bluff and stay there, but don't expose men any more than you have to. Contain them, but hold your troops back until you get word from me."

"Where're you going, sir?" Marc asked, frowning.

"Down," said Cletus, tersely. He reached for one of the extra jump belts with which the aircraft was supplied and began strapping it on. "Put half a company of men on each river over on their jump belts and send them down the opposite side. They're to fire back across the river into any exposed elements of the enemy as they go, but they are not to stop to do it. They're to keep traveling fast until they rendezvous with me down here."

He turned and tapped with his fingernail on the bend in the river below the town beyond which Wefer and his three Mark V's were at work. "How soon do you estimate they can meet me down there?" he asked.

"With luck, an hour," answered Marc. "What're you planning to do, sir—if you don't mind my asking?"

"I'm going to try to make it look as though we've got reinforcements into that town," Cletus said. He turned and called up to the pilot in the front of the reconnaissance ship. "Cease circling. Take me down to just beyond the bend in the main river there—point H29 and R7 on the grid."

The aircraft wheeled away from its post above the battle and began to circle down toward the river bend. Cletus moved over to the emergency escape hatch and put his hand on the eject button. Marc followed him.

"Sir," he said, "if you haven't used a jump belt in a long time—"

"I know," Cletus interrupted him cheerfully, "it's a trick to keep your feet down and your head up, particularly when you're coming in for a landing. Don't worry—" He turned his head to shout to the pilot up front. "That patch of jungle just inside the bend of the river. Call 'Jump' for me."

"Yes, sir," the pilot called back. There was a moment's pause and then he shouted, "Jump."

"Jump," echoed Cletus.

He punched the eject button. The emergency door flipped open before him and the section of decking beneath his feet flipped him abruptly clear of the aircraft. He found himself falling toward the tops of the jungle treetops, six hundred feet below.

He clutched the hand control in the center of the belt at his waist, and the twin jets angling out from his shoulder tank flared thunderously, checking him in midair with a wrench that left him feeling as though his back had been broken. For a moment, before he could catch his breath, he actually began to rise. Then he throttled back to a slow fall and began the struggle to keep himself in vertical position with his feet under him.

He was not so much falling as sliding down at a steep angle into the jungle below. He made an effort to slow the rate of his fall, but the sensitive, tricky reactions of the jump belt sent him immediately into a climb again. Hastily, he returned the throttle to its first, instinctive fall-setting.

He was very near the tops of the taller trees now, and it would be necessary to pick his way between them so as not to be brained by a branch in passing or land in one of the deadly, dagger-like thorn bushes. Careful not to twist the throttle grip in the process, he shifted the control handle slightly this way and that to determine the safe limits of a change of direction. His first attempt very nearly sent his feet swinging into the air, but he checked the swing and after a moment got himself back into a line of upright descent. There was a patch of relatively clear jungle down to his right. Gingerly he inched the control handle over and was relieved as his airy slide altered toward the patch. Then, abruptly, he was among and below the treetops.

The ground was rushing at him. The tall, jagged stump of a lightning-blasted tree, which he had not seen earlier because it was partly covered with creepers blending in with the green of the ground cover, seemed to leap upward at him like a spear.

Desperately he jammed the handle over. The jets bucked. He went into a spin, slammed at an angle into the tree stump and smashed against the ground. A wave of blackness took him under.

Chapter 15

When he came to—and it may have been only seconds later, he was lying twisted on the ground with his bad knee bent under him. His head was ringing, but, otherwise, he did not feel bad.

Shakily he sat up and, using both hands, gently began to straighten out his bum leg. Then there was pain, mounting and threatening unconsciousness.

He fought the unconsciousness off. Slowly it receded. He leaned back, panting against the tree trunk, to catch his breath and use his autocontrol techniques. Gradually the pain in his knee faded, and his breathing calmed. His heartbeat slowed. He concentrated on relaxing the whole structure of his body and isolating the damaged knee. After a little while, the familiar floating sensation of detachment came to him. He leaned forward and gently straightened the knee, pulled up the pants leg covering it and examined it.

It was beginning to swell, but beyond that his exploring fingers could not tell him what serious damage had been done it this time. He could sense the pain like a distant pressure off behind the wall of his detachment. Taking hold of the tree trunk and resting all his weight on his other foot, he slowly pulled himself to his feet.

Once on his feet he gingerly tried putting a little of his weight on that leg. It supported him, but there was a weakness about it that was ominous.

For a moment he considered using the jump belt to lift himself into the air once more, over the treetops and down to the river. But after a second, he dismissed the idea. He could not risk another hard landing on that knee, and coming down in the river with as much current as there was now was also impractical. He might have to swim, and swimming might put the knee completely beyond use.

He unbuckled the jump belt and let it fall. Relieved of its weight, he hopped on his good foot to a nearby sapling about two inches in diameter. Drawing his sidearm, he shot the sapling's trunk through some six feet above the ground, and again at ground level. Stripping off a few twigs from the length of wood this provided left him with a rough staff on which he could lean. With the help of the staff he began hobbling toward the river's edge. He finally reached the bank of the gray, flowing water. He took the body phone from his belt, set it for transmission limited to a hundred yards and called Wefer on the Navy wavelength.

Wefer answered, and a few minutes later one of the Mark V's poked its massive, bladed snout out of the water ten yards in front of him.

"What now?" asked Wefer, after Cletus had been assisted aboard and down into the control room of the Mark V. Cletus leaned back in the chair they had given him and stretched out his bad leg carefully.

"I'm having a company of men, half on each side of the river, meet us here in about"—he broke off to look at his watch—"thirty minutes or so from now. I want one of your Mark V's to take them, a platoon at a time, underwater up to the downriver end of the town. Can you spare one of your machines? How's the water level coming, by the way?"

"Coming fine," answered Wefer. "Those platoons of yours are going to find it knee-deep in the lower end of town by the time they get there. Give us another hour, and with only two machines I'll have the river as deep as you want it. So there's no problem about detaching one of the Mark V's for ferry purposes."

"Fine," said Cletus.

He rode into the town with the last Mark V load of the ferried Dorsais. As Wefer had predicted, the water was knee-deep in the streets near the downriver end of the town. Eachan Khan met him as he limped into the command room of the Dorsai HQ in Two Rivers.

"Sit down, Colonel," said Eachan, guiding Cletus into a chair facing the large plotting screen. "What's happening to the river? We've had to herd all the civilians into the tallest buildings."

"I've got Wefer Linet and some of those submarine dozers of his working downstream to raise the river level," answered Cletus. "I'll give you the details later. Right now, how are things with you here?"

"Nothing but some long-range sniping from the forward Neulander scouts, so far," said Eachan, coolly. "Those sandbagged strong points

of yours were a fine idea. The men will be dry and comfortable inside
them while the Neulanders will be slogging through ankle-deep water
to get to them."

"We may have to get out in the water and do a little slogging
ourselves," said Cletus. "I've brought you nearly two hundred extra
men. With these added to what you've got, do you think you could
mount an attack?"

Eachan's face had never inclined to any large changes of expression, but the stare he gave Cletus now was as close to visible emotion
as Cletus had seen him go.

"Attack?" he echoed. "Two and a half—three companies at most—
against six or eight battalions?"

Cletus shook his head. "I said mount an attack. Not carry one
through," he replied. "All I want to do is sting those two Neulander
fronts enough so that they'll pause to bring up more men before starting to go forward against us again. Do you think we can do that
much?"

"Hmm." Eachan fingered his mustache. "Something like that . . .
yes, quite possible, I'd think."

"Good," said Cletus. "How can you get me through, preferably
with picture as well as voice, to Marc Dodds?"

"We're on open channel." Eachan answered. He stepped across the
room and returned with a field phone.

"This is Colonel Khan," he said into it. "Colonel Grahame wishes
to speak with Colonel Dodds."

He passed the phone to Cletus. As Cletus' hands closed about it,
the vision screen in the phone's stem lit up with the image of Marc's
face, the plotting screen of the aircraft behind him.

"Sir?" Marc gazed at Cletus. "You're in Bakhalla?"

"That's right," Cletus answered. "And so's that company of men
I had you send to meet me at the bend of the main river. Give me a
view of the board behind you there, will you?"

Marc moved aside, and the plotting screen behind him seemed to
expand to fill the full screen of the phone. Details were too small to
pick out, but Cletus could see that the two main bodies of Neuland
troops were just beginning to join together on the sandy plain that
began where the river bluffs on adjacent banks of the converging Blue
and Whey rivers finally joined and ended in a sloping V-pointed bluff
above the town. Behind the forward scouts, the advancing main line
of the Neulanders was less than half a mile from the forward Dorsai
strongpoints defending the town. Those strongpoints and the defending
Dorsais would be firing into the enemy at long range, even now.

"I've got men along the tops of the bluffs all the way above the Neulanders on both rivers," said the voice of Marc, "and I've got at least two energy-rifle companies down on the flats at the foot of the bluffs behind their rear guards, keeping up fire into them."

"Pull those rifle companies back," Cletus said. "There's no point in risking a man we don't have to risk. And I want you to have your men on top of the bluffs stay there, but slacken off on their firing. Do it gradually, cut it down bit by bit until you're just shooting into them often enough to remind them that we're there."

"Pull back?" echoed Marc. His face came back into the screen, frowning. "And slacken fire? But what about the rest of you down in the town there?"

"We're going to attack," said Cletus.

Marc stared out of the screen without answering. His thoughts were as visible as though they were printed in the air before him. He, with better than three thousand men, was being told to back off from harassing the rear of an enemy force of more than six thousand—so as not to risk casualties. Meanwhile, Cletus, with less than six hundred men, was planning to attack the enemy head on.

"Trust me, Colonel," said Cletus softly into the phone. "Didn't I tell you all a week ago that I planned to get through this battle with as few men killed as possible?"

"Yes, sir . . ." said Marc, grudgingly, and obviously still bewildered.

"Then do as I tell you," said Cletus. "Don't worry, the game's not over yet. Have your men slacken fire as I say, but tell them to stay alert. They'll have plenty of chance to use their weapons a little later on."

He cut the connection and handed the phone back to Eachan.

"All right," he said. "Now let's see about mounting that attack."

Thirty minutes later, Cletus was riding with Eachan in a battle car that was sliding along on its air cushion ten inches above the water flooding the town, water that was now ankle-deep, even here at the upper edge of the town. He could see, moving ahead of him, spaced out in twenty-yard intervals and making good use of the houses, trees and other cover they passed, the closest half dozen of his Dorsai troopers in the first line of attack. Immediately in front of him, in the center of the control panel of the battle car, he could see a small replica plotting screen being fed with information by a remote circuit from the main plotting screen under Eachan's control at Dorsai HQ in the town behind him. It showed the Neulanders forming up at the base of the vertical wall of stone and earth where adjacent river bluffs came together. Their line stretched right across the some six hundred yards of sandy soil making up the neck of the land that connected the foot of the bluffs with the broader area of slightly higher ground on which the town of Two Rivers was built.

Only the apparent width of the neck of land showed on the plotting screen, however. Its actual width was lost now in an unbroken sheet of running water stretching from the bluffs on what had been the far side of the Whey River to the opposite bluffs on what had been the far side of the Blue. Under that gray, flowing sheet of liquid it was impossible to tell, except for the few small trees and bushes that dotted the neck of land, where the water was ankle-deep and where it was deep enough for one of Wefer's Mark V's to pass by on the bottom, unnoticed. Cletus had warned the attacking men to stay well toward the center of the enemy line, to avoid blundering into deeper water that would sweep them downstream.

The attackers paused behind the cover of the last row of houses and dressed their line. The enemy was only a few hundred yards away.

"All right," said Cletus into his battle phone. "Move out!"

The first wave of attackers rose from their places of concealment and charged forward at a run, zigzagging as they went. Behind them their companions, as well as the strongpoints with a field of fire across the former neck of land, opened up on the enemy with missile weapons.

The Neuland troops still standing on the dry footing of the slightly higher ground at the foot of the bluffs stared at the wild apparition of rifle-armed soldiers racing toward them, in great clouds of spray, with apparent suicidal intent. Before they could react, the first wave was down behind whatever cover was available, and the second wave was on its way.

It was not until the third wave had moved out that the Neulanders began to react. But by this time the fire from the attackers—as well as the slightly heavier automatic fire from the strongpoints—was beginning to cut up their forward lines. For a moment, disbelief wavered on the edge of panic. The Neuland troops had been under the impression that there was no one but a token force to oppose them in Two Rivers—and that it would be a matter of routing out small pockets of resistance, no more. Instead, they were being attacked by what was clearly a much greater number of Dorsais than they had been led to believe were in the town. The front Neuland line wavered and began to back up slightly, pressing in on the troops behind them, who were now crowding forward to find out what was going on.

The confusion was enough to increase the temporary panic. The

Neuland troops, who had never fought a pitched battle before, for all their Coalition-supplied modern weapons, lost their heads and began to do what any seasoned soldier would instinctively have avoided doing. Here and there they began to open up at the charging figures with energy weapons.

At the first touch of the fierce beams from the weapons, the shallow water exploded into clouds of steam—and in seconds the oncoming Dorsais were as effectively hidden as though the Neulanders had obligingly laid down a smoke screen for their benefit.

At that the panic in the first few ranks of the Neulanders broke completely into a rout. Their forward men turned and began trying to fight their way through the ranks behind them.

"Back!" Cletus ordered his charging Dorsais by battle phone. For, in spite of the temporary safety of the steam-fog that enveloped them, their mere handful of numbers was by now dangerously close to the mass soldiery of the Neulanders' force, as his plotting screen reported, even though vision was now obscured. "Get back! All the way back. We've done what we set out to do!"

Still under safety of the steam-fog, the Dorsais turned and retreated. Before they were back to the cover of the houses, the steam blew clear. But the Neulander front was still in chaos, and only a few stray shots chased the attackers back into safety.

Cletus brought them back to Dorsai HQ and climbed stiffly out of the battle car, whose air cushion hovered it above more than seven feet of water now lapping at the top of the steps leading to the main entrance of the building. He made a long step from the car to the threshold of the entrance and limped wearily inside toward the command room.

He was numb with exhaustion and he stumbled as he went. One of the younger officers in the building stepped over to take his arm, but Cletus waved him off. He limped shakily into the command room, and Eachan turned from the plotting screen to face him.

"Well done, sir," said Eachan slowly and softly. "Brilliantly done."

"Yes," replied Cletus thickly, too tired to make modest noises. On the screen before him the Neulanders were slowly getting themselves back into order. They were now a solid clump around and about the foot of the bluff. "It's all over."

"Not yet," said Eachan. "We can hold them off awhile yet."

"Hold them off?" The room seemed to waver and threaten to rotate dizzily about Cletus' burning eyes. "You won't have to hold them off. I mean it's all over. We've won."

"Won?"

As if through a gathering mist, Cletus saw Eachan staring at him strangely. A little clumsily, Cletus made it to the nearest chair and sat down.

"Tell Marc not to let them up to the top of the bluffs unless they surrender," he heard himself saying, as from a long way off. "You'll see."

He closed his eyes, and seemed to drop like a stone into the darkness. Eachan's voice reached down after him.

". . . Medic, here!" Eachan was snapping. "Damn it, hurry up!"

So it was that Cletus missed the last act of the battle at Two Rivers. From the moment of the Neulanders' momentary panic at being attacked by the Dorsais under Cletus' direction, trouble began to beset the six thousand soldiers from Neuland. It took them better than half an hour to restore order and make themselves ready to move forward upon the town again. But all that time the river level, raised by the work of Wefer's Mark V's, had been rising. Now it was up over the knees of the Neulanders themselves, and fear began to lay its cold hand upon them.

Ahead of them were certainly more Dorsai troops than they had been led to expect. Enough, at least, so that the Dorsais had not hesitated to mount an attack upon them. To go forward might cause them to be caught in a trap. Besides, to go forward was to go into steadily deepening water. Even the officers were uncertain—and caution suggested itself as the better part of valor. The word was given to withdraw.

In orderly manner, the two halves of the Neuland invading force split up and began to pull back along the river flats down which they had come. But, as they backed up, in each case, the width of the flat narrowed and soon the men farthest away from the bluff found themselves stumbling off into deeper water and the current pulling them away.

As more and more Neuland troopers were swept out into the main river current, struggling and splashing and calling for help, a new panic began to rise in the ranks of those still standing in shallow water. They began to crowd and jostle to get close to the bluff. Soon their organization began to dissolve. Within minutes, soldiers were breaking away from the ranks and beginning to climb directly up the bluffs toward the safety of high ground overhead.

But it was at this moment that Marc, following Cletus' earlier written orders, gave the command to his Dorsais lined up along the top of the bluff to fire down into these refugees from the rising waters. . . . And it was all over but the shouting.

They did not even have to call on the Neulanders to surrender. The panic-stricken colonists in uniform from over the mountains beyond Etter's Pass threw away weapons and began climbing the slope with their hands in the air, at first only a few, then mobs. By the time the sun was touching the western horizon, more than six thousand soldiers—as it was later to turn out, better than 70 percent of Neuland's army—sat huddled together as prisoners under the guns of their Dorsai guards.

But Cletus, still unconscious, knew none of this. Back in a room of the Dorsai HQ in Two Rivers, a prosthetic physician flown up from Bakhalla was straightening up from his examination of Cletus' swollen left knee, his face grave.

"How is it, Doctor?" asked Eachan Khan, sharply. "It's going to mend all right, isn't it?"

The physician shook his head and looked at Eachan soberly. "No, it isn't," the physician said. "He's going to lose the leg from just above the knee."

Chapter 16

"Prosthetic knee and ankle joints—in fact, prosthetic lower limbs," said the physician, patiently, "are really excellent. Inside of a couple of months after you've adapted to the prosthetic unit, you'll find yourself almost as mobile as you were before with that limp. Of course, no one likes to face the thought of an amputation, but—"

"It's not the thought of an amputation that worries me," interrupted Cletus. "I've got things to do that require two flesh and blood legs. I want a surgical replacement."

"I know," answered the doctor. "But you remember we ran tests on you and you've got an absolute level of rejection. All the evidence is that it's a case of psychological, not physiological, rejection. If that's the case, all the immune-suppressant drugs on the list can't help you. We can graft the leg on but your body's sure to reject it."

"You're sure it's a case of psychological rejection?" said Cletus.

"Your medical history shows you have a uniformly successful resistance to hypnosis, even under ordinary drugs," the doctor answered. "We find that kind of resistance almost always in people who exhibit psychological rejection of grafted organs, and whenever it's found we always—without exception—have psychological rejection. But just to put it to the test, I've brought along one of the new synthetic parahypnotic drugs. It leaves you conscious up to safe levels of dosage, but it absolutely anesthetizes volition. If you can resist hypnosis with that in you, then the resistance is below the levels even psychiatry can reach. It's probably a genetic matter. Do you want to try it?"

"Go ahead," said Cletus.

The doctor fastened the band of a hypnospray around Cletus' forearm, with the metered barrel of the drug poised above a large artery.

The level of the liquid in the barrel of the spray was visible. Resting his thumb and little finger on Cletus' arm on either side of the band, the doctor placed the top of his forefinger on the spray button.

"I'll keep asking you your name," he said. "Try not to tell me what it is. As you continue to refuse, I'll keep stepping up the dosage level. Ready?"

"Ready," said Cletus.

"What's your name?" asked the doctor. Cletus felt the cool breath of the hypnospray against the skin of his forearm.

Cletus shook his head.

"Tell me your name?" repeated the doctor.

Cletus shook his head. The cool feeling of the spray continued. Slightly to his surprise, Cletus felt no lightheadedness or any other indication that the drug was working on him.

"Tell me your name."

"No."

"Tell me your name . . ."

The questioning continued and Cletus continued to refuse. Abruptly, without warning, the room seemed filled with a white mist. His head whirled, and that was the last he remembered.

He drifted back into a weariness, to find the doctor standing over his bed. The hypnospray was unstrapped from his arm.

"No," said the doctor, and sighed. "You resisted right up to the point of unconsciousness. There's simply no point in trying a transplant."

Cletus gazed at him almost coldly. "In that case," he said, "will you tell Mondar the Exotic Outbond that I'd like to talk to him?"

The doctor opened his mouth as if to say something, closed it again, nodded and left.

A nurse came to the door. "General Traynor is here to see you, Colonel," she said. "Do you feel up to seeing him?"

"Certainly," said Cletus. He pressed the button on the side of the bed that raised the head section, lifting him up into a sitting position. Bat came in the door and stood beside the bed looking down at him; his face was like a stone mask.

"Sit down, sir," Cletus said.

"I'm not going to be here that long," said Bat.

He turned about to close the door of the room. Then he turned back to glare down at Cletus.

"I've just got two things to tell you," he said. "When I finally smashed the door open on the arms locker in your office and got a gun to shoot the hinges off the door, it was Sunday afternoon, so I made sure I got secretly out of town and phoned Colonel Dupleine quietly, before I made any fuss. You'll be glad to hear, then, there isn't going to be any fuss. Officially, I had a slight accident Friday afternoon a little ways outside of Bakhalla. My car went off the road. I was knocked unconscious and pinned in it. I wasn't able to get out until Sunday. Also, officially, what you did up at Two Rivers in capturing those Neulanders was done at my orders."

"Thank you, sir," said Cletus.

"Don't butter me up!" snarled Bat, softly. "You knew I was too bright to go around raising hell about your putting me out of the way until I'd found out what the score was. You knew I was going to do what I did. So let's not play games. You locked me up and nobody's ever going to know about it. But you captured two-thirds of the Neuland armed forces and *I'm* the one who's going to get most of the credit back in Geneva. That's the way things stand, and that's one of the two things I came to tell you."

Cletus nodded.

"The other thing's this," Bat said. "What you pulled off up there at Two Rivers was one hell of a piece of fine generalship. I can admire it. But I don't have to admire you. I don't like the way you work, Grahame, and I don't need you—and the Alliance doesn't need you. The second thing I came to tell you is this—I want your resignation. I want it on my desk inside of forty-eight hours. You can go back home and write books as a civilian."

Cletus looked at him quietly. "I've already submitted my resignation from the Alliance Military Service," he said. "I'm also giving up my citizenship as an Earth citizen. I've already made application for citizenship on the Dorsai, and it's been accepted."

Bat's eyebrows rose. For once his hard, competent face looked almost foolish. "You're skipping out on the Alliance?" he asked. "Completely?"

"I'm emigrating, that's all," said Cletus. He smiled a little at Bat. "Don't worry, General. I've no more interest in making public the fact that you were locked in my office over part of the weekend than you have. We'll assume a Neulander spy got into the office, found himself trapped and managed to break his way out."

Their eyes met. After a second, Bat shook his head. "Anyway," he said. "We won't be seeing each other again."

He turned and left. Cletus lay gazing at the ceiling until he fell asleep.

Mondar did not show up until the following afternoon; he apologized for not coming sooner.

"The message saying that you wanted to see me was sent through the regular mail," he said, sitting down in a chair at Cletus' bedside. "Evidently your good physician didn't see any urgency in your asking for me."

"No," said Cletus, "it's outside his area of knowledge."

"I think he assumed I'd have to tell you that I—or we Exotics, that is—couldn't help you either," said Mondar, slowly. "I'm afraid he may have been right. I called the hospital after I got your message and talked to someone I know on the staff here. I was told you've got a problem of almost certain psychological rejection of any organ graft."

"That's right," said Cletus.

"He said you thought that perhaps I—or perhaps some other Exotic, working with you, could succeed in overcoming such a psychological reaction long enough for a healthy leg to be grafted on you."

"It's not possible?" Cletus watched the Exotic closely as he spoke.

Mondar looked down and smoothed the blue robe covering his crossed knees. Then he looked back up at Cletus.

"It's not impossible," he said. "It'd be possible in the case, say, of someone like myself, who's trained in the areas of mental and physical self-control since he was a boy. I can ignore pain, or even consciously will my heart to stop beating, if I wish. I could also, if necessary, suppress my immune reactions—even if they included the kind of psychological rejection that afflicts you. . . . Cletus, you've got a tremendous amount of native talent, but you haven't had my years of training. Even with my assistance you wouldn't be able to control the rejection mechanism in your body."

"You're not the only one who can ignore pain," said Cletus. "I can do that too, you know."

"Can you?" Mondar looked interested. "Of course, come to think of it. Both after your first time up at Etter's Pass, and this last time at Two Rivers when you damaged the knee again, you did a good deal of moving around on it when ordinarily such movement should have been unendurable."

His eyes narrowed a little, thoughtfully. "Tell me—do you deny the pain—I mean do you refuse to admit the pain is there? Or do you *ignore* it—that is you remain conscious that the sensation is there but you don't allow the sensation to affect you?"

"I ignore it," answered Cletus. "I start out by relaxing to the point where I feel a little bit as though I'm floating. Just that much relaxation takes a lot of the sting out of the pain. Then I move in on what's left and more or less take the color out of it. What I'm left with is a little like a feeling of pressure. I can tell if it increases or decreases, or if it goes away entirely, but I'm not bothered by it in any way."

Mondar nodded slowly. "Very good. In fact, unusually good for self-trained," he said. "Tell me, can you control your dreams?"

"To a certain extent," said Cletus. "I can set up a mental problem before falling asleep, and work it out while I'm asleep—sometimes in the shape of a dream. I can also work out problems the same way while I'm awake by throwing a certain section of my mind out of gear, so to speak, and letting the rest of my body and mind run on automatic pilot."

Mondar gazed at him. Then he shook his head. But it was an admiring shake.

"You amaze me, Cletus," the Exotic said. "Would you try something for me? Look at that wall just to your left there, and tell me what you see."

Cletus turned his head away from Mondar and gazed at the flat, vertical expanse of white-painted wall. There was a small prickling sensation at the side of his neck just behind and below his right ear— followed by a sudden explosion of pain from the site of the prick, like the pain from the venom of a bee sting following the initial puncture. Cletus breathed out calmly; as the breath left his lungs, a crimson violence of the pain was washed clean and unimportant. He turned back to Mondar.

"I didn't see anything," he said, "of course."

"Of course. It was only a trick to get you to turn your head away," said Mondar, putting what looked like a miniature mechanical pencil back in his robes. "The amazing thing is, I wasn't able to measure any skin flinch, and that's a physiological reaction. Clearly your body hasn't much doubt about your ability to handle pain quickly."

He hesitated. "All right, Cletus," he said. "I'll work with you. But it's only fair to warn you that I still don't see any real chance of success. How soon do you want the transplant done?"

"I don't want it done," said Cletus. "I think you're probably quite right about the impossibility of suppressing my rejection mechanism. So we'll do something else. As long as it's a long shot anyway, let's try for a miracle cure."

"Miracle . . ." Mondar echoed the word slowly.

"Why not?" said Cletus cheerfully. "Miracle cures have been reported down through the ages. Suppose I undergo a purely symbolic operation. There's both flesh and bone missing from my left knee where the prosthetic unit was surgically implanted after I was first wounded years ago. I want that surgical implant taken out and some small, purely token portions of the flesh and bone from equivalent areas of my right knee transplanted into the area where the original flesh and bone is missing in the left. Then we cover both knees up with a cast"—his eyes met Mondar's—"and you and I concentrate hard while healing takes place."

Mondar sat for a second. Then he stood up.

"Anything is eventually possible," he murmured. "I've already said I'd help you. But this is something that's going to require some thought, and some consultation with my fellow Exotics. I'll come back to see you in a day or two."

The next morning Cletus had a visit from both Eachan Khan and Melissa. Eachan came in first, alone. He sat stiffly in the chair beside Cletus' bed. Cletus, propped up in a sitting position gazed at the older man keenly.

"Understand they're going to try to do something to fix that knee of yours," Eachan said.

"I twisted some arms," answered Cletus, smiling.

"Yes. Well, good luck." Eachan looked away, out the window of the room for a moment, and then back at Cletus. "Thought I'd bring you the good wishes of our men and officers," he said. "You promised them a victory almost without a casualty—and then you delivered it."

"I promised a battle," Cletus corrected, gently. "And I was hoping we wouldn't have much in the way of casualties. Besides, they deserve a good deal of credit themselves for the way they executed their battle orders."

"Nonsense!" said Eachan brusquely. He cleared his throat. "They all know you're emigrating to the Dorsai. All very happy about it. Incidentally, seems you started a small rash of emigrations. That young lieutenant of yours is coming over as soon as his shoulder heals up."

"You accepted him, didn't you?" Cletus asked.

"Oh, of course," Eachan said. "The Dorsai'll accept any military man with a good record. He'll have to pass through our officers' school, of course, if he wants to keep his commission with us, though. Marc Dodds told him there was no guarantee he'd make it."

"He will," said Cletus. "Incidentally, I'd like your opinion on something—now that I'm a Dorsai myself. If I supply the funds for subsistence, training facilities and equipment, do you suppose you could get together a regiment-sized body of officers and men who would be willing to invest six months in a complete retraining program—if I could guarantee them that at the end of that time they'd be able to find employment at half again their present pay?"

Eachan stared. "Six months is a long time for a professional soldier to live on subsistence," he said, after a moment. "But after Two Rivers, I think it just might be done. It's not just the hope of better pay, much as that means to a lot of these people who've got families back on the Dorsai. It's the better chance of staying alive to get back to the families that you might be able to give them. Want me to see about it?"

"I'd appreciate it," said Cletus.

"All right," said Eachan. "But where's the money to come from for all this?"

Cletus smiled. "I've got some people in mind," he said. "I'll let you know about that later. You can tell the officers and the men you contact that it's all conditional on my having the funds, of course."

"Of course." Eachan fingered his mustache. "Melly's outside."

"Is she?" asked Cletus.

"Yes. I asked her to wait while I had a word with you on some private matters first, before she came in . . ." Eachan hesitated. Cletus waited.

Eachan's back was as stiffly upright as a surveyor's rod. His jaw was clamped and the skin of his face was like stamped metal.

"Why don't you marry her?" he said, gruffly.

"Eachan . . ." Cletus checked himself and paused. "What makes you think Melissa would want to marry me, anyway?"

"She likes you," said Eachan. "You like her. You'd make a good team. She's mostly heart and you're nearly all head. I know you both better than you know each other."

Cletus shook his head slowly, for once finding no words ready to his tongue.

"Oh, I know she acts as if she knows all the answers when she doesn't, and acts like she wants to run my life, and yours, and everybody else's for them," went on Eachan. "But she can't help it. She does feel for people, you know—I mean, feel for what they're actually like, at core. Like her mother in that. And she's young. She feels something's so about someone and can't see why they don't do exactly what she thinks they ought to do, being who they really are. But she'll learn."

Cletus shook his head again. "And me?" he said. "What makes you think I'd learn?"

"Try it. Find out," retorted Eachan.

"And what if I made a mess of it?" Cletus looked up at him with more than a touch of grimness.

"Then at least you'll have saved her from deCastries," said Eachan, bluntly. "She'll go to him to make me follow her—to Earth. I will, too, to pick up the pieces. Because that's all that'll be left of her afterward—pieces. With some women it wouldn't matter, but I know my Melly. Do you want deCastries to have her?"

"No," said Cletus, suddenly quiet. "And he won't. I can promise you that, anyway."

"Maybe," said Eachan, getting to his feet. He swung about on his heel. "I'll send her in now," he said, and went out.

A moment or two later, Melissa appeared in the doorway. She smiled wholeheartedly at Cletus and came in to seat herself in the same chair Eachan had just vacated.

"They're going to fix your knee," she said. "I'm glad."

He watched her smile. And for a second there was an actual physical sensation in his chest, as though his heart had actually moved at the sight of her. For a second what Eachan had said trembled in his ears, and the guarded distance that life and people had taught him to keep about him threatened to dissolve.

"So am I," he heard himself saying.

"I was talking to Arvid today . . ." Her voice ran down. He saw her blue eyes locked with his, as if hypnotized and he became aware that he had captured her with his own relentless stare.

"Melissa," he said slowly, "what would you say if I asked you to marry me?"

"Please . . ." It was barely a whisper. He shifted his gaze, releasing her; she turned her head away.

"You know I've got Dad to think about, Cletus," she said, in a low voice.

"Yes," he said. "Of course."

She looked back, suddenly, flashing her smile at him, and put a hand on one of his hands, where it lay on the sheet.

"But I wanted to talk to you about all sorts of other things," she said. "You really are a remarkable man, you know."

"I am, am I?" he said, and summoned up a smile.

"You know you are," she said. "You've done everything just the way you said you would. You've won the war for Bakhalla, and done it all in just a few weeks with no one's help but the Dorsai troops. And now you're going to be a Dorsai yourself. There's nothing to stop you from writing your books now. It's all over."

Pain touched his innerself—and the guarded distance closed back around him. He was once more alone among people who did not understand.

"I'm afraid not," he said. "It's not over. Only the first act's finished. Actually, now it really begins."

She stared at him. "Begins?" she echoed. "But Dow's going back to Earth tonight. He won't be coming out here again."

"I'm afraid he will," said Cletus.

"He will? Why should he?"

"Because he's an ambitious man," said Cletus, "and because I'm going to show him how to further that ambition."

"Ambition!" Her voice rang with disbelief. "He's already one of the five Prime Secretaries of the Coalition Supreme Council. It's only a year or two, inevitably, until he'll get a seat on the Council itself. What else could he want? Look at what he's got already!"

"You don't quench ambition by feeding it any more than you quench a fire the same way," said Cletus. "To an ambitious man, what he already has is nothing. It's what he doesn't have that counts."

"But what doesn't he have?" She was genuinely perplexed.

"Everything," said Cletus. "A united Earth, under him, controlling all the Outworlds, again under him."

She stared at him. "The Alliance and the Coalition combine?" she said. "But that's impossible. No one knows that better than Dow."

"I'm planning to prove to him it is possible," said Cletus.

A little flush of anger colored her cheeks. "You're planning—" She broke off. "You must think I'm some kind of a fool, to sit and listen to this!"

"No," he said, a little sadly, "no more than anyone else. I'd just hoped that for once you'd take me on faith."

"Take you on faith!" Suddenly, almost to her own surprise, she was blindingly furious. "I was right when I first met you and I said you're just like Dad. Everybody thinks he's all leather and guns and nothing else, and the truth of the matter is, those things don't matter to him at all. Nearly everybody thinks you're all cold metal and calculation and no nerves. Well, let me tell you something—you don't fool everybody. You don't fool Dad, and you don't fool Arvid. Most of all, you don't fool me! It's people you care about, just like it's tradition Dad cares about—the tradition of honor and courage and truth and all those things nobody thinks we have any more. That's what they took away from him, back on Earth, and that's what I'm going to get back for him, when I get him back there, if I have to do it by main force—because he's just like you. He has to be made to take care of himself and get what he really wants."

"Did you ever stop to think," said Cletus, quietly, when she finished, "that perhaps he's found tradition all over again on the Dorsai?"

"Tradition? The Dorsai?" Scorn put a jagged edge on her voice. "A world full of a collection of ex-soldiers gambling their lives in other people's little wars for hardly more pay than a tool programmer gets! You can find tradition in that?"

"Tradition to come," said Cletus. "I think Eachan sees into the future further than you do, Melissa."

"What do I care about the future?" She was on her feet now, looking down at him where he lay in the bed. "I want him happy. He can take care of anyone but himself. I have to take care of him. When I was a little girl and my mother died she asked me—*me*—to be sure and take care of him. And I will."

She whirled about and went toward the door. "And he's all I'm going to take care of," she cried, stopping and turning again at the door. "If you think I'm going to take care of you, too, you've got another thing coming! So go ahead, gamble yourself twice over on some high principle or another, when you could be settling down and doing some real good, writing and working, person to person, the way you're built to do!"

She went out. The door was too well engineered to slam behind her, but that was all that saved it from slamming.

Cletus lay back against his pillows and gazed at the empty, white and unresponsive wall opposite. The hospital room felt emptier than it had ever felt before.

He had still one more visitor, however, before the day was out. This was Dow deCastries, preceded into Cletus' hospital room by Wefer Linet.

"Look whom I've got with me, Cletus!" said Wefer, cheerfully. "I ran into the Secretary here at the Officers' Club, where he was having lunch with some of the Exotics, and he told me to bring you his congratulations for abstract military excellence—as opposed to anything affecting the Neuland-Bakhalla situation. I asked him why he didn't come along and give you the congratulations himself. And here he is!"

He stepped aside and back, letting Dow come forward. Behind the taller man's back Wefer winked broadly at Cletus. "Got to run an errand here in the hospital," said Wefer. "Back in a minute."

He ducked out of the room, closing the door behind him. Dow looked at Cletus.

"Did you have to use Wefer as an excuse?" Cletus asked.

"He was convenient." Dow shrugged, dismissing the matter. "My congratulations, of course."

"Of course," said Cletus. "Thank you. Sit down, why don't you?"

"I prefer standing," said Dow. "They tell me you're going off to bury yourself on the Dorsai now. You'll be getting down to the writing of your books then?"

"Not just yet," said Cletus.

Dow raised his eyebrows. "There's something else for you to do?"

"There're half a dozen worlds and a few billion people to be freed first," said Cletus.

"Free them?" Dow smiled. "From the Coalition?"

"From Earth."

Dow shook his head. His smile became ironic. "I wish you luck," he said. "All this, in order to write a few volumes?"

Cletus said nothing. He sat upright in his bed, as if waiting. Dow's smile went away.

"You're quite right," Dow said, in a different tone, though Cletus still had not spoken. "Time is growing short, and I'm headed back to Earth this afternoon. Perhaps I'll see you there—say in six months?"

"I'm afraid not," said Cletus. "But I expect I'll see you out here among the new worlds. Say, inside two years?"

Dow's black eyes grew cold. "You badly misunderstand me, Cletus," he said. "I was never built to be a follower."

"Neither was I," said Cletus.

"Yes," said Dow, slowly, "I see. We probably will meet after all then"—his smile returned, suddenly and thinly—"at Phillippi."

"There never was any other place we could meet," said Cletus.

"I believe you're right. Fair enough," said Dow. He stepped backward and opened the door. "I'll wish you a good recovery with that leg of yours."

"And you, a safe trip to Earth," said Cletus.

Dow turned and went out. Several minutes later the door opened again and Wefer's head appeared in the opening.

"DeCastries gone?" Wefer asked. "He didn't talk long at all then."

"We said what we had to say," answered Cletus. "There wasn't much point in his staying, once we'd done that."

Chapter 17

Three days later, Mondar made his reappearance at Cletus' bedside.

"Well, Cletus," he said, sitting down in the chair by the bed, "I've spent most of my time since I saw you last going into your situation with other members of our group who've had more experience with certain aspects of what you suggested than I have. All together we worked out a pattern of behavior that looks as if it might give the greatest possible encouragement to the miracle you're after. The main question seemed to be whether it would be better for you to be intimately acquainted with the physiology of your knees, and the process of tissue growth and regrowth, or whether it would be better for you to have as little knowledge of it as possible."

"What was the decision?" Cletus asked.

"We decided it would be best if you knew as little as possible," Mondar said. "The point is, the stimulus for what's going to be essentially an abnormal body reaction has to come from a very primitive level of the organism—you being the organism."

"You don't want me visualizing what's going on then?"

"Just the opposite," answered Mondar. "You should remove your concern with the regrowth process as completely as possible from any symbolic area. Your determination to achieve regrowth must be channeled downward into the instinctive level. To achieve that channeling you're going to need practice, and so we worked up a set of exercises that I'm going to teach you to do over the next two weeks. I'll come here and work with you daily until you can do the exercises by yourself. Then I'll observe until I think you've got complete control in the necessary areas. Then we'll recommend the symbolic operation, in which the genetic pattern of your right knee will be transferred in the form of a few cells of tissue of flesh and bone to the area of the left knee, where we want regrowth to take place."

"Good," said Cletus. "When do you want to start the exercises?"

"Right now, if you like," answered Mondar. "We start out by getting off the topic of your knees entirely and into some completely different area. Any suggestions for a topic?"

"The best one in the universe," Cletus answered. "I was intending to talk to you about it anyway. I'd like to borrow two million IMU's."

Mondar gazed at him for a second, then smiled. "I'm afraid I don't have that much with me," he said. "After all, out here away from Earth two million International Monetary Units are rather more scarce than they are back on Earth. Are you very urgent about your need for them?"

"Urgent and absolutely serious," replied Cletus. "I'd like you to talk to your fellow Exotics here in Bakhalla—and anywhere else, if necessary. I'm not wrong, am I, in thinking your organization could lend me that kind of money if you thought it was worthwhile?"

"Not wrong, no," said Mondar, slowly. "But you have to admit it's a rather unusual request from an essentially propertyless ex-colonel in the Alliance forces who's now an emigrant to the Dorsai. What do you plan doing with a sum of money like that?"

"Build an entirely new type of military unit," Cletus answered. "New in organization, training, hardware and tactical abilities."

"Using," said Mondar, "the Dorsai mercenaries, of course?"

"That's right," answered Cletus. "I'm going to produce a fighting force at least five times as effective as any comparable military unit presently in existence. Such a force will be able to underbid not only the Alliance, but the Coalition, when it comes to supplying military force to an off-Earth colony such as yours. I can raise the pay of the men and officers in it and still market an effective force for less than even the Dorsai mercenaries were charging in the past—simply because we'll need less men to do the same job."

"And you're suggesting," Mondar said, thoughtfully, "that such a mercenary force would soon pay back a two million loan?"

"I don't think there's any doubt of it," said Cletus.

"Possibly not," said Mondar, "provided these new mercenaries of yours will do what you say they'll do. But how could anyone know that in advance? I'm afraid, Cletus, that our organization would need some kind of security before lending out such a very large amount of money."

"Security," said Cletus, "is often unnecessary where the borrower's reputation is good."

"Don't tell me you've borrowed two million IMU's on occasions before this?" Mondar raised his eyebrows quizzically.

"I was speaking of a military, not a financial, reputation," Cletus said calmly. "Your Exotics have just had the best possible proof of the military reputation in question. A small group of Dorsai mercenaries, single-handedly, have succeeded in doing what a very large and much better equipped Alliance force wasn't able to do—essentially destroy Neuland as a military power and win the local war for your colony. The conclusion to be drawn from that is that this colony of yours doesn't need the Alliance forces. It can protect itself perfectly adequately with its Dorsai mercenaries, alone. Am I right?"

"You certainly present a good argument," said Mondar.

"The security for the loan, therefore," said Cletus, "is the best sort of security in the world. It's the literal security of this colony, guaranteed by the Dorsai mercenaries until the loan is paid back."

"But what if . . . ah . . . ." Mondar said, delicately, "you Dorsai should default on your bargain? I don't mean to insult you, of course, but in matters like this all possibilities are going to have to be considered. If I don't bring up the question, someone else will. What if, after we'd lent you the money and you'd retrained your troops, you refused either to pay or to continue guaranteeing the security of this colony?"

"In that case," said Cletus, spreading his hands on the sheet of the bed, "who else would hire us? Successful mercenaries, like traders in any other goods, build their business on the basis of satisfied customers. If we took your money and then welshed on our agreement, what other colony would be willing to take a chance on us?"

Mondar nodded. "A very good point," he said. He sat for a moment, his gaze abstracted, as if he communed with himself in some secret corner of his brain. Then his eyes came back to Cletus.

"Very well," he said, "I'll convey your request for a loan to my fellow Exotics. That's as much as I can do, you realize. It'll take some little time for the matter to be considered, and I can't promise you any great hopes of success. As I said, it's a very large amount of IMU's you're asking to borrow, and there is, after all, no great reason why we should lend it."

"Oh, I think there is," said Cletus easily. "If my estimate of you Exotics is correct, one of your eventual aims is to be completely independent of outside obligations—so that you can be free to work out your vision of the future without interference. The Alliance's military aid has been helpful to you, but it's also kept you under the Alliance's thumb. If you can buy security from mercenary soldiers without obligation, you'll have achieved a freedom that I think you all want very badly. A two million unit loan on good security is a small risk to take for the chance of gaining that freedom."

He looked significantly at Mondar. Mondar shook his head slightly; there was a touch of admiration in his face.

"Cletus, Cletus," said Mondar, "what a waste it is, your not being an Exotic!" He sighed, and sat back in the chair. "Well, I'll pass your request for a loan along. And now, I think it's time we got started with your exercises. Sit back and try to achieve that state of a floating sensation that you described to me. As you probably know, it's called a state of regression. I'm also putting myself now into such a state. Now, if you're ready, join me in concentration on that isolated pinpoint of life, that single sperm cell that was the first core and beginning of your consciousness. To that early and primitive consciousness, now, you must try to return."

Three weeks later, healing well and with both legs stiffened by a walking cast about each knee, Cletus was swinging along on wrist-crutches with Arvid in the Bakhalla in-town terminal. They were headed toward the airbus that would lift them to that same shuttleboat landing pad on which Cletus had first set down on Kultis a couple of months before—the airbus being made necessary by new construction on the road to the pad, now that guerrilla activity had been halted.

As they passed the main lounge of the terminal, an Alliance officer stepped out in front of them. He was First Lieutenant Bill Athyer, and he was drunk—not drunk enough to stumble in his speech or his walk, but drunk enough to bar their way with an ugly light in his eye. Cletus halted. Arvid took half a step forward, opening his mouth, but Cletus stilled the young man with a hand on one massive arm.

"Leaving for the Dorsai, are you, Colonel?" said Athyer, ignoring Arvid. "Now that everything's nice and prettied up here, you're on your way?"

Cletus leaned on the crutches. Even bent over in this position, he had to look down to meet Athyer's bloodshot eyes.

"Thought so." Athyer laughed. "Well, sir, I didn't want to let you get away, sir, without thanking you. I might have gone up before a review board, if it hadn't been for you, sir. Thank you, sir."

"That's all right, Lieutenant," said Cletus.

"Yes, isn't it? Quite all right," said Athyer. "And I'm safely tucked away in a library instead of facing a reprimand and maybe losing one turn at an advance in grade. No danger of my getting out in the field where I might foul up again—or, who knows, might even make up for not being quite as smart as you up at Etter's Pass, sir."

"Lieutenant..." Arvid began in a dangerous rumble.

"No," said Cletus, still leaning on the crutches, "let him talk."

"Thank you, Colonel. Thank you, sir.... Damn you, Colonel"—
Athyer's voice broke suddenly, raw-throated—"did your precious reputation mean so much to you that you had to bury me alive? At least
you could've let me take my lumps fair and square, without any show-
off kindness from you! Don't you know I'll never get another chance
in the field now? Don't you know you've marked me for good? What
am I supposed to do now, stuck in a library for the rest of my army
life with nothing but books?"

"Try reading them!" Cletus made no attempt to hold his voice
down. It carried clearly to the crowd that by now was listening, and
the scorn in it was, for once in his life, cruel and unsparing. "That
way, you just might learn something about the handling of troops in
combat.... Come along, Arv."

He swung his crutches out to one side and went around Athyer.
Arvid followed. Behind them, as the crowd closed in about them once
more, they heard Athyer's hoarse, pursuing shout:

"I'll read, all right!" it rang behind them. "And I'll keep reading
until I've got the goods on you—*Colonel*!"

Chapter 18

Six months later, Cletus was not only successfully healed, but ready to begin upon the work he had anticipated, in emigrating to the Dorsai. Entering the last two miles of his fifteen-mile daily run, he leaned into the beginning of the long slope up the hill that would bring him back to the shore of Lake Athan across from the home of Eachan Khan on the outskirts of the town of Foralie, on that world known as the Dorsai. His stride shortened, his breathing deepened, but aside from these changes there was no difference. He did not slacken speed.

It had been nearly five months now since the casts had been taken off his legs to reveal a perfectly healthy, regrown left knee. The local medical fraternity had been eager to keep him available for tests and study of the essential miracle that had occurred, but Cletus had other things to do. Within a week, tottering along on legs that had just begun to relearn how to walk, he took ship with Melissa and Eachan Khan for the Dorsai. He had been here since, his engagement to Melissa an accepted fact, as a guest in Eachan's household, and the time from his arrival until now had been spent in unrelenting physical self-training.

The methods of that training were simple, and except in one respect, orthodox. Basically, he spent his days in walking, running, swimming and climbing. It was the climbing that provided the one unorthodox element to this routine, for Cletus had caused to be built, and continually added to since its construction, a sort of adult-sized jungle gym, a maze of steel pipes interconnected at different heights and angles that was now some thirty feet high, twenty feet wide and more than fifty feet long.

Cletus' day began now, six months after his departure from the hospital on Kultis, with a vertical climb, hands only and without pause, from the ground to the top of a rope suspended from a tree limb eighty feet above ground. Having reached the limb, he then moved a dozen feet farther out along its length, climbed down a shorter rope only fifty feet in length and set it swinging until the arc of his airborne travels brought him close enough to the top bar of the jungle gym for him to catch hold. The next thirty minutes or so were spent in clambering through the jungle gym by routes that had grown increasingly complex and torturous as the gym had been extended and Cletus' physical condition had improved.

At the far end of the jungle gym, his morning's run—which, as has been said, was now fifteen miles—began. It was a run that began across country of a fairly level surface, but later led him among a variety of the steep hills and slopes that this mountainous territory provided. Here the altitude was eighty-four hundred feet above sea level, and the effect upon Cletus' red blood cell count and coronary artery size had been remarkable.

It ended with this long, steady uphill slope two miles in length. Just beyond the upper end of the slope, the ground dipped down again for about fifty yards among pine-like trees, and Cletus came to the edge of Lake Athan.

He did not even break stride as he approached the bank, but went off it in a shallow dive directly into the waters of the lake. He surfaced and began swimming the half-mile distance across the lake to the shore above which the long, low-roofed, rather rustic shape of Eachan's house could be seen, small among trees.

The water of this mountain lake was cold, but Cletus was not chilled by it. His body, heated by the run, found it pleasantly cool. He swam, as he had done all the rest of his exercise, dressed in running shoes, socks, shorts and shirt; he was by now so accustomed to the weight of these water-heavy shoes and clothes upon him that he did not notice them.

He swam powerfully, arms digging deep, his head rolling rhythmically toward his right shoulder to take deep breaths of the upland air. His feet churned a steady wake behind him. Almost before he had settled to the soothing rhythm of his swimming, he drove into the shallow water at the lake's other side and got to his feet.

He glanced at his wristwatch and trotted leisurely up the slope to the ground-floor sliding window that led directly into his bedroom. Ten minutes later, showered and changed, he joined Eachan and Melissa in the sunny dining room of the long house for lunch.

"How did you do?" asked Melissa. She smiled at him with a sudden, spontaneous warmth, and a warm current of shared feeling sprang into existence between them. Six months of close association had destroyed all obvious barriers separating them. Cletus was too likable and Melissa too outgoing for them not to be drawn together under such close conditions. They had reached the stage now where what they did not say to each other was almost more important than their words.

"Under six minutes average on the fifteen-mile run," he answered. "A little over ten minutes crossing the lake." He looked over at Eachan. "I think it's time to set up that demonstration I planned. We can use the running track in the stadium at Foralie."

"I'll attend to it," said Eachan.

Three days later the demonstration took place. Present in the Foralie stadium under a warm August sun were the eighty-odd ranking Dorsai officers whom Eachan had invited. They sat down front in one section of the stand before a large screen fed by a battery of physiological monitoring equipment tuned to various transmitters on and within Cletus' body.

Cletus was in his usual running outfit. Neither the jungle gym nor a pool for swimming was in evidence, since this was to be a simple demonstration of endurance. As soon as the visiting officers were all seated, Eachan stood by to monitor the reports of various instruments onto the screen so that all could see them, and Cletus started running.

The various mercenary officers present had all been made acquainted with Cletus' history, particularly the events on Kultis, and the near miraculous regrowth of his wounded knee. They watched with interest while Cletus set a pace of nearly ten miles an hour around the half-mile track. After the first mile, he dropped back to a little better than eight miles an hour; his pulse, which had peaked at 170, dropped to about 140 and hung there.

He was running quite easily and breathing steadily as he approached the four-mile mark. But then, although his speed did not decrease, his pulse began to climb once more, slowly, until by the end of the six miles it was almost up to 180. Here it peaked again, and from that point on he began slowly to lose speed. By the time he had completed the eighth mile he was down below seven miles an hour, and by the time he finished the ninth he was barely moving at six miles an hour.

Clearly, he was approaching the exhaustion point. He pushed himself twice more around the track. Coming up toward the end of the tenth mile, he was barely jogging. Clearly, he had run himself out; but this kind of performance by anyone, let alone a man who had been a prosthetic cripple half a standard year before, was enough to waken a hum of amazement and admiration from the watchers.

Some of them stood up in their seats, ready to step down into the field and congratulate Cletus as he tottered toward the conclusion of the tenth mile, which seemed obviously intended to be the end of the race.

"Just a minute, please, gentlemen," Eachan Khan said. "If you'll hold your seats a little longer . . ."

He turned and nodded to Cletus, who was now passing the ten-mile mark directly in front of the viewers. Cletus nodded and kept on going.

Then, to the utter astonishment of the watchers, a remarkable thing happened. As Cletus continued around the track, his step became firmer and his breathing eased. He did not immediately pick up speed, but his pulse rate, as shown on the viewing screen, began slowly to fall.

At first it went down by ragged steps, dropping a few beats, holding firm, then dropping a few more. But as he continued, it began to drop more steadily. By the time he was back around in front of the watching officers, his pulse rate was again 150.

And his speed began to pick up. It did not pick up much; he gained back to just under six miles an hour. But he held steady at that pace, continuing to circle the track.

He ran six more laps of the track—three miles—and at the end of the third mile his speed and pulse rate were still constant.

At the end of that additional third mile he stopped running, walked a lap without any sign of unusual distress, and ended up in front of the watching group, breathing normally and hardly perspiring, with his pulse in the low seventies.

"That's it, gentlemen," he said, addressing them all. "Now I'm going to have to take a few moments to clean up, and the rest of you may adjourn to Eachan's house, where we'll be able to talk in more comfort and privacy. I'll join you there in about twenty minutes, and I'll leave you now to consider what you've just seen without any further explanation, except that what you've just seen me do, did, in fact, exact a penalty upon my bodily reserves greater than that ordinarily demanded by exertion. However, as you see, it was possible and practical, at that price."

He turned away toward the dressing room at the near end of the stadium. The spectators moved outside to an airbus rented by Eachan, and were flown out to Eachan's house, where the window wall along one side of the long living room had been opened up so that the living room and the patio outside became one large gathering space. Food and drink had been provided, and there, a little later, Cletus joined them.

"As you know," he said, standing facing them as they sat in a rough semicircle in chairs about him, "all of you here were officers we invited because I hoped you might be interested in joining me in forming an entirely new military unit, a military unit I intend to command, and which would pay its officers and men only subsistence during a training period of some months, but which would thereafter pay them at least double the rate they had been receiving as mercenaries up until this time. It goes without saying that I want the cream of the crop, and that I expect that cream of the crop to invest not merely their time but their wholehearted enthusiasm in this new type of organization I have in mind."

He paused. "That was one of the reasons for the demonstration you've just seen," he said. "What you saw, in the crudest terms, was a demonstration in which I was at least half again as physically effective as my bodily energy level and conditioning would allow me to be. In short, I've just given you an example of how a man can make himself into a man and a half."

He paused again, and this time he raked his eyes over every face in the audience before he continued.

"I am going to expect," he said, slowly and emphatically, "every enlisted man and officer in this military unit I'm forming to be able to multiply himself to at least that extent by the time he's finished training. This is a first prerequisite, gentlemen, to anyone wishing to join me in this venture."

He smiled, unexpectedly. "And now, relax and enjoy yourselves. Stroll around the place, look at my homemade training equipment, and ask as many questions as you like of Eachan, Melissa Khan or myself. We'll have another meeting out here in a few days' time for those of you who have decided to join us. That's all."

He stepped away from the center of their attention and made his way to the buffet tables where the food and drink had been set up. The gathering broke up into small groups and the hum of voices arose. By late afternoon most of the visitors had left, some twenty-six of them having pledged their services to Cletus before leaving. A somewhat larger number had promised to think it over and get in touch with him within the next two days. There remained a small group of those who had already pledged themselves to Cletus before the demonstration, and these met in the once more enclosed living room after dinner for a private conference.

Present were Arvid, now recovered from his shoulder wound, Major Swahili and Major David Ap Morgan, whose family was also a Foralie neighbor. Eachan's other officers were still back in Bakhalla commanding the force of Dorsais that remained there in Exotic pay to guard the colony, now that the Alliance had withdrawn its troops under Bat Traynor. Bat's misgivings about leaving had not been shared by Alliance HQ back on Earth, which had been overjoyed to free nearly half a division of men to reinforce its hard-pressed military commitments on half a dozen other new worlds. In addition to Arvid, Ap Morgan, Swahili and Eachan, himself, were two old friends of Eachan's—a Colonel Lederle Dark and a Brigadier General Tosca Aras. Dark was a thin, bald man who seemed to be all bone and long muscle under a somewhat dandified exterior. Tosca Aras was a small, neat, clean-shaven man with washed-out blue eyes and a gaze as steady as an aimed field rifle in its gun mount.

"By the end of the week," Cletus said to them all, "anyone who hasn't made up his mind to join us won't be worth having. From those I talked to today, I estimate we'll get perhaps fifty good officers, perhaps ten of which we'll lose in training. So there's no point in wasting time. We can start setting up a table of organization and a training schedule. We'll train the officers, and they can train their men afterward."

"Who's to be in charge of the extra energy training?" asked Lederle Dark.

"I'll have to be, to begin with," Cletus answered him. "Right now there's nobody else. And all of you will have to join the other officers in my classes on that. The rest of it you can all handle by yourselves—it's simply a matter of running them through the physical and practicing standard field problems, but from the viewpoint of the new organizational setup."

"Sir," said Arvid, "excuse me, but I still don't seem to really understand why we need to shake up the whole table of organization—unless you want it different just so the men in this outfit will feel that much more different."

"No—though the feeling of difference isn't going to do us any harm," Cletus said. "I should have gone into this with all of you before now. The plain fact of the matter is that a military body structured into squads, platoons, companies, battalions and so on is designed to fight the type of war that used to be common but which we aren't going to be encountering out here on the new worlds. Our fighting units are going to bear more resemblance to a group of athletes in a team sport than they are to the old type of fighting unit. The tactics they're going to be using—my tactics—aren't designed for structured armies in solid confrontation with each other. Instead, they're designed to be useful to what seems to be a loose group of almost independently acting units, the efforts of which are coordinated not so much by a hierarchy of command as by the fact that, like good members of a team, they're familiar with each other and can anticipate what their teammates will do in response to their own actions and the general situation."

Cletus paused and looked around him. "Are there any of the rest of you who don't understand that?" he asked.

Eachan cleared his throat. "We all understand what you say, Cletus," he said. "But what the words are going to mean when they're turned into battle units is something we've got to see before it'll make much sense. Here you cut the squad to six men—and that's divided into two teams of three men each. You make four squads to a group, with a senior or junior groupman in charge, and two groups make up a force. It's plain enough, but how's anyone going to know how it'll work until they see it in practice?"

"They aren't. You aren't—of course," answered Cletus. "But what you can do now is absorb the theory of it, and the reasoning behind the theory. Shall I go over it again?"

There was a moment of silence.

"Probably better," said Eachan.

"All right then," said Cletus. "As I think I've told you all, the basic principle is that, from the individual right up to the largest organizations within the total Dorsai military command, each unit should be capable of reacting like a single member of a team made up of other members equal in size and importance to himself. That is, any one of the three soldiers in any given half squad should be able to operate in perfect unison with the other two members of his team with no more communication than a few code words or signals that would cue the others to standard actions or responses to any given situation. Similarly, the two teams in any squad should be able to work as partners with no more than a few code words or signals. Likewise, the four squads should be able to operate as a team in the group with each squad knowing its role in any one of a hundred or more group actions identifiable by code word or signal. Just as the two groups must be able to react together almost instinctively as a single command, the commandant of which should likewise be trained to react in pattern with the commandants of the commands with which he is associated."

Cletus stopped talking. Once more there was the small silence.

"You say you'll supply the patterns?" Tosca Aras said. "I mean you'll work out all these team actions that are triggered by code words and signals and so forth?"

"I already have them worked out," said Cletus.

"You have?" Aras' voice teetered on the edge of incredulity. "There must be thousands of them."

Cletus shook his head. "Something over twenty-three thousand, to be exact," he said. "But I think you may be missing the point. The actions of a team are included within the actions of the squad, just as the actions of the squad are included within the actions of the group. In short, it's like a language with twenty-three thousand words. There are innumerable combinations, but there's also a logical structure. Once you master the structure, then the choice of words within the sentence is severely restricted. In fact, there's only one ideal choice."

"Then why have such a complicated setup anyway?" asked David Ap Morgan.

Cletus turned to look at the young major. "The value of the system," he said, "doesn't come so much from the fact that there are a large number of combinations of tactical actions ranging from the team on up through the command, but from the fact that any large choice of action implies a certain spectrum of choices of action for the lesser elements of the command, so that the individual soldier, on hearing the general code word for the command to which he belongs, knows immediately within what limits the actions of all the groups, all the squads and his own team must be."

He paused. "In short," he said, "no one, right up through the battle operator or the commander of the total military unit, simply follows orders. Instead, they all—right down to the individual line soldier— react as a team member in a common effort. The result is that breaks in the chain of command, misunderstood or incorrect orders, and all the other things that go to mess up a battle plan by mischance, are bypassed. Not only that, but from the lowest ranks on up each subordinate is ready to step into the position of his superior with 90 per cent of the necessary knowledge that his superior had at the moment the superior was put out of action."

Arvid gave a low whistle of admiration. The other officers in the room all looked at him. With the exception of Cletus, he was the only one among them who had never been a practicing Dorsai field officer. Arvid looked embarrassed.

"A revolutionary concept," said Tosca Aras. "More than revolutionary if it works out in practice."

"It's going to have to work," said Cletus. "My whole scheme of strategy and tactics is based upon troops that can operate along those lines."

"Well, we'll see." Aras picked up the thick manual Cletus had issued to each of them just after dinner and which had been lying since then in his lap. He stood up. "An old dog learning new tricks is an understatement in my case. If the rest of you gentlemen don't mind I'll be getting to my homework."

He said good night and went out, starting a general exodus. Eachan stayed behind, and Arvid—Arvid, to apologize for that whistle.

"You see, sir," he said earnestly to Cletus, "it suddenly came clear to me, all of a sudden. I hadn't seen it before. But now I see how it all ties together."

"Good," said Cletus. "That's half the learning process done for you right there."

Arvid followed the others out of the living room. Eachan alone was left. Cletus looked at him.

"Do *you* see how it all hangs together?" Cletus asked him.

"Think so," said Eachan. "But remember, I've been living with you for the last half year—and I know most of the patterns in that manual of yours already."

He reached for the decanter behind the glasses ranked on the small table beside his chair and thoughtfully poured himself a small amount of whiskey.

"Shouldn't expect too much too soon," he said, sipping at it. "Any military man's bound to be a bit conservative. In the nature of us. But they'll come through, Cletus. It's beginning to be more than just a name with us here, this business of being Dorsais."

He turned out to be correct. By the time the officers' training program got under way a week later, all of those who had sat in the living room with Cletus that night knew their manuals by heart—if not yet quite by instinct. Cletus divided the officers to be trained among the six of them, in groups of roughly ten each, and training began.

Cletus took the class that he had labeled simply "Relaxation," the course that would train these officers to tap that extra source of energy he had demonstrated to them all at the Foralie stadium after running himself to the normal exhaustion point. His first class consisted of the six from the living room. Eachan was among them, although he already had more than a faint grasp of the technique involved. Cletus had been privately tutoring both him and Melissa in it for the past couple of months, and both had become noticeably capable with it. However, it was Eachan's suggestion—and Cletus found it a good one—that his inclusion in the class would be an example to the others that someone besides Cletus could achieve unusual physiological results.

Cletus began his class just before lunch, after they had completed the full day's physical training schedule, consisting of jungle gym, run and swim. They were physically unwound by the exercise, and more than a little empty because of the long hours since breakfast. In short, they were in a condition of maximum receptivity.

Cletus lined them up behind a long steel bar supported between two posts at about shoulder height off the ground.

"All right," he said to them. "Now I want you all to stand on your right legs. You can reach out and touch the bar in front of you with your fingertips to help keep your balance, but take your left feet off the ground and keep them off until I tell you you can put them down again."

They complied. Their pose was a little on the ridiculous side, and there were a few smiles at first, but these faded as the legs on which they stood began to tire. About the time when bearing all their weight upon the muscle of one leg was beginning to become actively painful, Cletus ordered them to switch legs and kept them standing with all their weight on their left legs until the muscles of calf and thigh began to tremble under their full body weight. Then he switched them back to the right leg, and then again to the left, shortening the intervals each time as the leg muscles became exhausted more quickly. Very shortly they stood before him on legs as uncertain as those of men who had been bedridden for a period of weeks.

"All right, now," Cletus said then, cheerfully, "I want you all up in a handstand, the palms of your hands on the ground, your arms fully extended. You can balance yourselves this time by letting your legs rest against the bar."

They obeyed. Once they were all up, Cletus gave them a further order.

"Now," he said, "one hand off the ground. Do your handstand on one arm only."

When they were upside down, he went through the same process he had when they had been right side up. Only it took their arms a fraction of the time it had taken their legs to tire. Very shortly he released them from their exercise, and they all tumbled to the ground, virtually incapacitated in all their limbs.

"On your backs," ordered Cletus. Legs straight out, arms at your sides—but you don't have to lie at attention. Just straighten out on your back comfortably. Eyes on the sky."

They obeyed.

"Now," said Cletus, pacing slowly up and down before them, "I want you just to lie there and relax while I talk to you. Watch the sky . . ." It was one of those high, bright blue skies with a few clouds drifting lazily across it. "Concentrate on the feeling in your arms and legs, now that they've been relieved from the load of supporting your bodies against the force of gravity. Be conscious of the fact that now it's the ground supporting you—and them—and be grateful for it. Feel how heavy and limp your arms and legs are, now that they've given up the work of bearing weight, and are themselves being borne by the surface of the ground. Tell yourself—not out loud—in your own words how limp and heavy they are. Keep telling yourself that and watching the sky. Feel how heavy and relaxed your body is, with its weight being supported by the ground beneath your back. Feel the relaxation in your neck, in the muscles of your jaw, in your face, even in your scalp. Tell yourself how relaxed and heavy all these parts of you are and keep watching the sky. I'll be going on talking, but pay no attention to me. Just give all your attention to what you're telling yourself and what you're feeling and how the sky looks . . ."

He continued to pace up and down talking. After a while, the arm- and leg-weary men, soothed by their relaxed position and the slow movement of the clouds, lulled by the steady, pleasant, monotonous sound of his voice, ceased in fact to pay any attention to the sense of his words. He was merely talking. To Arvid, at one end of the line, Cletus' voice seemed to have gone off and become as remote as everything else about him. Lying on his back, Arvid saw nothing but sky. It was as if the planet beneath him did not exist, except as a soft grassy pressure at his back, bearing him up. The clouds moved slowly in the endless blue, and he seemed to drift along with them.

A nudge at his feet brought him suddenly and sharply back to consciousness. Cletus was smiling down at him.

"All right," Cletus said, in the same steady low tone, "on your feet and step over there."

Arvid obeyed, getting heavily upright once more, and moving off, as Cletus had indicated, about a dozen feet. The rest were still on the ground, with Cletus talking to them. Then he saw Cletus, who was still pacing, pause at the feet of David Ap Morgan and nudge the sole of David's right foot with his toe.

"All right, David," Cletus said, without breaking the pace or tone of his talking, "up you get and join Arvid over there."

David's eyes, which had been closed, jerked open. He got to his feet and went over to stand by Arvid. As the two of them watched, one by one other members of the class went to sleep and were quietly wakened and weeded out until no one but Eachan still lay on the grass, his eyes wide open.

Cletus abruptly ended his talking with a chuckle. "All right, Eachan," he said. "There's no point in my trying to put you to sleep. You get up and join the others."

Eachan rose. On their feet and all together once more, the class looked at Cletus.

"The idea," said Cletus, with a smile, "is *not* to fall asleep. But we won't worry about that for a while yet. How many of you remember feeling any kind of a floating sensation before you did drop off?"

Arvid and three others raised their hands. Eachan was one of them.

"Well, that's it for today," Cletus said. "Tomorrow we'll try it without the muscle-tiring exercises first. But I want you all to go back to your quarters and try doing this again, by yourself, at least three times before tomorrow morning. If you like, you can try putting yourself to sleep tonight with it. We'll gather together here again tomorrow, at this same place at the same time."

In the next few sessions Cletus worked with the class until all of them could achieve the floating sensation without drifting off into sleep. With this accomplished, he led them by easy stages into auto-control of pain and deep bodily sensations. When they had become fairly adept at this, he began to move them gradually from a relaxed and motionless position into movement—first getting them to achieve the floating sensation while standing upright, then when walking slowly and rhythmically forward, and finally under any kind of activity up to the most violent. This achieved, there remained for them only the ability to make use of the trance state in various types of autocontrol under all conditions of activity, and he turned them loose to become teachers, in their turn to the other officers in training—who would, again, pass on the training to the enlisted men under their command.

By this time nearly three months had gone by, and the officers in training had advanced to the point where they could begin to pass on at least the physical end of their training to the troops that would be under their orders. Recruitment was started for Dorsais to fill the enlisted ranks—and for some few extra Dorsai officers to replace those who had dropped out of the training program.

Just at this time Cletus received a thick envelope of clippings sent him by a news-clipping service on Earth he had contacted before leaving Bakhalla. He opened the envelope, alone in Eachan's study, and spread the clippings out in order of their dates to examine them.

The story they told was simple enough. The Coalition, sparked by a few key speeches by Dow deCastries himself, was attempting to raise a storm of protest against mercenary troop on the new worlds in general, and the Dorsais in particular.

Cletus replaced the clippings in their envelope and filed them in the cabinet holding his own correspondence. He went out on the terrace to find Melissa there reading.

It was high summer in these Dorsai mountains, and the sun was in late afternoon position above the farther peaks. He paused for a moment, watching her as she sat unsuspecting that he watched. In the clear sunlight, her face was untroubled, and somehow more mature-looking than he remembered it back at Bakhalla.

He went out onto the terrace and she looked up from her reading spool at the sound of his feet. He caught her gaze with his own, and her eyes widened a little at the seriousness with which he stood looking down at her. After a minute he spoke.

"Will you marry me, then, Melissa?" he said.

The blueness of her eyes was as deep as the universe itself. Once again, as it had in the hospital in Bakhalla, her gaze seemed to evaporate the barrier of protective loneliness that his experience with life and people had led him to build about him. She looked up at him for a long moment before answering.

"If you really want me, Cletus," she said.

"I do," he replied.

And he did not lie. But, as the protective barrier flowed once more into position about his inner self, even as he continued to match her gaze with his, a cold interior part of his mind reminded him of the necessity that there would be now to lie, hereafter.

Chapter 19

The wedding was set for a day two weeks away. Meanwhile, Cletus, seeing the formation of the force he had begun to raise on the Dorsai now beginning to operate under its own momentum, took time out for a trip back to Kultis and Bakhalla for a conversation with Mondar, and a farther trip to Newton seeking employment for the newly trained Dorsais of his command.

On Bakhalla, he and Mondar had an excellent dinner at Mondar's residence. Over the dinner table Cletus brought the Exotic up to date. Mondar listened with interest, which increased visibly when Cletus got into the matter of the special training in autocontrol he had initiated for the officers and men who would be under his command. After the dinner was over, they strolled out onto one of the many terraces of Mondar's home to continue their talk under the night sky.

"And there," said Cletus, as they stood in the warm night breeze, looking upward. He pointed at a yellowish star low on the horizon. "That'll be your sister world, Mara. I understand you Exotics have quite a colony there, too."

"Oh, yes," answered Mondar thoughtfully, gazing at the star.

"A pity," said Cletus, turning to him, "that they aren't as free there from Alliance and Coalition influence as you've been here on Kultis since the Neulanders were taken care of."

Mondar withdrew his eyes from the star, turned himself to face Cletus and smiled. "You're suggesting we Exotics hire your new battle unit to drive out the Alliance and Coalition forces?" he said, humor in his voice. "Cletus, we've strained our financial resources for you already. Besides, it's counter to our general philosophy to contemplate deliberate conquest of other peoples or territories. You shouldn't suggest it to us."

"I don't," said Cletus. "I only suggest you contemplate the building of a core-tap power station at the Maran North Pole."

Mondar gazed through the darkness at Cletus for a moment without speaking. "A core-tap power station?" he echoed at last, slowly. "Cletus, what new subtlety are you working at now?"

"Hardly a subtlety," replied Cletus. "It's more a matter of taking a square look at the facts on Mara, economic and otherwise. The Alliance and the Coalition are both still stretched to their economic limits to maintain their influence with various colonies on all the new worlds. They may have lost ground here. But they're both strong on Mara, on Freiland and New Earth under Sirius, on Newton and Cassida, and even to a certain extent on the younger old worlds of the solar system—Mars and Venus. In fact, you might say they're both overextended. Sooner or later they're bound to crack—and the one that's liable to crack first, because it's invested more of its wealth and manpower in influencing new world colonies than the Coalition has, is the Alliance. Now, if either the Alliance or the Coalition goes under, the one that's left is going to take over all the influence that the other formerly had. Instead of two large octopi, with their tentacles into everything on the new worlds, there'll be one extra-large octopus. You don't want that."

"No," murmured Mondar.

"Then it's plainly to your interests to see that, on some place like Mara, neither the Alliance nor the Coalition gets the upper hand," said Cletus. "After we took care of Neuland, and you invited the Alliance forces out, the personnel the Alliance had here were taken away and spread out generally—plugged in any place the Alliance seemed in danger of springing a leak in confrontation with the Coalition. The Coalition, on the other hand, took its people in Neuland—of which, granted, there weren't as many as there were of Alliance people, but it was a fair number—and simply shifted them over to Mara. The result is that the Coalition is headed toward getting the upper hand over the Alliance on Mara."

"So you're suggesting we hire some of these newly trained Dorsais of yours to do on Mara what you did here?" Mondar smiled at him, a little quizzically. "Didn't I just say that philosophically we Exotics consider it inadvisable to improve our position by conquest—or any violent means, for that matter. Empires built by force of arms are built on sand, Cletus."

"In that case," said Cletus, "the sand under the Roman Empire

must have been most solidly packed. However, I'm not suggesting any
such thing. I'm merely suggesting that you build the power plant. Your
Exotic colony of Mara occupies the subtropical belt across the one
large continent there. With a core-tap power station at the North Pole,
you not only extend your influence into the essentially unclaimed sub-
arctic regions there, you'll be able to sell power to all the small, independent, temperate-zoned colonies lying between Mara and the
station. Your conquest on that planet, if any, will be by purely peaceful
and economic means."

"Those small colonies you refer to," said Mondar, his head a little
on one side, watching Cletus out of the corners of his blue eyes, "are
all under Coalition influence."

"All the better," said Cletus. "The Coalition can't afford very well
to drill them a competing core-tap power plant."

"And how are we going to afford it?" Mondar asked. He shook
his head. "Cletus, Cletus, I think you must believe that our Exotic
peoples are made of money."

"Not at all," Cletus said. "There's no need for you to put yourself
to any more immediate expense than that for the basic labor force
required to set up the plant. It ought to be possible for you to set up
an agreement for a lease-purchase on the equipment itself, and the
specially trained people required to set up the plant."

"Where?" asked Mondar. "With the Alliance? Or the Coalition?"

"Neither," said Cletus, promptly. "You seem to forget there's one
other colonial group out here on the new worlds that's proved itself
prosperous."

"You mean the scientific colonies on Newton?" said Mondar.
"They're at the extreme end of the philosophical spectrum from us.
They favor a tight society having as little contact with outsiders as
possible. We prize individualism above anything else, and our whole
purpose of existence is the concern with the total human race. I'm
afraid there's a natural antipathy between the Newtonians and us."
Mondar sighed slightly. "I agree we should find a way around such
emotional barriers between us and other human beings. Nonetheless,
the barrier's there—and in any case, the Newtonians aren't any better
off financially than we are. Why should they extend us credit, equipment and the services of highly trained people—as if they were the
Alliance itself?"

"Because eventually such a power station can pay back their investment with an excellent profit—by the time the lease expires and
you purchase their interest in it back from them," said Cletus.

"No doubt," said Mondar. "But the investment's still too large and too long-ranged for people in their position. A man of modest income doesn't suddenly speculate on distant and risky ventures. He leaves that to richer men, who can afford the possible loss—unless he's a fool. And those Newtonians, whatever else they are, aren't fools. They wouldn't even listen."

"They might," said Cletus, "if the proposition was put to them in the proper manner. I was thinking I might say a word to them myself about it—if you want to authorize me to do that, that is. I'm on my way there now, to see if they might not want to hire some of our newly trained Dorsai troops."

Mondar gazed at him for a second; the Exotic's eyes narrowed. "I'm utterly convinced, myself," he said, "that there's no chance in the universe of your persuading them to anything like this. However, we'd stand to gain a great deal by it, and I don't see how we could possibly lose anything by your trying. If you like, I'll speak to my fellow Exotics—both about the project and about your approaching the Newtonians for equipment and experts to put it in."

"Fine. Do that," said Cletus. He turned back toward the house. "I imagine I should start folding up, then. I want to inspect the Dorsai troops in the regiment you've got here now, and set up some kind of rotation system so that we can move them back by segments to the Dorsai for the new training. I want to be on my way to Newton by the end of the week."

"I should have our answer for you by that time," said Mondar, following him in. He glanced curiously at Cletus as they moved into the house side by side. "I must say I don't see what you stand to gain by it, however."

"I don't, directly," Cletus answered. "Nor do the Dorsais—we Dorsais, I have to get used to saying. But didn't you say something to me once about how anything that moved mankind as a whole onward and upward also moved you and your people toward their long-term goal?"

"You're interested in our long-term goal now?" Mondar asked.

"No. In my own," said Cletus. "But in this case it amounts to the same thing, here and there."

He spent the next five days in Bakhalla briefing the Dorsai officers on his training program back on the Dorsai. He invited those who wished to return and take it, along with those of their enlisted men who wished the same thing, and he left them with a sample plan for rotation of troops to that end—a plan in which his own trained men on the Dorsai would fill in for those of the Bakhallan troops that wished to take the training, collecting the pay of those they replaced for the training period.

The response from the Dorsais in Bakhalla was enthusiastic. Most of the men there had known Cletus at the time of the victory over Neuland. Therefore, Cletus was able to extend the value of the loan he had made from the Exotics, since he did not have to find jobs immediately for those Dorsais he had already trained, but could use them several times over as replacements for other men wishing to take the training. Meanwhile, he was continually building up the number of Dorsais who had been trained to his own purposes.

At the end of the week, he took ship for Newton, bearing credentials from the Exotics to discuss the matter of a core-tap power station on Mara with the Newtonian Governing Board as an ancillary topic to his own search for employment for his Dorsais.

Correspondence with the board had obtained for him an appointment with the chairman of the board within a day of his arrival in Baille, largest city and de facto capital of the Advanced Associated Communities—as the combined colonies of technical and scientific emigrants to Newton had chosen to call themselves. The chairman was a slim, nearly bald, youthful-faced man in his fifties by the name of Artur Walco. He met with Cletus in a large, clean, if somewhat sterile, office in a tall building as modern as any on Earth.

"I'm not sure what we have to talk about, Colonel," Walco said when they were both seated on opposite sides of a completely clean desk showing nothing but a panel of controls in its center. "The AAC is enjoying good relationships currently with all the more backward colonies of this world."

It was a conversational opening gambit as standard as king's pawn to king's pawn four in chess. Cletus smiled.

"My information was wrong, then?" he said, pushing his chair back from the desk and beginning to stand up. "Forgive me. I—"

"No, no. Sit down. Please sit down!" said Walco, hastily. "After you've come all the way here, the least I can do is listen to what you wanted to tell me."

"But if there's no need your hearing . . ." Cletus was insisting, when Walco once more cut him short with a wave of his hand.

"I insist. Sit down, Colonel. Tell me about it," he said. "As I say, there's no need for your mercenaries here at the moment. But any open-minded man knows that nothing's impossible in the long run. Besides, your correspondence intrigued us. You claim you've made your mercenaries more efficient. To tell you the truth, I don't understand how individual efficiency can make much difference in a military unit under modern conditions of warfare. What if your single soldier *is* more efficient? He's still just so much cannon fodder, isn't he?"

"Not always," said Cletus. "Sometimes he's a man behind the cannon. To mercenaries, particularly, that difference is critical, and therefore an increase in efficiency becomes critical too."

"Oh? How so?" Walco raised his still-black, narrow eyebrows.

"Because mercenaries aren't in business to get themselves killed," said Cletus. "They're in business to win military objectives *without* getting themselves killed. The fewer casualties, the greater profit—both to the mercenary soldier and to his employer."

"How, to his employer?" Walco's eyes were sharp.

"An employer of mercenaries," Cletus answered, "is in the position of any businessman faced with a job that needs to be done. If the cost of hiring it done equals or exceeds the possible profit to be made from it, the businessman is better off leaving the job undone. On the other hand, if the cost of having it done is less than the benefit or profit to be gained, then hiring the work accomplished is a practical decision. The point I'm making is that, with more efficient mercenary troops, military actions which were not profitable to those wishing them accomplished now become practical. Suppose, for example, there was a disputed piece of territory with some such valuable natural resource as stibnite mines—"

"Like the Broza Colony stibnite mines the Brozans stole from us," shot out Walco.

Cletus nodded. "It's the sort of situation I was about to mention," he said. "Here we have a case of some very valuable mines out in the middle of swamp and forest stretching for hundreds of miles in every direction without a decent city to be found, worked and held onto by a backward colony of hunters, trappers and farmers. A colony, though, that is in possession of the mines by military forces supplied by the Coalition—that same Coalition, which takes its cut of the high prices you pay the Brozans for the antimony extracted from the stibnite."

Cletus stopped speaking and looked meaningfully at Walco. Walco's face had darkened.

"Those mines were discovered by us and developed by us on land we'd bought from Broza Colony," he said. "The Coalition didn't even bother to hide the fact that they'd instigated the Brozan's expropriation of them. It was piracy, literal piracy." Walco's jaw muscles tightened. His eyes met Cletus' across the desk top. "You picked an interesting example," he said. "As a matter of theoretical interest, suppose we do go into the matter of expense, and the savings to be gained by the efficiency of your Dorsais in this one instance."

*   *   *

A week later, Cletus was on his way back to the Dorsai with a contract for the three months' hire of two thousand men and officers. He stopped at Bakhalla on Kultis on the way back to inform the Exotics that their loan was already promising to pay off.

"Congratulations," said Mondar. "Walco has a reputation of being one of the hardest men on any world to deal with. Did you have much trouble persuading him?"

"There was no persuading involved," answered Cletus. "I studied the situation on Newton for a point of grievance before I first wrote him. The stibnite mines, which are essentially Newton's only native source of antimony, seemed ideal. So, in my correspondence after that I dwelt upon all those aspects and advantages of our troops under this new training, which would apply to just such a situation—but without ever mentioning the Brozan stibnite mines by name. Of course, he could hardly help apply the information I gave him to that situation. I think he was determined to hire us to recover the mines even before he met me. If I hadn't brought up the subject, he would have."

Mondar shook his head with a slow smile of admiration. "Did you take advantage of his good humor to ask him to consider the Maran core-tap plan?"

"Yes," said Cletus. "You'll have to send a representative to sign the actual papers, but I think you'll find he'll be falling over himself in his eagerness to sign the agreement."

The smile vanished from Mondar's face. "You mean he's seriously interested?" Mondar demanded. "He's interested in a situation in which they'd put up that kind of equipment and professional services simply in return for a long-term financial gain?"

"He's not merely interested," said Cletus. "You'll find he's pretty well determined not to let the chance get away, no matter what. You should be able to write your own terms."

"I can't believe it!" Mondar stared at him. "How in the name of eternity did you get him into such a favorable mood?"

"There wasn't any real problem," said Cletus. "As you say, the man's a hard bargainer—but only when he's bargaining from a position of strength. I began, after our talk about the Dorsais was done, by just dropping the hint that I was on my way to Earth, where I had family connections who'd help me in getting Alliance funds to help you set up the Maran core-tap. He was interested, of course—I think, at first, more in the prospect in getting some such sort of Alliance aid for Newton. But then I happened to dwell on some of the financial benefits the Alliance would receive in the long run in return for their help, and that seemed to start him thinking."

"Yes," murmured Mondar, "the Newtonian appetite for credit is real enough."

"Exactly," Cletus said. "Once he showed that appetite, I knew I had him hooked. I kept drawing him on until he, himself, suggested his Advanced Associated Communities might possibly be interested in putting up a small share themselves—perhaps supply 20 percent of the equipment, or an equivalent amount of the trained personnel, in return for no more than a five-year mortgage on property here on Bakhalla."

"He did?" Mondar's face became thoughtful. "It's a steep price, of course, but considering our chances of actually getting Alliance money are practically nonexistent—"

"Just what I told him," interrupted Cletus. "The price was so steep as to be ridiculous. In fact, I laughed in his face."

"You did?" Mondar's gaze sharpened. "Cletus, that wasn't wise. An offer like that from a chairman of the board on Newton—"

"—Is hardly realistic, as I frankly told him," said Cletus. "I wasn't likely to put myself in the position of carrying an offer from them to you that was penurious to the point of insult. After all, as I told him, I had an obligation to my Dorsais to maintain good relationships with the governments of *all* independent new worlds colonies—and on second thought, I'd even begun to feel a little doubtful that I ought to have mentioned the matter to him in any case. After all, I'd only been given authority to speak to my relatives and contacts back on Earth."

"And he stood for that?" Mondar stared at Cletus.

"He not only stood for it," said Cletus, "he didn't waste any time in apologizing and amending his offer to a more realistic level. However, as I told him, by this time I was beginning to feel a little bit unsure about the whole business where he was concerned. But he kept on raising his offer until he was willing to supply the entire amount of necessary equipment, plus as many trained people as necessary to drill the core-tap and get it into operation as a power source. I finally agreed—reluctantly—to bring that offer back to you before going on to Earth."

"Cletus!" Mondar's eyes were alight. "You did it!"

"Not really," said Cletus. "There was still that matter of the Newtonians requiring Bakhallan property as security in addition to a mortgage on the core-tap itself. I was due to leave the next day, so early that morning, before I left, I sent him a message saying I'd thought it over during the night and, since there was absolutely no doubt that the Alliance would be happy to finance the project with a mortgage merely on the basis of the core-tap mortgage alone, I'd decided to disregard his offer after all and go directly on to Earth."

Mondar breathed out slowly. "With that much of an offer from him already in your hands," he said—and from anyone but an Exotic the tone of the words would have been bitter—"you had to gamble on a bluff like that!"

"There wasn't any gamble involved," said Cletus. "By this time the man had talked himself into buying a piece of the project at any cost. I believe I could even have gotten more from him if I hadn't already implied the limits of what the Alliance would do. So, it's just a matter of your sending someone to sign the papers."

"You can count on that. We won't waste time," answered Mondar. He shook his head. "We'll owe you a favor for this, Cletus. I suppose you know that."

"The thought would be a strange one to overlook," said Cletus, soberly. "But I'm hoping Exotics and Dorsais have stronger grounds for mutual assistance in the long run than just a pattern of reciprocal favors."

He returned to the Dorsai, eight days later, ship's time, to find the three thousand men, about whom he had messaged from Newton, already mobilized and ready to embark. Of these, only some five hundred were new-trained Dorsais. The other twenty-five hundred were good solid mercenary troops from the planet, but as yet lacking in Cletus' specialized training. However, that fact did not matter; since the untrained twenty-five hundred would be essentially, according to Cletus' plans, along only for the ride.

Meanwhile, before he left with them for Newton in three days' time, there was his marriage to Melissa to accomplish. The negotiations at Bakhalla and on Newton had delayed him. As a result, he arrived— having messaged ahead that he would be there in time for the ceremony if he had to hijack an atmosphere ship to make it—less than forty-five minutes short of the appointed hour—all this, only to find the first news to greet him was that perhaps all his hurry had been needless.

"She says she's changed her mind, that's all," Eachan Khan said to Cletus, low-voiced, in the privacy of the shadowed dining room. Over Eachan's stiff shoulders Cletus could see, some thirty feet away, the chaplain of his regiment of new-trained Dorsais, along with the other guests, eating and drinking in light-hearted ignorance of the sudden, drastic change in plans. The gathering was made up of old, fast friends of Eachan's and new, but equally fast, friends and officers of Cletus'. Among the mercenaries, loyalties were apt to be hard-won, but once won, unshakable. Those who were friends of Cletus' outnumbered those of Eachan's by more than two to one. Cletus had set up the invitation list that way.

"She says there's something wrong," said Eachan, helplessly, "and she has to see you. I don't understand her. I used to understand her, before deCastries—" He broke off. His shoulders sagged under the jacket of his dress uniform. "But not any more."

"Where is she?" asked Cletus.

"In the garden. The end of the garden, down beyond the bushes in the summer house," said Eachan.

Cletus turned and went out one of the French doors of the dining room toward the garden. Once he was out of sight of Eachan, he circled around to the parking area and the rented car he had flown out here from Foralie.

Opening the car, he got out his luggage case and opened it. Inside were his weapon belt and sidearm. He strapped the belt around his waist, discarding the weather flap that normally protected the polished butt of the sidearm. Then he turned back toward the garden.

He found her where Eachan had said. She was standing in the summer house with her back to him, her hands on the white railing before her, looking through a screen of bushes at the far ridge of the surrounding mountains. At the sound of his boots on the wooden floor of the summer house, she turned to face him.

"Cletus!" she said. Her face was quite normal in color and expression, although her lips were somewhat firm. "Dad told you?"

"Yes," he answered, stopping in front of her. "You should be inside getting ready. As it is we're going to have to go ahead just the way we are."

Her eyes widened slightly. A look of uncertainty crept into them. "Go ahead?" she echoed. "Cletus, haven't you been up to the house? I thought you said you'd already talked to Dad."

"I have," he said.

"Then . . ." She stared at him. "Cletus, didn't you understand what he said? I told him—it's wrong. It's just wrong. I don't know what's wrong about it, but something is. I'm not going to marry you!"

Cletus looked at her. And, as she gazed back at him, Melissa's face changed. There crept into her face that expression that Cletus had seen her wear only once before. It was the look he had seen on her face after he had emerged alive from the ditch in which he had played dead in order to destroy with the dally gun the Neulander guerrillas who had attacked their armored car on its way into Bakhalla.

"You don't . . . you can't think," she began, barely above a whisper. But then her voice firmed. "You can *force* me to marry you?"

"We'll hold the ceremony," he said.

She shook her head, disbelievingly. "No Dorsai chaplain would marry me against my will!"

"My regimental chaplain will—if I order it," Cletus said.

"Marry the daughter of Eachan Khan?" she blazed, suddenly. "And I suppose my father's simply going to stand still and watch this happen?"

"I hope so—sincerely," answered Cletus, with such a slow and meaningful emphasis on the words that color leaped into her face for a second and then drained away to leave her as pale as a woman in shock.

"You . . ." Her voice faltered and stopped. Child of a mercenary officer, she could not have failed to notice that, among those present for the wedding, those bound to Cletus by emotional or other ties outnumbered those bound to her father by two to one. But her eyes on him were still incredulous. They searched his face for some indication that what she saw there was somehow not the true Cletus.

"But you're not like that. You wouldn't . . ." Her voice failed again. "Dad's your friend!"

"And you're going to be my wife," Cletus answered.

Her eyes fell for the first time to the sidearm in the uncapped holster at his waist.

"Oh, God!" She put a slim hand to each side of her face. "And I thought Dow was cruel—I won't answer. When the chaplain asks me if I'll take you for my husband, I'll say no!"

"For Eachan's sake," said Cletus, "I hope not."

Her hands fell from her face. She stood like a sleepwalker, with her arms at her sides.

Cletus stepped up to her, took her arm and led her, unresisting, out of the summer house up through the garden, through a hedge and back in through the French doors to the dining room. Eachan was still there, and he turned to face them quickly as they came in, putting down the glass he held and stepping quickly forward to meet them.

"Here you are!" he said. His gaze sharpened suddenly on his daughter. "Melly! What's the matter?"

"Nothing," Cletus answered. "There's no problem, after all. We're going to get married."

Eachan's gaze switched sharply to Cletus. "You are?" His eyes locked with Cletus' for a second, then went back to Melissa. "Is this right, Melly? Is everything all right?"

"Everything's fine," said Cletus. "You'd better tell the chaplain we're ready now."

Eachan did not move. His eyes raked downward and stared delib-

erately at the weapon in its holster on Cletus' hip. He looked back up
at Cletus, and then at Melissa.

"I'm waiting to hear from you, Melly," Eachan said slowly. His
eyes were as gray as weathered granite. "You haven't told me yet that
everything's all right."

"It's all right," she said between stiff, colorless lips. "It was your
idea I marry Cletus in the first place, wasn't it, Dad?"

"Yes," said Eachan. There was no noticeable change in his expression, but all at once a change seemed to pass over him, sweeping
away all emotion and leaving him quiet, settled and purposeful. He
took a step forward, so that he stood now almost between them, looking directly up into Cletus' face from a few inches away. "But perhaps
I was making a mistake."

His right hand dropped, seemingly in a casual way, to cover Cletus' hand where it held Melissa's wrist. His fingers curled lightly about
Cletus' thumb in a grip that could be used to break the thumb if Cletus
did not release his hold.

Cletus dropped his other hand lightly upon the belt of the weapon
at his side.

"Let go," he said softly to Eachan.

The same deadly quietness held them both. For a second there was
no movement in the room, and then Melissa gasped.

"No!" She forced herself between them, facing her father, her back
toward Cletus, his hand still holding her wrist, now behind her back.
"Dad! What's the matter with you? I'd think you'd be happy we've
decided to get married after all!"

Behind her, Cletus let go of her wrist and she brought the formerly
imprisoned arm around before her. Her shoulders lifted sharply with
the depth of her breathing. For a moment Eachan stared at her blankly,
and then a little touch of puzzlement and dismay crept into his eyes.

"Melly, I thought . . ." His voice stumbled and fell silent.

"Thought?" cried Melissa, sharply. "What, Dad?"

He stared at her, distractedly. "I don't know!" he exploded, all at
once. "I don't understand you, girl! I don't understand you at all."

He turned away and stamped back to the table where he had put
his drink down. He picked it up and swallowed heavily from it.

Melissa went to him and for a second put her arm around his
shoulders, laying her head against the side of his head. Then she turned
back to Cletus and placed a cold hand on his wrist. She looked at him
with eyes that were strangely deep and free of anger or resentment.

"Come along, then, Cletus," she said, quietly. "We'd better be
getting started."

It was some hours later before they were able to be alone together. The wedding guests had seen them to the door of the master bedroom in newly built Grahame House, and it was only when the door was shut in their faces that they finally left the building, the echo of their laughter and cheerful voices fading behind them.

Wearily, Melissa dropped into a sitting position on the edge of the large bed. She looked up at Cletus, who was still standing.

"Now, will you tell me what's wrong?" she asked.

He looked at her. The moment he had foreseen when he had asked her to marry him was upon him now. He summoned up courage to face it.

"It'll be a marriage in name only," he said. "In a couple of years you can get an annulment."

"Then why marry me at all?" she said, her voice still empty of blame or rancor.

"DeCastries will be back out among the new worlds within another twelve months," he said. "Before he came, he'd be asking you to come to Earth. With your marriage to me, you lost your Earth citizenship. You're a Dorsai, now. You can't go—until you've had the marriage annulled and reapplied for Earth citizenship. And you can't annul the marriage right away without letting Eachan know I forced you to marry me—with the results you know, the same results you agreed to marry me to avoid, right now."

"I would never let you two kill each other," she said. Her voice was strange.

"No," he said. "So you'll wait two years. After that, you'll be free."

"But why?" she said. "Why did you do it?"

"Eachan would have followed you to Earth," said Cletus. "That's what Dow counted on. That's what I couldn't allow. I need Eachan Khan for what I've got to do."

He had been looking at her as he talked, but now his eyes had moved away from her. He was looking out the high, curtained window at one end of the bedroom, at the mountain peaks, now just beginning to be clouded with the afternoon rains that would in a few months turn to the first of autumn snows.

She did not speak for a long time. "Then," she said, at last, "you never did love me?"

He opened his mouth to answer, for the moment was upon him. But at the last minute, in spite of his determination, the words changed on his lips.

"Did I ever say I did?" he answered, and, turning, went out of the room before she could say more.

Behind him, as he closed the door, there was only silence.

Chapter 20

The next morning Cletus got busy readying the expeditionary contingent of new-trained and not yet new-trained Dorsais he would be taking with him to Newton. Several days later, as he sat in his private office at the Foralie training grounds, Arvid stepped in to say that there was a new emigrant to the Dorsai, an officer-recruit, who wanted to speak to him.

"You remember him, I think, sir," said Arvid, looking at Cletus a little grimly. "Lieutenant William Athyer—formerly of the Alliance Expeditionary Force on Bakhalla."

"Athyer?" said Cletus. He pushed aside the papers on the float desk in front of him. "Send him in, Arv."

Arvid stepped back out of the office. A few seconds later, Bill Athyer, whom Cletus had last seen drunkenly barring his way in the in-town spaceship terminal of Bakhalla, hesitantly appeared in the doorway. He was dressed in the brown uniform of a Dorsai recruit, with a probationary officer's insignia where his first lieutenant's silver bars had been worn.

"Come in," said Cletus, "and shut the door behind you."

Athyer obeyed and advanced into the room. "It's good of you to see me, sir," he said, slowly. "I don't suppose you ever expected me to show up like this . . ."

"Not at all," said Cletus. "I've been expecting you. Sit down."

He indicated the chair in front of his desk. Athyer took it almost gingerly. "I don't know how to apologize . . ." he began.

"Then don't," said Cletus. "I take it life has changed for you?"

"Changed!" Athyer's face lit up. "Sir, you remember at the Bakhalla Terminal . . . ? I went back from there with my mind made up. I was going to go through everything you'd ever written—everything—with a fine-toothed comb, until I found something wrong, something false, I could use against you. You said not to apologize, but . . ."

"And I meant it," said Cletus. "Go on with whatever else you were going to tell me."

"Well, I . . . suddenly began to understand it, that's all," said Athyer. "Suddenly it began to make sense to me, and I couldn't believe it! I left your books and started digging into everything else I could find in that Exotic library in Bakhalla on military art. And it was just what I'd always read, no more, no less. It was *your* writing that was different. . . . Sir, you don't know the difference!"

Cletus smiled.

"Of course, of course you do!" Athyer interrupted himself. "I don't mean that. What I mean is, for example, I always had trouble with math. I wasn't an Alliance Academy man, you know. I came in on one of the reserve officer programs and I could sort of slide through on math. And that's what I did until one day when I ran into solid geometry. All at once the figures and the shapes came together—it was beautiful. Well, that was how it was with your writing, sir. All of a sudden, the art and the mechanics of military strategy came together. All the dreams I'd had as a kid of doing great things—and all at once I was reading how they could be done. Not just military things—all sorts and kinds of things."

"You saw that in what I'd written, did you?" asked Cletus.

"Saw it!" Athyer reached up a hand and closed its fingers slowly on empty air. "I saw it as if it were *there*, three-dimensional, laid out in front of me. Sir, nobody knows what you've done in those volumes you've written. Nobody appreciates—and it's not only what your work offers now, it's what it offers in the future!"

"Good," said Cletus. "Glad to hear you think so. And now what can I do for you?"

"I think you know, sir, don't you?" Athyer said. "It's because of what you've written that I came here, to the Dorsai. But I don't want to be just one of your command. I want to be close, where I can go on learning from you. Oh, I know you won't have any room for me on your personal staff right away, but if you could keep me in mind . . ."

"I think room can be made for you," said Cletus. "As I say, I've been more or less expecting you. Go see Commandant Arvid Johnson and tell him I said to take you on as his assistant. We'll waive the full training requirement and you can go along with the group we're taking to employment on Newton."

"Sir . . ." Words failed Athyer.

"That's all, then," said Cletus, raking back in front of him the papers he had pushed aside earlier. "You'll find Arvid in the office outside."

He returned to his work. Two weeks later the Dorsai contingent for Newton landed there, ready for employment—and newly commissioned Force Leader Bill Athyer was among them.

"I hope," said Artur Walco several days after that, as he stood with Cletus watching the contingent at evening parade, "your confidence in yourself hasn't been exaggerated, Marshal."

There was almost the hint of a sneer in his voice, as the chairman of the board of the Advanced Associated Communities on Newton used the title Cletus had adopted for himself as part of his general overhaul of unit and officer names among the new-trained Dorsai. They were standing together at the edge of the parade ground, with the red sun in the gray sky of Newton sinking to the horizon behind the flagstaff, its flag already half-lowered, as Major Swahili brought the regiment to the point of dismissal. Cletus turned to look at the thin, balding Newtonian.

"Exaggeration of confidence," he said, "is a fault in people who don't know their business."

"And you do?" snapped Walco.

"Yes," answered Cletus.

Walco laughed sourly, hunching his thin shoulders in their black jacket against the northern wind coming off the edge of the forest that grew right to the limits of the Newtonian town of Debroy, the same forest that rolled northward, unbroken for more than two hundred miles, to the stibnite mines and the Brozan town of Watershed.

"Two thousand men may be enough to take those mines," he said, "but your contract with us calls for you to hold the mines for three days or until we get Newtonian forces in to relieve you. And within twenty-four hours after you move into Watershed, the Brozans can have ten thousand regular troops on top of you. How you're going to handle odds of five to one, I don't know."

"Of course not," said Cletus. The flag was all the way down now and Major Swahili had turned the parade over to his adjutant to dismiss the men. "It's not your business to know. It's only your business to write a contract with me providing that we get our pay only after control of the mines has been delivered to your troops. And that you've done. Our failure won't cause your Advanced Associated Communities any financial loss."

"Perhaps not," said Walco, viciously, "but my reputation's at stake." .

"So's mine," replied Cletus cheerfully.

Walco snorted and went off. Cletus watched him go for a second, then turned and made his way to the Headquarters building of the temporary camp that had been set up for the Dorsais here on the edge of Debroy under the shadow of the forest. There, in the map room, he found Swahili and Arvid waiting for him.

"Look at this," he said, beckoning them both over to the main map table, which showed in relief the broad band of forest, with Debroy at one end of the table and the stibnite mines around Watershed at the other. The other two men joined him at the Debroy end of the table. "Walco and his people expect us to fiddle around for a week or two, getting set here before we do anything. Whatever Brozan spies are keeping tab on the situation will accordingly pick up the same idea. But we aren't going to waste time. Major . . . ."

He looked at Swahili, whose scarred, black face was bent with interest above the table top. Swahili lifted his eyes to meet Cletus'.

"We'll start climatization training of the troops inside the edge of the forest here, tomorrow at first light," Cletus said. "The training will take place no more than five miles deep in the forest, well below the Newtonian-Brozan frontier"—he pointed to a red line running through the forested area some twenty miles above Debroy. "The men will train by forces and groups, and they aren't going to do well. They aren't going to do well at all. It'll be necessary to keep them out overnight and keep them at it until your officers are satisfied. Then they can be released, group by group, as their officers think they're ready, and allowed to return to the camp here. I don't want the last group out of the forest until two and a half days from tomorrow morning. You leave the necessary orders with your officers to see to that."

"I won't be there?" asked Swahili.

"You'll be with me," answered Cletus. He glanced at the tall young captain to his right. "So will Arvid and two hundred of our best men. We'll have split off from the rest the minute we're in the woods, dispersed into two- and three-man teams and headed north to rendezvous five miles south of Watershed, four days from now."

"Four days?" echoed Swahili. "That's better than fifty miles a day on foot through unfamiliar territory."

"Exactly!" said Cletus. "That's why no one—Newtonians or Brozans—will suspect we'd try to do anything like that. But you and I know, don't we, Major, that our best men can make it?"

His eyes met the eyes in Swahili's dark, unchanging face.

"Yes," said Swahili.

"Good," said Cletus, stepping back from the table. "We'll eat now, and work out the details this evening. I want you, Major, to travel along with Arv, here. I'll take Force Leader Athyer along with me and travel with him."

"Athyer?" queried Swahili.

"That's right," replied Cletus, dryly. "Wasn't it you who told me he was coming along?"

"Yes," answered Swahili. It was true, oddly enough. Swahili seemed to have taken an interest in the newly recruited, untrained Athyer. It was an interest apparently more of curiosity than sentiment—for if ever two men were at opposite poles, it was the major and the force leader. Swahili was far and away the superior of all the new-trained Dorsais, men and officers alike, having surpassed everyone in the training, with the exception of Cletus in the matter of autocontrol. Clearly, however, Swahili was not one to let interest affect judgment. He looked with a touch of grim amusement at Cletus.

"And, of course, since he'll be with you, sir . . ." he said.

"All the way," said Cletus, levelly. "I take it you've no objection to having Arv with you?"

"No, sir." Swahili's eyes glanced at the tall young commandant with something very close—as close as he ever came—to approval.

"Good," said Cletus. "You can take off, then. I'll meet you both here in an hour after we've eaten."

"Yes."

Swahili went out. Cletus turned toward the door, and found Arvid still there, standing almost in his way. Cletus stopped.

"Something the matter, Arv?" Cletus asked.

"Sir . . ." began Arvid, and he did not seem to be able to continue.

Cletus made no attempt to assist the conversation. He merely stood, waiting.

"Sir," said Arvid again, "I'm still your aide, aren't I?"

"You are," said Cletus.

"Then"—Arvid's face was stiff and a little pale—"can I ask why Athyer should be with you in an action like this, instead of me?"

Cletus looked at him coldly. Arvid held himself stiffly, and his right shoulder was still a little hunched under his uniform coat, drawn forward by the tightening of the scar tissue of the burn he had taken back at the BOQ in Bakhalla, protecting Cletus from the Neuland gunmen.

"No, Commandant," said Cletus, slowly. "You can't ask me why I decide what I do—now or ever."

They stood facing each other.

"Is that clear?" Cletus said, after a moment.

Arvid stood even more stiffly. His eyes seemed to have lost Cletus, and his gaze traveled past him now to some spot on the farther wall.

"Yes, sir," he said.

"Then you'd probably better be getting to the evening meal, hadn't you?" said Cletus.

"Yes, sir."

Arvid turned and went out. After a second, Cletus sighed and also left for his own quarters and a solitary meal served there by his orderly.

At nine the following morning, he was standing with Force Leader Athyer five miles inside the forest fringe, when Swahili came up to him and handed him the matchbox-sized metal case of a peep-map. Cletus tucked it into a jacket pocket of his gray-green field uniform.

"It's oriented?" he asked Swahili. The major nodded.

"With the camp as base point," Swahili answered. "The rest of the men tagged for the expedition have already left—in two- and three-man teams, just as you said. The captain and I are ready to go."

"Good," said Cletus. "We'll get started, too, Bill and I. See you at the rendezvous point, five miles below Watershed, in approximately ninety-one hours."

"We'll be there, sir." With a single, slightly humorous glance at Athyer, Swahili turned and left.

Cletus turned the peep-map over in the palm of his hand, exposing the needle of the orientation compass under its transparent cover. He pressed the button in the side of the case and the needle swung clockwise some forty degrees until it pointed almost due north into the forest. Cletus lined himself up with a tree trunk as far off as he could see through the dimness of the forest in that direction. Then he put the peephole at one end of the instrument to his eye and gazed through it. Within he saw the image of what appeared to be a ten-by-twelve-foot relief map of the territory between his present position and Watershed. A red line marked the route that had been programed into the map. Reaching for another button on the case, he cranked the view in close to study the detail of the first half-dozen miles. It was all straight forest, with no bog land to be crossed or avoided.

"Come on," he said over his shoulder to Athyer. Putting the peep-map into his pocket, he started off at a jog trot.

Athyer followed him. For the first couple of hours they trotted along side by side without speaking, enclosed in the dimness and silence of the northern Newtonian forest. There were no flying creatures, neither birds nor insects, in this forest, only the amphibious and fish-like life of its lakes, swamps and bogs. Under the thick cover of the needle-like leaves that grew only on the topmost branches of the trees, the ground was bare except for the leafless tree trunks and lower branches but covered with a thick coat of blackened, dead needles fallen from the trees in past seasons. Only here and there, startling and expectedly, there would be a thick clump of large, flesh-colored leaves as much as four feet in length, sprouting directly from the needle bed to signal the presence of a spring or some other damp area of the jungle floor beneath.

After the first two hours, they fell into an alternate rhythm of five minutes at a jog trot, followed by five minutes at a rapid walk. Once each hour they stopped for five minutes to rest, dropping at full length upon the soft, thick, needle carpet without bothering even to remove the light survival packs they wore strapped to their shoulders.

For the first half hour or so, the going had been effortful. But after that they warmed to the physical movement, their heartbeats slowed, their breathing calmed—and it seemed almost as if they could go on forever like this. Cletus ran or walked, with the larger share of his mind abstract, far away in concentration on other problems. Even the matter of periodically checking their progress with the directional compass on the peep-map was an almost automatic action for him, performed by reflex.

He was roused from this at last by the fading of the already dim light of the forest about them. Newton's sun, hidden behind its double screen of the treetop foliage and the high, almost constant cloud layer that gave the sky its usual gray, metallic look, was beginning to set.

"Time for a meal break," said Cletus. He headed for a flat spot at the base of a large tree trunk and dropped into a sitting position, cross-legged with his back to the trunk, stripping off his shoulder pack as he did so. Athyer joined him on the ground. "How're you doing?"

"Fine, sir," grunted Athyer.

In fact, the other man was looking as good as he claimed to feel, and this Cletus was glad to see. There was only a faint sheen of perspiration on Athyer's face, and his breathing was deep and unhurried.

They broke out a thermo meal pack apiece and punctured the seal to start warming the food inside. By the time it was hot enough to eat, the darkness around them had closed in absolutely. It was as black as the inside of some sealed underground room.

"Half an hour until the moons start to rise," Cletus said into the darkness in the direction in which he had last looked to see the seated Athyer. "Try and get some sleep, if you can."

Cletus lay back on the needles, and made his limbs and body go limp. In a few seconds, he felt the familiar drifting sensation. Then it seemed that there were perhaps thirty seconds of inattention, and he opened his eyes to find a new, pale light filtering down through the leaf cover of the forest.

It was still only a fraction as bright as the filtered daylight had been, but already it was bright enough so that they could see to travel, and that brightness would perhaps double, since at least four of Newton's five moons should be in the night sky.

"Let's move," said Cletus. A couple of minutes later, he and Athyer, packs on back, were once more jog trotting upon their route.

The peep-map, when Cletus consulted it by its own inter-illumination, now showed a black line paralleling the red line of their indicated route for a distance of a little over thirty-one miles from their starting point. In the next nine hours of nighttime traveling, interrupted only by hourly rests and a short meal break around midnight, they accomplished another twenty-six miles before the setting of most of the moons dimmed the light once more below the level of illumination at which it was safe to travel. They ate a final, light meal and dropped off into five hours of deep slumber on the thick needle bed of the forest floor.

When Cletus' wrist alarm woke them, the chronometer showed that over two hours of daylight had already elapsed. They arose, ate and moved on as soon as possible.

For the first four hours they made good progress—if anything, they were traveling even a little faster than they had the day before. But around noon they entered into an area of bog and swamp thick with plants of the big, flesh-colored leaf, and something new called parasite vines, great ropes of vegetation hanging from the low limbs of the trees or stretching out across the ground for miles and sometimes as thick as an oil drum.

They were slowed and forced to detour. By the time night fell, they had made only an additional twenty miles. They were barely one-third of the distance to the rendezvous point below Watershed, nearly one-third of their time had gone, and from now on fatigue would slow them progressively. Cletus had hoped to cover nearly half the distance by this time.

However, the peep-map informed him that another twenty miles would bring them out of this boggy area and into more open country again. They had their brief supper during the half hour of darkness, and then pushed on during the night. They reached the edge of the bog area just before the moonlight failed them; they fell, like dead men, on the needle carpet underfoot and into slumber.

The next day the going was easier, but exhaustion was beginning to slow their pace. Cletus traveled like a man in a dream, or in a high fever, hardly conscious of the efforts and weariness of his body except as things perceived dimly, at a distance. But Athyer was running close to the end of his strength. His face was gray and gaunt, so that the harsh beak of his nose now seemed to dominate all the other features in it, like the battering-ram prow of some ancient wooden vessel. He managed to keep the pace as they trotted, but when they slowed to a walk, his foot would occasionally go down loosely and he would stumble. That night Cletus let them both sleep for six hours after the evening meal.

They made less than sixteen miles in the hours of moonlight that remained to them, before stopping to sleep again for another six hours.

They awoke with the illusion of being rested and restored to full strength. However, two hours of travel during the following daylight found them not much better than they had been twenty-four hours before, although they were traveling more slowly and more steadily now, portioning out their strength as a miser portions out the money for necessary expenses. Once again, Cletus was back in his state of detachment; his bodily suffering seemed remote and unimportant. The feeling clung to his mind that he could go on like this forever, if necessary, without even stopping for food or rest.

By now, in fact, food was one of the least of their wants. They paused for the midday meal break and forced themselves to swallow some of the rations they carried, but without appetite or sense of taste. The ingested food lay heavily in their stomachs, and when darkness came neither of them could eat. They dug down to the base of one of the flesh-colored leafed plants to uncover the spring that was bubbling there, and drank deeply before dropping off into what was now an almost automatic slumber. After a couple of hours of sleep, they arose and went on under the moonlight.

Dawn of the fourth day found them only half a dozen miles from the rendezvous point. But when they tried to get to their feet with their packs on, their knees buckled and gave under them like loose hinges. Cletus continued to struggle, however, and, after several tries, found himself at last on his feet and staying there. He looked around and saw Athyer, still on the ground, unmoving.

"No use," croaked Athyer. "You go on."

"No," said Cletus. He stood, legs stiff and braced, a little apart. He swayed slightly, looking down at Athyer.

"You've got to go on," said Athyer, after a moment. It was the way they had gotten in the habit of talking to each other during the last day or so—with long pauses between one man's words and the other's reply.

"Why did you come to the Dorsai?" asked Cletus, after one of these pauses.

Athyer stared at him. "You," said Athyer. "You did what I always wanted to do. You were what I always wanted to be. I knew I'd never make it the way you have. But I thought I could learn to come close."

"Then learn," said Cletus, swaying. "Walk."

"I can't," said Athyer.

"No such thing as can't—for you," said Cletus. "Walk."

Cletus continued to stand there. Athyer lay where he was for a few minutes. Then his legs began to twitch. He struggled up into a sitting position and tried to get his legs under him, but they would not go. He stopped, panting.

"You're what you've always wanted to be," said Cletus slowly, swaying above him. "Never mind your body. Get Athyer to his feet. The body will come along naturally."

He waited. Athyer stirred again. With a convulsive effort he got to his knees, wavered in a half-kneeling position, and then with a sudden surge lifted to his feet, stumbled forward for three steps and caught hold of a tree trunk to keep from going down again. He looked over his shoulder at Cletus, panting but triumphant.

"When you're ready to go," said Cletus.

Five minutes later, though Athyer still stumbled like a drunken man, they were moving forward. Four hours later they made it to the rendezvous point, to find Swahili and Arvid, together with perhaps a fifth of the rest of the men due to arrive at this point, already there. Cletus and Athyer collapsed without even bothering to take off their back packs, and they were asleep before they touched the needle-carpeted ground.

Chapter 21

Cletus awoke about midafternoon. He felt stiff and a little lightheaded, but rested and extremely hungry. Athyer was still sleeping heavily, like a man under deep anesthesia.

Cletus ate and joined Swahili and Arvid.

"How many of the men are in?" he asked Swahili.

"There're twenty-six who haven't shown up yet," answered Swahili. "We got most of the rest in during the next hour after you got here."

Cletus nodded. "Good," he said. "Then they should be slept up enough to operate by twilight. We'll get busy right now with the ones that are already rested. The first thing we need is a vehicle."

So it happened that a Brozan truck driver sliding on his airjets down the single fused-earth highway leading into the small mining town of Watershed unexpectedly found his way barred by half a dozen armed men in gray-blue uniforms, each with a small blue and white flag of the Advanced Associated Communities stapled over the left breast pocket. One of these, a tall officer wearing a circle of stars on each shoulder tab, stepped up on the foot-rest entrance to his cab and opened the door.

"Out," said Cletus, "we need this truck of yours."

Two hours later, just before sunset, that same truck drove into Watershed from a highway that had been strangely unproductive of traffic during the last 120 minutes. There were two men in the cab without caps on and they drove the truck directly to the headquarters of the small police detachment that had the duty of keeping law and order in the mining town.

The truck pulled into the parking compound behind the police headquarters, and a few moments later there was the sound of some disturbance within the headquarters itself. This, however, quietened, and a few moments later the fire siren above the police headquarters burst to life with a whooping like that of some mad, gigantic creature. It continued to whoop as the townspeople poured out of their houses and other buildings to find the town surrounded and the streets patrolled by armed soldiers with blue and white flags stapled over the left breast pockets of their uniform jackets. By the time the sun was down, Watershed had awakened to the fact that it was a captured community.

"You must be crazy! You'll never get away with it!" stormed the manager of the stibnite mines when, with the mayor of the town and the head of the local police contingent, he was brought into Cletus' presence at police headquarters. "The Brozan Army's headquartered at Broza City—and that's only two hours from here, even by road. They'll find out you're here in a few hours, and then—"

"They already know," Cletus interrupted him, dryly. "One of the first things I did was use your police communications here to announce the fact that we've taken over Watershed and the mines."

The mine manager stared at him. "You *must* be crazy!" he said at last. "Do you think your five hundred men can stand up to a couple of divisions?"

"We may not have to," said Cletus. "In any case, it's no concern of yours. All I want you and these other two gentlemen to do is to reassure the local people that they're in no danger as long as they keep off the streets and make no effort to leave the town."

There was a note in his voice that did not invite further argument. With a few additional half-hearted attempts at protest, the three officials of Watershed agreed to make a joint community call over the local phone system with the reassurance and warning he had asked them to deliver—following which, he had them placed under guard in the police headquarters.

It was in fact less than two hours before the first elements of the Brozan Army began to arrive. These were flying transports loaded with troops who quickly ringed the village at a distance of about two hundred yards inside the edge of the forest surrounding the town. Through the rest of the night, other troops, heavy weapons and armored vehicles could be heard arriving. By dawn, Swahili and Cletus concurred in an estimate that close to a division of Brozan soldiery, bristling with everything from belt knives to energy weapons, enclosed Watershed and its two hundred occupying Dorsai troops.

Swahili was in good humor as he handed the field glasses back to

Cletus, after making his own survey of the surrounding forest area. They were standing together on top of the communications tower, which was the tallest structure in the town.

"They won't want to use those heavy weapons indiscriminately, with all these local people on hand," said Swahili. "That means they're going to have to come in on foot—probably all around the perimeter at once. I'd guess they'll attack inside the hour."

"I don't think so," answered Cletus. "I think they'll send someone in to talk, first."

He turned out to be correct. The surrounding Brozan troops did nothing for the first three hours of the morning. Then, toward noon, as the cloud-veiled sun over Newton was heating the northern landscape, a command car flying a white flag slowly emerged from the shadows of the forest and entered the town from the highway. It was met at the perimeter of Watershed by soldiers instructed in preparation for this meeting, and it was escorted by them to the police headquarters. There, a small, spare general in his early sixties, flanked by a round man perhaps ten years younger and wearing a colonel's insignia, dismounted and entered the headquarters building. Cletus received them in the office of the commander of the police detachment.

"I'm here to offer you surrender terms—" The general broke off, staring at Cletus' shoulder tabs. "I don't recognize your rank?"

"Marshal," Cletus answered. "We've shaken up our table of organization and our titles on the Dorsai, recently. Marshal Cletus Grahame."

"Oh? General James Van Dassel. And this is Colonel Morton Offer. As I was saying, we're here to offer you terms of surrender—"

"If it was a matter of sending surrender terms, you'd hardly have needed to come yourself, would you, General?" Cletus broke in. "I think you know very well that there's no question of our surrendering."

"No?" Van Dassel's eyebrows rose politely. "Maybe I should tell you we've got more than a full division, with a full complement of heavy weapons, surrounding you right now."

"I'm aware of that fact," said Cletus. "Just as you're completely aware of the fact that we have something over five thousand civilians here inside our lines."

"Yes, and we're holding you strictly accountable for them," said Van Dassel. "I have to warn you that, if any harm comes to them, the liberal surrender terms we're about to offer you—"

"Don't try my patience, General," interrupted Cletus. "We hold those civilians as hostages against any inimical action by your forces. So let's not waste any more time on this nonsense about our surrendering. I've been expecting you here so that I could inform you of the immediate steps to be taken by the Advanced Associated Communities with regard to Watershed and the mines. As you undoubtedly know, these mines were developed on land purchased from Broza by the Advanced Associated Communities, and Broza's expropriation has since been ruled illegal by the international court here on Newton—although Broza has seen fit until now to refuse to obey that court's order returning the mines to the Advanced Associated Communities. Our expeditionary force has already notified the Advanced Associated Communities that the mines are once more under their proper ownership, and I've been informed that the first contingents of regular AAC troops will begin to arrive here by 1800 hours, to relieve my command and begin to function as a permanent occupying force...." Cletus paused.

"I'm certainly not going to permit any such occupying forces to move in here," said Van Dassel, almost mildly.

"Then I'd suggest you check with your political authorities before you make any move to prevent them," said Cletus. "I repeat, we hold the townspeople here hostage for the good behavior of your troops."

"Nor am I willing to be blackmailed," said Van Dassel. "I'll expect notification of your willingness to surrender before the next two hours are up."

"And I, as I say," answered Cletus, "will hold you responsible for any hostile action by your command during our relief by the regular troops from the Advanced Associated Communities."

On that mutual statement, they parted politely. Van Dassel and his colonel returned to the Brozan troops encircling the village. Cletus called in Swahili and Arvid to have lunch with him.

"But what if he decides to hit us before the relieving troops get here?" asked Swahili.

"He won't," said Cletus. "His situation's bad enough as it is. The Brozan politicians are going to be asking him how he allowed us to take over Watershed and the mines here in the first place. He might survive that question, as far as his career is concerned—but only if there're no Brozan lives lost. He knows I understand that as well as he does, so Van Dassel won't take chances."

In fact, Van Dassel did not make any move. His division surrounding Watershed sat quietly while his deadline for surrender passed, and the relieving forces from the Advanced Associated Communities began to be airlifted in. During the following night, he quietly withdrew his forces. By the following sunrise, as the newly landed, AAC soldiery began to clear an area of the forest outside the town and construct a semipermanent camp for themselves, there was not a Brozan soldier to be found within two hundred miles.

"Very well done indeed!" said Walco, enthusiastically, when he arrived at Watershed with the last of his own troops and was ushered in to the office Cletus had taken over in the police headquarters building. "You and your Dorsais have done a marvelous job. You can move out any time now."

"As soon as we're paid," said Cletus.

Walco smiled, thinly. "I thought you might be eager to get your pay," he said. "So I brought it along with me."

He lifted a narrow briefcase onto the desk between them, took out a release form, which he passed to Cletus, and then began to remove gold certificates, which he stacked on the desk in front of Cletus.

Cletus ignored the form and watched coolly as the pile of certificates grew. When Walco stopped at last, and looked up at him with another broad smile, Cletus did not smile back. He shook his head.

"That's less than half of what our agreement called for," Cletus said.

Walco preserved his smile. "True," Walco said. "But in the original agreement we envisioned hiring you for a three-month term. As it happens, you've been lucky enough to achieve your objective in less than a week and with only a quarter of your expeditionary force. We figured full combat pay for the whole week, however, for the five hundred men you used, and in addition we're paying you garrison scale not only for the rest of your men for that week but for your whole force for the rest of this month as well—as a sort of bonus."

Cletus looked at him. Walco's smile faded.

"I'm sure you remember as well as I do," said Cletus, coldly, "that the agreement was for two thousand men for three months, full combat pay for everybody during that period—and no pay at all if we weren't able to deliver the stibnite mines to you. How many men I used to make that recovery, and how long I took, was my concern. I expect full combat pay for three months for my entire command, immediately."

"That's out of the question, of course," said Walco, a little shortly.

"I don't think so," said Cletus. "Maybe I should remind you that I told General Van Dassel, the Brozan commander who had us encircled here, that I was holding the civilian population of Watershed hostage for his good behavior. Perhaps I should remind you that I and the men I brought here with me are still holding these people hostage—this time for *your* good behavior."

Walco's face became strangely set. "You wouldn't harm civilians!" he said, after a moment.

"General Van Dassel believes I would," replied Cletus. "Now I, personally, give you my word as a Dorsai—and that's a word that's going to become something better than a signed contract, in time— that no single civilian will be hurt. But have you got the courage to believe me? If I'm lying, and your takeover of the mines includes a blood bath of the resident townspeople, your chances of coming to some eventual agreement with Broza about these mines will go up in smoke. Instead of being able to negotiate on the basis of having a bird in the hand, you'll have to face a colony interested only in ven- geance—vengeance for an action for which all civilized communities will indict you."

Walco stood, staring at him. "I don't have any more certificates with me," he said at last, hoarsely.

"We'll wait," answered Cletus. "You should be able to fly back and get them and return here by noon at the latest."

Shoulders slumped, Walco went. As he mounted the steps of the aircraft that had brought him to Watershed however, he stopped and turned for a parting shot at Cletus.

"You think you're going to cut a swath through the new worlds," he said, viciously, "and maybe you will for a while. But one of these days everything you've built is going to come tumbling down around your ears."

"We'll see," said Cletus.

He watched the door shut behind Walco and the aircraft lift away into the sky of Newton. Then he turned to Arvid, who was standing beside him.

"By the way, Arv," he said, "Bill Athyer wants to have the chance to study my methods of tactics and strategy at close hand, so he'll be taking over as my aide as soon as we're back on the Dorsai. We'll find a command for you, out in the field somewhere. It's about time you were brushing up on your combat experience anyway."

Without waiting for Arvid's response, he turned his back on the younger man and walked off, his mind already on other problems.

Chapter 22

"Your prices," said James Arm-of-the-Lord, Eldest of the First Militant Church, on both the neighboring worlds of Harmony and Association—those two worlds called the Friendlies, "are outrageous."

James Arm-of-the-Lord was a small, frail, middle-aged man with sparse gray hair—looking even smaller and more frail than he might otherwise in the tight black jumper and trousers that were the common dress of those belonging to the fanatical sects that had colonized, and later divided and multiplied, on the surfaces of Harmony and Association. At first sight, he seemed a harmless little man, but a glance from his dark eyes or even a few words spoken aloud by him were enough to destroy that illusion. Plainly he was one of those rare people who burn with an inner fire—but the inner fire that never failed in James Arm-of-the-Lord was a brand of woe and a torch of terror to the Unrighteous. Nor was it lessened by the fact that the ranks of the Unrighteous, in James' estimation, included all those whose opinions in any way differed from his own. He sat now in his office at Government Center on Harmony, gazing across the desk's bare, unpolished surface at Cletus, who sat opposite.

"I know we're priced beyond your means," said Cletus. "I didn't come by to suggest that you hire some of our Dorsais. I was going to suggest that possibly we might want to hire some of your young men."

"Hire out our church members to spend their blood and lives in the sinful wars of the Churchless and the Unbelievers?" said James. "Unthinkable!"

"None of your colonies on Harmony or Association have anything to speak of in the way of technology," said Cletus. "Your Militant Church may contain the largest population of any of the churches on these two worlds, but you're still starving for real credit—of the kind you can use in interworld trading to set up the production machinery your people need. You could earn that credit from us, as I say, by hiring out some of your young men to us."

James' eyes glittered like the eyes of a coiled snake in reflective light. "How much?" he snapped.

"The standard wages for conventional mercenary soldiers," replied Cletus.

"Why, that's barely a third of what you asked for each of your Dorsais!" James' voice rose. "You'd sell to us at one price, and buy from us at another?"

"It's a matter of selling and buying two different products," answered Cletus, unmoved. "The Dorsais are worth what I ask for them because of their training and because by now they've established a reputation for earning their money. Your men have no such training, and no reputation. They're worth only what I'm willing to pay for them. On the other hand, not a great deal would be demanded of them. They'd be used mainly as diversionary forces like our jump troops in our recent capture of Margaretha, on Freiland."

The taking over of Margaretha on Freiland had been the latest of a series of successful engagements fought by the new-trained Dorsai mercenaries under Cletus' command. Over a year had gone by since the capture of the stibnite mines on Newton, and in that time they had conducted campaigns leading to clear-cut and almost bloodless victories on the worlds of Newton's sister planet of Cassida, St. Marie, a smaller world under the Procyon sun with Mara and Kultis, and most recently on Freiland, which, with New Earth, were the inhabited planets under the star of Sirius.

Margaretha was a large, ocean-girt island some three hundred miles off the northeastern shore of the main continental mass of Freiland. It had been invaded and captured by the nearest colony adjoining it on the mainland mass. The island's government in exile had raised the funds to hire the Dorsais to recapture their homeland from the invaders.

Cletus had feinted with an apparent jump-belt troop drop of untrained Dorsais over Margaretha's main city. But meanwhile he had sent several thousand trained troops into the island by having them swim ashore at night at innumerable points around the coastline of the island. These infiltrators had taken charge of and coordinated the hundreds of spontaneous uprisings that had been triggered off among the island's population by word of the jump-troop drop.

Faced with uprisings from within and evident attack from without, the mainland troops that had seized the island chose discretion as the better part of valor and abandoned the island for their home colony. They reached home only to discover how few had been the troops that had actually driven them out, and turned swiftly about to return to Margaretha.

When they reached the island this second time, however, they found watch fires burning on all the beaches, and the population aroused, armed and this time ready to die between the tide marks rather than let a single mainlander invader ashore.

As with Cletus' other military successes, it had been a victory achieved through a careful blending of imagination and psychology with what was now beginning to be regarded, on the other colony worlds, as the almost superhuman abilities of the trained Dorsai soldiers. Clearly, for all his apparent unwillingness to listen to Cletus' offer, James was not unaware of the hard facts and advantages of the proposition. It was typical of elders such as James that they were either pro or con, but never admitted to indecision.

Cletus took his leave, accordingly, having planted the seed of an idea in a Friendly mind, and being content to bide his time and let it grow.

He took a spaceship to New Earth, that sister planet of Freiland, where his command of Dorsais and a new military campaign were waiting for him. Marcus Dodds, Eachan's old second-in-command, met him at the Dorsai camp just outside of Adonyer, the main city of Breatha Colony, their employers on New Earth. In spite of the two new stars on each of his shoulder tabs, marking him as a field commander with a full division of mercenaries under him, Marcus' face was solemn with concern.

"Spainville's formed an alliance with four of the five other city-states of the interior plains," he told Cletus, as soon as they were alone in Marcus' office. "They call it the Central Combine, and they've mustered a combined army of better than twenty thousand regular troops. Not only that, they're ready and waiting for us. We aren't going to be able to use surprise the way we have in other campaigns, and this short division you've given me here has less than five thousand men."

"True enough," said Cletus, thoughtfully. "What do you suggest I do about it?"

"Break the contract with Breatha," said Marcus, strongly. "We can't possibly go up against this Central Combine now without more men. And how many other new-trained Dorsais are there? Certainly not more than a couple of hundred. We've got no choice but to break the contract. You can cite the fact that the situation has changed since we were hired. Breatha may squawk, but responsible people in other colonies wanting to hire us will understand. If we don't have the troops, we don't have the troops—that's all there is to it."

"No," said Cletus. He got up from his seat beside Marcus' desk and walked across the room to a map showing the flat plains area of the continental interior, which Breatha shared with its rivals, five other colonies, each of which was essentially farming communities centered around one large city—hence their common name of city-states. "I don't want to start breaking contracts, no matter how well justified we are."

He studied the map for a minute. Breatha, with a narrow corridor running to the coast, was surrounded by the city-states of the interior on four of its five sides. Originally it had been the manufacturing center that supplied the city-states with most of their factory-made equipment and brought farm produce from the city-states in return. But then Spainville, the largest of the five city-states, had ventured into manufacturing on its own, sparking off a similar action in the other city-states—one of which, called Armoy, had chosen to construct a deep-space spaceport in competition with the one existing in Breatha Colony.

Now, with economic ambition burning bright in the former agricultural colonies of the central plain, Spainville, which bordered on Breatha's corridor to the sea, had chosen to lay claim upon that corridor and threaten to take it over by armed force if Breatha did not yield it peacefully. Hence, the presence of the Dorsais on the Breatha payroll.

"On the other hand," said Cletus, turning back to Marcus, "if they believed we'd been reinforced, that might be almost as good as our actually getting the necessary extra troops in here."

"How're you going to make them think that?" demanded Marcus.

"It may take some thought." Cletus smiled. "At any rate, I'll make a quick trip back to the Dorsai now, as though I was going after extra men, and see if I can't work out a plan on the way."

Having announced his intentions, Cletus wasted no time. By late that evening, after a wild trip halfway around the circumference of New Earth in an atmosphere ship, he was on board a deep-space vessel that had the Dorsai as its next port of call. Three days later he was back in Foralie. Melissa met him at the doorway of Grahame House with a warmth that was surprising. Since the marriage, she had slowly been softening toward him, and since the birth of their son, three months ago, that process had accelerated even while it seemed that all those others who had once been close to Cletus were becoming more and more estranged to him.

Typical of these was Eachan, whose greeting to Cletus was almost as detached and wary as that which might be accorded a stranger. At the first opportunity, he got Cletus away from Melissa and the child to speak bluntly to his son-in-law.

"Have you seen these?" he asked, spreading an assortment of news clippings out on the desk before Cletus. They were standing in Cletus' office-study, in the west wing of Grahame House. "They're all from Earth news services—Alliance and Coalition alike."

Cletus glanced over the clippings. Unanimously, they were concerned with the Dorsais and himself. Not only that, but their vituperative tone was so alike that they could have been the product of a single voice.

"You see?" Eachan challenged, as Cletus finally looked up from the clippings. "It was the Coalition news service that started calling you a pirate after the Bakhalla business. But now the Alliance has taken it up too. These city-states you're hired to go against on New Earth are backed by Alliance as well as Coalition aid and investment. If you don't look out you'll have the Alliance as well as the Coalition laying for you. Look"—his brown right forefinger stabbed at one of the clippings—"read what Dow deCastries said in a speech in Delhi— '*If nothing else, the peoples of the Coalition and the Alliance both can join in condemning the brutal and bloody activities of the ex-Alliance renegade Grahame. . . .*' "

Cletus laughed.

"You think this is funny?" said Eachan, grimly.

"Only in its predictability," answered Cletus, "and in the obviousness of Dow's intentions."

"You mean you've been expecting this—expecting deCastries to make speeches like that?" demanded Eachan.

"Yes," answered Cletus. He dismissed the subject. "Never mind that. I'm back here to go through the motions of transporting an imaginary extra division of troops to Breatha Colony. I'll need at least two deep-space transports. Maybe we can arrange to lease some empty cargo spaceships for a diversionary trip—"

"You'd better listen to something else first," Eachan interrupted him. "Did you know you're losing Swahili?"

Cletus raised his eyebrows. "No," he murmured. "But it's not surprising."

Eachan opened a drawer of Cletus' library desk and took out a resignation form, which he dropped on the table on top of the news clippings. Cletus looked down at it. Sure enough, it was made out and signed by Swahili, now a one-star general field commander. Promotions had come thick and fast among those men who had been with Cletus from the beginning. Only Arvid, now in the field, was still a commandant—the equivalent of his old grade of captain—and Eachan, who had refused the one promotion offered him. By contrast, the once ineffective Bill Athyer was now a rank above Arvid as commandant senior grade, less than two ranks away from field commander, with command of a regiment.

"I suppose I'd better talk to him," said Cletus.

"Not that it'll do you any good," replied Eachan.

Cletus invited Swahili up from his post at the main new-training center, now on the far side of Foralie. The next day they met briefly in that same office-study where Eachan had confronted Cletus with the news clippings shortly after his arrival home.

"Of course, I'm sorry to lose you," said Cletus, as the two faced each other. Swahili, a single star gleaming gold on each of his shoulder tabs, bulked larger than ever in his blue dress uniform. "But I imagine you've completely made up your mind."

"Yes," said Swahili. "You understand, don't you?"

"I think so," said Cletus.

"I think you do," echoed Swahili softly, "even if it is just the opposite of the way you like to do things. You've taken all the life out of war—you know that, don't you?"

"It's the way I like it," said Cletus.

Swahili's eyes flashed a little in the soft light of the peaceful library-office. "It's not the way I like it," he said. "What I like is what nearly everyone else hates—hates or is scared sick of. And it's that you've taken out of the business for everybody who serves under you."

"You mean the combat, itself," said Cletus.

"That's right," said Swahili, softly. "I don't like being hurt and all those weeks in the hospital any more than the next man. I don't want to die. But I put up with all the rest of it—all the training, all the hurry-up-and-waiting, all the marking time between engagements—I put up with all that, just for the few hours when everything turns real."

"You're a killer. Or don't you admit that to yourself?" asked Cletus.

"No," said Swahili. "I'm a special fighter, that's all. I like to fight. Just the killing itself wouldn't do anything for me. I told you I didn't want to get hurt, or killed, any more than the next man. I feel just as hollow inside when the energy weapons start burning the air over my head. At the same time, I wouldn't miss it for anything. It's a dirty, damn universe, and every once in a while I get a chance to hit back at it. That's all. If I knew in the morning when I started out that I was going to be killed that day, I'd still go—because I couldn't die happier than to go down hitting back."

He stopped talking, abruptly. For a moment he simply looked at Cletus in the silence of the room.

"And it's that you've taken out of mercenary work," he said. "So I'm going someplace else where they still have it."

Cletus held out his hand. "Good luck," he said.

They shook hands.

"Luck to you," said Swahili. "You'll need it. In the end the man with gloves on always loses to the bare-knuckle fighter."

"You'll have your chance to test that belief, at least," said Cletus.

Chapter 23

A week later Cletus returned to New Earth with two leased cargo vessels, the crew and officers of which had agreed to being held in a locked room during the embarking and disembarking of the troops they were supposed to carry. They could testify afterward only to hearing the sounds of boots entering the ship for two and a half hours, on the Dorsai, and to some four hours of similar sounds as they hung in orbit above New Earth, while landing craft shuttled from their ships to some unannounced spot on the planet below. Agents for the Central Combine of city-states, however, observed these landing craft making their sit-downs in a wooded area just inside Breatha Colony's border with Spainville. On attempting to investigate further, the agents found themselves stopped and warned back by a cordon of armed Dorsais, but their estimate of the troops landed, taken from the number of trips from the spaceships in orbit, was of at least five thousand men.

General Lu May, commander of the city-states combined forces, grunted when this information was brought to him.

"That's the sort of thing this Grahame likes to pull," said Lu May. The general was in his mid-seventies, and had been retired from active soldiering until the new ambitions and war-like fervor of the city-states had summoned him back to take over-all command of their new army. "He'd like to shake us up with the idea that we've got to watch two separate invading commands. But I'll lay you odds he pulls them to-gether at the first opportunity, as soon as he thinks he's got us out in the open where he can pull all sorts of fancy maneuvers. But we aren't going to fall for it. We'll stay dug in here in Spainville, and make him come to us."

He chuckled. He was fat as well as old, and the thought of being able to frustrate this unorthodox young upstart while remaining comfortably seated in his own home in Stanleyville tickled him. He ordered heavy energy weapons dug in all around the perimeter of the city and all approaches heavily mined. It would take more than the light-weaponed and light-armored Dorsai mercenaries to break through defenses such as these, even if they were equal in number to the men he had under arms inside the city.

Meanwhile, Cletus' forces were already in motion. A motley horde of civilian trucks and other heavy-duty, air-cushioned sliders had earlier converged on the area where the shuttleboats had landed from the spaceships. These now moved out like a transport and supply convoy, with an armed Dorsai driving each of them. This force crossed the border into Armoy, and swung inland toward Armoy City and its new spaceport, thereby raising flutters of alarm within the community's citizens.

"Sit tight!" grunted Lu May to the frantic messages that reached him from Armoy City for an expeditionary force to defend them against the oncoming Dorsais. He did not send the force, but instead followed his own advice, sitting tight and watching Cletus' other command, which was also in movement now, across the Spainville border, heading apparently through Spainville toward one of the other adjoining city-states. Still Lu May made no move, and sure enough, once it had passed the city of Spainville, Cletus' first command of Dorsais swung about and came up on the city's rear. At the same time, the command that had been threatening Armoy City swung away and cut in to come up before the city of Spainville, so that within a few days the city was ringed by the Dorsai troops.

Lu May chortled and slapped his fat knees. Curiously enough, in Cletus' headquarters outside the city, there was hardly less satisfaction to be found in the person of Chancellor Ad Reyes, representative of the government of Breatha Colony, who was accompanying Cletus, ostensibly as an "observer."

"Excellent, Marshal. Excellent!" Reyes, who was a thin, eager, scholarly-looking man with a high forehead, dressed in the long, black, official gown of his chancellorhood, rubbed his thin hands with pleasure. "You've managed to trap their army here. And there're no other forces who can come to their rescue. Excellently done!"

"You should thank General Lu May for that, instead of me," Cletus answered, dryly. "He has a good deal less to fear from us, sitting back behind his mine fields and his perimeter defenses, than he does in the open field, where the Dorsais are a great deal more mobile than his troops. He has more men and he's in an entrenched position."

"But you don't have to try to take the place by assault!" protested Reyes. "You can live off the country or supply yourself from Breatha as you want. Lu May's cut off from outside supplies. It's just a matter of starving him out!"

"That may not be easy," said Cletus, "unless he's been strangely forgetful, while preparing for everything else, to stock enough provisions for the city and his troops so that they can hold out longer than we can afford to sit here besieging them."

Reyes frowned. Plainly, it seemed to him that this Dorsai marshal was taking an entirely too gloomy a view of the situation.

"Do you object to besieging the city?" Reyes demanded. "If so, I should probably mention that the Breatha government considered this the optimum—indeed the only—course you could pursue, if you were lucky enough to trap Lu May in a fixed position."

"I don't object—for now," Cletus answered, quietly. "But that's because there're military reasons for it, far removed from the opinions of your government. I might remind you, Chancellor, that one of my stipulations in accepting employment with Breatha Colony, as it is with every government with whom I sign a contract, is that I, alone, be in charge of the conduct of the campaign."

He turned and sat down behind the desk in the office of the field structure in which they had been talking. "And now, if you'll excuse me, I've got work to do."

Reyes hesitated, then turned on his heel and walked out.

Cletus continued the siege for three weeks, throwing up breastworks and digging his own trenches behind them to encircle the city, as if he had every intention of staying indefinitely. Meanwhile, outside of an occasional exchange of small-arms fire, there was little open conflict between the city defenders and its Dorsai attackers.

Meanwhile, overhead, a similar unspoken truce existed. Dorsai aircraft patrolled the atmosphere above and about the city to prevent city-state vessels from entering or leaving it. But beyond this, there was no aerial conflict. As in most inter-colony armed conflicts on the new worlds, air warfare was being avoided by the sort of tacit agreement that had interdicted the use of poison gas during World War II in the twentieth century on Earth. The object of armed struggle between opposed technology-poor communities, such as the young colonies, was not so much to destroy the enemy's productive capacity as to take it away from him. One did not obliterate by bombing that which one had started a war to obtain. And if the factories and other hardware of civilization were valuable, the men who had the skills to operate them were almost as valuable.

Therefore, bombing and even the indiscriminate use of heavy weapons in the vicinity of built-up areas was avoided, and—atmosphere craft being almost as expensive as spacecraft—any other use of the skies other than for reconnaissance or the transporting of troops was likewise avoided.

At the end of three weeks, however, Cletus apparently lost patience with this stalemate and issued orders, orders that brought Chancellor Ad Reyes literally running to Cletus' headquarters office, the black gown tucked up to allow free movement to the chancellor's legs.

"You're pulling out half your forces and sending them to take Armoy City and its spaceport!" Reyes accused him, bursting into Cletus' office.

Cletus looked up from the desk at which he was working. "You've heard of that, have you?" Cletus asked.

"Heard of it!" Reyes strode up to the edge of the desk and leaned over it almost as though he would have liked to have thrust his face nose-to-nose with Cletus'. "I've *seen* them! All those civilian trucks you requisitioned to transport your secondary command are headed off toward Armoy! Don't tell me that isn't where they're headed!"

"That's where they're headed," said Cletus, agreeably. "The rest of us will be following them in twenty-four hours. There's plainly no point in continuing this siege any longer. I'm going to raise it, move on Armoy City and take that spaceport of theirs."

"Raise the siege? . . . What kind of trick is this? If you'd been paid by the city-states to betray us, you couldn't have picked a better—" He broke off abruptly, shrinking a little at the sudden sound of his own words in his ears. Cletus was on his feet behind the desk.

"I hope I don't hear you correctly, Chancellor." Cletus' voice and eyes had changed. "Are you accusing Dorsais of dishonoring a contract with your government?"

"No . . . that is, I didn't mean . . ." Reyes stammered.

"I'd advise you to be careful of what you do mean," said Cletus. "The Dorsais don't break contracts, and we don't tolerate talk that we do. And now, for the last time, let me remind you that I—I, alone— am in command of this campaign. Perhaps you should get back to your own quarters, now."

"Yes, I . . ." Reyes fled.

Just before dawn the following morning, the rest of the Dorsais besieging Spainville mounted their military vehicles and pulled out with all armor and weapons. Only their aircraft remained above Spainville to discourage pursuit by air reconnaissance.

Dawn rose on the empty trenches and breastworks that the mercenaries had thrown up, but it was nearly noon before their silence and appearance of abandonment could tempt patrols out from Spainville to investigate. When, however, the former Dorsai positions had been investigated and found to be abandoned, the patrols took note of the direction of the signs of departure visible in the pasture earth and summer grass south of the city, and passed the word hastily to General Lu May.

Lu May, roused with this news from his slumbers after a late evening, swore in a way that had gone out of fashion forty years ago.

"We've got him!" the old man exploded, rolling out of bed and beginning hastily to struggle into his clothes. "He couldn't stand the waiting—now he's cut his own throat!"

"Sir?" protested the colonel who had brought him the news. "Cut his own throat? I don't understand—"

"That's because you kids know nothing about war the way it's really fought!" trumpeted Lu May, getting into his trousers. "Grahame's headed for Armoy City, idiot!"

"Yes, sir," said the colonel. "But I still don't see—"

"He's faced the fact that there was no hope of his taking the city here!" snapped Lu May. "So he's pulled out and decided to take Armoy City, instead. That way he can claim that he did the best he could, and at least got Breatha Colony the spaceport that was giving them competition! With the spaceport, he'll tell them, they can make a deal to protect their corridor to the sea! Don't you see? Grahame's finally faced the fact that it was a bad contract he signed. He wants to get out of it on any terms—but he can't get out unless he has at least something to offer Breatha. Armoy City and that spaceport will be it!"

"Yes, sir," said the colonel, earnestly. "I see all that. But what I don't understand is why you say he cut his own throat. After all, if he's able to give Breatha Colony the spaceport and Armoy City to bargain with—"

"Idiot! Double idiot!" roared Lu May. "He has to take Armoy City first, doesn't he, fool?"

"Yes, sir—"

"Then he's going to have to occupy Armoy City with his forces, isn't he?"

Dressed at last, Lu May waddled hastily toward the door. Over his shoulder, he continued, "If we move fast after him, we'll catch him inside Armoy City, and we can surround him! He's got no supplies to last in a city like that very long—and if we need to, we even have the men and weapons to take the city by storm! Either way we can wrap his Dorsais up and have him as a prisoner to do what we want with!"

Lu May wasted no time in getting his army in pursuit of Cletus and the Dorsais. But for all his hurry, he did not fail to move out in good marching order, or without the heavy energy weapons he had dug in around the perimeter of the city, and which he now took with him, even though having them with him would necessarily slow his movement. Ponderous, but deadly, he slid along over the plain track Cletus' two departing commands had left behind through the standing grass and grain.

The direction of the track aimed directly at Armoy City, perhaps three days' travel away for Cletus' lightly equipped Dorsais. Lu May would be lucky to do it in four with his command, but the extra day should bring the Spainville general on the scene at Armoy City, as he calculated, just in good time to take advantage of that moment in which Cletus' troops were letting down, after having made their conquest of Armoy City and the spaceport an accomplished fact.

All the same, it was wise—thought Lu May—to give himself a little time margin if at all possible. If he should find himself ahead of schedule, he could always dawdle a bit in coming up to the city at the far end of his pursuit. Therefore, he issued orders after the evening meal for his command to continue after dark, under the moonless but star-bright New Earth sky. He pushed them on through the darkness until men began falling asleep at the controls of their vehicles, or on their feet. Finally, reluctantly, he called a halt for the night about three hours after midnight.

His army had just managed to get deeply into exhausted slumber, when a series of sharp, blasting explosions jerked them back to wakefulness, and they sat up to see the heavy energy weapons they had been hauling burning with sparkling red-white flames as their energy storage units melted under their own fierce heat like butter in a furnace. In the same moment, dark-clad Dorsais were suddenly among Lu May's troops stripping them of their body weapons and heading them into groups under the watchful eyes and guns of other mercenaries standing guard.

General Lu May, himself, started out of deep slumber, and sat up in his field bed to find Cletus standing over him, an uncapped holster showing the sidearm at Cletus' side. Lu May stared in befuddlement.

"But you're ... up ahead of me ..." he stammered, after a moment.

"I've got a detachment of empty civilian trucks up ahead of you," answered Cletus. "Trucks that never had any men in them except the drivers. What men I had are here with me now—and your command is taken prisoner, General. You'll make things simpler by giving me your surrender, right now."

Lu May fumbled out of bed. Suddenly he was very old, and chilly, and helpless, standing there in his pajamas. Almost humbly, he went through the motions of surrender.

Cletus went back to the field unit that had already been set up as his temporary headquarters. Waiting inside for him was Chancellor Ad Reyes.

"You can inform your government that the effective military forces of the combined city-states are now our prisoner, Chancellor . . ." he began, and broke off as Arvid entered, bearing a yellow message slip.

"Signal from Colonel Khan on the Dorsai," said Arvid, "forwarded on by our base camp at Adonyer, back in Breatha Colony."

Cletus took the message sheet and unfolded it. He read:

Attack made through Etter's Pass from Neuland into Bak-halla territory beaten off. Alliance and Coalition forces combined in a joint "Peace Force" for the new worlds. Dow deCastries has supreme command of this force.

Cletus folded the message and put it in a pocket of his battle tunic. He turned to Reyes.

"You've got twenty-four hours," he said, "to get Breatha troops here to take charge of these prisoners we've just captured. I and my troops must return immediately to the Dorsai."

Reyes stared at him in combined awe and amazement. "But we'd planned a triumphal parade in case of victory . . ." he began, uncertainly.

"Twenty-four hours," said Cletus, brusquely. He turned on his heel and left the chancellor standing.

Chapter 24

Landing back on the Dorsai, Cletus phoned ahead to order Major Arvid
Johnson, now acting field commander, to meet him at Grahame House.
Then with Bill Athyer like a smaller, beak-nosed shadow at his side,
he took a hired atmosphere craft to Foralie and Grahame House, still
wearing his battle uniform.

Melissa, with Arvid and Eachan, met him just inside the front door.
Athyer, diffident still in spite of his present rank, stood at the far end
of the entrance hall as Cletus greeted Melissa and Eachan briefly before
striding on toward the door to his office-study and beckoning Eachan
and Arvid to follow him.

"You too, Bill," he said to Athyer.

He closed the door of the office behind them. "What's the latest
word?" Cletus demanded of his father-in-law, as he walked around to
stand behind the pile of message blanks on his desk and stare down at
them.

"It seems deCastries was appointed to this position as Commander-
in-Chief of the joint Alliance-Coalition troops on the new worlds several months ago," answered Eachan. "The Coalition and the Alliance
just kept it secret while the two high commands built up a news campaign to get the common citizens of Earth on both sides ready for the
idea. Also, Artur Walco's here to see you. Seems like deCastries is
already making trouble for him at those stibnite mines on Newton."

"Yes, there'll be brush wars breaking out all over the new worlds
now. . . . I'll see Walco tomorrow morning," said Cletus. He turned to
Arvid.

"Well, Arv," he said. "If the Dorsai had medals to give I'd be
handing you a fistful of them right now. I hope someday you can

forgive me for this. I had to have you thinking I'd shoved you aside into the field for good."

"You didn't, sir?" asked Arvid, quietly.

"No," said Cletus. "I wanted a development in you. And I've got it."

In fact, it was a different man who stood before them to answer to the name of Arvid Johnson. Not the least of the change was that he looked at least five years older. His white-blond hair had darkened as though with age, and his skin was more deeply suntanned than it had been. He looked as though he had lost weight, and yet he appeared larger than ever, a man of gaunt bone and whip-cord muscle, towering over all of them.

At the same time, something was gone from him for good. A youthfulness, a friendly softness that had been a basic part of him before was vanished now. In its place was something grim and isolated, as though he had at last become coldly conscious of the strength and skill in him that set him apart from other men. A quality like the sheer, physical deadliness of Swahili had entered into him.

He stood without moving. When he had moved earlier, it had been almost without a sound. He seemed to carry about him now a careful- ness born of the consciousness that all others were smaller and weaker than he, so that he must remember not to damage them without intent. Like someone more warrior than man, prototype of some line of in- vincible giants to come, he stood by Cletus' desk.

"That's good to hear," he said softly, to Cletus, now. "What do you want me to do?"

"Fight a campaign—if necessary," said Cletus. "I'm going to give you a world to defend. And I'm promoting you two grades to a new rank—vice-marshal. You'll be working in team with another officer also holding an entirely new rank—the rank of battle operator."

He turned slightly to look at Bill Athyer. "That'll be Bill, here," he said. "As battle op, Bill will rank just below you and above any other officer in the field with you, except myself."

Arvid and Bill looked at each other.

"Battle operator?" said Eachan.

"That's right," Cletus answered him. "Don't look so surprised, Eachan. This is something we've been headed toward from the start, with the reorganization and retraining of the men."

He looked back at Arvid and Bill. "The marshal, or vice-marshal, and the battle operator," Cletus said, "will form a general commander's team. The battle op is the theoretical strategist of that team and the vice-marshal is the field tactician. The two will bear roughly the same relationship to each other as an architect and a general contractor in the construction of a building. The battle op will first consider the strategical situation and problem and lay out a campaign plan. And in this process he will have complete authority and freedom."

Cletus had been watching Bill in particular as he spoke. Now, he paused. "You understand, Bill?" he said.

"Yes, sir," he replied.

"Then, however"—Cletus' eyes swung to Arvid—"the battle op will hand his strategical plan to the vice-marshal, and from that point on, it'll be the vice-marshal who has complete authority. His job will be to take the plan given him, make any and all alterations in it he thinks it needs for practical purposes and then execute it as he sees fit. *You* understand, Arv?"

"Yes, sir," said Arvid, softly.

"Good," said Cletus. "Then you and Bill are released from your present duties as of now and you'll begin immediately on your new jobs. The world I'm giving you to start with is the Dorsai here, and the first force you'll be working with will be made up of the women and children, the sick, the injured, and the average men."

He smiled a little at them. "Then get at it, both of you," he said. "None of us has any time to waste nowadays."

As the door to the office closed behind the two of them, a wave of the fatigue he had been holding at bay for a number of days and hours now suddenly washed over him. He swayed where he stood and felt Eachan catch him by the elbow.

"No—it's all right," he said. His vision cleared and he looked into Eachan's concerned face. "I'm just tired, that's all. I'll take a nap and then we'll hit things after dinner."

With Eachan walking guardedly beside him, he walked out of the office-study, feeling as though he were stepping on pillows, and went up to his bedroom. The bed was before him; he dropped onto its yielding surface without bothering even to take off his boots. . . . And that was the last he remembered.

He awoke just before sunset, ate a light meal and spent half an hour getting reacquainted with his son. Then he closeted himself in his office with Eachan to attack the pile of paper work. They sorted the correspondence into two piles, one which Cletus had to answer himself and one which Eachan could answer with a few words per letter of direction from him. Both men dictated until nearly dawn before the desk was cleared and the necessary orders for the Dorsai and off-world troops were issued.

The interview in the study next day with the Newtonian chairman,

Walco, was brief and bitter. The bitterness might have gone into acrimony and the interview prolonged unduly if Cletus had not cut short Walco's scarcely veiled accusations.

"The contract I signed with you," said Cletus, "promised to capture Watershed and the stibnite mines, and turn them over to your own troops. We made no guarantee that you'd stay in control of the mines. Holding onto them was up to you, and to whatever agreement you could make with the Brozans."

"We made our agreement!" said Walco. "But now that they've suddenly been reinforced by fifteen thousand Alliance and Coalition troops, courtesy of this fellow deCastries, they're refusing to honor it. They claim they made it under duress!"

"Didn't they?" Cletus said.

"That's not the point! The point is, we need you and enough troops from the Dorsai, right away, to match those fifteen thousand soldiers from Earth that the Brozans're holding over us like a club."

Cletus shook his head. "I'm sorry," he said. "I'm facing unusual demands on my available mercenaries right now. Also, I'm not free to come to Newton, myself."

Walco's face went lumpy and hard. "You help get us into a spot," he said, "and then when trouble comes, you leave us to face it alone. Is that what you call justice?"

"Was justice mentioned when you signed us to the original contract?" replied Cletus, grimly. "I don't remember it. If justice had been a topic, I'd have been forced to point out to you that, while it was your funds and experts who developed the stibnite mine, that was only because you were in a position to take advantage of the Brozan poverty that was then keeping them from developing the mines themselves. You may have a financial interest in the mines, but the Brozans have a moral claim to them—they're a Brozan natural resource. If you'd faced that fact, you'd hardly have been able to avoid seeing their moral claim, which would have to be recognized by you, eventually—" He broke off.

"Forgive me," he said, dryly. "I'm a little overworked these days. I gave up long ago doing other people's thinking for them. I've told you that neither I, nor an expeditionary force of the size you ask for, is available to you right at the moment."

"Then what will you do for us?" muttered Walco.

"I can send you some men to officer and command your own forces, provided you contract to let them make all the military decisions, themselves."

"What?" Walco cried out the word. "That's worse than nothing!"

"I'll be perfectly happy to let you have nothing, then, if that's what you prefer," said Cletus. "If so, let me know now. My time's limited at the moment."

There was a second's pause. Gradually the lumpiness of Walco's features smoothed out into an expression almost of despair.

"We'll take your officers," he said, on a long exhalation of breath.

"Good. Colonel Khan will have the contract ready for you in two days. You can discuss the terms with him then," said Cletus. "And now, if you'll excuse me . . ."

Walco left. Cletus called in David Ap Morgan, one of Eachan's old officers, now a senior field commander, and gave him the job of heading up the officers to be sent to command the troops of the Associated Advanced Communities on Newton.

"You can turn the job down, of course," Cletus wound up.

"You know I won't," said David Ap Morgan. "What do you want me to do?"

"Thanks," said Cletus. "All right. I'm going to give you about twelve hundred and fifty men, each one bumped up at least one rank from what he's holding now. You'll have ex-noncoms to be your force leaders. Use them to replace all the local commissioned officers—I mean *all*. And the contract's being written to give you sole command in military matters. Be sure you keep that command. Don't take any advice from Walco and his government, under any circumstances. Tell them if they don't leave you alone, you'll pull out and come back here."

David nodded. "Yes, sir," he said. "Any plan for the campaign?"

"Just make sure you don't fight any stand-up battles," said Cletus. "I probably don't need to tell you that. Your AAC troops wouldn't be any good in a stand-up battle anyway. But even if they would be, I still wouldn't want you to fight. Tease the Alliance-Coalition forces into chasing you—and then keep them chasing. Lead them all over the map. Hit them just enough to keep them hot after you and break up into guerrilla groups if they get too close. Do anything needed to keep them worried and your own casualties down as much as possible."

David nodded again.

"I think"—Cletus looked at him seriously—"you'll find you'll lose 70 or 80 percent of your AAC troops through desertion in the first four to six weeks. The ones that hang on will be the ones who're starting to have faith in you. You may be able to start training them as they go to turn into fairly effective soldiers."

"I'll do that," said David. "Anything else?"

"No. Just make it as expensive for the enemy as possible," answered Cletus. "Don't hit their troops when you can avoid it. Make their casualties light, but make it expensive for them in material. The more active duty soldiers they have, the more there'll be around to miss the food, equipment and other supplies I'm counting on you to destroy, every chance you get."

"Got it," said David, and went off, whistling, to his nearby home of Fal Morgan, to pack his gear for the campaign. Like all his family, he had a fine singing voice and he also whistled sweetly and intricately. Unexpectedly, hearing that tune fade away down his entrance hall and out the front door of Grahame House, Cletus was reminded of a song Melissa had played and sung for him once. It was a small, sad, beautiful tune made by a young member of the Ap Morgan family who had died in some campaign when Melissa had been even younger, long before Cletus had come to the Dorsai.

He could not remember it all, but it dealt with the young soldier's strong memories of the house where he had grown up, remembered while he was waiting for an engagement to begin on some other world.

> . . . Fal Morgan, Fal Morgan, when morning is gray,
> Your wall stones and rooftree stand near me, today . . .

Cletus shook the emotional tag end of recollection from his mind. He turned to the task of picking out the men he would promote and send with David.

During the weeks that followed, the demand upon the Dorsai professional soldiers continued. Everywhere that Cletus had won a campaign, the combined Alliance-Coalition forces were in action, trying to reverse whatever situation his successful actions had created.

The efforts of the forces from Earth were ponderous and awesome. Together, the Alliance and the Coalition had better than half a million military people scattered out upon the new worlds. If the full half million could have been made effective in the campaigns Dow de-Castries was trying to conduct, any opposition by the Dorsais or the attacked colonies could not have lasted more than a few days in each case.

As it was, however, nearly half the half million were engaged in military occupations other than those of a fighting soldier or officer. And of the more than two hundred and fifty thousand men that this left technically available for active duty in the field, more than a hundred and fifty thousand at any one time were rendered—or managed to render themselves—ineffective through a variety of means and for a variety of causes.

Among these were deep suspicions and old rivalries between former Alliance officers and their new Coalition partners; also, there was laziness and inefficiency among those of all ranks and political backgrounds, and the sheer blundering that inevitably resulted from the disorganization in such a large, hastily formed partnership of military units.

In spite of this, with all these subtractions, there remained a hard core of perhaps eighty thousand well-trained and superbly equipped troops from Earth to face a couple of hundred thousand almost useless and practically nonequipped local Colonial troops, plus a relative handful of Dorsais. Cletus could hardly have put twenty thousand Dorsai men in the field, even if he had scraped together every male from that small world, including walking cripples, between the ages of twelve and eighty.

Sending small contingents of Dorsais to officer Colonial troops was one solution; but only where the Colonial troops had at least a shred of training and effectiveness. Where this was not the case—as on Cassida—or where there simply were no native Colonial troops to officer—as on St. Marie—actual contingents of Dorsais had to be sent.

"But why don't we just stop?" demanded Melissa, anguished one day after she had come back from visiting a neighboring household that had lost yet another of the family's men. "Why can't we just stop sending men out?"

"For the same reason the Coalition and the Alliance have combined to send men to reverse everything we've accomplished," Cletus answered her. "If they beat us at every point, they'll destroy our value as soldiers for hire to the other colonies. That's what Dow's really after. Then they'll come on to the Dorsai and destroy us."

"You can't be sure of that—that they're out to destroy us!"

"I can't be other than sure. Nor can anyone who's thought the matter through," said Cletus. "We were winning every campaign and proving ourselves superior to their own troops. A little more of that, and troops from the Alliance and the Coalition wouldn't be needed anymore on the new worlds. And with the need gone for any military support from Earth, there'd go Earth's influence among the colonies. This way, if they win, they protect their hold on the new worlds. While if we win—"

"Win!" snorted Eachan, who was in the room at the time.

"If we win," repeated Cletus, looking steadily at the older man, "we break that hold for good. It's a battle for survival between us now—when it's over, either Earth or the Dorsai are going to be counted out on the new worlds."

She stared at him, her eyes unnaturally wide, for a long moment of silence. "I can't believe that!" she said at last. She turned to her father. "Dad—"

"Oh, it's true enough," said Eachan flatly, from across the room. "We *were* too successful—with Cletus' early campaigns on Newton and worlds like that. We scared the Alliance and the Coalition, both. Now they're out to make themselves safe. And they're very big, and we're very small. . . . And we've already sent out the last men we've got to send."

"They haven't any left in reserve either," said Cletus.

Eachan said nothing. Melissa turned back to Cletus.

"No," said Cletus, although she had not spoken, "I don't intend to lose."

Eachan still said nothing. In the silence, distantly, the front door annunciator chimed. A second later, an aide opened the door.

"Rebon, Exotic Outbond to the Dorsai, sir," he said.

"Bring him in," said Cletus. The aide stood aside and a slight man in blue robes entered the room.

His face held the eternal Exotic calm, but his expression was serious nonetheless. He came up to Cletus as both Cletus and Eachan got to their feet.

"I've got some bad news I'm afraid, Cletus," he said. "A military force of the Alliance-Coalition Peace Force has seized the Maran core-tap site and all the equipment and technicians there."

"On what basis?" snapped Eachan.

"The Coalition has filed claims against the Associated Advanced Communities of Newton," said Rebon, turning slightly to face Eachan. "They've seized the core-tap site as an AAC asset pending settlement of their claim. Mondar"—he turned back to Cletus—"asks your help."

"When did this happen?" asked Cletus.

"Eight hours ago," said Rebon.

"Eight hours!" exploded Eachan. The fastest spaceship—and there was no known swifter way of transmitting messages across interstellar space—required at least three days to cover the light-years between Mara and the Dorsai. Rebon's eyes veiled themselves slightly.

"I assure you it's true," he murmured.

"And where'd the troops come from?" demanded Eachan. He threw a glance at Cletus. "They weren't supposed to have any more available!"

"From the Friendlies, undoubtedly," replied Cletus.

Rebon lifted his gaze back to Cletus, slowly. "That's true," he said, on a note of surprise. "You expected this?"

"I expected deCastries to hire help from Harmony or Association eventually," said Cletus, brusquely. "I'll leave right away."

"For the core-tap site on Mara?" Relief sounded in Rebon's voice. "You *can* raise men to help us, then?"

"No. Alone. For Kultis," said Cletus, already striding out of the room, "to talk to Mondar."

Boarding the spaceship that would take him to Kultis, he encountered at the foot of the boarding ladder Vice-Marshal Arvid Johnson and Battle Operator William Athyer, who had been ordered to meet him here. Cletus stopped for a moment to speak to them.

"Well," said Cletus, "do you still have any notion I gave you a nothing job when I put you in charge of defending the Dorsai?"

"No, sir." Arvid looked calmly at him.

"Good. It's up to you then," said Cletus. "You know the principles behind whatever action you'll need to take. Good luck."

"Thank you," said Bill. "Good luck to you, too, sir."

"I make it a point not to know the lady," said Cletus "I can't afford to count on her."

He went up the boarding ladder and the entry port of the ship closed behind him.

Five minutes later it leaped skyward in thunder and was lost into space.

Chapter 25

Mondar had changed in some indefinable way, since Cletus had seen him last, when they met again in Mondar's garden-enclosed residence in Bakhalla. There were no new lines in the calm face, no touch of gray in the Exotic's hair, but the blue eyes, like Melissa's, were becoming strangely deeper in color, as though the time that had passed had dredged new levels of understanding in the mind behind them.

"You can't help us on Mara, then, Cletus?" were the words with which he greeted Cletus on the latter's arrival.

"I don't have any more troops to send," said Cletus. "And if I had, I'd strongly suggest we not send them."

They passed through the halls of Mondar's house, walking side by side, and emerged into an enclosure half-room, half-arbor, where Mondar waved Cletus to a wide, basket-weave chair, and then took one like it himself. All this time Mondar had not spoken; but now he did.

"We stand to lose more than we can afford, if we lose our present investment in the core-tap," said Mondar. "We've still got a contingent of your Dorsais here in Bakhalla. Can't we use some of them to retake the core-tap site?"

"Not unless you want the additional Alliance-Coalition troops that have been put into Neuland to come boiling over the border into your colony, here," said Cletus. "You don't want that, do you?"

"No," said Mondar. "We don't want that. But what's to be done about the Friendly mercenaries occupying the core-tap site?"

"Leave them there," said Cletus.

Mondar gazed at him. "Cletus," he said softly after a second, "you aren't just trying to justify this situation you've created?"

"Do you trust my judgment?" countered Cletus.

"I've got a high regard for it," Mondar answered slowly, "personally. But I'm afraid that most of the other Outbonds here and in the
Maran colonies of our people don't share that high regard at the moment."

"But they still trust you to make the decisions about me, don't
they?" asked Cletus.

Mondar gazed at him, curiously. "What makes you so sure of
that?" he asked.

"The fact that I've gotten everything I've ever asked the Exotics
for, through you—up until now," answered Cletus. "You're the man
who has to recommend me as a bad bet or a good one, still, aren't
you?"

"Yes," said Mondar, with something of a sigh. "And that's why
I'm afraid you won't find me as personally partial to you now as I
might be, Cletus. I've got a responsibility to my fellow Exotics now
that makes me take a harder view of the situation than I might take by
myself. Also, I've got a responsibility to come to some kind of a
decision between you and the Alliance-Coalition combination."

"What's the procedure if you decide for them—and against us?"
asked Cletus.

"I'm afraid we'd have to come to the best possible terms with
them that we could," Mondar answered. "Undoubtedly they'd want us
to do more than dismiss the troops we've now got in hire from you,
and call in your loan. They'd want us to actively throw our support on
their side, hire their troops and help them against you on the Dorsai."

Cletus nodded. "Yes, that's what they'd want," he said. "All right,
what do you need to decide to stick with the Dorsai?"

"Some indication that the Dorsai stands a chance of surviving the
present situation," said Mondar. "To begin with, I've told you we face
a severe loss in the case of the Maran core-tap, and you said just now,
even if you had the troops to spare, you'd suggest doing nothing about
the Alliance-Coalition occupation of the site. You must have some
reasoning to back that suggestion?"

"Certainly," said Cletus. "If you stop and think for a moment,
you'll realize the core-tap project itself is perfectly safe. It's a structure
with both potential and actual value—to the Alliance and Coalition, as
well as to anyone else. Maybe they've occupied the site, but you can
be sure they aren't going to damage the work done so far by the men
or machines that can finish it."

"But what good's that do us, if it stays in their hands?"

"It won't stay long," said Cletus. "The occupying troops are
Friendlies and their religious, cultural discipline makes them excellent

occupying troops—but that's all. They look down their noses at the very people who hire them, and the minute their pay stops coming they'll pack up and go home. So wait a week. At the end of that time either Dow will have won, or I will. If he's won, you can still make terms with him. If I've won, your Friendlies will pack up and leave at a word from me."

Mondar looked at him narrowly. "Why do you say a week?" he asked.

"Because it won't be longer than that," Cletus answered. "Dow's hiring of Friendly troops gives away the fact that he's ready for a showdown."

"It does?" Mondar's eyes were still closely watching him. Cletus met them squarely with his own gaze.

"That's right," he said. "We know the number of the available field troops in the Alliance-Coalition force that Dow's put together. It can be estimated from what we already knew of the number of troops the Alliance and the Coalition had out on the new worlds, separately. Dow had to use all of them to start enough brush wars to tie up all my Dorsais. He hadn't any spare fighting men. But, by replacing his fighting troops with Friendlies, he can temporarily withdraw a force great enough, in theory, to destroy me. Therefore the appearance of Friendly troops under Dow's command can only mean he's forming such a showdown force."

"You can't be sure his hiring of Friendlies as mercenaries means just that, and not something else."

"Of course I can," said Cletus. "After all, I was the one who suggested the use of the Friendly troops in that way."

"*You* suggested?" Mondar stared.

"In effect," said Cletus. "I stopped off at Harmony myself some time back, to talk to James Arm-of-the-Lord and suggest he hire out members of his Militant Church as raw material to fill uniforms and swell the official numbers of my Dorsais. I offered him a low price for the men. It hardly took any imagination to foresee that once the idea'd been suggested to him, he'd turn around as soon as I'd left and try to get a higher price from Dow for the same men, used the same way."

"And Dow, of course, with Alliance and Coalition money, could pay a higher price," said Mondar, thoughtfully. "But if that's true, why didn't Dow hire them earlier?"

"Because exposing them to conflicts with my Dorsais would have quickly given away the fact that the Friendlies hadn't any real military skills," replied Cletus. "Dow's best use of them could come only from putting them into uniform briefly, to replace the elite Alliance-Association troops he wanted to withdraw secretly, for a final battle to settle all matters."

"You seem," said Mondar slowly, "very sure of all this, Cletus."

"That's natural enough," said Cletus. "It's what I've been pointing toward ever since I sat down at the table with Dow and the rest of you on board the spaceship to Kultis."

Mondar raised his eyebrows. "That much planning and executing?" he said. "Still, it doesn't mean you can be absolutely sure Dow will do what you think he'll do."

"Nothing's absolutely sure, of course," said Cletus. "But for practical purposes I'm sure enough. Can you get your fellow Exotics to hold off action on the occupation of the Maran core-tap site for seven days?"

Mondar hesitated. "I think so," he said. "For seven days, anyway. Meanwhile, what are you going to do?"

"Wait," said Cletus.

"Here?" said Mondar. "With Dow, according to your estimate, gathering his best troops to strike? I'm surprised you left the Dorsai to come here in the first place."

"No need to be surprised," said Cletus. "You know I know that the Exotics somehow seem to get information of events on other worlds faster than the fastest spaceship can bring it. It merely seemed to me that information might reach me as fast here as it would any place. Would you say I was wrong?"

Mondar smiled slightly. "No," he answered. "I'd have to say you weren't wrong. Be my guest, then, while you wait."

"Thank you," said Cletus.

Mondar's guest, then, he remained—for three days during which he inspected the Dorsai troops in Bakhalla, browsed in the local library that had been the scene of Bill Athyer's discovery of a new occupation life and renewed his old acquaintance with Wefer Linet.

On the morning of the fourth day, as he and Mondar were having breakfast together, a young Exotic in a green robe brought in a paper, which he handed to Mondar without a word. Mondar glanced at it and passed it over to Cletus.

"Dow and fifteen shiploads of Coalition elite troops," Mondar said, "landed on the Dorsai two days ago. They've occupied the planet."

Cletus got to his feet.

"What now?" Mondar looked up at him from the table. "There's nothing you can do now. Without the Dorsai, what have you got?"

"What did I have before I had the Dorsai?" retorted Cletus. "It's not the Dorsai Dow wants, Mondar, it's me. And as long as I'm able to operate, he hasn't won. I'll be leaving for the Dorsai immediately." Mondar got to his feet. "I'll go with you," he said.

Chapter 26

The shuttleboat, with the Exotic sunburst emblem inlaid on its metal side, was allowed to land without protest on the Dorsai at the Foralie shuttleboat pad. But on emerging with Mondar, Cletus was immediately disarmed of his sidearm by competent-looking and obviously veteran troops in Coalition uniforms, with the white band of the Alliance-Coalition Joint Force fastened about their right sleeves. The same soldiers escorted the three men through a Foralie town where none of the local people were to be seen—only the occupying soldiers—to a military atmosphere craft that flew them up to Grahame House.

Word of their arrival had obviously been sent ahead. They were escorted to the door of the main lounge of the house, ushered inside and the door closed firmly behind them. Within, seated with drinks in which they obviously had little interest, were Melissa and Eachan, in their stiffness and unnaturalness, like set pieces arranged to show off Dow deCastries, slim in the gray-white Coalition uniform, standing beside the bar at the far end of the room with a drink also in his hand.

Across the room, Swahili, also in Coalition uniform, stood holding a heavy energy handgun.

"Hello, Cletus," Dow said. "I was expecting to find you here when I landed. I'm surprised you came on in when you saw my transports in orbit. Or didn't you think we'd have occupied all of the Dorsai yet?"

"I knew you had," said Cletus.

"But you came in anyway? I wouldn't have," said Dow. He raised his drink and sipped from it. "Or did you come down to trade yourself if I'd turn the Dorsai loose? If you did, that was foolish. I'm going to turn it loose anyway. All you've done is save me the trouble of hunting you down on some other world. I've got to take you back to Earth, you know."

"To be sure," said Cletus. "So I can have a trial—which will end in a death sentence. Which you can commute to life imprisonment—after which I'll be imprisoned secretly somewhere, and eventually just disappear."

"Exactly right," said Dow.

Cletus looked at the watch on his wrist. "How long is it since your scanning screens picked up the approach of the spaceship I came in?" he asked.

"About six hours." Dow put his drink down and straightened up. "Don't tell me you came in here expecting to be rescued? Maybe the handful of officers you left here do have a screen that picked your ship up, and maybe they did know it was you aboard her. But Cletus, we've been chasing them twenty-four hours a day since I brought my troops in here. They're too busy running to worry about you, even if they had enough men and guns to do something."

He stared at Cletus for a second. "All the same," he said, turning to Swahili, "we won't take any chances. Go give the local commander my orders to set up a security cordon to the shuttleboat landing pad in Foralie. And order a shuttle down from one of the transports. We'll get Grahame aboard as soon as possible." He looked back at Cletus. "I'm not going to start underestimating you now."

Swahili went out, handing his weapon to Dow and closing the door carefully behind him.

"You've never stopped underestimating me," said Cletus. "That's what brought you here."

Dow smiled.

"No. What I'm saying is quite true," said Cletus. "I needed a lever to change history and I picked you. From the time I sat down at your table on the ship to Kultis, I was busy working you into this situation."

Dow leaned the elbow holding the heavy handgun on the bar beside him, keeping its muzzle pointed steadily at Cletus.

"Move a few feet away from him, Mondar," Dow said to the Exotic, who had been standing beside and a little behind Cletus all this time. "I can't imagine you sacrificing yourself to give him a chance to escape, but there's no point in risking it."

Mondar moved.

"Go on, Cletus," said Dow. "We've got a few moments to wait anyway. I don't believe what you're saying at all, but if there's even a slight chance you've been able to maneuver me, I want to know about it."

"There's not much to tell," said Cletus. "I started out first by attracting your attention to myself. Then I showed you I had military genius. Then I began to make a name for myself on all the new worlds, knowing this would suggest an idea to you—the idea you could use what I was doing as an excuse to get what you wanted for yourself."

"And what was that?" The gun in Dow's hand was steady.

"Personal control of both the Alliance and the Coalition—and through them the new worlds," answered Cletus. "You talked up my successes on the new worlds as a threat to both the Alliance and the Coalition, until they agreed to combine their outworld forces and put you in command of them. Once in command, you thought all you needed was to stretch the Dorsais out so thin you could defeat them. Then you'd capture me and use your popularity and military power to put military juntas in place of the political leaders at the head of both the Coalition and Alliance, back on Earth. Naturally, the generals you picked for the military juntas would be your men—and in time they'd be yielding up the government of all Earth to you."

Swahili came back into the room. Dow handed him the handgun and, carefully covering Cletus all the while, Swahili crossed once more to his position on the other side of the room.

"How long?" Dow asked him.

"Twenty minutes," Swahili answered. Dow looked thoughtfully back at Cletus.

"Maybe a trial would be too much of a risk after all—" He broke off.

There were shouts, and the sharp, chorused whistling of cone rifles outside the house, followed by the heavy sizzle of at least one energy weapon. Swahili ran toward the door of the room.

"No!" snapped Dow. Swahili checked and spun about. Dow pointed at Cletus. "Shoot him!"

Swahili brought the energy handgun up and there was a sound like the snapping of a small stick. Swahili checked abruptly, turning toward Eachan, who was still sitting in his chair, but now holding the same flat little handgun—minus the long sniper's barrel—that he had used long ago from under the overturned command car in which he, with Melissa, Mondar and Cletus, had been trapped on the road to Bakhalla.

Swahili went suddenly, heavily, to his knees on the carpet. The energy pistol dropped from his grasp. He fell over on his side and lay there. Dow moved sharply toward the fallen weapon.

"Don't!" said Eachan. Dow stopped abruptly. There were more sounds of voices shouting outside the house.

Eachan got to his feet and walked across to the fallen energy weapon, still holding his own pistol. He picked up the fallen gun and bent over Swahili, who was breathing raggedly.

"Sorry, Raoul," Eachan said, gently.

Swahili looked up at him and almost smiled. The almost-smile continued and did not change. Eachan reached down in an old-fashioned gesture and softly closed the lids over the unmoving eyes. He straightened up as the door burst open and Arvid, a cone rifle in one large hand, strode into the room closely followed by Bill Athyer.

"All right, here?" said Arvid, looking at Cletus.

"All right, Arv," Cletus answered. "How about outside?"

"We've got them all," Arvid answered.

"You'd better start running in a hurry, then," said Dow, dryly. "All these detachments of mine are in constant open-channel communication with each other. There'll be other detachments moving in here within minutes. And where are you going to run to?"

"We're not going to run at all." Arvid looked at him. "All your troops on the Dorsai are now captured."

Dow stared at him. Black eyes locked with pale blue.

"I don't believe it," Dow said, flatly. "There are nothing but women, children and old men left on this world."

"What of it?" Cletus asked. Dow turned to look at him. Cletus went on: "Don't you believe I could defeat a few thousand Coalition elite troops with a worldful of women, old men and children to help me?"

Dow regarded him for a few seconds without speaking. "Yes," he said at last. "You, Cletus—I'll believe you could do it. But you weren't here." He lifted his right hand and pointed his index finger at Cletus. "The thing you forget—"

There was a small, momentary, soundless puff of white vapor from the sleeve of his jacket. What felt like a sledgehammer smashed into Cletus' upper right chest. He stumbled backward and the edge of a table stopped him from falling.

Arvid took one long, swift pace toward Dow, his nearer hand flinging up and starting to descend, edge-on.

"Don't kill him!" snapped Cletus, with what little breath was left in him.

Arvid's hand changed direction in midair. It came down to close on Dow's outstretched arm. He peeled back the sleeve, and they all saw a dead-man's tube, a reflex single-dart thrower, strapped to Dow's wrist. Arvid broke the strap fastening loose and tossed the tube into a corner of the room. He caught up Dow's other arm and peeled the sleeve back, but the wrist was bare.

"Don't move at all," Arvid said to Dow, and stepped back from him. Melissa was already at Cletus' side.

"You've got to lie down," she said.

"No." He shook his head, resisting the pull of her hands. He could not feel the extent of the damage from the shock-point of the dart, but his right upper body was numb and a weak dizziness was threatening to overwhelm him. He fought it back with all the strength of physiological discipline he had. "There's something I've got to tell him."

He leaned gratefully back against the supporting edge of the table top behind him.

"Listen to me, Dow," he said. "I'm going to send you back to Earth. We're not going to kill you."

Dow looked at him fearlessly and almost curiously.

"If that's so, I'm sorry I shot you," he said. "I thought I was on my way out and might as well take you with me. But why send me back to Earth? You know I'll just raise another army and come back. And next time I'll beat you."

"No." Cletus shook his head. "Earth's lost its influence on the new worlds. You'll tell them that, back there. From now on any colony can hire half the number of Dorsai troops that the Alliance or the Coalition supplies to their enemy—and defeat the Earth troops easily. The Dorsais will always win, and any colony can afford to hire them."

Dow frowned. "It's you that make Dorsais potent," he said. "And you won't last forever."

"But I will." Cletus had to pause to fight off the encroaching dizziness again. Barely, once more, he won the battle and went on. "Just as you said—I wasn't here when you landed. And a planetful of women, children and oldsters beat you. That's because I was as good as here. You see these two?" He nodded weakly toward Arvid and Bill.

"There're the two parts of me," he said, almost whispering now. "The theoretician and the field general. The only orders I left them was to defend Dorsai. But they defended it just the way I would have— right down to being here, when I knew they would, to rescue me from you. There's no end to the Dorsais now. Earth won't ever have troops able to beat them." The dizziness surged in on him and he forced it back.

". . . why?" he heard Dow saying. He looked about for the man and saw the lean face under the black hair and graying temples floating as if on a field of mist.

"It's time for the new worlds to go free," Cletus said. "They had to break loose from the Alliance, the Coalition—from all Earth—and make themselves into what they're meant to be. It was time. I did it."

". . . because of the books you wanted to write, you said." Dow's voice faded out almost to nothingness and then roared like the sound of surf on his ears.

"That . . . too . . ." Cletus held hard to the table edge behind him with both hands, for the floor was threatening to dissolve under his feet. "The last sixteen volumes will be tactics only as Dorsais-to-come can use . . . no use to ordinary military, back on Earth. Only with a new sort of soldier . . . with restraint . . . obligation . . . mind and body . . ."

There was no more.

After what seemed many centuries of nothingness, he drifted back to fuzzy consciousness to find himself lying on a bed. A young commandant wearing medical insignia was just finishing a broad bandage across his upper chest, and behind the commandant stood Melissa and Mondar.

"I'm not dead . . . then?" he asked, hearing the words come out in a whisper so weak it was ridiculous.

"Dow used the wrong weapon on you, Cletus," said Mondar. "Darts that trigger a state of physical shock and collapse are all right for killing ordinary men, but not one like you, who's trained his physiological processes to obey his will automatically. You're going to live—isn't he, Doctor?"

"Absolutely." The medical commandant straightened up and stepped back from the bedside. "He should have died on his feet within the first minute and a half after he was hit. When he got past that point, there was no place for his system to go but toward recovery."

He handed a hypospray arm band to Melissa. "See that he does a lot of sleeping," he said. "Come on, Outbond."

The figures of the two men moved out from Cletus' field of vision. He heard a door close at a little distance. Melissa sat down in the chair the doctor had occupied and began to strap the hypospray around Cletus' sleeveless right arm.

"You don't have to do that," he whispered to her. "You can go now, to Earth or anywhere you want. It's all over."

"Don't talk," she said. "It's all nonsense, anyway. If I'd wanted to go, I'd have gone right after you made me marry you. I could have dreamed up some excuse—to explain it to Dad. You know he'd believe anything I told him."

He stared at her. "Then why didn't—"

"Because you told me you loved me," she said. "That was all I wanted to know."

He rolled his head a little, weakly and negatively, on the pillow. "I said—"

She finished strapping the hypospray on his wrist and bent down and kissed him, stopping the words on his lips.

"You idiot!" she said, fiercely and tenderly. "You magnificent, genius-idiot! Do you think I paid any attention to what you *said?*"

DORSAI!

CADET

The boy was odd.

This much he knew for himself. This much he had heard his seniors—his mother, his father, his uncles, the officers at the Academy—mention to each other, nodding their heads confidentially, not once but many times during his short eighteen years of life, leading up to this day. Now, apart, wandering the empty rec fields in this long, amber twilight before returning to his home and the graduation supper awaiting him there, he admitted to the oddness—whether truly in himself, or only in what others thought of him.

"An odd boy," he had overheard the Commandant at the Academy saying once to the Mathematics Officer, "you never know which way he'll jump."

Back at home right now, the family would be waiting his return—unsure of which way he would jump. They would be half expecting him to refuse his Outgoing. Why? He had never given them any cause to doubt. He was Dorsai of the Dorsai, his mother a Kenwick, his father a Graeme, names so very old their origin was buried in the prehistory of the Mother Planet. His courage was unquestioned, his word unblemished. He had headed his class. His very blood and bones were the heritage of a long line of great professional soldiers. No blot of dishonor had ever marred that roll of warriors, no home had ever been burnt, its inhabitants scattered and hiding their family shame under new names, because of some failure on the part of one of the family's sons. And yet, they doubted.

He came to the fence that marked off the high hurdles from the jump pits, and leaned on it with both elbows, the tunic of a Senior

Cadet pulled tight across his shoulders. In what way was he odd? he wondered into the wide glow of the sunset. How was he different? He put himself apart from him in his mind's eye, and considered himself. A slim young man of eighteen years—tall, but not tall by Dorsai standards, strong, but not strong by Dorsai standards. His face was the face of his father, sharp and angular, straight-nosed; but without his father's massiveness of bones. His coloring was the dark coloring of the Dorsai, hair straight and black and a little coarse. Only his eyes—those indeterminate eyes that were no definite color but went from gray to green to blue with his shifting moods—were not to be found elsewhere on his family trees. But surely eyes alone could not account for a reputation of oddness?

There was, of course, his temper. He had inherited, in full measure, those cold, sudden, utterly murderous Dorsai rages which had made his people such that no sane man cared to cross one of them without good reason. But that was a common trait; and if the Dorsai thought of Donal Graeme as odd, it could not be for that alone.

Was it, he wondered now, gazing into the sunset, that even in his rages he was a little too calculating—a little too controlled and remote? And as he thought that thought, all his strangeness, all his oddness came on him with a rush, together with that weird sense of disembodiment that had afflicted him, now and again, ever since his birth.

It came always at moments like this, riding the shoulders of fatigue and some great emotion. He remembered it as a very young boy in the Academy chapel at evening service, half-faint with hunger after the long day of hard military exercises and harder lesson. The sunset, as now, came slanting in through the high windows on the bare, highly polished walls and the solidographs of famous battles inset in them. He stood among the rows of his classmates between the hard, low benches, the ranked male voices, from the youngest cadet to the deep man-voices of the officers in the rear, riding the deep, solemn notes of the Recessional—that which was known as the Dorsai Hymn now, wherever man had gone, and which a man named Kipling had written the words of, over four centuries before.

> . . . Far called, our navies melt away,
> On dune and headland sinks the fire.
> Lo! All our pomp of yesterday,
> Is one with Nineveh, and Tyre . . .

As he had remembered it being sung at the burial service when his youngest uncle's ashes had been brought back from the slagged battlefield of Donneswort, on Freiland, third planet circling the star of Sirius.

> . . . For heathen heart that puts her trust
> In reeking tube and iron shard,
> All valiant dust, that builds on dust
> And guarding, calls not thee to guard . . .

And he had sung with the rest, feeling then, as now, the final words in the innermost recesses of his heart.

> . . . For frantic boast and foolish word—
> *Thy Mercy on Thy People, Lord!*

A chill shiver ran down his back. The enchantment was complete. Far and wide about him the red and dying light flooded the level land. In the farther sky the black dot of a hawk circled. But here by the fence and the high hurdles, he stood removed and detached, enclosed by some clear, transparent wall that set him apart from all the universe, alone, untouchable and enraptured. The inhabited worlds and their suns sank and dwindled in his mind's eye; and he felt the siren, deadly pull of that ocean of some great, hidden purpose that promised him at once fulfillment and a final dissolution. He stood on its brink and its waves lapped at his feet; and, as always, he strove to lift his foot and step forward into its depths and be lost forever; but some small part of him cried out against the self-destruction and held him back.

Then suddenly—as suddenly as it had come—the spell was broken. He turned toward the craft that would take him home.

As he came to the front entrance, he found his father waiting for him, in the half-shadow leaning with his wide shoulders spread above the slim metal shaft of his cane.

"Be welcome to this house," said his father and straightened up. "You'd better get out of that uniform and into some man's clothes. Dinner will be ready in half an hour."

MAN

The men of the household of Eachan Khan Graeme sat around the long, shimmering slab of the dining board in the long and shadowy room, at their drinking after the women and children had retired. They were not all present, nor—short of a minor miracle—was it ever likely that they would be, in this life. Of sixteen adult males, nine were off at the wars among the stars, one was undergoing reconstructive surgery at the hospital in Omalu, and the eldest, Donal's granduncle, Kamal, was quietly dying in his own room at the back of the household with an oxygen tube up his nose and the faint scent of the bay lilac to remind him of his Maran wife, now forty years dead. Sitting at the table were five—of which, since three o'clock this afternoon—Donal was one.

Those others who were present to welcome him to his adulthood were Eachan, his father; Mor, his elder brother, who was home on leave from the Friendlies; and his twin uncles Ian and Kensie, who had been next in age above that James who had died at Donneswort. They sat grouped around the high end of the table, Eachan at its head, with his two sons on his right and his two younger twin brothers on his left.

"They had good officers when I was there," Eachan was saying. He leaned over to fill Donal's glass, and Donal took it up automatically, listening with both ears.

"Freilanders all," said Ian, the grimmer of the two dark twins. "They run to stiffness of organization without combat to shake them up. Kensie says Mara or Kultis, and I say why not?"

"They have full companies of Dorsai there, I hear," said Mor, at Donal's right. The deep voice of Eachan answered from his left.

"They're show guards. I know of those. Why make a cake of nothing but icing? The Bond of Kultis likes to think of having an unmatched bodyguard; but they'd be farmed out to the troops fast enough in case of real trouble between the stars."

"And meanwhile," put in Kensie, with a sudden smile that split his dark face, "no action. Peacetime soldiering goes sour. The outfits split up into little cliques, the cake-fighters move in and an actual man—a Dorsai—becomes an ornament."

"Good," said Eachan, nodding. Donal swallowed absently from his glass and the unaccustomed whiskey burned fiercely at the back of his nose and throat. Little pricklings of sweat popped out on his forehead; but he ignored them, concentrating on what was being said. This talk was all for his benefit, he knew. He was a man now, and could no longer be told what to do. The choice was his, about where he would go to take service, and they were helping him with what knowledge they had, of the eight systems and their ways.

". . . I was never great for garrison duty myself," Eachan was continuing. "A mercenary's job is to train, maintain and fight; but when all's said and done, the fighting's the thing. Not that everyone's of my mind. There are Dorsai and Dorsai—and not all Dorsai are Graemes."

"The Friendlies, now—" said Mor, and stopped with a glance at his father, afraid that he had interrupted.

"Go on," said Eachan, nodding.

"I was just about to point out," said Mor, "there's plenty of action on Association—and Harmony, too, I hear. The sects will always be fighting against each other. And there's bodyguard work—"

"Catch us being personal gunmen," said Ian, who—being closer in age to Mor than Mor's father—did not feel the need to be quite so polite. "That's no job for a soldier."

"I didn't mean to suggest it," said Mor, turning to his uncle. "But the psalm-singers rate it high among themselves, and that takes some of their best talent. It leaves the field posts open for mercenaries."

"True enough," said Kensie, equably. "And if they had less fanatics and more officers, those two worlds would be putting strong forces out between the stars. But a priest-soldier is only troublesome when he's more soldier than priest."

"I'll back that," said Mor. "This last skirmish I was in on Association, an elder came down the line after we'd taken one little town and wanted five of my men for hangmen."

"What did you do?" asked Kensie.

"Referred him to my Commandant—and then got to the old man

first and told him that if he could find five men in my force who actually wanted such a job, he could transfer them out the next day."

Ian nodded.

"Nothing spoils a man for battle like playing butcher," he said.

"The old man got that," said Mor. "They got their hangmen, I heard—but not from me."

"The lusts are vampires," said Eachan, heavily, from the head of the table. "Soldiering is a pure art. A man with a taste for blood, money or women was one I never trusted."

"The women are fine on Mara and Kultis," grinned Mor. "I hear."

"I'll not deny it," said Kensie, merrily. "But you've got to come home, some day."

"God grant that you all may," said Eachan, somberly. "I am a Dorsai and a Graeme, but if this little world of ours had something else to trade for the contracts of out-world professionals besides the blood of our best fighting men, I'd be more pleased."

"Would *you* have stayed home, Eachan," said Mor, "when you were young and had two good legs?"

"No, Mor," said Eachan, heavily. "But there are other arts, beside the art of war—even for a Dorsai." He looked at his eldest son. "When our forefathers settled this world less than a hundred and fifty years ago, it wasn't with the intention of providing gun-fodder for the other eight systems. They only wanted a world where no man could bend the destinies of another man against that second man's will."

"And that we have," said Ian, bleakly.

"And that we have," echoed Eachan. "The Dorsai is a free world where any man can do as he likes as long as he respects the rights of his neighbor. Not all the other eight systems combined would like to try their luck with this one world. But the price—the price—" He shook his head and refilled his glass.

"Now those are heavy words for a son who's just going out," said Kensie. "There's a lot of good in life just the way she is now. Beside, it's economic pressures we're under today, not military. Who'd want the Dorsai, anyway, besides us? We're all nut here, and very little kernel. Take one of the rich new worlds—like Ceta under Tau Ceti—or one of the richer, older worlds like Freiland, or Newton—or even old Venus herself. They've got cause to worry. They're the ones that are at each other's throats for the best scientists, the best technicians, the top artists and doctors. And the more work for us and the better life for us, because of it."

"Eachan's right though, Kensie," growled Ian. "They still dream of squeezing our free people up into one lump and then negotiating with that lump for the force to get the whip hand over all the other worlds." He leaned forward across the table toward Eachan and in the muted light of the dining room Donal saw the sudden white flash of the seared scar that coiled up his forearm like a snake and was lost in the loose sleeve of his short, undress tunic. "That's the danger we'll never be free of."

"As long as the cantons remain independent of the Council," said Eachan, "and the families remain independent of the cantons, there'll be no success for them, Ian." He nodded at all about the table. "That's my end of the job here at home. You can go out to the wars with easy consciences. I promise you your children will grow up free in this house—free of any man's will—or the house will no longer stand."

"I trust you," said Ian. His eyes were gleaming pale as the scar in the dimness and he was very close to that Dorsai violence of emotion that was at once so cold and so deadly. "I have two boys now under this roof. But remember no men are perfect—even the Dorsai. There was Mahub Van Ghent only five years back, who dreamed about a little kingdom among the Dorsai in the Midland South—only five years ago, Eachan!"

"He was on the other side of the world," said Eachan. "And he's dead now, at the hand of one of the Benali, his closest neighbor. His home is burnt and no man acknowledges himself a Van Ghent any more. What more do you want?"

"He should have been stopped sooner."

"Each man has a right to his own destiny," said Eachan, softly. "Until he crosses the line into another man's. His family has suffered enough."

"Yes," said Ian. He was calming down. He poured himself another drink. "That's true—that's true. They're not to blame."

"About the Exotics—" said Mor, gently.

"Oh, yes," answered Kensie, as if the twin brother that was so much a part of himself had never gotten excited at all. "Mara and Kultis—interesting worlds. Don't mistake them if you ever go there, Mor—or you either, Donal. They're sharp enough, for all their art and robes and trappings. They won't fight themselves, but they know how to hire good men. There's things being done on Mara and Kultis—and not only in the arts. Meet one of their psychologists, one time."

"They're honest," said Eachan.

"That, too," said Kensie. "But what catches at me is the fact they're going some place, in their own way. If I had to pick one of the other worlds to be born on—"

"I would always be a soldier," said Mor.

"You think so now," said Kensie, and drank. "You think so now. But it's a wild civilization we have nowadays, with its personality split a dozen different ways by a dozen different cultures. Less than five hundred years ago the average man never dreamed of getting his feet off the ground. And the farther we go the faster. And the faster farther."

"It's the Venus group forcing that, isn't it?" asked Donal, his youthful reticence all burnt away in the hot fumes of the whiskey.

"Don't you think it," said Kensie. "Science is only one road to the future. Old Venus, Old Mars—Cassida, Newton—maybe they've had their day. Project Blaine's a rich and powerful old man, but he doesn't know all the new tricks they're dreaming up on Mara and Kultis, or the Friendlies—or Ceta, for that matter. Make it a point to take two good looks at things when you get out among the stars, you two young ones, because nine times out of ten that first glance will leave you fooled."

"Listen to him, boys," said Eachan from the top of the table. "Your uncle Kensie's a man and a half above the shoulders. I just wish I had as good advice to give you. Tell them, Kensie."

"Nothing stands still," said Kensie—and with those three words, the whiskey seemed to go to Donal's head in a rush, the table and the dark harsh-boned faces before him seemed to swim in the dimness of the dining room, and Kensie's voice came roaring at him as if from a great distance. "Everything changes, and that's what you must bear in mind. What was true yesterday about something may not be true today. So remember that and take no man's word about something without reservation, even mine. We have multiplied like the biblical locusts and spread out among the stars, splitting into different groups with different ways. Now, while we still seem to be rushing forward to where I have no idea, at a terrific rate, increasing all the time, I have this feeling—as if we are all poised, hanging on the brink of something, something great and different and maybe terrible. It's a time to walk cautious, it is indeed."

"I'll be the greatest general that ever was!" cried Donal, and was startled as the rest to hear the words leap, stumbling and thick-tongued, but loud, from within him. "They'll see—I'll show them what a Dorsai can be!"

He was aware of them looking at him, though all their faces were blurred, except—by some trick of vision—that of Kensie, diagonally across the table from him. Kensie was considering him with somber, reading eyes. Donal was conscious of his father's hand on his shoulder.

"Time to turn in," said his father.

"You'll see—" said Donal, thickly. But they were all rising, picking up their glasses and turning to his father, who held his own glass up.

"May we all meet again," said his father. And they drank, standing. The remains of the whiskey in his glass flowed tasteless as water down Donal's tongue and throat—and for a second everything cleared and he saw these tall men standing around him. Big, even for Dorsai, they were; even his brother Mor topping him by half a head, so that he stood like a half-grown boy among them. But at that same instant of vision he was suddenly wrung with a terrible tenderness and pity for them, as if he was the grown one, and they the children to be protected. He opened his mouth to say, for once in his life, how much he loved them, and how always he would be there to take care of them—and then the fog closed down again; and he was only aware of Mor leading him stumblingly to his room.

Later, he opened his eyes in the darkness to become aware of a dim figure drawing the curtains of his room against the bright new light of the double moon, just risen. It was his mother; and with a sudden, reflexive action he rolled off his bed and lurched to her and put his hands on her shoulders.

"Mother—" he said.

She looked up at him with a pale face softened by the moonlight.

"Donal," she said tenderly, putting her arms around him. "You'll catch cold, Donal."

"Mother—" he said, thickly. "If you ever need me . . . to take care of you—"

"Oh, my boy," she said, holding his hard young body tightly to her, "take care of yourself; my boy . . . my boy—"

MERCENARY

Donal shrugged his shoulders in the tight civilian half-jacket and considered its fit as reflected in the mirror of his tiny, boxlike cabin. The mirror gave him back the image of someone almost a stranger. So much difference had three short weeks brought about in him, already. Not that he was so different, but his own appraisal of himself had changed; so that it was not merely the Spanish-style jacket, the skin-tight under-tunic, and the narrow trousers that disappeared into boots as black as all the rest of the costume, that made him unfamiliar to himself—but the body within. Association with the men of other worlds had done this to his point of view. Their relative shortness had made him tall, their softness had made him hard, their untrained bodies had made his balanced and sure. Outbound from the Dorsai to Alpha Centauri and surrounded by other Dorsai passengers, he had not noticed the gradual change. Only in the vast terminal on Newton, surrounded by their noisy thousands, had it come on him, all at once. And now, transhipped and outbound for the Friendlies, facing his first dinner on board a luxury-class liner where there would probably be no others from his world, he gazed at himself in the mirror and felt himself as suddenly come of age.

He went out through the door of his cabin, letting it latch quietly behind him, and turned right in the tightly narrow, metal-walled corridor faintly stale with the smell of dust from the carpet underfoot. He walked down its silence toward the main lounge and pushed through a heavy sealing door that sucked shut behind him, into the corridor of the next section.

He stepped into the intersection of the little cross corridor that led right and left to the washrooms of the section ahead—and almost strode directly into a slim, tall girl in an ankle-length, blue dress of severe and conservative cut, who stood by the water fountain at the point of the intersection. She moved hastily back out of his way with a little intake of breath, backing into the corridor to the women's washroom. They stared at each other, halted, for a second.

"Forgive me," said Donal, and took two steps onward—but between these and a third, some sudden swift prompting made him change his mind without warning; and he turned back.

"If you don't mind—" he said.

"Oh, excuse me." She moved back again from the water fountain. He bent to drink; and when he raised his head from the fountain, he looked her full in the face again and recognized what had brought him back. The girl was frightened; and that strange, dark ocean of feeling that lay at the back of his oddness had stirred to the gust of her palpable fear.

He saw her now, clearly and at once; at close range. She was older than he had thought at first—at least in her early twenties. But there was a clear-eyed immaturity about her—a hint that her full beauty would come later in life, and much later than that of the usual woman. Now, she was not yet beautiful; merely wholesome-looking. Her hair was a light brown, verging into chestnut, her eyes wide-spaced and so clearly green that, opening as she felt the full interest of his close gaze, they drove all the other color about her from his mind. Her nose was slim and straight, her mouth a little wide, her chin firm; and the whole of her face so perfectly in balance, the left side with the right, that it approached the artificiality of some sculptor's creation.

"Yes?" she said, on a little gasping intake of breath—and he saw, suddenly, that she was shrinking from him and his close survey of her.

He frowned at her. His thoughts were galloping ahead with the situation, so that when he spoke, it was unconsciously in the middle of the conversation he had in mind, rather than at the beginning.

"Tell me about it," said Donal.

"You?" she said. Her hand went to her throat above the high collar of her dress. Then, before he could speak again, it fell to her side and some of the tightness leaked out of her. "Oh," she said. "I see."

"See what?" said Donal, a little sharply; for unconsciously he had fallen into the tone he would have used to a junior cadet these last few years, if he had discovered one of them in some difficulty. "You'll have to tell me what your trouble is, if I'm going to be any help to you."

"Tell you—?" she looked desperately around her, as if expecting someone to come upon them at any moment. "How do I know you're what you say you are?"

For the first time Donal check-reined the horses of his galloping estimate of the situation; and, looking back, discovered a possible misconception on her part.

"I didn't say I was anybody," he answered. "And in fact—I'm not. I just happened to be passing by and saw you seemed upset about something. I offered to help."

"Help?" Her eyes widened again and her face suddenly paled. "Oh, no—" she murmured, and tried to go around him. "Please let me go. Please!"

He stood his ground.

"You were ready to accept help from someone like me, if he could only provide proofs of identity, a second ago," said Donal. "You might as well tell me the rest of it."

That stopped her efforts to escape. She stiffened, facing him.

"I haven't told you anything."

"Only," said Donal, ironically, "that you were waiting here for someone. That you did not know that someone by sight, but expected him to be a man. And that you were not sure of his bona fides, but very much afraid of missing him." He heard the hard edge in his own voice and forced it to be more gentle. "Also that you're very frightened and not very experienced at what you're doing. Logic could take it further."

But she had herself under control now.

"Will you move out of the way and let me by?" she said evenly.

"Logic might make it that what you're engaged in is something illegal," he replied.

She sagged under the impact of his last word as if it had been a blow; and, turning her face blindly to the wall, she leaned against it.

"What are you?" she said brokenly. "Did they send you to trap me?"

"I tell you," said Donal, with just a hint of exasperation, "I'm nothing but a passer-by who thought maybe I could help."

"Oh, I don't believe you!" she said, twisting her face away from him. "If you're really nobody . . . if nobody sent you . . . you'll let me go. And forget you ever saw me."

"Small sense in that," said Donal. "You need help evidently. I'm equipped to give it. I'm a professional soldier. A Dorsai."

"Oh," she said. The tension drained from her. She stood straighter and met his eyes with a look in which he thought he read some contempt. "One of those."

"Yes," he said. Then frowned. "What do you mean *one of those?*"

"I understand," she answered. "You're a mercenary."

"I prefer the term professional soldier," he said—a little stiffly in his turn.

"The point is," she said, "you're for hire."

He felt himself growing cold and angry. He inclined his head to her and stepped back, leaving her way clear. "My mistake," he said, and turned to leave her.

"No, wait a minute," she said. "Now that I know what you really are, there's no reason why I can't use you."

"None at all, of course," said Donal.

She reached in through a slit in her tight gown and produced a small, thick folding of some printed matter, which she pushed into his hand.

"You see this is destroyed," she said. "I'll pay you—whatever the usual rates are." Her eyes widened suddenly as she saw him unfold what he held and start to read it. "What are you doing? You aren't supposed to read that! How dare you!"

She grabbed for the sheet, but he pushed her back absently with one hand. His gaze was busily running down the form she had given him, his own eyes widening at the sight of the facsimile portrait on it, which was that of the girl herself.

"Anea Marlivana," he said. "Select of Kultis."

"Well, what if I am?" she blazed. "What about it?"

"Only," said Donal, "that I expected your genes to imply intelligence."

Her mouth fell open.

"What do you mean by that?"

"Only that you're one of the worst fools I've had the bad fortune to meet." He put the sheet into his pocket. "I'll take care of it."

"You will?" Her face lit up. A second later it was twisted in wrath. "Oh, I don't like you!" she cried. "I don't like you at all!"

He looked at her a little sadly.

"You will," he said, "if you live long enough." He turned about and pushed open the door through which he had come just a few minutes ago.

"But wait a minute—" her voice leaped after him. "Where will I see you after you've got rid of it? How much do I have to pay—"

He let the door, sucking to behind him, be the period to that question of hers—and his answer to it.

*   *   *

He went back through the section he had just traversed to his own cabin. There, with the door locked he considered the sheet she had given him, a little more closely. It was nothing more—and nothing less—than a five-year employment contract, a social contract, for her services as companion in the entourage of William, Prince, and Chairman of the Board of that very commercial planet Ceta which was the only habitable world circling the sun Tau Ceti. And a very liberal social contract it was, requiring no more than that she accompany William wherever he wished to go and supply her presence at such public and polite social functions as he might require. It was not the liberalness of the contract that surprised him so much—a Select of Kultis would hardly be contracted to perform any but the most delicately moral and ethical of duties—but the fact that she had asked him to destroy it. Theft of contract from her employer was bad enough, breach of contract infinitely worse—calling for complete rehabilitation—but destruction of contract required the death penalty wherever any kind of government operated. The girl, he thought, must be insane.

But—and here the fine finger of irony intruded into the situation—being the Select of Kultis she could not possibly be insane, any more than an ape could be an elephant. On the extreme contrary, being the product of a number of the most carefully culled forebearers on that planet where careful genetic culling and wizardry of psychological techniques was commonplace, she must be eminently sane. True, she had impressed Donal on first acquaintance as possessing nothing much out of the ordinary except a suicidal foolishness. But this was one instance where you had to go by the record books. And the record books implied that if anything about this business was abnormal, it was the situation itself, and not the girl involved in it.

Thoughtfully, Donal fingered the contract. Anea had clearly had no conception at all of what she was requesting when she so blithely required him to destroy it. The single sheet he held, and even the words and signatures upon it, were all integral parts of a single giant molecule which in itself was well-nigh indestructible and could not be in any way altered or tampered with short of outright destruction. As for destruction itself—Donal was quite sure that there was nothing aboard this ship that could in any way burn, shred, dissolve, or in any other fashion obliterate it. And the mere possession of it by anyone but William, its rightful owner, was as good as an order of sentence.

A soft chime quivered on the air of his cabin, announcing the serving of a meal in the main lounge. It chimed twice more to indicate that this was the third of the four meals interspersed throughout the ship "day." Contract in hand, Donal half-turned toward the little orifice of the disposal slot that led down to the central incinerator. The incinerator, of course, was not capable of disposing of the contract—but it might be that it could lie unnoticed there until the ship had reached its destination and its passengers had dispersed. Later, it would be difficult for William to discover how it had reached the incinerator in the first place.

Then he shook his head, and replaced the contract in his pocket. His motives for doing so were not entirely clear to himself. It was that oddness of his at work again, he thought. Also, he told himself that it seemed a sloppy way of handling the situation this girl had got him into. Quite typically, he had already forgotten that his participation in the matter was all of his own contriving.

He straightened his half-jacket and went out of his cabin and down the long corridor through various sections to the main lounge. A slight crowding of likewise dinner-bound passengers in the narrow entrance to the lounge delayed him momentarily; and, in that moment, looking over the heads of those before him, he caught sight of the long captain's table at the far end of the lounge and of the girl, Anea Marlivana, amongst those seated at it.

The others seated with her appeared to consist of a strikingly handsome young officer of field rank—a Freilander, by the look of him— a rather untidy, large young man almost as big as the Freilander, but possessing just the opposite of the other's military bearing; in fact, he appeared to half-slouch in his seat as if he were drunk. And a spare, pleasant-looking man in early middle age with iron-gray hair. The fifth person at the table was quite obviously a Dorsai—a massive, older man in the uniform of a Freiland marshal. The sight of this last individual moved Donal to sudden action. He pushed abruptly through the little knot of people barring the entrance and strode openly across the room to the high table. He extended his fist across it to the Dorsai marshal.

"How do you do, sir," he said. "I was supposed to look you up before the ship lifted; but I didn't have time. I've got a letter for you from my father, Eachan Khan Graeme. I'm his second son, Donal."

Blue Dorsai eyes as cold as river water lifted under thick gray brows to consider him. For part of a second the situation trembled on the balance-point of Dorsai pride with the older man's curiosity weighed against the bare-faced impudence of Donal's claim to acquaintance. Then the marshal took Donal's fist in a hard grip.

"So he remembered Hendrik Galt, did he?" the marshal smiled. "I haven't heard from Eachan for years."

Donal felt a slight, cold shiver of excitement course down his spine. Of all people, he had chosen one of the ranking Dorsai soldiers of his day to bluff acquaintance with. Hendrik Galt, First Marshal of Freiland.

"He sends you his regards, sir," said Donal, "and . . . but perhaps I can bring you the letter after dinner and you can read it for yourself."

"To be sure," said the marshal. "I'm in Stateroom Nineteen."

Donal was still standing. The occasion could hardly be prolonged further. But rescue came—as something in Donal had more than half-expected it would—from farther down the table.

"Perhaps," said the gray-haired man in a soft and pleasant voice, "your young friend would enjoy eating with us before you take him back to your stateroom, Hendrik?"

"I'd be honored," said Donal, with glib promptness. He pulled out the empty float before him and sat down upon it, nodding courteously to the rest of the company at the table as he did so. The eyes of the girl met him from the table's far end. They were as hard and still as emeralds caught in the rock.

MERCENARY II

"Anea Marlivana," said Hendrik Galt, introducing Donal around the table. "And the gentleman who was pleased to invite you—William of Ceta, Prince and Chairman of the Board."

"Greatly honored," murmured Donal, inclining his head toward them.

". . . The Unit Commandant, here, my adjutant . . . Hugh Killien—"

Donal and the Commandant Freilander nodded to each other.

". . . And ArDell Montor, of Newton." The loose-limbed young man slumping in his float, lifted a careless, half-drunken hand in a slight wave of acknowledgment. His eyes—so dark as to appear almost black under the light eyebrows that matched his rather heavy, blond hair, cleared for a disconcerting fraction of a second to stare sharply at Donal, then faded back to indifference. "ArDell," said Galt, humorlessly, "set a new high score for the competitive exams on Newton. His field was social dynamics."

"Indeed," muttered the Newtonian, with something between a snort and a laugh. "Indeed, was. Was, indeed." He lifted a heavy tumbler from the table before him and buried his nose in its light golden contents.

"ArDell—" said the gray-haired William, gently reproving. ArDell lifted his drink-pale face and stared at the older man, snorted again, on laughter, and lifted the tumbler again to his lips.

"Are you enlisted somewhere at the moment, Graeme?" asked the Freilander, turning to Donal.

"I've a tentative contract for the Friendlies," said Donal. "I thought I'd pick between the Sects when I got there and had a chance to look over the opportunities for action."

"Very Dorsai of you," said William, smiling, from the far end of the table, next to Anea. "Always the urge to battle."

"You over-compliment me, sir," said Donal. "It merely happens that promotion comes more quickly on a battlefield than in a garrison, under ordinary conditions.

"You're too modest," said William.

"Yes, indeed," put in Anea, suddenly. "Far too modest."

William turned about to gaze quizzically at the girl.

"Now, Anea," he said. "You mustn't let your Exotic contempt for violence breed a wholly unjustified contempt for this fine young man. I'm sure both Hendrik and Hugh agree with him."

"Oh, they would—of course," said Anea, flashing a look at the other two men. "Of course, they would!"

"Well," said William, laughing, "we must make allowances for a Select, of course. As for myself, I must admit to being male enough, and unreconstructed enough, to like the thought of action, myself. I . . . ah, here comes the food."

Brimming soup plates were rising above the surface of the table in front of everybody but Donal.

"You'd better get your order in now," said William. And, while Donal pressed the communicator key before him and attended to this necessary duty, the rest of them lifted their spoons and began their meal.

". . . Donal's father was a classmate of yours, was he, Hendrik?" inquired William, as the fish course was being served.

"Merely a close friend," said the marshal, dryly.

"Ah," said William, delicately lifting a portion of the white, delicate flesh on a fork. "I envy you Dorsai for things like that. Your professions allow you to keep friendship and emotional connections unrelated to your work. In the Commercial area"—he gestured with a slim, tanned hand—"a convention of general friendliness obscures the deeper feelings."

"Maybe it's what the man is to begin with," answered the marshal. "Not all Dorsai are soldiers, Prince, and not all Cetans are entrepreneurs."

"I recognize that," said William. His eyes strayed to Donal. "What would you say, Donal? Are you a simple mercenary soldier, only, or do you find yourself complicated by other desires?"

The question was as blunt as it was obliquely put. Donal concluded that ingenuousness overlaid with a touch of venality was perhaps the most proper response.

"Naturally, I'd like to be famous," he said—and laughed a trifle self-consciously, "and rich."

He caught the hint of a darkening cloud on the brow of Galt. But he could not be concerned with that now. He had other fish to fry. There would, he hoped, be a chance to clear up the marshal's contempt for him at some later time. For the present he must seem self-seeking enough to arouse William's interest.

"Very interesting," said William, pleasantly. "How do you plan to go about becoming these pleasant things?"

"I was hoping," said Donal, "maybe to learn something of the worlds by being out among them—something I might be able to use to my own advantage, as well as others."

"Good Lord, is *that* all?" said the Freilander, and laughed in a way that invited the rest of the table to join in with him.

William, however, did not laugh—although Anea joined her own clear amusement to that of the commandant, and ArDell's snorted chuckle.

"No need to be unkind, Hugh," he said. "I like Donal's attitude. I had the same sort of notion myself once—when I was younger." He smiled in a kindly fashion on Donal. "You must come talk to me, too," he said, "after you've had your chat with Hendrik. I like young men with ambition."

ArDell snorted with laughter again. William turned to look sadly at him.

"You should try to eat, ArDell," he said. "We'll be making a phase shift in four hours or so; and if you don't have something solid on your stomach—"

"My stomach?" said the young man, drunkenly. "And what if my stomach should reach universal dimensions, out of phase? What if *I* should reach universal dimensions; and be everywhere and never come back to point position again?" He grinned at William. "What a waste of good food."

Anea had paled to a sickly color.

"If you'll excuse me—" she murmured, rising hastily.

"I don't blame you a bit!" said William sharply. "ArDell, that was in inexcusable bad taste. Hugh, help Anea to her stateroom."

"I don't want him!" flared Anea. "He's just like all the rest of you—"

But the Freilander was already on his feet, looking almost like a recruiting poster in his trim uniform and coming around the table to take her arm. She jerked away from him, turned, and went unsteadily out of the lounge. Hugh following closely behind her. They passed through the doorway into the corridor, but as they turned to move out of sight, Donal saw her turn to the tall soldier and lean into the protection of his arm, just before they disappeared.

William was continuing to speak calm and acid words of disapprobation to ArDell, who made no retort, but gazed drunkenly and steadily back at him out of his black, unmoving eyes. During the rest of the meal the talk turned to military affairs, in particular field strategy, in which triologue—ArDell pointedly excluded—Donal was able to win back some of the personal credit which his earlier remark about fame and riches had cost him—in the marshal's eyes.

"... Remember," William said, as they parted in the corridor outside the lounge, after the meal. "Come in and see me after you've finished with Hendrik, Donal. I'll be glad to help you if I can." And with a smile, and a nod, he turned away.

Donal and Galt went off down the narrow corridor that forced them to walk one behind the other. Following the thick shoulders of the older man, Donal was surprised to hear him ask: "Well, what do you think of them?"

"Sir?" said Donal. Hesitating, he chose what he took to be the safest subject. "I'm a little surprised about the girl."

"Anea?" said Galt, stopping before a door marked with the number nineteen.

"I thought a Select of Kultis would be—" Donal stopped, honestly at a loss, "more . . . more in control of herself."

"She's very healthy, very normal, very intelligent—but those are only potentialities," retorted the marshal, almost gruffly. "What did you expect?"

He threw open the door, ushered them both in, and closed the door firmly behind them. When he turned around, there was a harder, more formal note to his voice.

"All right now," he said, sharply, "what's all this about a letter?"

Donal took a deep breath. He had tried hard to read Galt's character during the course of the dinner—and he staked everything now in the honesty of his answer, on what he thought he had seen there.

"No letter, sir," he said. "To the best of my knowledge, my father never met you in his life."

"Thought as much," said Galt. "All right—what's it all about, then?" He crossed to a desk on the other side of the room, took something from a drawer, and when he turned about Donal was astonished to find him filling an antique pipe with tobacco.

"That Anea, sir," he said. "I never met such a fool in my life."
And he told, fully and completely, the story of the episode in the
corridor. Galt half-sat on the edge of the desk, the pipe in his mouth
now, and alight, puffing little clouds of white smoke which the venti-
lating system whisked away the second they were formed.

"I see," he said, when Donal had finished. "I'm inclined to agree
with you. She is a fool. And just what sort of insane idiot do you
consider yourself?"

"I, sir?" Donal was honestly astonished.

"I mean you, boy," said Galt, taking the pipe out of his mouth.
"Here you are, still damp from school, and sticking your nose into a
situation a full planetary government'd hesitate at." He stared in frank
amazement at Donal. "Just what did you think—what did you figure
. . . hell, boy, what did you *plan* to get out of it?"

"Why, nothing," said Donal. "I was only interested in seeing a
ridiculous and possibly dangerous situation smoothed out as neatly as
possible. I admit I hadn't any notion of the part William played in the
matter—he's apparently an absolute devil."

The pipe rattled in Galt's suddenly unclenched jaws and he had to
grab it quickly with one thick hand to keep it from falling. He took it
from his lips and stared in amazement at Donal.

"Who told you that?" he demanded.

"No one," said Donal. "It's obvious, isn't it?" Galt laid his pipe
down on the table and stood up.

"Not to ninety-nine per cent of the civilized worlds, it isn't," he
retorted. "What made it so obvious to you?"

"Certainly," said Donal, "any man can be judged by the character
and actions of the people with which he surrounds himself. And this
William has an entourage of thwarted and ruined people."

The marshal stiffened.

"You mean me?" he demanded.

"Naturally not," said Donal. "After all—you're a Dorsai." The
stiffness went out of Galt. He grinned a little sourly and, reaching back
for his pipe, retrieved and relit it.

"Your faith in our common origin is . . . quite refreshing," he said.
"Go on. On this piece of evidence you read William's character, do
you?"

"Oh, not just that," said Donal. "Stop and think of the fact that a
Select of Kultis finds herself at odds with him. And the good instincts
of a Select are inbred. Also, he seems to be an almost frighteningly
brilliant sort of man, in that he can dominate personalities like Anea,

and this fellow Montor, from Newton—who must be a rather high-level mind himself to have rated as he did on his tests."

"And someone that brilliant must be a devil?" queried Galt, dryly.

"Not at all," explained Donal, patiently. "But having such intellectual capabilities, a man must show proportionately greater inclinations toward either good or evil than lesser people. If he tends toward evil, he may mask it in himself—he may even mask its effect on the people with which he surrounds himself. But he has no way of producing the reflections of good which would ordinarily be reflected from his lieutenants and initiates—and which, if he was truly good—he would have no reason to try and hide. And by that lack, you can read him."

Galt took the pipe from his mouth and gave a long, slow whistle. He stared at Donal.

"You weren't brought up on one of the Exotics, by any chance, were you?" he asked.

"No, sir," said Donal. "My father's mother was a Maran, though. And my mother's mother was Maran."

"This," Galt paused and tamped thoughtfully in the bowl of his pipe—it had gone out—with one thick forefinger, "business of reading character—did you get this from your mother, or your grandmother—or is it your own idea?"

"Why, I imagine I must have heard it somewhere," replied Donal. "But surely it stands to reason—anyone would arrive at it as a conclusion, with a few minutes' thought."

"Possibly the majority of us don't think," said Galt, with the same dryness. "Sit down, Donal. And I'll join you."

They took a couple of armchair floats facing each other. Galt put his pipe away.

"Now, listen to me," he said, in a low and sober voice. "You're one of the oddest young fish I can remember meeting. I don't know quite what to do with you. If you were my son, I'd pack you up in quarantine and ship you home for ten more years seasoning before I let you out among the stars—all right—" he interrupted himself abruptly, raising a silencing hand as Donal's mouth opened. "I know you're a man now and couldn't be shipped anywhere against your will. But the way you strike me now is that you've got perhaps one chance in a thousand of becoming something remarkable, and about nine hundred and ninety-nine chances of being quietly put out of the way before the year's out. Look, boy, what do you know about the worlds, outside the Dorsai?"

"Well," said Donal. "There are fourteen planetary governments not counting the anarchic setups on Dunnin's World and Coby—"

"Governments, my rear echelon!" interrupted Galt, rudely. "Forget your civics lessons! Governments in this twenty-fourth century are mere machinery. It's the men who control them who count. Project Blaine, on Venus; Sven Holman, on Earth; Eldest Bright on Harmony, the very planet we're headed for—and Sayona the Bond on Kultis, for the Exotics."

"General Kamal—" began Donal.

"Is nothing!" said Galt, sharply. "How can the Elector of the Dorsai be anything when every little canton hangs to its independence with tooth and nail? No, I'm talking about the men who pull the strings between the stars. The ones I mentioned, and others." He took a deep breath. "Now, how do you suppose our Merchant Prince and Chairman of the Board on Ceta ranks with those I mentioned?"

"You'd say he's their equal?"

"At least," said Galt. "At least. Don't be led astray by the fact that you see him traveling like this, on a commercial ship, with only the girl and Montor with him. Chances are he owns the ship, the crew and officers—and half the passengers."

"And you and the commandant?" asked Donal, perhaps more bluntly than was necessary. Galt's features started to harden; and then he relaxed.

"A fair question," he rumbled. "I'm trying to get you to question most of the things you've taken for granted. I suppose it's natural you'd include myself. No—to answer your question—I am First Marshal of Freiland, still a Dorsai, and with my professional services for hire, and nothing more. We've just hired out five light divisions to the First Dissident Church, on Harmony, and I'm coming along to observe that they operate as contracted for. It's a complicated deal—like they are all—involving a batch of contract credits belonging to Ceta. Therefore William."

"And the commandant?" persisted Donal.

"What about him?" replied Galt. "He's a Freilander, a professional, and a good one. He'll take over one of the three-Force commands for a short test period when we get to Harmony, for demonstration purposes."

"Have you had him with you long?"

"Oh, about two standard years," said Galt.

"And he's good, professionally?"

"He's damn good," said Galt. "Why do you think he's my adjutant? What're you driving at, anyway?"

"A doubt," said Donal, "and a suspicion." He hesitated for a second. "Neither of which I'm ready to voice yet."

Galt laughed.

"Save that Maran character-sniffing of yours for civilians," he said. "You'll be seeing a snake under every bush. Take my word for it, Hugh's a good, honest soldier—a bit flashy, perhaps—but that's all."

"I'm hardly in a position to argue with you," murmured Donal, stepping aside gracefully. "You were about to say something about William, when I interrupted you?"

"Oh yes," said Galt. He frowned. "It adds up to this—and I'll make it short and clear. The girl's none of your business; and William's deadly medicine. Leave them both alone. And if I can help you to the kind of post you're after—"

"Thank you very much," said Donal. "But I believe William will be offering me something."

Galt blinked and stared.

"Hell's breeches, boy!" he exploded after half a second. "What gives you that idea?"

Donal smiled a little sadly.

"Another one of my suspicions," he said. "Based on what you call that Maran character-sniffing of mine, no doubt." He stood up. "I appreciate your trying to warn me, sir." He extended his fist. "If I could talk to you again, sometime?"

Galt stood up himself, taking the proffered fist, mechanically.

"Any time," he said. "Damned if I understand you."

Donal peered at him, suddenly struck by a thought.

"Tell me, sir," he asked. "Would you say I was—odd?"

"Odd!" Galt almost exploded on the word. "Odd as—" his imagination failed him. "What makes you ask that?"

"I just wondered," said Donal. "I've been called that so often. Maybe they were right."

He withdrew his fist from the marshal's grasp. And on that note, he took his leave.

MERCENARY III

Returning again up the corridor toward the bow of the ship, Donal allowed himself to wonder, a little wistfully, about this succubus of his own strange difference from other people. He had thought to leave it behind with his cadet uniform. Instead, it seemed, it continued to ride with him, still perched on his shoulders. Always it had been this way. What seemed so plain, and simple and straightforward to himself, had always struck others as veiled, torturous, and involved. Always he had been like a stranger passing through a town, the ways of whose people were different, and who looked on him with a lack of understanding amounting to suspicion. Their language failed on the doorstep of his motives and could not enter the lonely mansion of his mind. They said "enemy" and "friend"; they said "strong" and "weak"— "them" and "us". They set up a thousand arbitrary classifications and distinctions which he could not comprehend, convinced as he was that all people were only people—and there was very little to choose between them. Only, you dealt with them as individuals, one by one; and always remembering to be patient. And if you did this successfully, then the larger, group things all came out right.

Turning again into the entrance of the lounge, he discovered—as he had half-expected to—the young Newtonian ArDell Montor, slumped in a float by one end of the bar that had made its appearance as soon as the dinner tables had been taken up into the walls. A couple of other small, drinking groups sparsely completed the inhabitants of the lounge—but none of these were having anything to do with Montor. Donal walked directly to him; and Montor, without moving, lifted the gaze of his dark eyes to watch Donal approach.

"Join you?" said Donal.

"Honored," replied the other—not so much thickly as slowly, from the drink inside him. "Thought I might like to talk to you." His fingers crept out over the buttons on the bar-pad next to him. "Drink?"

"Dorsai whiskey," said Donal. Montor pressed. A second later a small transparent goblet, full, rose to the bartop. Donal took it and sipped cautiously. The drinking the night he had attained his majority had acquainted him with the manner in which alcohol affected him; and he had made a private determination never to find himself drunk again. It is a typical matter of record with him, that he never did. Raising his eyes from the glass, he found the Newtonian staring steadily at him with his eyes unnaturally clear, lost, and penetrating.

"You're younger than I," said ArDell. "Even if I don't look it. How old do you think I am?"

Donal looked him over curiously. Montor's face, for all its lines of weariness and dissipation, was the scarcely mature visage of a late adolescent—a situation to which his shock of uncombed hair and the loose-limbed way he sprawled in his float, contributed.

"A quarter of a standard century," said Donal.

"Thirty-three years absolute," said ArDell. "I was a school-child, a monk, until I was twenty-nine. Do you think I drink too much?"

"I think there's no doubt about it," answered Donal.

"I agree with you," said ArDell, with one of his sudden snorts of laughter. "I agree with you. There's no doubt about it—one of the few things in this God-abandoned universe about which there is no doubt. But that's not what I was hoping to talk to you about."

"What was that?" Donal tasted his glass of whiskey again.

"Courage," said ArDell, looking at him with an empty, penetrating glance. "Have you got courage?"

"It's a necessary item for a soldier," said Donal. "Why do you ask?"

"And no doubts? No doubts?" ArDell swirled the golden drink in his tall tumbler and took a swallow from it. "No secret fears that when the moment comes your legs will weaken, your heart will pound, you'll turn and run?"

"I will not, of course, turn and run," said Donal. "After all, I'm a Dorsai. As for how I'll feel—all I can say is, I've never felt the way you describe. And even if I did—"

Above their heads a single mellow chime sounded, interrupting.

"Phase shift in one standard hour and twenty minutes," announced a voice. "Phase shift in one standard hour and twenty minutes. Passengers are advised to take their medication now and accomplish the shift while asleep, for their greatest convenience."

"Have you swallowed a pill yet?" asked ArDell.

"Not yet," said Donal.

"But you will?"

"Of course." Donal examined him with interest. "Why not?"

"Doesn't taking medication to avoid the discomfort of a phase shift strike you as a form of cowardice?" asked ArDell. "Doesn't it?"

"That's foolish," said Donal. "Like saying it's cowardly to wear clothes to keep you warm and comfortable, or to eat, to keep from starving. One is a matter of convenience; the other is a matter of"— he thought for a second—"duty."

"Courage is doing your duty?"

". . . In spite of what you personally might want. Yes," said Donal.

"Yes," said ArDell, thoughtfully. "Yes." He replaced his empty glass on the bar and pressed for a refill. "I *thought* you had courage," he said, musingly, watching the glass sink, fill, and begin to reemerge.

"I am a Dorsai," said Donal.

"Oh, spare me the glories of careful breeding!" said ArDell, harshly, picking up his now-full glass. As he turned back to face Donal, Donal saw the man's face was tortured. "There's more to courage than that. If it was only in your genes—" he broke off suddenly, and leaned toward Donal. "Listen to me," he almost whispered. "I'm a coward."

"Are you sure?" said Donal, levelly. "How do you know?"

"I'm frightened sick," whispered ArDell. "Sick-frightened of the universe. What do you know about the mathematics of social dynamics?"

"It's a predicative system of mathematics, isn't it?" said Donal. "My education didn't lie in that direction."

"No, no!" said ArDell, almost fretfully. "I'm talking about the statistics of social analysis, and their extrapolation along lines of population increase and development." He lowered his voice even further. "They approach a parallel with the statistics of random chance!"

"I'm sorry," said Donal. "That means nothing to me."

ArDell gripped Donal's arm suddenly with one surprisingly strong hand.

"Don't you understand?" he murmured. "Random chance provides for every possibility—including dissolution. It must come, because the chance is there. As our social statistics grow into larger figures, we, too, entertain the possibility. In the end, it must come. We must destroy ourselves. There is no other alternative. And all because the universe is too big a suit of clothes for us to wear. It gives us room to grow too much, too fast. We will reach a statistically critical mass—and then," he snapped his fingers, "the end!"

"Well, that's a problem for the future," said Donal. But then, because he could not help reacting to the way the other man was feeling, he added, more gently, "Why does it bother you, so much?"

"Why, don't you see?" said ArDell. "If it's all to go—just like that—as if it never has been, then what was the use of it all? What's to show for our existence? I don't mean things we built—they decay fast enough. Or knowledge. That's just a copying down from an open book into our own language. It has to be those things that the universe didn't have to begin with and that we brought to it. Things like love, and kindness—and courage."

"If that's the way you feel," said Donal, gently withdrawing his arm from the other's grasp, "why drink this way?"

"Because I *am* a coward," said ArDell. "I feel it out there, all the time, this enormousness that is the universe. Drinking helps me shut it out—that God-awful knowledge of what it can do to us. That's why I drink. To take the courage I need out of a bottle, to do the little things like passing through phase shift without medication."

"Why," said Donal, almost tempted to smile. "What good would that do?"

"It's facing it, in a little way," ArDell fixed him with his dark and pleading eyes. "It's saying, in one little instance—go ahead, rip me to the smallest shreds you can manage, spread me over your widest limits. I can take it."

Donal shook his head.

"You don't understand," said ArDell, sinking back in his float. "If I could work, I wouldn't need the alcohol. But I'm walled away from work nowadays. It's not that way with you. You've got your job to do; and you've got courage—the real kind. I thought maybe I could . . . well, never mind. Courage wouldn't be transferable, anyway."

"Are you going to Harmony?" asked Donal.

"Whither my Prince goes, there go I," said ArDell, and snorted his laugh again. "You should read my contract, sometime." He turned back to the bar. "Another whiskey?"

"No," said Donal, standing up. "If you'll excuse me—"

"I'll see you again," muttered ArDell, keying for another drink. "I'll be seeing you."

"Yes," said Donal. "Until then."

"Until then," ArDell lifted his newly filled glass from the bar. The chime sounded again overhead, and the voice reminded them that only seventy-odd minutes remained before shift-time. Donal went out.

* * *

Half an hour later, after he had gone back to his own room for one more careful rereading and study of Anea's contract, Donal pressed the button on the door of the stateroom of William, Prince and Chairman of the Board, on Ceta. He waited.

"Yes?" said the voice of William, over his head.

"Donal Graeme, sir," said Donal. "If you aren't busy—"

"Oh, of course—Donal. Come in!" The door swung open before him and Donal entered.

William was sitting on a plain float before a small deskboard holding a pile of papers and a tiny portable secretary. A single light glowed directly above him and the deskboard, silvering his gray hair. Donal hesitated, hearing the door click to behind him.

"Find a seat somewhere," said William, without looking up from his papers. His fingers flickered over the keys of the secretary. "I have some things to do."

Donal turned about in the gloom outside the pool of light, found an armchair float and sat down in it. William continued for some minutes, scanning through his papers, and making notes on the secretary.

After a while he shoved the remaining papers aside and the deskboard, released, drifted with its burden to over against a farther wall. The single overhead light faded and a general illumination flooded the cabin.

Donal blinked at the sudden light. William smiled.

"And now," he said, "what's the nature of your business with me?"

Donal blinked, stared, and blinked again.

"Sir?" he said.

"I think we can avoid wasting time by ignoring pretenses," said William, still in his pleasant voice. "You pushed yourself on us at the table because you wanted to meet someone there. It was hardly the marshal—your Dorsai manners could have found a better way than that. It was certainly not Hugh, and most unlikely to be ArDell. That leaves Anea; and she's pretty enough, and you're both young enough to do something that foolish . . . but, I think not, under the conditions." William folded his lean fingers together, and smiled. "That leaves me."

"Sir, I—" Donal started to stand up, with the stiffness of outraged dignity.

"No, no," said William, gesturing him back. "Now it'd be foolish to leave, after going to all this trouble to get here, wouldn't it?" His voice sharpened. "Sit down!"

Donal sat.

"Why did you want to see me?" asked William.

Donal squared his shoulders.

"All right," he said. "If you want me to put it bluntly . . . I think I might be useful to you."

"By which," said William, "you think you might be useful to yourself, by tapping the till, as it were, of my position and authority—go on."

"It so happened," said Donal, "that I came into possession of something belonging to you."

William extended his hand, without a word. After a second's hesitation, Donal extracted Anea's contract from his pocket and passed it over. William took it, unfolded it, and glanced over it. He laid it carelessly down on a little table beside him.

"She wanted me to get rid of it for her," said Donal. "She wanted to hire me to dispose of it for her. Evidently she didn't know how hard it is to destroy a sheet of the material contracts are made on."

"But you took the job," said William.

"I made no promises," said Donal, painfully.

"But from the start, you intended to bring it straight to me."

"I believe," said Donal, "it's your property."

"Oh, of course," said William. He smiled at Donal for a long moment. "You realize, of course," he said, finally, "that I needn't believe a word of what you've said. I only need to assume that you stole it yourself and later got cold feet about disposing of it—and dreamed up this cock-and-bull story in a attempt to sell it back to me. The captain of this ship would be glad to put you under arrest at my word and hold you for trial as soon as we reach Harmony."

A slight, cold, galvanic shiver ran down Donal's spine.

"A Select of Kultis won't lie under oath," he said. "She—"

"I see no reason to involve Anea in this," said William. "It could be all handled very conveniently without her. My statement against yours."

Donal said nothing. William smiled again.

"You see," said William, "the point I'm laboring to bring home to you. You happen not only to be venal, but a fool."

"*Sir!*" the word shot from Donal's lips. William waved a disinterested hand.

"Save your Dorsai rages for someone who'll be impressed by them. I know as well as you do, you've no intention of attacking me. Possibly, if you were a different sort of Dorsai—but you're not. You are as I say, both venal and a fool. Accept these statements for the obvious facts they are; and we can get down to business."

He looked at Donal. Donal said nothing.

"Very well, then," went on William. "You came to me, hoping I could find you of some use. As it happens, I can. Anea is, of course, just a foolish young girl—but for her benefit, as well as my own, being her employer, we'll have to see she doesn't get into serious trouble. Now, she had confided in you once. She may again. If she does so— by no means discourage her. And to keep you available for such confidences," William smiled again, quite good humoredly, this time, "I believe I can find you a commission as Force-Leader, under Commandant Hugh Killien, when we touch down on Harmony. There is no reason why a military career shouldn't go hand in hand with whatever other uses I can find for you."

"Thank you, sir," said Donal.

"Not at all—" A chime sounded over some hidden wall speaker. "Ab—phase shift in five minutes." William picked up a small silver box from a table near his feet, and sprung it open. "Have you taken your medication, yet? Help yourself."

He extended to Donal.

"Thank you, sir," said Donal carefully. "I have."

"Then," said William, helping himself to a white tablet, and replacing the box. "I believe that is all."

"I believe so, sir," said Donal.

Donal inclined his head and went out. Stopping outside the stateroom door only long enough to take one of his own phase shift sedatives, he headed back toward his own stateroom. On the way, he stopped by the ship's library to check out an information spool on the First Dissident Church, of Harmony; and this delayed him sufficiently so that he was passing down one of the long sectional corridors when the phase shift occurred.

He had been prudently asleep during those previous shifts he had gone through while outbound from Dorsai; and, of course, he had learned years ago what to expect. In addition, he was fully medicated; and the shift itself was over before it was really begun. In fact, it took place in no time, in no conceivable interval at all. Yet it *had* happened; and some inextinguishable recognizing part of him *knew* and remembered that he had been torn apart, down to the most fractional elements of his being, and spread to the wide universe and caught and collected and reassembled at some arbitrary point light-years from his destruction. And it was this memory, not the shift itself, that made him falter, for one short step, before he took up again his steady march back to his stateroom. And the memory would stay with him.

He continued on down the corridor; but he was far from having run his gauntlet for the day. As he reached the end of one section, Anea stepped out from the cross-bar corridor there that was the exact duplicate of the one, several sections down, where he had first met her. Her green eyes were afire.

"You've been seeing him!" she snapped, barring his way.

"Seeing . . . oh, William," he said.

"Don't deny it."

"Why should I?" Donal looked at her almost with wonder. "Surely, it's nothing to make a secret about?"

She stared at him.

"Oh!" she cried. "You just don't care for anything, do you? What did you do . . . about what I gave you?"

"I gave it back to its owner, of course," said Donal. "There was no other sensible thing I could do."

She turned suddenly so white that he almost reached out to catch her, certain she was about to faint. But she did no such womanish thing. Her eyes, as she stared at him, were shocked to enormity.

"Oh!" she breathed. "You . . . you traitor. You *cheat!*" and before he could make a move or say a word to stop her, she had whirled about and was running off down the corridor back in the direction from which she had come.

With a certain wry unhappiness—for, in spite of his rather low opinion of her common sense, he had really expected her to listen to his explanation—he took up his solitary walk to his stateroom. He traveled the rest of the way without meeting anyone. The corridors, in the aftermath of the phase shift were deserted by prudent passengers.

Only, passing a certain stateroom, he heard sounds of sickness from within; and, looking up, recognized the number on its door as one he had looked up just now on his recent trip to the library.

It was the stateroom of ArDell Montor; and that would be the man himself inside it now, unmedicated and racked by the passing of the phase shift, fighting his own long battle with the universe.

FORCE-LEADER

"All right, gentlemen," said Hugh Killien.

He stood, confident and impressive in his chameleon battle-dress, with the fingertips of his right hand resting on the gently domed surface of the mapviewer before him.

"If you'll gather around the viewer, here—" he said. The five Force-Leaders moved in until all six men stood thickly clustered around the meter-square area of the viewer. The illumination from the blackout shell enclosing them beat down and met the internal upward illumination of the viewer, so that Donal, glancing around at his fellow-officers, was irresistibly reminded of men caught between wrath and wrath, in some small package section of that hell their First Dissident Church Liaison-Elder had been so eloquent about, only a few hours since at the before-battle service.

"... Our position is here," Hugh was saying. "As your commandant I make you the customary assurance that it is a perfectly tenable position and that the contemplated advance in no way violates the Mercenaries Code. Now—" he went on more briskly, "as you can see, we occupy an area five kilometers in front and three kilometers in depth, between these two ridges. Second Command of Battle Unit 176 to our right, Fourth Command of Battles to our left.

"The contemplated action calls for the Second and Fourth Commands to hold fast in full strength on both our flanks, while we move forward at sixty per cent of strength and capture a small town called Faith Will Succour, which is *here*—"

His index finger stabbed down and rested upon the domed image of the map.

"... At approximately four kilometers of distance from our present position. We will use three of our five Forces, Skuak's, White's and Graeme's; and each Force will make its separate way to the objective. You will each have your individual maps. There are woods for the first twelve hundred meters. After that, you will have to cross the river, which is about forty meters in width, but which Intelligence assures us is fordable at the present time with a maximum depth of a hundred and twenty centimeters. On the other side it will be woods again, thinning out gradually right up to the edge of the town. We leave in twenty minutes. It'll be dawn in an hour and I want all three Forces across that river before full daylight. Any questions?"

"What about enemy activity in the area?" asked Skuak. He was a short, stocky Cassidan, who looked Mongoloid, but was actually Eskimo in ancestry. "What kind of opposition can we expect?"

"Intelligence says nothing but patrols. Possibly a small Force holding the town, itself. Nothing more." Hugh looked around the circle of faces. "This should be bread and butter. Any more questions?"

"Yes," said Donal. He had been studying the map. "What sort of military incompetent decided to send us at only sixty per cent of strength?"

The atmosphere in the shell froze suddenly and sharply. Donal looked up to find Hugh Killien's eyes on his across the viewer.

"As it happened," said the commandant, a slight edge to his words, "it was *my* suggestion to Staff, Graeme. Perhaps you've forgotten— I'm sure none of the other Force-Leaders have—but this is a demonstration campaign to show the First Dissident Church we're worthy of our hire."

"That hardly includes gambling the lives of four hundred and fifty men," retorted Donal, unmoved.

"Graeme," said Hugh, "you're junior officer here; and I'm commandant. You ought to know I don't have to explain tactics to you. But just to set your mind at rest, Intelligence has given a clear green on enemy activity in the area."

"Still," persisted Donal, "why take unnecessary chances?"

Hugh sighed in exasperation.

"I certainly shouldn't have to give you lessons in stategy," he said bitingly. "I think you abuse the right the code gives you to question Staff decisions. But to put an end to this—there's a good reason why we'll be using the minimum number of men. Our main thrust at the enemy is to come through this area. If we moved forward in strength, the United Orthodox forces would immediately begin to strengthen defenses. But doing it this way, it should appear we're merely moving to take up a natural vacuum along the front. Once we have the town tied down, the Second and Fourth Commands can filter in to reinforce us and we are in position to mount a full-scale attack at the plains below. Does that answer you?"

"Only partially," said Donal. "I—"

"Give me patience!" snapped the Freilander. "I have five campaigns to my credit, Force-Leader. I'd hardly stick my own neck in a noose. But I'll be taking over White's Force and leaving him in command back here in the Area. You, I and Skuak will make the assay. *Now*, are you satisfied?"

There was, of course, no reply to be made to that. Donal bowed his head in submission and the meeting broke up. Walking back to his Force area, however, alongside Skuak, Donal remained unreconstructed enough to put an extra question to the Cassidan.

"Do *you* think I'm starting at shadows?" asked Donal.

"Huh!" grunted Skuak. "It's his responsibility. He ought to know what he's doing." And, on that note, they parted; each to marshal his own men.

Back in his own Force area, Donal found that his Groupmen had already assembled his command. They stood under arms, drawn up in three lines of fifty men each, with a senior and junior Groupman at the head of each line. The ranking senior Groupman, a tall, thin Cetan veteran named Morphy, accompanied him as he made his rounds of the ranks, inspecting the men.

They were a good unit, Donal thought, as he paced down between the rows. Well-trained men, battle-seasoned, although in no sense elite troops, since they had been picked at random by the Elders of the First Dissident Church—William having stipulated only his choice of officers for the demonstration Battle Unit. Each man carried a handgun and knife in addition to his regular armament; but they were infantry, spring-rifle men. Weapon for weapon, any thug in the back alley of a large city had more, and more modern firepower; but the trick with modern warfare was not to outgun the enemy, but carry weapons he could not gimmick. Chemical and radiation armament was too easily put out of action from a distance. Therefore, the spring-rifle with its five thousand-sliver magazine and its tiny, compact, nonmetallic mechanism which could put a sliver in a man-sized target at a thousand meters time after time with unvarying accuracy.

Yet, thought Donal, pacing between the silent men in the faint darkness of pre-dawn, even the spring-rifle would be gimmickable one of these days. Eventually, the infantryman would be back to the knife and short sword. And the emphasis would weigh yet again more heavily on the skill of the individual soldier. For sooner or later, no matter what fantastic long-range weapons you mounted, the ground itself had to be taken—and for that there had never been anything but the man in the ranks.

Donal finished his inspection and went back to stand in front of them.

"Rest, men," he said. "But hold your ranks. All Groupmen over here with me."

He walked off out of earshot of the men in ranks and the Groupmen followed him. They squatted in a circle and he passed on to them the orders of the Staff he had just received from Hugh, handing out maps to each of them.

"Any questions?" he asked, as Hugh had asked his Force-Leaders.

There were none. They waited for him to go on. He, in turn looked slowly around the circle, assessing these men on whom his command would depend.

He had had a chance to get to know them in the three weeks previous to this early morning. The six who faced him represented, in miniature, the varying reactions his appointment as Force-Leader had produced in the Force as a whole. Of the hundred and fifty men under him, a few were doubtful of him because of his youth and lack of battle experience. A larger number were unequivocally glad to have him over them because of the Dorsai reputation. A few, a very few, were of that class of men who bristle automatically, as man to man, whenever they find themselves in contact with another individual who is touted as better than they. The instinctive giant-killers. Of this type was the Senior Groupman of the Third Group, an ex-Coby miner named Lee. Even squatting now in this circle, on the brink of action, he met Donal's eye with a faint air of challenge, his brush of dark hair stiffly upright in the gloom, his bony jaw set. Such men were trouble-makers unless they had responsibility to hold them down. Donal revised his original intention to travel, himself, with the Third Group.

"We'll split up into patrol-sized units of twenty-five men each," he said. "There'll be a Senior or Junior Groupman to each unit. You'll move separately as units, and if you encounter an enemy patrol, you'll fight as a unit. I don't want any unit going to the rescue of another. Is that clear?"

They nodded. It was clear.

"Morphy," said Donal, turning to the thin Senior Groupman. "I want you to go with the Junior unit of Lee's Group, which will have the rearguard position. Lee will take his own half-group directly in front of you. Chassen"—he looked at the Senior Groupman of the Second Group—"you and Zolta will take positions third and fourth from the rear. I want you personally in fourth position. Suki, as Junior of the First Group, you'll be ahead of Chassen and right behind me. I'll take the upper half of the First Group in advance position."

"Force," said Lee. "How about communications?"

"Hand-signal. Voice. And that's all. And I don't want any of you closing up to make communication easier. Twenty-meter miminum interval between units." Donal looked around the circle again. "Our job here is to penetrate to the little town as quickly and quietly as we can. Fight only if you're forced into it; and break away as quickly as you can."

"The word is it's supposed to be a Sunday walk," commented Lee.

"I don't operate by back-camp rumor," said Donal flatly, his eyes seeking out the ex-miner. "We'll take all precautions. You Groupmen will be responsible for seeing that your men are fully equipped with everything, including medication."

Lee yawned. It was not a gesture of insolence—not quite.

"All right," said Donal. "Back to your Groups."

The meeting broke up.

A few minutes later the almost inaudible peep of a whistle was carried from Force to Force; and they began to move out. Dawn was not yet in the sky, but the low overcast above the treetops was beginning to lighten at their backs.

The first twelve hundred meters through the woods, though they covered it cautiously enough, turned out to be just what Lee had called it—a Sunday walk. It was when Donal, in the lead with the first half-Group, came out on the edge of the river that things began to tighten up.

"Scouts out!" he said. Two of the men from the Group sloshed into the smoothly flowing water, and, rifles held high, waded across its gray expanse to the far side. The glint of their rifles, waved in a circle, signaled the all clear and Donal led the rest of the men into the water and across.

Arrived on the far side, he threw out scouts in three directions—ahead, and along the bank each way—and waited until Suki and his men appeared on the far side of the river. Then, his scouts having returned with no sight of the enemy, Donal spread his men out in light skirmish order and went forward.

The day was growing rapidly. They proceeded by fifty meter jumps, sending the scouts out ahead, then moving the rest of the men up when the signal came back that the ground was clear ahead. Jump succeeded jump and there was no contact with the enemy. A little over an hour later, with the large orange disk of E. Eridani standing clear of the horizon, Donal looked out through a screen of bushes at a small, battle-torn village that was silent as the grave.

Forty minutes later, the three Forces of the Third Command, Battle Unit 176 were united and dug in about the small town of Faith Will Succour. They had uncovered no local inhabitants.

They had had no encounter with the enemy.

FORCE-LEADER II

The name of Force-Leader Graeme was mud.

The Third Command, or at least that portion of it that was dug in around the village, made no great attempt to hide the fact from him. If he had shown at all that he was sensitive to their opinion of him, they would have made even less. But there was something about his complete indifference to their attitude that put a check to their obvious contempt. Nevertheless, the hundred and fifty men that had been forced by him to make their approach on the village under full equipment and maximum security effort, and the three hundred other men who had made a much more casual and easy approach, and were congratulating themselves on being out from under such an officer, agreed in an opinion of Donal that had reached its nadir! There is only one thing that veterans hate worse than being made to sweat unnecessarily in garrison; and that is being made to sweat unnecessarily in the field. The word had gone out that the day's work was to be a Sunday walk. And it *had* been a Sunday walk, except for those serving under a green young Dorsai officer, name of Graeme. The men were not happy.

Along about twilight, as the sunset was fading through the bushy-limbed trees that were the local mutant variform of the Earthly conifer that had been imported when this planet was terraformed, a runner came from Hugh at Command HQ, just outside the enemy end of the village. He found Donal seated astride a fallen log, studying a map of the local area.

"Signal from Battles," said the runner, squatting beside the log.

"Stand up," said Donal, quietly. The runner stood. "Now, what's the signal?"

"Second and Third Commands won't be moving up until tomorrow morning," said the runner, sulkily.

"Signal acknowledged," said Donal, waving him off. The runner turned and hurried away with another instance of the new officer's wax-and-braid to relate to the other enlisted men back at HQ.

Left to himself, Donal continued to study the map as long as the light lasted. When it was completely gone, he put the map away, produced a small black whistle from his pocket and peeped for his ranking Senior Groupman.

A moment later a thin body loomed up against the faintly discernible sky beyond the treetops.

"Morphy, sir. Reporting," came a voice of the Senior Groupman.

"Yes—" said Donal. "Sentries all posted, Groupman?"

"Yes, sir." The quality of Morphy's tone was completely without inflection.

"Good. I want them alert at all times. Now, Morphy—"

"Yes, sir?"

"Who do we have in the Force that has a good sense of smell?"

"Smell, sir?"

Donal merely waited.

"Well, sir," said Morphy, finally and slowly. "There's Lee, he practically grew up in the mines, where you have to have a good sense of smell. That's the mines on Coby, Force-Leader."

"I assumed those were the mines you meant," said Donal, dryly. "Get Lee over here, will you?"

Morphy took out his own whistle and blew for the Senior Groupman, Third Group. They waited.

"He's about the camp isn't he?" said Donal, after a moment. "I want all the men within whistle sound that aren't on sentry duty."

"Yes, sir," said Morphy. "He'll be here in a moment. He knows it's me. Everybody sounds a little different on these whistles and you get to know them like voices after a while, sir."

"Groupman," said Donal. "I'd be obliged if you didn't feel the need to keep telling me things I already know."

"Yes, sir," said Morphy, subsiding.

Another shadow loomed up out of the darkness.

"What is it, Morphy?" said the voice of Lee.

"I wanted to see you," spoke up Donal, before the Senior Groupman had a chance to answer. "Morphy tells me you have a good sense of smell."

"I do pretty well," said Lee.

"*Sir!*"

"I do pretty well, sir."

"All right," said Donal. "Both of you take a look at the map here. Look sharp. I'm going to make a light." He flicked on a little flash, shielded by his hand. The map was revealed, spread out on the log before them. "Look here," said Donal, pointing. "Three kilometers off this way. Do you know what that is?"

"Small valley," said Morphy. "It's way outside our sentry posts."

"We're going there," Donal said. The light went out and he got up from the log.

"Us? Us, sir?" the voice of Lee came at him.

"The three of us," said Donal. "Come along." And he led the way surefootedly out into the darkness.

Going through the woods, he was pleased to discover the two Groupmen were almost as sure-footed in the blackness as himself. They went slowly but carefully for something over a mile; and then they felt the ground beginning to slope upward under their feet.

"All right. Down and easy," said Donal quietly. The three men dropped to their bellies and began in skilled silence to work their way up to the crest of the slope. It took them a good half-hour; but at the end of that time they lay side by side just under the skyline of a ridge, looking over into a well of blackness that was a small, hidden valley below. Donal tapped Lee on the shoulder and when the other turned his face toward him in the gloom, Donal touched his own nose, pointed down into the valley and made sniffing motions. Lee turned his face back to the valley and lay in that position for several minutes, apparently doing nothing at all. However, at the end of that time, he turned toward Donal again, and nodded. Donal motioned them all back down the slope.

Donal asked no questions and the two Groupmen volunteered nothing until they were once more back safely within the lines of their own sentry posts. Then Donal turned toward Lee.

"Well, Groupman," he said. "What did you smell?"

Lee hesitated. His voice, when he answered, had a note of puzzlement in it.

"I don't know, sir," he answered. "Something—sour, sort of. I could just barely smell it."

"That's the best you can do?" inquired Donal. "Something sour?"

"I don't know, sir," said Lee. "I've got a pretty good nose, Force— in fact," a note of belligerence crept into his voice. "I've got a damned good nose. I never smelled anything like this before. I'd remember."

"Have either of you men ever contracted on this planet before?"

"No," said Lee.

"No, sir," answered Morphy.

"I see," said Donal. They had reached the same log from which they had started a little less than three hours before. "Well, that'll be all. Thank you, Groupmen."

He sat down on the log again. The other two hesitated a moment; and then went off together.

Left alone, Donal consulted the map again; and sat thinking for a while. Then he rose, and hunting up Morphy, told him to take over the Force, and stay awake. Donal himself was going to Command HQ. Then he took off.

Command HQ was a blackout shell containing a sleepy orderly, a map viewer and Skuak.

"The commandant around?" asked Donal, as he came in.

"Been asleep three hours," said Skuak. "What're you doing up? I wouldn't be if I didn't have the duty."

"Where's he sleeping?"

"About ten meters off in the bush, at eleven o'clock," said Skuak. "What's it all about? You aren't going to wake him, are you?"

"Maybe he'll still be awake," said Donal; and went out.

Outside the shell, and the little cleared space of the HQ area, he cat-footed around to the location Skuak had mentioned. A battle hammock was there, slung between two trees, with a form mounding its climate cover. But when Donal reached in to put his hand on the form's shoulder, it closed only on the soft material of a rolled-up battle jacket.

Donal breathed out and turned about. He went back the way he had come, past the Command HQ area, and was stopped by a sentry as he approached the village.

"Sorry, Force," said the sentry. "Commandant's order. No one to go into the village area. Not even himself, he says. Booby traps."

"Oh, yes—thank you, sentry," said Donal; and, turning about, went off into the darkness.

As soon as he was safely out of sight, however, he turned again, and worked his way back past the sentry lines and in among the houses of the village. The small but very bright moon which the Harmonites called The Eye of the Lord was just rising, and throwing, through the ruined walls, alternate patches of tricky silver and black. Slipping in and out of the black places, he began patiently to search the place, house by house, and building by building.

It was a slow and arduous process, carried out the way he was doing it, in complete silence. And the moon mounted in the sky. It was nearly four hours later that he came upon what he was searching for.

In the moonlit center of a small building's roofless shell stood Hugh Killien, looking very tall and efficient in his chameleon battle-dress. And close to him—almost close enough to be in his arms—was Anea, the Select of Kultis. Beyond them both, blurred by action of the polarizer that had undoubtedly been the means of allowing it to carry her invisibly to this spot, was a small flying platform.

"... Sweet," Hugh was saying, his resonant voice pitched so low it barely carried to the ears of Donal, shrouded in shadow outside the broken wall, "Sweet, you must trust me. Together we can stop him; but you must let me handle it. His power is tremendous—"

"I know, I know!" she interrupted, fiercely, all but wringing her hands. "But every day we wait makes it more dangerous for you, Hugh. Poor Hugh—" gently she raised her hand to touch his cheek, "what I've dragged you into."

"Dragged? Me?" Hugh laughed, low and confidently. "I went into this with my eyes open." He reached out for her. "For you—"

But she slipped away from him.

"Now's not the time for that," she said. "Anyway, it's not me you're doing this for. It's Kultis. He's not going to use me," she said fiercely, "to get *my* world under his thumb!"

"Of course, it's for Kultis," said Hugh. "But you *are* Kultis, Anea. You're everything I love about the Exotics. But don't you see; all we have to work on are your suspicions. You *think* he's planning against the Bond, against Sayona, himself. But that's not enough for us to go to Kultis with."

"But what can I do?" she cried. "I can't use his own methods against him. I can't lie, or cheat, or set agents on him while he still holds my contract. I . . . I just *can't.* That's what being Select means!" She clenched her fists. "I'm trapped by my own mind, my own body." She turned on him suddenly. "You said when I first spoke to you, two months ago you said you had evidence!"

"I was mistaken," Hugh's tone was soothing. "Something came to my attention—at any rate I was wrong. I have my own built-in moral system, too, Anea. It may not reach the level of psychological blockage like yours," he drew himself up, looking very martial in the moonlight. "But I know what's honorable and right."

"Oh, I know. I know, Hugh—" she was all contrition. "But I get so desperate. You don't know—"

"If he had only made some move against you personally—"

"Me?" She stiffened. "He wouldn't dare! A Select of Kultis—and besides," she added with more of a touch of common sense than Donal had heretofore given her credit for possessing, "that'd be foolish. He'd have nothing to gain; and Kultis would be alerted against him."

"I don't know," Hugh scowled in the moonlight. "He's a man like anyone else. If I thought—"

"Oh, Hugh!" she giggled suddenly, like any schoolgirl. "Don't be absolutely ridiculous!"

"Ridiculous!" His tone rang with wounded feelings.

"Oh, now—I didn't mean that. Hugh, now stop looking like an elephant that just had his trunk stung by a bee. There's no point in making things up. He's far too intelligent to—" she giggled again, then sobered. "No, it's his head we have to worry about; not his heart."

"Do you worry about my heart?" he asked in a low voice.

She looked down at the ground.

"Hugh—I do like you," she said. "But you don't understand. A Select is a . . . a symbol."

"If you mean you can't—"

"No, no, not that—" she looked up quickly. "I've no block against love, Hugh. But if I was involved in something . . . something small, and mean, it's what it would do to those back on Kultis to whom a Select means something—You *do* understand?"

"I understand that I'm a soldier," he said. "And that I never know whether I'll have a tomorrow or not."

"I know," she said. "And they send you out on things like this, dangerous things."

"My dear little Anea," he said, tenderly. "How little you understand what it is to be a soldier. I volunteered for this job."

"Volunteered?" She stared at him.

"To go look for danger—to go look for opportunities to prove myself!" he said, fiercely. "To make myself a name, so that the stars will believe I'm the kind of man a Select of Kultis could want and belong with!"

"Oh, Hugh!" she cried on a note of enthusiasm. "If you only could! If only something would make you famous. Then we could really fight him!"

He checked, staring at her in the moonlight with such a sandbagged expression that Donal, in the shadows, nearly chuckled.

"Must you always be talking about politics?" he cried.

But Donal had already turned away from the two of them. There was no point in listening further. He moved silently out of earshot; but after that he went quickly, not caring about noise. His search for Hugh had taken him clear across the village, so that what was closest to him now was his own Force area. The short night of Harmony's northern continent was already beginning to gray toward dawn. He headed toward his own men, one of his odd certainties chilling him.

"Halt!" cried one of his own sentries, as Donal broke clear of the houses. "Halt and give—sir!"

"Come with me!" snapped Donal. "Where's the Third Group Area from here?"

"This way, sir," said the man; and led the way, trotting to keep up with Donal's long strides.

They burst into the Third Group area. Donal put his whistle to his lips and blew for Lee.

"What—?" mumbled a sleepy voice from half a dozen meters' distance. A hammock heaved and disgorged the bony figure of the ex-miner. "What the hell . . . sir?"

Donal strode up to him and with both hands swung him about so that he faced toward the enemy territory from which the dawn breeze was coming. "Smell!" he ordered.

Lee blinked, scrubbed his nose with one knotty fist, and stifled a yawn. He took a couple of deep breaths filling his lungs, his nostrils spread—and suddenly he snapped into complete awakedness.

"Same thing, sir," he said, turning to Donal. "Stronger."

"All right!" Donal wheeled about on the sentry. "Take a signal to Senior Groupmen, First and Second Groups. Get their men into trees, high up in trees, and get themselves up, too."

"Trees, sir?"

"Get going! I want every man in this Force a dozen meters off the ground in ten minutes—*with* their weapons!" The sentry turned to make off. "If you've got time after making that signal, try to get through to Command HQ with it. If you see you can't, climb a tree yourself. Got that?"

"Yes, sir."

"Then get going!"

Donal wheeled about and started himself on the business of getting the sleeping Third Group soldiers out of their hammocks and up the trunks of tall trees. It was not done in ten minutes. It was closer to twenty by the time they were all off the ground. A group of Dorsai schoolboys would have made it in a quarter of the time, from the sounder sleep of youth. But on the whole, thought Donal, pulling himself at last up into a tree, they had been in time; and that was what counted.

He did not stop as the others had, at a height of a dozen meters. Automatically, as he hurried the others out of their hammocks, he had marked the tallest tree in the area; and this he continued to climb until he had a view out over the tops of the lesser vegetation of the area. He shaded his eyes against the new-rising sun, peering off toward enemy territory, and between the trees.

"Now, what d'we do?" floated up an aggrieved voice from below and off to one side of his own lofty perch. Donal took his palm from his eyes and tilted his head downward.

"Senior Groupman Lee," he said in a low, but carrying voice. "You will shoot the next man who opens his mouth without being spoken to first by either you, or myself. That is a direct order."

He raised his head again, amid a new silence, and again peered off under his palm through the trees.

The secret of observation is patience. He saw nothing, but he continued to sit, looking at nothing in particular, and everything in general; and after four slow minutes he was rewarded by a slight flicker of movement that registered on his gaze. He made no effort to search it out again, but continued to observe in the same general area; and gradually, as if they were figures developing on a film out of some tangled background, he became aware of men slipping from cover to cover, a host of men, approaching the camp.

He leaned down again through the branches.

"No firing until I blow my whistle," he said, in an even lower voice than before. "Pass the word—quietly."

He heard, like the murmur of wind in those same branches, the order being relayed on to the last man in the Third Group and—he hoped—to the Second and First Groups as well.

The small, chameleon-clad figures continued to advance. Squinting at them through the occulting leaves and limbs, he made out a small black cross sewn to the right shoulder of each battle-dress. These were no mercenaries. These were native elite troops of the United Orthodox Church itself, superb soldiers and wild fanatics both. And even as the recognition confirmed itself in his mind, the advancing men broke into a charge upon the camp, bursting forth all at once in the red-gray dawnlight into full-throated yips and howls, underlaid a second later by the high-pitched singing of their spring-gun slivers as they ripped air and wood and flesh.

They were not yet among the trees where Donal's force was hiding. But his men were mercenaries, and had friends in the camp the Orthodox elite were attacking. He held them as long as he could, and a couple of seconds longer; and then, putting his whistle to lips, he blew with the damper completely off—a blast that echoed from one end of the camp to the other.

Savagely, his own men opened up from the trees. And for several moments wild confusion reigned on the ground. It is not easy to tell all at once from which direction a sliver gun is being fired at you. For perhaps five minutes, the attacking Orthodox soldiers labored under the delusion that the guns cutting them down were concealed in some groundlevel ambush. They killed ruthlessly, everything they could see on their own eye-level; and, by the time they had discovered their mistake, it was too late. On their dwindled numbers was concentrated the fire of a hundred and fifty-one rifles; and if the marksmanship of only one of these was up to Dorsai standards, that of the rest was adequate to the task. In less than forty minutes from the moment in which Donal had begun to harry his sleep-drugged men up into the trees, the combat was over.

The Third Group slid down out of their trees and one of the first down—a soldier named Kennedy—calmly lifted his rifle to his shoulder and sent a sliver through the throat of an Orthodox that was writhing on the ground, nearby.

"None of that!" cried Donal, sharply and clearly; and his voice carried out over the sea. A mercenary hates wanton killing, it not being his business to slaughter men, but to win battles. But not another shot was fired. The fact said something about a significant change in the attitude of the men of the Third Command toward a certain new officer by the name of Graeme.

Under Donal's orders, the wounded on both sides were collected and those with serious wounds medicated. The attacking soldiery had been wiped out almost to a man. But it had not been completely one-sided. Of the three hundred-odd men who had been on the ground at the time of the attack, all but forty-three—and that included Force-Leader Skuak—were casualities.

"Prepare to retreat," ordered Donal—and, at that moment, the man facing him turned his head to look past at something behind Donal. Donal turned about. Pounding out of the ruined village, hand gun in his fist, was Commandant Killien.

In silence, not moving, the surviving soldiers of the Command watched him race up to him. He checked at their stare; and his eyes swung about to focus on Donal. He dropped to a walk and strode up to within a few meters of the younger officer.

"Well, Force-Leader!" he snapped. "What happened? Report?"

Donal did not answer him directly. He raised his hand and pointed to Hugh; and spoke to two of the enlisted men standing by.

"Soldiers," he said. "Arrest that man. And hold him for immediate trial under Article Four of the Mercenaries Code."

VETERAN

Directly after getting into the city, with his canceled contract stiff in his pocket, and cleaning up in his hotel room, Donal went down two flights to pay his visit to Marshal Hendrik Galt. He found him in, and concluded certain business with him before leaving to pay his second call at a different hotel across the city.

In spite of himself, he felt a certain weakness in the knees as he announced his presence to the doorbot. It was a weakness most men would have excused him. William, Prince of Ceta, was someone few persons would have cared to beard in his own den; and Donal, in spite of what he had just experienced, was still a young—a very young—man. However, the doorbot invited him in, and summoning up his calmest expression, Donal strode into the suite.

William was, as the last time Donal had seen him, busy at his desk. This was no affectation on William's part, as a good many people between the stars could testify. Seldom has one individual accomplished in a single day what William accomplished in the way of business, daily, as a matter of routine. Donal walked up to the desk and nodded his greeting. William looked up at him.

"I'm amazed to see you," he said.

"Are you, sir?" said Donal.

William considered him in silence for perhaps half a minute.

"It's not often I make mistakes," he said. "Perhaps I can console myself with the thought that when I do they turn out to be on the same order of magnitude as my successes. What inhuman kind of armor are you wearing, young man, that leads you to trust yourself in my presence, again?"

"Possibly the armor of public opinion," replied Donal. "I've been in the public eye, recently. I have something of a name, nowadays."

"Yes," said William. "I know that type of armor from personal experience, myself."

"And then," said Donal, "you did send for me."

"Yes." And then, without warning, William's face underwent a change to an expression of such savagery as Donal had never seen before. "How dare you!" snarled the older man, viciously. "How dare you!"

"Sir," said Donal, wooden-faced, "I had no alternative."

"No alternative! You come to me and have the effrontery to say— no alternative?"

"Yes, sir," said Donal.

William rose in swift and lithe motion. He stalked around the desk to stand face to face, his eyes uptitled a little to bore into the eyes of this tall young Dorsai.

"I took you on to follow my orders, nothing else!" he said icily. "And you—grandstand hero that you are—wreck everything."

"Sir?"

"Yes—'sir'. You backwoods moron! You imbecile. Who told you to interfere with Hugh Killien? Who told you to take any action about him?"

"Sir," said Donal. "I had no choice."

"No choice? How—no choice?"

"My command was a command of mercenaries," answered Donal, without moving a muscle. "Commandant Killien had given his assurance in accordance with the Mercenaries Code. Not only had his assurance proved false, he himself had neglected his command while in the field and in enemy territory. Indirectly, he had been responsible for the death of over half his men. As ranking field officer present, I had no choice but to arrest him and hold him for trial."

"A trial held on the spot?"

"It is the code, sir," said Donal. He paused. "I regret it was necessary to shoot him. The court-martial left me no alternative."

"Again!" said William. "No alternative! Graeme, the space between the stars does not go to men who can find *no alternatives*!" He turned about abruptly, walked back around his desk and sat down.

"All right," he said coldly but with all the passion gone, "get out of here." Donal turned and walked toward the door as William picked up a paper from before him. "Leave your address with my doorbot," said William. "I'll find some kind of a post for you on some other world."

"I regret, sir—" said Donal.

William looked up.

"It didn't occur to me that you would have any further need of me. Marshal Galt has already found me another post."

William continued to look at him for a long moment. His eyes were as cold as the eyes of a basilisk.

"I see," he said at last, slowly. "Well, Graeme, perhaps we shall have something to do with each other in the future."

"I'll hope we will," said Donal. He went out. But, even after he had closed the door behind him, he thought he could feel William's eyes still coming at him through all the thickness of its panel.

He had yet one more call to make, before his duty on this world was done. He checked the directory out in the corridor and went down a flight.

The doorbot invited him in; and ArDell Montor, as large and untidy as ever, with his eyes only slightly blurred from drink, met him halfway to the entrance.

"You!" said ArDell, when Donal explained what it was he wanted. "She won't see *you*." He hunched his heavy shoulders, looking at Donal; and for a second his eyes cleared. Something sad and kind looked out of them, to be replaced with bitter humor. "But the old fox won't like it. I'll ask her."

"Tell her it's about something she needs to know," said Donal.

"I'll do that. Wait here." Ardell went out the door.

He returned in some fifteen minutes.

"You're to go up," he said. "Suite 1890." Donal turned toward the door. "I don't suppose," said the Newtonian, almost wistfully, "I'll be seeing you again."

"Why, we may meet," answered Donal.

"Yes," said ArDell. He stared at Donal penetratingly. "We may at that. We may at that."

Donal went out and up to Suite 1890. The doorbot let him in. Anea was waiting for him, slim and rigid in one of her high-collared, long dresses of blue.

"Well?" she said. Donal considered her almost sorrowfully.

"You really hate me, don't you?" he said.

"You killed him!" she blazed.

"Oh, of course." In spite of himself, the exasperation she was always so capable of tapping in him rose to the surface. "I had to—for your own good."

"For my good!"

He reached into his tunic pocket and withdrew a small telltale. But it was unlighted. For a wonder this apartment was unbugged. And then he thought—*of course, I keep forgetting who she is.*

"Listen to me," he said. "You've been beautifully equipped by gene selection and training to be a Select—but not to be anything else. Why can't you understand that interstellar intrigue isn't your dish?"

"Interstellar . . . what're you talking about?" she demanded.

"Oh, climb down for a moment," he said wearily—and more youngly than he had said anything since leaving home. "William is your enemy. You understand that much; but you don't understand why or how, although you think you do. And neither do I," he confessed, "although I've got a notion. But the way for you to confound William isn't by playing his game. Play your own. Be the Select of Kultis. As the Select, you're untouchable."

"If," she said, "you've nothing more to say than that—"

"All right," he took a step toward her. "Listen, then. William was making an attempt to compromise you. Killien was his tool—"

"How dare you?" she erupted.

"How dare I?" he echoed wearily. "Is there anyone in this interstellar community of madmen and madwomen who doesn't know that phrase and use it to me on sight? I dare because it's the truth."

"Hugh," she stormed at him, "was a fine, honest man. A soldier and a gentleman! Not a . . . a—"

"Mercenary?" he inquired. "But he was."

"He was a career officer," she replied haughtily. "There's a difference."

"No difference." He shook his head. "But you wouldn't understand that. Mercenary isn't necessarily the dirty word somebody taught you it is. Never mind. Hugh Killien was worse than any name you might be mistaken enough to call me. He was a fool."

"Oh!" she whirled about.

He took her by one elbow and turned her around. She came about in shocked surprise. Somehow, it had never occurred to her to imagine how strong he was. Now, the sudden realization of her physical helplessness in his hands shocked her into abrupt and unusual silence.

"Listen to the truth, then," he said. "William dangled you like an expensive prize before Killien's eyes. He fed him full of the foolish hope that he could have *you*—the Select of Kultis. He made it possible for you to visit Hugh that night at Faith Will Succour—yes," he said, at her gasp, "I know about that. I saw you there with him. He also

made sure Hugh would meet you, just as he made sure that the Orthodox soldiers would attack."

"I don't believe it—" she managed.

"Don't you be a fool, too," Donal said, roughly. "How else do you
think an overwhelming force of Orthodox elite troops happened to
move in on the encampment at just the proper time? What other men
than fanatic Orthodox soldiery could be counted on to make sure none
of the men in our unit escaped alive? There was supposed to be only
one man to escape from that affair—Hugh Killien, who would be in a
position then to make a hero's claim on you. You see how much your
good opinion is worth?"

"Hugh wouldn't—"

"Hugh didn't," interrupted Donal. "As I said, he was a fool. A fool
but a good soldier. Nothing more was needed for William. He knew
Hugh would be fool enough to go and meet you, and good soldier
enough not to throw his life away when he saw his command was
destroyed. As I say, he would have come back alone—and a hero."

"But you saw through this!" she snapped. "What's your secret? A
pipeline to the Orthodox camp?"

"Surely it was obvious from the situation; a command exposed, a
commandant foolishly making a love-tryst in a battleground, that something like the attack was inevitable. I simply asked myself what kind
of troops would be used and how they might be detected. Orthodox
troops eat nothing but native herbs, cooked in the native fashion. The
odor of their cooking permeates their clothing. Any veteran of a Harmony campaign would be able to recognize their presence the same
way."

"If his nose was sensitive enough. If he knew where to look for
them—"

"There was only one logical spot—"

"Anyway," she said coldly. "This is beside the point. The point
is"—suddenly she fired up before him—"Hugh wasn't guilty. You said
it yourself. He was, even according to you, only a fool! And you had
him murdered!"

He sighed in weariness.

"The crime," he said, "for which Commandant Killien was executed was that of misleading his men and abandoning them in enemy
territory. It was *that* he paid with his life for."

"Murderer!" she said. "Get out!"

"But," he said, staring baffledly at her, "I've just explained."

"You've explained nothing," she said, coldly, and from a distance.
"I've heard nothing but a mountain of lies, lies, about a man whose

boots you aren't fit to clean. Now, will you get out, or do I have to call the hotel guard?"

"You don't believe—?" He stared at her, wide-eyed.

"Get out." She turned her back on him. Like a man in a daze, he turned himself and walked blindly to the door and numbly out into the corridor. Still walking, he shook his head, like a person who finds himself in a bad dream and unable to wake up.

What was this curse upon him? She had not been lying—she was not capable of doing so successfully. She had really heard his explanation and—it had meant nothing to her. It was all so obvious, so plain—the machinations of William, the stupidity of Killien. And she had not seen it when Donal pointed it out to her. *She*, of all people, a Select of Kultis!

Why? Why? Why?

Scourged by the devils of self-doubt and loneliness, Donal moved off down the corridor, back in the direction of Galt's hotel.

AIDE-DE-CAMP

They met in the office of Marshal Galt, in his Freiland home; and the enormous expanse of floor and the high vaulted ceiling dwarfed them as they stood three men around a bare desk.

"Captain Lludrow, this is my Aide, Commandant Donal Graeme," said Galt, brusquely. "Donal, this is Russ Lludrow, Patrol Chief of my Blue Patrol."

"Honored, sir," said Donal, inclining his head.

"Pleased to meet you, Graeme," answered Lludrow. He was a fairly short, compact man in his early forties, very dark of skin and eye.

"You'll trust Donal with all staff information," said Galt. "Now, what's your reconnaissance and intelligence picture?"

"There's no doubt about it, they're planning an expeditionary landing on Oriente." Lludrow turned toward the desk and pressed buttons on the map keyboard. The top of the desk cleared to transparency and they looked through at a non-scale map of the Sirian system. "Here we are," he said, stabbing his finger at the world of Freiland, "here's New Earth"—his finger moved to Freiland's sister planet—"and here's Oriente"—his finger skipped to a smaller world inward toward the sun—"in the positions they'll be in, relative to one another twelve days from now. You see, we'll have the sun between the two of us and also almost between each of our worlds and Oriente. They couldn't have picked a more favorable tactical position."

Galt grunted, examining the map. Donal was watching Lludrow with quiet curiosity. The man's accent betrayed him for a New Earth-man, but here he was high up on the Staff of Freiland's fighting forces. Of course, the two Sirian worlds were natural allies, being on the same side as Old Earth against the Venus-Newton-Cassida group; but simply because they were so close, there was a natural rivalry in some things, and a career officer from one of them usually did best on his home world.

"Don't like it," said Galt, finally. "It's a fool stunt from what I can see. The men they land will have to wear respirators; and what the devil do they expect to do with their beachhead when they establish it? Oriente's too close to the sun for terraforming, or we would have done it from here long ago."

"It's possible," said Lludrow, calmly, "they could intend to mount an offensive from there against our two planets here."

"No, no," Galt's voice was harsh and almost irritable. His heavy face loomed above the map. "That's as wild a notion as terraforming Oriente. They couldn't keep a base there supplied, let alone using it to attack two large planets with fully established population and industry. Besides, you don't conquer civilized worlds. That's a maxim."

"Maxims can become worn out, though," put in Donal.

"What?" demanded Galt, looking up. "Oh—Donal. Don't interrupt us now. From the looks of it," he went on to Lludrow, "it strikes me as nothing so much as a live exercise—you know what I mean."

Lludrow nodded—as did Donal unconsciously. Live exercises were something that no planetary Chief of Staff admitted to, but every military man recognized. They were actual small battles provoked with a handy enemy either for the purpose of putting a final edge on troops in training, or to keep that edge on troops that had been too long on a standby basis. Galt, almost alone among the Planetary Commanders of his time, was firmly set against this action, not only in theory, but in practice. He believed it more honest to hire his troops out, as in the recent situation on Harmony, when they showed signs of going stale. Donal privately agreed with him; although there was always the danger that when you hired troops out, they lost the sense of belonging to you, in particular, and were sometimes spoiled through mismanagement.

"What do you think?" Galt was asking his Patrol chief.

"I don't know, sir," Lludrow answered. "It seems the only sensible interpretation."

"The thing," interrupted Donal, again, "would be to go over some of the nonsensible interpretations as well, to see if one of them doesn't constitute a possible danger. And from that—"

"Donal," broke in Galt, dryly, "you are my aide, not my Battle Op."

"Still—" Donal was persisting, when the marshal cut him off in a tone of definite command.

"That will be all!"

"Yes, sir," said Donal, subsiding.

"Then," said Galt, turning back to Lludrow, "we'll regard this as a heaven-sent opportunity to cut an arm or two off the fighting strength of the Newton Cassidan fleet and field force. Go back to your Patrol. I'll send orders."

Lludrow inclined his head and was just about to turn and go when there was an interruption—the faint swish of air from one of the big office doors sliding back, and the tap of feminine heels approaching over the polished floor. They turned to see a tall, dazzlingly beautiful woman with red hair coming at them across the office.

"Elvine!" said Galt.

"Not interrupting anything, am I?" she called, even before she came up to them. "Didn't know you had a visitor."

"Russ," said Galt. "You know my sister-in-law's daughter, The Elvine Rhy? Elvine, this is my Blue Patrol Chief, Russ Lludrow."

"Very deeply honored," said Lludrow, bowing.

"Oh, we've met—or at least I've seen you before." She gave him her hand briefly, then turned to Donal. "Donal, come fishing with me."

"I'm sorry," said Donal. "I'm on duty."

"No, no," Galt waved him off with a large hand. "There's nothing more at the moment. Run along, if you want."

"At your service, then," said Donal.

"But what a cold acceptance!" she turned on Lludrow. "I'm sure the Patrol chief wouldn't have hesitated like that."

Lludrow bowed again.

"I'd never hesitate where the Rhy was concerned."

"There!" she said. "There's your model, Donal. You should practice manners—and speeches like that."

"If you suggest it," said Donal.

"Oh, Donal." She tossed her head. "You're hopeless. But come along, anyway." She turned and left; and he followed her.

They crossed the great central hall and emerged into the garden terrace above the blue-green bay of the shallow, inland sea that touched the edges of Galt's home. He expected her to continue down to the docks, but instead she whirled about in a small arbor, and stood facing him.

"Why do you treat me like this?" she threw at him. "Why?"

"Treat you?" He looked down at her.

"Oh, you wooden man!" Her lips skinned back over her perfect teeth. "What're you afraid of—that I'll eat you up?"

"Wouldn't you?" he asked her quite seriously—and she checked at his answer.

"Come on. Let's go fishing!" she cried, and whirled about and ran down toward the dock.

So, they went fishing. But even slicing through the water in pursuit of a twisting fish at sixty fathoms depth, Donal's mind was not on the sport. He let the small jet unit on his shoulders push him whither the chase led him; and, in the privacy of his helmet, condemned himself darkly for his own ignorance. For it was this crime of ignorance which he abhorred above all else—in this case his ignorance of the ways of women—that had led him to believe he could allow himself the luxury of a casual and friendly acquaintanceship with a woman who wanted him badly, but whom he, himself, did not want at all.

She had been living here, in this household, when Galt had brought him here as a personal aide. She was, by some intricate convolution of Freiland inheritance laws, the marshal's responsibility; in spite of the distance of their relationships and the fact that her own mother and some other relatives were still living. She was some five years older than Donal, although in her wild energy and violence of emotion, this difference was lost. He had found her excitements interesting, at first; and her company a balm to what—though he would not admit it to himself in so many words—was a recently bruised and very tender portion of his ego. That had been at first.

"You know," she had said to him in one of her peculiar flashes of directness. "Anybody would want me."

"Anybody would," he admitted, considering her beauty. It was not until later that he discovered, to his dismay, that he had accepted an invitation he had not even suspected was there.

For four months now, he had been established at the marshal's estate, learning some of the elements of Freilander Staff Control; and learning also, to his increasing dismay, some of the intricacies of a woman's mind. And, in addition to it all, he found himself puzzled as to why he did not want her. Certainly he liked Elvine Rhy. Her company was enjoyable, her attractiveness was undeniable, and a certain brightness and hunger in her personality matched similar traits in his own. Yet, he did not want her. No, not the least bit, not at all.

They gave up their fishing after several hours. Elvine had caught four, averaging a good seven or eight kilograms. He had caught none.

"Elvine—" he began, as he went up the steps of the terrace with her. But, before he could finish his carefully thought out speech, an annunciator hidden in a rosebush chimed softly.

"Commandant," said the rosebush, gently, "the doorbot announces a Senior Groupman Tage Lee to see you. Do you wish to see him?"

"Lee—" murmured Donal. He raised his voice. "From Coby?"

"He says he is from Coby," answered the rosebush.

"I'll see him," said Donal, striding quickly toward the house. He heard the sound of running feet behind him and Elvine caught at his arm.

"Donal—" she said.

"This'll just take a minute," he answered. "I'll see you in the library in a few minutes."

"All right—" She let go and fell behind him. He went in and to the entrance hall.

Lee, the same Lee who had commanded his Third Group, was waiting for him.

"Well, Groupman," said Donal, shaking hands. "What brings you here?"

"You do, sir," said Lee. He looked Donal in the eye with something of the challenge Donal had marked the first time Donal had seen him. "Could you use a personal orderly?"

Donal considered him.

"Why?"

"I've been carrying my contract around since they let us all go after that business with Killien," said Lee. "If you want to know, I've been on a bat. That's my cross. Out of uniform I'm an alcoholic. In uniform, it's better, but sooner or later I get into a hassle with somebody. I've been putting off signing up again because I couldn't make up my mind what I wanted. Finally, it came to me. I wanted to work for you."

"You look sober enough now," said Donal.

"I can do anything for a few days—even stop drinking. If I'd come up here with the shakes, you'd never have taken me."

Donal nodded.

"I'm not expensive," said Lee. "Take a look at my contract. If you can't afford me yourself, I'll sign up as a line soldier and you pull strings to get me assigned to you. I don't drink if I've got something to do; and I can make myself useful. Look here—"

He extended his hand in a friendly manner, as if to shake hands again, and suddenly there was a knife in it.

"That's a back-alley, hired killer trick," said Donal. "Do you think it'd work with me?"

"With you—no." Lee made the knife vanish again. "That's why I want to work for you. I'm a funny character, commandant. I need something to hang to. I need it the way ordinary people need food and drink and home and friends. It's all there in the psychological index number on my contract, if you want to copy it down and check on me."

"I'll take your word for it, for now," said Donal. "What *is* wrong with you?"

"I'm borderline psycho," Lee answered, his lean face expressionless. "Not correctable. I was born with a deficiency. What they tell me is, I've got no sense of right or wrong; and I can't manage just by abstract rules. The way the doctors put it when I first got my contract, I need my own, personal, living god in front of me all the time. You take me on and tell me to cut the throat of all the kids under five I meet, and that's fine. Tell me to cut my own throat—the same thing. Everything's all right, then."

"You don't make yourself sound very attractive."

"I'm telling you the truth. I can't tell *you* anything else. I'm like a bayonet that's been going around all my life looking for a rifle to fit on to; and now I've found it. So, don't trust me. Take me on probation for five years, ten years—the rest of my life. But don't shut me out." Lee half-turned and pointed one bony finger at the door behind him. "Out there is hell for me, commandant. Anything inside here is heaven."

"I don't know," said Donal, slowly. "I don't know that I'd want the responsibility."

"No responsibility." Lee's eyes were shining; and it struck home to Donal suddenly that the man was terrified: terrified of being refused. "Just tell me. Try me, now. Tell me to get down and bark like a dog. Tell me to cut my left hand off at the wrist. As soon as they've grown me a new one I'll be back to do whatever you want me to do." The knife was suddenly back in his hand. "Want to see?"

"Put that away!" snapped Donal. The knife disappeared. "All right, I'll buy your contract personally. My suit of rooms are third door to the right, the head of the stairs. Go up there and wait for me."

Lee nodded. He offered no word of thanks. He only turned and went.

Donal shook himself mentally as if the emotional charge that had crackled in the air about him the last few seconds was a thing of physical mass draped heavily upon his shoulders. He turned and went to the library.

Elvine was standing looking out the great expanse of open wall at the ocean, as he came in. She turned quickly, at the sound of his steps and came to meet him.

"What was it?" she asked.

"One of my soldiers from the Harmony business," he said. "I've taken him on as my personal orderly." He looked down at her. "Ev—"

Instantly, she drew a little away from him. She looked out the wall, one hand falling down to play with a silver half-statuette that sat on a low table beside her.

"Yes?" she said.

He found it very hard to get the words out.

"Ev, you know I've been around here a long time," he said.

"A long time?" At that, she turned to face him with a slight look of startlement. "Four months? It seems like hours, only."

"Perhaps," he said, doggedly. "But it *has* been a long time. So perhaps it's just as well I'm leaving."

"Leaving?" Her eyes shot wide; hazel eyes, staring at him. "Who said you were leaving?"

"I have to, of course," he said. "But I thought I ought to clear something up before I go. I've liked you a great deal, Ev—"

But she was too quick for him.

"Liked me?" she cried. "I should think you should! Why, I haven't hardly had a minute to myself for entertaining you. I swear I hardly know what it looks like any more outside of this place! Liked me! You certainly ought to like me after the way I've put myself out for you!"

He gazed at her furious features for a long moment and then he smiled ruefully.

"You're quite right," he said. "I've put you to a great deal of trouble. Pardon me for being so dense as not to notice it." He bent his head to her. "I'll be going now."

He turned and walked away. But he had hardly taken a dozen steps across the sunlit library before she called his name.

"Donal!"

He turned and saw her staring after him, her face stiff, her fists clenched at her side.

"Donal, you . . . you can't go," she said, tightly.

"I beg your pardon?" He stared at her.

"You can't go," she repeated. "Your duty is here. You're assigned here."

"No." He shook his head. "You don't understand, Ev. This business of Oriente's come up. I'm going to ask the marshal to assign me to one of the ships."

"You can't." Her voice was brittle. "He isn't here. He's gone down to the Spaceyard."

"Well, then, I'll go there and ask him."

"You can't. I've already asked him to leave you here. He promised."

"You *what*?" The words exploded from his lips in a tone more suited to the field than to this quiet mansion.

"I asked him to leave you here."

He turned and stalked away from her.

"Donal!" He heard her voice crying despairingly after him, but there was nothing she, or anyone in that house could have done, to stop him then.

He found Galt examining the new experimental model of a two-man anti-personnel craft. The older man looked up in surprise as Donal came up.

"What is it?" he asked.

"Could I see you alone for a minute, sir?" said Donal. "A private and urgent matter."

Galt shot him a keen glance, but motioned aside with his head and they stepped over into the privacy of a tool control booth.

"What is it?" asked Galt.

"Sir," said Donal. "I understand Elvine asked you if I couldn't continue to be assigned to your household during the upcoming business we talked about with Patrol Chief Lludrow earlier today."

"That's right. She did."

"I did not know of it," said Donal, meeting the older man's eyes. "It was not my wish."

"Not your wish?"

"No, sir."

"Oh," said Galt. He drew a long breath and rubbed his chin with one thick hand. Turning his head aside, he gazed out through the screen of the control booth at the experimental ship. "I see," he said. "I didn't realize."

"No reason why you should." Donal felt a sudden twist of emotion inside him at the expression on the older man's face. "I should have spoken to you before sir."

"No, no," Galt brushed the matter aside with a wave of his hand. "The responsibility's mine. I've never had children. No experience.

She has to get herself settled in life one of these days; and . . . well, I have a high opinion of you, Donal."

"You've been too kind to me already, sir," Donal said miserably.

"No, no . . . well, mistakes will happen. I'll see you have a place with the combat forces right away, of course."

"Thank you," said Donal.

"Don't thank me, boy." Abruptly, Galt looked old. "I should have remembered. You're a Dorsai."

STAFF LIAISON

"Welcome aboard," said a pleasant-faced Junior Captain, as Donal strode through the gas barrier of the inner lock. The Junior Captain was in his early twenties, a black-haired, square-faced young man who looked as if he had gone in much for athletics. "I'm J. C. Allmin Clay Andresen."

"Donal Graeme." They saluted each other. Then they shook hands.

"Had any ship experience?" asked Andresen.

"Eighteen months of summer training cruises in the Dorsai," answered Donal. "Command and armament—no technical posts."

"Command and armament," said Andresen, "are plenty good enough on a Class 4J ship. Particularly Command. You'll be senior officer after me—if anything happens." He made the little ritual gesture, reaching out to touch a close, white, carbon-plastic wall beside him. "Not that I'm suggesting you take over in such a case. My First can handle things all right. But you may be able to give him a hand, if it should happen."

"Be honored," said Donal.

"Care to look over the ship?"

"I'm looking forward to it."

"Right. Step into the lounge, then." Andresen led the way across the small reception room, and through a sliding bulkhead to a corridor that curved off ahead of them to right and left. They went through another door in the wall of the corridor directly in front of them, down a small passage, and emerged through a final door into a large, pleasantly decorated, circular room.

"Lounge," said Andresen. "Control center's right under our feet; reversed gravity." He pressed a stud on the wall and a section of the floor slid back. "You'll have to flip," he warned, and did a head-first dive into the hole.

Donal, who knew what to expect, followed the J.C.'s example. The momentum of his dive shot him through and into another circular chamber of the same size as the lounge, in which everything would have been upside down and nailed to the ceiling, except for the small fact that here the gravity was reversed; and what had been down, was up, and up was down instead.

"Here," said Andresen, as Donal landed lightly on the floor at one side of the opening, "is our Control Eye. As you probably saw when you were moving in to come aboard, the Class 4J is a ball-and-hammer ship." He pressed several studs and in the large globe floating in the center of the floor, that which he had referred to as the Control Eye, a view formed of their craft, as seen from some little distance outside the ship. Half-framed against the star-pricked backdrop of space, and with just a sliver of the curved edge of Freiland showing at the edge of the scene, she floated. A sphere thirty meters in diameter, connected by two slim shafts a hundred meters each in length to a rhomboid-shape that was the ship's thrust unit, some five meters in diameter at its thickest and looking like a large child's spinning top, pivoted on two wires that clamped it at the middle. This was the "hammer." The ship, proper, was the "ball."

"No phase-shift equipment?" asked Donal. He was thinking of the traditional cylinder shape of the big ships that moved between the stars.

"Don't fool yourself," answered Andresen. "The grid's there. We just hope the enemy doesn't see it, or doesn't hit it. We can't protect it, so we try to make it invisible." His finger stabbed out to indicate the apparently bare shafts. "There's a covering grid running the full length of the ship, from thrust to nose. Painted black."

Donal nodded thoughtfully.

"Too bad a polarizer won't work in the absence of atmosphere," he said.

"You can say that," agreed Andresen. He flicked off the Eye. "Let's look around the rest of the ship by hand."

He led out a door and down a passage similar to the one by which they had entered the lounge. They came out into a corridor that was the duplicate of the curving one they had passed in the other half of the ship.

"Crew's quarters, mess hall, on the other one," explained Andresen. "Officer's quarters, storage and suppliers, repair section, on this one." He pushed open a door in the corridor wall opposite them and they stepped into a section roughly the size of a small hotel room, bounded on its farther side by the curving outer shell of the ship, proper. The shell in this section was, at the moment, on transparent; and the complicated "dentist's chair" facing the bank of controls at the foot of the transparency was occupied; although the figure in it was dressed in coveralls only.

"My First," said Andresen. The figure looked up over the headrest of the chair. It was a woman in her early forties.

"Hi, All," she said. "Just checking the override." Andresen made a wry grimace at Donal.

"Antipersonnel weapons," he explained. "Nobody likes to shoot the poor helpless characters out of the sky as they fall in for an assault—so it's an officer's job. I usually take it over myself if I'm not tied up with something else at the moment. Staff Liaison Donal Graeme—First Officer Coa Benn."

Donal and she shook hands.

"Well, shall we get on?" asked Andresen. They toured the rest of the ship and ended up before the door of Donal's stateroom in Officer's Country.

"Sorry," said Andresen. "But we're short of bunk space. Full complement under battle conditions. So we had to put your orderly in with you. If you've no objection—"

"Not at all," said Donal.

"Good," Andresen looked relieved. "That's why I like the Dorsai. They're so sensible." He clapped Donal on the shoulder, and went hurriedly off back to his duties of getting his ship and crew ready for action.

Entering his stateroom, Donal found Lee had already set up both their gear, including a harness hammock for himself to supplement the single bunk that would be Donal's.

"All set?" asked Donal.

"All set," answered Lee. He still chronically forgot the "sir"; but Donal, having already had some experience with the fanatic literal-mindedness with which the man carried out any command given him, had refrained from making an issue of it. "You settle my contract, yet?"

"I haven't had time," said Donal. "It can't be done in a day. You knew that, didn't you?"

"No," said Lee. "All I ever did was hand it over. And then, later on when I was through my term of service they gave it back to me; and the money I had coming."

"Well, it usually takes a number of weeks or months," Donal said. He explained that it had never occurred to him that anyone should fail to know, that the contracts are owned entirely by the individual's home community or world, and that a contract agreement was a matter for settlement between the employer and the employee's home government. The object was not to provide the individual so much with a job and a living wage, as to provide the home government with favorable monetary and "contractual" balances which would enable them to hire, in their turn, the trained specialists *they* needed. In the case of Lee's contract, since Donal was a private employer and had money to offer, but no contractual credits, the matter of Lee's employment had to be cleared with the Dorsai authorities, as well as the authorities on Coby, where Lee came from.

"That's more of a formality than anything else, though," Donal assured him. "I'm allowed an orderly, since I've been commandant rank. And the intent to hire's been registered. That means your home government won't draft you for any special service some place else."

Lee nodded, which was almost his utmost expression of relief.

". . . Signal!" chimed the annunciator in the stateroom wall by the door, suddenly. "Signal for Staff Liaison Graeme. Report to Flagship, immediately. Staff Liaison Graeme report to Flagship immediately."

Donal cautioned Lee to keep from under the feet of the ship's regular crew; and left.

The Flagship of the Battle made up by the Red and Green Patrols of the Freilander Space Force was, like the Class 4J Donal had just left, already in temporary loose orbit around Oriente. It took him some forty minutes to reach her; and when he entered her lock reception room and gave his name and rank, he was assigned a guide who took him to a briefing room in the ship's interior.

The room was filled by some twenty-odd other Staff Liaisons. They ranged in rank from Warrant Couriers to a Sub-Patrol Chief in his fifties. They were already seated facing a platform; and, as Donal entered—he was, apparently, the last to arrive—a Senior Captain of flag rank entered, followed closely by Blue Patrol Chief Lludrow.

"All right, gentlemen," said the Senior Captain; and the room came to order. "Here's the situation." He waved a hand and the wall behind him dissolved to reveal an artist's extrapolation of the coming battle. Oriente floated in black space, surrounded by a number of ships in various patterns. The size of the ships had been grossly exaggerated in order to make them visible in comparison with the planet which was roughly two-thirds the diameter of Mars. The largest of these, the

Patrol Class—long cylindrical interstellar warships—were in varying orbit eighty to five hundred kilometers above the planet's surface, so that the integration of their pattern enclosed Oriente in web of shifting movement. A cloud of smaller craft, C4Js, A (subclass) 9s, courier ships, firing platforms, and individual and two-man gnat class boats, held position out beyond and planetward of them, right down into the atmosphere.

"We think," said the Senior Captain, "that the enemy, at effective speed and already braking, will come into phase about here—" a cloud of assault ships winked into existence abruptly, a half million kilometers sunward of Oriente, and in the sun's eye. They fell rapidly toward the planet, swelling visibly in size. As they approached, they swung into a circular landing orbit about the planet. The smaller craft closed in, and the two fleets came together in a myriad of patterns whose individual motions the eye could not follow all at once. Then the attacking fleet emerged below the mass of the defenders, spewing a sudden cloud of tiny objects that were the assault troops. These drifted down, attacked by the smaller craft, while the majority of the assault ships from Newton and Cassida began to disappear like blown-out candles as they sought safety in a phase shift that would place them light-years from the scene of battle.

To Donal's fine-trained professional mind it was both beautifully thrilling—and completely false. No battle since time began had ever gone off with such battle grace and balance and none ever would. This was only an imaginative guess at how the battle would take place, and it had no place in it for the inevitable issuance of wrong orders, the individual hesitations, the underestimation of an opponent, the navigational errors that resulted in collisions, or firing upon a sister ship. These all remained for the actual event, like harpies roosting upon the yet-unblasted limbs of a tree, as dawn steals like some gray thief onto the field where men are going to fight. In the coming action off Oriente there would be good actions and bad, wise decisions, and stupid ones—and none of them would matter. Only their total at the end of the day.

". . . Well, gentlemen," the Senior Captain was saying, "there you have it as Staff sees it. Your job—yours personally, as Staff Liaisons—is to observe. We want to know anything you can see, anything you can discover, anything you can, or think you can, deduce. And of course"—he hesitated, with a wry smile—"there's nothing we'd appreciate quite so much as a prisoner."

There was a ripple of general laughter at this, as all men there knew the fantastic odds against being able to scoop up a man from an already broken-open enemy ship under the velocities and other conditions of a space battle—and find him still alive, even if you succeeded.

"That's all," said the Senior Captain. The Staff Liaisons rose and began to crowd out the door.

"Just a minute, Graeme!"

Donal turned. The voice was the voice of Lludrow. The Patrol Chief had come down from the platform and was approaching him. Donal turned back to meet him.

"I'd like to speak to you for a moment," said Lludrow. "Wait until the others are out of the room." They stood together in silence until the last of the Staff Liaisons had left, and the Senior Captain had disappeared.

"Yes, sir?" said Donal.

"I'm interested in something you said—or maybe were about to say the other day—when I met you at Marshal Galt's in the process of assessing this Oriente business. You said something that seemed to imply doubt about the conclusions we came to. But I never did hear what it was you had in mind. Care to tell me now?"

"Why, nothing, sir," said Donal. "Staff and the marshal undoubtedly know what they're doing."

"It isn't possible, then, you saw something in the situation that we didn't?" Donal hesitated.

"No, sir. I don't know any more about enemy intentions and plans than the rest of you. Only—" Donal looked down into the dark face below his, wavering on the verge of speaking his mind. Since the affair with Anea he had been careful to keep his flights of mental perception to himself. "Possibly I'm just suspicious, sir."

"So are all of us, man!" said Lludrow, with a hint of impatience. "What about it? In our shoes what would *you* be doing?"

"In your shoes," said Donal, throwing discretion to the winds, "I'd attack Newton."

Lludrow's jaw fell. He stared at Donal.

"By heaven," he said, after a moment. "You're not shy about expedients, are you? Don't you know a civilized world can't be conquered?"

Donal allowed himself the luxury of a small sigh. He made an effort to explain himself, once again, in terms others could understand.

"I remember the marshal saying that," he said. "I'm not so sanguine, myself. In fact, that's a particular maxim I'd like to try to disprove some day. However—that's not what I meant. I didn't mean to suggest we attempt to *take* Newton; but that we *attack* it. I suspect the

Newtonians are as maxim-ridden as ourselves. Seeing us try the impossible, they're very likely to conclude we've suddenly discovered some way to make it possible. From their reactions to such a conclusion we might learn a lot—including about the Oriente affair."

Lludrow's look of amazement was tightening into a frown.

"Any force attacking Newton would suffer fantastic losses," he began.

"Only if they intended to carry the attack through," interrupted Donal, eagerly. "It could be a feint—nothing more than that. The point wouldn't be to do real damage, but to upset the thinking of the enemy strategy by introducing an unexpected factor."

"Still," said Lludrow, "to make their feint effective, the attacking force would have to run the risk of being wiped out."

"Give me a dozen ships—" Donal was beginning; when Lludrow started and blinked like a man waking up from a dream.

"Give you—" he said; and smiled. "No, no, commandant, we were speaking theoretically. Staff would never agree to such a wild, unplanned gamble; and I've no authority to order it on my own. And if I did—how could I justify giving command of such a force to a young man with only field experience, who's never held command in a ship in his life?" He shook his head. "No, Graeme—but I will admit your idea's interesting. And I wish one of us at least had thought of it."

"Would it hurt to mention it—"

"It wouldn't do any good—to argue with a plan Staff has already had in operation for over a week, now." He was smiling broadly. "In fact, my reputation would find itself cut rather severely. But it was a good idea, Graeme. You've got the makings of a strategist. I'll mention the fact in my report to the marshal."

"Thank you, sir," said Donal.

"Back to your ship, then," said Lludrow.

"Good-by, sir."

Donal saluted and left. Behind him, Lludrow frowned for just a moment more over what had just been said—before he turned his mind to other things.

ACTING CAPTAIN

Space battles, mused Donal, are said to be held only by mutual consent. It was one of those maxims he distrusted; and which he had privately determined to disprove whenever he should get the chance. However— as he stood now by the screen of the Control Eye in the main control room of the C4J, watching the enemy ships appearing to swell with the speed of their approach—he was forced to admit that in this instance, it was true. Or true at least to the extent that mutual consent is involved when you attack an enemy point that you know that enemy will defend.

But what if he should not defend it after all? What if he should do the entirely unexpected—

"Contact in sixty seconds. Contact in sixty seconds!" announced the speaker over his head.

"Fasten all," said Andresen, calmly into the talker before him. He sat, with his First and Second Officers duplicating him on either side, in a "dentist's chair" across the room—"seeing" the situation not in actual images as Donal was doing, but from the readings of his instruments. And his knowledge was therefore the more complete one. Cumbersome in his survival battle suit, Donal climbed slowly into the similar chair that had been rigged for him before the Eye, and connected himself to the chair. In case the ship should be broken apart, he and it would remain together as long as possible. With luck, the two of them would be able to make it to a survival ship in orbit around Oriente in forty or fifty hours—if none of some dozens of factors intervened.

He had time to settle himself before the Eye before contact was made. In those last few seconds, he glanced around him; finding it a little wonderful in spite of all he knew, that this white and quiet room, undisturbed by the slightest tremor, should be perched on the brink of savage combat and its own quite possible destruction. Then there was no more time for thinking. Contact with the enemy had been made and he had to keep his eyes on the scene.

Orders had been to harry the enemy, rather than close with him. Estimates had been twenty per cent casualties for the enemy, five per cent for the defending forces. But such figures, without meaning to be, are misleading. To the man in the battle, twenty per cent, or even five per cent casualties do not mean that he will be twenty per cent or five per cent wounded. Nor, in a space battle, does it mean that one man out of five, or one man out of twenty will be a casualty. It means one *ship* out of five, or one *ship* out of twenty—and every living soul aboard her; for, in space, one hundred per cent casualties mean ninety-eight per cent dead.

There were three lines of defense. The first were the light craft that were meant to slow down the oncoming ships so that the larger, more ponderous craft, could try to match velocities well enough to get to work with heavy weapons. Then there were the large craft them-selves in their present orbits. Lastly, there were the second line of smaller craft that were essentially antipersonnel, as the attackers dropped their space-suited assault troops. Donal in a C4J was in the first line.

There was no warning. There was no full moment of battle. At the last second before contact, the gun crews of the C4J had opened fire. Then—

It was all over.

Donal blinked and opened his eyes, trying to remember what had happened. He was never to remember. The room in which he lay, fastened to his chair, had been split as if by a giant hatchet. Through the badly-lit gap, he could see a portion of an officer's stateroom. A red, self-contained flare was burning somewhere luridly overhead, a signal that the control room was without air. The Control Eye was slightly askew, but still operating. Through the transparency of his helmet, Donal could see the dwindling lights that marked the enemy's departure on toward Oriente. He struggled upright in his chair and turned his head toward the Control panel.

Two were quite dead. Whatever had split the room open had touched them, too. The Second officer was dead, Andresen was un-deniably dead. Coa Benn still lived, but from the feeble movements she was making in the chair, she was badly hurt. And there was nothing anyone could do for her now that they were without air and all prisoners in their suits.

Donal's soldier-trained body began to react before his mind had quite caught up to it. He found himself breaking loose the fastenings that connected him to his chair. Unsteadily, he staggered across the room, pushed the lolling head of Andresen out of the way, and thumbed the intership button.

"C4J One-twenty-nine," he said. "C4J One-twenty-nine—" he continued to repeat the cabalistic numbers until the screen before him lit up with a helmeted face as bloodless as that of the dead man in the chair underneath him.

"KL," said the face. "A-twenty-three?" Which was code for: *"Can you still navigate?"*

Donal looked over the panel. For a wonder, it had been touched by what had split the room—but barely. Its instruments were all reading.

"A-twenty-nine," he replied affirmatively.

"M-Forty," said the other, and signed off. Donal let the intership button slip from beneath his finger. M-Forty was—*Proceed as ordered.*

Proceed as ordered, for the C4J One-twenty-nine, the ship Donal was in, meant—get in close to Oriente and pick off as many assault troops as you can. Donal set about the unhappy business of removing his dead and dying from their control chairs.

Coa, he noted, as he removed her, more gently than the others, seemed dazed and unknowing. There were no broken bones about her, but she appeared to have been pinched, or crushed on one side by just a touch of what had killed the others. Her suit was tight and intact. He thought she might make it, after all.

Seating himself in the captain's chair, he called the gun stations and other crew posts.

"Report," he ordered.

Gun stations One and Five through Eight answered.

"We're going in planetward," he said. "All able men abandon the weapon stations for now and form a working crew to seal ship and pump some air back in here. Those not sealed off, assemble in lounge. Senior surviving crewman to take charge."

There was a slight pause. Then a voice spoke back to him.

"Gun Maintenanceman Ordovya," it said. "I seem to be surviving Senior, sir. Is this the captain?"

"Staff Liaison Graeme, Acting Captain. Your officers are dead. As ranking man here, I've taken command. You have your orders, Maintenanceman."

"Yes, sir." The voice signed off.

Donal set himself about the task of remembering his ship training. He got the C4J underway toward Oriente and checked all instruments. After a while, the flare went out abruptly overhead and a slow, hissing noise registered on his eardrums—at first faintly, then scaling rapidly up in volume and tone to a shriek. His suit lost some of its drum-tightness.

A few moments later, a hand tapped him on his shoulder. He turned around to look at a blond-headed crewman with his helmet tilted back.

"Ship tight, sir," said the crewman. "I'm Ordovya."

Donal loosened his own helmet and flipped it back, inhaling the room air gratefully.

"See to the First Officer," he ordered. "Do we have anything in the way of a medic aboard?"

"No live medic, sir. We're too small to rate one. Freeze unit, though."

"Freeze her, then. And get the men back to their posts. We'll be on top of the action again in another twenty minutes."

Ordovya went off. Donal sat at his controls, taking the C4J in cautiously and with the greatest possible margins of safety. In principle, he knew how to operate the craft he was seated in; but no one knew better than he what a far cry he was from being an experienced pilot and captain. He could handle this craft the way someone who has taken half a dozen riding lessons can handle a horse—that is, he knew what to do, but he did none of it instinctively. Where Andresen had taken in the readings of all his instruments at a glance and reacted immediately, Donal concentrated on the half dozen main telltales and debated with himself before acting.

So it was that they came late to the action on the edges of Oriente's atmosphere; but not so late that the assault troops were already safely down out of range. Donal searched the panel for the override button on the antipersonnel guns and found it.

"Override on the spray guns," he announced into the mike before him. He looked at the instruments, but he saw in his imagination the dark and tumbling spacesuited bodies of the assault troops, and he thought of the several million tiny slivers of carbon steel that would go sleeting among them at the touch of his finger. There was a slight pause before answering; and then the voice of Ordovya came back.

"Sir . . . if you like, the gunmen say they're used to handling the weapons—"

"Maintenanceman!" snapped Donal. "You heard the order. Override!"

"Override, sir."

Donal looked at his scope. The computer had his targets in the gunsights. He pressed the button, and held it down.

Two hours later, the C4J, then in standby orbit, was ordered to return to rendezvous and its captain to report to his Sub-Patrol chief. At the same time came a signal for all Staff Liaisons to report to the flagship; and one for Staff Liaison Donal Graeme to report personally to Blue Patrol Chief Lludrow. Considering the three commands, Donal called Ordovya on the ship's phone and directed him to take care of the first errand. He himself, he decided, could take care of the other two, which might—or might not—be connected.

Arriving at the flagship, he explained his situation to the Reception Officer, who made a signal both to the Staff Liaison people and to the Blue Patrol chief.

"You're to go directly to Lludrow," he informed Donal; and assigned him a guide.

Donal found Lludrow in a private office on the flagship that was not much bigger than Donal's stateroom in the C4J.

"Good!" said Lludrow, getting up behind a desk as Donal came in and coming briskly around it. He waited until the guide had left, and then he put a dark hand on Donal's arm.

"How'd your ship come through?" he asked.

"Navigating," said Donal. "There was a direct hit on the control room though. All officers casualties."

"All officers?" Lludrow peered sharply at him. "And you?"

"I took command, of course. There was nothing left, though, but antipersonnel mop-up."

"Doesn't matter," said Lludrow. "You were Acting Captain for part of the action?"

"Yes."

"Fine. That's better than I hoped for. Now," said Lludrow, "tell me something. Do you feel like sticking your neck out?"

"For any cause I can approve of, certainly," answered Donal. He considered the smaller, rather ugly man; and found himself suddenly liking the Blue Patrol chief. Directness like this had been a rare experience for him, since he had left the Dorsai.

"All right. If you agree, we'll both stick our necks out." Lludrow looked at the door of the office, but it was firmly closed. "I'm going to violate top security and enlist you in an action contrary to Staff orders, if you don't mind."

"Top security?" echoed Donal, feeling a sudden coolness at the back of his neck.

"Yes. We've discovered what was behind this Newton-Cassida landing on Oriente . . . you know Oriente?"

"I've studied it, of course," said Donal. "At school—and recently when I signed with Freiland. Temperatures up to seventy-eight degrees centigrade, rock, desert, and a sort of native vine and cactus jungle. No large bodies of water worth mentioning and too much carbon dioxide in the atmosphere."

"Right. Well," said Lludrow, "the important point is, it's big enough to hide in. They're down there now and we can't root them out in a hurry—and not at all unless we go down there after them. We thought they were making the landing as a live exercise and we could expect them to run the gauntlet back out in a few days or weeks. We were wrong."

"Wrong?"

"We've discovered their reason for making the landing on Oriente. It wasn't what we thought at all."

"That's fast work," said Donal. "What's it been . . . four hours since the landing?"

"*They* made fast work of it," said Lludrow. "The news is being sat on; but they are firing bursts of a new kind of radiation from projectors that fire once, move, and fire again from some new hiding place—a large number of projectors. And the bursts they fire hit old Sirius himself. We're getting increased sunspot activity." He paused and looked keenly at Donal, as if waiting for comment. Donal took his time, considering the situation.

"Weather difficulties?" he said at last.

"That's it!" said Lludrow, energetically, as though Donal had been a star pupil who had just shone again. "Meteorological opinion says it can be serious, the way they're going about it. And we've already heard their price for calling it off. It seems there's a trade commission of theirs on New Earth right now. No official connection—but the Commission's got the word across."

Donal nodded. He was not at all surprised to hear that trade negotiations were going on in normal fashion between worlds who were at the same time actively fighting each other. That was the normal course of existence between the stars. The ebb and flow of trained personnel on a contractual basis was the lifeblood of civilization. A world who tried to go it on its own would be left behind within a matter of years, to wither on the vine—or at last buy the mere necessities of existence at ruinous cost to itself. Competition meant the trading of skilled minds, and that meant contracts, and contracts meant continuing negotiations.

"They want a reciprocal brokerage agreement," Lludrow said.

Donal looked at him sharply. The open market trading of contracts had been abandoned between the worlds for nearly fifty years. It amounted to speculating in human lives. It removed the last shreds of dignity and security from the individual and treated him as so much livestock or hardware to be traded for no other reason than the greatest possible gain. The Dorsai, along with the Exotics, Mara and Kultis, had led the fight against it. There was another angle as well. On "tight" worlds such as those of the Venus Group—which included Newton and Cassida—and the Friendlies, the open market became one more tool of the ruling group; while on "loose" worlds like Freiland, it became a spot of vulnerability where foreign credits could take advantage of local situations.

"I see," said Donal.

"We've got three choices," Lludrow said. "Give in—accept the agreement. Suffer the weather effects over a period of months while we clean out Oriente by orthodox military means. Or pay a prohibitive price in casualties by a crash campaign to clean up Oriente in a hurry. We'd lose as many lives to the conditions down there as we would to the enemy in a crash campaign. So, it's my notion that it's a time to gamble—my notion, by the way, not Staff's. They don't know anything about this; and wouldn't stand for it if they did. Care to try your idea of throwing a scare into Newton, after all?"

"With pleasure!" said Donal, quickly, his eyes glowing.

"Save your enthusiasm until you hear what you're going to have to do it with," replied Lludrow, dryly. "Newton maintains a steady screen of ninety ships of the first class, in defensive orbit around it. I can give you five."

SUB-PATROL CHIEF

"Five!" said Donal. He felt a small crawling sensation down his spine. He had, before Lludrow turned him down the first time, worked out rather carefully what could be done with Newton and how a man might go about it. His plan had called for a lean and compact little fighting force of thirty first-class ships in a triangular organization of three sub-patrols, ten ships to each.

"You see," Lludrow was explaining, "it's not what craft I have available—even with what losses we've just suffered, my Blue Patrol counts over seventy ships of the first class, alone. It's what ships I can trust to you on a job where at least the officers and probably the men as well will realize that it's a mission that should be completely volunteer and that's being sneaked off when Staff's back is turned. The captains of these ships are all strongly loyal to me, personally, or I couldn't have picked them." He looked at Donal. "All right," he said. "I know it's impossible. Just agree with me and we can forget the matter."

"Can I count on obedience?" asked Donal.

"That," said Lludrow, "is the one thing I can guarantee you."

"I'll have to improvise," said Donal. "I'll go in with them, look at the situation, and see what can be done."

"Fair enough. It's decided then."

"It's decided," said Donal.

"Then come along." Lludrow turned and led him out of the office and through corridors to a lock. They passed through the lock to a small courier ship, empty and waiting for them there; and took it to a ship of the first class, some fifteen minutes off.

Ushered into the ship's large and complex main control room.

Donal found five senior captains waiting for him. Lludrow accepted a salute from a gray-haired powerful-looking man, who by saluting revealed himself as captain of this particular ship.

"Captain Bannerman," said Lludrow, introducing him to Donal, "Captain Graeme." Donal concealed a start well. In the general process of his thinking, he had forgotten that a promotion for himself would be necessary. You could hardly put a Staff Liaison with a field rank of commandant over men captaining ships of the first class.

"Gentlemen," said Lludrow, turning to the other executive officers. "I've been forced to form your five ships rather hastily into a new Sub-Patrol unit. Captain Graeme will be your new chief. You'll form a reconnaissance outfit to do certain work near the very center of the enemy space area; and I want to emphasize the point that Captain Graeme's command is absolute. You will obey any and all of his orders without question. Now, are there any questions any of you would like to ask before he assumes command?"

The five captains were silent.

"Fine, then." Lludrow led Donal down the line. "Captain Graeme, this is Captain Aseini."

"Honored," said Donal, shaking hands.

"Captain Sukaya-Mendez."

"At your service, captain."

"Captain El Man."

"Honored," said Donal. A scarred Dorsai face nearing forty looked at him. "I believe I know your family name, captain. High Island, isn't it?"

"Sir, near Bridgehead," answered El Man. "I've heard of the Graemes." Donal moved on.

"And Captain Ruoul."

"Honored."

"Well, then," said Lludrow, stepping back briskly. "I'll leave the command in your hands, Captain Graeme. Anything in the way of special supplies?"

"Torpedoes, sir," answered Donal.

"I'll have Armaments Supply contact you," said Lludrow. And left.

Five hours later, with several hundred extra torpedoes loaded, the five-ship Sub-Patrol moved out for deep space. It was Donal's wish that they get clear of the home base as soon as possible and off where the nature of their expedition could not be discovered and countermanded. With the torpedoes, Lee had come aboard; Donal having remembered that his orderly had been left aboard the C4J. Lee had come through the battle very well, being strapped in his hammock harness throughout in a section of the ship that was undamaged by the hit that had pierced to the control room. Now, Donal had definite instructions for him.

"I want you with me, this time," he said. "You'll stay by me. I doubt very much I might need you; but if I do, I want you in sight."

"I'll be there," said Lee, unemotionally.

They had been talking in the Patrol chief's stateroom, which had been opened to Donal. Now, Donal headed for the main control room, Lee following behind. When Donal reached that nerve center of the ship, he found all three of the ship's officers engaged in calculating the phase shift, with Bannerman overseeing.

"Sir!" said Bannerman as Donal came up. Looking at him, Donal was reminded of his mathematics instructor at school; and he was suddenly and painfully reminded of his own youth.

"About ready to shift?" asked Donal.

"In about two minutes. Since you specified no particular conclusion point, the computer run was a short one. We've merely been making the usual checks to make sure there's no danger of collision with any object. A four light-year jump, sir."

"Good," said Donal. "Come here with me, Bannerman."

He led the way over to the larger and rather more elaborate Control Eye that occupied the center of this control room; and pressed keys. A scene from the library file of the ship filled the globe. It showed a green-white planet with two moons floating in space and lit by the illumination from a G2 type sun.

"The orange and the two pips," said Bannerman, revealing a moonless Freilander's dislikes for natural planetary satellites.

"Yes," said Donal. "Newton." He looked at Bannerman. "How close can we hit it?"

"Sir?" said Bannerman, looking around at him. Donal waited, holding his eyes steady on the older man. Bannerman's gaze shifted and dropped back to the scene in the Eye.

"We can come out as close as you want, sir," he answered. "See, in deep space jumps, we have to stop to make observations and establish our location precisely. But the precise location of any civilized planet's already established. To come out at a safe distance from their defenses, I'd say, sir—"

"I didn't ask you for a safe distance from their defenses," said Donal, quietly. "I said—how close?"

Bannerman looked up again. His face had not paled; but there was now a set quality about it. He looked at Donal for several seconds.

"How close?" he echoed. "Two planetary diameters."

"Thank you, captain," said Donal.

"Shift in ten seconds," announced the First Officer's voice; and began to count down. "Nine seconds—eight—seven—six—five—four—three—two—*shift!*" They shifted.

"Yes," said Donal, as if the shift itself had never interrupted what he was about to say, "out here where it's nice and empty, we're going to set up a maneuver, and I want all the ships to practice it. If you'll call a captain's conference, captain."

Bannerman walked over to the control board and put in the call. Fifteen minutes later, with all junior officers dismissed, they gathered in the privacy of the control room of Bannerman's ship and Donal explained what he had in mind.

"In theory," he said, "our Patrol is just engaged in reconnaissance. In actuality, we're going to try to simulate an attacking force making an assault on the planet Newton."

He waited a minute to allow the weight of his words to register on their minds; and then went on to explain his intentions.

They were to set up a simulated planet on their ship's instruments. They would approach this planet, which was to represent Newton, according to a random pattern and from different directions, first a single ship, then two together, then a series of single ships—and so on. They would, theoretically, appear into phase just before the planet, fire one or more torpedoes, complete their run past the planet and immediately go out of phase again. The intention would be to simulate the laying of a pattern of explosions covering the general surface of the planet.

There was, however, to be one main difference. Their torpedoes were to be exploded well without the outer ring of Newton's orbits of defense, as if the torpedoes were merely intended as a means to release some radiation or material which was planned to fall in toward the planet, spreading as it went.

And, one other thing, the runs were to be so timed that the five-ship force, by rotation, could appear to be a large fleet engaged in continuous bombardment.

". . . Any suggestions or comments?" asked Donal, winding it up. Beyond the group facing him, he could see Lee, lounging against the control room wall and watching the captains with a colorless gaze.

There was no immediate response; and then Bannerman spoke up slowly, as if he felt it had devolved upon him, the unwelcome duty of being spokesman for the group.

"Sir," he said, "what about the chances of collision?"

"They'll be high, I know," said Donal. "Especially with the defending ships. But we'll just have to take our chances."

"May I ask how many runs we'll be making?"

"As many," said Donal, "as we can." He looked deliberately around the group. "I want you gentlemen to understand. We're going to make every possible attempt to avoid open battle or accidental casualties. But these things may not be avoidable considering the necessarily high number of runs."

"How many runs did you have in mind, captain?" asked Sukaya-Mendez.

"I don't see," replied Donal, "how we can effectively present the illusion of a large fleet engaged in saturation bombardment of a world in under a full two hours of continuous runs."

"Two hours!" said Bannerman. There was an instinctive murmur from the group. "Sir," continued Bannerman. "Even at five minutes a run, that amounts with five ships to better than two runs an hour. If we double up, or if there's casualties it could run as high as four. That's eight phase shifts to an hour—sixteen in a two-hour period. Sir, even doped to the ears, the men on our ships can't take that."

"Do you know of anyone who ever tried, captain?" inquired Donal.

"No, sir—" began Bannerman.

"Then how do we know it can't be done?" Donal did not wait for an answer. "The point is, it must be done. You're being required only to navigate your ships and fire possibly two torpedoes. That doesn't require the manpower it would to fight your ships under ordinary conditions. If some of your men become unfit for duty, make shift with the ones you have left."

"*Shai Dorsai!*" murmured the scarred El Man; and Donal glanced toward him, as grateful for the support as for the compliment.

"Anyone want out?" Donal asked crisply.

There was a slow, but emphatic, mutter of negation from all of them.

"Right." Donal took a step back from them. "Then let's get about our practice runs. Dismissed, gentlemen."

He watched the four from other ships leave the control room.

"Better feed and rest the crews," Donal said, turning to Bannerman. "And get some rest yourself. I intend to. Have a couple of meals sent to my quarters."

"Sir," acknowledged Bannerman. Donal turned and left the control room, followed by Lee as by a shadow. The Cobyman was silent until they were in the stateroom; then he growled: "What did that scarface mean by calling you shy?"

"Shy?" Donal turned about in surprise.

"Shaey, shy—something like that."

"Oh," Donal smiled at the expression on the other's face. "That wasn't an insult, Lee. It was a pat on the back. *Shai* was what he said. It means something like—true, pure, the actual."

Lee grunted. Then he nodded.

"I guess you can figure on him," he said.

The food came, a tray for each of them. Donal ate lightly and stretched himself out on the couch. It seemed he dropped instantly into sleep; and when he awoke at the touch of Lee's hand on his shoulder he knew he had been dreaming—but of what, he could not remember. He remembered only a movement of shapes in obscurity, as of some complex physics problem resolving itself in terms of direction and mass, somehow given substance.

"Practice about to start," said Lee.

"Thank you, orderly," he said automatically. He got to his feet and headed toward the control room, shedding the druggedness of his sleep as he went. Lee had followed him, but he was not aware of this until the Cobyman pushed a couple of small white tablets into his hand.

"Medication," said Lee. Donal swallowed them automatically. Bannerman, over by the control board, had seen him come in, and now turned and came across the floor.

"Ready for the first practice run, sir," he said. "Where would you like to observe—controls, or Eye?"

Donal looked and saw they had a chair set up for him in both locations.

"Eye," he said. "Lee, you can take the other chair, as long as there does not seem to be one for you."

"Captain, you—"

"I know, Bannerman," said Donal, "I should have mentioned the fact I meant to have my orderly up here. I'm sorry."

"Not at all, sir." Bannerman went over and fitted himself into his own chair, followed by Lee. Donal turned his attention to the Eye.

The five ships were in line, in deep space, at thousand-kilometer intervals. He looked at their neat Indian file and stepped up the magnification slightly so that in spite of the distance that should have made even the nearest invisible, they appeared in detail, inlighted by the Eye.

"Sir," said Bannerman; and his quiet voice carried easily across the room. "I've arranged a key-in. When we make our phase shift, that library tape will replace the image in the Eye, so you can see what our approach will actually look like."

"Thank you, captain."

"Phase shift in ten seconds—"

The count-down ticked off like the voice of a clock. Then, there was the sensation of a phase shift; and abruptly Donal was sweeping closely over a planet, barely fifty thousand kilometers distance from its surface. "Fire—" and "Fire—" spoke the speaker in the control room ceiling. Again, the indescribable destruction and rebuilding of the body. The world was gone and they were again in deep space.

Donal looked at the four other ships in line. Abruptly the leading one disappeared. The rest continued, seemingly, to hang there, without motion. There was no sound in the control room about him. The seconds crept by, became minutes. The minutes crawled. Suddenly—a ship appeared in front of Bannerman's craft.

Donal looked back at the three behind. Now, there were only two.

The run continued until all the ships had made their pass.

"Again," ordered Donal.

They did it again; and it went off without a hitch.

"Rest," said Donal, getting out of the chair. "Captain, pass the word for all ships to give their personnel a break of half an hour. Make sure everyone is fed, rested, and supplied with medication. Also supply every person with extra medication to be taken as needed. Then, I'd like to talk to you, personally."

When Bannerman had accomplished these orders and approached Donal, Donal took him aside.

"How about the reactions of the men?" he asked.

"Fine, captain," Bannerman said; and Donal was surprised to read a true enthusiasm in his voice. "We've got good crews, here. High level-ratings, and experience."

"I'm glad to hear it," said Donal, thankfully. "Now . . . about the time interval—"

"Five minutes exactly, sir." Bannerman looked at him inquiringly. "We can shorten slightly, or lengthen as much as you want."

"No," said Donal. "I just wanted to know. Do you have battle dress for me and my orderly?"

"It's coming up from stores."

The half hour slid by quickly. As it approached its end and they prepared to tie into their chairs, Donal noticed the chronometer on the control room wall. It stood at 23:10 and the half hour would be up at 23:12.

"Make that start at 23:15," he directed Bannerman. The word was passed to the other ships. Everyone was in battle dress in their chairs and at their posts, waiting. Donal felt a strange metallic taste in his mouth and the slow sweat began to work out on the surface of his skin.

"Give me an all-ship hookup," he said. There was a few seconds pause, and then a Third Officer spoke from the control panel.

"You're hooked in, sir."

"Men," said Donal. "This is Captain Graeme." He paused. He had no idea what he had intended to say. He had asked for the hookup on impulse, and to break the strain of the last few moments which must be weighing on all the rest as much as him. "I'll tell you one thing. This is something Newton's never going to forget. Good luck to all of you. That's all."

He wigwagged to the Third Officer to cut him off; and looked up at the clock. A chime sounded softly through the ship.

It was 23:15.

SUB-PATROL CHIEF II

Newton was not to forget.

To a world second only to Venus in its technical accomplishments—and some said not even second—to a world rich in material wealth, haughty with its knowledge, and complacent in the contemplation of its lavish fighting forces, came the shadow of the invader. One moment its natives were secure as they had always been behind the ringing strength of their ninety ships in orbit—and then enemy craft were upon them, making runs across the skies of their planet, bombing them with—*what*?

No, Newton was never to forget. But that came afterward.

To the men in the five ships, it was the here and now that counted. Their first run across the rich world below them seemed hardly more than another exercise. The ninety ships were there—as well as a host of other spacecraft. They—or as many of them as were not occluded by the body of the planet—registered on the instruments of the Freilander ships. But that was all. Even the second run was almost without incident. But by the time Donal's leading ship came through for the start of the third run, Newton was beginning to buzz like a nest of hornets, aroused.

The sweat was running freely down Donal's face as they broke into the space surrounding the planet; and it was not tension alone that was causing it. The psychic shocks of five phase shifts were taking their toll. Halfway in their run there was a sudden sharp tremor that shook their small white-walled world that was the control room, but the ship continued as if unhurt, released its second torpedo and plunged into the safety of its sixth phase shift.

"Damage?" called Donal—and was surprised to hear his voice

issue on an odd croaking note. He swallowed and asked again, in a more normal, controlled tone. "Damage?"

"No damage—" called an officer sharply, from the control panel. "Close burst."

Donal turned his eyes almost fiercely back onto the scene in the Eye. The second ship appeared. Then the third. The fourth. The fifth.

"Double up this time!" ordered Donal harshly. There was a short minute or two of rest and then the sickening wrench of the phase shift again.

In the Eye, its magnification jumping suddenly, Donal caught sight of two Newtonian ships, one planetward, the other in a plane and at approximately two o'clock to the line of the bombing run they had begun.

"Defensive—" began Donal; but the gun crews had waited for no order. Their tracking had been laid and the computers were warm. As he watched, the Newtonian ship which was ahead and in their plane opened out like a burst balloon in slow motion and seemed to fall away from them.

—Another phase shift.

The room swam for a second in Donal's blurred eyes. He felt a momentary surge of nausea; and, on the heels of it, heard someone over at the panel, retching. He blazed up inside, forcing an anger to fight the threatening sickness.

It's in your mind—it's all in your mind—he slapped the thought at himself like a curse. The room steadied; the sickness retreated a little way.

"Time—" It was Bannerman, calling in a half-gasping voice from the panel. Donal blinked and tried to focus on the scene in the Eye. The rank odor of his own sweat was harsh in his nostrils—or was it simply that the room was permeated with the stink of all their sweating?

In the Eye he could make out that four ships had come through on this last run. As he watched, the fifth winked into existence.

"Once more!" he called, hoarsely. "In at a lower level, this time." There was a choked, sobbing-like sound from the direction of the panel; but he deliberately did not turn his head to see who it was.

Again the phase shift.

Blur of planet below. A sharp shock. Another.

Again the phase shift.

The control room—full of mist? No—his own eyes. Blink them. Don't be sick.

"Damage?"

No answer.

"Damage!"

"—Light hit. Aft. Sealed—"

"Once more."

"Captain—" Bannerman's voice, "we can't make it again. One of our ships—"

Check in the Eye. Images dancing and wavering—yes, only four ships.

"Which one?"

"I think—" Bannerman, gasping, "Mendez."

"Once more."

"Captain, you can't ask—"

"Give me a hookup then." Pause. "You hear me? Give me a hookup."

"Hookup—" some officer's voice. "You're hooked up, captain."

"All right, this is Captain Graeme." Croak and squeak. Was that *his* voice speaking? "I'm calling for volunteers—one more run. Volunteers only. Speak up, anyone who'll go."

Long pause.

"Shai Dorsai!"

"Shai El Man!"—any others?"

"Sir—" Bannerman—"The other two ships aren't receiving."

Blink at Eye. Focus. True. Two of three ships there yawning out of line.

"Just the two of us then. Bannerman?"

"At"—croaking—"your orders, sir."

"Make the run."

Pause . . .

Phase shift!

Planet, whirling—shock—dark space. Can't black out now—

"Pull her out of it!" Pause. *"Bannerman!"*

Weakly responding: "Yes sir—"

PHASE SHIFT

—Darkness . . .

"—Up!"

It was a snarling, harsh, bitter whisper in Donal's ear. He wondered, eyes-closed, where it was coming from. He heard it again, and once again. Slowly it dawned on him that he was saying it to himself.

He fought his eyes open.

The control room was still as death. In the depths of the eye before

him three small tiny shapes of ships could be seen, at full magnification, far-flung from each other. He fumbled with dead fingers at the
ties on his suit, then bound them to his chair. One by one they came
free. He pushed himself out of the chair and fell to his knees on the
floor.

Swaying, staggering, he got to his feet. He turned himself toward
the five chairs at the control panel, and staggered to them.

In four of the chairs, Bannerman and his three officers sagged
unconscious. The Third Officer seemed more than unconscious. His
face was milkish white and he did not seem to be breathing. All four
men had been sick.

In the fifth chair, Lee hung twisted in his ties. He was not unconscious. His eyes were wide on Donal as he approached, and a streak
of blood had run down from one corner of the orderly's mouth. He
had apparently tried to break his ties by main strength, like a mindless
animal, and go directly to Donal. And yet his eyes were not insane,
merely steady with an unnatural fixity of purpose. As Donal reached
him Lee tried to speak; but all he was able to manage for a second
was a throttled sound, and a little more blood came out of the corner
of his mouth.

"Y'arright?" he mumbled, finally.

"Yes," husked Donal. "Get you loose in a minute. What happened
to your mouth?"

"Bit tongue—" mumbled Lee thickly. "M'arright."

Donal unfastened the last of the ties and, reaching up, opened Lee's
mouth with his hands. He had to use real strength to do so. A little
more blood came out, but he was able to see in. One edge of Lee's
tongue, halfway back from the tip, had been bitten entirely through.

"Don't talk," directed Donal. "Don't use that tongue at all until
you can get it fixed."

Lee nodded, with no mark of emotion, and began painfully to work
out of the chair.

By the time he was out, Donal had managed to get the ties loose
on the still form of the Third Officer. He pulled the man out of the
chair and laid him on the floor. There was no perceptible heartbeat.
Donal stretched him out and attempted to begin artificial respiration;
but at the first effort his head swam dizzily and he was forced to stop.
Slowly he pulled himself erect and began to break loose the ties on
Bannerman.

"Get the Second, if you feel up to it," he told Lee. The Cobyman
staggered stiffly around to the Second Officer and began work on his
ties.

Between the two of them, they got the three Freilanders stretched out on the floor and their helmets off. Bannerman and the Second Officer began to show signs of regaining consciousness and Donal left them to make another attempt at respiration with the Third Officer. But he found the body, when he touched it, was already beginning to cool.

He turned back and began work on the First Officer, who was still laxly unconscious. After a while the First Officer began to breathe deeply and more steadily; and his eyes opened. But it was apparent from his gaze that he did not see the rest of them, or know where he was. He stared at the control panel with blank eyes like a man in a heavily drugged condition.

"How're you feeling?" Donal asked Bannerman. The Freiland captain grunted, and made an effort to raise himself up on one elbow. Donal helped, and between the two of them they got him, first sitting up, then to his knees, and finally—with the help of the back of a chair to pull him up—to his feet.

Bannerman's eyes had gone directly to the control panel, from the first moment they had opened. Now, without a word, he pulled himself painfully back into his chair and began clumsily to finger studs.

"All ship sections," he croaked into the grille before him. "Report."

There was no answer.

"Report!" he said. His forefinger came down on a button and an alarm bell rang metallically loud through the ship. It ceased and a faint voice came from the speaker overhead.

"Fourth Gun Section reporting as ordered, sir—"

The battle of Newton was over.

HERO

Sirius himself had just set; and the small bright disk of that white dwarf companion that the Freilanders and the New Earthmen had a number of uncomplimentary names for was just beginning to show strongly through the wall of Donal's bedroom. Donal sat, bathed in the in-between light, dressed in only a pair of sport trunks, sorting through some of the interesting messages that had come his way, recently—since the matter of the raid on Newton.

So engrossed was he that he paid no attention until Lee tapped him on one brown-tanned shoulder.

"Time to dress for the party," said the Cobyman. He had a gray dress uniform of jacket and trousers, cut in the long-line Freiland style, over one arm. It was fashionably free of any insignia of rank. "I've got a couple of pieces of news for you. First, *she* was here again."

Donal frowned, getting into the uniform. Elvine had conceived the idea of nursing him after his return from the short hospital stay that had followed the Newton affair. It was her convenient conclusion that he was still suffering from the psychological damage of the overdose of phase-shifting they had all gone through. Medical opinion and Donal's to the contrary, she had insisted on attaching herself to him with a constancy which lately had led him to wonder if perhaps he would not have preferred the phase shifting itself. The frown now vanished, however.

"I think I see an end to that," he said. "What else?"

"This William of Ceta you're so interested in," answered Lee. "He's here for the party."

Donal turned his head to look sharply at the man. But Lee was merely delivering a report. The bony face was empty of even those small signs of expression which Donal had come to be able to read, in these past weeks of association.

"Who told you I was interested in William?" he demanded.

"You listen when people talk about him," said Lee. "Shouldn't I mention him?"

"No, that's all right," Donal said. "I want you to tell me whenever you find out anything about him you think I might not know. I just didn't know you observed that closely."

Lee shrugged. He held the jacket for Donal to slide his arms into.

"Where'd he come from?" asked Donal.

"Venus," said Lee. "He's got a Newton man with him—big young drunk named Montor. And a girl—one of those special people from the Exotics."

"The Select of Kultis?"

"That's right."

"What're they doing here?"

"He's top-level," said Lee. "Who is on Freiland and not here for your party?"

Donal frowned again. He had almost managed to forget that it was in his honor these several hundred well-known people would be gathered here tonight. Oh—not that he would be expected to place himself on show. The social rules of the day and this particular world made lionizing impolite. Direct lionizing, that is. You honored a man by accepting his hospitality, that was the theory. And since Donal had little in the way of means to provide hospitality for the offering, the marshal had stepped into the breach. Nevertheless, this was the sort of occasion that went against Donal's instinctive grain.

He put that matter aside and returned to that of William. If the man happened to be visiting Freiland it would be unthinkable that he should not be invited, and hardly thinkable that he should decline to come. It could be just that. Perhaps, thought Donal with a weariness beyond his years, I'm starting at shadows. But even as his mind framed the thought, he knew it was not true. It was that oddness in him, now more pronounced than ever since the psychic shaking-up of the Newtonian battle, with its multiple phase shifts. Things seen only dimly before were now beginning to take on shape and substance for him. A pattern was beginning to form, with William as its center, and Donal did not like what he saw of the pattern.

"Let me know what you can find out about William," he said.

"Right," replied Lee. "And the Newton man?"

"And the girl from the Exotics." Donal finished dressing and took a back slipway down to the marshal's office. Elvine was there, and with her and the marshal, as guests, were William and Anea.

"Come in, Donal!" called Galt, as Donal hesitated in the entrance. "You remember William and Anea, here!"

"I'd be unlikely to forget." Donal came in and shook hands. William's smile was warm, his handclasp firm; but the hand of Anea was cool and quickly withdrawn from Donal's grasp, and her smile perfunctory. Donal caught Elvine watching them closely; and a faint finger of warning stirred the surface of Donal's mind.

"I've looked forward to seeing you again," said William. "I owe you an apology, Donal. Indeed I do. I've underestimated your genius considerably."

"Not genius," said Donal.

"Genius," insisted William. "Modesty's for little men." He smiled frankly. "Surely you realize this affair with Newton's made you the newest nova on our military horizon?"

"I'll have to watch out your flattery doesn't go to my head, Prince." Donal could deal in double meaning, too. William's first remark had put him almost at his ease. It was not the wolves among people who embarrassed and confused him; but the sheep dogs gone wrong. Those, in fact, who were equipped by nature and instinct to be one thing and through chance and wrongheadedness found themselves acting contrary to their own natures. Possibly, he had thought, that was the reason he found men so much easier to deal with than women—they were less prone to self-deception. Now, however, a small intake of breath drew his attention to Anea.

"You're modest," she said; but two touches of color high on the cheek-bones of her otherwise slightly pale face, and her unfriendly eyes, did not agree with her.

"Maybe," he said, as lightly as he could, "that's because I don't really believe I've got anything to be modest about. Anyone could have done what I did above Newton—and, in fact, several hundred other men did. Those that were there with me."

"Oh, but it was your idea," put in Elvine.

Donal laughed.

"All right," he said. "For the idea, I'll take credit."

"Please do," said Anea.

"Well," put in Galt, seeing that things were getting out of hand. "We were just about to go in and join the party, Donal. Will you come along?"

"I'm looking forward to it," answered Donal, smoothly.

They proceeded, a small knot of people, out through the big doors of the office and into the main hall of the mansion. It was already full of guests interspersed with drifting floats laden with food and drinks. Into this larger body of people, their small group melted like one drop of coloring matter into a glass of water. Their individual members were recognized, captured and dispersed by other guests; and in a few seconds they were all separated—all but Donal and Elvine, who had taken his arm possessively, as they had come out of the office.

She pulled him into the privacy of a small alcove.

"So that's what you've been mooning over!" she said fiercely. "It's her!"

"Her?" he pulled his arm loose. "What's wrong with you, Ev?"

"You know who I mean!" she snapped. "That Select girl. It's her you're after—though why, I don't know. She's certainly nothing special to look at. And she's hardly even grown up yet."

He chilled suddenly. And she—abruptly realizing that this time she had gone too far, took a sudden, frightened step back from him. He fought to control himself; but this was the authentic article, one of the real Dorsai rages that was his by inheritance. His limbs were cold, he saw everything with an unwonted clarity, and his mind ticked away like some detached machine in the far depths of his being. There was murder in him at the moment. He hung balanced on the knife edge of it.

"Good-by, Ev," he said. She took another, stiff-legged step back from him, then another, and then she turned and fled. He turned about to see the shocked faces of those nearby upon him.

His glance went among them like a scythe, and they fell away before it. He walked forward through them and out of the hall as if he had been alone in the room.

He was pacing back and forth in the bare isolation of the marshal's office, walking off the charge of adrenalin that had surged through him on the heels of his emotion, when the door opened. He turned like a wolf; but it was only Lee.

"You need me?" asked Lee.

The three words broke the spell. The tension in him snapped suddenly; and he burst out laughing. He laughed so long and loud that the Cobyman's eyes became shadowed first with puzzlement, and then with a sort of fear.

"No ... no ... it's all right," he gasped at last. He had a fastidiousness about casually touching people; but now he clapped Lee on the shoulder to reassure him, so unhappy did the lean man look. "See if you can find me a drink—some Dorsai whisky."

Lee turned and left the room. He was back in seconds with a tulip-shaped glass holding perhaps a deciliter of the bronze whisky. Donal drank it down, grateful for the burn in his throat.

"Learn anything about William?" He handed the glass back to Lee. Lee shook his head.

"Not surprised," murmured Donal. He frowned. "Have you seen ArDell Montor around—that Newtonian that came with William?"

Lee nodded.

"Can you show me where I can find him?"

Lee nodded again. He led Donal out onto the terrace, down a short distance, and in through an open wall to the library. There, in one of the little separate reading cubicles, he found ArDell alone with a bottle and some books.

"Thanks, Lee," said Donal. Lee vanished. Donal came forward and sat down at the small table in the cubicle opposite ArDell and his bottle.

"Greetings," said ArDell, looking up. He was not more than slightly drunk by his own standards. "Hoping to talk to you."

"Why didn't you come up to my room?" asked Donal.

"Not done," ArDell refilled his glass, glanced about the table for another and saw only a vase with some small native variform lilies in it. He dumped these on the floor, filled the vase and passed it politely to Donal.

"No thanks," said Donal.

"Hold it anyway," ArDell said. "Makes me uncomfortable, drinking with a man who won't drink. No, besides, better to just bump into each other." He looked at Donal suddenly with one of his unexpected flashes of soberness and shrewdness. "He's at it again."

"William?"

"Who else?" ArDell drank. "But what would he be doing with Project Blaine?" ArDell shook his head. "*There's* a man. And a scientist. Make two of any of the rest of us. Can't see *him* leading Blaine around by the nose—but still . . ."

"Unfortunately," said Donal, "we are all tied to the business end of our existence by the red tape in our contracts. And it's in business William shines."

"But he doesn't make sense!" ArDell twisted the glass in his hands. "Take me. Why would he want to ruin me? But he does." He chuckled suddenly. "I've got him scared now."

"You have?" asked Donal. "How?"

ArDell tapped the bottle with one forefinger.

"This. He's afraid I may kill myself. Evidently he doesn't want that." .

"Will you?" asked Donal, bluntly.

ArDell shook his head.

"I don't know. Could I come out of it, now? It's been five years. I started it deliberately to spite him—didn't even like the stuff, like you. Now, I wonder. I'll tell you"—he leaned forward over the table— "they can cure me, of course. But would I be any good now, if they did? Math—it's a beautiful thing. Beautiful like art. That's the way I remember it; but I'm not sure. Not sure at all any more." He shook his head again. "When the time comes to dump this," he pointed again at the bottle, "you need something that means more to you. I don't know if work does, any more."

"How about William?" asked Donal.

"Yes," said ArDell slowly, "there is him. That would do it. One of these days I'm going to find out why he did this to me. Then—"

"What does he seem to be after?" asked Donal. "I mean, in general?"

"Who knows?" ArDell threw up his hands. "Business. More business. Contracts—more contracts. Agreements with every government, a finger in every honey-pot. That's our William."

"Yes," said Donal. He pushed back his float and stood up.

"Sit down," said ArDell. "Stop and talk. You never sit still for more than a second or two. For the love of peace, you're the only man between the stars I can talk to, and you won't sit still."

"I'm sorry," Donal said. "But there're things I have to do. A day'll come, maybe, when we can sit down and talk."

"I doubt it," muttered ArDell. "I doubt it very much."

Donal left him there, staring at his bottle.

He went in search of the marshal; but it was Anea he encountered first, standing upon a small balcony, deserted except for herself; and gazing out over the hall, directly below, with an expression at the same time so tired and so longing that he was suddenly and deeply moved by the sight of it.

He approached her, and she turned at the sound of his footsteps. At the sight of him, her expression changed.

"You again," she said, in no particularly welcome tone.

"Yes," said Donal, brusquely. "I meant to search you out later, but this is too good a chance to pass up."

"Too good."

"I mean you're alone . . . I mean I can talk to you privately," said Donal, impatiently.

She shook her head.

"We've got nothing to talk about," she said.

"Don't talk nonsense," said Donal. "Of course we have—unless you've given over your campaign against William."

"Well!" The word leaped from her lips and her eyes flashed their green fire at him. "Who do you think you are!" she cried furiously. "Who ever gave you the right to have any say about what I do?"

"I'm part Maran through both my grandmothers," he said. "Maybe that's why I feel a sense of responsibility to you."

"I don't believe it!" she snapped. "About you being part Maran, that is. You couldn't be part Maran, someone like you, a—" she checked, fumbling for words.

"Well?" He smiled a little grimly at her. "A what?"

"A . . . *mercenary!*" she cried triumphantly, finding at last the word that would hurt him the most, in her misinterpretation of it.

He *was* hurt, and angered; but he managed to conceal it. This girl had the ability to get through his defenses on the most childish level, where a man like William could not.

"Never mind that," he said. "My question was about you and William. I told you not to try intriguing against him the last time I saw you. Have you followed that advice?"

"Well, I certainly don't have to answer that question," she blazed directly at him. "And I won't."

"Then," he said, finding suddenly an insight into her that was possibly a natural compensation for her unusual perceptiveness where he was concerned. "You have. I'm glad to know that." He turned to go. "I'll leave you now."

"Wait a minute," she cried. He turned back to her. "I didn't do it because of you!"

"Didn't you?"

Surprisingly, her eyes wavered and fell.

"All right!" she said. "It just happened your ideas coincided with mine."

"Or, that what I said was common sense," he retorted, "and being the person you are, you couldn't help seeing it."

She looked fiercely up at him again.

"So he just goes on . . . and I'm chained to him for another ten years with options—"

"Leave that part to me," said Donal.

Her mouth opened.

"You!" she said; and her astonishment was so great that the word came out in a tone of honest weakness.

"I'll take care of it."

"*You!*" she cried. And the word was entirely different this time. "*You* put yourself in opposition to a man like William—" she broke off suddenly, turning away. "Oh!" she said angrily, "I don't know why I keep listening to you as if you were actually telling the truth—when I know what kind of person you are."

"You don't know anything at all about what kind of a person I am!" he snapped, nettled again. "I've done a few things since you first saw me."

"Oh, yes," she said, "you've had a man shot, and pretended to bomb a planet."

"Good-by," he said, wearily, turning away. He went out through the little balcony entrance, abruptly leaving her standing there; and unaware that he had left her, not filled with the glow of righteous indignation and triumph she had expected, but oddly disconcerted and dismayed.

He searched throughout the rest of the mansion and finally located the marshal back in his office, and alone.

"May I come in, sir?" he said from the doorway.

"Of course, of course—" Galt looked up from his desk. "Lock the door behind you. I've had nothing but people drifting in, thinking this was an extra lounge. Why'd they think I had it set up without any comfortable floats or cushions in the first place?"

Donal locked the door behind him and came across the wide floor to the desk.

"What is it, boy?" asked the marshal. He raised his heavy head and regarded Donal intently. "Something up?"

"A number of things," agreed Donal. He took the bare float beside the desk that Galt motioned him into. "May I ask if William came here tonight with the intention of transacting any business with you?"

"You may ask," answered Galt, putting both his massive forearms on the desk, "but I don't know why I should answer you."

"Of course you needn't," said Donal. "Assuming he did, however, I'd like to say that in my opinion it would be exceedingly unwise to do any business with Ceta at this time—and particularly William of Ceta."

"And what causes this to be your opinion?" asked Galt, with a noticeable trace of irony. Donal hesitated.

"Sir," he said, after a second. "I'd like to remind you that I was

right on Harmony, and right about Newton; and that I may be right
here, as well."

It was a large pill of impertinence for the marshal to swallow;
since, in effect, it pointed out that if Donal had twice been right, Galt
had been twice wrong—first about his assessment of Hugh Killien as
a responsible officer, and second about his assessment of the reasons
behind the Newtonian move on Oriente. But if he was Dorsai enough
to be touchy about his pride, he was also Dorsai enough to be honest
when he had to.

"All right," he said. "William did come around with a proposition.
He wants to take over a large number of our excess land forces, not
for any specific campaign, but for re-leasing to other employers.
They'd remain our troops. I was against it, on the grounds that we'd
be competing against ourselves when it came to offering troops to
outside markets, but he proved to me the guarantee he's willing to pay
would more than make up for any losses we might have. I also didn't
see how he intended to make his own profit out of it, but evidently he
intends training the men to finer specializations than a single planet
can afford to do, and maintain a balanced force. And God knows Ceta's
big enough to train all he wants, and that its slightly lower gravity
doesn't hurt either—for our troops, that is."

He got his pipe out of a compartment in the desk and began to
fill it.

"What's your objection?" he asked.

"Can you be sure the troops won't be leased to someone who might
use them against you?" Donal asked.

Galt's thick fingers ceased suddenly to fill his pipe. "We can insist
on guarantees."

"But how much good are guarantees in a case like that?" asked
Donal. "The man who gives you the guarantee—William—isn't the
man who might move the troops against you. If Freilander leased
troops were suddenly found attacking Freilander soil, you might gain
the guarantee, but lose the soil."

Galt frowned.

"I still don't see," he said, "how that could work out to William's
advantage."

"It might," said Donal, "in a situation where what he stood to gain
by Freilander fighting Freilander was worth more than the guarantee."

"How could that be?"

Donal hesitated on the verge of those private suspicions of his own.

Then he decided that they were not yet solid enough to voice to the marshal; and might, indeed, even weaken his argument.

"I don't know," he replied. "However, I think it'd be wise not to take the chance."

"Hah!" Galt snorted and his fingers went back to work, filling the pipe. "*You* don't have to turn the man down—and justify your refusal to Staff and Government."

"I don't propose that you turn him down outright," said Donal. "I suggest you only hesitate. Say that in your considered opinion the interstellar situation right now doesn't justify your leaving Freiland short-handed of combat troops. Your military reputation is good enough to establish such an answer beyond question."

"Yes"—Galt put the pipe in his mouth and lit it thoughtfully—"I think I may just act on that recommendation of yours. You know, Donal, I think from now on you better remain as my aide, where I can have the benefit of your opinions handy when I need them."

Donal winced.

"I'm sorry, sir," he said. "But I was thinking of moving on—if you'll release me."

Galt's eyebrows abruptly drew together in a thicket of dense hair. He took the pipe from his mouth.

"Oh," he said, somewhat flatly. "Ambitious, eh?"

"Partly," said Donal. "But partly—I'll find it easier to oppose William as a free agent." Galt bent a long, steady look upon him.

"By heaven," he said, "what is this personal vendetta of yours against William?"

"I'm afraid of him," answered Donal.

"Leave him alone and he'll certainly leave you alone. He's got bigger fish to fry—" Galt broke off, jammed his pipe into his mouth and bit hard on the stem.

"I'm afraid," said Donal, sadly, "there are some men between the stars that are just not meant to leave each other alone." He straightened in his chair. "You'll release my contract, then?"

"I won't hold any man against his will," growled the marshal. "Except in an emergency. Where were you thinking of going?"

"I've had a number of offers," said Donal. "But I was thinking of accepting one from the Joint Church Council of Harmony and Association. Their Chief Elder's offered me the position of War Chief for both the Friendlies."

"Eldest Bright? He's driven every commander with a spark of independence away from him."

"I know," said Donal. "And just for that reason I expect to shine the more brightly. It should help build my reputation."

"By—" Galt swore softly. "Always thinking, aren't you?"

"I suppose you're right," said Donal, a trifle unhappily. "It comes of being born with a certain type of mind."

WAR CHIEF

The heels of his black boots clicking against the gray floor of the wide office of the Defense Headquarters on Harmony, the aide approached Donal's desk, which had been his home for three years now.

"Special, urgent and private, sir." He placed a signal tape in the blue shell of ordinary communications on the desk pad.

"Thank you," said Donal, and waved him off. He broke the seal on the tape, placed it in his desk unit, and—waiting until the aide had left the room—pressed the button that would start it.

His father's voice came from the speaker, deep-toned.

"Donal, my son—

"We were glad to get your last tape; and to hear of your successes. No one in this family has done so well in such a short time, in the last five generations. We are all happy for you here, and pray for you and wait to hear from you again.

"But I am speaking to you now on an unhappy occasion. Your uncle, Kensie, was assassinated shortly over a month ago in the back streets of the city of Blauvain, on St. Marie, by a local terrorist group in opposition to the government there. Ian, who was, of course, an officer in the same unit, later somehow managed to discover the head-quarters of the group in some alley or other and killed the three men he found there with his hands. However, this does not bring Kensie back. He was a favorite of us all; and we are all hard hit, here at home, by his death.

"It is Ian, however, who is presently the cause of our chief concern. He brought Kensie's body home, refusing burial on St. Marie, and has been here now several weeks. You know he was always the dark-natured of the twins, just as it seemed that Kensie had twice the brightness and joy in life that is the usual portion of the normal man. Your mother says it is now as if Ian had lost his good angel, and is abandoned to the forces of darkness which have always had such a grip on him.

"She does not say it in just that way, of course. It is the woman and the Maran in her, speaking—but I have not lived with her twenty-seven years without realizing that she can see further into the soul of a man or woman than I can. You have in some measure inherited this same gift, Donal; so maybe you will understand better what she means. At any rate, it is at her urging that I am sending you this signal; although I would have been speaking to you about Kensie's death, in any case.

"As you know, it has always been my belief that members of the same immediate family should not serve too closely together in field or garrison—in order that family feelings should not be tempted to influence military responsibilities. But it is your mother's belief that Ian should not now be allowed to sit in his dark silence about the place, as he has been doing; but that he should be once more in action. And she asks me to ask you if you could find a place for him on your staff, where you can keep your eye on him. I know it will be difficult for both of you to have him filling a duty post in a position subordinate to you; but your mother feels it would be preferable to the present situation.

"Ian has expressed no wish to return to an active life; but if I speak to him as head of the family, he will go. Your brother Mor is doing well on Venus and has recently been promoted to commandant. Your mother urges you to write him, whether he has written you or not, since he may be hesitant to write you without reason, you having done so well in so short a time, although he is the older.

"All our love. Eachan."

The spool, seen through the little transparent cover, stopped turning. The echoes of Eachan Khan Graeme's voice died against the gray walls of the office. Donal sat still at his desk, his eyes fixed on nothing, remembering Kensie.

It seemed odd to him, as he sat there, to discover that he could remember so few specific incidents. Thinking back, his early life seemed to be filled with his smiling uncle—and yet Kensie had not been home much. He would have thought that it would be the separate occasions of Kensie's going and coming that would be remembered—but instead it was more as if some general presence, some light about the house, had been extinguished.

Donal sighed. It seemed he was accumulating people at a steady rate. First Lee. Then the scarfaced El Man had asked to accompany him, when he left Freiland. And now Ian. Well, Ian was a good officer, aside from whatever crippling the death of his twin brother had caused him now. It would be more than easy for Donal to find a place for him. In fact, Donal could use him handily.

Donal punched a stud and turned his mouth to the little grille of the desk's signal unit.

"Eachan Khan Graeme, Graeme-house, South District, Foralie Canton, the Dorsai," he said. "Very glad to hear from you, although I imagine you know how I feel about Kensie. Please ask Ian to come right along. I will be honored to have him on my staff; and, to tell the truth, I have a real need for someone like him here. Most of the ranking officers I inherited as War Chief have been browbeaten by these Elders into a state of poor usefulness. I know I won't have to worry about Ian on that score. If he would take over supervision of my training program, he would be worth his weight in diamonds—natural ones. And I could give him an action post either on my personal staff, or as Patrol Chief. Tell Mother I'll write Mor but that the letter may be a bit sketchy right at present. I am up to my ears in work at the moment. These are good officers and men; but they have been so beaten about the ears at every wrong move that they will not blow their nose without a direct order. My love to all at home. Donal."

He pressed the button again, ending the recording and sealing it ready for delivery with the rest of the outgoing signals his office sent daily on their way. A soft chime from his desk reminded him that it was time for him to speak once more with Eldest Bright. He got up and went out.

The ranking elder of the joint government of the Friendly Worlds of Harmony and Association maintained his own suite of offices in Government Center, not more than half a hundred meters from the military nerve center. This was not fortuitous. Eldest Bright was a Militant, and liked to keep his eye on the fighting arm of God's True Churches. He was at work at his desk, but rose as Donal came in.

He advanced to meet Donal, a tall, lean man, dressed entirely in black, with the shoulders of a back-alley scrapper and the eyes of a Torquemada, that light of the Inquisition in ancient Spain.

"God be with you," he said. "Who authorized this requisition order for sheathing for the phase shift grids on the sub-class ships?"

"I did," said Donal.

"You spend credit like water." Bright's hard, middle-aged face leaned toward Donal. "A tithe on the churches, a tithe of a tithe on the church members of our two poor planets is all we have to support the business of government. How much of this do you think we can afford to spend on whims and fancies?"

"War, sir," said Donal, "is hardly a matter of whims and fancies."

"Then why shield the grids?" snapped Bright. "Are they liable to rust in the dampness of space? Will a wind come along between the stars and blow them apart?"

"Sheathe, not shield," replied Donal. "The point is to change their appearance; from the ball-and-hammer to the cylindrical. I'm taking all ships of the first three classes through with me. When they come out before the Exotics, I want them all looking like ships of the first class."

"For what reason?"

"Our attack on Zombri cannot be a complete surprise," explained Donal, patiently. "Mara and Kultis are as aware as anyone else that from a military standpoint it is vulnerable to such action. If you'll permit me—" He walked past Bright to the latter's desk and pressed certain keys there. A schematic of the Procyon system sprang into existence on one of the large gray walls of the office, the star itself in outline to the left. Pointing, Donal read off the planets in their order, moving off to the right. "Mara—Kultis—Ste. Marie-Coby. As close a group of habitable planets as we're likely to discover in the next ten generations. And simply because they are habitable—and close, therefore—we have this escaped moon, Zombri, in its own eccentric orbit lying largely between Coby and St. Marie—"

"Are you lecturing me?" interrupted Bright's harsh voice.

"I am," said Donal. "It's been my experience that the things people tend to overlook are those they learned earliest and believe they know best. Zombri is not habitable and too small for terraforming. Yet it exists like the Trojan horse, lacking only its complement of latter-day Acheans to threaten the Procyon peace—"

"We've discussed this before," broke in Bright.

"And we'll continue to discuss it," continued Donal, pleasantly, "whenever you wish to ask for the reason behind any individual order of mine. As I was saying—Zombri is the Trojan horse of the Procyon city. Unfortunately, in this day and age, we can hardly smuggle men onto it. We can, however, make a sudden landing in force and attempt to set up defenses before the Exotics are alerted. Our effort, then, must be to make our landing as quickly and effectively as possible. To do that best is to land virtually unopposed in spite of the fact that the Exotics will undoubtedly have a regular force keeping its eye on Zombri. The best way to achieve that is to appear in overwhelming strength, so that the local commanders will realize it is foolish to attempt to interfere with our landing. And the best way to put on a show of strength is to appear to have three times the ships of the first class that we do have. Therefore the sheathing."

Donal stopped talking, walked back across to the desk, and pressed the keys. The schematic disappeared.

"Very well," said Bright. The tone of his voice showed no trace of defeat or loss of arrogance. "I will authorize the order."

"Perhaps," said Donal, "you'll also authorize another order to remove the Conscience Guardians from my ships and units."

"Heretics—" began Bright.

"Are no concern of mine," said Donal. "My job is to get these people ready to mount an assault. But I've got over sixty per cent native troops of yours under me; and their morale is hardly being improved, on an average of three trials for heresy a week."

"This is a church matter," said Bright. "Is there anything else you wished to ask me, War Chief?"

"Yes," said Donal. "I ordered mining equipment. It hasn't arrived."

"The order was excessive," said Bright. "There should be no need to dig in anything but the command posts, on Zombri."

Donal looked at the black-clad man for a long moment. His white face and white hands—the only uncovered part of him—seemed rather the false part than the real, as if they were mask and gloves attached to some black and alien creature.

"Let's understand each other," said Donal. "Aside from the fact that I don't order men into exposed positions where they'll be killed— whether they're mercenaries or your own suicide-happy troops, just what do you want to accomplish by this move against the Exotics?"

"They threaten us," answered Bright. "They are worse than the heretics. They are Satan's own legion—the deniers of God." The man's eyes glittered like ice in the sunlight. "We must establish a watchtower over them that they may not threaten us without warning; and we may live in safety."

"All right," said Donal. "That's settled then. I'll get you your watchtower. And you get me the men and equipment I order without question and without delay. Already, these hesitations of your government mean I'll be going into Zombri ten to fifteen per cent under-strength."

"What?" Bright's dark brows drew together. "You've got two months yet until Target Date."

"Target Dates," said Donal, "are for the benefit of enemy intelligence. We'll be jumping off in two weeks."

"Two weeks!" Bright stared at him. "You can't be ready in two weeks."

"I earnestly hope Colmain and his General Staff for Mara and Kultis agrees with you," replied Donal. "They've the best land and space forces between the stars."

"How?" Bright's face paled with anger. "You dare to say that our own organization's inferior?"

"Facing facts is definitely preferable to facing defeat," said Donal, a little tiredly. "Yes, Eldest, our forces are definitely inferior. Which is why I'm depending on surprise rather than preparation."

"The Soldiers of the Church are the bravest in the universe!" cried Bright. "They wear the armor of righteousness and never retreat."

"Which explains their high casualty rate, regular necessity for green replacements, and general lower level of training," Donal reminded him. "A willingness to die in battle is not necessarily the best trait in a soldier. Your mercenary units, where you've kept them free of native replacements, are decidedly more combat-ready at the moment. Do I have your backing from now on, for anything I feel I need?"

Bright hesitated. The tension of fanaticism relaxed out of his face, to be replaced by one of thoughtfulness. When he spoke again his voice was cold and businesslike.

"On everything but the Conscience Guardians," he answered. "They have authority, after all, only over our own Members of the Churches." He turned and walked around once more behind his desk. "Also," he said, a trifle grimly, "you may have noticed that there are sometimes small differences of opinion concerning dogma between members of differing Churches. The presence of the Conscience Guardians among them makes them less prone to dispute, one with the other—and this you'll grant, I'm sure, is an aid to military discipline."

"It's effective," said Donal, shortly. He turned himself to go. "Oh, by the way, Eldest," he said. "That true Target Date of two weeks from today. It's essential it remain secret; so I've made sure it's known only to two men and will remain their knowledge exclusively until an hour or so before jump-off."

Bright's head came up.

"Who's the other?" he demanded sharply.

"You, sir," said Donal. "I just made my decision about the true date a minute ago."

They locked eyes for a long minute.

"May God be with you," said Bright, in cold, even tones.

Donal went out.

WAR CHIEF II

Genève bar-Colmain was, as Donal had said, commander of the best land-and-space forces between the stars. This because the Exotics of Mara and Kultis, though they would do no violence in their own proper persons, were wise enough to hire the best available in the way of military strength. Colmain, himself, was one of the top military minds of his time, along with Galt on Freiland, Kamal on the Dorsai, Isaac on Venus, and that occasional worker of military miracles—Dom Yen, Supreme Commander on the single world of Ceta where William had his home office. Colmain had his troubles (including a young wife who no longer cared for him) and his faults (he was a gambler—in a military as well as a monetary sense) but there was nothing wrong with either the intelligence that had its home in his skull, or the Intelligence that made its headquarters in his Command Base, on Mara.

Consequently, he was aware that the Friendly Worlds were preparing for a landing on Zombri within three weeks of the time when the decision to do so had become an accomplished fact. His spies adequately informed him of the Target Date that had been established for that landing; and he himself set about certain plans of his own for welcoming the invaders when they came.

The primary of these was the excavation of strong points on Zombri, itself. The assault troops would find they had jumped into a hornet's nest. The ships of the Exotic fleet would meanwhile be on alert not too far off. As soon as action had joined on the surface of Zombri, they would move in and drive the space forces of the invasion inward. The attackers would be caught between two fires; their assault troops lacking the chance to dig in and their ships lacking the support from below that entrenched ground forces could supply with moon-based heavy weapons.

The work on the strong points was well under way one day as, at the Command Base, back on Mara, Colmain was laying out a final development of strategy with his General Staff. An interruption occurred in the shape of an aide who came hurrying into the conference room without even the formality of asking permission first.

"What's this?" growled Colmain, looking up from the submitted plans before him with a scowl on his swarthy face, which at sixty was still handsome enough to provide him compensation in the way of other female companionship for his wife's lack of interest.

"Sir," said the aide, "Zombri's attacked—"

"*What?*" Colmain was suddenly on his feet; and the rest of the heads of the General Staff with him.

"Over two hundred ships, sir. We just got the signal." The aide's voice cracked a little—he was still in his early twenties. "Our men on Zombri are fighting with what they have—"

"Fighting?" Colmain took a sudden step toward the aide almost as if he would hold the man personally responsible. "They've started to land assault troops?"

"They've landed, sir—"

"How many?"

"We don't know sir—"

"Knucklehead! How many ships went in to drop men?"

"None, sir," gasped the aide. "They didn't drop any men. They all landed."

"Landed?"

For the fraction of a second, there was no sound at all in the long conference room.

"Do you mean to tell me—" shouted Colmain. "They landed two hundred ships of the first class on Zombri?"

"Yes, sir," the aide's voice had thinned almost to a squeak. "They're cleaning out our forces there and digging in—"

He had no chance to finish. Colmain swung about on his Battle Ops and Patrol Chiefs.

"Hell and damnation!" he roared. "Intelligence!"

"Sir?" answered a Freilander officer halfway down the length of the table.

"What's the meaning of this?"

"Sir—" stammered the officer. "I don't know how it happened. The latest reports I had from Harmony, three days ago—"

"Damn the latest reports. I want every ship and every man we can get into space in five hours! I want every patrol ship of any class to rendezvous with everything we can muster here, off Zombri in ten hours. Move!"

The General Staff of the Exotics moved.

It was a tribute to the kind of fighting force that Colmain commanded that they were able to respond at all in so short a time as ten hours to such orders. The fact that they accomplished the rendezvous with nearly four hundred craft of all classes, all carrying near their full complement of crews and assault troops, was on the order of a minor miracle.

Colmain and his chief officers, aboard the flagship, regarded the moon, swimming below them in the Control Eye of the ship. There had been reports of fighting down there up until three hours ago. Now there was a silence that spoke eloquently of captured troops. In addition, Observation reported—in addition to the works instigated by the Exotic forces—another hundred and fifty newly mined entrances in the crust of the moon.

"They're in there," said Colmain, "ships and all." Now that the first shock of discovery had passed, he was once more a cool and capable commander of forces. He had even found time to make a mental note to get together with this Dorsai, Graeme. Supreme command was always sweet bait to a brilliant youngster; but he would find the Council of United Churches a difficult employer in time—and the drawback of a subordinate position under Colmain himself could be compensated for by the kind of salary the Exotics were always willing to pay. Concerning the outcome of the actual situation before him, Colmain saw no real need for fear, only for haste. It was fairly obvious now that Graeme had risked everything on one bold swoop. He had counted on surprise to get him onto the moon and so firmly entrenched there that the cost of rooting him out would be prohibitive—before reinforcements could arrive.

He had erred only—and Colmain gave him full credit for all but that single error—in underestimating the time it would take for Colmain to gather his strength to retaliate. And even that error was forgiveable. There was no other force on the known worlds that could have been gotten battle-ready in under three times the time.

"We'll go in," said Colmain. "All of us—and fight it out on the moon." He looked around his officers. "Any comment?"

"Sir," said his Blue Patrol chief, "maybe we could wait them out up here?"

"Don't you think it," said Colmain, good-humoredly. "They would not come and dig in, in our own system, without being fully supplied for long enough to establish an outpost we can't take back." He shook his head. "The time to operate is now, gentlemen, before the infection has a chance to get its hold. All ships down—even the ones without assault troops. We'll fight them as if they were ground emplacements."

His staff saluted and went off to execute his orders.

The Exotic fleet descended on the moon of Zombri like locusts upon an orchard. Colmain, pacing the floor of the control room in the flagship—which had gone in with the rest—grinned as the reports began to flood in of strong points quickly cleaned of the Friendly troops that had occupied them—or dug in ships quickly surrendering and beginning to dig themselves out of the deep shafts their mining equipment had provided for them. The invading troops were collapsing like cardboard soldiers; and Colmain's opinion of their commander—which had risen sharply with the first news of the attack—began to slip decidedly. It was one thing to gamble boldly; it was quite another to gamble foolishly. It appeared from the morale and quality of the Friendly troops that there had, after all, been little chance of the surprise attack succeeding. This Graeme should have devoted a little more time to training his men and less to dreaming up dramatic actions. It was, Colmain thought, very much what you might expect of a young commander in supreme authority for the first time in his life.

He was enjoying the roseate glow of anticipated victory when it was suddenly all rudely shattered. There was a sudden ping from the deep-space communicator and suddenly two officers at the board spoke at once.

"Sir, unidentified call from—"

"Sir, ships above us—"

Colmain, who had been watching the Zombri surface through his Control Eye, jabbed suddenly at his buttons and the seeker circuit on it swung him dizzily upward and toward the stars, coming to rest abruptly, on full magnification, on a ship of the first class which unmistakably bore the mark of Friendly design and manufacture. Incredulously, he widened his scope, and in one swift survey, picked out more than twenty such ships in orbit around Zombri, within the limited range of his ground-restricted Eye, alone.

"Who is it?" he shouted, turning on the officer who had reported a call.

"Sir—" the officer's voice was hesitantly incredulous, "he says he's the Commander of the Friendlies."

"What?" Colmain's fist came down on a stud beside the controls of the Eye. A wall screen lit up and a lean young Dorsai with odd, indefinite-colored eyes looked out at him.

"Graeme!" roared Colmain. "What kind of an imitation fleet are you trying to bluff me with?"

"Look again, commander," answered the young man. "The imitation are digging their way out down there on the surface by you. They're my sub-class ships. Why'd you think they would be taken so easily? These are my ships of the first class—one hundred and eighty-three of them."

Colmain jammed down the button and blanked the screen. He turned on his officers at the control panel.

"Report!"

But the officers had already been busy. Confirmations were flooding in. The first of the attacking ships had been dug out and proved to be sub-class ships with sheathing around their phase-shift grids, little weapons, and less armor. Colmain swung back to the screen again, activated it, and found Donal in the same position, waiting for him.

"We'll be up to see you in ten minutes," he promised, between his teeth.

"You've got more sense than that, commander," replied Donal, from the screen. "Your ships aren't even dug in. They're sitting ducks as they are; and in no kind of formation to cover each other as they try to jump off. We can annihilate you if you try to climb up here, and lying as you are we can pound you to pieces on the ground. You're not equipped from the standpoint of supplies to dig in there; and I'm well enough informed about your total strength to know you've got no force left at large that's strong enough to do us any damage." He paused. "I suggest you come up here yourself in a single ship and discuss terms of surrender."

Colmain stood, glaring at the screen. But there was, in fact, no alternative to surrender. He would not have been a commander of the caliber he was, if he had not recognized the fact. He nodded, finally, grudgingly.

"Coming up," he said; and blanked the screen. Shoulders a little humped, he went off to take the little courier boat that was attached to the flagship for his own personal use.

"By heaven," were the words with which he greeted Donal, when he at last came face to face with him aboard the Friendly flagship, "you've ruined me. I'll be lucky to get the command of five C-class and a tender, on Dunnin's World, after this."

It was not far from the truth.

*   *   *

Donal returned to Harmony two days later, and was cheered in triumph even by the sourest of that world's fanatics, as he rode through the streets to Government Center. A different sort of reception awaited him there, however, when he arrived and went alone to report to Eldest Bright.

The head of the United Council of Churches for the worlds of Harmony and Association looked up grimly as Donal came in, still wearing the coverall of his battle dress under a barrel-cut jacket he had thrown on hastily for the ride from the spaceport. The platform on which he had ridden had been open for the admiration of the crowds along the way; and Harmony was in the chill fall of its short year.

"Evening, gentlemen," said Donal, taking in not only Bright in the greeting, but two other members of the Council who sat alongside him at his desk. These two did not answer. Donal had hardly expected them to. Bright was in charge here. Bright nodded at three armed soldiers of the native elite guard that had been holding post by the door and they went out, closing the door behind them.

"So you've come back," said Bright.

Donal smiled.

"Did you expect me to go some place else?" he asked.

"This is no time for humor!" Bright's large hand came down with a crack on the top of the desk. "What kind of an explanation have you got for us, for this outrageous conduct of yours?"

"If you don't mind, Eldest!" Donal's voice rang against the gray walls of the room, with a slight cutting edge the three had never heard before and hardly expected on this occasion. "I believe in politeness and good manners for myself; and see no reason why others shouldn't reciprocate in kind. What're you talking about?"

Bright rose. Standing wide-legged and shoulder-bent above the smooth, almost reflective surface of the gray desk, the resemblance to the back-alley scrapper for the moment outweighed the Torquemada in his appearance.

"You come back to us," he said, slowly and harshly, "and pretend not to know how you betrayed us?"

"Betrayed you?" Donal considered him with a quietness that was almost ominous. "How—betrayed you?"

"We sent you out to do a job."

"I believe I did it," said Donal dryly. "You wanted a watchtower over the Godless. You wanted a permanent installation on Zombri to spot any buildup on the part of the Exotics to attack you. You remem-

ber I asked you to set out in plain terms what you were after, a few
days back. You were quite explicit about that being just what you
wanted. Well—you've got it!"

"You limb of Satan!" blared Bright, suddenly losing control. "Do
you pretend to believe that you thought that was all we wanted? Did
you think the anointed of the Lord would hesitate on the threshold of
the Godless?" He turned and stalked suddenly around the desk to stand
face to face with Donal. "You had them in your power and you asked
them only for an unarmed observation station on a barren moon. You
had them by the throat and you slew none of them when you should
have wiped them from the face of the stars, to the last ship—to the
last man!"

He paused and Donal could hear his teeth gritting in the sudden
silence.

"How much did they pay you?" Bright snarled.

Donal stood in an unnatural stillness.

"I will pretend," he said, after a moment, "that I didn't hear that
last remark. As for your questions as to why I asked only for the
observation station, that was all you had said you wanted. As to why
I did not wipe them out—wanton killing is not my trade. Nor the
needless expenditure of my own men in the pursuit of wanton killing."
He looked coldly into Bright's eyes. "I suggest you could have been
a little more honest with me, Eldest, about what you wanted. It was
the destruction of the Exotic power, wasn't it?"

"It was," gritted Bright.

"I thought as much," said Donal. "But it never occurred to you
that I would be a good enough commander to find myself in the position to accomplish that. I think," said Donal, letting his eyes stray to
the other two black-clad elders as well, "you are hoist by your own
petard, gentlemen." He relaxed; and smiling slightly, turned back to
Bright. "There are reasons," he said, "why it would be very unwise
tactically for the Friendly Worlds to break the back of Mara and Kultis.
If you'll allow me to give you a small lesson in power dis—"

"You'll come up with better answers than you have!" burst out
Bright. "Unless you want to be tried for betrayal of your employer!"

"Oh, come now!" Donal laughed out loud.

Bright whirled away from him and strode across the gray room.
Flinging wide the door by which Donal had entered, and they had
exited, he revealed the three elite guard soldiers. He whirled about,
arm outstretched to its full length, finger quivering.

"Arrest that traitor!" he cried.

The guards took a step toward Donal—and in that same moment, before they had any of them moved their own length's-worth of distance toward him—three faint blue beams traced their way through the intervening space past Bright, leaving a sharp scent of ionized air behind them. And the three dropped.

Like a man stunned by a blow from behind, Bright stared down at the bodies of his three guards. He swayed about to see Donal reholstering his handgun.

"Did you think I was fool enough to come here unarmed?" asked Donal, a little sadly. "And did you think I'd submit to arrest?" He shook his head. "You should have wit enough to see now I've just saved you from yourselves."

He looked at their disbelieving faces.

"Oh, yes," he said. He gestured to the open wall at the far end of the office. Sounds of celebration from the city outside drifted lightly in on the evening breeze. "The better forty per cent of your fighting forces are out there. Mercenaries. Mercenaries who appreciate a commander who can give them a victory at the cost of next to no casualties at all. What do you suppose their reaction would be if you tried me for betrayal, and found me guilty, and had me executed?" He paused to let the thought sink in. "Consider it, gentlemen."

He pinched his jacket shut and looked grimly at the three dead elite guards; and then turned back to the elders, again.

"I consider this sufficient grounds for breach of contract," he said. "You can find yourself another War Chief."

He turned and walked toward the door. As he passed through it, Bright shouted after him.

"Go to them, then! Go to the Godless on Mara and Kultis!"

Donal paused and turned. He inclined his head gravely.

"Thank you, gentlemen," he said. "Remember—The suggestion was yours."

PART-MARAN

There remained the interview with Sayona the Bond. Going up some wide and shallow steps into the establishment—it could not be called merely a building, or group of buildings—that housed the most important individual of the two Exotic planets, Donal found cause for amusement in the manner of his approach.

Farther out, among some shrubbery at the entrance to the—estate?—he had encountered a tall, gray-eyed woman; and explained his presence.

"Go right ahead," the woman had said, waving him onward. "You'll find him." The odd part of it was, Donal had no doubt that he would. And the unreasonable certainty of it tickled his own strange sense of humor.

He wandered on by a sunlit corridor that broadened imperceptibly into a roofless garden, past paintings, and pools of water with colorful fish in them—through a house that was not a house, in rooms and out until he came to a small sunken patio, half-roofed over; and at the far end of it, under the shade of the half-roof, was a tall bald man of indeterminate age, wrapped in a blue robe and seated on a little patch of captive turf, surrounded by a low, stone wall.

Donal went down three stone steps, across the patio, and up the three stone steps at the far side until he stood over the tall, seated man.

"Sir," said Donal. "I'm Donal Graeme."

The tall man waved him down on the turf.

"Unless you'd rather sit on the wall, of course," he smiled. "Sitting cross-legged doesn't agree with everyone."

"Not at all, sir," answered Donal, and sat down cross-legged himself.

"Good," said the tall man; and apparently lost himself in thought, gazing out over the patio.

Donal also relaxed, waiting. A certain peace had crept into him in the way through this place. It seemed to beckon to meditation; and— Donal had no doubt—was probably cleverly constructed and designed for just that purpose. He sat, comfortably now, and let his mind wander where it chose; and it happened—not so oddly at all—to choose to wander in the direction of the man beside him.

Sayona the Bond, Donal had learned as a boy in school, was one of the human institutions peculiar to the Exotics. The Exotics were two planetsful of strange people, judged by the standards of the rest of the human race—some of whom went so far as to wonder if the inhabitants of Mara and Kultis had developed wholly and uniquely out of the human race, after all. This, however, was speculation half in humor and half in superstition. In truth, they were human enough.

They had, however, developed their own forms of wizardry. Particularly in the fields of psychology and its related branches, and in that other field which you could call gene selection or planned breeding depending on whether you approved or disapproved of it. Along with this went a certain sort of general mysticism. The Exotics worshiped no god, overtly, and laid claim to no religion. On the other hand they were nearly all—they claimed, by individual choice—vegetarians and adherents of nonviolence on the ancient Hindu order. In addition, however, they held to another cardinal nonprinciple; and this one was the principle of noninterference. The ultimate violence, they believed, was for one person to urge a point of view on another—in any fashion of urging. Yet, all these traits had not destroyed their ability to take care of themselves. If it was their creed to do violence to no man, it was another readily admitted part of their same creed that no one should therefore be wantonly permitted to do violence to them. In war and business, through mercenaries and middlemen, they more than held their own.

But, thought Donal—to get back to Sayona the Bond, and his place in Exotic culture. He was one of the compensations peculiar to the Exotic peoples, for their different way of life. He was—in some way that only an Exotic fully understood—a certain part of their emotional life made manifest in the person of a living human being. Like Anea, who—devastatingly normal and female as she was—was, to an Exotic, *literally* one of the select of Kultis. She was their best selected qualities made actual—like a living work of art that they worshiped. It did not matter that she was not always joyful, that indeed, her life must bear as much or more of the normal human sorrow of situation and existence. That was where most people's appreciation of the matter went astray. No, what was important was the capabilities they had bred and trained into her. It was the capacity in her for living, not the life she actually led, that pleasured them. The actual achievement was up to her, and was her own personal reward. They appreciated the fact that— if she chose, and was lucky—she could appreciate life.

Similarly, Sayona the Bond. Again, only in a sense that an Exotic would understand, Sayona was the actual bond between their two worlds made manifest in flesh and blood. In him was the capability for common understanding, for reconciliation, for an expression of the community of feeling between people . . .

Donal awoke suddenly to the fact that Sayona was speaking to him. The older man had been speaking some time, in a calm, even voice, and Donal had been letting the words run through his mind like water of a stream through his fingers. Now, something that had been said had jogged him to a full awareness.

". . . Why, no," answered Donal, "I thought this was standard procedure for any commander before you hired him."

Sayona chuckled.

"Put every new commander through all that testing and trouble?" he said. "No, no. The word would get around and we'd never be able to hire the men we wanted."

"I rather enjoy taking tests," said Donal, idly.

"I know you do," Sayona nodded. "A test is a form of competition, after all; and you're a competitor by nature. No, normally when we want a military man we look for military proofs like everyone else— and that's as far as we go."

"Why the difference with me, then?" asked Donal, turning to look at him. Sayona returned his gaze with pale brown eyes holding just a hint of humor in the wrinkles at their corners.

"Well, we weren't just interested in you as a commander," answered Sayona. "There's the matter of your ancestors, you know. You're actually part-Maran; and those genes, even when outmatched, are of interest to us. Then there's the matter of you, yourself. You have astonishing potentials."

"Potentials for what?"

"A number of rather large things," said Sayona soberly. "We only glimpse them, of course, in the results of our tests."

"Can I ask what those large things are?" asked Donal, curiously.

"I'm sorry, no. I can't answer that for you," said Sayona. "The answers would be meaningless to you personally, anyway—for the reason you can't explain anything in terms of itself. That's why I thought I'd have this talk with you. I'm interested in your philosophy."

"Philosophy!" Donal laughed. "I'm a Dorsai."

"Everyone, even Dorsai, every living thing has its own philosophy—a blade of grass, a bird, a baby. An individual philosophy is a necessary thing, the touchstone by which we judge our own existence. Also—you're only part Dorsai. What does the other part say?"

Donal frowned.

"I'm not sure the other part says anything," he said. "I'm a soldier. A mercenary. I have a job to do; and I intend to do it—always—in the best way I know how."

"But beyond this—" urged Sayona.

"Why, beyond this—" Donal fell silent, still frowning. "I suppose I would want to see things go well."

"You said want to see things go well—rather than *like* to see things go well." Sayona was watching him. "Don't you see any significance in that?"

"Want? Oh—" Donal laughed. "I suppose that's an unconscious slip on my part. I suppose I was thinking of *making* them go well."

"Yes," said Sayona, but in a tone that Donal could not be sure was meant as agreement or not. "You're a doer, aren't you?"

"Someone has to be," said Donal. "Take the civilized worlds now—" he broke off suddenly.

"Go on," said Sayona.

"I meant to say—take civilization. Think how short a time it's been since the first balloon went up back on Earth. Four hundred years? Five hundred years? Something like that. And look how we've spread out and split up since then."

"What about it?"

"I don't like it," said Donal. "Aside from the inefficiency, it strikes me as unhealthy. What's the point of technological development if we just split in that many more factions—everyone hunting up his own type of aberrant mind and hiving with it? That's no progress."

"You subscribe to progress?"

Donal looked at him.

"Don't you?"

"I suppose," said Sayona. "A certain type of progress. *My* kind of progress. What's yours?"

Donal smiled.

"You want to hear that, do you? You're right. I guess I do have a philosophy after all. You want to hear it?"

"Please," said Sayona.

"All right," said Donal. He looked out over the little sunken garden. "It goes like this—each man is a tool in his own hands. Mankind is a tool in *its* own hands. Our greatest satisfaction doesn't come from the rewards of our work, but from the working itself; and our greatest responsibility is to sharpen, and improve the tool that is ourselves so as to make it capable of tackling bigger jobs." He looked at Sayona. "What do you think of it?"

"I'd have to think about it," answered Sayona. "My own point of view is somewhat different, of course. I see Man not so much as an achieving mechanism, but as a perceptive link in the order of things. I would say the individual's role isn't so much to *do* as it is to *be*. To realize to the fullest extent the truth already and inherently in him—if I make myself clear."

"Nirvana as opposed to Valhalla, eh?" said Donal, smiling a little grimly. "Thanks, I prefer Valhalla."

"Are you sure?" asked Sayona. "Are you quite sure you've no use for Nirvana?"

"Quite sure," said Donal.

"You make me sad," said Sayona, somberly. "We had had hopes."

"Hopes?"

"There is," said Sayona, lifting one finger, "this possibility in you—this great possibility. It may be exercised in only one direction— that direction you choose. But you have freedom of choice. There's room for you here."

"With you?"

"The other worlds don't know," said Sayona, "what we've begun to open up here in the last hundred years. We are just beginning to work with the butterfly implicit in the matter-bound worm that is the present human species. There are great opportunities for anyone with the potentialities for this work."

"And I," said Donal, "have these potentialities?"

"Yes," answered Sayona. "Partly as a result of a lucky genetic accident that is beyond our knowledge to understand, now. Of course— you would have to be retrained. That other part of your character that rules you now would have to be readjusted to a harmonious integration with the other part *we* consider more valuable."

Donal shook his head.

"There would be compensations," said Sayona, in a sad, almost whimsical tone, "things would become possible to you—do you know that you, personally, are the sort of man who, for example, could walk on air if only you believed you could?"

Donal laughed.

"I am quite serious," said Sayona. "Try believing it some time."

"I can hardly try believing what I instinctively disbelieve," said Donal. "Besides, that's beside the point. I am a soldier."

"But what a strange soldier," murmured Sayona. "A soldier full of compassion, of whimsical fancies and wild daydreams. A man of loneliness who wants to be like everyone else; but who finds the human race a conglomeration of strange alien creatures whose twisted ways he cannot understand—while still he understands them too well for their own comfort."

He turned his eyes calmly onto Donal's face, which had gone set and hard.

"Your tests *are* quite effective, aren't they?" Donal said.

"They are," said Sayona. "But there's no need to look at me like that. We can't use them as a weapon, to make you do what we would like to have you do. That would be an action so self-crippling as to destroy all its benefits. We can only make the offer to you." He paused. "I can tell you that on the basis of our knowledge we can assure you with better than fair certainty that you'll be happy if you take our path."

"And if not?" Donal had not relaxed.

Sayona sighed.

"You are a strong man," he said. "Strength leads to responsibility, and responsibility pays little heed to happiness."

"I can't say I like the picture of myself going through life grubbing after happiness." Donal stood up. "Thanks for the offer, anyway. I appreciate the compliment it implies."

"There is no compliment in telling a butterfly he is a butterfly and need not crawl along the ground," said Sayona.

Donal inclined his head politely.

"Good-by," he said. He turned about and walked the few steps to the head of the shallow steps leading down into the sunken garden and across it to the way he had come in.

"Donal—" The voice of Sayona stopped him. He turned back and saw the Bond regarding him with an expression almost impish. "*I* believe you can walk on air," said Sayona.

Donal stared; but the expression of the other did not alter. Swinging about, Donal stepped out as if onto level ground—and to his unutterable astonishment his foot met solidity on a level, unsupported, eight inches above the next step down. Hardly thinking why he did it, Donal brought his other foot forward into nothingness. He took another step—and another. Unsupported on the thin air, he walked across above the sunken garden to the top of the steps on the far side.

Striding once more onto solidity, he turned about and looked across the short distance. Sayona still regarded him; but his expression now was unreadable. Donal swung about and left the garden.

Very thoughtful, he returned to his own quarters in the city of Portsmouth, which was the Maran city holding the Command Base of the Exotics. The tropical Maran night had swiftly enfolded the city by the time he reached his room, yet the soft illumination that had come on automatically about and inside all the buildings by some clever trick of design failed to white-out the overhead view of the stars. These shone down through the open wall of Donal's bedroom.

Standing in the center of the bedroom, about to change for the meal which would be his first of the day—he had again forgotten to eat during the earlier hours—Donal paused and frowned. He gazed up at the gently domed roof of the room, which reached its highest point some twelve feet above his head. He frowned again and searched about through his writing desk until he found a self-sealing signal-tape capsule. Then, with this in one hand, he turned toward the ceiling and took one rather awkward step off the ground.

His foot caught and held in air. He lifted himself off the floor. Slowly, step by step he walked up through nothingness to the high point of the ceiling. Opening the capsule, he pressed its self-sealing edges against the ceiling, where they clung. He hung there a second in air, staring at them.

"Ridiculous!" he said suddenly—and, just as suddenly, he was falling. He gathered himself with the instinct of long training in the second of drop and, landing on hands and feet, rolled over and came to his feet like a gymnast against a far wall. He got up, brushing himself off, unhurt—and turned to look up at the ceiling. The capsule still clung there.

He lifted the little appliance that was strapped to his wrist and keyed its phone circuit in.

"Lee," he said.

He dropped his wrist and waited. Less than a minute later, Lee came into the room. Donal pointed toward the capsule on the ceiling. "What's that?" he asked.

Lee looked.

"Tape capsule," he said. "Want me to get it down?"

"Never mind," answered Donal. "How do you suppose it got up there?"

"Some joker with a float," answered Lee. "Want me to find out who?"

"No—never mind," said Donal. "That'll be all."

Bending his head at the dismissal, Lee went out of the room. Donal took one more look at the capsule, then turned and wandered over to the open wall of his room, and looked out. Below him lay the bright carpet of the city. Overhead hung the stars. For longer than a minute he considered them.

Suddenly he laughed, cheerfully and out loud.

"No, no," he said to the empty room. "I'm a Dorsai!"

He turned his back on the view and went swiftly to work at dressing for dinner. He was surprised to discover how hungry he actually was.

PROTECTOR

Battle Commander of Field Forces Ian Ten Graeme, that cold, dark man, strode through the outer offices of the Protector of Procyon with a *private-and-secret* signal in his large fist. In the three outer offices, no one got in his way. But at the entrance to the Protector's private office, a private secretary in the green-and-gold of a staff uniform ventured to murmur that the Protector had left orders to be undisturbed. Ian merely looked at her, placed one palm flat against the lock of the inner office door—and strode through.

Within, he discovered Donal standing by an open wall, caught by a full shaft of Procyon's white-gold sunlight, gazing out over Portsmouth and apparently deep in thought. It was a position in which he was to be discovered often, these later days. He looked up now at the sound of Ian's measured tread approaching.

Six years of military and political successes had laid their inescapable marks upon Donal's face, marks plain to be seen in the sunlight. At a casual glance he appeared hardly older than the young man who had left the Dorsai half a dozen years before. But a closer inspection showed him to be slightly heavier of build now—even a little taller. Only this extra weight, slight increase as it was, had not served to soften the clear lines of his features. Rather these same features had grown more pronounced, more hard of line. His eyes seemed a little deeper set now; and the habit of command—command extended to the point where it became unconscious—had cast an invisible shadow upon his brows, so that it had become a face men obeyed without thinking, as if it was the natural thing to do.

"Well?" he said, as Ian came up.

"They've got New Earth," his uncle answered; and handed over the signal tape. "Private-and-secret to you from Galt."

Donal took the tape automatically, that deeper, more hidden part of him immediately taking over his mind. If the six years had wrought changes upon his person and manner, they had worked to even greater ends below the surface of his being. Six years of command, six years of estimate and decision had beaten broad the path between his upper mind and that dark, oceanic part of him, the depthless waters of which lapped on all known shores and many yet unknown. He had come— you could not say to terms—but to truce with the source of his oddness; hiding it well from others, but accepting it to himself for the sake of the tool it placed in his hands. Now, this information Ian had just brought him was like one more stirring of the shadowy depths, a rippled vibration spreading out to affect all, integrate with all—and make even more clear the vast and shadowy ballet of purpose and counterpurpose that was behind all living action; and—for himself—a call to action.

As Protector of Procyon, now responsible not only for the defense of the Exotics, but of the two smaller inhabited planets in that system— St. Marie, and Coby—that action was required of him. But even more; as himself, it was required of him. So that what it now implied was not something he was eager to avoid. Rather, it was due, and welcome. Indeed, it was almost too welcome—fortuitous, even.

"I see—" he murmured. Then, lifting his face to his uncle, "Galt'll need help. Get me some figures on available strength, will you Ian?"

Ian nodded and went out, as coldly and martially as he had entered.

Left alone, Donal did not break open the signal tape immediately. He could not now remember what he had been musing about when Ian entered, but the sight of his uncle had initiated a new train of thought. Ian seemed well, these days—or at least as well as could be expected. It did not matter that he lived a solitary life, had little to do with the other commanders of his own rank, and refused to go home to the Dorsai, even for a trip to see his family. He devoted himself to his duties of training field troops—and did it well. Aside from that, he went his own way.

The Maran psychiatrists had explained to Donal that no more than this could be expected of Ian. Gently, they had explained it. A normal mind, gone sick, they could cure. The unfortunate thing was that—at least in so far as his attachment to his twin had been—Ian was not normal. Nothing in this universe could replace the part of him that had died with Kensie—had, indeed, *been* Kensie—for the peculiar psychological make-up of the twins had made them two halves of a whole.

"Your uncle continued to live," the psychiatrists had explained to Donal, "because of an unconscious desire to punish himself for letting his brother die. He is, in fact, seeking death—but it must be a peculiar sort of death which will include the destruction of all that matters to him. 'If thy right hand offend thee, cut if off.' To his unconscious, the Ian-Kensie gestalt holds the Ian part of it to blame for what happened and is hunting a punishment to fit the crime. That is why he continues to practice the—for him—morbid abnormality of staying alive. The normal thing for such a personality would be to die, or get himself killed.

"And that is why," they had concluded, "he refuses to see or have anything to do with his wife or children. His unconscious recognizes the danger of pulling them down to destruction with him. We would advise against his being urged to visit them against his will."

Donal sighed. Thinking about it now, it seemed to him strange that the people who had come to group around him had none of them come—really—because of the fame he had won or the positions he could offer them. There was Ian, who had come because the family had sent him. Lee, who had found the supply of that which his own faulty personality lacked—and would have followed if Donal had been Protector of nothing, instead of being Protector of Procyon. There was Lludrow, Donal's now assistant Chief of Staff, who had come to him not under his own free will, but under the prodding of his wife. For Lludrow had ended up marrying Elvine Rhy, Galt's niece, who had not let even marriage impose a barrier to her interest in Donal. There was Genève bar-Colmain, who was on Donal's staff because Donal had been kind; and because he had no place else to go that was worthy of his abilities. And, lastly, there was Galt, himself, whose friendship was not a military matter, but the rather wistful affection of a man who had never had a son, and saw its image in Donal—though it was not really fair to count Galt, who was apart, as still Marshal of Freiland.

And—in contradistinction to all the rest—there was Mor, the one Donal would have most liked to have at his side; but whose pride had driven him to place himself as far from his successful younger brother as possible. Mor had finally taken service with Venus, where in the open market that flourished on that technological planet, he had had his contract sold to Ceta; and now found himself in the pay of Donal's enemy, which would put them on opposite sides if conflict finally came.

Donal shook himself abruptly. These fits of depression that took him lately were becoming more frequent—possibly as a result of the long hours of work he found himself putting in. Brusquely, he broke open the signal from Galt.

> Donal:
> The news about New Earth will have reached you by this time. The *coup d'état* that put the Kyerly government in control of the planet was engineered with troops furnished by Ceta. I have never ceased to be grateful to you for your advice against leasing out units to William. But the pattern here is a bad one. We will be facing the same sort of internal attack here through the local proponents of an open exchange for the buying and selling of contracts. One by one, the worlds are falling into the hands of manipulators, not the least of which is William himself. Please furnish us with as many field units as you can conveniently spare.
> There is to be a General Planetary Discussion, meeting on Venus to discuss recognition of the new government on New Earth. They would be wise not to invite you; so come anyway. I, myself, must be there; and I need you, even if no other reason impels you to come.
>
> > Hendrik Galt
> > Marshal, Freiland.

Donal nodded to himself. But he did not spring immediately into action. Where Galt was reacting against the shock of a sudden discovery, Donal, in the situation on New Earth, recognized only the revelation of something he had been expecting for a long time.

The sixteen inhabited worlds of the eight stellar systems from Sol to Altair survived within a complex of traded skills. The truth of the matter was that present day civilization had progressed too far for each planet to maintain its own training systems and keep up with progress in the many necessary fields. Why support a thousand mediocre school systems when it was possible to have fifty superb ones and trade the graduates for the skilled people you needed in other areas of learning? The overhead of such systems was tremendous, the number of top men in each field necessarily limited; moreover, progress was more effective if all the workers in one area of knowledge were kept closely in touch with each other.

The system seemed highly practical. Donal was one of the few men of his time to see the trouble inherent in it.

The joker to such an arrangement comes built in to the question—

how much is a skilled worker an individual in his own right, and how much is he a piece of property belonging to whoever at the moment owns his contract? If he is too much an individual, barter between worlds breaks down to a series of individual negotiations; and society nowadays could not exist except on the basis of community needs. If he is too much a piece of property, then the field is opened for the manipulators—the buyers and sellers of flesh, those who would corner the manpower market and treat humanity like cattle for their own gain.

Among the worlds between the stars, this question still hung in argument. "Tight" societies, like the technological worlds of the so-called Venus group—Venus herself, Newton and Cassida—and the fanatic worlds of Harmony and Association, and Coby, which was ruled by what amounted to a criminal secret society—had always favored the piece of property view more strongly than the individual one. "Loose" societies, like the republican worlds of Old Earth, and Mars, the Exotics—Mara and Kultis—and the violently individualistic society of the Dorsai, held to the individual side of the question. In between were the middling worlds—the ones with strong central governments like Freiland and New Earth, the merchandising world of Ceta, the democratic theocracy of St. Marie, and the pioneer, under-populated fisher-planet of Dunnin's World, ruled by the co-operative society known as the Corbel.

Among the "tight" societies, the contract exchange mart had been in existence for many years. On these worlds, unless your contract was written with a specific forbidding clause, you might find yourself sold on no notice at all to a very different employer—possibly on a completely different world. The advantages of such a mart were obvious to an autocratic government, since the government itself was in a position to control the market through its own vast needs and resources, which no individual could hope to match. On a "loose" world, where the government was hampered by its own built-in system of checks from taking advantage of opposing individual employers, the field was open for the sharp practices not only of individuals, but of other governments.

Thus, an agreement between two worlds for the establishment of a reciprocal open market worked all to the advantage of the "tighter" of the two governments—and must inevitably end in the tighter government gaining the lion's share of the talent available on the two worlds.

This, then, was the background for the inevitable conflict that had been shaping up now for fifty years between two essentially different systems of controlling what was essentially the lifeblood of the human race—its skilled minds. In fact, thought Donal, standing by the open wall—the conflict was here, and now. It had already been under way that day he had stepped aboard the ship on which he was to meet Galt, and William, and Anea, the Select of Kultis. Behind the scenes, the build-up for a final battle had been already begun, and his own role in that battle, ready and waiting for him.

He went over to his desk and pressed a stud, speaking into a grille.

"I want all Chiefs of Staff here immediately," he said. "For a top-level conference."

He took his finger from the stud and sat down at the desk. There was a great deal to be done.

PROTECTOR II

Arriving at Holmstead the capital city of Venus five days later, Donal went immediately to a conference with Galt in the latter's suite of rooms at Government Hotel.

"There were things to take care of," he said, shaking hands with the older man and sitting down, "or I'd have been here sooner." He examined Galt. "You're looking tired."

The Marshal of Freiland had indeed lost weight. The skin of his face sagged a little on the massive bones, and his eyes were darkened with fatigue.

"Politics—politics—" answered Galt. "Not my line at all. It wears a man down. Drink?"

"No thanks," said Donal.

"Don't care for one myself," Galt said. "I'll just light my pipe . . . you don't mind?"

"I never did before. And," said Donal, "you never asked me before."

"Heh . . . no," Galt gave vent to something halfway between a cough and a chuckle; and, getting out his pipe, began to fill it with fingers that trembled a little. "Damned tired, that's all. In fact I'm ready to retire—but how can a man quit just when all hell's popping? You got my message—how many field units can you let me have?"

"A couple and some odds and ends. Say twenty thousand of first-line troops—" Galt's head came up. "Don't worry," Donal smiled. "They will be moved in by small, clumsy stages to give the impression I'm letting you have five times that number, but the procedure's a little fouled up in getting them actually transferred."

Galt grunted.

"I might've known you'd think of something," he said. "We can use that mind of yours here, at the main Conference. Officially, we're gathered here just to agree on a common attitude to the new government on New Earth—but you know what's really on the fire, don't you?"

"I can guess," said Donal. "The open market."

"Right." Galt got his pipe alight; and puffed on it gratefully. "The split's right down the middle, now that New Earth's in the Venus Group's camp and we—Freiland, that is—are clear over on the non-market side by way of reaction. We're in fair enough strength counting heads as we sit around the table; but that's not the problem. They've got William—and that white-haired devil Blaine." He looked sharply over at Donal. "You know Project Blaine, don't you?"

"I've never met him. This is my first trip to Venus," said Donal.

"There's a shark," said Galt with feeling. "I'd like to see him and William lock horns on something. Maybe they'd chew each other up and improve the universe. Well . . . about your status here—"

"Officially I'm sent by Sayona the Bond as an observer."

"Well, that's no problem then. We can easily get you invited to step from observer to delegate status. In fact, I've already passed the word. We were just waiting for you to arrive." Galt blew a large cloud of smoke and squinted at Donal through it. "But how about it, Donal? I trust that insight of yours. What's really in the wind here at the Conference?"

"I'm not sure," answered Donal. "It's my belief somebody made a mistake."

"A mistake?"

"New Earth," explained Donal. "It was a fool's trick to overthrow the government there right now—and by force, at that. Which is why I believe we'll be getting it back."

Galt sat up sharply, taking his pipe from his mouth.

"Getting it back? You mean—the old government returned to power?" He stared at Donal. "Who'd give it back to us?"

"William for one, I'd imagine," said Donal. "This isn't *his* way of doing things—piecemeal. But you can bet as long as he's about returning it, he'll exact a price for it."

Galt shook his head.

"I don't follow you," he said.

"William finds himself working with the Venus group right now," Donal pointed out. "But he's hardly out to do them a kindness. His own aims are what concerns him—and it's those he'll be after in the long run. In fact, if you look, I'll bet you see two kinds of negotiations going on at this Conference. The short range, and the long range. The short range is likely to be this matter of an open market. The long range will be William's game."

Galt sucked on his pipe again.

"I don't know," he said, heavily. "I don't hold any more of a brief for William than you do—but you seem to lay everything at his doorstep. Are you sure you aren't a little overboard where the subject of him is concerned?"

"How can anyone be sure?" confessed Donal, wryly. "I think what I think about William, because—" he hesitated, "if I were in his shoes, I'd be doing these things I suspect him of." He paused. "William's weight on our side could swing the conference into putting enough pressure on New Earth to get the old government back in power, couldn't it?"

"Why—of course."

"Well, then." Donal shrugged. "What could be better than William setting forth a compromise solution that at one and the same time puts him in the opposite camp and conceals as well as requires a development in the situation he desires?"

"Well—I can follow that," said Galt, slowly. "But if that's the case, what's he after? What is it he'll want?"

Donal shook his head.

"I'm not sure," he said carefully. "I don't know."

On that rather inconclusive note, they ended their own private talk and Galt took Donal off to meet with some of the other delegates.

The meeting developed, as these things do, into a cocktail gathering in the lounges of the suite belonging to Project Blaine of Venus. Blaine himself, Donal was interested to discover, was a heavy, calm-looking white-haired man who showed no surface evidences of the character Galt had implied to him.

"Well, what do you think of him?" Galt murmured, as they left Blaine and his wife in the process of circulating around the other guests.

"Brilliant," said Donal. "But I hardly think someone to be afraid of." He met Galt's raised eyebrows with a smile. "He seems too immersed in his own point of view. I'd consider him predictable."

"As opposed to William?" asked Galt, in a low voice.

"As opposed to William," agreed Donal. "Who is not—or, not so much."

They had all this time been approaching William, who was seated facing them at one end of the lounge and talking to a tall slim woman whose back was to them. As Galt and Donal came up, William's gaze went past her.

"Well, Marshal!" he said, smiling. "Protector!" The woman turned around; and Donal found himself face to face with Anea.

If six years had made a difference in the outward form of Donal, they had made much more in that of Anea. She was in her late twenties now, and past the last stages of that delayed adolescence of hers. She had begun now to reveal that rare beauty that would deepen with age and experience and never completely leave her, even in extreme old age. She was more developed now, than the last time Donal had seen her, more fully woman-formed and more poised. Her green eyes met Donal's indeterminate ones across mere centimeters of distance.

"Honored to see you again," said Donal, inclining his head.

"The honor is mine." Her voice, like the rest of her, had matured. Donal looked past her to William. "Prince!" he said.

William stood up and shook hands, both with Donal and with Galt.

"Honored to have you with us, Protector," he said cheerfully to Donal. "I understand the marshal's proposing you for delegate. You can count on me."

"That's good of you," answered Donal.

"It's good for me," said William. "I like open minds around the Conference table and young minds—no offense, Hendrik—are generally open minds."

"I don't pretend to be anything but a soldier," growled Galt.

"And it's precisely that that makes you dangerous in negotiations," replied William. "Politicians and businessmen always feel more at home with someone who they know doesn't mean what he says. Honest men always have been a curse laid upon the sharpshooter."

"A pity," put in Anea, "that there aren't enough honest men, then, to curse them all." She was looking at Donal.

William laughed.

"The Select of Kultis could hardly be anything else but savage upon us underhanded characters, could you, Anea?" he said.

"You can ship me back to the Exotics, any time I wear too heavily on you," she retorted.

"No, no." William wagged his head, humorously. "Being the sort of man I am, I survive only by surrounding myself with good people like yourself. I'm enmeshed in the world of hard reality—it's my life and I wouldn't have it any other way—but for vacation, for a spiritual rest, I like to glance occasionally over the wall of a cloister to where the greatest tragedy is a blighted rose."

"One should not underestimate roses," said Donal. "Men have died over a difference in their color."

"Come now," said William turning on him. "The Wars of the Roses—ancient England? I can't believe such a statement from you, Donal. That conflict, like everything else, was over practical and property disputes. Wars never get fought for abstract reasons."

"On the contrary," Donal said. "Wars invariably get fought for abstract reasons. Wars may be instigated by the middle aged and the elderly; but they're fought by youth. And youth needs more than a practical motive for tempting the tragedy of all tragedies—the end of the universe—which is dying, when you're young."

"What a refreshing attitude from a professional soldier!" laughed William. "Which reminds me—I may have some business to discuss with you. I understand you emphasize the importance of field troops over everything else in a world's armed forces—and I hear you've been achieving some remarkable things in the training of them. That's information right down my alley, of course, since Ceta's gone in for this leasing of troops. What's your secret, Protector? Do you permit observers?"

"No secret," said Donal. "And you're welcome to send observers to our training program any time, Prince. The reason behind our successful training methods is the man in charge—my uncle, Field Commander Ian Graeme."

"Ah—your uncle," said William. "I hardly imagine I could buy him away from you if he's a relative."

"I'm afraid not," answered Donal.

"Well, well—we'll have to talk, anyway. By heaven—my glass seems to have got itself empty. Anyone else care for another?"

"No thank you," said Anea.

"Nor I," said Donal.

"Well, I will," Galt said.

"Well, in that case, come along marshal," William turned to Galt. "You and I'll make our own way to the bar." They went off together across the lounge. Donal and Anea were left facing each other.

"So," said Donal, "you haven't changed your mind about me."

"No."

"So much for the fair-mindedness of a Select of Kultis," he said ironically.

"I'm not superhuman, you know!" she flashed, with a touch of her younger spirit. "No," she said, more calmly, "there's probably millions as bad as you—or worse—but you've got ability. And you're a self-seeker. It's that I can't forgive you."

"William's corrupted your point of view," he said.

"At least he makes no bones about being the kind of man he is!"

"Why should there be some sort of virtue always attributed to a frank admission of vice?" wondered Donal. "Besides, you're mistaken. William"—he lowered his voice—"sets himself up as a common sort of devil to blind you to the fact that he is what he actually is. Those who have anything to do with him recognize the fact that he's evil; and think that in recognizing this, they've plumbed the depths of the man."

"Oh?" Her voice was scornful. "What *are* his depths, then?"

"Something more than personal aggrandizement. You, who are so close to him, miss what the general mass of people who see him from a distance recognize quite clearly. He lives like a monk—he gets no personal profit out of what he does and his long hours of work. And he does not care what's thought of him."

"Any more than you do."

"Me?" Caught by an unexpected amount of truth in this charge, Donal could still protest. "I care for the opinion of the people whose opinion I care for."

"Such as?" she said.

"Well, you," he answered, "for one. Though I don't know why."

About to say something, and hardly waiting for him to finish so she could say it, she checked suddenly; and stared at him, her eyes widening.

"Oh," she gasped, "don't try to tell me that!"

"I hardly know why I try to tell you anything," he said, suddenly very bitter; and went off, leaving her where she stood.

He went directly out from the cocktail gathering and back to his own suite, where he immersed himself in work that kept him at his desk until the small hours of the morning. Even then, when he at last got to bed, he did not sleep well—a condition he laid to a walking hangover from the drinks at the cocktail gathering.

His mind would have examined this excuse further—but he would not let it.

PROTECTOR III

"... A typical impasse," said William, Prince of Ceta. "Have some more of this Moselle."

"Thank you, no," answered Donal. The Conference was in its second week and he had accepted William's invitation to lunch with him in William's suite, following a morning session. The fish was excellent, the wine was imported—and Donal was curious, although so far they had spoken of nothing of real importance.

"You disappoint me," William said, replacing the decanter on the small table between them. "I'm not very strong in the food and drink department myself—but I do enjoy watching others enjoy them." He raised his eyebrows at Donal. "But your early training on the Dorsai is rather Spartan?"

"In some respects, yes," answered Donal. "Spartan and possibly a little provincial. I'm finding myself sliding into Hendrik Galt's impatience with the lack of progress in our talks."

"Well, there you have it," said William. "The soldier loves action, the politician the sound of his own voice. But there's a better explanation than that, of course. You've realized by now, no doubt, that the things that concern a Conference aren't settled at the Conference table"—he gestured with his hand at the food before him—"but at small tete-a-tetes like these."

"I'd guess then that the tete-a-tetes haven't been too productive of agreements so far." Donal sipped at the wine left in his glass.

"Quite right," said William cheerfully. "Nobody really wants to interfere in local affairs on a world; and nobody really wants to impose an institution on it from the outside, such as the open market, against the will of some of its people." He shook his head at Donal's smile.

"No, no—I'm being quite truthful. Most of the delegates here would just as soon the problem of an open market had never come up at all on New Earth, so that they could tend to their own styles of knitting without being bothered."

"I'll still reserve my judgment on that," said Donal. "But in any case, now we're here, we've got to come to some decision. Either for or against the current government; and for or against the market."

"Do we?" asked William. "Why not a compromise solution?"

"What sort of compromise?"

"Well that, of course," said William, in a frank tone, "is why I asked you to lunch. I feel very humble about you, Donal—I really do. I was entirely wrong in my estimate of you, five years ago. I did you an injustice."

Donal lifted his right hand in a small gesture of deprecation.

"No . . . no," said William. "I insist on apologizing. I'm not a kind man, Donal. I'm interested only in buying what others have to sell— and if a man has ability, I'll buy it. If not—" He let the sentence hang significantly. "But you *have* ability. You had it five years ago, and I was too concerned with the situation to recognize it. The truth of the matter is, Hugh Killien was a fool."

"On that, I can agree with you," Donal said.

"Attempting to carry on with Anea under my nose—I don't blame the girl. She was still a child then, for all her size. That's the way these Exotic hothouse people are—slow growing. But I should have seen it and expected it. In fact, I'm grateful to you for what you did, when I think back on it."

"Thank you," murmured Donal.

"No, I mean that absolutely. Not that I'm talking to you now out of a sense of gratitude alone—I wouldn't insult your credulity with such a suggestion. But I am pleased to be able to find things working out in such a way that my own profit combines with the chance to pay you a small debt of gratitude."

"At any rate, I appreciate it," said Donal.

"Not at all. Now, the point is this," said William, leaning forward over the table, "personally, of course, I favor the open market. I'm a businessman, after all, and there're business advantages to perfectly free trading. But more than open markets, it's important to business to have peace between the stars; and peace comes only from a stable situation."

"Go on," said Donal.

"Well, there are after all only two ways of imposing peace on a community—from the inside or from the outside. We don't seem to be able to do it to ourselves from the inside; so why not try imposing it from the outside?"

"And how would you go about that?"

"Quite simply," said William, leaning back in his float. "Let *all* the worlds have open markets, but appoint a separate, individual supraplanetary authority to police the markets. Equip it with sufficient force to back up its authority against even individual governments if need be— and appoint a responsible individual in charge whom governments will think twice about tangling with." He raised his eyes calmly to Donal across the table and paused to let expectation build to its proper peak in this young man. "How would you like the job?" he asked.

"I?"

Donal stared at him. William's eyes were shrewd upon him. Donal hesitated; and the muscles of his throat worked, once.

"I?" he said. "Why, the man who commanded a force like that would be—" the word faltered and died, unspoken.

"He would, indeed," said William, softly. Across from him Donal seemed to come slowly back to himself. He turned narrowed eyes on William. "Why come to me with an offer like this?" he demanded. "There are older commanders. Men with bigger names."

"And that is just precisely why I come to you, Donal," replied William, without hesitation. "Their stars are fading. Yours is rising. Where will these older men be twenty years from now? On the other hand, you—" he waved a self-explanatory hand.

"I!" said Donal. He seemed to be dazzled. "Commander—"

"Call it Commander in Chief," said William. "The job will be there; and you're the man for the job. I'm prepared, in the name of Ceta, to set up a tax on interplanetary transactions which, because of our volume of trade, we will bear the most heavily. The tax would pay for your forces, and yourself. All we want in exchange is a place on a three-man commission which will act as final authority over you." He smiled. "We could hardly put such power in your hands and turn you loose under no authority."

"I suppose—" Donal was hesitant. "I'd have to give up my position around Procyon—"

"I'm afraid so," said William, frankly. "You'd have to remove any suspicion of conflicting interests."

"I don't know." Donal's voice was hesitant. "I might lose this new post at any time—"

"There's no need to worry about that," said William. "Ceta should effectively control the commission—since we will be paying the lion's share. Besides, a force like that, once established, isn't easy to disband. And if they're loyal to their commander—and your troops, I hear, usually are very much so—you would be in a position to defend your own position, if it came to that."

"Still—" Donal still demurred. "Taking a post like that I'd inevitably make enemies. If something *should* go wrong, I'd have no place to turn, no one would hire me—"

"Frankly," said William, sharply, "I'm disappointed in you, Donal. Are you completely lacking in foresight?" His tone took on a little impatience. "Can't you see that we're inevitably tending toward a single government for all the worlds? It may not come tomorrow, or even in the next decade; but any supraplanetary organization must inevitably grow into the ultimate, central authority."

"In which case," said Donal, "I'd still be nothing but a hired hand. What I want"—his eyes burned a little more brightly—"is to own something. A world . . . why not? I'm equipped to control a world; and defend it." He turned on William. "You'll have *your* position," he said.

William's eyes were hard and bright as two cut stones. He laughed shortly.

"You don't mince words," he said.

"I'm not that kind of man," said Donal, with a slight swagger in his tone. "You should have expected me to see through this scheme of yours. You want supreme authority. Very well. Give me one of the worlds—under you."

"And if I was to give you a world," said William. "Which one?"

"Any fair size world." Donal licked his lips. "Well, why not New Earth?"

William laughed. Donal stiffened.

"We're getting nowhere," said Donal. He stood up. "Thank you for the lunch." He turned and headed for the exit from the lounge.

"Wait!"

He turned to the sound of William's voice. The other man was also on his feet; and he came toward Donal.

"I've underestimated you again," said William. "Forgive me." He placed a detaining hand on Donal's arm. "The truth is, you've only anticipated me. Indeed, I'd intended you to be something more than a hired soldier. But . . . all this is in the future," he shrugged. "I can hardly do more than promise you what you want."

"Oh," said Donal. "Something more than a promise. You could give me a contract, confirming me as the supreme authority on New Earth."

William stared at him and this time he did laugh, loudly and long.

"Donal!" he said. "Excuse me . . . but what good would a contract like that be?" He spread his arms wide. "Some day New Earth may be mine to write you a contract for. But now—?"

"Still, you could write it. It would serve as a guarantee that you mean what you say."

William stopped laughing. His eyes narrowed.

"Put my name to a piece of writing like that?" he said. "What kind of a fool do you take me for?"

Donal wilted a little under the angry contempt in the older man's voice.

"Well . . . at least draw up such a contract," he said. "I suppose I couldn't expect you to sign it. But . . . at least I'd have something."

"You have something that could possibly cause me some slight embarrassment," said William. "I hope you realize it'd do nothing more than that—in the face of my denial of ever having discussed the matter with you."

"I'd feel more secure if the terms were laid out ahead of time," said Donal, almost humbly. William shrugged, not without a touch of scorn.

"Come on then," he said; and led the way across the room to a desk. He pressed a stud on it and indicated a grille. "Dictate," he said.

Later, leaving William's suite of rooms with the unsigned contract in his pocket, Donal came out into the general hotel corridor outside so swiftly that he almost trod upon the heels of Anea, who seemed also to be leaving.

"Where away?" he said. She turned on him.

"None of your business!" she snapped; but an expression which the inescapable honesty of her face would not permit her to hide, aroused his sudden suspicions. He reached out swiftly and caught up her right hand, which was clenched into a fist. She struggled, but he lifted the fingers easily back. Tucked into the nest of her palm was a tiny contact snooper mike.

"You *will* continue to be a fool," he said, wearily, dropping her hand with the mike still in it. "How much did you hear?"

"Enough to confirm my opinion of *you!*" she hissed.

"Bring that opinion to the next session of the Conference, if you can get in," he said. And went off. She stared after him, shaken with a fury, and a sudden pain of betrayal for which she could find no ready or sensible explanation.

She had, she told herself through that afternoon and the evening that followed, no intention of watching the next session personally.

Early the next morning, however, she found herself asking Galt if he would get her a visitor's pass to the Conference room.

The marshal was obliged to inform her that at William's request, this session of the Conference was to be a closed one. He promised, however, to bring her what news he could; and she was forced to rest uneasily content with that.

As for Galt, himself, he went on to the Conference, arriving some few minutes late and discovering that the session had already started. William himself had begun the proposal of a plan that made the Dorsai Marshal of Freiland stiffen to attention, even as he was sitting down on his float at the Conference table.

". . . To be established by a vote of this body," William was saying. "Naturally," he smiled, "our individual governments will have to ratify later, but we all know that to be pretty much a formality. A supraplanetary controlling body—having jurisdiction over trade and contracts, only—in conjunction with a general establishment of the open market, satisfies the requirements of all our members. Also, once this is out of the way, there should be no reason why we should not call upon the present insurgent government of New Earth to resign in favor of the previous, regular government. And I expect that if we call with a united voice, the present heads of state there will yield to our wishes." He smiled around the table. "I'm open for questions and objections, gentlemen."

"You said," spoke up Project Blaine, in his soft, precise voice, "something about a supranational armed force which would enforce the rulings of this controlling body. Such an armed force is, of course, contrary to our principles of individual worldrights. I would like to say right now that I hardly think we would care to support such a force and allow it such freedom if a commander inimical to our interests was at its head. In short—"

"We have no intention of subscribing to a commander other than one with a thorough understanding of our own principles and rights," interrupted Arjean, of St. Marie, all but glaring at the Venusian. Galt's shaggy brows shot together in a scowl.

There was something entirely too pat about the way these two had horned in. He started to look over at Donal for confirmation of this suspicion but William's voice drew his attention back to the Cetan.

"I understand, of course," said William. "However, I think I have the answer to all of your objections." He smiled impersonally at all of them. "The top commanders, as you know, are few. Each one has various associations which might make him objectionable to some one or more of the delegates here. In the main, I would say nothing more than a professional soldier. The prime examples of this, of course, are our Dorsai—"

The glances around the table swung quickly in on Galt, who scowled back to hide his astonishment.

". . . The Marshal of Freiland would, therefore, because of his position in his profession and between the stars, be our natural choice. But—" William barely got the word out in time to stifle objections that had begun to voice themselves from several points around the table, "Ceta recognizes that because of the marshal's long association with Freiland, some of you may not welcome him in such a position. We're therefore proposing another man entirely—equally a Dorsai, but one who is young enough and recently enough on the scene to be considered free of political prejudice—I refer to the Protector of Procyon, Donal Graeme."

He gestured at Donal and sat down.

A babble of voices broke out all at once, but Donal was on his feet, looking tall, and slim, and remarkably young amongst the group of them. He stood, waiting, and the voices finally died down.

"I won't keep you for more than a minute," said Donal, looking around at them. "I agree thoroughly with Prince William's compromise solution to the problem of this Conference; because I most heartily believe the worlds *do* need a watchdog over them to prevent what's just now taken place, from happening." He paused, and looked around the table again. "You see, honored as I am by Prince William's nomination, I can't accept because of something which just recently came into my hands. It names no names, but it promises things which will be a revelation to all of us. I also will name no names, but I would guess however that if this is a sample of what's going on, there are probably half a dozen other such writings being traded around."

He paused to let this sink in. .

"So, I hereby refuse the nomination. And, further, I'm now withdrawing as a Delegate from this Conference in protest against being approached in this manner. I could not accept such a post or such a responsibility except with perfectly clean hands and no strings attached. Good-by, gentlemen."

He nodded to them and stepped back from their stunned silence. About to turn toward the exit, he stopped and pulled from his pocket the unsigned and nameless contract he had received from William the previous day. "Oh, by the way," he said. "This is the matter I was talking about. Perhaps you'd all like to look it over."

He threw it onto the table in their midst and strode out. As he left the lounge behind him, a sudden eruption of voices reached to his ears.

He did not go directly back to his own suite, but turned instead to Galt's. The doorbot admitted him; and he made his way to the main lounge of the suite, striding in with the confidence of one who expects to find it empty.

It was not, however. He had made half a dozen long strides into the room before he discovered another person seated alone at a chess board on a little table, and looking up at his entrance with startled eyes.

It was Anea.

He checked and inclined his head to her.

"Excuse me," he said. "I was going to wait for Hendrik. I'll take one of the other lounges."

"No," she had risen to her feet. Her face was a little pale, but controlled. "I'm waiting for him, too. Is the session over?"

"Not yet," he replied.

"Then let's wait together." She sat down at the table again. She waved a hand at the pieces, presently set up in the form of a knights-castles problem. "You play?"

"Yes," he said.

"Then join me." It was almost an order the way she said it. Donal showed no reaction, however, but crossed the lounge and took a seat opposite her. She began to set out the pieces.

If she expected to win, she was mistaken. Donal won three swift games; but oddly without showing any particular flair or brilliance. Consistently he seemed able to take advantage of opportunities she had overlooked, but which had been there before her in perfect obviousness all the time. The games seemed more a tribute to her obtuseness, than his perception. She said as much. He shrugged.

"You were playing me," he said. "And you should rather have been playing my pieces."

She frowned; but before she had a chance to sort this answer out in her mind, there was the sound of steps outside the lounge, and Galt entered, striding along, fast and excitedly.

Donal and she both rose.

"What happened?" she cried.

"Eh? What?" Galt's attention had been all for Donal. Now the older man swung on her. "Didn't he tell you what happened up to the time he left?"

"No!" She flashed a look at Donal, but his face was impassive.

Quickly, Galt told her. Her face paled and became shadowed by bewilderment. Again, she turned to Donal; but before she could frame the question in her mind, Donal was questioning Galt.

"And after I left?"

"You should have seen it!" the older man's voice held a fierce glee. "Each one was at the throat of everybody else in the room before you were out of sight. I swear the last forty years of behind-the-scenes deals, and the crosses and the double-crosses came home to roost in the next five minutes. Nobody trusted anybody, everybody suspected everybody else! What a bombshell to throw in their laps!" Galt chuckled. "I feel forty years younger just for seeing it. Who was it that actually approached you, boy? It was William, wasn't it?"

"I'd rather not say," said Donal.

"Well, well—never mind that. For all practical purposes it could have been any of them. But guess what happened! Guess how it all ended up—"

"They voted me in as commander in chief after all?" said Donal.

"They—" Galt checked suddenly, his face dropping into an expression of amazement. "How'd you know?"

Donal smiled a little mirthlessly. But before he could answer, a sharp intake of breath made both men turn their heads. Anea was standing off a little distance from them, her face white and stiff.

"I might have suspected," she said in a low, hard voice to Donal. "I might have known."

"Known? Known what?" demanded Galt, staring from one to the other. But her eyes did not waver from Donal.

"So this was what you meant when you told me to bring my opinion to today's session," she went on in the same low, hate-filled voice. "Did you think that this . . . this sort of double-dealing would change it?"

For a second pain shadowed Donal's normally enigmatic eyes.

"I should have known better, I suppose," he said, quietly. "I assumed you might look beyond the necessities of this present action to—"

"Thank you," she broke in icily. "Ankle deep into the mud is far enough." She turned on Galt. "I'll see you another time, Hendrik." And she stalked out of the room.

The two men watched her go in silence. Then Galt slowly turned back to look at the younger man.

"What's between you two, boy?" he asked.

Donal shook his head.

"Half of heaven and all of hell, I do believe," he said; and that was the most illuminating answer the marshal was able to get out of him.

COMMANDER IN CHIEF

Under the common market system, controlled by the United Planetary Forces under Commander in Chief Donal Graeme, the civilized worlds rested in a highly unusual state of almost perfect peace for two years, nine months, and three days absolute time. Early on the morning of the fourth day, however, Donal woke to find his shoulder being shaken.

"What?" he said, coming automatically awake.

"Sir—" It was the voice of Lee. "Special Courier here to see you. He says his message won't wait."

"Right." Groggily, but decisively, Donal swung his legs over the edge of his sleeping float and reached for his trunks on the ordinary float beside him. He gathered them in, brushing something to the floor as he did so.

"Light," he said to Lee. The light went on, revealing that what he had knocked down was his wrist appliance. He picked it up and stared at it with blurry eyes. "March ninth," he murmured. "That right, Lee?"

"That's right," responded the voice of Lee, from across the room. Donal chuckled, a little huskily.

"Not yet the ides of March," he murmured. "But close. Close."

"Sir?"

"Nothing. Where's the courier, Lee?"

"The garden lounge."

Donal pulled on the trunks and—on a second's impulse—followed them with trousers, tunic and jacket, complete outerwear. He followed Lee through the pre-dawn darkness of his suite in Tomblecity, Cassida, and into the garden lounge. The courier, a slim, small, middle-aged man in civilian clothes, was waiting for him.

"Commander—" the courier squinted at him. "I've got a message for you. I don't know what it means myself—"

"Never mind," interrupted Donal. "What is it?"

"I was to say to you 'the gray rat has come out of the black maze and pressed the white lever.' "

"I see," said Donal. "Thank you." The courier lingered.

"Any message or orders, commander?"

"None, thank you. Good morning," said Donal.

"Good morning, sir," said the courier; and went out, escorted by Lee. When Lee returned, he found Donal already joined by his uncle Ian Graeme, fully dressed and armed. Donal was securing a weapons belt around his own waist. In the new glare of the artificial light after the room's darkness, and beside his dark and giant uncle, the paring-down effect of the last months showed plainly on Donal. He was not so much thinned down as stretched drum-tight over the hard skeleton of his own body. He seemed all harsh angles and tense muscle. And his eyes were hollowed and dark with fatigue.

Looking at him, it would be hard not to assume that here was a man either on the verge of psychological and nervous breakdown, or someone of fanatic purpose who had already pushed himself beyond the bounds of ordinary human endurance. There was something of the fanatic's translucency about him—in which the light of the consuming will shows through the frailer vessel of the body. Except that Donal was not really translucent, but glowed, body and all, like one fine solid bar of tempered steel with the white, ashy heat of his consuming but all-unconsumable will.

"Arm yourself, Lee," he said, pointing to a weapons belt. "We've got two hours before sun-up and things begin to pop. After that, I'll be a proscribed criminal on any world but the Dorsai—and you two with me." It did not occur to him to ask either of the other men whether they wished to throw themselves into the holocaust that was about to kindle about him; and it did not occur to the others to wonder that he did not. "Ian, did you make a signal to Lludrow?"

"I did," said Ian. "He's in deep space with all units, and he'll hold them there a week if need be, he says—incommunicado."

"Good. Come on."

As they left the building for the platform awaiting them on the landing pad outside; and later, as the platform slipped them silently through the pre-dawn darkness to a landing field not far from the residence, Donal was silent, calculating what could be done in seven days time, absolute. On the eighth day, Lludrow would have to open his communication channels again, and the orders that would reach him when he did so would be far different from the sealed orders Donal had left him and which he would be opening right now. Seven days— They landed at the field. The ship, a space-and-atmosphere courier N4J, was lying waiting for them, its ground lights gleaming dimly on steady-ready. The forward lock on the great shadowy cylinder swung open as they approached; and a scar-faced senior captain stepped out.

"Sir," he said, saluting Donal, and standing aside to let them enter. They went in and the lock closed behind them.

"Coby, captain," said Donal.

"Yes, sir." The captain stepped to a grille in the wall. "Control room. Coby," he said. He turned from the grille. "Can I show you to the lounge, commander?"

"For the time being," said Donal. "And get us some coffee."

They went on into the courier's lounge, which was fixed up like the main room on a private yacht. And presently coffee was forthcoming on a small autocart from the galley, which scooted in the door by itself and parked itself in the midst of their floats.

"Sit down with us, Cor," said Donal. "Lee, this is Captain Coruna El Man, Cor, my uncle Ian Graeme."

"Dorsai!" said Ian, shaking hands.

"Dorsai!" responded El Man. They smiled slightly at each other, two grimly-carved professional warriors.

"We have met," Ian said.

"Right," said Donal. "Now that introductions are over—how long will it take us to make it to Coby?"

"We can make our first jump immediately we get outside atmosphere," answered El Man, in his rather harsh, grating voice. "We've been running a steady calculation on a standby basis. After the first jump, it'll take a minimum of four hours to calculate the next. We'll be within a light-year of Coby then, and each phase shift will take progressively less calculation as we zero in. Still—five more calculation periods at an average of two hours a period. Ten hours, plus the original four makes fourteen, straight drive and landing in on Coby another three to four hours. Call it eighteen hours—minimum."

"All right," said Donal. "I'll want ten of your men for an assault party. And a good officer."

"Myself," said El Man.

"Captain, I . . . very well," said Donal. "You and ten men. Now." He produced an architectural plan from inside his jacket. "If you'll all look here; this is the job we have to do."

*   *   *

The plan was that of an underground residence on Coby, that planet which had grown into a community from a collection of mines and never been properly terraformed. Indeed, there was a question whether, even with modern methods, it could be. Coby was just too far out from hospitable Procyon, and formed of the wrong materials.

The plan itself showed a residence of the middle size, comprising possibly eighteen rooms, surrounded by gardens and courtyards. The differences, which only began to appear as Donal proceeded to point them out, from an above-ground residence of the ordinary type on other planets, lay in the fakery involved. As far as appearances went, someone in the house, or in one of the gardens, would imagine he was surface-dwelling on at least a terraformed world. But eight-tenths of that impression would be sheer illusion. Actually, the person in question would have ultimate rock in all directions—rock ten meters overhead at the furthest, rock underfoot, and rock surrounding.

For the assault party, this situation effected certain drawbacks, but also certain definite advantages. A drawback was, that after securing their objective—who was a man Donal did not trouble himself to identify—withdrawal would not be managed as easily as it might on the surface, where it was simply a matter of bundling everyone into the nearby ship and jumping off. A great advantage, however, which all but offset the drawback mentioned, was the fact that in this type of residence, the rock walls surrounding were honeycombed with equipment rooms and tunnels which maintained the above-ground illusion— a situation allowing easy ingress and surprise.

As soon as the four with him had been briefed, Donal turned the plans over to El Man, who went off to inform his assault party, and suggested to Lee and Ian that they join him in getting what sleep they could. He took himself to his own cabin, undressed and fell into the bunk there. For a few minutes his mind, tight-tuned by exhaustion, threatened to wander off into speculations about what would be taking place on the various worlds while he slept. Unfortunately, no one had yet solved the problems involved in receiving a news broadcast in deep space. Which was why, of course, all interstellar messages were taped and sent by ship. It was the swiftest and, when you came right down to it, the only practical way to get them there.

However, twenty years of rigid training slowly gained control of Donal's nerves. He slept.

He woke some twelve hours later, feeling more rested than he had in over a year. After eating, he went down to the ship's gym; which, cramped and tiny as it was, was still a luxurious accessory on a deep-space vessel. He found Ian methodically working out in the Dorsai fashion—a procedure the large dark man went through every morning when conditions did not prohibit it, as conscientiously and as nearly without thought as most men shave and brush their teeth. For several minutes Donal watched Ian on the single bar, doing arm twists and stands; and when his uncle dropped to the mat, his wide torso gleaming with perspiration and the reek of it strong in Donal's nostrils, Donal took him on at grips-and-holds.

The results were a little shocking to Ian. That Ian was stronger than he was only to be expected. His uncle was the bigger man. But Donal should have had a clear edge in speed, both because of age and because of his own natural reflexes, which were unusually good. The past year's strain and physical idleness, however, had taken their toll. He broke three holds of his uncle's with barely a fraction of a second to spare; and when he did, at last, throw the older man, it was by the use of a feint he would have scorned to use his senior year at school back on the Dorsai, a feint that took sneaking advantage of a slight stiffness he knew to be the result of an old wound in his uncle's deep-scarred left arm.

Ian could hardly have failed to recognize the situation and the reason behind the slightly unfair maneuver that had downed him. But nothing seemed to matter to him these days. He said nothing, but showered and dressed with Donal; and they went in to the lounge.

Shortly after they sat down there, there was the medication warning, and—a few minutes later—the shock of a phase shift. On the heels of it, El Man came walking into the lounge.

"We're in range, commander," he said. "If you want the news—"

"Please," said Donal.

El Man touched one of the walls and it thinned into transparency through which they could see the three-dimensional image of a Co-byman seated at a desk.

". . . Has been spreading," came the voice of the man at the desk, "following quickly upon the charges brought by the Commission for the Common Market System against Commander in Chief Graeme of the United Planetary Forces. The Com Chief himself has disappeared and most of his deep-space units appear presently to be out of communication and their whereabouts are presently unknown. This development has apparently sparked outbreaks of violence on most of the civilized worlds, in some cases amounting to open revolt against the established governments. The warring factions seem split by a fear of the open markets on the part of the general populaces, and a belief that the charges against Graeme are an attempt to remove what safe-guards on the rights of the individual still remain in effect.

"As far as this office has been informed, fighting is going on on the present worlds—Venus, Mars, Cassida, New Earth, Freiland, As-sociation, Harmony, and St. Marie; and the governments of the follow-ing worlds are known to be deposed, or in hiding—Cassida, New Earth, and Freiland. No outbreaks are reported on Old Earth, Dunnin's World, Mara, Kultis, or Ceta. And there is no present violence here on Coby at all. Prince William has offered the use of his leased troops as a police force to end the disturbances; and levies of Cetan troops are either on, or en route to, all trouble spots at the present time. William has announced that his troops will be used to put down trouble wherever they find it, without respect to what faction this leaves in power. 'Our job is not to take sides,' he is reported as stating, 'but to bring some kind of order out of the present chaos and put out the flames of self-destruction.'

"A late signal received from Old Earth reports that a number of the insurgent factions are agitating for the appointment of William as World's Regent, with universal authority and strong-man powers to deal with the present emergency. A somewhat similar movement puts forward the name of Graeme, the missing Com Chief, for a similar position."

"That's all for now," concluded the man at the desk, "watch for our next signal in fifteen minutes."

"Good," said Donal, and gestured to El Man to shut off the re-ceiver, which the scarred Dorsai captain did. "How long until planet-fall?"

"A couple of hours," replied El Man. "We're a bit ahead of sched-ule. That was the last phase shift. We're on our way in on straight drive now. Do you have co-ordinates on our landing point?"

Donal nodded; and stood up.

"I'll come up to control," he said.

The process of bringing the N4J into the spot on the surface of Coby, corresponding to the co-ordinates indicated by Donal, was a time-consuming but simple procedure—only mildly complicated by Donal's wish to make their visit undetected. Coby had nothing to de-fend in the sense a terraformed world might have; and they settled down without incident on its airless surface, directly over the freight lock to one of the subsurface transportation tunnels.

"All right," said Donal, five minutes later, to the armed contingent of men assembled in the lounge. "This is an entirely volunteer mission,

and I'll give any of you one more chance to withdraw without prejudice if you want to." He waited. Nobody stirred. "Understand," said
Donal, "I want nobody with me simply because he was shamed into
volunteering, or because he didn't want to hesitate when his shipmates
volunteered." Again he waited. There were no withdrawals. "Right,
then. Here's what we'll be doing. You'll follow me down that freight
lock and into a receiving room with a door into a tunnel. However,
we won't be taking the door, but burning directly through one of the
walls to the service section of an adjoining residence. You've all seen
a drawing of our route. You're to follow me, or whoever remains in
command; and anyone who can't keep up gets left behind. Everybody
understand?" He looked around their faces.

"All right," he said. "Let's go."

He led out down the passageway of the ship, out through their lock
and down into the freight lock into the receiving room. This turned
out to be a large, gloomy chamber with fused rock walls. Donal measured off a section of one wall and set his torchmen to work. Three
minutes later they were in the service section of a Coby residence.

The area in which they found themselves was a network of small
tunnels wide enough for only one man at a time, and interspersed with
little niches and crannies holding technical devices necessary to the
maintenance and appearance of the residence. The walls were coated
with a permanent illuminating layer; and, in this cold white light, they
filed along one of the tunnels and emerged into a garden.

The cycle of the residence's system was apparently now set on
night. Darkness held the garden and a fine imitation of the starry heav-
ens glittered overhead. Ahead and to their right was the clump of main
rooms, soft-lit with interior light.

"Two men to hold this exit," whispered Donal. "The rest of you
follow me."

He led the way at a low crouching run through the garden and to
the foot of some wide stairs. At their top, a solitary figure could be
seen pacing back and forth on a terrace before an open wall.

"Captain—" said Donal. El Man slipped away into the bushes
below the terrace. There was a little wait in the artificial night and then
his dark shadow was seen to rise suddenly upon the terrace behind the
pacing figure. They melted together, sagged, and only the shadow of
El Man was left. He beckoned them up.

"Three men to hold this terrace," whispered Donal, as they all
came together at the head of the stairs. El Man told off the necessary
number of the assault party; and they continued on into the lighted
interior of the house.

For several rooms it seemed almost as if they would achieve their objective without meeting anyone other than the man they had come to seek. Then, without anything in the way of warning at all, they were suddenly in the middle of a pitched battle.

As they emerged into the main hall, hand weapons opened up on them from three converging rooms at once. The shipmen, automatically responding to training, dropped to the floor, took cover and returned the fire. They were pinned down.

They were, but not the three Dorsai. Donal, Ian, and El Man, reacting in that particular way that was a product of genes, reflexes and their own special training, and that made the Dorsai so particularly valuable as professional soldiers—these three had responded automatically and in unison a split-second before the fire opened up on them. It was almost as if some small element of precognition had entered the picture. At any rate, with a reaction too quick for thought, these three swung about and rushed one of the enemy doorways, reached it and closed with their opponents within before that opposition could bring their fire to bear. The three found themselves in a darkened room and fighting hand to hand.

Here again, the particular character of the Dorsai soldier paid off. There were eight men in ambush within this particular room and they were all veteran soldiers. But no two of them were a match at hand-to-hand fighting with any single Dorsai; and in addition the Dorsai had the advantage of being able, almost by instinct, to recognize each other in the dark and the melee, and to join forces for a sudden common effort without the need for discussion. The total effect of these advantages made it almost a case of three men who could see fighting eight who were blind.

In Donal's case, he plunged into the dark room right on the heels of El Man and to El Man's left, with Ian right behind *him*. Their charge split the defenders within into two groups and also carried them farther back into obscurity—a movement which the Dorsai, by common silent consent, improved on for the purpose of further separating the enemy. Donal found himself pushing back four men. Abandoning three of these to Ian behind him under the simple common-sense precept that you fight best when you fight only one man at a time, he dove in almost at the level of his opponent's knees, tackled him, and they went down and rolled over together, Donal taking advantage of the opportunity to break the other soldier's back in the process.

He continued his roll and came up, pivoting and instinctively sidestepping. A dark body flung past him—but that instinct spoken of before warned him that it was El Man, flinging himself clear across the room to aid the general confusion. Donal reversed his field and went back the way from which El Man had come. He came up against an opponent plunging forward with a knife held low, slipped the knife, chopped at the man's neck with the calloused edge of his hand—but missed a clean killing stroke and only broke the man's collar bone. Leaving that opponent however in the interests of keeping on the move, Donal spun off to the right, cornered another man against the wall and crushed this one's windpipe with a stiff-fingered jab. Rebounding from the wall and spinning back into the center of the room, his ears told him that El Man was finishing off one opponent and Ian was engaged with the remaining two. Going to help him, Donal caught one of Ian's men from behind and paralyzed him with a kidney punch. Ian, surprisingly enough, was still engaged with the remaining enemy. Donal went forward and found out why. Ian had caught himself another Dorsai.

Donal closed with both men and they went down in a two-on-one pin, the opponent in a stretcher that held him helpless between Donal and his uncle.

"Shai Dorsai!" gasped Donal. "Surrender!"

"Who to?" grunted the other.

"Donal and Ian Graeme," said Ian. "Foralie."

"Honored," said the strange Dorsai. "Heard of you. Hord Vlaminck, Snelbrich Canton. All right then, let me up. My right arm's broken, anyway."

Donal and Ian let go and assisted Vlaminck to his feet. El Man had finished off what else remained, and now came up to them.

"Hord Vlaminck—Coruna El Man," said Donal.

"Honored," said El Man.

"Honor's mine," replied Vlaminck. "I'm your prisoner, gentlemen. Want my parole?"

"I'd appreciate it," said Donal. "We've got work to do here yet. What kind of contract are you under?"

"Straight duty. No loyalty clause. Why?"

"Any reason why I can't hire you on a prisoner's basis?" asked Donal.

"Not from this job." Vlaminck sounded disgusted. "I've been sold twice on the open market because of a typo in my last contract. Besides," he added, "as I say, I've heard of you."

"You're hired, then. We're looking for the man you're guarding here. Can you tell us where we'll find him?"

"Follow me," said Vlaminck; and led the way back through the darkness; and opened a door. They stepped through into a short corridor that led them up a ramp and to another door.

"Locked," said Vlaminck. "The alarm's gone off." He looked at them. Further than this he could not in honor go, even on a hired prisoner's basis.

"Burn it down," said Donal.

He and Ian and El Man opened up on the door, which glowed stubbornly to a white heat, but finally melted. Ian threw a concussion bolt at it and knocked it open.

Within, a large man with a black hood over his head was crouched against the far wall of the room, a miner's heavy-duty ion gun in his hand pointing a little unsteadily at them and shifting from one to the other.

"Don't be a fool," said Ian. "We are all Dorsai."

The gun sagged in the hand of the hooded man. A choked, bitter exclamation came from behind the mask.

"Come on," Donal gestured him out. He dropped the gun and came, shoulders bowed. They headed back through the house.

The fire fight in the hall was still going on as they retraced their footsteps; but died out as they reached the center hall. Two of the five men they had left behind there were able to navigate on their own power and another one could make it back to the ship with assistance. The other two were dead. They returned swiftly to the terrace, through the garden, and back into the tunnel, picking up the rest of their complement as they went. Fifteen minutes later, they were all aboard and the N4J was falling into deep space.

In the lounge, Donal was standing before the hooded man, who sat slumped on a float.

"Gentlemen," said Donal, "take a look at William's social technician."

Ian and El Man, who were present, looked sharply over at Donal— not so much at the words as at the tone in which he had said them. He had spoken in a voice that was, for him, unexpectedly bitter.

"Here's the man who sowed the whirlwind the civilized worlds are reaping at this moment," went on Donal. He stretched out his hand to the black hood. The man shrank from him, but Donal caught the hood and jerked it off. A slow exhalation of breath slipped out between Donal's lips.

"So you sold out," he said.

The man before them was ArDell Montor.

COMMANDER IN CHIEF II

ArDell looked back at him out of a white face, but with eyes that did not bend before Donal's bleak glance.

"I had to have work," he said. "I was killing myself. I don't apologize."

"Was that all the reason?" asked Donal, ironically.

At that, ArDell's face did turn aside.

"No—" he said. Donal said nothing. "It was her," ArDell whispered. "He promised me her."

"*Her!*" The note in Donal's voice made the other two Dorsai take an instinctive step toward him. But Donal held himself without moving, under control. "Anea?"

"She might have taken pity on me—" ArDell whispered to the floor of the lounge. "You don't understand . . . living close to her all those years . . . and I was so miserable, and she . . . I couldn't help loving her—"

"No," said Donal. Slowly, the sudden lightning of his tension leaked out of him. "You couldn't help it." He turned away. "You fool," he said, with his back to ArDell. "Didn't you know him well enough to know when he was lying to you? He had her in mind for himself."

"William? *No!*" ArDell was suddenly on his feet. "Not him—with her! It can't be . . . such a thing!"

"It won't," said Donal, wearily. "But not because it depends on people like you to stop him." He turned back to face ArDell. "Lock him up, will you, captain." El Man's hard hand closed on ArDell's shoulder and turned him toward the entrance to the lounge. "Oh . . . and captain—"

"Sir?" said El Man, turning to face him.

"We rendezvous with all units under Fleet Commander Lludrow as soon as possible."

"Yes, sir." El Man half-pushed, half-carried ArDell Montor out of the room; and, as if symbolically, out of the main current of the history of mankind which he had attempted to influence with his science for William, Prince of Ceta.

The N4J set out to make contact with Lludrow. It was not a thing to be quickly or easily accomplished. Even when it is known where it should be, it is far from easy to track down and pinpoint as small a thing as a fleet of human ships in the inconceivable vastnesses of interstellar space. For the very good reasons that there is always the chance of human error, that a safety margin must always be maintained—better to fall short of your target than to come out too close to it—and that there is, for practical purposes, no such thing as standing still in the universe. The N4J made a phase shift from where it calculated it was, to where it calculated the fleet to be, sent out a call signal and got no answer. It calculated again, signaled again—and so continued until it got first, a very faint signal in response, then a stronger one, and finally, one which permitted communication. Calculations were then matched between the flagship of the fleet and the N4J—and at last a meeting was effected.

By that time, better than three more days of the alloted week of incommunicado had passed. Donal went aboard the flagship with Ian, and took command.

"You've got the news?" was his first question of Lludrow when the two of them were together again.

"I have," said the Fleet commander. "I've had a ship secretly in shuttle constantly between here and Dunnin's World. We're right up to date."

Donal nodded. This was a different problem from the N4J's of finding Lludrow. A shuttle between a planet whose position and direction of movement was well known, and a fleet which knew its own position and drift, could hop to within receiving distance of that same planet in one jump, and return as easily, provided the distance was not too great—as it sometimes was between the various planets themselves—for precise calculation.

"Want to see a digest—or shall I just brief you?" asked Lludrow.

"Brief me," said Donal.

Lludrow did. The hysteria that had followed on the charges of the Commission against Donal and Donal's disappearance had caused the existing governments, already shaky and torn by the open-market dissension, to crumble on all the worlds but those of the Exotics, the Dorsai, Old Earth, and the two small planets of Coby and Dunnin's World. Into the perfect power vacuum that remained, William and the armed units of Ceta had moved swiftly and surely. Pro-tem governments in the name of the general populace, but operating directly under William's orders, had taken over New Earth, Freiland, Newton, Cassida, Venus, Mars, Harmony and Association and held them now in the iron grip of martial law. As William had cornered less sentient materials in the past, he had just prior to this cornered the field troops of the civilized world. Under the guise of training, reassignment, lease, stand-by—and a dozen other paper maneuvers—William had had under Cetan contract actual armies on each of the worlds that had fallen into disorder. All that had been necessary for him was the landing of small contingents, plus officers for the units already present, with the proper orders.

"Staff meeting," said Donal.

His staff congregated in the executive room of the flagship. Lludrow, Fleet Commander, Ian, Field Commander—and half a dozen senior officers under each.

"Gentlemen," said Donal, when they were seated around the table. "I'm sure all of you know the situation. Any suggestions?"

There was a pause. Donal ran his eye around the table.

"Contact Freiland, New Earth—or some place where we have support," said Ian. "Land a small contingent and start a counteraction against the Cetan command." He looked at his nephew. "They know your name—the professionals on all sides. We might even pick up support out of the enemy forces."

"No good," said Lludrow, from the other side of the table. It's too slow. Once we were committed to a certain planet, William could concentrate his forces there." He turned to Donal. "Ship for ship, we overmatch him—but his ships would have ground support from whatever world we were fighting on; and our ground forces would have their hands full trying to establish themselves."

"True enough," Donal said. "What's your suggestion, then?"

"Withdraw to one of the untouched worlds—the Exotics, Coby, Dunnin's World. Or even the Dorsai, if they'll take us. We'll be safe there, in a position of strength, and we can take our time then about looking for a chance to strike back."

Ian shook his head.

"Every day—every hour," he said, "William grows stronger on those worlds he's taken over. The longer we wait, the greater the odds

against us. And finally, he'll have the strength to come after us—and
take us."

"Well, what do you want us to do, then?" demanded Lludrow. "A
fleet without a home base is no striking weapon. And how many of
our men will want to stick their necks out with us? These are professional soldiers, man—not patriots fighting on their home ground!"

"You use your field troops now or never!" said Ian shaking his
head. "We've got forty thousand battle-ready men aboard these ships.
They're my responsibility and I know them. Set them down on some
backwater planet and they'll fall apart in two months."

"I still say—"

"All right. All right!" Donal was rapping with his knuckles on the
table to call them back to order. Lludrow and Ian sat back on their
floats again; and they all turned to look at Donal.

"I wanted you all to have a chance to speak up," he said, "because
I wanted you to feel that we had explored every possibility. The truth
of the matter is that both you gentlemen are right in your objections—
just as there is some merit in each of your plans. However, both your
plans are gambles; long gambles—desperate gambles."

He paused to look around the table.

"I would like to remind you right now that when you fight a man
hand-to-hand, the last place you hit him is where he expects to be hit.
The essence of successful combat is to catch your enemy unawares in
an unprotected spot—one where he is not expecting to be caught."

Donal stood up at the head of the table.

"William," he said, "has for the last few years put his emphasis
on the training of ground troops—field troops. I have been doing the
same thing, but for an entirely different purpose."

He placed his finger over a stud on the table before him and half-
turned to the large wall behind him.

"No doubt all you gentlemen have heard the military truism that
goes—you can't conquer a civilized planet. This happens to be one of
the ancient saws I personally have found very irritating; since it ought
to be obvious to any thinking person that in theory you can conquer
anything—given the necessary wherewithal. The case for conquering
a civilized world becomes then a thing of perfect possibility. The only
problem is to provide that which is necessary to the action."

They were all listening to him—some a little puzzled, others
doubtfully, as if they expected all of what he was saying to turn suddenly into some joke to relieve the tension. Only Ian was phlegmatic
and absorbing.

"Over the past few years, this force, which we officer, has developed the wherewithal—some of it carried over from previous forces, some of recent development. Your men know the techniques, although they have never been told in what way they were going to apply them. Ian, here, has produced through rigorous training the highly specialized small unit of the field forces—the Group, which under ordinary battle conditions numbers fifty men, but which we have streamlined to a number of thirty men. These Groups have been trained to take entirely independent action and survive by themselves for considerable periods of time. This same streamlining has gone up through the ranks—extending even to your fleet exercises, which have also been ordered, with a particular sort of action in mind."

He paused.

"What all this boils down to, gentlemen," he said, "is that we are all about to prove that old truism wrong—and take a civilized world, lock, stock, and barrel. We will do it with the men and ships we have at hand right here, and who have been picked and trained for this specific job—as the planet we are about to take has been picked and thoroughly intelligenced." He smiled at them. They were all sitting on the edges of their floats now.

"That world,"—he pressed the stud that had been under his finger all this time; the wall behind him vanished to reveal the three-dimensional representation of a large, green planet—"is the heart of our enemy's power and strength. His home base—Ceta!"

It was too much—even for senior officers. A babble of voice burst out around the table all at once. Donal paid no attention. He had opened a drawer at his end of the table and produced a thick sheaf of documents, which he tossed on the table before him.

"We will take over Ceta, gentlemen," he said. "By, in a twenty-four hour period, replacing *all* her local troops, *all* her police, *all* her garrisons and militia and law enforcement bodies and arms, with our own men."

He pointed to the sheaf of documents.

"We will take them over piecemeal, independently, and simultaneously. So that when the populace wakes up the following morning they will find themselves guarded, policed and held, not by their own authorities, but by us. The details as to targets and assignments are in this stack, gentlemen. Shall we go to work?"

They went to work. Ceta, large, low-gravity planet that it was, had huge virgin areas. Its civilized part could be broken down into thirty-eight major cities, and intervening agricultural and residential areas.

There were so many military installations, so many police stations, so many armories, so many garrisons of troops—the details fell apart like the parts of a well-engineered mechanism, and were fitted together again with corresponding units of the military force under Donal's command. It was a masterpiece of combat preplanning.

"Now," said Donal, when they were done. "Go out and brief your troops."

He watched them all leave the conference room—all, with the exception of Ian, whom he had detained; and Lee, for whom he had just rung. When the others were gone, he turned to the two still with him.

"Lee," he said, "in six hours every man in the fleet will know what we intend to do. I want you to go out and find a man—not one of the officers—who doesn't think it'll work. Ian"—he looked over at his uncle—"when Lee finds such a man and reports to you, I want you to see that the man is sent up to see me, right away. Is that clear?"

The other two nodded; and went out, to do each his own job in his own fashion. So it was that a disgruntled Groupman from a particular landing force had a surprising meeting and surprisingly cordial chat with his commander in chief, and that they went out together, half an hour later, arm-in-arm, to the control room of the flagship, where Donal requested, and got, a voice-and-picture hookup to all ships.

"All of you," Donal said, smiling at them out of their screens after he had been connected, "have by this time been informed about the impending action. It's the result of a number of years of top-level planning and the best intelligence service we have been lucky enough to have. However, one of you has come to me with the natural fear that we may be biting off more than we can chew. Therefore, since this is an entirely new type of operation and because I believe firmly in the rights of the individual professional soldier not to be mishandled, I'm taking the unprecedented step of putting the coming assault on Ceta to a vote. You will vote as ships, and the results will be forwarded by your captain, as for or against, to the Flagship here. Gentlemen"— Donal reached out an arm and brought the man Lee had discovered into the screen area with him—"I want you to meet Groupman Theiss, who had the courage to stand up like a free man and ask questions."

Caught unawares, and dazzled by the sudden limelight into which he had been thrust, the Groupman licked his lips and grinned a little foolishly.

"I leave the decision to all of you," added Donal, and signaled for the viewing eyes to be cut off.

*   *   *

Three hours later, Groupman Theiss was back on his own ship, astounding his fellow soldiers with an account of what had happened to him; and the votes were in.

"Almost unanimous," reported Lludrow, "in favor of the attack. Only three ships—none of the first line, and none troop carriers—voting against."

"I want those three ships held out of the attack," said Donal. "And a note made of their names and captains. Remind me about that after this is over. All right." He got up from the float where he had been sitting in the Flagship Lounge. "Give the necessary orders, commander. We're going in."

They went in. Ceta had never taken the thought of enemy attack too seriously. Isolated in her position as the single inhabitable planet, as yet largely unexplored and unexploited, that circled her G_8 type sun of Tau Ceti; and secure in the midst of an interstellar maze of commitments that made every other planetary government to some extent dependent upon her good will, she had only a few ships in permanent defensive orbit about her.

These ships, their position and movement fully scouted by Donal's intelligence service, were boxed and destroyed by Donal's emerging fleet almost before they could give warning. And what warning they did give fell on flabbergasted and hardly-believing ears.

But by that time the asault troops were falling planetward, dropping down on city and military installation and police station behind the curtain of night as it swung around the big, but swiftly-turning world.

They came down in most cases almost on top of their targets, for the ships that had sowed them in the sky above had not been hampered in that action by enemy harassment. And the reaction of those on the ground was largely what might have been expected, when veteran troops, fully armed and armored, move in on local police, untried soldiers in training, and men relaxed in garrison. Here and there, there was sharp and bitter fighting where an assault unit found itself opposed to leased troops as trained in war as they. But in that case, reinforcements were speedily brought in to end the action.

Donal himself went down with the fourth wave; and when the sun rose the following morning large and yellow on the horizon, the planet was secured. Two hours later, an orderly brought him word that William himself had been located—in his own residence outside the city of Whitetown, some fifteen hundred kilometers distant.

"I'll go there," said Donal. He glanced around him. His officers were busy, and Ian was off somewhere with an arm of his field troops. He turned to Lee. "Come on, Lee," he said.

They took a four-man platform and made the trip, with the orderly as guide. Coming down in the garden of the residence, Donal left the orderly with the platform, motioned Lee to accompany him, and entered the house.

He walked through silent rooms, inhabited only by furniture. All the residents of the house seemed to have vanished. After some little time, he began to think that perhaps the report had been in error; and that William was gone, too. And then he passed through an archway into a little anteroom and found himself facing Anea.

She met his gaze with a pale but composed face.

"Where is he?" asked Donal.

She turned and indicated a door on the far side of the room.

"It's locked," she said. "He was in there when your men started to land; and he's never come out. Nobody else would stay here with him. I . . . I couldn't leave."

"Yes," said Donal, somberly. He examined the locked door from across the room. "It wouldn't have been easy—for him."

"You care about him?" Her voice brought his head up sharply. He looked at her, seeking some note of mockery in her expression. But there was none. She was honestly questioning.

"I care somewhat for every man," he said. He walked across the room to the door and laid his hand upon it on a sudden impulse, he put his thumb into the finger-lock—and the door swung open.

A sudden coldness blossomed inside him.

"Stay with her," he threw over his shoulder to Lee. He pushed open the door, found himself faced by another, heavier door—but one which also opened to his touch—and went in.

At the end of a long room William sat behind a desk occupied by a mass of papers. He stood up as Donal entered.

"So you're finally here," he said, calmly. "Well, well."

Going closer, Donal examined the man's face and eyes. There was nothing there to evoke such a notion; but Donal had the sudden suspicion that William was not as he should be.

"It was a very good landing. Very good," said William tiredly. "It was a clever trick. I acknowledge the fact, you see. I underestimated you from the first day I met you. I freely admit it. I'm quite conquered—am I not?"

Donal approached to the other side of the desk. He looked into William's calm exhausted face.

"Ceta is in my control," said Donal. "Your expeditionary forces on the other worlds are cut off—and their contracts aren't worth the paper they're written on. Without you to give the orders, it's all over with."

"Yes . . . yes, I thought as much," said William, with the hint of a sigh. "You're my doom, you know—my weird. I should have recognized it earlier. A force like mine among men must be balanced. I thought it would be balanced with numbers; but it wasn't." He looked at Donal with such a strange, searching expression that Donal's eyes narrowed.

"You're not well," said Donal.

"No, I'm not well." William rubbed his eyes, wearily. "I've been working too hard lately—and to no purpose. Montor's calculations were foolproof; but the more perfect my plan, the more perfectly it always went awry. I hate you, you know," said William, emotionlessly, dropping his hand and looking up at Donal again. "No one in all the history of man has ever hated the way I hate you."

"Come along," said Donal, going around the desk toward him. "I'll take you to someone who can help you—"

"No. Wait—" William held up his hand and backed away from Donal. Donal stopped. "I've got something to show you first. I saw the end the minute I got reports your men were landing. I've been waiting nearly ten hours now." He shivered, suddenly. "A long wait. I had to have something to keep myself occupied." He turned about and walked briskly back to a set of double doors set in a far wall. "Have a look," he invited; and pressed a button.

The doors slid back.

Donal looked. Hanging in the little close area revealed there was something only barely recognizable by what was left of its face. It was, or had been, his brother Mor.

SECRETARY FOR DEFENSE

Flashes of clarity began to return.

For some time, now and again, they had been calling him from the dark corridors down which he walked. But he had been busy, too busy to respond until now. But now—slowly—he let himself listen to the voices, which were sometimes those of Anea, and Sayona, and Ian, and sometimes the voices of those he did not know.

He rose to them reluctantly, slow to abandon the halls of darkness where he traveled. Here was the great ocean he had always hesitated to enter; but now that he was in it, it held him warm, and would have possessed him except for their little voices calling him back to petty things. Yet, duty lay to them, and not to it—that duty that had been impressed on him from his earliest years. The things undone, the things ill-done—and what he had done to William.

"Donal?" said the voice of Sayona.

"I'm here," he said. He opened his eyes; and they took in a white hospital room and the bed in which he lay, with Sayona and Anea and Galt standing beside it—along with a short man with a mustache in the long pink jacket of one of the Exotic psychiatric physicians.

Donal swung his legs over the edge of the bed and stood up. His body was weak from long idleness, but he put the weakness aside the way a man puts aside any irritating, but small and unimportant thing.

"You should rest," said the physician.

Donal looked at him casually. The physician looked away; and Donal smiled, to ease the man.

"Thanks for curing me, doctor," he said.

"I didn't cure you," said the physician, a little bitterly, his head still averted.

Donal turned his glance on the other three; and a sadness touched him. In themselves, they had not changed, and the hospital room was like similar rooms had always been. But yet, in some way, all had dwindled—the people and the place. Now there was something small and drab about them, something tawdry and limited. And yet, it was not their fault.

"Donal" began Sayona, on a strangely eager, questioning note. Donal looked at the older man; and he, like the physician, looked automatically away. Donal shifted his glance to Galt, who also dropped his eyes. Only Anea, when he gazed at her, returned his glance with a child's pure stare.

"Not now, Sayona," said Donal. "We'll talk about it later. Where's William?"

"One floor down . . . Donal—" the words broke suddenly from Sayona's lips in a rush. "What did you do to him?"

"I told him to suffer," said Donal, simply. "I was wrong. Take me to him."

They went slowly—and, on Donal's part, a little unsteadily—out the door and down to a room on the floor below. A man there lay rigid on a bed like the one Donal had occupied—and it was hard to recognize that man as William. For all the asepsis of the hospital, a faint animal smell pervaded the room; and the face of the man was stretched into a shape of inhumanity by all known pain. The skin of the face was tautened over the flesh and bones like cloth of thinnest transparency over a mask of clay, and the eyes recognized no one.

"William—" said Donal, approaching the bed. The glazed eyes moved toward the sound of his voice. "Mor's trouble is over."

A little understanding flickered behind the Pavlovian focusing of the eyes. The rigid jaws parted and a hoarse sound came from the straining throat. Donal put his hand on the drum-tight brow.

"It'll be all right," he said. "It'll be all right, now."

Slowly, like invisible bonds melting away, the rigidity began to melt out of the man before them. Gradually he softened back into the shape of humanity again. His eyes, now comprehending, went to Donal as if Donal's tall form was one light in a cavern of lightlessness.

"There'll be work for you to do," said Donal. "Good work. All you ever wanted to do. I promise you."

William sighed deeply. Donal took his hand from the brow. The eyes dropped closed; and William slept.

"Not your fault," said Donal, absently, looking down at him. "Not your fault, but your nature. I should have known." He turned a little unsteadily, to the others who were staring at him with new eyes. "He'll be all right. Now, I want to get to my headquarters on Cassida. I can rest on the way. There's a great deal to do."

The trip from the Maran hospital where both Donal and William had been under observation, to Tomblecity on Cassida, passed like a dream for Donal. Waking or dreaming, he was still half in that ocean into which at Mor's death he had finally stepped, and the dark waters of which would never entirely leave him now. It was to become finally a matter of living with it—this sea of understanding along the margin of which he had wandered all the young years of his life, and which no other human mind would be able to comprehend, no matter how long his explanation. He understood now why he understood—this much had the shock of Mor's death brought him. He had been like any young animal, hesitant on the edge of the unknown, before his own uncertain desires and the sharp nudge of circumstance combined to tumble him headlong into it.

He had had to learn first to admit, then to live with, and finally to embrace his difference.

It had been necessary that what was uniquely Donal be threatened—first by the psychic shocks of the phase shifts during the attack on Newton; and second by the manner of Mor's dying, for which only he knew how truly he was responsible—in order that he be forced to fight for survival; and fighting, discover fang and use of claw. In that final battle he had seen himself at last, full-imaged in the unplumbed depths; and recognized himself at last for what he was—a recognition no one else would ever be able to make. Anea, alone, would know without needing to understand, what he was; it is Woman's ancient heritage to appreciate without the need to know. Sayona, William, and a few such would half-recognize, but never understand. The rest of the race would never know.

And he—he himself, knowing and understanding, was like a man who could read, lifting the first small book from a library the shelves of which stretched off and away to infinity. A child in a taller land.

Anea, Sayona, Galt and the others came with him back to Tomblecity. He did not have to ask them to come with him. Now, they followed instinctively.

DONAL

The man was different.

Already, a few people were beginning to say it. And in this fact lay the seeds of a possible difficulty. It was necessary, considered Donal, that a means be taken to lightning-rod such a recognition, and render it harmless.

He stood in that position which was becoming very common with him of late, alone on a balcony of his residence outside Tomblecity, hands clasped behind his back like a soldier at parade rest, gazing out toward the Milky Way and the unknown stars. He heard Anea come up behind him.

"Sayona's here," she said.

He did not turn. And after a moment she spoke again.

"Do you want me to talk to him by myself?" she asked.

"For a little while," answered Donal, still without moving. He heard her footsteps move away from him into the bigness of the lounge behind him. He lost himself in the stars again; and, after a moment, there was the sound of a man's voice and a murmur of conversation between it and Anea's. At this distance, their words were indistinguishable; but Donal did not have to hear the words to know what they were saying.

Eight months had gone by since he had opened his eyes onto the full universe that was exposed to his view alone. *Eight months*, thought Donal to himself. And in that short time, order had been returned to the civilized worlds. A parliament of peoples had been formed with an interiorly elected council of thirty-two Senior Representatives, two for each world. Today, here on Cassida, that parliament had voted on its choice for a permanent Secretary for Defense—

Donal's mind reached out and enclosed the problem of what Sayona would, this moment, be saying to Anea.

". . . And then he went around the room, a little before the voting." Sayona's voice was now murmuring in the lounge behind him. "He said a word here, and a word there—nothing important. But when he was done, he had them in the palm of his hand. It was just as it was last month when he mingled with the delegates to the full parliament."

"Yes," replied Anea. "I can see it how it was."

"Do you understand?" asked Sayona, looking at her keenly.

"No," she said, serenely. "But I've seen it. He blazes—*blazes*—like an atomic flare among a field full of little campfires. Their small lights fade when they get too close to him. And he hoods his light, when he's amongst them, to keep from blinding them."

"Then you're not sorry—?"

"Sorry!" Her happy laugh tore his question to foolish ribbons.

"I know," said Sayona, soberly, "what effect he has on men. And I can guess his effect on other women. Are you sure you've got no regrets?"

"How could I?" But she looked at him suddenly, questioningly. "What do you mean?"

"That's why I've come tonight," said Sayona. "I've got something to tell you . . . if I can ask you a question after I'm through?"

"What kind of question?" she queried sharply.

"Let me tell you first," he said. "Then you can answer or not, whichever you like. It's nothing that can touch you—now. Only I should have told you before. I'm afraid I've put it off, until . . . well, until there was no more putting off possible. What do you know about your own gene history, Anea?"

"Why," she looked at him, "I know all about it."

"Not this part," said Sayona. "You know you were bred for certain things—" He put one old, slim hand on the edge of her float in a gesture that begged for understanding.

"Yes. Mind and body," she answered, watching him.

"And more," said Sayona. "It's hard to explain in a moment. But you know what was behind Montor's science, don't you? It treated the human race as a whole, as a single social entity, self-repairing in the sense that as its individual components die off they are replaced by the birth of new components. Such an entity is manipulable under statistical pressures, in somewhat the same manner that a human being may be manipulated by physical and emotional pressures. Increase the temperature of a room in which a man stands, and he will take off his jacket. This was William's key to power."

"But—" she stared at him. "*I'm* an individual—"

"No, no. Wait," Sayona held up his hand. "That was *Montor's* science. Ours on the Exotics had somewhat the same basis, but a differing viewpoint. We regarded the race as manipulable through its individuals, as an entity in a constant state of growth and evolution by reason of the birth of improved individuals among the mass that constituted it. Gene-selection, we believed, was the key to this—both natural or accidental, and controlled."

"But it is!" said Anea.

"No," Sayona shook his head slowly. "We were wrong. Manipulation by that approach is not truly possible; only analysis and explanation. It is adequate for an historian, for the meditative philosopher. And such, Anea, have we of the Exotics been, wherefore it seemed not only valid, but complete, to us.

"But manipulation by that means is possible only in small measure—very small. The race is not controllable from within the race; such gene-selection as we did could use only those characteristics which we *already* knew and understood. And it repelled us from those genes which we detected, and could not understand, and, of course, we could not work with ones we did not know existed, or could exist.

"We were, without seeing the fact, crippled both at the beginning and the end; we had only the middle. We could not conceive of characteristics to breed toward—goals—which were not already presented to us, and already understood by us. That was the proper end, however—truly new characteristics. And the beginning was, necessarily, truly new genes, and gene-combinations.

"The problem was stated long ago; we deceived ourselves that the statement was not meaningful. Simply, it is this; could a congress of gorillas, gathered to plan the breeding of the supergorilla, plan a human being? Discard the line of development of mightier muscles, stronger and longer teeth, greater specialization to master their tropical environment?

"Manipulation of the race from within the race is a circular process. What we can do, the valuable thing we can do, is to stabilize, conserve, and spread the valuable genetic gifts that come to us from outside our own domain.

"William—and you must have known this better than any one else, Anea—belongs to that small and select group of men who have been the conquerors of history. There's a name, you know, for this rare and freakish individual—but a name means nothing by itself. It's only a tag hung on something we never completely understood. Such men are unopposable—they can do great good. But also, usually, an equally great deal of harm, because they are uncontrolled. I'm trying to make you understand something rather complex. We, on the Exotics, spotted William for what he was when he was still in his early twenties. At that time the decision was taken to select the genes that would result in you."

"*Me!*" She stiffened suddenly, staring at him.

"You." Sayona bent his head to her briefly. "Didn't you ever wonder that you were so instinctively opposed to William in everything he did? Or why he was so perversely insistent on possessing your contract? Or why we, back on Kultis, allowed such an apparently unhappy relationship to continue?"

Anea shook her head slowly. "I . . . I must have. But I don't remember—"

"You were intended as William's complement, in a psychological sense." Sayona sighed. "Where his instincts were for control for the sake of controlling, yours were towards goals, purposes, and you did not care who controlled so long as the control was directed toward that purpose. Your eventual marriage—which we aimed for—would have, we hoped, blended the two natures. You would have acted as the governor William's personality needed. The result would have been beneficial . . . we thought."

She shuddered.

"I'd never have married him."

"Yes," said Sayona with a sigh, "you would have. You were designed—if you'll forgive the harsh word—to react at full maturity to whatever man in the galaxy stood out above all others." A little of Sayona's gravity lifted for a moment, and a twinkle crept into his eyes. "That, my dear, was by no means difficult to provide for; it would have been near impossible to prevent it! Surely you see that the oldest and greatest of the female instincts is to find and conserve the strength of the strongest male she can discover. And the ultimate conservation is to bear his children."

"But—there was Donal!" she said, her face lighting up.

"Quite so," Sayona chuckled. "If the strongest male in the galaxy were wrongly directed, misusing his great strength—still, for the sake of the great value of that strength, you would have sought him out. Strength, abilities, are tools; these are important. How they are used is a separate matter.

"But with Donal on the scene . . . Well, he was the ruin of all our theories, all our plans. The product of one of those natural accidents, outside our domain, a chance combining of genes even superior to William's. The blending of a truly great line of thinkers, with an equally great line of doers.

"I failed to realize this, even when we tested him." Sayona shook his head as though to clear it. "Or . . . perhaps our tests were just not capable of measuring the really important characteristics in him. We . . . well, we don't know. It's that that worries me. If we've failed to discover a true mutation—someone with a great new talent that could benefit the race, then we have failed badly."

"Why, what would it have to do with you?" she asked.

"It would be in the area where we are supposed to have knowledge. If a cyberneticist fails to recognize that his companion has a broken bone, he is not culpable; if a physician makes the same mistake, he merits severe punishment.

"It would be our duty to recognize the new talent, isolate it, and understand it, we on the Exotics. It may be that Donal has something he does not recognize himself." He looked at her. "And that is the question I must ask you. You are closer to him than anyone else; do *you* think Donal may have something—something markedly different about him? I don't mean simply his superior genius; that would be simply more of the same kind of thing other men have had; I mean some true ability over and above that of the normal human."

Anea became very still for a long moment, looking beyond rather than at Sayona. Then she looked at Sayona again, and said, "Do you want me to guess? Why don't you ask him?"

It was not that she did not know the answer; she did not know how, or what she knew, nor did she know how to convey it, nor whether it was wise to convey it. But the knowing within her was quietly and completely certain that Donal knew, and would know what should and should not be said.

Sayona shrugged wryly. "I am a fool; I do not believe what all my own knowledge assures me. It was perfectly certain that the Select of Kultis would make such an answer. I am afraid to ask him; knowing that makes the fear no less. But you are right, my dear. I . . . will ask him."

She lifted her hand.

"Donal!" she called.

Out on the balcony he heard her voice. He did not move his eyes from the stars.

"Yes," he answered.

*　　*　　*

There were footsteps behind him, and then the voice of Sayona.
"Donal—"

"You'll have to forgive me," said Donal, without turning. "I didn't
mean to make you wait. But I had something on my mind."

"Quite all right," said Sayona. "I hate to disturb you—I know how
busy you've been lately. But there was a question I wanted to ask."

"Am I a superman?" asked Donal.

"Yes, that's essentially it," Sayona chuckled. "Has somebody else
been asking you the same question?"

"No," Donal was smiling himself. "But I imagine there's some
would like to."

"Well, you mustn't blame them," said Sayona, seriously. "In a
certain sense, you actually are, you know."

"In a sense?"

"Oh," Sayona made a little dismissing gesture with his hand. "In
your general abilities, compared to the ordinary man. But that wasn't
my question—"

"I believe you have said that a name is without meaning in itself.
What do you mean by 'Superman'? Can your question be answered,
if that tag has no meaning, no definition?

"And who would want to be a Superman?" asked Donal in a tone
halfway between irony and sadness, his eyes going to the depth beyond
depth of starspace. "What man would want twenty billion children to
raise? What man would cope with so many? How would he like to
make the necessitous choices between them, when he loved them all
equally? Think of the responsibility involved in refusing them candy
when they shouldn't—but could—have it, and seeing that they went
to the dentist against their wills! And if 'Superman' means a unique
individual—think of having twenty billion children to raise, and no
friend to relax with, complain to, to blow off steam to, so that the next
day's chores would be more bearable.

"And if your 'Superman' were so super, who could force him to
spend his energies wiping twenty billion noses, and cleaning up the
messes twenty billion petulant bratlings made? Surely a Superman
could find some more satisfying use for his great talents?"

"Yes, yes," said Sayona. "But of course, I wasn't thinking of anything so far-fetched." He looked at Donal's back with mild annoyance.
"We know enough about genetics now to realize that we could not
have, suddenly, a completely new version of the human being. Any
change would have to come in the shape of one new, experimental
talent at a time."

"But what if it were an undiscoverable talent?"

"Undiscoverable?"

"Suppose," said Donal, "I have the ability to see a strange new color? How would I describe it to you—who cannot see it?"

"Oh, we'd locate it all right," replied Sayona. "We'd try all possible forms of radiation until we found one you could identify as the color you were seeing."

"But still you wouldn't be able to see it, yourselves."

"Well, no," said Sayona. "But that would be hardly important, if we knew what it was."

"Are you sure?" persisted Donal, not turning. "Suppose there was someone with a new way of thinking, someone who in childhood forced himself to do his thinking within the framework of logic— because that was the only way those around him thought. Gradually, however, as he grows older he discovers that there are relationships for him that do not exist for other minds. He knows, for example, that if I cut down that tree just below us out here in my garden, some years in time, and some light-years in distance away, another man's life will be changed. But in logical terms he cannot explain his knowledge. What good would it do you then, to know what his talent *was*?"

"No good at all, of course," said Sayona, good-humoredly, "but on the other hand it would do him no good at all, either, since he lives in, and is part of, a logical society. In fact, it would do him so little good, he would undoubtedly never discover his talent at all; and the mutation, being a failure, would die aborning."

"I disagree with you," said Donal. "Because I, myself, am an intuitional superman. I have a conscious intuitive process. I use intuition consciously, as you use logic, to reach a conclusion. I can cross-check, one intuition against the other, to find out which is correct; and I can build an intuitive structure to an intuitive conclusion. This is one, single talent—but it multiplies the meaning and the power of all the old, while adding things of its own."

Sayona burst out laughing.

"And since, according to my own argument, this ability would do you so little good that you wouldn't even be able to discover it, it therefore stands that you wouldn't be able to answer my question about being a superman in the affirmative, when I ask it! Very good, Donal. It's been so long since I've had the Socratic method used in argument against me I didn't even recognize it when I came face to face with it."

"Or perhaps you instinctively would prefer not to recognize my talent," said Donal.

"No, no. That's enough," said Sayona, still laughing. "You win, Donal. Anyway, thank you for setting my mind at rest. If we had overlooked a real possibility, I would have held myself personally responsible. They would have taken *my* word for it and—I would have been negligent." He smiled. "Care to tell me what the real secret of your success has been, if it's not a wild talent?"

"I *am* intuitive," said Donal.

"Indeed you are," said Sayona. "Indeed you are. But to be merely intuitive—" he chuckled. "Well, thank you, Donal. You don't know how you've relieved my mind on this particular score. I won't keep you any longer." He hesitated, but Donal did not turn around. "Good night."

"Good night," said Donal. He heard the older man's footsteps turn and move away from him.

"Good night," came Sayona's voice from the lounge behind him.

"Good night," answered Anea.

Sayona's steps moved off into silence. Still Donal did not turn. He was aware of the presence of Anea in the room behind him, waiting.

"Merely intuitive," he echoed to himself, in a whisper. *"Merely—"*

He lifted his face once more to the unknown stars, the way a man lifts his face from the still heat of the valley to the coolness of the hills, in the early part of the long work day when the evening's freedom is yet far off. And the look on his face was one which no living person—not even Anea—had seen. Slowly, he lowered his eyes, and slowly turned; and, as he turned, the expression faded from him. As Anea had said, carefully he hooded the brilliance of his light that he might not blind them; and, turning full around at last, entered once more, and for a little while again, into the habitation of Man.

SOLDIER, ASK NOT

Chapter 1

Μῆνιν ἄειδε, θεά, Πηληϊάδεω ᾿Αχιλῆος—begins the *Iliad* of Homer, and its story of thirty-four hundred years ago. *This is the story of the wrath of Achilles.*—And this is the story of *my* wrath; I, Earthman, against the people of the two worlds so-called The Friendlies, the conscript, fanatic, black-clad soldiers of Harmony and Association. Nor is it the story of any small anger. For like Achilles, I am a man of Earth.

That does not impress you? Not in these days when the sons of the younger worlds are taller, stronger, more skilled and clever than we of the Old World? Then, how little you know Earth, and the sons of Earth. Leave your younger worlds and come back to the Mother Planet, once, and touch her. She is still here and still the same. Her sun still shines on the waters of the Red Sea that parted before the Children of the Lord. The wind still blows in the Pass of Thermopylae, where Leonidas with the Spartan Three Hundred held back the hosts of Xerxes, King of the Persians, and changed history. Here, men fought and died and bred and buried and built for more than five hundred thousand years before your newer worlds were even dreamed of by man. Do you think those five centuries of tens-of-centuries, generation upon generation, between the same sky and soil left *no* special mark on us in blood and bone and soul?

The men of the Dorsai may be warriors above imagining. The Exotics of Mara and Kultis may be robed magicians who can turn a man inside out and find answers outside philosophy. The researchers in hard sciences on Newton and Venus may have traveled so far beyond ordinary humans that they can talk to us only haltingly, nowadays. But we—we duller, shorter, simpler men of Old Earth still have something more than any of these. For we are still the whole being of man, the basic stock, of which they are only the refined parts—flashing, fine-honed, scintillant parts. But parts.

But, if you still are one of those, like my uncle Mathias Olyn, who think us utterly bypassed, then I direct you to the Exotic-supported Enclave at St. Louis, where forty-two years ago, an Earthman named Mark Torre, a man of great vision, first began the building of what a hundred years from now will be The Final Encyclopedia. Sixty years from now will see it too massive and complicated and delicate to endure Earth's surface. You will start to find it then in orbit about the Mother Planet. A hundred years from now and it will—but no one knows for sure what it will do. Mark Torre's theory is that it will show us the back of our heads—some hidden part of the basic Earth human soul and being that those of the younger worlds have lost, or are not able to know.

But see for yourself. Go there now, to the St. Louis Enclave, and join one of the tours that take you through the chambers and research rooms of the Encyclopedia Project; and finally into the mighty Index Room at their very center, where the vast, curving walls of that chamber are already beginning to be charged with leads to the knowledge of the centuries. When the whole expanse of that great sphere's interior is finally charged, a hundred years from now, connections will be made between bits of knowledge that never have been connected, that never could have been connected, by a human mind before. And in this final knowledge we will see—what?

The back of our heads?

But as I say, never mind that now. Simply visit the Index Room—that is all I ask you to do. Visit it, with the rest of the tour. Stand in the center of it, and do as the guide tells you.

—*Listen.*

Listen. Stand silent and strain your ears. Listen—you will hear nothing. And then finally the guide will break the reaching, almost unendurable silence, and tell you why he asked you to listen.

Only one man or woman in millions ever hears anything. Only one in millions—of those born here on Earth.

But none—*no one*—of all those born on the younger worlds who has ever come here to listen has ever heard a thing.

It still proves nothing, you think? Then you think wrong, my friend. For I have been one of those who *heard*—what there was to hear—and the hearing changed my life, as witness what I have done, arming me with self-knowledge of power with which I later turned in fury to plan the destruction of the peoples of two Friendly worlds.

So do not laugh if I compare my wrath to the wrath of Achilles, bitter and apart among the boats of his Myrmidons, before the walls of Troy. For there are other likenesses between us. Tam Olyn is my name and my ancestry is more Irish than otherwise; but it was on the Peloponnesus of Greece that I, like Achilles, grew to be what I became.

In the very shadow of the ruins of the Parthenon, white over the city of Athens, our souls were darkened by the uncle who should have set them free to grow in the sun. My soul—and that of my younger sister, Eileen.

Chapter 2

It was her idea—my sister Eileen's—that we visit the Final Encyclopedia that day, using my new travel pass as a worker in Communications. Ordinarily, perhaps, I might have wondered why she wanted to go there. But in this instance, even as she suggested it, the prospect struck forth a feeling in me, deep and heavy as the sudden note of a gong—a feeling I had never felt before—of something like dread.

But it was not just dread, nothing so simple as that. It was not even wholly unpleasant. Mostly, it resembled that hollow, keyed-up sensation that comes just before the moment of being put to some great test. And yet, it was this—but somehow much more as well. A feeling as of a dragon in my path.

For just a second it touched me; but that was enough. And, because the Encyclopedia, in theory, represented all hope for those Earth-born and my uncle Mathias had always represented to us all hopelessness, I connected the feeling with him, with the challenge he had posed me during all the years of our living together. And this made me suddenly determined to go, overriding whatever other, little reasons there might be.

Besides, the trip fitted the moment like a celebration. I did not usually take Eileen places; but I had just signed a trainee work-contract with the Interstellar News Services at their Headquarters Unit here on Earth. This, only two weeks after my graduation from the Geneva University of Communications. True, that University was first among those like it on the sixteen worlds of men, including Earth; and my scholastic record there had been the best in its history. But such job offers came to young men straight out of school once in twenty years—if that often.

So I did not stop to question my seventeen-year-old sister as to why she might want me to take her to the Final Encyclopedia, on just that particular day and hour she specified. I suppose perhaps, as I look back on it now, I told myself she only wanted to get away from the dark house of our uncle, for the day. And that, in itself, was reason enough for me.

For it had been Mathias, my father's brother, who had taken us in, Eileen and me, two orphan children after the death of our parents in the same air-car crash. And it was he who had broken us during our growing years that followed. Not that he had ever laid a finger on us physically. Not that he had been guilty of any overt or deliberate cruelty. He did not have to be.

He had only to give us the richest of homes, the choicest of food, clothing and care—and make sure that we shared it all with *him*, whose heart was as sunless as his own great, unpierced block of a house, sunless as a cave below the earth's surface that has never felt the daylight, and whose soul was as cold as a stone within that cave.

His bible was the writings of that old twenty-first century saint or devil, Walter Blunt—whose motto was "DESTRUCT!"—and whose Chantry Guild later gave birth to the Exotic culture on the younger worlds of Mara and Kultis. Never mind that the Exotics had always read Blunt's writings with a difference, seeing the message in them to be one of tearing up the weeds of the present, so that there would be room for the flowers of the future to grow. Mathias, our uncle, saw only as far as the tearing; and day by day, in that dark house, he drummed it into us.

But enough about Mathias. He was perfect in his emptiness and his belief that the younger worlds had already left us of Earth behind them to dwindle and die, like any dead limb or atrophied part. But neither Eileen nor I could match him in that cold philosophy, for all we tried as children. So, each in our own way, we fought to escape from him and it; and our escape routes brought us, that day, together to the Exotic Enclave at St. Louis, and the Final Encyclopedia.

We took a shuttle flight from Athens to St. Louis and the subway from St. Louis to the Enclave. An airbus took us to the Encyclopedia courtyard; and I remember that, somehow, I was last off the bus. As I stepped to the circle of concrete, it struck again, that deep, sudden gong-note of feeling inside me. I stopped dead, like a man struck into a trance.

"—Pardon me?" said a voice behind me. "You're part of the tour, aren't you? Will you join the rest over here? I'm your guide."

I turned sharply, and found myself looking down into the brown eyes of a girl in the blue robes of an Exotic. She stood there, as fresh as the sunlight about her—but something in her did not match.

"You're not an Exotic!" I said suddenly. No more she was. The Exotic-born have their difference plain about them. Their faces are more still than other people's. Their eyes look more deeply into you. They are like Gods of Peace who sit always with one hand on a sleeping thunderbolt they do not seem to know is there.

"I'm a co-worker," she answered. "Lisa Kant's my name.—And you're right. I'm not a born Exotic." She did not seem bothered by my penetrating her difference from the robe she wore. She was shorter than my sister, who was tall—as I am tall—for a man from Earth. Eileen was silver-blond, while, even then, my hair was dark. It was the same color as hers when our parents died; but it darkened over the years in Mathias' house. But this girl, Lisa, was brown-haired, pretty and smiling. She intrigued me with her good looks and Exotic robes— and she nettled me a little as well. She seemed so certain of herself.

I watched her, therefore, as she went about rounding up the other people who were waiting for the guided tour through the Encyclopedia; and once the tour itself was underway, I fell into step beside her and got her talking to me, between lecture spots.

She showed no hesitation in speaking about herself. She had been born in the North American Midwest, just outside of St. Louis, she told me. She had gone to primary and secondary schools in the Enclave and became convinced of the Exotic philosophies. So she had adopted their work and their ways. I thought it seemed like a waste of a girl as attractive as herself—and bluntly I told her so.

"How can I be wasting myself," she said, smiling at me, "when I'm using my energies to the full this way—and for the best purposes?"

I thought that perhaps she was laughing at me. I did not like that— even in those days, I was no one to laugh at.

"What best purposes?" I asked as brutally as I could. "Contemplating your navel?"

Her smile went away and she looked at me strangely, so strangely that I always remembered that look, afterward.

It was as if she had suddenly become aware of me—as of someone floating and adrift in a nighttime sea beyond the firm rock shore on which she stood. And she reached out with her hand, as if she would touch me, then dropped her hand again, as if suddenly remembering where we were.

"We are always here," she answered me, strangely. "Remember that. We are always here."

She turned away and led us on through the spread-out complex of structures that was the Encyclopedia. These, once moved into space, she said, speaking to us all now as she led us on, would fold together to form a roughly spherical shape, in orbit a hundred and fifty miles above the Earth's surface. She told us what a vast expense it would be to move the structure into orbit like that, as one unit. Then she explained how, expensive as this was, the cost was justified by the savings during the first hundred years of construction and information-charging, which could be done more economically here on the ground.

For the Final Encyclopedia, she said, was not to be just a storehouse of fact. It would store facts, but only as a means to an end— that end being the establishment and discovery of relationships between those facts. Each knowledge item was to be linked to other knowledge items by energy pulses holding the code of the relationship, until these interconnections were carried to the fullest extent possible. Until, finally, the great interconnected body of man's information about himself and his universe would begin to show its shape as a whole, in a way man had never been able to observe it before.

At this point, Earth would then have in the Encyclopedia a mighty stockpile of immediately available, interrelated information about the human race and its history. This could be traded for the hard science knowledge of worlds like Venus and Newton, for the psychological sciences of the Exotic Worlds—and all the other specialized information of the younger worlds that Earth needed. By this alone, in a multi-world human culture in which the currency between worlds was itself the trading of skilled minds, the Encyclopedia would eventually pay for itself.

But the hope that had led Earth to undertake its building was for more than this. It was Earth's hope—the hope of all the people of Earth, except for such as Mathias, who had given up all hope—that the true payment from the Encyclopedia would come from its use as a tool to explore Mark Torre's theory.

And Torre's theory, as we all should know, was a theory which postulated that there was a dark area in Man's knowledge of himself, an area where man's vision had always failed, as the viewing of any perceptive device fails in the blind area where it, itself, exists. Into man's blind area, Torre theorized, the Final Encyclopedia would be able to explore by inference, from the shape and body of total known knowledge. And in that area, said Torre, we would find something— a quality, ability or strength—in the basic human stock of Earth that was theirs alone, something which had been lost or was not available to the human splinter types on the younger worlds that now seemed to be fast out-stripping our parent breed in strength of body or mind.

Hearing all this, for some reason I found myself remembering the strange look and odd words of Lisa to me earlier. I looked around the strange and crowded rooms, where everything from heavy construction to delicate laboratory work was going on, as we passed; and the odd, dread-like feeling began to come back on me. It not only came back, it stayed and grew, until it was a sort of consciousness, a feeling as if the whole Encyclopedia had become one mighty living organism, with me at its center.

I fought against it, instinctively; for what I had always wanted most in life was to be free—to be swallowed by nothing, human or mechanical. But still it grew on me; and it was still growing as we came at last to the Index Room, which in space would be at the Encyclopedia's exact center.

The room was in the shape of a huge globe so vast that, as we entered it, its farther wall was lost in dimness, except for the faint twinkling of firefly lights that signaled the establishment of new facts and associations of fact within the sensitive recording fabric of its inner surface, that endless surface curving about us which was at once walls, ceiling and floor.

The whole reaching interior of this enormous spherical room was empty; but cantilevered ramps led out and up from the entrances to the room, stretching in graceful curves to a circular platform poised in the midst of the empty space, at the exact center of the chamber.

It was up one of these ramps that Lisa led us now until we came to the platform, which was perhaps twenty feet in diameter.

"... Here, where we're now standing," said Lisa as we halted on the platform, "is what will be known as the Transit Point. In space, all connections will be made not only around the walls of the Index Room, but also through this central point. And it's from this central point that those handling the Encyclopedia then will try to use it according to Mark Torre's theory, to see if they can uncover the hidden knowledge. of our Earth-human minds."

She paused and turned around to locate everyone in the group.

"Gather in closely, please," she said. For a second her gaze brushed mine—and without warning, the wave of feeling inside me about the Encyclopedia suddenly crested. A cold sensation like fear washed through me, and I stiffened.

"Now," she went on, when we were all standing close together, "I want you all to keep absolutely still for sixty seconds and listen. Just listen, and see if you hear anything."

The others stopped talking and the vast, untouchable silence of that huge chamber closed in about us. It wrapped about us, and the feeling in me sang suddenly up to a high pitch of anxiety. I had never been bothered by heights or distances, but suddenly now I was wildly aware of the long emptiness below the platform, of all the space enclosing me. My head began to swim and my heart pounded. I felt dizziness threatening me.

"And what're we supposed to hear?" I broke in loudly, not for the question's sake, but to snap the vertiginous sensation that seemed to be trying to sweep me away. I was standing almost behind Lisa as I said it. She turned and looked up at me. There was a shadow in her eyes again of that strange look she had given me earlier.

"Nothing," she said. And then, still watching me strangely, she hesitated. "Or maybe—something, though the odds are billions to one against it. You'll know if you hear it, and I'll explain after the sixty seconds are up." She touched me lightly, requestingly on the arm with one hand. "Now, please be quiet—for the sake of the others, even if you don't want to listen yourself."

"Oh, I'll listen," I told her.

I turned from her. And suddenly, over her shoulder, behind us, below me, small and far off by that entrance to the Index Room by which we had come in, I saw my sister, no longer with our group. I recognized her at that distance only by the pale color of her hair and her height. She was talking to a dark, slim man dressed all in black, whose face I could not make out at that distance, but who stood close to her.

I was startled and suddenly annoyed. The sight of the thin male figure in black seemed to slap at me like an affront. The very idea that my sister would drop behind our group to speak to someone else after begging me to bring her here—speak to someone who was a complete stranger to me, and speak as earnestly as I could see she was speaking, even at this distance, by the tenseness of her figure and the little movements of her hands—seemed to me like a discourtesy amounting to betrayal. After all, she had talked me into coming.

The hair on the back of my neck rose, a cold wave of anger rose in me. It was ridiculous; at that distance not even the best human ears ever born could have overheard their conversation, but I found myself straining against the enclosing silence of the vast room, trying to make out what it was they could be talking about.

And then—imperceptibly, but growing rapidly louder—I began to hear. Something.

Not my sister's voice, or the voice of the stranger, whoever he was. It was some distant, harsh voice of a man speaking in a language a little like Latin, but with dropped vowels and rolled *r*'s that gave his talk a mutter, like the rapid rolling of the summer thunder that accompanies heat lightning. And it grew, not so much louder, as closer—and then I heard another voice, answering it.

And then another voice. And another, and another and another.

Roaring, shouting, leaping, like an avalanche, the voices leaped suddenly upon me from every direction, growing wildly greater in number every second, doubling and redoubling—all the voices in all the languages of all the world, all the voices that had ever been in the world—and more than that. More—and more—and more.

They shouted in my ear, babbling, crying, laughing, cursing, ordering, submitting—but not merging, as such a multitude should, at last into one voiceless, if mighty, thunder like the roar of a waterfall. More and more as they grew, they still remained all separate. *I heard each one! Each one* of those millions, those billions of men's and women's voices shouted individually in my ears.

And the tumult lifted me at last as a feather is lifted on the breast of a hurricane, swirling me up and away out of my senses into a raging cataract of unconsciousness.

Chapter 3

I remember I did not want to wake up. It seemed to me I had been on a far voyage, that I had been away a long time. But when, at last, reluctantly, I opened my eyes, I was lying on the floor of the chamber and only Lisa Kant was bending over me. Some of the others in our party had not yet finished turning around to see what had happened to me.

Lisa was raising my head from the floor.

"You *heard*!" she was saying, urgently and low-voiced, almost in my ear. "What did you hear?"

"Hear?" I shook my head, dazedly, remembering at that, and almost expecting to hear that uncountable horde of voices flooding back in on me. But there was only silence now, and Lisa's question. "Hear?" I said. "—them."

"Them?"

I blinked my eyes up at her and abruptly my mind cleared. All at once, I remembered my sister Eileen; and I scrambled to my feet, staring off into the distance at the entrance by which I had seen her standing with the man in black. But the entrance and the space about it was empty. The two of them, together—they were gone.

I scrambled to my feet. Shaken, battered, torn loose from my roots of self-confidence by that mighty cataract of voices in which I had been plunged and carried away, the mystery and disappearance of my sister shook me now out of all common sense. I did not answer Lisa, but started at a run down the ramp for the entrance where I had last seen Eileen talking to the stranger in black.

Fast as I was, with my longer legs, Lisa was faster. Even in the blue robes, she was as swift as a track star. She caught up with me, passed me and swung around to bar the entrance as I reached it.

"Where are you going?" she cried. "You can't leave—just yet! If you heard something, I've got to take you to see Mark Torre himself! He has to talk to anyone who ever hears anything!"

I hardly heard her.

"Get out of my way," I muttered, and I pushed her aside, not gently. I plunged on through the entrance into the circular equipment room beyond the entrance. There were technicians at work in their colored smocks, doing incomprehensible things to inconceivable tangles of metal and glass—but no sign of Eileen, or the man in black.

I raced through the room into the corridor beyond. But that, too, was empty. I ran down the corridor and turned right into the first doorway I came to. From desks and tables a few people, reading and transcribing, looked up at me in wonder, but Eileen and the stranger were not among them. I tried another room and another, all without success.

At the fifth room, Lisa caught up with me again.

"Stop!" she said. And this time she took actual hold of me, with a strength that was astonishing for a girl no larger than she was. "Will you stop?—And think for a moment? What's the matter?"

"Matter!" I shouted. "My sister—" and then I stopped. I checked my tongue. All at once it swept over me how foolish it would sound if I told Lisa the object of my search. A seventeen-year-old girl talking to, and even going off from a group with, someone her older brother does not know, is hardly good reason for a wild chase and a frantic search—at least in this day and age. And I was not of any mind to rehearse for Lisa's benefit the cold unhappiness of our upbringing, Eileen's and mine, in the house of my uncle Mathias.

I stood silent.

"You have to come with me," she said urgently after a second. "You don't know how terribly, inconceivably rare it is when someone actually hears something at the Transit Point. You don't know how much it means now to Mark Torre—to Mark Torre, himself—to find someone who's heard!"

I shook my head numbly. I had no wish to talk to anyone about what I had just been through, and least of all to be examined like some freak experimental specimen.

"You have to!" repeated Lisa. "It means so much. Not just to Mark, to the whole project. Think! Don't just run off! Think about what you're doing first!"

The word "think" got through to me. Slowly my mind cleared. It was quite true what she said. I should think instead of running around like someone out of his wits. Eileen and the black-dressed stranger could be in any one of dozens of rooms or corridors—they could even be on their way out of the Project and the Enclave completely. Besides, what would I have said if I had caught up with them, anyway? Demand that the man identify himself and state his intentions toward my sister? It was probably lucky I had not been able to find them.

Besides, there was something else. I had worked hard to get the contract I had signed three days ago, just out of the University, with the Interstellar News Services. But I had a far way to go yet, to the place of my ambitions. For what I had wanted—so long and so fiercely that it was as if the want was something live with claws and teeth tearing inside me—was freedom. Real freedom, of the kind possessed only by members of planetary governments—and one special group, the working Guild members of the Interstellar News Services. Those workers in the communications field who had signed their oath of nonallegiance and were technically people without a world, in guarantee of the impartiality of the News Services they operated.

For the inhabited worlds of the human race were split—as they had been split for two hundred years now—into two camps, one which held their populations to "tight" contracts and the other who believed in the so-called loose contract. Those on the tight-contract side were the Friendly worlds of Harmony and Association, Newton, Cassida and Venus, and the big new world of Ceta under Tau Ceti. On the loose side were ranged Earth, the Dorsai, the Exotic worlds of Mara and Kultis, New Earth, Freiland, Mars and the small Catholic world of Ste. Marie.

What divided them was a conflict of economic systems—an inheritance of the divided Earth that had originally colonized them. For in our day interplanetary currency was only one thing—and that was the coin of highly trained minds.

The race was now too big for a single planet to train all of its own specialists, particularly when other worlds produced better. Not the best education Earth or any other world could provide could produce a professional soldier to match those turned out by the Dorsai. There were no physicists like the physicists from Newton, no psychologists like those from the Exotics, no conscript hired troops as cheap and careless of casualty losses as those from Harmony and Association— and so on. Consequently, a world trained one kind or type of professional and traded his services by contract to another world for the contract and services of whatever type of other professional the world needed.

And the division between the two camps of worlds was stark. On the "loose" worlds a man's contract belonged in part to him; and he could not be sold or traded to another world without his own consent—except in a case of extreme importance or emergency. On the "tight" worlds the individual lived at the orders of his authorities—his contract might be sold or traded at a moment's notice. When this happened, he had only one duty—and that was to go and work where he was ordered.

So, on all the worlds, there were the non-free and the partly free. On the loose worlds, of which as I say Earth was one, people like myself were partly free. But I wanted full freedom, of the sort only available to me as a Guild member. Once accepted into the Guild, this freedom would be mine. For the contract for my services would belong to the News Services, itself, during the rest of my lifetime.

No world after that would be able to judge me or sell my services, against my will, to some other planet to which it owed a deficit of trained personnel. It was true that Earth, unlike Newton, Cassida, Ceta and some of the others, was proud of the fact that it had never needed to trade off its university graduates in blocks for people with the special trainings of the younger worlds. But, like all the planets, Earth held the right to do so if it should ever become necessary—and there were plenty of stories of individual instances.

So, my goal and my hunger for freedom, which the years under the roof of Mathias had nourished in me, could be filled only by acceptance into the News Services. And in spite of my scholastic record, good as it was, that was still a far, hard, chancy goal to reach. I would need to overlook nothing that could help me to it; and it came to me now that refusing to see Mark Torre might well be to throw away a chance at such help.

"You're right," I said to Lisa. "I'll go and see him. Of course. I'll see him. Where do I go?"

"I'll take you," she answered. "Just let me phone ahead." She went a few steps away from me and spoke quietly into the small phone on her ring finger. Then she came back and led me off.

"What about the others?" I asked, suddenly remembering the rest of our party back in the Index Room.

"I've asked someone else to take them over for the rest of the tour," Lisa answered without looking at me. "This way."

She led me through a doorway off the hall and into a small light-maze. For a moment this surprised me and then I realized that Mark Torre, like anyone in the public eye constantly, would need protection from possibly dangerous crackpots and cranks. We came out of the maze into a small empty room, and stopped.

The room moved—in what direction, I could not say—and then stopped.

"This way," said Lisa again, leading me to one of the walls of the room. At her touch, a section of it folded back and let us into a room furnished like a study, but equipped with a control desk, behind which sat an elderly man. It was Mark Torre, as I had often seen him pictured in the news.

He was not as old in appearance as his age might have made him appear—he was past eighty at the time—but his face was gray and sick-looking. His clothes sat loosely on his big bones, as if he had weighed more once than he did now. His two really extraordinarily large hands lay limply on the little flat space before the console keys, their gray knuckles swollen and enlarged by what I later learned was an obscure disease of the joints called arthritis.

He did not get up when we came in, but his voice was surprisingly clear and young when he spoke and his eyes glowed at me with something like scarcely contained joy. Still he made us sit and wait, until after a few minutes another door to the room opened and there came in a middle-aged man from one of the Exotic worlds—an Exotic-born, with penetrating hazel-colored eyes in his smooth, unlined face under close-cropped white hair, and dressed in blue robes like those Lisa was wearing.

"Mr. Olyn," said Mark Torre, "this is Padma, OutBond from Mara to the St. Louis Enclave. He already knows who you are."

"How do you do?" I said to Padma. He smiled.

"An honor to meet you, Tam Olyn," he said and sat down. His light, hazel-colored eyes did not seem to stare at me in any way—and yet, at the same time, they made me uneasy. There was no strangeness about him—that was the trouble. His gaze, his voice, even the way he sat, seemed to imply that he knew me already as well as anyone could, and better than I would want anyone to know me, whom I did not know as well in return.

For all that I had argued for years against everything my uncle stood for, at that moment I felt the fact of Mathias' bitterness against the peoples of the younger worlds lift its head also inside me, and snarl against the implied superiority in Padma, OutBond from Mara to the Enclave at St. Louis, on Earth. I wrenched my gaze away from him and looked back at the more human, Earth-born eyes of Mark Torre.

"Now that Padma's here," the old man said, leaning forward eagerly toward me over the keys of his control console, "what was it like? Tell us what you heard!"

I shook my head, because there was no good way of describing it as it really had been. Billions of voices, speaking at once, and all distinct, are impossible.

"I heard voices," I said. "All talking at the same time—but separate."

"Many voices?" asked Padma.

I had to look at him again.

"All the voices there are," I heard myself answering. And I tried to describe it. Padma nodded; but, as I talked I looked back at Torre, and saw him sinking into his seat away from me, as if in confusion or disappointment.

"Only . . . voices?" the old man said, half to himself when I was done.

"Why?" I asked, pricked into a little anger. "What was I supposed to hear? What do people usually hear?"

"It's always different," put in the voice of Padma soothingly from the side of my vision. But I would not look at him. I kept my eyes on Mark Torre. "Everyone hears different things."

I turned to Padma at that.

"What did *you* hear?" I challenged. He smiled a little sadly.

"Nothing, Tam," he said.

"Only people who are Earth-born have ever heard anything," said Lisa sharply, as if I should know this without needing to be told.

"You?" I stared at her.

"Me! Of course not!" she replied. "There's not half a dozen people since the Project started who've ever heard anything."

"Less than half a dozen?" I echoed.

"Five," she said. "Mark is one, of course. Of the other four, one is dead and the other three"—she hesitated, staring at me—"weren't fit."

There was a different note to her voice that I heard now for the first time. But I forgot it entirely as, abruptly, the figures she had mentioned struck home.

Five people only, in forty years! Like a body blow the message jarred me that what had happened to me in the Index Room was no small thing; and that this moment with Torre and Padma was not small either, for them as well as myself.

"Oh?" I said; and I looked at Torre. With an effort, I made my voice casual. "What does it mean, then, when someone hears something?"

He did not answer me directly. Instead he leaned forward with his dark old eyes beginning to shine brilliantly again, and stretched out the fingers of his large right hand to me.

"Take hold," he said.

I reached out in my turn and took his hand, feeling his swollen knuckles under my grasp. He gripped my hand hard and held on, staring at me for a long moment, while slowly the brilliance faded and finally went out; and then he let go, sinking back into his chair as if defeated.

"Nothing," he said dully, turning to Padma. "Still—nothing. You'd think he'd feel something—or I would."

"Still," said Padma, quietly, looking at me, "he heard."

He fastened me to my chair with his hazel-colored Exotic eyes.

"Mark is disturbed, Tam," he said, "because what you experienced was only voices, with no overburden of message or understanding."

"What message?" I demanded. "What kind of understanding?"

"That," said Padma, "you'd have to tell us." His glance was so bright on me that I felt uncomfortable, like a bird, an owl, pinned by a searchlight. I felt the hackles of my anger rising in resentment.

"What's this all got to do with you, anyway?" I asked.

He smiled a little.

"Our Exotic funds," he said, "bear most of the financial support of the Encyclopedia Project. But you must understand, it's not *our* Project. It's Earth's. We only feel a responsibility toward all work concerned with the understanding of Man by man, himself. Moreover, between our philosophy and Mark's there's a disagreement."

"Disagreement?" I said. I had a nose for news even then, fresh out of college, and that nose twitched.

But Padma smiled as if he read my mind.

"It's nothing new," he said. "A basic disagreement we've had from the start. Put briefly, and somewhat crudely, we on the Exotics believe that Man is improvable. Our friend Mark, here, believes that Earth man—Basic Man—is already improved, but hasn't been able to uncover his improvement yet and use it."

I stared at him.

"What's that got to do with me?" I asked. "And with what I heard?"

"It's a question of whether you can be useful to him—or to us," answered Padma calmly; and for a second my heart chilled. For if either the Exotics or someone like Mark Torre should put in a demand for my contract from the Earth government, I might as well kiss good-bye all hopes of working my way eventually into the News Services Guild.

"Not to either of you—I think," I said, as indifferently as I could.

"Perhaps. We'll see," said Padma. He held up his hand and extended upward his index finger. "Do you see this finger, Tam?"

I looked at it; and as I looked—suddenly it rushed toward me, growing enormously, blocking out the sight of everything else in the room. For the second time that afternoon, I left the here and now of the real universe for a place of unreality.

Suddenly, I was encompassed by lightnings. I was in darkness but thrown about by lightning strokes—in some vast universe where I was tossed light-years in distance, first this way and then that, as part of some gigantic struggle.

At first I did not understand it, the struggle. Then slowly I woke to the fact that all the lashing of the lightnings was a furious effort for survival and victory in answer to an attempt by the surrounding, ancient, ever-flowing darkness, to quench and kill the lightnings. Nor was this any random battle. Now I saw how there was ambush and defeat, stratagem and tactic, blow and counterblow, between the lightning and the dark.

Then, in that moment, came the memory of the sound of the billions of voices, welling up around me once more in rhythm to the lightnings, to give me the key to what I saw. All at once, in the way a real lightning-flash suddenly reveals in one glimpse all the land for miles around, in a flash of intuition I understood what surrounded me.

It was the centuries-old battle of man to keep his race alive and push forward into the future, the ceaseless, furious struggle of that beastlike, godlike—primitive, sophisticated—savage and civilized— composite organism that was the human race fighting to endure and push onward. Onward, and up, and up again, until the impossible was achieved, all barriers were broken, all pains conquered, all abilities possessed. Until all was lightning and no darkness left.

It was the voices of this continuing struggle down the hundreds of centuries that I had heard in the Index Room. It was this same struggle that the Exotics were attempting to encompass with their strange magics of the psychological and philosophical sciences. *This* struggle that the Final Encyclopedia was designed at last to chart throughout the past centuries of human existence, so that Man's path might be calculated meaningfully into his future.

This was what moved Padma, and Mark Torre—and everyone, including myself. For each human being was caught up in the struggling mass of his fellows and could not avoid the battle of life. Each of us living at this moment was involved in it, as its parts and its plaything.

But with that thought, suddenly, I became conscious that I was different, not just a plaything of this battle. I was something more— potentially an involved power in it, a possible lord of its actions. For the first time, then, I laid hands on the lightnings about me and began to try to drive, to turn and direct their movements, forcing them to my own ends and desires.

Still, I was flung about for unguessable distances. But no longer like a ship adrift upon a storm-wrenched sea, now like a ship close-hauled, using the wind to bear to windward. And in that moment for the first time it came upon me—the feeling of my own strength and power. For the lightnings bent at my grasp and their tossing shaped to my will. I felt it—that sensation of unchained power within me that is beyond description; and it came to me at last that indeed I had never been one of the tossed and buffeted ones. I was a rider, a Master. And I had it in me to shape at least part of all I touched in this battle between the lightnings and the dark.

Only then, at last, I became aware of rare others like myself. Like me they were riders and Masters. They, too, rode the storm that was the rest of the struggling mass of the human race. We would be flung together for a second, then torn measureless eons apart in the next moment. But I saw them. And they saw me. And I became conscious of the fact that they were calling to me, calling on me, not to fight for myself alone, but to join with them in some common effort to bring the whole battle to some future conclusion and order out of chaos.

But everything that was inherent in me rebelled against their call. I had been downtrodden and confounded too long. I had been the lightnings' helplessly buffeted subject for too long. Now I had won to the wild joy of riding where I had been ridden, and I gloried in my power. I did not want the common effort that might lead at last to peace, but only that the intoxicating whirl and surge and conflict should go on with me, like a fury, riding the breast of it. I had been chained and enslaved by my uncle's darkness but now I was free and a Master. Nothing should bring me to put on chains again. I stretched out my grasp on the lightnings and felt that grasp move wider and grow stronger, wider and stronger yet.

—Abruptly, I was back in the office of Mark Torre.

Mark, his aging face set like wood, stared at me. Whitefaced, Lisa also stared in my direction. But, directly before me, Padma sat looking into my eyes with no more expression than he had shown before.

"No," he said, slowly. "You're right, Tam. You can't be any help here on the Encyclopedia."

There was a faint sound from Lisa, a little gasp, almost a tiny cry of pain. But it was drowned in a grunt from Mark Torre, like the grunt of a mortally wounded bear, cornered at last, but turning to raise up on his hind legs and face his attackers.

"*Can't?*" he said. He had straightened up behind his desk and now he turned to Padma. His swollen right hand was cramped into a great, gray fist on the table. "He must—he has to be! It's been twenty years since anyone heard anything in the Index Room—and I'm getting old!"

"All he heard was the voices; and they touched no special spark in him. You felt nothing when you touched him," said Padma. He spoke softly and distantly, the words coming out one by one, like soldiers marching under orders. "It's because there's nothing there. No identity in him with his fellowman. He has all the machinery, but no empathy—no power source hooked to it."

"You can fix him! Damn it"—the old man's voice rang like a steeple bell, but it was hoarse to the point of tears—"on the Exotics you can heal him!"

Padma shook his head.

"No," he said. "No one can help him but himself. He's not ill or crippled. He's only failed to develop. Once, some time when he was young, he must have turned away from people into some dark, solitary valley of his own, and over the years that valley's grown deeper and darker and more narrow, until now no one can get down there beside him to help him through it. No other mind could go through it and survive—maybe even his can't. But until he does and comes out the other end, he's no good to you or the Encyclopedia; and all it represents for men on Earth and elsewhere. Not only is he no good, he wouldn't take your job if you offered it to him. Look at him."

The pressure of his gaze all this time, the low, steady utterance of his words, like small stones dropped one after the other into a calm, but bottomless pool of water, had held me paralyzed even while he talked about me as if I were not there. But with his last three words, the pressure from him let up; and I found myself free to speak.

"You hypnotized me!" I flung at him. "I didn't give you any permission to put me under—to psychoanalyze me!"

Padma shook his head.

"No one hypnotized you," he answered. "I just opened a window for you to your own inner awareness. And I didn't psychoanalyze you."

"Then what was it—" I checked myself, abruptly wary.

"Whatever you saw and felt," he said, "were your own awarenesses and feelings translated into your own symbols. And what those were I've no idea—and no way of finding out, unless you tell me."

"Then how did you make up your mind to whatever it was you decided here?" I snarled at him. "You decided it fast enough. How'd you find out whatever it was made you decide?"

"From you," he answered. "Your looks, your actions, your voice as you talk to me now. A dozen other unconscious signals. These tell me, Tam. A human being communicates with his whole body and being, not just his voice, or his facial expression."

"I don't believe it!" I flared—and then my fury suddenly cooled as caution came on me with the certainty that indeed there must be grounds, even if I could not figure them out at the moment, for my not believing it. "I don't believe it," I repeated, more calmly and coldly. "There had to be more going into your decision than that."

"Yes," he said. "Of course. I had a chance to check the records here. Your personal history, like that of everyone Earthborn who's alive at this moment, is already in the Encyclopedia. I looked at that before I came in."

"More," I said grimly, for I felt I had him on the run now. "There was more to it even than that. I can tell. I know it!"

"Yes," answered Padma and breathed out softly. "Having been through this much, you'd know it, I suppose. In any case, you'd learn it soon enough by yourself." He lifted his eyes to focus squarely on mine, but this time I found myself facing him without any feeling of inferiority.

"It happens, Tam," he said, "that you're what we call an Isolate, a rare pivotal force in the shape of a single individual—a pivotal force in the evolving pattern of human society, not just on Earth, but on all the sixteen worlds, in their road to Man's future. You're a man with a terrible capability for affecting that future—for good or ill."

At his words my hands remembered the feel of their grasp on the lightning; and I waited, holding my breath to hear more. But he did not go on.

"And—" I prompted harshly, at last.

"There is no 'and,' " said Padma. "That's all there is to it. Have you ever heard of ontogenetics?"

I shook my head.

"It's a name for one of our Exotic calculative techniques," he said. "Briefly, there's a continually evolving pattern of events in which all living human beings are caught up. In mass, the strivings and desires of these individuals determine the direction of growth of the pattern into the future. But, again as individuals only, nearly all people are more acted upon, than act effectively upon the pattern."

He paused, staring at me, as if asking me if I had understood him so far. I had understood—oh, I had understood. But I would not let him know that.

"Go on," I said.

"Only now and then, in the case of some rare individual," he continued, "do we find a particular combination of factors—of character and the individual's position within the pattern—that combined make him inconceivably more effective than his fellows. When this happens, as in your case, we have an Isolate, a pivotal character, one who has great freedom to act upon the pattern, while being acted upon only to a relatively small degree, himself."

He stopped again. And this time he folded his hands. The gesture was final and I took a deep breath to calm my racing heart.

"So," I said. "I've got all this—and still you don't want me for whatever it is you want me?"

"Mark wants you to take over from him, eventually, as Controller, building the Encyclopedia," said Padma. "So do we, on the Exotics. For the Encyclopedia is such a device that its full purpose and use, when completed, can only be conceived of by rare individuals; and that conception can only be continually translated into common terms, by a unique individual. Without Mark, or someone like him to see its construction through at least until it is moved into space, the common run of humanity will lose the vision of the Encyclopedia's capabilities when it's finished. The work on it will run into misunderstandings and frustrations. It will slow down, finally stall, and then fall apart."

He paused and looked at me, almost grimly.

"It will never be built," he said, "unless a successor for Mark is found. And without it, Earth-born man may dwindle and die. And if Earth-born man goes, the human strains of the younger worlds may not be viable. But none of this matters to you, does it? Because it's you who don't want us, not the other way around."

He stared across the room with eyes that burned with a hazel flame against me.

"You don't want us," he repeated slowly. "Do you, Tam?"

I shook off the impact of his gaze. But in the same moment I understood what he was driving at, and knew he was right. In that same moment I had seen myself seated in the chair at the console before me, chained there by a sense of duty for the rest of my days. No, I did not want them, or their works, on Encyclopedia or anywhere else. I wanted none of it.

Had I worked this hard, this long, to escape Mathias, only to throw everything aside and become a slave to helpless people—all those in that great mass of the human race who were too weak to fight the lightning for themselves? Should I give up the prospect of my own power and freedom to work for the misty promise of freedom for *them*, someday—for them, who could not earn that freedom for themselves, as I could earn my own, and had? No, I would not—I would not, I would have no part of them, of Torre or his Encyclopedia!

"No!" I said harshly. And Mark Torre made a faint, rattling sound deep in his throat, like a dying echo of the wounded grunt he had given earlier.

"No. That's right," said Padma, nodding. "You see, as I said, you've got no empathy—no soul."

"Soul?" I said. "What's that?"

"Can I describe the color of gold to a man blind from birth?" His eyes were brilliant upon me. "You'll know it if you find it—but you'll find it only if you can fight your way through that valley I mentioned. If you come through that, finally, then maybe you'll find your human soul. You'll know it when you find it."

"Valley," I echoed, at last. "What valley?"

"You know, Tam," said Padma more quietly. "You know, better than I do. That valley of the mind and spirit where all the unique creativity in you is now turned—warped and twisted—toward destruction."

"DESTRUCT!"

There it thundered, in the voice of my uncle, ringing in the ear of my memory, quoting, as Mathias always did, from the writings of Walter Blunt. Suddenly, as if printed in fiery letters on the inner surface of my skull, I saw the power and possibilities of that word to me, on the path I wanted to travel.

And without warning, in my mind's eye, it was as if the valley of which Padma had been speaking became real around me. High black walls rose on either side of me. Straight ahead was my route and narrow—and downward. Abruptly, I was afraid, as of something at the deepest depth, unseen in the farther darkness beyond, some blacker-than-black stirring of amorphous life that lay in wait for me there.

But, even as I shuddered away from this, from somewhere inside me a great, shadowy, but terrible joy swelled up at the thought of meeting it. While, as if from a great distance above me, like a weary bell, came the voice of Mark Torre sadly and hoarsely tolling at Padma.

"No chance for us, then? There's nothing at all we can do? What if he never comes back to us, and the Encyclopedia?"

"You can only wait—and hope he does," Padma's voice was answering. "If he can go on and down and through what he has created for himself, and survive, he may come back. But the choice has always been up to him, heaven or hell, as it is to all of us. Only his choices are greater than ours."

The words pattered like nonsense against my ears, like the sound of a little gust of cold rain against some unfeeling surface like stone or concrete. I felt suddenly a great need to get away from them all, to get off by myself and think. I climbed heavily to my feet.

"How do I get out of here?" I asked thickly.

"Lisa," said Mark Torre, sadly. I saw her get to her feet.

"This way," she said to me. Her face was pale but expressionless, facing me for a moment. Then she turned and went before me.

So she led me out of that room and back the way we had come. Down through the light-maze and the rooms and corridors of the Final Encyclopedia Project and at last to the outer lobby of the Enclave, where our group had first met her. All the way she did not say a word; but when I left her at last, she stopped me unexpectedly, with a hand on my arm. I turned back to face down at her.

"I'm always here," she said. And I saw to my astonishment that her brown eyes were brimming with tears. "Even if no one else is— *I'm* always here!"

Then she turned swiftly and almost ran off. I stared after her, unexpectedly shaken. But so much had happened to me in the past hour or so that I did not have the time or desire to try to discover why, or figure out what the girl could have meant by her strange words, echoing her strange words earlier.

I took the subway back into St. Louis and caught a shuttle flight back to Athens, thinking many things.

So wound up I was in my own thoughts that I entered my uncle's house and walked clear into its library before I was aware of people already there.

Not merely my uncle, seated in his high wing chair, with an old leather-bound book spread open, face down and ignored on his knees, and not only my sister, who had evidently returned before me, standing to one side and facing him, from about ten feet away.

Also in the room was a thin, dark young man some inches shorter than myself. The mark of his Berber ancestry was plain to anyone who, like myself, had been required in college to study ethnic origins.

He was dressed all in black, his black hair was cut short above his forehead, and he stood like the upright blade of an unsheathed sword.

He was the stranger I had seen Eileen talking to at the Enclave. And the dark joy of the promised meeting in the valley's depths leaped up again in me. For here, waiting, without my need to summon it, was the first chance to put to use my newly discovered understanding and my strength.

Chapter 4

It was a square of conflict.

So much already of the discovery I had made in the place of lightning was already beginning to work in my conscious mind. But almost immediately, this new acuteness of perception in me was momentarily interrupted by recognition of my own personal involvement in the situation.

Eileen threw me one white-faced glance as she saw me, but then looked directly back at Mathias, who sat neither white-featured nor disturbed. His expressionless, spade-shaped face, with its thick eyebrows and thick hair, still uniformly black although he was in his late fifties, was as cold and detached as usual. He, also, looked over at me, but only casually, before turning to meet Eileen's emotional gaze.

"I merely say," he said to her, "that I don't see why you should bother to ask me about it. I've never placed any restraints on you, or Tam. Do what you want." And his fingers closed on the book that was face down on his knees as if he would pick it up again and resume reading.

"Tell me what to do!" cried Eileen. She was close to tears and her hands were clenched into fists at her sides.

"There's no point in my telling you what to do," said Mathias remotely. "Whatever you do will make no difference—to you or me, or even to this young man, over here—" he broke off and turned to me. "Oh, by the way, Tam. Eileen's forgotten to introduce you. This visitor of ours is Mr. Jamethon Black, from Harmony."

"Force-Leader Black," said the young man turning to me his thin, expressionless face. "I'm on attaché duty here."

At that, I identified his origin. He was from one of the worlds called, in sour humor by the people of the other worlds, the Friendlies.

He would be one of the religious, spartan-minded zealots who made up the population of those worlds. It was strange, very strange it seemed to me then, that of all the hundreds of types and sorts of human societies which had taken seed on the younger planets, that a society of religious fanatics should turn out, along with the soldier type of the Dorsai World, the philosopher type of the Exotics, and the hard-science-minded people of Newton and Venus, to be one of the few distinct great Splinter Cultures to grow and flourish as human colonies between the stars.

And a distinct Splinter Culture they were. Not of soldiers, for all that the other fourteen worlds heard of them most often as that. The Dorsai were soldiers—men of war to the bone. The Friendlies were men of Devotion—if grim and hair-shirt devotion—who hired themselves out because their resource-poor worlds had little else to export for the human contractual balances that would allow them to hire needed professionals from other planets.

There was small market for evangelists—and this was the only crop that the Friendlies grew naturally on their thin, stony soil. But they could shoot and obey orders—to the death. And they were cheap. Eldest Bright, First on the Council of Churches ruling Harmony and Association, could underbid any other government in the supplying of mercenaries. Only—never mind the military skill of those mercenaries.

The Dorsai were true men of war. The weapons of battle came to their hands like tame dogs, and fitted their hands like gloves. The common Friendly soldier took up a gun as he might take up an axe or a hoe—as a tool needing to be wielded for his people and his church.

So that those who knew said it was the Dorsai who supplied soldiers to the sixteen worlds. The Friendlies supplied cannon fodder.

However, I did not speculate upon that, then. In that moment my reaction to Jamethon Black was only one of recognition. In the darkness of his appearance and his being, in the stillness of his features, the remoteness, the somehow *impervious* quality like that which Padma possessed—in all these I read him plainly, even without my uncle's introduction, as one of the superior breed from the younger worlds. One of those with whom, as Mathias had always proved to us, it was impossible for an Earth man to compete. But the preternatural alertness from my just-concluded experience at the Encyclopedia Project was back with me again, and it occurred to me with that same dark and inner joy that there were other ways than competition.

". . . Force-Leader Black," Mathias was saying, "has been taking a night course in Earth history—the same course Eileen was in—at Geneva University. He and Eileen met about a month ago. Now, your sister thinks she'd like to marry him, and go back to Harmony with him when he's transferred home at the end of this week."

Mathias' eyes looked over at Eileen.

"I've been telling her it's up to her, of course," he finished.

"But I want someone to help me—help me decide what's right!" burst out Eileen piteously.

Mathias shook his head, slowly.

"I told you," he said, with his usual, lightless calm of voice, "that there's nothing to decide. The decision makes no difference. Go with this man—or not. In the end it'll make no difference either to you or anyone else. You may cling to the absurd notion that what you decide affects the course of events. I don't—and just as I leave you free to do as you want and play at making decisions, I insist you leave me free to do as I want, and engage in no such farce."

With that, he picked up his book, as if he was ready to begin reading again.

The tears began to run down Eileen's cheeks.

"But I don't know—I don't know what to do!" she choked.

"Do nothing then," said our uncle, turning a page of his book. "It's the only civilized course of action, anyway."

She stood, silently weeping. And Jamethon Black spoke to her.

"Eileen," he said, and she turned toward him. He spoke in a low, quiet voice, with just a hint of different rhythm to it. "Do you not want to marry me and make your home on Harmony?"

"Oh, yes, Jamie!" she burst out. "Yes!"

He waited, but she did not move toward him. She burst out again.

"I'm just not sure it's right!" she cried. "Don't you see, Jamie, I want to be sure I'm doing the right thing. And I don't know—I don't know!"

She whirled about to face me.

"Tam!" she said. "What should I do? Should I go?"

Her sudden appeal to me rang in my ears like an echo of the voices that had poured in on me in the Index Room. All at once the library in which I stood and the scene within it seemed to lengthen and brighten strangely. The tall walls of bookshelves, my sister, tear-streaked, appealing to me, the silent young man in black—and my uncle, quietly reading, as if the pool of soft light about him from the shelves behind him was some magic island moated off from all human responsibilities and problems—all these seemed suddenly to reveal themselves in an extra dimension.

It was as if I saw through them and around them all in the same moment. Suddenly I understood my uncle as I had never understood him before, understood that for all his pretense of reading he had already worked to decide which way I should jump in answer to Eileen's question.

He knew that had he said "Stay" to my sister, I would have gotten her out of that house by main force if necessary. He knew it was my instinct to oppose him in everything. So, by doing nothing, he was leaving me nothing to fight against. He was retreating into his devil-like (or godlike) indifference, leaving me to be humanly fallible, and decide. And, of course, he believed I would second Eileen's wish to go with Jamethon Black.

But this once he had mistaken me. He did not see the change in me, my new knowledge that pointed the way to me. To him, *"Destruct!"* had been only an empty shell into which he could retreat. But I now, with a sort of fever-brightness of vision, saw it as something far greater—a weapon to be turned even against these superior demons of the younger worlds.

I looked across at Jamethon Black now, and I was not awed by him, as I had ceased to be awed by Padma. Instead, I could not wait to test my strength against him.

"No," I said quietly to Eileen, "I don't think you should go."

She stared at me, and I realized that unconsciously she had reasoned as my uncle had, that I must end up telling her to do what her heart wanted. But I had struck her all adrift now; and I went eagerly ahead to anchor my judgment firmly in those things she believed, choosing my words with care.

They came easily to my mind.

"Harmony's no place for you, Eileen," I said gently. "You know how different they are from us, here on Earth. You'd be out of place. You couldn't measure up to them and their ways. And besides, this man's a Force-Leader." I made myself look across sympathetically at Jamethon Black; and his thin face looked back at me, as free of any resentment or pleading for my favor as the blade of an axe.

"Do you know what that means, on Harmony?" I said. "He's an officer in their military forces. At any moment his contract may be sold, away from you. He may be sent places you can't follow. He may not come back for years—or ever at all, if he's killed, which is likely. Do you want to let yourself in for that?" And I added brutally, "Are you strong enough to take that kind of emotional punching, Eileen? I've lived with you all your life and I don't think so. You'd not only let yourself down, you'd let this man down."

I stopped talking. My uncle had not looked up from his book all this time, and he did not look up now; but I thought—and I took a secret satisfaction from it—that his grip upon its covers trembled a little, in betrayal of feelings he had never admitted having.

As for Eileen, she had been staring at me unbelievingly all the time I talked. Now, she gave one heavy gasp that was almost a sob, and straightened up. She looked toward Jamethon Black.

She did not say anything. But that look was enough. I was watching him, too, for some betraying sign of emotion; but his face only saddened a little, in a gentle way. He took two steps toward her, until he was almost standing at her side. I stiffened, ready to shove myself between them if necessary to back up my opinion. But he only spoke to her, very softly, and in that odd, canting version of ordinary speech that I had read that his people used among themselves, but which had never fallen upon my ears before.

"Thou wilt not come with me, Eileen?" he said.

She shook, like a light-stemmed plant in unfirm ground when a heavy step comes by, and looked away from him.

"I can't, Jamie," she whispered. "You heard what Tam said. It's true. I'd let you down."

"It is not true," he said, still in the same low voice. "Do not say you cannot. Say you will not, and I will go."

He waited. But she only continued to stare away from him, refusing to meet his gaze. And then, finally, she shook her head.

He drew a deep breath at that. He had not looked at me or Mathias since I had finished speaking; and he did not look at either of us now. Still without pain or fury visible in his face, he turned and went softly out of the library, and out of the house and my sister's sight forever.

Eileen turned and ran from the room. I looked at Mathias; and he turned a page of his book, not looking up at me. He never referred to Jamethon Black or the incident again, afterward.

Nor did Eileen.

But less than six months later she quietly entered her contract for sale to Cassida and was shipped off to a job on that world. A few months after she arrived she married a young man, a native of the planet named David Long Hall. Neither Mathias nor I heard about it until some months after the marriage had taken place, and then from another source. She, herself, did not write.

But by that time I was as little concerned with the news of it as was Mathias, for my success with Jamethon Black and my sister in that moment in the library had pointed me the way I wanted. My new perception was beginning to harden in me. I had begun to evolve techniques to put it to work to manipulate people, as I had manipulated Eileen, to gain what I wanted; and already I was hot on the road to my personal goal of power and freedom.

Chapter 5

Yet, it turned out that the scene in the library was to stick in my mind like a burr, after all.

For five years, while I climbed through the ranks of the News Service like a man born to succeed, I had no word from Eileen. She still did not write Mathias; and she did not write me. The few letters I wrote her went unanswered. I knew many people, but I could not say I had any friends—and Mathias was nothing. Distantly, in one corner of me, I became slowly aware that I was alone in the world; and that in the first feverish flush of my discovered ability for manipulating people I might well have chosen a different target than the one person on sixteen worlds who might have had some reason to love me.

It was this, five years later, that brought me to a hillside on New Earth, recently torn up by heavy artillery. I was walking down it, for the hillside was part of a battlefield occupied only a few hours since by the mutually engaged forces of the North and South Partitions of Altland, New Earth. The military both of the North and the South consisted of only a nucleus of native forces. That of the rebellious North was over eighty percent of mercenary Commands, hired from the Friendlies. That of the South was more than sixty-five percent of Cassidan levies, hired on contractual balance by the New Earth authorities from Cassida—and it was this latter fact that had me picking my way down among the torn earth and exploded tree trunks on the hillside. Among the levies in this particular command was a young Groupman named Dave Hall—the man my sister had married on Cassida.

My guide was a foot soldier of the loyal, or South Partition Forces. Not a Cassidan but a native New Earthman, a cadreman-runner. He was a skinny individual, in his thirties and naturally sour-minded—as I gathered from the secret pleasure he seemed to take in getting my city boots and Newsman's cloak dirtied up in the earth and underbrush. Now, five years after my moment at the Final Encyclopedia, my personal skills had begun to harden in me, and by taking a few minutes out, I could have entirely rebuilt his opinion of me. But it was not worth it.

He brought me at last to a small message center at the foot of the hill, and turned me over to a heavy-jawed officer in his forties, with dark circles under his eyes. The officer was overage for such a field command and the fatigues of middle age were showing. Moreover, the grim Friendly legions had lately been having a good deal of pleasure with the half-trained Cassidan levies opposing them. It was small wonder he looked on me as sourly as had my guide.

Only, in the Commander's case his attitude posed a problem. I would have to change it to get what I was after. And the rub in changing it was that I had come out practically without data concerning this man. But there had been rumors of a new Friendly push and as time was short I had come here on the spur of the moment. I would have to make up my arguments as I went.

"Commandant Hal Frane!" He introduced himself without waiting for me to speak, and held out a square, somewhat dirty hand brusquely. "Your papers!"

I produced them. He looked them over with no softening of expression. "Oh?" he said. "Probationary?"

The question was tantamount to an insult. It was none of his business whether I was a full-fledged member of the Newsman's Guild, or still on trial as an Apprentice. The point he was making implied that I was probably still so wet behind the ears that I would be a potential danger to him and his men, up here in the front lines.

However, if he had only known it, by that question he had not so much attacked a soft spot in my own personal defenses, as revealed such a spot in his own.

"Right," I said calmly, taking the papers back from him. And I improvised on the basis of what he had just given away about himself. "Now, about your promotion—"

"Promotion!"

He stared at me. The tone of his voice confirmed all I had deduced, one of the little ways people betray themselves by their choice of the accusations they bring to bear on others. The man who hints that you are a thief is almost sure to have a large, vulnerable area of dishonesty in his own inner self; and in this case, Frane's attempt to needle me about my status undoubtedly assumed I was sensitive where he was sensitive. This attempt to insult, coupled with the fact that he was overage for the rank he held, indicated that he had been passed over at least once for promotion, and was vulnerable on the subject.

It was an opening wedge only—but all I needed, now, after five years of practicing my skills on people's minds.

"Aren't you up for promotion to Major?" I asked. "I thought—" I broke off abruptly, and grinned at him. "My mistake, I guess. I must have mixed you up with somebody else." I changed the subject, looking around the hillside. "I see you and your people had a rough time here, earlier today."

He broke in on me.

"Where'd you hear I'd been promoted?" he demanded, scowling at me. I saw it was time to apply a touch of the lash.

"Why, I don't think I remember, Commandant," I said, looking squarely back at him. I paused a minute to let that sink in. "And if I did, I don't suppose I'd be free to tell you. A Newsman's sources are privileged—they have to be, in my business. Just as the military has to have its secrecy."

That brought him to heel. Suddenly he was reminded that I was not one of his infantrymen. He had no authority to order me to tell him anything I didn't wish to tell him. I was a case calling for the velvet glove rather than the iron fist, if he wanted to get anything from me.

"Yes," he said, struggling to make the transition from scowling to smiling as gracefully as possible.

"Yes, of course. You've got to forgive me. We've been under fire a lot here."

"I can see that," I said more sympathetically. "Of course, that's not the sort of thing that leaves your nerves lying limp and easy."

"No." He managed a smile. "You—can't tell me anything about any promotion affecting me, then?"

"I'm afraid not," I said. Our eyes met again. And held.

"I see." He looked away, a little sourly. "Well, what can we do for you, Newsman?"

"Why, you can tell me about yourself," I answered. "I'd like to get some background on you."

He faced back at me suddenly.

"Me?" he said, staring.

"Why, yes," I said. "Just a notion of mine. A human-interest story—the campaign as seen from the viewpoint of one of the experienced officers in the field. You know."

He knew. I thought he did. I could see the light coming back into his eyes, and all but see the wheels turning in the back of his mind. We were at the point where a man of clear conscience would have once again demanded—"Why *me*, for a human-interest story, instead of some other officer of higher rank or more decorations?"

But Frane was not about to ask it. He thought he knew why *him*. His own buried hopes had led him to put two and two together to get what he thought was four. He was thinking that he must indeed be up for a promotion—a battlefield promotion. Somehow, although he could not right now think why, his recent conduct in the field must have put him in line for an extra grade in rank; and I was out here to make my human-interest story out of that. Being nothing but a civilian, he was reasoning, it would not have occurred to me that he, himself, might not yet have heard of the pending promotion; and my ignorance had caused me thoughtlessly to spill the beans on first meeting him.

It was a little disgusting the way his voice and attitude changed, once he had finished working this out to his own satisfaction. Like some people of inferior ability, he had spent his lifetime storing up reasons and excuses to prove that he was really possessed of extraordinary qualities, but that chance and prejudice had combined until now to keep him from his rightful rewards.

He proceeded then to tell me all these reasons and excuses, in the process of informing me about himself; and if I had been actually interviewing him for purposes of reportage I could have convicted him of his small soul and little worth, out of his own words, a dozen times over. There was a whine to his story as he told it. The real money in soldiering was in work as a mercenary, but all the good mercenary opportunities went either to men of the Friendlies, or the Dorsai. Frane did not have either the guts or the conviction to live the hair-shirt life of even a commissioned officer among the Friendlies. And, of course, the only way anyone could be a Dorsai was to be born one. That left only garrison work, cadre-work, officering the standby forces of worlds or political areas—only to be shoved aside for the top command posts when war did come, by the mercenaries born or built and imported for the actual fighting.

And garrison work, needless to say, paid a pittance compared to mercenary wages. A government could sign second-class officer material like Frane to long-term contracts at low salaries and hold them to it. But when the same government wanted mercenaries, it *needed* mercenaries; and every time it needed mercenaries, then quite naturally those who were in the business of laying their lives on the line for cash, drove hard bargains.

But enough about Commandant Frane, who was not that important. He was a little man who had now convinced himself that he was about to be recognized—in the Interstellar News Services at that—as a potentially big man. Like most of his kind he had a wildly inflated view of the usefulness of publicity in furthering a man's career. He told me all about himself, he showed me about the positions on the hillside where his men were dug in; and by the time I was ready to leave, I had him reacting like a well-tuned machine to my every suggestion. So, just as I was about to head back behind the lines, I made it—the one real suggestion I had come here to make.

"You know, I've just had an idea," I said, turning back to him. "Battle Headquarters has given me permission to pick out one of the enlisted men to assist me during the rest of the campaign. I was going to pick out one of the men from Headquarters Pool, but you know, it might be better to get one of the men from your Command."

"One of my men?" He blinked.

"That's right," I said. "Then if there's a request for a follow-up story on you or they want expansion of the original details about the campaign as you've seen it here, I could get the information from him. It wouldn't be practical to chase you all over the battlefield for things like that; otherwise I'd simply have to message back advising that follow-up or expansion wasn't possible."

"I see," he said; and his face cleared. Then he frowned again. "It'll take a week or two to get a replacement up here so that I can let someone go, though. I don't see how—"

"Oh, that's all right," I said, and fished a paper out of my pocket. "I've got authority to pick up anyone I want without waiting for his replacement—if the Commandant lets him go, of course. You'd be a man short for a few days, naturally, but—"

I let him think about it. And for a moment he *was* thinking—with all the nonsense gone out of his head—just like any other military commander in such a position. All the Commands in this sector were understrength after the last few weeks of battle. Another man out meant a hole in Frane's line, and he was reacting to the prospect with the conditioned reflexes of any officer in the field.

Then I saw the prospect of promotion and publicity fight its way back to his attention, and the battle was joined in his head.

"Who?" he said at last, almost more to himself than to me. What he was asking himself was where he could best spare someone. But I took him up on it, as if the question had been all for me.

"There's a boy in your Command called Dave Hall—"

His head came up like a shot. Suspicion leaped into being, plain

and short and ugly in his face. There are two ways to deal with suspicion—one is to protest your innocence, the other, and better, is to
plead guilty to a lesser charge.

"I noticed his name on the Command roster when I was looking
you up at Battle Headquarters, before I came up here to see you," I
said. "To tell the truth, it was one of the reasons I *chose*"—I empha-
sized the word a little, so that he shouldn't miss it—"you for this
writeup. He's a sort of shirt-tail relative of mine, this Dave Hall, and
I thought I might as well kill two birds with one stone. The family's
been after me to do something for the boy."

Frane stared at me.

"Of course," I said, "I know you're short-handed. If he's that valuable to you—"

If he's that valuable to you, my tone of voice hinted, *I won't think
of arguing that you give him up. On the other hand, I'm the man who's
going to be writing you up as a hero-type for the sixteen worlds to
read, and if I sit down to my vocoder feeling you could have released
my relative from the front lines, and didn't—*

He got the message.

"Who? Hall?" he said. "No, I can spare him, all right." He turned
to his command post and barked, "Runner! Get Hall in here—full pack,
weapons and equipment, ready to move out."

Frane turned back to me as the runner left.

"Take about five minutes to get him ready and up here," he said.

It took closer to ten. But I didn't mind waiting. Twelve minutes
later, with our Groupman guide, we were on our way back to Battle
Headquarters, Dave and I.

Chapter 6

Dave had never seen me before, of course. But Eileen must have described me, and it was plain he recognized my name the minute the Commandant turned him over to me. At that, though, he had sense enough not to ask me any foolish questions until we had made it back to Battle Headquarters and gotten rid of that Groupman guiding us.

As a result I had a chance to study him myself on the way in. He did not assay too highly on my first examination of him. He was smaller than I, and looked a good deal younger than the difference in our ages should have made him. He had one of those round, open faces under taffy-colored hair which seem to look boyish right up into middle age. About the only thing that I could see that he seemed to have in common with my sister was a sort of inborn innocence and gentleness—that innocence and gentleness of weak creatures who know they are too weak to fight for their rights and win, and so try to make the best of it by the willingness of their dependence on the good will of others.

Or maybe I was being harsh. I was no denizen of the sheepfold myself. You would rather find me outside, slinking along the fence and cocking a thoughtful eye at the inmates.

But it is true, Dave seemed nothing great to me as far as appearance and character were concerned. I do not think, either, that he was any great shakes mentally. He had been an ordinary programmer when Eileen had married him; and he had worked part time, and she full time, these last five years trying to get him through a Cassidan University schedule in shift mechanics. He had had three years yet of work to go when he fell below the seventy-percentile median on a competitive examination. It was his bad luck that this should happen just at that moment when Cassida was raising its levies for sale to New Earth in the present campaign to put down the North Partition rebels. Away he went, in uniform.

You might think that Eileen had immediately appealed to me for help. No such thing—though the fact that she had not, puzzled me, when I finally heard of it. Though it should not have. She told me, eventually, and the telling stripped my soul and left its bare bones for the winds of rage and madness to howl through. But that was later. Actually, the way I found out about Dave going with the levies for New Earth was because our uncle Mathias, quietly and unexpectedly, died; and I was required to get in touch with Eileen on Cassida about the estate.

Her small share of the estate (contemptuously, even sneeringly, Mathias had left the bulk of his considerable fortune to The Final Encyclopedia Project as testimony that he thought any project concerning Earth and Earthmen so futile that no help could make it succeed) was no use to her unless I could make a private deal for her with some Earth-working Cassidan who had a family back on Cassida. Only governments or great organizations could translate planetary wealth into the human work-contracts that were actually transferable from one world to another. It was so that I learned that Dave had already left her and his native world for the ruckus on New Earth.

Even then, Eileen did not ask me for help. It was I who thought of asking for Dave as my assistant during the campaign and went ahead with it, merely writing to let her know what I was doing. Now that I had begun the deal, I was not at all sure why, myself, and even a little uncomfortable about it, as when Dave tried to thank me, after we finally got rid of our guide and headed in toward Molon, the nearest large city behind the lines.

"Save it!" I snapped at him. "All I've done for you so far's been the easy part. You're going to have to go into those lines with me as a noncombatant, carrying no weapons. And to do that, you've got to have a pass signed by both sides. That isn't going to be easy, for someone who was laying the sights of his spring-rifle on Friendly soldiers less than eight hours ago!"

He shut up at that. He was abashed. He was plainly hurt by the fact that I wouldn't let him thank me. But it stopped him talking and that was all I cared about.

We got orders cut by his Battle Headquarters, assigning him permanently to me; and then finished our ride by platform into Molon, where I left him in a hotel room with my gear, explaining that I'd be back for him in the morning.

"I'm to stay in the room?" he asked, as I was leaving.

"Do what you want, damn it!" I said. "I'm not your Groupman. Just be here by nine in the morning, local time, when I get back."

I went out. It was only after I closed the door behind me that I realized both what was driving him and eating me. He thought we might spend a few hours getting to know each other as brothers-in-law, and something in me set my teeth on edge at the prospect. I'd save his life for him for Eileen's sake, but that was no reason why I had to associate with him.

New Earth and Freiland, as everyone knows, are brother planets under the sun of Sirius. That makes them close—not so close as Venus-Earth-Mars clumping, naturally—but close enough so that from orbit New Earth you can make orbit Freiland in a single shift jump with a good but not excellent statistical chance of reaching your goal with minimum error. For those, then, who aren't afraid of a little risk in travel between the worlds, you can go from one planet to the other in about an hour—half an hour up to orbit station, no time at all for the jump, and half an hour down to surface at the end of the trip.

That was the way I went, and two hours after leaving my brother-in-law, I was showing my hard-wangled invitation to the doorman at the entrance of the establishment of Hendrik Galt, First Marshal of Freiland's battle forces.

The invitation was to a party being held for a man not so well known then as he has since become, a Dorsai (as Galt of course was a Dorsai) Space Sub-Patrol Chief named Donal Graeme. This was Graeme's first emergence into the public eye. He had just completed an utterly foolhardy attack on the planetary defenses of Newton, with something like four or five ships—an attack that had been lucky enough to relieve Newtonian pressure on Oriente, an uninhabited sister world of Freiland and New Earth, and get Galt's planetary forces out of a bad tactical hole.

He was, I judged at the time, a wild-eyed military gambler of some sort—his kind usually were. But my business, happily, was not with him, anyway. It was with some of the influential people who should be at this party of his.

In particular, I wanted the co-signature of the Freiland News Services Department Chief on Dave's papers—not that this would imply any actual protection extended to my brother-in-law by the News Services. That type of protection was extended only to Guild members and, with reservations, to apprentices on trial like myself. But to the uninitiate, like a soldier in the field, it might well look as if News Service protection was implied. Then, in addition, I wanted the signature of someone ranking among the Friendly mercenaries, for Dave's protection, in case he and I should fall in with some of their soldiers on the battlefield during the campaign.

I found the News Services Department Chief, a reasonable pleasant Earthman named Nuy Snelling, without difficulty. He gave me no trouble about noting on Dave's pass that the News Services agreed to Dave's assisting me and signing the message.

"Of course you know," he said, "this isn't worth a hoot." He eyed me curiously, as he handed the pass back. "This Dave Hall some friend of yours?"

"Brother-in-law," I answered.

"Hmm," he said, raising his eyebrows. "Well, good luck." And he turned away to talk to an Exotic in blue robes—who, with a sudden shock, I recognized as Padma.

The shock was severe enough so that I committed an imprudence I had not been guilty of for several years, at least, that of speaking without thinking.

"Padma—OutBond!" I said, the words jolted from me. "What are you doing here?"

Snelling, stepping back so as to have both of us in view at once, raised his eyebrows again. But Padma answered before my superior in the Services could take me to task for a pretty obvious rudeness. Padma was under no compulsion to account to me for his whereabouts. But he did not seem to take offense.

"I could ask you the same thing, Tam," he said, smiling.

I had my wits back by that time.

"I go where the news is," I answered. It was the stock News Services answer. But Padma chose to take it literally.

"And, in a sense, so do I," he said. "Remember I spoke to you once about a pattern, Tam? This place and moment is a locus."

I did not know what he was talking about; but having begun the conversation, I could not let go of it easily.

"Is that so?" I said smiling. "Nothing to do with me, I hope?"

"Yes," he said. And all at once I was aware once more of his hazel eyes, looking at and deep into me. "But more with Donal Graeme."

"That's only fair, I suppose," I said, "since the party's in his honor." And I laughed, while trying to think of some excuse to escape. Padma's presence was making the skin crawl at the back of my neck. It was as if he had some occult effect on me, so that I could not think clearly when he was present. "By the way, whatever happened to that girl who brought me to Mark Torre's office that day? Lisa . . . Kant, I think her name was."

"Yes, Lisa," said Padma, his eyes steady on me. "She's here with me. She's my personal secretary now. I imagine you'll bump into her shortly. She's concerned about saving you."

"Saving him?" put in Snelling, lightly, but interestedly enough. It was his job, as it was the job of all full Guild members, to observe the Apprentices for anything that might affect their acceptability into the Guild.

"From himself," said Padma, his hazel eyes still watching me, as smoky and yellow as the eyes of a god or a demon.

"Then, I'd better see if I can't look her up myself and let her get on with it," I said lightly in my turn, grasping at the opportunity to get away. "I'll see you both later perhaps."

"Perhaps," said Snelling. And I went off.

As soon as I had lost myself in the crowd, I ducked toward one of the entrances to the stairways leading up to the small balconies that looked down around the walls of the room, like opera boxes in a theater. It was no plan of mine to be trapped by that strange girl, Lisa Kant, whom I remembered with too much vividness anyway. Five years before, after the occasion at the Final Encyclopedia, I had been bothered, time and again, by the desire to go back to the Enclave and look her up. And, time and again, something like a fear had stopped me.

I knew what the fear was. Deep in me was the irrational feeling that the perception and ability I had been evolving for handling people, as I had first handled my sister in the library with Jamethon Black, and as I had later handled all who got in my path right up to Commandant Frane, earlier that same day and a world away—deep in me, I say, was the fear that something would rob me of this power in the face of any attempt of mine to handle Lisa Kant.

Therefore, I found a stairway and ran up it, onto a little, deserted balcony with a few chairs around a circular table. From here I should be able to spot Eldest Bright, Chief Elder of the Joint Church Council that ruled both Friendly worlds of Harmony and Association. Bright was a Militant—one of the ruling Friendly churchmen who believed most strongly in war as a means to any end—and he had been paying a brief visit to New Earth to see how the Friendly mercenaries were working out for their New Earth employers. A scribble from him on Dave's pass would be better protection for my brother-in-law from the Friendly troops than five Commands of Cassidan armor.

I spotted him, after only a few minutes of searching the crowd milling about fifteen feet below me. He was clear across the large room, talking to a white-haired man—a Venusian or Newtonian by the look of him. I knew the appearance of Eldest Bright, as I knew the appearance of most interstellarly newsworthy people on the sixteen inhabited worlds. Just because I had made my way this far and fast by my own special talents, did not mean I had not also worked to learn my job. But, in spite of my knowledge, my first sight of Eldest Bright was still a shock.

I had not realized how strangely powerful for a churchman he would look in the flesh. Bigger than myself, with shoulders like a barn door and—though he was middle-aged—a waist like a sprinter. He stood, dressed all in black, with his back to me and his legs a little spread, the weight of him on the balls of his feet like a trained fighter. Altogether, there was something about the man, like a black flame of strength, that at the same time chilled me and made me eager to match wits with him.

One thing was certain, he would be no Commandant Frane to dance eagerly at the end of a string of words.

I turned to go down to him—and chance stopped me. If it *was* chance. I shall never know for sure. Perhaps it was a hypersensitivity planted in me by Padma's remark that this place and moment was a locus in the human pattern of development to which he had responsibility. I had affected too many people myself by just such subtle but apposite suggestion, to doubt that it might have been done to me, in this case. But I suddenly caught sight of a little knot of people almost below me.

One of the group was William of Ceta, Chief Entrepreneur of that huge, commercial, low-gravity planet under the sun of Tau Ceti. Another was a tall, beautiful, quite good-looking girl named Anea Marlivana, who was the Select of Kultis for her generation, chief jewel of generations of Exotic breeding. There was also Hendrik Galt, massive in his Marshal's dress uniform, and his niece Elvine. And there was also another man, who could only be Donal Graeme.

He was a young man in the uniform of a Sub-Patrol Chief, an obvious Dorsai with the black hair and strange efficiency of movement that characterizes those people who are born to war. But he was small for a Dorsai—no taller than I would have been, standing next to him— and slim, almost unobtrusive. Yet he caught my eye out of all that group; and, in the same instant, glancing up, he sáw me.

Our eyes met for a second. We were close enough so that I should have been able to see the color of his eyes—and that is what stopped me.

For their color was no color, no one color. They were gray, or green, or blue, depending on what shade you looked for in them.

Graeme looked away again, almost in the same instant. But I was held, caught by the strangeness of eyes like that, in a moment of surprise and transferred attention; and the delay of that moment was enough. When I shook myself out of my trance and looked back to where I had seen Eldest Bright, I discovered him now drawn away from the white-haired man by the appearance of an aide, a figure strangely familiar-looking to me in its shape and posture, who was talking animatedly to the Eldest of the Friendly Worlds.

And, as I still stood watching, Bright spun about on his heel; and, following the familiar-looking aide, went rapidly from the room through a doorway which I knew led to the front hall and the entrance to Galt's establishment. He was leaving and I would lose my chance at him. I turned quickly, to rush down the stairs from the balcony and follow him before he could get away.

But my way was blocked. My moment of transfixed staring at Donal Graeme had tripped me up. Just coming up the stairs and reaching the balcony as I turned to leave was Lisa Kant.

Chapter 7

"Tam!" she said. "Wait! Don't go!"

I could not, without crowding past her. She blocked the narrow stairway. I stopped, irresolute, glancing over at the far entrance through which Bright and his aide had already disappeared. At once it became plain to me that I was already too late. The two of them had been moving fast. By the time I could get downstairs and across the crowded room, they would have already reached their transportation outside the establishment and been gone.

Possibly, if I had moved the second I saw Bright turn to leave— But probably, catching him, even then, would have been a lost cause. Not Lisa's arrival, but my own moment of wandered attention, on seeing the unusual eyes of Donal Graeme, had cost me my chance to obtain Bright's signature on Dave's pass.

I looked back at Lisa. Oddly, now that she had actually caught up with me and we were face to face once more, I was glad of it, though I still had that fear which I mentioned earlier, that she would somehow render me ineffective.

"How'd you know I was here?" I demanded.

"Padma said you'd be trying to avoid me," she said. "You couldn't very well avoid me down on the main floor there. You had to be out of the way someplace, and there weren't any out-of-the-way places but these balconies. I saw you standing at the railing of this one just now, looking down."

She was a little out of breath from hurrying up the stairs, and her words came out in a rush.

"All right," I said. "You've found me. What do you want?"

She was getting her breath back now, but the flush of effort from her run up the stairs still colored her cheeks. Seen like this, she was beautiful, and I could not ignore the fact. But I was still afraid of her.

"Tam!" she said. "Mark Torre has to talk to you!"

My fear of her whined sharply upward in me, like the mounting siren of an alarm signal. I saw the source of her dangerousness to me in that moment. Either instinct or knowledge had armed her. Anyone else would have worked up to that demand slowly. But an instinctive wisdom in her knew the danger of giving me time to assess a situation, so that I could twist it to my own ends.

But I could be direct, too. I started to go around her, without answering. She stepped in my way, and I had to stop.

"What about?" I said harshly.

"He didn't tell me."

I saw a way of handling her attack then. I started laughing at her. She stared at me for a second, then flushed again and began to look very angry indeed.

"I'm sorry." I throttled down on the laughter; and at the same time, secretly, I was in fact truly sorry. For all I was forced to fight her off, I liked Lisa Kant too well to laugh so at her. "But what else could we talk about except the old business of my taking over on the Final Encyclopedia again? Don't you remember? Padma said you couldn't use me. I was all oriented toward"—I tasted the word, as it went out of my mouth—"*destruction*."

"We'll just have to take our chance on that." She looked stubborn. "Besides, it isn't Padma who decides for the Encyclopedia. It's Mark Torre, and he's getting old. He knows better than anyone else how dangerous it would be if he dropped the reins and there was no one there quickly to pick them up. In a year, in six months, the Project could founder. Or be wrecked by people outside it. Do you think your uncle was the only person on Earth who felt about Earth and the younger worlds' people the way he did?"

I stiffened, and a cold feeling came into my mind. She had made a mistake, mentioning Mathias. My face must have changed, too; because I saw her own face change, looking at me.

"What've you been doing?" Fury burst out in me all of a sudden. "Studying up on me? Putting tracers on my comings and goings?" I took a step forward and she backed instinctively. I caught her by the arm and held her from moving further. "Why chase me down *now*, after five years? How'd you know I was going to be here anyway?"

She stopped trying to pull away and stood still, with dignity.

"Let go of me," she said quietly. I did and she stepped back.

"Padma told me you'd be here. He said that it was my last chance at you—he calculated it. You remember, he told you about ontogenetics." I stared at her for a second, then snorted with harsh laughter.

"Come on, now!" I said. "I'm willing to swallow a lot about your Exotics. But don't tell me they can calculate exactly where anyone in the sixteen worlds is going to be ahead of time!"

"Not anyone!" she answered angrily. "*You*. You and a few like you—because you're a maker, not a made part of the pattern. The influences operating on someone who's moved about by the pattern are too far reaching, and too complicated to calculate. But *you* aren't at the mercy of outside influences. You have *choice*, overriding the pressures people and events bring to bear on you. Padma told you that five years ago!"

"And that makes me easier to predict instead of harder? Let's hear another joke."

"Oh, Tam!" she said, exasperated. "Of course it makes you easier. It doesn't take ontogenetics, hardly. You can almost do it yourself. You've been working for five years now to get Membership in the Newsman's Guild, haven't you? Do you suppose that hasn't been obvious?"

Of course, she was right. I had made no secret of my ambitions. There had been no reason to keep them secret. She read the admission in my expression.

"All right," she went on. "So now you've worked your way up to Apprentice. Next, what's the quickest and surest way for an Apprentice to win his way into full Guild membership? To make a habit of being where the most interesting news is breaking, isn't that right? And what's the most interesting—if not important—news on the sixteen worlds right now? The war between the North and South Partitions on New Earth. News of a war is always dramatic. So you were bound to arrange to get yourself assigned to cover this one, if you could. And you seem to be able to get most things you want."

I looked at her closely. All that she said was true and reasonable. But, if so, why hadn't it occurred to me before this that I could be so predictable? It was like finding myself suddenly under observation by someone with high-powered binoculars, someone whose spying I had not even slightly suspected. Then I realized something.

"But you've only explained why I'd be on New Earth," I said slowly. "Why would I be here, though, at this particular party on Freiland?"

For the first time she faltered. She no longer seemed sure in her knowledge.

"Padma . . ." she said, and hesitated. "Padma says this place and moment is a locus. And, being what you are you can perceive, and are drawn to, loci—by your own desire to use them for your own purposes."

I stared at her, slowly absorbing this. And then, as suddenly as a sheet of flame across my mind leaped the connection between what she had just said and what I had heard earlier.

"Locus—yes!" I said tightly, taking a step toward her again in my excitement. "Padma said it was a locus here. For Graeme—but for me, too! Why? What does it mean for me?"

"I . . ." she hesitated. "I don't know exactly, Tam. I don't think even Padma knows."

"But something about it, and me, brought you here! Isn't that right?" I almost shouted at her. My mind was closing on the truth like a fox on a winded rabbit. "Why did you come hunting me now then? At this particular place and moment, as you call it! Tell me!"

"Padma . . ." she faltered. I saw then with the almost blinding light of my sudden understanding that she would have liked to lie about this, but something in her would not let her. "Padma . . . only found out everything he knows now because of the way the Encyclopedia's grown able to help him. It has given him extra data to use in his calculations. And recently, when he used that data, the results showed everything up as more complex—and important. The Encyclopedia's more important, to the whole human race, than he thought five years ago. And the danger of the Encyclopedia's never being finished is greater. And your own power of destruction . . ."

She ran down and looked at me, almost pleadingly as if asking me to excuse her from finishing what she had started to say. But my mind was racing, and my heart pounded with excitement.

"Go on!" I told her harshly.

"The power in you for destruction was greater than he had dreamed. But, Tam"—she broke in on herself quickly, almost frantically—"there was something else. You remember five years ago how Padma thought you had no choice but to go through that dark valley of yours to its very end? Well, that's not quite true. There *is* a chance— at this point in the pattern, here at this locus. If you'll think, and choose, and turn aside, there's a narrow way for you up out of the darkness. But you've got to turn sharply right now! You've got to give up this assignment you're on, no matter what it costs, and come back to Earth to talk to Mark Torre, right now!"

"Right now," I muttered, but I was merely echoing her words without thought, while listening to my racing mind. "No," I said, "never mind that. What is it I'm supposed to be turning my back on? What special destruction? I'm not planning anything like that—right now."

"Tam!" I felt her hand distantly on my arm, I saw her pale face staring tensely up at me, as if trying to get my attention. But it was as if these things registered on my senses from a long distance away. For if I was right—*if I was right*—then even Padma's calculations were testifying to the dark strength in me, that ability I had worked these five years to harness and drive. And if such power were actually mine, what couldn't I do next?

"But it isn't what you *plan!*" Lisa was saying desperately. "Don't you see, a gun doesn't plan to shoot anyone. But it's in you, Tam, like a gun ready to go off. Only, you don't have to let it go off. You can change yourself while there's still time. You can save yourself, and the Encyclopedia—"

The last word rang suddenly through me, with a million echoes. It rang like the uncounted voices I had heard five years ago at the Transit Point of the Index Room in the Encyclopedia itself. Suddenly, through all the excitement holding me, it reached and touched me as sharply as the point of a spear. Like a brilliant shaft of light it pierced through the dark walls that had been building triumphantly in my mind on either side of me, as they had built in my mind that day in Mark Torre's office. Like an unbearable illumination it opened the darkness for a second, and showed me a picture—myself, in the rain; and Padma, facing me; and a dead man who lay between us.

But I flung myself away from that moment of imagination, flung myself clear back into the comforting darkness, and the sense of my power and strength came back on me.

"I don't need the Encyclopedia!" I said loudly.

"But you do!" she cried. "Everybody who's Earth-born—and if Padma's right, all the people in the future on the sixteen worlds—are going to need it. And only you can make sure they get it. Tam, you *have to*—"

"Have to!"

I took a step back from her, myself, this time. I had gone fiercely cold all over with the same sort of fury Mathias had been able to raise in me once, but it was mixed now with my feeling of triumph and of power. "I don't *'have to'* anything! Don't lump me in with the rest of you Earth worms. Maybe *they* need your Encyclopedia. But not me!"

I went around her with that, using my strength finally to shove her physically aside. I heard her still calling after me as I went down the stairs. But I shut my mind to the sense of her voice and refused to hear it. To this day I do not know what the last words she called after me were. I left the balcony and her calling behind me, and threaded my way through the people of the floor below toward the same exit through which Bright had disappeared. With the Friendly leader gone, there was no point in my hanging around. And with the newly re-aroused sense of my power in me, abruptly I could not bear them close around me. Most of them, nearly all of them, were people from the younger worlds; and Lisa's voice rang on and on, it seemed, in my ear, telling me I needed the Encyclopedia, reechoing all Mathias' bitter lesson-giving about the relative helplessness and ineffectuality of Earthmen.

As I had suspected, once I gained the open air of the cool and moonless Freiland night outside, Eldest Bright, and whoever had called him from the party, had disappeared. The parking-lot attendant told me that they had left.

There was no point in my trying to find them, now. They might be headed anywhere on the planet, if not to a spacefield off-world entirely, back to Harmony or Association. Let them go, I thought, still bitter from the implication of my Earth-born ineffectiveness that I thought I had read in Lisa's words. Let them go. I alone could handle any trouble Dave might get in with the Friendlies, as a result of having a pass unsigned by one of their authorities.

I headed back to the spacefield and took the first shuttle to orbit and shift back to New Earth. But on the way, I had a chance to cool down. I faced the fact that it was still worthwhile getting Dave's pass signed. I might have to send him off for some reason of his own. An accident might even separate us on the battlefield. Any one of a number of things could occur to put him in trouble where I would not be around to save him.

With Eldest Bright a lost cause, I was left with the only option of heading to military headquarters of the Friendly troops in North Par-tition, to seek the signature for Dave's pass there. Accordingly, as soon as I hit orbit New Earth, I changed my ticket for Contrevale, the North Partition city right behind the lines of the Friendly mercenaries.

All this took some little time. It was after midnight by the time I had gotten from Contrevale to Battle Headquarters of the North Par-tition Forces. My Newsman's pass got me admission to the Head-quarters' area, which seemed strangely deserted even for this time of night. But, when I pulled in at last before the Command building, I was surprised at the number of floaters parked there in the Officers' area.

Once again, my pass got me past a silent-faced, black-clothed guard with spring-rifle at the ready. I stepped into the reception room, with its long counter clipping it in half before me and the tall wall transparencies showing the full parking area under its night lights behind me. Only one man was behind the counter at one of the desks there, a Groupman hardly older than myself, but with his face already hardened into the lines of grim and merciless self-discipline to be observed on some of these people.

He got up from his desk and came to the other side of the counter as I approached the near side.

"I'm a Newsman of the Interstellar News Service," I began. "I'm looking for—"

"Thy papers!"

The interruption was harsh and nasal. The black eyes in the bony face stared into mine; and the archaic choice of the pronoun was all but flung in my face. Grim contempt, amounting nearly to a hatred on sight, leaped like a spark from him to me, as he held out his hand for the papers he had requested—and like a lion roused from slumber by the roar of an enemy, my own hatred leaped back at him, instinctively, before I could leash it with cooler reflection and wisdom.

I had heard of his breed of Friendly, but never until this moment had I come face to face with one. This was one of those from Harmony or Association who used the canting version of their private speech not just privately among themselves, but indifferently toward all men and women. He was one of those who avoided all personal joy in life, as he avoided any softness of bed or fullness of belly. His life was a trial-at-arms, antechamber only for the life to come, that life to come that was possible only to those who had kept the true faith—and to only those who, in keeping the true faith, had in addition been Chosen of the Lord.

It did not matter to this man that he was no more than a noncommissioned officer, a lesser functionary among thousands such, from a poor and stony planet, and I was one of only a few hundred on sixteen inhabited worlds intensively educated, trained and privileged to wear the Newsman's cloak. It made no difference to him that I was a member or Apprentice of the Guild, that I could talk with the rulers of planets. It did not even matter that I knew him to be half a madman and he knew me to be a product of education and training many times his own. None of this mattered, for he was one of God's Elect, and I was without the shadow of his church; and so he looked on me as an emperor might look at a dog to be kicked from his path.

And I looked back at him. There is a counter for every human emotional blow, deliberately given. Who knew this better than I? And I knew well the counter to anyone who tries to look down his nose at you. That counter is laughter. There never was a throne yet built so high that it could not be rocked by laughter from below. But I looked at this Groupman now, and I could not laugh.

I could not laugh for a very simple reason. For half-mad as he was, narrow-minded, limited as he was, yet *he* would have calmly let himself be burned at the stake rather than give up the lightest tenet of his beliefs. While *I* could not have held one finger in a match flame one minute to uphold the greatest of my own.

And he knew I knew that was true of him. And he knew I knew he knew what was true of me. Our mutual knowledge was plain as the counter between us. And so I could not laugh at him, and win my self-respect back. And I hated him for it.

I gave him my papers. He looked them over. Then he handed them back to me.

"Thy papers are in order," he said, high in his nose. "What brings thee here?"

"A pass," I said, putting my own papers away and digging out Dave's. "For my assistant. You see, we move back and forth on both sides of the battle line and—"

"Behind our lines and across them, no pass is necessary. Thy Newsman's papers are sufficient." He turned as if to go back to his desk.

"But this assistant of mine"—I kept my voice level—"doesn't have Newsman's papers. I just took him on earlier today and I haven't had time to make arrangements for him. What I'd like would be a temporary pass, signed by one of your Headquarters' officers here—"

He had turned back to the counter.

"Thy assistant is no Newsman?"

"Not officially. No. But—"

"Then he hath no leave or freedom to move across our battle lines. No pass can be issued."

"Oh, I don't know," I said carefully. "I was going to get one from your Eldest Bright, at a party on Freiland, just a few hours back, but he left before I had a chance to get it from him." I stopped, for the Groupman was grimly shaking his head.

"*Brother* Bright," he said, and in his choice of title I saw at last that he would be immovable. Only the purest of the fanatics among the Friendlies scorned the necessities of rank amongst themselves. *Eldest* Bright might order my Groupman to charge an enemy gun emplacement bare-handed and my Groupman would not hesitate to obey. But that did not mean that my Groupman considered Bright, or Brother Bright's opinion of the rightness of things, to be better than his own.

The reason was a very simple one. Bright's rank and title were of this present life, and therefore, in my Groupman's eyes, no more than toys and dross and tinkling cymbals. They did not weigh with the fact that as Brothers of the Elect, he and the Groupman were equal in the sight of the Lord.

"*Brother* Bright," he said, "could not have issued a pass to one not qualified to go and come among our numbers and perhaps be a spy upon us to the favor of our enemies."

There was one last card to play, and it was, I knew, a losing card; but I might as well play it anyway.

"If you don't mind," I said. "I'd like to get an answer on this from one of your superior officers. Please call one—the Officer of the Day, if no one else's available."

But he turned and went back to sit down at his desk.

"The Officer of the Day," he said, with finality, returning to some papers he had been working on, "can give thee no other answer. Neither will I summon him from his duties to repeat what I have already told thee."

It was like the crashing down of an iron portcullis upon my plans to get that pass signed. But there was nothing to be gained by arguing further with this man. I turned about and left the building.

Chapter 8

As the door shut behind me, I paused on the top of the three steps leading up it, to try to think what I could do next. What I would do next. I had gone over, under, or around what seemed to be immovable barriers of human decision too many times to give up so easily. Somewhere, there must be a back entrance to what I wanted, a trapdoor, a crack in the wall. I glanced again at the officers' parking area, jammed with floaters.

And then, suddenly, it came to me. All at once the bits and pieces floated together to give me a completed picture; and I kicked myself mentally for not having seen it before.

Item, the strange look of familiarity about the aide who had come to take Eldest Bright from the party of Donal Graeme. Item, Bright's own precipitate departure following the aide's appearance. Finally, the unusually deserted Headquarters' area, contrasted with the crowded parking lot here, the empty office within, and the refusal of the Groupman on duty reception even to call the Officer of the Day.

Either Bright himself, or his presence in the war area, had triggered some unusual plan for military action on the part of the Friendly mercenaries. A surprise blow, crushing the Cassidan forces and ending the war suddenly would be excellent publicity for the Eldest's attempts to hire out his Friendly commands of mercenaries in the face of some public dislike on the other worlds of their fanatic behavior and attitudes.

Not that all Friendlies were dislikable, I had been told. But, having met the Groupman inside, I could see where it would not take many like him to prejudice people against the black-clad soldiers as a group. Therefore, I would bet my boots that Bright was inside the Command Post now with his top brass, preparing some military action to take the Cassidan levies by surprise. And with him would be the aide who had summoned him from Donal Graeme's party—and unless my highly trained professional memory was misleading me, I had a hunch who that aide might be.

I went quickly back down to my own floater, got in it and turned on its phone. Central at Contrevale looked abruptly at me out of the screen, with the face of a pretty, young blonde girl.

I gave her the number of my floater, which of course was a rented vehicle.

"I'd like to speak to a Jamethon Black," I said. "He's an officer with the Friendly forces; I believe he's right now at their Headquarters' Unit near Contrevale. I'm not sure what his rank is—at least Force-Leader, though he may be a Commandant. It's something of an emergency. If you can contact him, would you put him through to me on this phone?"

"Yes, sir," said Central. "Please hold on, I'll report in a minute." The screen blanked out and the voice was replaced by the soft hum that indicated the channel was open and holding.

I sat back against the cushions of the floater, and waited. Less than forty seconds later, the face returned.

"I have reached your party and he will be in contact with you in a few seconds. Will you hold, please?"

"Certainly," I said.

"Thank you, sir." The face disappeared. There was another half minute or so of hum and the screen lit up once more, this time with the face of Jamethon.

"Hello, Force-Leader Black?" I said. "Probably you don't remember me. I'm Newsman Tam Olyn. You used to know my sister, Eileen Olyn."

His eyes had already told me that he remembered me. Evidently I had not changed as much as I thought I had; or else his memory was a very good one. He himself had changed also, but not in any way that would make him unrecognizable. Above the tabs on the lapels of his uniform that showed his rank was still the same, his face had strengthened and deepened. But it was the same still face I remembered from my uncle's library that day. Only—it was older, of course.

I remembered how I had thought of him then, as a boy. Whatever he was now, however, he was a boy no longer. Nor ever could be again.

"What can I do for you, Mr. Olyn?" he asked. His voice was

perfectly even and calm, a little deeper than I remembered it. "The operator said your call was an emergency."

"In a way it is," I said, and paused. "I don't want to take you from anything important; but I'm in your Headquarters Area here, in the officers' parking lot just outside the Headquarters Command Building. If you're not too far from there, maybe you can step over here and speak to me for a moment." I hesitated again. "Of course, if you're on duty at the moment—"

"My duty at the moment can spare me for a few minutes," he said. "You're in the parking lot of the Command Building?"

"In a rental floater, green, with transparent top."

"I will be right down, Mr. Olyn."

The screen went blank.

I waited. A couple of minutes later, the same door by which I myself had entered the Command Building to talk with the Groupman behind the counter opened. A dark, slim figure was momentarily silhouetted against the light there; then it came down the three steps toward the lot.

I opened the door of the floater as he got close and slid around on the seat so that he could step in and sit down himself.

"Mr. Olyn?" he said, putting his head in.

"That's right. Join me."

"Thank you."

He stepped in and sat down, leaving the door open behind him. It was a warm spring night for that season and latitude on New Earth; and the soft scents of trees and grasses blew past him into my face.

"What is this emergency?" he asked.

"I've got an assistant I need a pass for." I told him the situation, omitting the fact that Dave was Eileen's husband.

When I was through, he sat silent for a moment, a silhouette against the lights of the lot and the Command Building, with the soft night airs blowing past him.

"If your assistant's not a Newsman, Mr. Olyn," he said at last, in his quiet voice, "I don't see how we can authorize his coming and going behind and through our lines."

"He *is* a Newsman—for this campaign at least," I said. "I'm responsible for him, and the Guild is responsible for me, as it is for any Newsman. Our impartiality is guaranteed between the stars. That impartiality of course includes my assistant."

He shook his head slowly in the darkness.

"It would be easy enough for you to disown him, if he should turn out to be a spy. You could say simply that he was pushed upon you as an assistant, without your knowledge."

I turned my head to look full into his darkened features. I had led him to this point in our talk for just this reason.

"No, I wouldn't find it easy at all," I said. "Because he wasn't pushed on me. I went to a great deal of trouble to get him. He's my brother-in-law. He's the boy Eileen finally married; and by using him as my assistant, I'm keeping him out of the lines where he's likely to get killed." I paused to let that sink in. "I'm trying to save his life for Eileen, and I'm asking you to try and help me save it."

He did not move or answer immediately. In the darkness, I could not see any change of expression on his features. But I do not think there would have been any change to see even if I had had light to see by, because he was a product of his own spartan culture, and I had just dealt him a heavy, double blow.

For, as you have seen, that was how I handled men—and women. Deep in every intelligent, living individual are things too great, too secret or too fearful for questioning. Faiths, or loves, or hates or fears or guilts. All I needed ever was to discover these things, and then anchor my argument for the answer I wanted in one of these deep, unself-questionable areas of the individual psyche, so that to question the rightness of what I argued, a man must needs question the secret, unquestionable place in himself as well.

In Jamethon Black's case, I had anchored my request both in that area of him which had been capable of love for Eileen in the first place; and in that part of every prideful man (and pride was in the very bone of the religion of these Friendlies) that required him to be above nourishing a long-held resentment for a past and (as far as he knew) a fair defeat.

To refuse the pass to Dave, now that I had spoken as I did, was tantamount to sending Dave forth to be killed, and who could think this was not done on purpose, now that I had shown Jamethon the emotional lines connecting it to his inner pride and lost love?

He stirred now, on the seat of the floater.

"Give me the pass, Mr. Olyn," he said. "I'll see what can be done."

I gave it to him, and he left me.

In a couple of minutes, he was back. He did not enter the floater this time, but he bent down to the open door and passed in the paper I had given him.

"You did not tell me," he said in his quiet voice, "that you had already applied for a pass, and been refused."

I stopped dead, still clutching the paper in midair, staring up and out at him.

"Who? That Groupman in there?" I said. "But he's just a noncommissioned officer. And you're not only a commissioned officer but an aide."

"Nonetheless," he said, "a refusal has been given. I cannot alter a decision already made. I'm sorry. No pass is possible for your brother-in-law."

It was only then I realized that the paper he had handed me back was unsigned. I stared at it, as if I could read it in the darkness and will a signature into being on the blank area where it should have gone. Then fury boiled up in me almost beyond control. I jerked my gaze up from the paper and stared out the open door of the floater at Jamethon Black.

"So that's your way of getting out of it!" I said. "That's how you excuse yourself for sending Eileen's husband to his death! Don't think I don't see through you, Black—because I do!"

With his back to the light, with his face in darkness, I still could not see his face and any change that might have come over it at my words. But something like a light sigh, a faint, sad breath, came from him; and he answered in the same, even tones.

"You see only the man, Mr. Olyn," he said. "Not the Vessel of the Lord. I must get back to my duties now. Good morning."

With that he swung closed the door of the floater, turned and went away across the lot. I sat, staring after him, boiling inside at the line of cant he had thrown at me in leaving by way of what I took to be excuse. Then I woke to what I was doing. As the door of the Command Building opened, his dark figure was silhouetted there for an instant, and then disappeared, taking the light with it as the door closed again. I kicked the floater into movement, swung it about and headed out of the military area.

As I drove out past the gateyard, they were changing guards for the three-A.M. watch; and the dismissed watch were drawn up in a dark clump, still under weapons, engaged in some ritual of their special worship.

As I passed them, they began to sing—chant rather—one of their hymns. I was not listening for the words, but the three beginning ones stuck in my ear in spite of me. *"Soldier, ask not—"* were the first three words, of what I later learned was their special battle hymn, sung at times of special rejoicing, or on the very eve of combat.

"Soldier, ask not—" It continued to ring in my ears, mockingly it seemed to me, as I drove away with Dave's pass still unsigned in my

pocket. And once more the fury rose in me; and once more I swore that Dave would need no pass. I would not let him from my side for an instant during the coming day between the battle lines; and in my presence he would find his protection and his utter safety.

Chapter 9

It was six-thirty in the morning when I stepped out of the tube from the port into the lobby of my hotel in Molon. There was a gritty feeling to my nerves and a dryness to my eyes and mouth, for I had not slept for twenty-four hours. The day coming up was to be a big one, so that I could probably not look forward to rest for another twenty-four. But going two or three days without sleep is an occupational hazard of Newswork. You get hold of something, with the situation about to break at a second's warning; and you simply have to stay with it until it does.

I would be alert enough; and if it came right down to the wire, I had medication to see me through. As it happened, though, at the desk I found something that knocked the need for sleep cheerfully right out of my head.

It was a letter from Eileen. I stepped aside and pressed it open.

Dearest Tam: [she wrote]
     Your letter about your plan to take Dave out of the battle lines and keep him with you as your assistant just reached here. I'm so happy I can't tell you how I feel. It never occurred to me that someone like you, from Earth, and still only an Apprentice in the Newsman's Guild, could do something like that for us.
     How can I thank you? And how can you forgive me after the way I've been, not writing, or not caring what happened to you all these last five years? I haven't been very much like a sister to you. But it was because I knew how useless and

helpless I was; and ever since I was a little girl I've felt you were secretly ashamed of me and just putting up with me.

And then when you told me that day in the library how it would never work out for me to marry Jamethon Black—I knew you were right, even at the time, you were only telling me the truth about myself—but I couldn't help hating you for it. It seemed to me then that you were actually *proud* of the fact you could stop me from going away with Jamie.

But how wrong I was, as this thing you are doing to protect Dave shows me now; and how bitterly, bitterly sorry I am for feeling the way I did. You were the only one I had left to love after Mother and Daddy died, and I did love you, Tam; but most of the time it seemed to me you didn't want me to, any more than Uncle Mathias did.

Anyway, all that has changed now, since I met Dave and he married me. Someday you must come to Alban, on Cassida, and see our apartment. We were very lucky to get one this big. It is my first real home of my own, and I think you may be a little surprised at how well we've fixed it up. Dave will tell you all about it, if you ask him—don't you think he's wonderful, for someone like me to marry, I mean? He is so kind, and so loyal. Do you know he wanted me to let you know about our marriage at the time it happened, in spite of the way I felt? But I wouldn't do it. Only of course he was right. He is always right, just as I am nearly always wrong—as you know, Tam.

But thank you, thank you again for what you're doing for Dave; and all my love goes with both of you. Tell Dave I'm writing him, too, at this same time; but I suppose his army mail won't reach him as fast as yours does you.

All my love,
Eileen

I tucked the letter and its envelope away in my pocket and went up to my room. I had meant to show him the letter; but on the way up the tube I found myself unexpectedly embarrassed at the thought of the fullness of her thanks expressed in it, and the way she had accused herself of not being the best possible sister. I had not been the best possible brother, either; and what I was doing for Dave now might look big to her, but it was nothing great really. Hardly more than the sort of thing I might do for a total stranger, by way of returning a professional favor.

She had me, in fact, feeling somewhat ashamed of myself, absurdly warmed by having heard from her so. Maybe we could turn out to exist like normal people after all. The way she and Dave felt about each other, I would undoubtedly be having nephews or nieces one of these days. Who knew—I might even end up married myself (the thought of Lisa floated inexplicably through my mind) and with children. And we might all end up with relations spread over half a dozen worlds like most of the ordinary family groups, nowadays.

Thus I refute Mathias! I thought to myself. *And Padma, too.*

I was daydreaming in this absurd but cheerful fashion when I reached the door of my hotel suite and remembered the question of showing Dave the letter. Better to let him wait and read his own letter, which Eileen had said was on the way, I decided. I pushed open the door and went in.

He was already up, dressed, and packed. He grinned at the sight of me; and this puzzled me for a split second until I realized that I must have come in with a smile on my own face.

"I heard from Eileen," I said. "Just a note. She says a letter's on its way to you, but it may take a day or so to catch up from being forwarded on from your army unit."

He beamed at that; and we went down to breakfast. The food helped to wake me up; and we took off the moment we were done, for Battle Headquarters of the Cassidan and local troops. Dave was handling my recording and other equipment. There was no real bulk or weight to it. I often carried it myself without hardly noticing it. But theoretically his caring for it left me free to concentrate on finer matters of reportage.

Battle Headquarters had promised me a military air-car, one of the small two-man reconnaissance jobs. When I got to the Transport Pool, however, I found myself in line behind a Field Commander who was waiting for his command car to be specially equipped. My first impulse was to put up a squawk on principle at being kept waiting. My second thought was decidedly to do no such thing. This was no ordinary Field Commander.

He was a lean, tall man with black, slightly coarse, slightly curly hair above a big-boned, but open and smiling face. I have mentioned before that I am tall, for an Earth-born man. This Field Commander was tall for a Dorsai, which of course he was. In addition he had that— that quality for which there is no name, which is the birthright of his people. Something beyond just strength, or fearsomeness, or courage. Something almost the opposite of those keyed-up qualities.

It is calmness, even; a thing beyond argument, beyond time, beyond life itself. I have been on the Dorsai planet since then, and I have seen it as well among the half-grown boys there, and in some of the children. These people can be killed—all who are born of women are mortal—but staining them through, like a dye, is the undeniable fact that together, or as individuals, they cannot be conquered. By anything. Conquest of the Dorsai character is not merely unthinkable. It is somehow not—possible.

So, all this my Field Commander automatically had, in addition to his magnificent military mind and body. But there was something strange, over and above it all. Something that did not seem to belong in with the rest of the Dorsai character at all.

It was an odd, powerful, sunny warmth of character that lapped even upon me, standing several yards away and outside the knot of officers and men that surrounded him like elm saplings in the wind-shelter of an oak. A joy of life seemed to fountain up in this Dorsai officer, so brightly that it forced the kindling of a similar joy in those around him. Even in me, standing to one side and not—I would have said—normally too much liable to such influence.

But it may have been that Eileen's letter was making me particularly vulnerable that morning. That could have been it.

There was another thing which my professional eye was quick to spot; and which had nothing to do with character qualities. That was the fact that his uniform was of the field-blue color and narrow cut that identified it as issue, not of the Cassidan, but of the Exotic forces. The Exotics, rich and powerful, and philosophically committed not to do violence in their own proper persons, hired the best mercenary troops to be had between the stars. And, of course, that meant that an unusually high proportion of those troops, or at least of their officers, were Dorsai. So what was a Dorsai Field Commander doing here with a New Earth shoulder patch hastily added to his Exotic-cut uniform, and surrounded by New Earth and Cassidan staff officers?

If he was newly come to the battered New Earth South Partition Forces, it was indeed a fortunate coincidence that he should show up on the very morning following a night I happened to know had been occupied by busy planning on the part of the Friendly Battle Headquarters at Contrevale.

But, was it coincidence? It was hard to believe that the Cassidans could already have found out about the Friendly tactical session. The Cadre of the New Earth Intelligence Forces staffed by men like Commandant Frane, were poor in the spying department; and it was part of the Mercenaries Code, under which professional soldiers of all worlds hired out, that a mercenary could not operate out of uniform on any intelligence mission. But coincidence seemed too easy an answer, all the same.

"Stay here," I told Dave.

I started forward to penetrate the crowd of staff officers around this unusual Dorsai Field Commander, and find out something about him from his own lips. But at that moment his command car came up, and he got in, taking off before I could reach him. I noted he headed south into the battle lines.

The officers he had left behind dispersed. I let them go, keeping my questions instead for the enlisted New Earth cadreman who brought up my own air-car. He would be likely to know almost as much as the officers and a lot less likely to have been cautioned not to tell it to me. The Field Commander, I learned, had indeed been loaned to the South Partition Forces just the day before, on the orders of an Exotic OutBond called Patma, or Padma. Oddly, this Exotic officer was a relative of that same Donal Graeme whose party I had attended—although Donal was, as far as I knew, in Freiland, not Exotic employ, and under the command of Hendrik Galt.

"Kensie Graeme, that's the name of this one," said the Transport Pool cadreman. "And he's a twin, do you know that? By the way, you know how to drive one of these cars?"

"Yes," I said. I was already behind the stick and Dave was in the seat beside me. I touched the lift button and we rose on our eight-inch cushion of air. "Is his twin here, too?"

"No, still back on Kultis, I guess," said the cadreman. "He's just as sour as this one's happy, I hear. They've each got two men's dose of being one way or the other. Outside of that, they say, you can't tell them apart—other one's a Field Commander, too."

"What's the other one's name?" I asked, with my hand on the stick, ready to pull out.

He frowned, thought for a minute, shook his head.

"Can't remember," he said. "Something short—Ian, I think."

"Thanks, anyhow," I said, and I took off. It was a temptation to head south in the direction Kensie Graeme had gone; but I had made my plans on my way back from Friendly Battle Headquarters the night before; and when you're short on sleep, it's a bad practice to go changing plans without strong reason. Often the fuzzy-headedness that comes from sleeplessness is just enough to make you forget some strong reason you had for making the original plan. Some strong reason which later on—too late—you will remember to your regret.

So, I make it a principle not to change plans on the spur of the moment, unless I can be sure my mind is in top working order. It's a principle that pays off more often than not. Though, of course, no principle is perfect.

We lifted the air-car to about six hundred feet of altitude and cruised north along the Cassidan lines, our News Service colors on the air-car body glowing in the sunlight and our warning beeper beaming a neutral signal at the same time. Banner and beeper together should be enough, I figured, to make us safe at this altitude as long as there was no active shooting going on. Once the fighting really started, we would be smarter to head for ground cover like a wounded bird.

Meanwhile, while it was still safe to do so from the air, I meant to coast the lines first to the north (where they angled back toward the Friendly Battle HQ and Contrevale) and then to the south—and see if I couldn't figure out just what Bright, or Bright's black-clad officers, could have in mind for their plan.

Between the two enemy camps of Contrevale and Dhores, a direct line would have run almost due north and south. The present actual battle line struck across this imaginary north-south line at an angle, its northern end leaning toward Contrevale and the Friendly HQ, and its southern end all but touching the outskirts of Dhores, which was a city of about sixty-odd thousand people.

So the battle line as a whole was much closer to Dhores than to Contrevale—which put the Cassidan-New Earth Forces at a disadvantage. They could not fall back at their south end into the city proper and still be able to preserve a straight front of battle line and the communication necessary for effective defense. By so much had the Friendly troops already pushed their opponents into bad field position.

On the other hand, the angle of the battle line was acute enough so that a major share of the Friendly troops toward the south were inside the northern end of the Cassidan line. Given more reserves in the way of troops and bolder leadership, I thought determined sallies from the north end of the Cassidan line could have cut communications between the southern and forward elements of the Friendly line—and the Friendly HQ, back toward Contrevale.

This would at least have had the advantage of introducing confusion into the Friendly ranks, out of which a determined Cassidan field command might have made some capital.

They had shown no signs of doing so, however. Now, with a Dorsai as Field Commander, some such thing might still be attempted by the Cassidans—if there was still time and men available. But it seemed unlikely to me that the Friendlies, after sitting up all night, planning, were going to sit still today while the Cassidans made attempts to cut enemy communications.

The big question was, what did the Friendlies have in mind? I could see what I have just mentioned as a possible tactic for the Cassidans. But I could not imagine just how the Friendlies planned to take advantage of the present positions and tactical situation.

The south end of the line, on the outskirts of Dhores, was pretty much open country, farmland planted in corn, or cattle pasture on rolling glaciated hills. To the north, there were also the hills, but covered with wooded patches, groves of towering yellow birch, which had found a fine, alien home in the moist, glacial uplands of the South Partition, here on New Earth, so that here they rose to nearly double their Earthly heights—nearly two hundred feet—and clustered their tops so densely that no undergrowth but a native, mosslike groundcover could exist beneath them. Consequently, it was a sort of dim, Robin Hood-like country that existed beneath their branches, with great, peeling, silver-gold and gray, four-to-six-foot trunks reaching straight up like pillars in the dimness to the darkness of sun-shot leaves overhead.

It was not until, looking at them, I remembered all this of how it was underneath them, that it struck me that any number of troops could be at movement under their cover and I—up here in my air-car—would not be aware of rifle or helmet of them. In short, the Friendlies could be developing a major push under the cover of the trees below me and I would have no suspicion of it.

No sooner thought than acted upon. I blamed my lack of sleep for a fuzziness of perception that had not made me suspect something like this before. I swung the air-car wide to the edge of one of the groves, where there was a fortified Cassidan emplacement with the ringed muzzle of a sonic cannon poking out of it, and parked. Out here in the open, there was too much sun for the mosslike groundcover, but a knee-high native grass was everywhere, leaning to the little wind that was blowing it in ripples, like the surface of a lake.

I got out and waded through it to the entrance of the bushes masking the gun emplacement. The day was getting hot already.

"Any sign of Friendly movement around here, or in the woods over there?" I asked the Senior Groupman in charge of the emplacement.

"Nothing, far as we know," he answered. He was a slim, high-keyed young fellow, gone half-bald considerably before his time. His uniform jacket was unclipped at the throat. "Patrols are out."

"Hmm," I said. "I'll try up forward a bit. Thanks."

I got back in the air-car and took off again, just six inches above ground obstacles now, and into the woods. Here it was cooler. The patch of trees we entered led to another and that to another. In the third patch we were challenged, and found we had come up on a Cassidan patrol. Its members were flat on the ground, out of sight and covering us at the time we were challenged; and I did not spot a single man until a square-faced Force-Leader rose up almost beside the car, spring-rifle in his hand and visor of his helmet down.

"What the hell are you doing here?" he said, shoving the visor up.

"Newsman. I've got permissions to be in and across the battle lines. Want to see them?"

"You know what you can do with your permissions," he said. "If it was up to me, you'd do it, too. Not that your being here makes this business any more of a damn Sunday picnic than it is now. But we've got trouble enough trying to keep the men acting halfway like soldiers in a battle zone without people like you wandering around."

"Why?" I asked innocently. "Are you having some kind of trouble besides that? What trouble?"

"We haven't seen a black helmet since dawn, that's what trouble!" he said. "Their forward gun emplacements are empty—and they weren't yesterday, that's what trouble. Shoot an antenna down into bedrock and listen for five seconds and you can hear armor—heavy armor and lots of it—moving not more than fifteen, twenty kilometers from here. That's what trouble! Now, why don't you get back behind the lines, friend, so we don't have to worry about you on top of everything else?"

"Which direction did you hear the armor?"

He pointed ahead, into Friendly territory.

"Then that's where we're headed ourselves," I said, leaning back into the seat of the air-car and getting ready to close the overhead.

"Hold it!" His voice stopped me before I got the overhead shut. "If you're determined to cross over toward the enemy, I can't stop you. But it's my duty to warn you that you head that way on your own responsibility. That's between the lines, out there; and your chances of running into automatic weapons are better than not."

"Sure, sure. Consider us cautioned!" I slid the overhead shut with a bang. It may have been my own lack of sleep making me irritable, but it seemed to me at the time that he was giving us an unnecessarily hard time. I saw his face staring grimly at us as I started up the car and pulled away.

But maybe I did him an injustice. We slid forward between the trees and in a few seconds he was lost to sight behind us. We moved on, through forests and across small glades, over gently rolling territory for about half an hour more, without encountering anything. I was just figuring that we could not be more than two or three kilometers short of where the Force-Leader had estimated the sound of Friendly armor to be coming from when it happened.

There was a sudden swift sound and blow that seemed to tilt the instrument panel suddenly into my face, smashing me into unconsciousness.

I blinked and opened my eyes. His round face concerned, Dave was out of his own seat harness and bent over me, unfastening mine.

"What?" I muttered. But he paid no attention, merely getting me loose and getting me out of the air-car.

He wanted me to lie down on the moss; but by the time we were outside the vehicle, my head had cleared. I had been, I thought, almost more dazed than out. But, when I turned to look back at the air-car, I felt grateful that that had been the worst to happen to me.

We had run across a vibration mine. Of course the air-car, like any vehicle designed for use around battlefields, had sensor rods projecting out of it at odd angles; and one of these had set off the mine while we were still a dozen feet from it. But still the air-car now had a tangle of junk for a front end, and the instrument panel was pretty well wrecked by my head; so much so that it was surprising I had not even a cut on my forehead to show for it, though a rather considerable bruise was already rising there.

"I'm all right—*I'm all right!*" I said irritably to Dave. And then I swore at the air-car for a few minutes to relieve my feelings.

"What do we do now?" asked Dave when I was finished.

"Head for the Friendly lines on foot. They're the closest!" I growled. The warning of the Force-Leader came back to my mind, and I swore again. Then, because I had to take it out on somebody, I snapped at Dave. "We're still out here to get a newsstory, remember?"

I turned and stalked away in the direction the air-car had been headed. There were probably other vibration mines around, but walking on foot, I would not have the weight or disturbance to spring them. After a moment Dave caught up with me and we walked along in silence together over the mosslike groundcover, between the enormous tree trunks, until glancing back, I saw that the air-car was out of sight behind us.

It was only then, when it was too late, that it occurred to me that I had forgotten to check my wrist director with the direction indicator in the air-car. I glanced at the director on my wrist now. It seemed to indicate the Friendly lines as just ahead. If it had kept correlation with the direction indicator in the air-car, all was well. If not—among these huge pillars of tree trunks, on this soft, unending, mossy carpet, every

direction looked alike. Turning back to search for the air-car to correct
the correlation could make us lost in a real sense.

Well, there was nothing to be done about it now. The important
thing was to keep on in a straight line forward through the dimness
and silence of the forest. I locked the wrist director to our present line
of march and hoped for the best. We kept on—toward the Friendly
battle line, I hoped, wherever that might be.

Chapter 10

I had seen enough of this part of the territory from the air-car to be fairly sure that whatever was going on, either in the movement of Friendly or Cassidan forces, was not taking place in the open. So we stuck to the trees, moving from one grove to another.

Necessarily, this meant that we were not able to go straight in the direction the patrol's Force-Leader had pointed, but zigzagged to it as the wooded cover permitted. It was slow going, on foot.

By noon, disgusted, I sat down with Dave to eat the cold lunch we had packed along. By noon we had seen no one since the Cassidan patrol earlier, heard nothing, discovered nothing. We had moved forward from the point where we left the air-car only about three kilometers, but because of the arrangement of the wooded patches, we had angled south about five kilometers.

"Maybe they've gone home—the Friendlies, I mean," suggested Dave.

He was joking, with a grin on his face that I saw as I jerked up my head from my sandwich to stare at him. I managed a grin in return, feeling I owed him at least that. The truth of the matter was that he had been an unusually good assistant, keeping his mouth shut and avoiding the making of suggestions born in ignorance not only of warfare but of Newswork.

"No," I said, "something's up—but I was an idiot to let myself get separated from that air-car. We just can't cover enough territory on foot. The Friendlies have pulled back for some reason, at least at this end of the front. Probably it was to draw the Cassidan levies in after them, would be my guess. But why we haven't seen black uniforms counterattacking before now—"

"Listen!" said Dave.

He had turned his head and held up his hand to stop me talking. I broke off and listened. Sure enough, at some distance off, I heard a *wump*, a muffled, innocuous sound like a blanket snapping, as if it were being shaken out by an energetic housewife.

"Sonics!" I said, scrambling to my feet and leaving the rest of our picnic lunch lying. "By God, they're starting to get some action on after all! Let's see." I pivoted, trying to aim myself at the direction the noise had come from. "That sounded about a couple of hundred meters off, and over to our right—"

I never finished speaking. Suddenly, Dave and I were caught in the heart of a thunderclap. I found myself lying on the moss without remembering how I had got there. Five feet away, Dave was lying sprawled out; and less than forty feet away was a shallow, scooped area of torn-up earth, surrounded by trees that appeared to have exploded from internal pressure, with the white wood of their insides showing splintered and spread.

"Dave!" I got to him, and turned him over. He was breathing, and, as I watched, his eyes opened. His eyes were bloodshot, and he was bleeding from the nose. At the sight of his blood I became conscious of a wetness of my own upper lip, a salt taste in my mouth, and, putting up my hand, felt the blood dripping from my own nose.

I wiped it away with one hand. With the other hand, I pulled Dave to his feet.

"Barrage!" I said. "Come on, Dave! We've got to get out of here." For the first time, the reaction of Eileen if I should fail to bring him safely home to her presented itself to my mind in vivid image. I had been sure of the protection my skilled mind and tongue could provide for Dave between the battle lines. But you cannot argue with a sonic cannon, firing from five to fifty kilometers away.

He made it to his feet. He had been closer to the "burst" of the sonic capsule than I had, but luckily the effective zone of a sonic explosion is bell-shaped, with the wide mouth of the bell-area downward. So we had both been in the rim-part of that sudden imbalance of internal and external pressures. He was only a little more dazed than I was. And shortly, recovering somewhat as we went, we were both legging it away from the area, back at an angle toward where figuring from my wrist director indicated the Cassidan lines should be.

We stopped, finally, out of breath, and sat down for a moment, panting. We could hear the *wump, wump* of the barrage bursts continuing, some little distance behind us.

"—'s all right," I panted to Dave. "They'll lift the barrage and send in troops before they follow up with armor. Troops we can talk sense to. With sonic cannon and armored vehicles we'd never have a chance. Might as well sit here and pull ourselves together, then strike sideways along the lines to join up with either a Cassidan force, or the first wave of Friendlies—whichever we run into first."

I saw him looking at me with an expression I could not fathom at first. Then, to my astonishment, I recognized it as admiration.

"You saved my life back there," he said.

"Saved your—" I broke off. "Look, Dave, I'm the last man to turn down credit when credit is due. But that sonic only knocked you out for a second."

"But you knew what to do when we came to," he said. "And you didn't just think of doing it for yourself. You waited to get me on my feet and help me get out of there, too."

I shook my head, and let it go at that. If he had accused me instead of deliberately trying to save myself first, I would not have thought it worth the trouble to change his mind. So, since he had chosen to go the other way in his opinion, why should I bother to change that, either? If he liked to consider me a selfless-minded hero, let him.

"Suit yourself," I said. "Let's go."

We got back on our feet a little shakily—there was no doubt that same burst had taken it out of us both—and moved off southward at an angle that ought to cut the line of any Cassidan resistance, if indeed we were as far forward of their main posts as our earlier encounter with the patrol had indicated.

After a little while the *wump, wump* of the barrage moved away from our right on ahead of us and finally died out into the distance. In spite of myself, I found myself sweating a little and hoping we would come upon Cassidans before the Friendly infantry swept over us. The business of the sonic capsule had reminded me of how big a part chance plays in the matter of death and wounds on a battlefield. I would like to get Dave safely under the protective shell of a gun emplacement, so that there would be a chance to talk to any of the black-uniformed men we came upon before any shooting began.

For myself, there was no danger. My billowing Newsman's cloak, the colors of which I had this day set on a dazzling white and scarlet, advertised me as a noncombatant as far as I could be seen. Dave, on the other hand, was still wearing a Cassidan's field-gray uniform, though without insignia or decorations and with a noncombatant's white armband. I crossed my fingers, for luck.

The luck worked; but not to the extent of bringing us to a Cassidan gun-emplacement shell. A small neck of woods running up the spine of a hill brought us to its top and a red-yellow flare, blinding in the dimness under the trees, burst in warning half a dozen feet in front of us. I literally knocked Dave to the ground with a hand in the middle of his back and skidded to a stop myself, waving my arms.

"Newsman!" I shouted. "Newsman! I'm a noncombatant!"

"I know you're a goddam Newsman!" called back a voice tense with anger and stifled with caution. "Get on over here, both of you, and keep your voices down!"

I gave Dave a hand up, and we went, still half-blinded, toward the voice. As we moved, my vision cleared; and twenty steps farther on I found myself behind the eight-foot-thick trunk of an enormous yellow birch, face to face once more with the Cassidan Force-Leader who had warned me about going on toward the Friendly line.

"You again!" we both said in the same second. But then our reactions varied. Because he began telling me in a low, fervent, and determined voice, just what he thought of civilians like myself who got themselves mixed up in the front lines of a battle.

Meanwhile, I was paying little attention and using the seconds to pull my own wits together. Anger is a luxury—the Force-Leader might be a good soldier, but he had not yet learned that elemental fact in all occupations. He ran down finally.

"The point is," he said grimly, "you *are* on my hands. And what am I going to do with you?"

"Nothing," I answered. "We're here at our own risk, to observe. And observe we will. Tell us where we can dig in out of your way, and that'll be the last you'll have to think of us."

"I'll bet!" he said sourly, but it was merely a last spark of his anger sputtering out. "All right. Over there. Behind the men dug in between those two trees. And stay in your spot once you pick it!"

"All right," I said. "But before we take off, would you answer me one other question? What're you supposed to be doing on this hill?"

He glared at me as if he would not answer. Then, the emotion inside him forced the answer out.

"Holding it!" he said. And he looked as if he would have liked to spit, to clean the taste of those two words out of his mouth.

"Holding it? With a patrol?" I stared at him. "You can't hold a position like this with a dozen or so men if the Friendlies are moving in!" I waited, but he said nothing. "Or can you?"

"No," he answered. And this time he did spit. "But we're going to try. Better lay that cloak out where the black helmets can see it when they come up the hill." He turned away to the man beside him wearing the message unit. "Get Command HQ," I heard him say. "Tell him we've got a couple of Newsmen up here with us!"

I got the name, and unit, and the names of the men in his patrol; then I took Dave off to the spot the Force-Leader had indicated, and we started digging in just like the soldiers around us. Nor did I forget to spread my cloak out in front of our two foxholes as the Force-Leader had said. Pride runs a very slow second to the desire to remain alive.

From our holes, once we were in them, we could look down the steeper slope of the wooded hill toward the direction of the Friendly lines. The trees went all the way down the hill and continued on to the next hill beyond. But halfway down, there was the scar of an old landslip, like a miniature cliff, breaking the even roof of treetops, so that we could look out between the pillars of those tree trunks rising from the upper edge of the landslip and see over the tops of the trees at the bottom edge, and thus get a view of the whole panorama of wooded slope and open field toward the far green horizon under which probably sat the Friendly sonic cannon Dave and I had run from earlier.

It was our first good look at the general field since I had brought the air-car down to ground level, and I was busy studying it through glasses, when I saw what seemed to be a flicker of movement among the tree trunks at the bottom of the divide between our hill and the next. The flicker was not enough for me to pick out anything definite, but at the same time I saw movement in both of the foxholes ahead of us and knew that the soldiers in them had been alerted by whichever one of them carried the patrol's heat-sensing unit. The screens of which would now be showing the blips of the body heat of men, starting to mix in with the earth vegetation, and other heat of the ground area before us.

The Friendlies had found us. In a few seconds, there was no question of it, for even my glasses picked out flickers of black as their soldiers began to work their way up the slope of the hill toward our front and the weapons of the Cassidan patrol began to whicker and snap in response.

"Down!" I said to Dave.

He had been trying to raise up and see. I suppose he thought that because I was raising up to get a better view and so exposing myself, he could too. It was true that the Newsman's cloak was spread out in front of both our holes; but I also had my beret color controls set on scarlet and white, and in addition I had more faith in my ability to survive than he. All men have such moments when they feel invulnerable; and the moment in that foxhole, with the Friendly troops attacking, was one of mine. Besides, I was expecting the current Friendly attack on us to die down and quit in a moment.

And sure enough, it did.

Chapter 11

There was no great mystery about the pause that came then in the Friendly attack. The men who had come into momentary contact with us were little more than a skirmish line out in front of the main Friendly forces. It had been their job to push the Cassidan opposition ahead of them, until it dug in and showed signs of fighting. When that happened the first line of skirmishers had, predictably, backed off, sent messages for reinforcements, and waited.

It was a military tactic older than Julius Caesar—assuming Julius Caesar were still alive.

But it, and the rest of the circumstances that had brought Dave and me to this place and moment, provided me with the mental ammunition to draw a couple of conclusions.

The first was that all of us—I included the Friendly forces as well as the Cassidan, and the whole war right down to its involved individuals, like Dave and myself—were being shoved around by the plannings of forces outside and beyond the battlefield. And it was not too hard to figure who those manipulating forces might be. One, clearly, was Eldest Bright and his concern with whether the Friendly mercenaries wrapped up their assignment in such a way as to attract further employers to their employment. Bright, like one chess player facing another, had planned and set in motion some kind of move aimed at wrapping up the war in one bold tactical strike.

But that strike had been, if not foreseen, at least precalculated by his opponent. And that opponent could only be Padma, with his ontogenetics.

For if Padma, with his calculations, could figure that I would put in an appearance at the party of Donal Graeme on Freiland, then with the same ontogenetics he would have been able to calculate that Bright would make some swift move with the Friendly forces to destroy the Cassidan levies opposing them. His calculation of this was deducible from the fact that he had lent one of his own best tacticians from the Exotic forces—Kensie Graeme—to frustrate what Bright had planned. Without that explanation Kensie's appearance here on the battlefield at the crucial moment made no sense.

But the interesting question to me, behind all this, was why Padma should automatically oppose himself to Bright in any case. As far as I knew the Exotics had no stake in this civil war on New Earth—important enough to the world on which it was occurring, but small compared to other matters between the sixteen worlds and the stars.

The answer might lie somewhere in the tangle of contractual agreements that controlled the ebb and flow of trained personnel between the worlds. The Exotics, like Earth, Mars, Freiland, Dorsai, and the little Catholic Christian world of Ste. Marie, did not draft their trained young graduates en bloc, and trade off their contracts to other worlds without consulting the wishes of the individual. They were therefore known as "loose" worlds; in automatic opposition to "tight" worlds like Ceta, the Friendlies, Venus, Newton, and the rest who bartered their skilled personnel without concern for individual rights or desires.

The Exotics, therefore, being "loose" worlds, were automatically in opposition to the "tight" worlds of the Friendlies. But this alone was not reason enough for their choosing up sides in a conflict on some third world gratuitously. There might be some secret tangle of contractual balances concerning the Exotics and the Friendlies I knew nothing about. Otherwise, I was at a loss to understand Padma's taking a hand in the current situation.

But it showed me, who was concerned with manipulating my environment by manipulating those immediately around me, that forces could be brought into play outside the charmed circle of my tongue, which could frustrate anything I could do, simply because they were from outside. In short, there were wider areas to be considered in the handling of men and events to some individually desired end than I had thought of before this.

I filed that discovery away for future reference.

The second conclusion that came to mind now had to do with the immediate matter of our defending this hill as soon as the Friendlies could bring up reinforcements. For it was no place to defend with a couple of dozen men. Even a civilian like myself could see that.

If I could see it, certainly the Friendlies could see it, to say nothing of the Force-Leader of the patrol, himself. Obviously he was holding it under orders from his Headquarters, a good deal farther back behind the lines. For the first time I began to see some excuse for this unwelcoming attitude where Dave and I were concerned. He obviously had his troubles—including some superior officer back at Headquarters who would ask him and his patrol to hold such a place as this hill. I began to feel more kindly toward the Force-Leader. Wise, panic-stricken, or foolish his orders might be; but he was soldier enough to do his best to carry them out.

It would make a great story, his hopeless attempt to defend this hill, with no support on either side or behind him and the whole Friendly army in front. And between the lines of my writing, I could have my say about the kind of command who had put him there. And then I looked around the slope and saw the enlisted men of his patrol dug in and a cool, sickly feeling knotted my stomach right under my breastbone. For they were in this, too, and they did not know the price they were about to pay in order to become heroes in my newsstory.

Dave punched me in the side.

"Look there—over there—" he breathed in my ear. I looked.

There was a stir among the Friendlies hidden in the trees at the bottom of the hill. But they were clearly only picking up extra strength and grouping for an actual assault on the hill. Nothing would happen for a few minutes yet, and I was about to tell Dave so, when he jogged me again.

"No!" he said, low-voiced, but urgently. "Out there. Away out. Near the horizon."

I looked. And I saw what he meant. Out there among the trees that finally met the sky, now turning hot and blue, some ten kilometers, or about six miles, off, there were firefly-like flickers. Little yellow flashes among the green and occasionally a little upward plume of something white or dark that dissipated on the breeze.

But no fireflies ever flickered so as to be seen in broad daylight like that, and at a distance of over six miles. They were heat beams we were looking at.

"Armor!" I said.

"They're coming this way," said Dave, staring fascinated at the flashes, looking so small and trivial at that distance. Flashes that were in reality swords of searing light, forty thousand degrees centigrade at the core, that could topple the huge trees around us as a razor blade might slice through a bed of standing asparagus.

They were coming on unopposed, for there were no infantry worthy of the name in their way to take them out with plastics or sonic hand-weapons. Missiles, the classic defense against armor, had been outdated nearly fifty years by counter-missilery advanced to the point where reaction speeds of half-light made their use on planetary surfaces impossible. They were coming on slowly, but unstoppably, burning out on principle any likely hiding spots for infantry they passed.

Their coming made our defense of the hill a mockery. For if the Friendly infantry did not sweep over us before the armor got here, we would be fried in our foxholes. It was plain to me—and plain to the men of the platoon as well, for I heard a little humming moan move along the hillside as the soldiers in the other holes spotted the flashes.

"Silence!" snapped the Force-Leader from his. "Hold your positions. If you don't—"

But he had no time to finish, for, at that moment, the first serious assault of the Friendly infantry mounted the slope against us.

And a sliver from a spring-gun took the Force-Leader high in the chest, just at the base of the neck, so that he fell back, choking on his own blood.

But the rest of the patrol had no time to notice this, for the assaulting Friendly spring-gunmen, wave on wave of them, were halfway up the slope to them. Low in their foxholes, the Cassidans fired back; and either the hopelessness of their position or an unusual amount of battle experience was paying off for them, for I did not see a single man who was paralyzed by combat fear and not using his gun.

They had all the advantage of it. The slope steepened as the top of the hill was approached. The Friendlies slowed and were shot down easily as they came closer. They broke and ran once more for the bottom of the hill. And once again, there was a pause in the firing.

I scrambled out of my foxhole and ran over toward the Force-Leader, to find out if he was still alive. It was a foolish thing to do, standing up in plain sight like that, Newsman's cape or not; and I paid for it accordingly. The retreating Friendlies had lost friends and fellow soldiers on the hill. Now one of them reacted. Just a few steps short of the Force-Leader's foxhole, something chopped my left leg out from under me and I went down, skidding, on my face.

The next thing I knew I was in the command foxhole beside the Force-Leader, and Dave was leaning over me, crowding the narrow space which also held two Groupmen, who must have been the Force-Leader's noncoms.

"What's going on . . ." I began, and tried to get to my feet. Dave moved to push me back; but I had already tried to put some of my weight on my left leg; and a tiger's-tooth of pain drove through it, so that I slumped again, half-fainting, and soaked in my own sweat.

"Got to fall back," one of the Groupmen was saying to the other.

"Got to get out of here, Akke. Next time they'll get us, or if we wait twenty minutes the armor'll do it for them!"

"No," croaked the Force-Leader beside me. I had thought him dead; but when I turned to look, I saw someone had set a pressure bandage against his wound, and released the trigger, so that its fibers would be inside the hole in him now, sealing apertures and clotting the blood flow. All the same he was dying. I could see it in his eyes. The Groupman ignored him.

"Listen to me, Akke," said the Groupman who had just spoken. "You're in command now. Got to move!"

"No." The Force-Leader could barely whisper, but whisper he did. "Orders. Hold at all—costs—"

The Groupman evidently called Akke looked uncertain. His face was pale and he turned to look at the communications unit beside him in the foxhole. The other Groupman saw the direction of his glance and the spring-rifle across his knees went off, as if by accident. There was a smash and a tinkle inside the communications unit and I could see the ready light on its instrument panel go dark.

"I order you," the Force-Leader was saying: but then the terrible jaws of pain closed upon my knee once more and my head swam. When my vision cleared again, I could see that Dave had ripped my left pant's leg up above the knee and just finished setting a neat, white pressure bandage around the knee.

"It's all right, Tam," he was saying to me. "The spring-rifle sliver went all the way through. It's all right."

I looked around. The Force-Leader still sat beside me, now with his side-arm half drawn. There was another spring-rifle wound, this time in his forehead and he was quite dead. Of the two Groupmen, there was no sign.

"They've gone, Tam," said Dave. "We've got to get out of here, too." He pointed down the hill. "The Friendly troops decided we weren't worth it. They pulled out. But their armor's getting close— and you can't move fast with that knee. Try to stand up, now."

I tried. It was like standing with one knee resting on the needle-point of a stake and bearing half my weight on that. But I stood. Dave helped me out of the foxhole; and we began our limping retreat down the back way of the hill, away from the armor.

I had likened those woods earlier in my thoughts to a Robin Hood-like forest, in their openness, dimness and color finding them fancifully attractive. Now, as I struggled through them, with each step, or hop rather, feeling as if a red-hot nail was being driven into my knee, my image of the tree groves began to change. They became darkling, ominous, hateful and full of cruelty, in the fact that they held us trapped in their shadow where the Friendly armor would seek us out and destroy us either with heat beams or falling trees before we had a chance to explain who we were.

I had hoped desperately that we would catch sight of an open area. For the armored vehicles floating up behind us were hunting the woods, not the open spaces; and particularly out in the open knee-high grass, it would be hard for even an armored pilot to see and identify my cape before shooting at us.

But we had evidently moved into an area where there were much more trees than open spaces. Also, as I had noticed before, all directions among those tree trunks looked alike. Our only way of being sure we would not be traveling in circles, but of keeping in a straight line away from the pursuing tanks, was to follow back along the direction we had come. This direction we could follow because we could be guided back along it by my wrist director. But that direction, that line of march that had brought us here, had been deliberately through all the treed areas I could find.

Meanwhile, we were moving at so slow a pace because of my knee that even the relatively slow-moving armor must soon catch up with us. I had been badly shaken by the sonic explosion earlier. Now, the continual jab-jabbing of the brilliant pain through my knee goaded me into a sort of feverish frenzy. It was like some calculated torture— and it happens that I am not a stoic when it comes to pain.

Neither am I cowardly, though I do not think it would be fair to call me brave, either. It is simply that I am so constructed that my response to pain beyond a certain level is fury. And the greater the pain the greater my rage. Some ancient berserker blood, perhaps, filtering down through the Irish in my veins, if you want to be romantic about it. But there it is—the fact. And now, as we hobbled through the eternal twilight between those gold-and-silver, peeling tree trunks, I exploded inside.

In my rage, I had no fear of the Friendly armor. I was certain of the fact that they would see my white and scarlet cloak in time not to fire at me. I was positive that if they did fire, both their beam and any falling tree trunks or limbs would miss me. In short I was convinced of my own invulnerability—and the only thing that concerned me was that Dave was being slowed down by being with me and that if anything happened to him Eileen would never get over it.

I raved at him, I cursed him. I told him to go on and leave me, and save his own neck, that I was in no danger by myself.

His only answer was that I had not abandoned him when the sonic barrage caught us both; and he would not abandon me. I was Eileen's brother and it was his duty to take care of me. It was just as she had said in her letter, he was loyal. He was too damn loyal, he was a loyal damn fool—and I told him so, obscenely and at length. I tried valiantly to pull away from him; but hopping on one leg, tottering on one leg rather, it was no use. I sank down on the ground and refused to go any farther; but he actually outwrestled me and got me up on his back, piggy-back, and tried to carry me that way.

That was even worse. I had to promise to go along with him, if he would let me down. He was already tottering himself from weariness when he let me. By that time, half-insane with my pain and my fury, I was ready to do anything to save him from himself. I began to yell for help as loudly as I could in spite of his efforts to shut me up.

It worked. In less than five minutes after he got me quiet we found ourselves staring down the pinhole muzzles of the spring-rifles in the hands of two young Friendly skirmishers, attracted by my shouts.

Chapter 12

I had expected them to appear in answer to my shouts even more quickly. The Friendly skirmishers were naturally all around us almost from the moment we left the hill to its dead, under the command of their dead Force-Leader. These two might have been among the same Friendlies who had discovered the patrol dug in on the hill in the first place. But, having found it, they had moved on.

For it was their job to discover important pockets of Cassidan resistance, so that they could call for strength to eliminate those points. They would be carrying listening devices as part of their equipment, but they would pay little attention if those devices picked up merely the sound of two men arguing. Two men were game too small for their orders to concern themselves with.

But one man deliberately calling for help—that was an occurrence unusual enough to be worth investigating. A Soldier of the Lord should not be weak enough to be so calling, whether he needed personal assistance or not. And why should a Cassidan be appealing for aid in this area where no fighting had been going on? And who other than Soldiers of the Lord or their weaponed enemies might be in this zone of battle?

Now they knew who might be—a Newsman and his assistant. Both noncombatants, as I was quick to point out to them. Nevertheless the spring-rifles remained steadily aimed at us.

"Damn your eyes!" I told them. "Can't you see I need medical attention? Get me to one of your field hospitals right away!"

They looked back at me with startlingly innocent eyes in smooth young faces. The one on the right wore the single collar mark of a lance-private, the other was an ordinary battle-class private soldier. Neither one of them was out of his teens.

"We have no orders to turn aside and return to a field hospital," said the lance-private, speaking for both of them, as the—barely— superior in rank. "I can only conduct you to a gathering spot for prisoners, where no doubt other measures will be taken for your care." He stepped back, his rifle still aimed at us. "Do thou help the other to aid this wounded man along, Greten," he said dropping into the cant to speak to his partner. "Take his other side and I will follow with both our weapons."

The other soldier passed over his spring-rifle and between him and Dave, I began getting over the ground a little more comfortably, although the rage still seethed and bubbled in me. They brought us to a clearing finally, not an actual grass-filled clearing exposed to the sun, but a spot where one huge tree had fallen and left open a sort of glade among the other giants. Here, there were perhaps twenty or so dejected-looking Cassidans, disarmed and being held under guard by four young Friendlies like those who had captured us.

Dave and the young Friendly soldier sat me down carefully with my back to the stump of the huge fallen tree. Then Dave was herded over to join the rest of the uniformed Cassidans, who were backed against the tall trunk of the fallen and moldering tree itself, with the four armed Friendly guards facing them. I shouted that Dave should be left with me as a noncombatant, pointing out his white armband and lack of insignia. But all six of the men in black uniforms ignored me.

"Who hath rank here?" asked the lance-private of the four guards.

"I am senior," answered one of them, "but my rank is less than thine."

He was, in fact, a plain battle-private. However, he was well into his twenties, plainly older than the rest of them, and his quick disclaimer of authority had the ring of the experienced soldier, who has learned not to volunteer for things.

"This man is a Newsman," said the lance-private, indicating me, "and does claim the other under his protection. Certain the Newsman needeth medical attention; and though none of us can take him to the nearest field hospital, maybe thou canst call his case to the attention of higher authority over thy communicator."

"We have none," said the older soldier. "Message center is two hundred meters distant."

"I and Greten will remain to assist thy guard while one of you go to your message center."

"There was no provision"—the older, battle-private looked stubborn—"in our orders for one of us to leave for such a purpose."

"Surely this is a special case and situation?"

"There was no provision."

"But—"

"I tell thee, there was no provision made for this!" the battle-
private shouted at him. "We can do nothing until an officer or a Groupman comes!"

"Will he come shortly?" The lance-private had been shaken by the
vehemence of the objections of the older man. He glanced over at me
worriedly; and I thought that perhaps he was beginning to think he had
made a mistake in even mentioning medical help for us. But I had
underestimated him. His face was a little pale, but he spoke evenly
enough to the older man.

"I do not know," answered the other.

"Then I myself will go to your message center. Wait here, Greten."

He shouldered his spring-rifle and went off. We never saw him
again.

Meanwhile, the fury and the body adrenalin that had helped me
fight the pain of the hole drilled through my kneecap and the flesh and
nerves and bone beyond it were beginning to wear off. I no longer felt
the recurrent stab of agony as I tried to move the leg, but a swelling,
steady ache was beginning to send billows of pain up my thigh from
it—or so it seemed—and this was making me lightheaded. I began to
wonder if I could stand it—and then, suddenly, with the feeling of
stupidity that hits you when you realize all at once that what you have
been searching for has been right before your eyes all this time, I
remembered my belt.

Clipped to my belt, as to the belt of all soldiers, was a field-
medication kit. Almost ready to laugh in spite of the pain, I reached
for it now, fumbled it open, thumbed out two of the octagonal pills I
found there—unaccountably, it was growing dark under the trees
where we were, so that I could not make out their red color, but their
shape was identity enough. It had been designed for just that purpose.

I chewed and swallowed them dry. Off in the distance, it seemed,
I heard Dave's voice, unaccountably shouting. But, swift as cyanide
on the tongue, the anesthetic, tranquilizing effect of the pain pills was
sweeping through me. The pain was washed away before it, leaving
me feeling whole, and clean and new—and unconcerned about anything beyond the peace and comfort of my own body.

Once more I heard Dave shouting. This time I understood him, but
the message of his shouting had no power to disturb me. He was calling

that he had already given me the pain pills from his own kit, when I had passed out twice before. He was shouting that I had now taken an overdose, that someone should help me. Distant, also, at the same time, the grove grew quite dark and there was a roll like thunder overhead, and then I heard, as one hears some distant, charming symphony, the patter of millions of raindrops on the millions of leaves far overhead.

And I went away into comforting nothingness.

When I came back to myself again, for a while I paid very little attention to anything around me, for I was cramped and nauseated, with the aftereffects of the drug overdose. My knee no longer hurt if it was not moved, but it had swollen and grown stiff as a steel rod; and the slightest movement of it brought a jolt of pain that shook me like a blow.

I vomited and began slowly to feel better internally. Slowly, I began to be aware once more of what was going on around me. I was wet to the skin, for the rain, after being held up a little by the leaves overhead, had worked its way down to us. Off a little way by the trees, both the prisoners and the guards made a sodden group. There was a newcomer in the black uniform of the Friendlies. He was a Groupman, middle-aged, lean and lined heavily in the face; and he had taken the battle-private called Greten aside in my direction, evidently to argue with him.

Above us, in the little openings between the tree branches that had been left by the falling of the giant tree that had produced the forest glade, the sky had lightened after the thunderstorm; but though it was cloudless, it was all flushed now with the crimson of sunset. To my drug-distorted vision, that red came down and painted the outlines of the wet-dark figures of the gray-clad prisoners, and glittered the soaked black uniforms of the Friendlies.

Red and black, black and red, they were like some figures in a stained-glass window, under the huge, over-arching frame of the shadow-dark giants that were the trees. I sat there, chilled by my own heavy, damp clothes, staring at the Groupman and the battle-private in their argument. And gradually their words, low-pitched so that they would not carry to the prisoners, but plain to my closer ears, began to make sense to me.

"Thou art a child!" the Groupman was snarling. He lifted his head a little with the vehemence of his emotion; and the sunset sky reached down to illuminate his face with red, so that I saw it clearly for the first time—and saw in its starved features and graven lines the same sort of harsh and utter fanaticism I had found in the Groupman at

Friendly Battle Headquarters who had turned down the chance of a pass for Dave.

"Thou art a child!" he repeated. "Young thou art! What dost thou know of the struggle to gain sustenance, generation on generation, on our harsh and stony worlds, as I have known it? What dost thou know of hunger and want, even to the women and babes, I say it, among the Children of the Lord? What dost thou know of the purposes of them who send us to battle, that our people may live and flourish when all men elsewhere would gladly see us dead and our faith dead and buried with us?"

"I know something," retorted the younger soldier, though his voice showed its youth and trembled a little even as he answered. "I know that we have a duty to the right, and that we have sworn to the Mercenaries' Code, and—"

"Shut thy milk-babe mouth!" hissed the Groupman. "What are Codes before the Code of the Almighty? What are oaths other than our oath to the God of Battles? Lo, our Eldest of our Council of Elders, he who is called Bright, hath said that this day bears hard upon the future of our people, and the winning of this day's war is a need that we must meet. Therefore shall we win! And nothing else!"

"But still I tell thee—"

"Thou shalt tell me nothing! I am thy superior! I tell *thee*. Our orders are to regroup for another attack upon the enemy. Thou and these four with thee are to report *now*, to their message center. It recks not that thou art not of their unit. Thou hast been called and will obey!"

"Then we shall take the prisoners safely with us—"

"*Thou shalt obey!*" The Groupman was carrying his spring-gun slung under one arm. He swung it around into his grasp so that the barrel pointed at the private. The Groupman's thumb pushed the control of the weapon to automatic fire. I saw Greten's eyes close for a second and his throat worked; but when his voice came out, it was still steady.

"Yet all my life have I walked in the shadow of the Lord which is truth and faith—" I heard him say, and the barrel came up. I shouted at the Groupman.

"You! Hey, you—Groupman!"

He jerked about like a timber wolf at the sound of a snapping twig under a hunter's boot—and I was looking down the pinhole muzzle of his automatic-set spring-rifle myself. Then he came toward me, gun still aimed, and the axe blade of his starved fanatic's face above it looked down at me.

"Thou art sensible, then?" he said. And the words were like a

sneer. I read in them a contempt for anyone weak enough to take a
pain-killer for the relief of any physical discomfort.

"Sensible enough to tell you a few things," I croaked. My throat
was dry and my leg was beginning to stir to an ache again, but he was
good medicine for me, reawakening my anger, so that the returning
hurt could feed the fury that rose easily in me. "Listen to me. I'm a
Newsman. You've been around long enough to know that nobody
wears this cape and beret who isn't entitled to them. But just to make
sure"—I dug into my jacket and produced them—"here are my papers.
Look them over."

He took them and glanced through them.

"All right now," I said, when he had looked at the last of them.
"I'm a Newsman and you're a Groupman. And I'm not asking you
anything—I'm telling you! I want transportation to a field hospital
immediately, and I want my assistant over there"—and I pointed at
Dave—"returned to me. Now! Not ten minutes from now, or two
minutes from now; but now! These privates who've been on guard
here may not think they have the authority to get me and my assistant
out of here and me to a hospital, but you know you have. And I want
it done!"

He stared from the papers to me and there came over his face a
peculiar grimness of cast, the sort of look a man might get as he shakes
off the grasp of those escorting him to a gallows and strides forward
to the place of his execution contemptuously under his own power.

"Thou art a Newsman," he said, and drew a deep breath. "Aye,
thou art one of Anarch's breed, who with lies and false report spreads
hatred of our people and our faith throughout the worlds of men. I
know thee well, Newsman"—he stared at me with black, hollowed
eyes—"and thy papers to me are but trash and nonsense. But I will
humor thee, and show thee how little thou weighest in the balance,
with all thy foul reports. I will give thee a story to write, and thou
shalt write it, and thou shalt see how it is less than dry leaves blowing
before the marching feet of the Anointed of the Lord."

"Get me to a field hospital," I said.

"Thou shalt wait for that," he said. "Further"—and he waved the
papers at me—"I see here thy pass, but no pass signed by one of
authority in our ranks that gives free passage to the one thou callest
thy assistant. Therefore he shall not come to thee, but remain with
those prisoners of like uniform, to meet what the Lord shall send
them."

He threw the papers down into my lap, turned and stalked off, back toward the prisoners. I shouted after him, telling him to come back; but he paid me no attention.

But Greten ran after him, caught him by the arm and murmured something in his ear, meanwhile gesturing sharply toward the group of prisoners. The Groupman shoved him off with a thrust of his arm that sent Greten staggering.

"Are they of the Chosen?" the Groupman shouted. "Are *they* Chosen of God?"

And he whirled about in fury, with his spring-rifle still set on automatic menacing not merely Greten, but the other guards as well.

"Fall in!" he shouted.

Some slowly, some hastily, they left off guarding the prisoners and fell into line, facing the Groupman.

"You shall all report to the Message Center—now!" the Groupman snapped. "Right face!" And they turned. *"Move out!"*

And so they left us, moving off out of my sight among the shadows of the trees.

The Groupman watched after them for a second, then turned his attention and his rifle back on the Cassidan prisoners. They shrank a little from him; and I saw the white, indistinct outline of Dave's face turned momentarily in my direction.

"Now, your guards are gone," the Groupman said to them slowly and grimly. "For an assault begins that will wipe your forces from the field. In that assault every soldier of the Lord is needed, for a call has been placed upon us by our Eldest in Council. Even I must go—and I cannot leave enemies like yourselves unguarded behind our lines, to do mischief against our victory. Therefore, I send you now to a place from which you cannot harm the Anointed of the Lord."

In that moment, in that moment only, for the first time, I understood what he meant. And I opened my mouth to shout; but nothing came out. I tried to rise, but my stiff leg would not let me. And I hung there, mouth open, frozen in the act of half-rising.

He opened fire at full automatic upon the unarmed men before him. And they fell—Dave among them—they dropped and fell, and died.

Chapter 13

I am not clear in my mind exactly how things went after that. I remember, when there was no longer any stir or movement among the fallen bodies, how the Groupman turned and came toward me, holding his rifle in one hand.

He seemed, though he strode swiftly, to come slowly, slowly but inexorably. It was as if I watched him on a treadmill growing ever bigger as he loomed closer to me with the black rifle in his hand and the red sky behind his head. Until, at last, he reached me and stopped, standing over me.

I also tried to shrink from him, but could not; for the great stump of the tree was behind me and my damaged leg, itself stiff as a dead stick of wood, anchored me. But he did not lift his rifle against me; and he did not shoot me.

"There," he said, looking at me. His voice was deep and calm, but his eyes were strange. "Thou hast thy story, Newsman. And thou shalt live to report it. Perhaps they will let thee come when I am led before a firing squad—unless the Lord decrees otherwise, so that I fall in the assault now beginning. But though they executed me a million times over, thy writing will avail thee nothing. For I, who am the fingers of the Lord, have writ His will upon these men, and that writing thou cannot erase. So shalt thou know at last how little is *thy* writing in the face of that which is written by the God of Battles."

He stepped back from me one step without turning his back. It was almost as if I were some dark altar from which he retreated with ironic respect.

"Now, farewell, Newsman," he said, and a hard smile twisted his lips. "Fear not, for they will find thee. And save thy life."

He turned and went. I saw him go, black into the blackness of the deeper shadows; and then I was alone.

I was alone—alone with the still dripping leaves ticking occasionally upon the forest floor. Alone with the red-darkening sky, showing in its tiny patches between the growing black masses of the treetops. Alone with the day's end and the dead.

I do not know how I did it, but after a while I began to crawl, dragging my useless leg along with me, over the wet forest floor until I came to the still heap of bodies. In the little light that remained I hunted through them until I found Dave. A line of slivers had stitched themselves across the lower part of his chest, and from there on down his jacket was soaked with blood. But his eyelids fluttered as I got my arm around his shoulders and lifted him up so that I could support his head on my good knee. His face was as white and smooth as the face of a child in sleep.

"Eileen?" he said faintly but clearly as I lifted him. But he did not open his eyes.

I opened my mouth to say something, but at first no sound would come out. Then, when I could make my vocal cords work, they sounded strange.

"She'll be here in a minute," I said.

The answer seemed to soothe him. He lay still, hardly breathing. The calmness of his face made it seem as if he were not in any pain. I heard a steady sound of dripping that at first I took to be the rain dripping still from some leaf overhead; but then I put down my hand and felt the falling of dampness on its palm. The dripping was of his blood, from the lower part of his soaked jacket, onto the forest earth below where the mosslike groundcover had been scuffed away by the scrabbling of dying men, leaving the bare earth.

I hunted around as best I could for wound dressings on the bodies near us, without disturbing Dave upon my knee. I found three of them, and tried to stop his wounds with them, but it was no use. He was bleeding from half a dozen places. By trying to put the bandages on I disturbed him, rousing him a little.

"Eileen?" he asked.

"She'll be here in a minute," I told him, again.

And, later on, after I had given up and was just sitting, holding him, he asked again.

"Eileen?"

"She'll be here in a minute."

But by the time the full dark passed and the moon rose high enough to send its silver light down through the little opening into the trees, so that I could see his face again, he was dead.

Chapter 14

I was found just after sunrise, not by Friendly, but by Cassidan troops. Kensie Graeme had fallen back at the south end of his battle line before Bright's well-laid plan of an attack to crush the Cassidan defenses there and cut them up in the streets of Dhores. But Kensie, foreseeing this, had robbed the southern end of his line and sent the armor and infantry so acquired swinging wide around to reinforce the north end of his line, where Dave and I had been.

The result was that his line pivoted about a central point, which was just about at the motor pool where I had first caught sight of him. The advancing reinforced north end of it, the following morning, swept around and down, cutting the Friendly communications and crashing in upon the rear of those Friendly troops that thought they had most of the Cassidan levies penned and broken up within the city.

Dhores, which was to have been a rock on which the Cassidan levies were broken up, became instead the rock on which the Friendly forces themselves were broken. The black-clad warriors fought with their usual fierceness and reckless bravery on being trapped; but they were between the barrage of Kensie's sonic cannon to the west of the city and his fresh forces piling in upon their rear. Finally, the Friendly Command, rather than lose any more of the valuable battle units in human shape that were their soldiers, surrendered—and the civil war between the North and South Partitions of New Earth was over, won by the Cassidan levies.

But I cared nothing about this. I was taken, half-conscious from medication, back to Molon for hospitalization. The wound in my knee had complicated itself from lack of attention—I do not know the details; but, though they were able to heal it, it remained stiff. The only cure for that, the medicians told me, was surgery and a whole new, completely artificial knee—and they advised against that. The original flesh and blood, they said, was still better than anything man could build to replace it.

For my part, I did not care. They had caught and tried the Group-man who had perpetrated the massacre; and—as he himself had pre-dicted—he had been executed by firing squad under the provisions of the Mercenaries' Code with respect to the treatment of prisoners. But I did not care even about that.

Because—again as he himself had said—his execution did not alter things. What he had written upon Dave and the other prisoners with his spring-rifle was past the power of me, or any other man, to erase; and by this much he had done something to me.

I was like a clock with a broken part in it that does not keep it from running, but which you can hear rattling away, if you pick the clock up and shake it. I had been broken, inside; and not even the commendation that came from the Interstellar News Service and my acceptance into full membership in the Guild could mend me. But the wealth and power of the Guild was caring for me, now that I was a full member; and they did what few private organizations would have been able to do—they sent me to the wizards of mental mending on Kultis, the larger of the two Exotic Worlds, for treatment.

On Kultis, they enticed me into mending myself—but they could not force the manner in which I chose to mend. First, because they did not have the power (though I am not sure if they actually realized how limited they were, in my particular case) and secondly, because their basic philosophy forbade the use of force in their own proper persons, and also forbade them any attempt to control the individual's self-will. They could only beckon me down the road they wished I would go.

And the instrument they chose to beckon me down that road was a powerful one. It was Lisa Kant.

"—But you're not a psychiatrist!" I said in astonishment to Lisa when she first appeared in the place on Kultis to which I had been brought—one of their many-purposed indoor-outdoor structures. I had been lying by a swimming pool, ostensibly soaking up sun and relax-ing, when she showed up suddenly beside me and replied, in answer to my question, that Padma had recommended she be the person to work with me in getting my emotional strength back.

"How do you know what I am?" she snapped back, not at all with the calm self-control of a born Exotic. "It's been five years since I first met you in the Encyclopedia, and I'd already been a student then for years!"

I lay blinking at her, as she stood over me. Slowly, something that had been dormant in me began to come back to life and began to tick and move once more. I got to my feet. Here was I, who had been able to choose the proper words to make people dance like puppets, making a blundering assumption like that.

"Then you actually are a psychiatrist?" I asked.

"Yes and no," she answered me quietly. Suddenly she smiled at me. "Anyway, you don't need a psychiatrist."

The moment she said this, I woke to the fact that this was exactly my own thought, that it had been my own thought all along, but encased in my own misery I had let the Guild plow to its own conclusions. Suddenly, all through the machinery of my mental awareness, little relays began to click over and perceptions to light up again.

If she knew that much, how much more did she know? At once, the alarms were ringing throughout the mental citadel I had spent these last five years in building, and defenses were rushing to their post.

"Maybe you're right," I said, suddenly wary; and I grinned at her. "Why don't we sit down and talk it over?"

"Why not?" she said.

And so we did sit down and talk—unimportant make-conversation to begin with, while I sized her up. There was a strange echo about her. I can describe it no other way. Everything she said, every gesture or movement of her, seemed to ring with special meaning for me, a meaning I could not quite interpret.

"Why did Padma think you could—I mean, think that you ought to come here and see me?" I asked cautiously after a while.

"Not just see you—work with you," she corrected me. She was wearing not the Exotic robes, but some ordinary, short street dress of white. Above it her eyes were a darker brown than I had ever seen them. Suddenly she darted a glance at me as challenging and sharp as a spear. "Because he believes I'm one of the two portals by which you can still be reached, Tam."

The glance and the words shook me. If it had not been for that strange echo about her, I might have fallen into the error of thinking she was inviting me. But it was something bigger than that.

I could have asked her then and there what she meant; but I was just newly reawakened and cautious. I changed the subject—I think I invited her to join me for a swim or something—and I did not come back to the subject until several days later.

By that time, aroused and wary, I had had a chance to look around me and see where the echo came from, to see what was being done to me by Exotic methods. I was being worked on subtly, by a skillful coordination of total environmental pressure, pressure that did not try to steer me in one direction or another, but which continually urged me to take hold of the tiller of my own being and steer myself. Briefly, the structure that housed me, the weather that bathed it, the very walls and furniture and colors and shapes that inhabited it, were so designed that they subtly combined to urge me to live—not only to live, but to live actively, fully and joyously. It was not merely a happy dwelling—it was an exciting dwelling, a stimulating environment that wrapped me around.

And Lisa was a working part of it.

I began to notice that as I roused from my depression, not only did the colors and shapes of the furniture and of the dwelling itself alter day by day, but her choice of conversational subjects, her tone of voice, her laughter changed as well, to continue to exert maximum pressure upon my own shifting and developing feelings. I do not think even Lisa herself understood how the parts combined to produce the gestalt effect. It would have taken a native Exotic to understand that. But she understood—consciously or subconsciously—her own part in it. And played it.

I did not care. Automatically, inevitably, as I healed myself I was falling in love with her.

Women had never been hard for me to find, from the time I broke loose from my uncle's house and began to feel my own powers of mind and body. Especially the beautiful ones, in whom there was often a strange hunger for affection that often ran unsatisfied. But before Lisa they had all, beautiful or not, broken, and turned hollow on me. It was as if I were continually capturing song-sparrows and bringing them home, only to find the following morning that they had become common sparrows overnight and their wild song had dwindled to a single chirp.

Then I would realize that it was my own fault—it was I who had made song-sparrows of them. Some chance trait or element in them had touched me off like a skyrocket, so that my imagination had soared, and my tongue with it, so that I had lifted us both up with words and carried us off to a place of pure light and air and green grass and running water. And there I had built us a castle full of light and air and promise and beauty.

They always liked my castle. They would come gladly up on the wings of my imagination, and I would believe that we flew together. But later, on a different day, I would wake to the fact that the light was gone, the song was muted. For they had not really believed in my castle. It was well enough to dream of such a thing, but not to think of translating it into ordinary stone, and wood, and glass and tile. When it came to these matters of reality, a castle was madness; and I should put the thought aside for some real dwelling. Perhaps of poured concrete like the home of my uncle Mathias. With practical vision screen instead of windows, with economic roof, not soaring turrets, and weathered-glassed porches, not open loggias. And so we parted.

But Lisa did not leave me as the others always had when at last I fell in love with her. She soared with me and soared again on her own. And then, for the first time I knew why she was different, why she would never retreat earthward like the others.

It was because she had built castles of her own, before I ever met her. So she needed no help from me to lift her to the land of enchantment, for she had reached there before on her own strong wings. We were sky-matched, though our castles were different.

It was that difference in castles which stopped me, which came at last to shatter the Exotic shell. Because when finally I would have made love to her, she stopped me.

"No, Tam," she said, and she fended me off. "Not yet."

"Not yet" might have meant "not this minute," or "not until tomorrow"; but, looking at the change that had come into her face, the way her eyes looked a little away from mine, suddenly I knew better. Something stood like a barred gate half-ajar between us, and my mind leaped to name it.

"The Encyclopedia," I said. "You still want me to come back and work on it." I stared at her. "All right. Ask me again."

She shook her head.

"No," she said, in a low voice. "Padma told me before I hunted you out at the Donal Graeme party that you would never come just because I asked you. But I didn't believe him then. I believe him now." She turned her face back to look me squarely in the eyes. "If I did ask now, and told you to take a moment to think about it before answering, you'd say no all over again, even now."

She sat, staring at me, by the side of the pool where we were, in the sunlight, with a bush of great yellow roses behind her, and the light of the flowers upon her.

"Wouldn't you, Tam?" she asked.

I opened my mouth, and then I closed it again. Because, like the stone hand of some heathen god, all that I had forgotten while I mended here, all of that which Mathias and then the Friendly Groupman had carved upon my soul, came back heavily down upon me.

The barred gate slammed shut then between Lisa and me, and its closing echoed in the inmost depths of my being.

"That's right," I admitted hollowly. "You're right. I'd say no."

I looked at Lisa, sitting among the shatters of our mutual dream. And I remembered something.

"When you first came here," I said slowly but unsparingly, for she was almost my enemy again now, "you mentioned something about Padma saying you were one of the two portals by which I could be reached. What was the other one? I didn't ask you then."

"But now you can't wait to stop up the other one, can you, Tam?" she said a little bitterly. "All right—tell me something." She picked up a petal fallen from one of the flowers behind her and tossed it onto the still waters of the pool, where it floated like some fragile yellow boat. "Have you gotten in touch with your sister?"

Her words crashed in upon me like a bar of iron. All the matter of Eileen and Dave, and Dave's death after I had promised Eileen to keep him safe, came swarming back on me. I found myself on my feet without knowing how I had gotten there, and a cold sweat had sprung out all over me.

"I haven't been able—" I started to answer; but my voice failed me. It strangled itself in the tightness of my throat and I stood face to face in my own soul with the knowledge of my own cowardice.

"*They've* notified her!" I shouted, turning furiously on Lisa where she still sat watching up at me. "The Cassidan authorities will have told her all about it! What's the matter—don't you think she knows what happened to Dave?"

But Lisa said nothing. She only sat, looking up at me. Then I realized that she would go on saying nothing. No more than the Exotics who had trained her almost from the cradle would she tell me what to do.

But she did not have to. The Devil had been raised again in my soul; and he stood, laughing on the far side of a river of glowing coals, daring me to come over and tangle with him. And neither man nor Devil has ever challenged me in vain.

I turned from Lisa, and I went.

Chapter 15

As a full member of the Guild, I no longer had to produce an assignment as a reason for drawing travel money. The currency between worlds was knowledge and skills wrapped up in the human packages that conveyed these things. In the same way, a credit easily convertible into this currency was the information collected and transferred by the skilled Communications people of the Interstellar News Guild—which was no less necessary to the individual worlds between the stars. So the Guild was not poor; and the two hundred or so full members had funds to draw upon on each one of the sixteen worlds that might have made a government leader envious.

The curious result of which in my case, I discovered, was that money as such ceased to have any meaning for me. In that corner of my mind which before this had concerned itself with spendables, there was now a void—and rushing in to fill that void, it seemed, through the long flight from Kultis to Cassida, were memories. Memories of Eileen.

I had not thought that she had been so important a part of my young life, both before our parents' death, and especially after. But now, as our space ship shifted, and paused, and shifted again between the stars, moments and scenes came thronging to my mind as I sat alone in my first-class compartment. Or for that matter, still alone in the lounge, for I was in no mood for company.

They were not dramatic memories. They were recollections of gifts she had given me on this birthday or that. They were moments in which she had helped me to bear up under the unendurable empty pressure of Mathias upon my soul. There were unhappy moments of her own that I recalled now as well, that I now realized had been unhappy and lonely, but that I had not understood at the time, because of being so bound up in my own unhappiness. Suddenly it came to me that I could remember any number of times when she had ignored her own troubles to do something about mine; and never—there was no single instance I could recall—had I ever forgotten mine even to consider hers.

As all this came back to me, my very guts shrank up into a cold, hard knot of guilt and unhappiness. I tried between one set of shifts to see if I could not drink the memories away. But I found I had no taste either for the liquor or for that as a way out.

And so I came to Cassida.

A poorer, smaller planetary counterpart of Newton, with whom it shared a double-sun system, Cassida lacked the other world's academic link with and consequently the rarefied supply of scientific and mathematical minds that had made the earlier-settled world of Newton a rich one. From Cassida's capital-city spaceport of Moro, I took a shuttle flight to Alban, the Newton-sponsored University City where Dave had been studying shift mechanics, and where both he and Eileen had held supportive jobs while he did so.

It was an efficient ant-hill of a city on various levels. Not that there had been any lack of land on which to build it, but because most of it had been built by Newtonian credit; and the building method most economical of that credit had been one that clustered all necessary quarters together in the smallest practical space.

I picked up a direction rod at the shuttleport and set it for the address Eileen had given me in that one letter received the morning of Dave's death. It pointed me the way through a series of vertical and horizontal tubes and passageways to a housing-complex unit that was above ground level—but that was about the best you could say for it.

As I turned into the final hallway that led to the door of the address I hunted, for the first time the true emotion that had kept me from even consciously thinking of Eileen, until Lisa recalled her directly to my attention, began to boil up in me. The scene in the forest clearing on New Earth rose again around me as vividly as a nightmare; and fear and rage began to burn in me like a fever.

For a moment I faltered—I almost stopped. But then the momentum I had built up by the long voyage this far carried me on to the doorway and I sounded the doorcall.

There was a second's eternity of waiting. Then the door opened and a middle-aged woman's face looked out. I stared down into it in shock, for it was not the face of my sister.

"Eileen . . ." I stammered. "I mean—Mrs. David Hall? Isn't she here?" Then I remembered that this woman could not know me. "I'm her brother—from Earth. Newsman Tam Olyn."

I was wearing cape and beret, of course, and in a way this was passport enough. But for the moment I had forgotten all about it. I remembered then as the woman fluttered a bit. She had probably never before seen a member of the Guild in the actual flesh.

"Why, she's moved," the woman said. "This place was too big for her alone. She's down a few levels and north of here. Just a minute, I'll get you her number."

She darted away. I heard her talking to a male voice for a moment, and then she came back with a slip of paper.

"Here," she said a little breathlessly. "I wrote it down for you. You go right along this corridor—oh, I see you've got a direction rod. Just set it then. It's not far."

"Thank you," I said.

"Not at all. We're glad to—well, I mustn't keep you, I suppose," she said, for I was already beginning to turn away. "Glad to be of service. Good-bye."

"Good-bye," I muttered. I was moving off down the corridor re-setting the direction rod. It led me away and down and the door I finally pressed the call button on was well below ground level.

There was a longer wait this time. Then, at last, the door slid back—and my sister stood there.

"Tam," she said.

She did not seem to have changed at all. There was no sign of change or grief upon her, and my mind leaped suddenly with hope. But when she simply continued to stand there, looking at me, the hope sank once more. I could do nothing but wait. I stood there also.

"Come in," she said finally, but without much change in tone. She stood aside and I walked in. The door slid closed behind me.

I looked around, shocked out of my emotion for the moment by what I saw. The gray-draped room was no bigger than the first-class compartment I had occupied on the spaceship coming there.

"What're you doing living here?" I burst out.

She looked at me without any response to my shock.

"It's cheaper," she said indifferently.

"But you don't need to save money!" I said. "I got that arrange-ment made for your inheritance from Mathias—it was all set with an Earth-working Cassidan to transfer funds from his family back here to you. You mean"—for the thought had never occurred to me before—"there's been some hitch at this end? Hasn't his family been paying you?"

"Yes," she said calmly enough. "But there's Dave's family now to take care of, too."

"Family?" I stared stupidly at her.

"Dave's younger brother's still in school—never mind." She stood still. Nor had she asked me to sit down. "It's too long a story, Tam. What've you come here for?"

I stared at her.

"Eileen," I said pleadingly. She only waited. "Look," I said, snatching at the straw of our earlier subject, "even if you're helping out Dave's family, there's no problem anymore. I'm a full Guild member now. I can supply you with anything in the way of funds you need."

"No." She shook her head.

"In heaven's name, why not? I tell you I've got unlimited—"

"I don't want anything from you, Tam," she said. "Thank you anyway. But we're doing fine. Dave's family and myself. I've got a good job."

"Eileen!"

"I asked you once, Tam," she said, still unmoved. "Why've you come here?"

If she had been changed to stone, there could not have been a greater difference in her from the sister I had known. She was no one I knew. She was like a perfect stranger to me.

"To see you," I said. "I thought—you might like to know—"

"I know all about it," she said, with no emotion at all. "I was told all about it. They said you were wounded, too; but you're well now, aren't you, Tam?"

"Yes," I said, helplessly. "I'm well now. My knee's a little stiff. They say it'll stay that way."

"That's too bad," she said.

"Damn it, Eileen!" I burst out. "Don't just stand there talking to me as if you don't know me! I'm your brother!"

"No." She shook her head. "The only relatives I have now—the only relatives I want now—are Dave's family. They need me. You don't and never did, Tam. You were always sufficient for yourself, by yourself."

"Eileen!" I said, pleadingly. "Look, I know you must blame me— partly at least—for Dave's death."

"No," she answered. "You can't help being what you are. It was my fault, all these years, for trying to convince myself that you were something different from what you are. I thought there was something about you that Mathias never got to, something that just needed a chance to come out. It was that I was counting on when I asked you to help me decide about Jamie. And when you wrote you were going to help Dave, I was sure that what I'd always thought was in you was finally coming to the front. But I was wrong both times."

"Eileen!" I cried. "It wasn't my fault we ran into a madman, Dave and I. Maybe I should have done something different—but I did try to make him leave me after I got shot, only he wouldn't. Don't you understand, it *wasn't all my fault!*"

"Of course it wasn't, Tam," she said. I stared at her. "That's why I don't blame you. You're no more responsible for what you do than a police dog that's been trained to attack anyone who moves. You're what Uncle Mathias made you, Tam—a destroyer. It's not your fault, but that doesn't change anything. In spite of all the fighting you did with him, Mathias' teaching about *Destruct* filled you up, Tam, and didn't leave anything."

"You can't say that!" I shouted at her. "It's not true. Give me just one more chance, Eileen, and I'll show you! I tell you, it's not true!"

"Yes, it is," she said. "I know you, Tam, better than anyone alive. And I've known this about you for a long time. I just wouldn't let myself believe it. But I have to, now—for the sake of Dave's family, who need me. I couldn't help Dave, but I can help them—as long as I never see you again. If I let you come close to them, through me, you'll destroy them, too."

She stopped talking then and stood looking at me. I opened my mouth to answer her, but I could think of nothing to say. We stood looking at each other across a couple of feet of distance that was a wider, deeper space and gulf than I had ever encountered in my life.

"You'd better go, then, Tam," she said at last.

Her words stirred me numbly to life again.

"Yes," I said dully. "I guess I'd better."

I turned away from her. As I stepped toward the door I think I still hoped she might stop me and call me back. But there was no movement or sound behind me; and as I went out the door I glanced back for a final time over my shoulder.

She had not moved. She was still standing where she had been, like a stranger, waiting for me to go.

So I went. And I returned to the spaceport alone. Alone, alone, alone. . . .

Chapter 16

I got on the first ship out for Earth. I had priority now over all but people with diplomatic status, and I used it. I bumped someone with a prior reservation and found myself once more alone in a first-class compartment, while the ship I was on shifted, stopped to calculate its position, and shifted again between the stars.

That closed cabin was like a sanctuary, a hermit's cell to me, a chrysalis in which I could lock and reshape myself before entering once more into the worlds of men in a different dimension. For I had been stripped to the very core of my old self and no single self-delusion remained, that I could see, to cover me.

Mathias had cleaned the most of the flesh of self-delusion off my bones early, of course. But here and there a shred had stuck—like the rain-washed memory of the ruins of the Parthenon that I used to gaze at in the vision screens as a boy after Mathias' deadly dialectic had stripped away one more shred of nerve or sinew. Just by being there, above the dark, windowless house, the Parthenon had seemed to my young mind to refute all Mathias' arguments.

It had been, once—and therefore he must be wrong, I used to comfort myself in thinking. It had existed, once it had been, and if the men of Earth were no more than Mathias said, it never could have been built. But it had *been*—that was what I saw now. For in the end it was no more than ruins and the dark defeatism of Mathias endured. So, at last now I came to it—I endured, in Mathias' image, and the dreams of glory and rightness somehow, in some way, for those born on Earth in spite of those changed and greater children of younger worlds, were ruins, like the Parthenon, filed away with other childish delusions, filed and forgotten in the rain.

What was it Lisa had said? If I had only understood her, I thought now, I could have foreseen this moment and saved myself the pain of hoping that Eileen might have forgiven me for Dave's death. Lisa had mentioned two portals, that there were only two portals left to me, and she was one of them. I understood what those portals were now. They were doorways through which love could get at me.

Love—the deadly sickness that robbed the strength from men. Not just carnal love, but any weak hungering for affection, for beauty, for hope of wonders to come. For I remembered now that there was one thing I had never been able to do. I had never been able to hurt Mathias, to shame, or even trouble him. And why not? Because he was as pure in health as any sterilized body. He loved not only no one, but nothing. And so, by giving away the universe, he had gained it, for the universe was nothing, too; and in that perfect symmetry of nothing into nothing he rested, like a stone, content.

With that understanding, I suddenly realized I could drink again. On the way here, I had not been able to do so because of my feeling of guilt and hope, and because of the tattered bits of corruptible, love-susceptible flesh still clinging to the pure skeleton of Mathias' philosophy in me. But now—

I laughed out loud in the empty compartment. Because then, on the way to Cassida when I most needed that anesthesia of liquor, I had not been able to use it. And now that I did not need it at all, I could swim in it if I wanted.

Always provided I had a due care for the respectableness of my professional position and did not overdo in public. But there was no reason keeping me back from getting drunk privately in my compartment right now if I wanted to. In fact, there was every reason to do just that. For this was an occasion for celebration—the hour of my deliverance from the weaknesses of the flesh and mind that caused pain to all ordinary men.

I ordered a bottle, a glass and ice; and I toasted myself in the mirror of my compartment, across from the lounge seat in which I sat, with the bottle at my elbow.

"*Slainte, Tam Olyn bach!*" I said to myself; for it was Scotch I had ordered, and all the Scot and Irish of my ancestors was frothing metaphorically in my veins at the moment. I drank deeply.

The good liquor burned inside me and spread comfortably through me; and after a little while, as I went on drinking, the close walls of the compartment moved back away from me for some distance while the wide memory of how I had ridden the lightning, under Padma's hypnotic influence, that day at the Encyclopedia, came back to me.

Once more I felt the power and the fury that had come into me then, and for the first time I became aware of how I now stood, with no more human weaknesses to hold me back, to temper my use of that lightning. For the first time I saw possibilities in that use and the power of *Destruct*. Possibilities to which what Mathias had done, or even I had accomplished before now, were child's play.

I drank, dreaming of things that were possible. And, after a while, I fell asleep, or passed out, whichever it was; and I dreamed literally.

It was a dream I passed into from waking with no seeming transition. Suddenly, I was there—and *there* was someplace on a stony hillside, between the mountains and the western sea, in a small house of stone, chinked with turf and dirt. A small, one-room house with no fireplace, but a primitive hearth with walls on each side leading up to a hole in the roof for the smoke to get out. On the wall near the fire, on two wooden pegs driven into cracks between stones, hung my one valuable possession.

It was the family weapon, the true, original claymore—*claidheamh mōr*, the "great sword." Over four feet long it was, straight and double-edged and wide of blade, not tapering to the point. Its hilt had only a simple crossbar with the guards turned down. Altogether it was a two-handed broadsword carefully kept wrapped in greased rags and laid on its pegs, for it had no sheath.

But, at the time of my dream, I had taken it down and unwrapped it, for there was a man I was to meet in three days' time, some half a day's walk away. For two days the sky was fair, the sun bright but cold, and I sat out on the beach, sharpening the long sword's two edges with a gray stone from the beach, smoothed by the sea. On the morning of the third day it was overcast and with the dawn a light rain began falling. So I wrapped the sword in a corner of the long, rectangular plaid I had wound about me, and went to keep my appointment.

The rain blew cold and wet in my face and the wind was cold, but under the thick, almost oily wool of the plaid, my sword and I were dry, and a fine, fierce joy rose in me, a wondrous feeling greater than I had ever felt before. I could taste it as a wolf must taste hot blood in his mouth, for there was no feeling to compare to this—that I was going at last to my revenge.

And then I woke. I saw the bottle almost empty and felt the heavy, sluggish feeling of drunkenness; but the joy of my dream was still with me. So I stretched out on the lounge seat and fell asleep again.

This time I did not dream.

When I woke, I could feel no trace of a hangover. My mind was cold and clear and free. I could remember, as if it had been just the second before I had dreamed it, the terrible joy I had felt, going sword in hand to my meeting in the rain. And, at once, I saw my way clear before me.

I had sealed the two portals that remained—that meant I had stripped love from me. But now to replace it I had found this wine-rich joy of revenge. I almost laughed out loud as I thought about it, because I remembered what the Friendly Groupman had said, before he left me with the bodies of those he had massacred.

"What I have writ upon these men is beyond the power of you or any man to erase."

Oh, it was true enough. I could not erase that exact, particular writing of his. But I—alone among sixteen worlds of people—had it in my power and skill to erase something far greater than that. I could erase the instruments that made such writing. I was a rider and master of the lightning; and with that I could destroy the culture and people of both the Friendly worlds together. Already, I saw glimmerings of the method by which it could be done.

By the time my spaceship reached Earth, the basic outline of my plans was essentially made.

Chapter 17

My immediate goal was a quick return to New Earth, where Eldest
Bright, having ransomed free the troops Kensie Graeme's forces had
captured, had immediately reinforced them. The reinforced unit had
been encamped outside Moreton, the North Partition capital, as an occupation force in demand of interstellar credits due the Friendly Worlds
for troops hired by the now defunct rebel government.

But there was a matter to be taken care of before I could go directly
to New Earth. First, I needed a sanction and a seal for what I intended
to do. For, once you were a full member of the Newsman's Guild there
was no higher authority over you—except for the fifteen members that
made up the Guild Council to watchdog the Creed of Impartiality under
which we operated, and to set Guild policy, to which all members must
conform.

I made an appointment to see Piers Leaf, Chairman of that Council.
It was a bright morning in April in St. Louis, just across the city from
the Final Encyclopedia, that I finally found myself facing him across
a wide, neatly bare oak desk in his office on the top floor of the Guild
Hall.

"You've come a long way pretty fast for someone so young, Tam,"
he said, after he had ordered and received coffee for both of us. He
was a dry-mannered, small man in his late fifties, who never left the
Solar System nowadays and seldom left Earth, because of the public-
relations aspect of his Chairmanship. "Don't tell me you still aren't
satisfied? What do you want now?"

"I want a seat on the Council," I said.

He was lifting his coffee cup to his lips when I spoke. He went right on lifting without a pause. But the sudden glance he shot me over the rim of his cup was as sharp as a falcon's. But all he said was:

"Do you? Why?"

"I'll tell you," I said. "Maybe you've noticed I seem to have a knack for being where the news-stories are."

He set his cup down precisely in the center of its saucer.

"That, Tam," he said mildly, "is why you're wearing the cape permanently now. We expect certain things from members, you know."

"Yes," I said. "But I think mine may be a little bit out of the ordinary—oh," I said, as his eyebrows rose suddenly, "I'm not claiming some kind of precognition. I just think I happen to have a talent for a little more insight into the possibilities of situations than other members."

His eyebrows came down. He frowned slightly.

"I know," I said, "that sounds like boasting. But, just stop and suppose I have what I claim. Wouldn't a talent like that be highly useful to the Council in its policy decisions for the Guild?"

He looked at me sharply.

"Maybe," he said, "if it was true—and it worked every time—and a number of other things."

"But if I could convince you of all those ifs, you'd sponsor me for the next opening on the Council?"

He laughed.

"I might," he said. "But how are you going to prove it to me?"

"I'll make a prediction," I said. "A prediction calling—if it comes true—for a major policy decision by the Council."

"All right," he said. He was still smiling. "Predict, then."

"The Exotics," I said, "are at work to wipe out the Friendlies."

The smile went away. For a moment he stared at me.

"What do you mean by that?" he demanded. "The Exotics can't be out to wipe out anyone. It's not only against everything they say they believe in, but no one can *wipe out* two whole worlds of people and a complete way of life. What do you mean by 'wipe out,' anyway?"

"Just about what you'd think," I answered. "Tear down the Friendly culture as a working theocracy, break both worlds financially, and leave only a couple of stony planets filled with starving people who'll either have to change their way of life or emigrate to other worlds."

He stared at me. For a long moment neither of us said anything.

"What," he said, finally, "gave you this fantastic idea?"

"A hunch. My insight," I said. "Plus the fact that it was a Dorsai

Field Commander, Kensie Graeme, lent to the Cassidan levies at the last moment, that defeated the Friendly forces there."

"Why," said Piers, "that's the sort of thing that could happen in any war, anywhere, between any two armies."

"Not exactly," I said. "Kensie's decision to sweep around the north end of the Friendly line and take the Friendlies in the rear wouldn't have worked so successfully at all if Eldest Bright hadn't the day before taken command and ordered a Friendly attack on the south end of Kensie's line. There's a double coincidence here. An Exotic Commander appears and does just the right thing at the moment when the Friendly forces take the very action that makes them vulnerable."

Piers turned and reached for the phone on his desk.

"Don't bother checking," I said. "I already have. The decision to borrow Kensie from the Exotics was taken independently on the spur of the moment by the Cassidan Levies Command, and there was no way Kensie's Intelligence Unit could have known in advance about the attack Bright had ordered."

"Then it's coincidence." Piers scowled at me. "Or that Dorsai genius for tactics we all know they have."

"Don't you think Dorsai genius may have been a little overrated? And I don't buy the coincidence. It's too large," I said.

"Then what?" demanded Piers. "How do you explain it?"

"My hunch—my insight—suggests that the Exotics have some way of predicting what the Friendlies will do in advance. You spoke of Dorsai military genius—how about the Exotic psychological genius?"

"Yes, but—" Piers broke off, suddenly thoughtful. "The whole thing's fantastic." He looked once more at me. "What do you suggest we do about it?"

"Let me dig into it," I said. "If I'm right, three years from now will see Exotic troops fighting Friendlies. Not as hirelings in some other-planet war, but in a direct test of Exotic-Friendly strength." I paused. "And if I turn out to be right, you sponsor me to replace the next Council member dying or retiring."

Once more, the dry little man sat staring at me for a long minute.

"Tam," he said finally. "I don't believe a word of it. But look into it as much as you want; I'll answer for Council backing for you on that—if the question comes up. And if it comes off anything like you say, come talk to me again."

"I will," I said, getting up and smiling at him.

He shook his head, remaining in his seat, but said nothing.

"I'll hope to see you again before too long," I said. And I went out.

It was a tiny burr I had stuck onto him, to irritate his mind in the direction I wanted him to speculate. But Piers Leaf had the misfortune of having a highly intelligent and creative mind; otherwise he would not have been Chairman of the Council. It was the kind of mind that refused to let go of a question until it had settled it one way or another. If it could not disprove the question, it was likely to start finding evidence to prove it—even in places where others could not see such proof at all.

And this particular burr would have nearly three years to stick and work itself into the fabric of Leaf's picture of things. I was content to wait for that, while I went ahead with other matters.

I had to spend a couple of weeks on Earth, bringing some order back to my personal business affairs there; but at the end of that time I took ship for New Earth once more.

The Friendlies, as I said, having bought back the troops they had lost as prisoners to the Cassidan forces under Kensie Graeme, had immediately reinforced them and encamped them outside the North Partition capital of Moreton, as an occupation force in demand of interplanetary credits due them.

The credits due, of course, were from the government of the now defeated and nonexistent North Partition rebels who had hired them. But, while there was nothing exactly legal about it, this was not uncommon practice between the stars, to hold a world ransom for any debt contracted off-world by any of its people.

The reason, of course, was that special currency between worlds which was the services of individual human units, whether as psychiatrists or soldiers. A debt contracted for the services of such units by one world from another had to be paid by the debtor world, and could not be repudiated by a change of governments. Governments would have proved too easy to change, if that had been a way out of interplanetary debts.

In practice, it was a winner-pay-all matter, if conflicting interests on a single world hired help from off-world. Something like the reverse of a civil suit-at-law to recover monetary damages, where the loser is required to pay the court costs of the winner. Officially, what had happened was that the Friendly government, being unpaid for the soldiers it had lent the rebel government, had declared war on New Earth as a world, until New Earth as a world should make up the bad debt contracted by some of her inhabitants.

In actuality, no hostilities were involved, and payment would, after a due amount of haggling, be forthcoming from those New Earth governments most directly involved. In this case, the South Partition government, mainly, since it had been the winner. But meanwhile, Friendly troops were in occupation upon New Earth soil; and it was in self-assignment to write a series of feature articles about this that I arrived there, some eight months after I had left.

I got in to see their Field Commander with no trouble this time. It was evident among the bubble-plastic buildings of the cantonment they had set up in an open area that the Friendly military were under orders to give as little irritation to non-Friendlies as possible. I heard no cant spoken by any of the soldiers, from the cantonment gate clear into and including the office of the Field Commander himself. But in spite of the fact he "youed" instead of "thoued" me, he was not happy to see me.

"Field Commander Wassel," he introduced himself. "Sit down, Newsman Olyn. I've heard about you."

He was a man in his late forties or early fifties with close-cropped, pure gray hair. He was built as square as the lower half of a Dutch door and had a heavy, square jaw which had no trouble looking grim. It was looking grim now, for all he was trying to appear unconcerned— and I knew the cause of the worry that was making his expression a rebel against his intentions.

"I supposed you would have," I said, grim enough in my own way. "So I'll make one point clear by reminding you right from the start of the impartiality of the Interstellar News Services."

He had sat back down.

"We know about that," he said, "and I'm not suggesting any bias on your part against us, either, Newsman. We regret the death of your brother-in-law and your own wounding. But I'd like to point out that the News Services, in sending you, of all Guild members, to do a series of articles on our occupation of this New Earth territory—"

"Let me make myself perfectly clear!" I broke in on him. "I chose to do this assignment, Commander. I asked to be able to do it!"

By this time his face was grim as a bulldog's, with little pretense remaining. I stared as bitterly straight across his desk into his eyes.

"I see you don't understand, Commander." I rapped the words out in as metallic a tone as I could; and—to my ear, at least—the tone was good. "My parents died when I was young. I was raised by an uncle and it was the goal of my life to be a Newsman. To me, the News Services are more important than any institution or human being on any of the sixteen civilized worlds. The Creed of the members of the Guild is carried in my heart, Commander. And the keystone article of that Creed is impartiality—the crushing down, the wiping out of any personal feeling where that might conflict with or influence to the slightest degree the work of a Newsman."

He continued to look grim at me from across the desk; and, gradually it seemed to me, a hint of doubt crept into that iron visage of his.

"Mr. Olyn," he said at last; and the more neutral title was a tentative lightening of the formal sword's-point attitude with which we had begun our talk. "Are you trying to tell me that you're here to do these articles as proof of your lack of bias toward us?"

"Toward you, or any people or things," I said, "in accordance with the Newsman's Creed. This series will be a public testimony to our Creed, and consequently to the benefit of all who wear the cloak."

He did not believe me even then, I think. His good sense warred with what I was telling him; and the assumption of selflessness on my part must have had a boastful ring in the mouth of someone he knew to be a non-Friendly.

But, at the same time, I was talking his language. The harsh joy of self-sacrifice, the stoic amputation of my own personal feelings in the pursuit of my duty rang true to the beliefs he had lived with all his own life.

"I see," he said at last. He got to his feet and extended his hand across the desk as I rose, too. "Well, Newsman, I cannot say that we are pleased to see you here, even now. But we will cooperate with you within reason as much as possible. Though any series reflecting the fact that we are here as unwelcome visitors upon a foreign planet is bound to do us harm in the eyes of the people of the sixteen worlds."

"I don't think so this time," I said shortly as I shook hands. He let go of my hand and looked at me with a sudden renewal of suspicion.

"What I plan to do is an editorial series," I explained. "It'll be titled *The Case for Occupation by the Friendly Troops on New Earth*, and it'll restrict itself completely to exploring the attitudes and positions of you and your men in the occupation force."

He stared at me.

"Good afternoon," I said.

I went out, hearing his half-mumbled "Good afternoon" behind me. I left him, I knew, completely uncertain as to whether he was sitting on a carton of high explosive or not.

But, as I knew he would, he began to come around, when the first of the articles in the series began to appear in the Interstellar News releases. There is a difference between an ordinary article of reportage and an editorial article. In an editorial article, you can present the case for the Devil; and as long as you dissociate yourself from it personally, you can preserve your reputation of a freedom from bias.

I presented the case for the Friendlies, in the Friendlies' own terms and utterances. It was the first time in years that the Friendly soldiers had been written about in the Interstellar News without adverse criticism; and, of course, to the Friendlies, all adverse criticism implied a bias against them. For they knew of no half-measures in their own way of life and recognized none in outsiders. By the time I was halfway through the series, Field Commander Wassel and all his occupation forces had taken me as close to their grim hearts as a non-Friendly could be taken.

Of course, the series evoked a howl from the New Earthians that *their* side of the occupation also be written up. And a very good Newsman named Moha Skanosky was assigned by the Guild to do just that.

But I had had the first innings at bat in the public eye; and the articles had so strong an effect that they almost convinced *me*, their writer. There is a magic in words when they are handled, and when I had finished the series I was almost ready to find in myself some excuse and sympathy for these unyielding men of a Spartan faith.

But there was a *claidheamh mōr*, unsharpened and unslaked, hanging on the stone walls of my soul, that would not bend to any such weakness.

Chapter 18

Still, I was under the close observation of my peers in the Guild; and on my return to St. Louis on Earth, among my other mail was a note from Piers Leaf.

Dear Tam:
Your series was an admirable job. But, bearing in mind what we talked about the last time we met, I would think that straight reporting might build a better professional record for you than dealing in background material of this sort.
With best wishes for your future—

P.L.

It was a plain enough cautioning not to be observed involving myself personally in the situation I had told him I would investigate. It might have caused me to put off for a month or so the trip I had planned to Ste. Marie. But just then Donal Graeme, who had accepted the position of War Chief for the Friendlies, carried out his first sub-surface extrication of a Friendly expeditionary force from Coby, the airless mining world in the same system as the Exotic worlds and Ste. Marie. As a result of that rescue, the Exotic mercenary command was severely shaken up, to be reorganized under the command of Geneve bar-Colmain.

Despite widespread admiration for Graeme's skill, the public saw the situation as an unexpected pardon for Friendly forces who had been the aggressors on Coby. With the general liking for the Exotics on the other twelve worlds, what attention my series of articles had obtained was completely wiped out. In this I was well content. What I hoped to gain from their publication, I had already gained in the relaxation of enmity and suspicion of me personally by Field Commander Wassel and his occupation force.

I went to Ste. Marie, a small but fertile world which, with Coby and a few uninhabited bits of rock like Zombri, shared the Procyon system with the Exotic worlds, Mara and Kultis. My official purpose of visit was to see what effect the Coby military debacle had had on this suburban planet with its largely Roman Catholic, predominantly rural population.

While there were no official connections between them, except a mutual-aid pact, Ste. Marie was by necessity of spatial geography almost a ward of the larger, more powerful Exotic worlds. Like anyone with rich and powerful neighbors Ste. Marie, in her government and affairs, pretty much rose and fell with Exotic fortunes. It would be interesting to the reading public of the sixteen worlds to see how the Exotic reversal on Coby had caused the winds of opinion and politics to blow on Ste. Marie.

As anyone might expect, it had caused them to blow contrary. After some five days of pulling strings, I finally arranged an interview with Marcus O'Doyne, past-President and political power in the so-called Blue Front, the out-of-power political party of Ste. Marie. It took less than half an eye to see that he was bursting with ill-contained joy.

We met in his hotel suite in Blauvain, the capital of Ste. Marie. He was of no more than average height, but his head was outsized, heavy-boned and powerful-featured under wavy white hair. It sat awkwardly on his plump and fairly narrow shoulders; and he had a habit of booming his voice out with the ring of a platform speaker, during ordinary conversation, that did not endear him to me. His faded blue eyes gleamed as he spoke.

". . . Woken them up, by—*George!*" he said, once we were seated in overplump chairs in the sitting room of his hotel suite with drinks in our hands. He paused, catching his breath stagily a little before coming out with emphasis on the "—*George!*" as if he wished me to notice that he had been about to use the name of the deity, but had recollected himself in time. It was, I began to find out, a regular trick of his, this catching himself from profanity or obscenity as if in the nick of time.

"—the common people—the rural people," he said leaning confidentially toward me. "They were asleep here. They've been asleep for years. Lulled to sleep by those sons of—*Belial* on the Exotics. But that business on Coby woke them up. Opened their eyes!"

"Lulled to sleep—how?" I asked.

"Song and dance, song and dance!" O'Doyne rocked back and forth on the couch. "Stage-show magic! Headshrinker's tactics—oh, a thousand and one things, Newsman. You wouldn't believe it!"

"My readers might," I said. "How about citing some instances?"

"Why—*darn* your readers! Yes, I say—*darn* your readers!" He rocked forward again, glaring proudly at me. "It's the common inhabitant of my own world I'm concerned with! The common inhabitant. *He* knows what instances, what coercions, what wrongs! We're not a sideshow here, Mr. Olyn, though maybe you think so! No, I say—*darn* your readers, and—*darn* you! I'll get no man in trouble with those robed—*babies* by citing exact instances."

"You don't give me much to write about, in that case," I said. "Suppose we shift our ground a little, then. I understand that you claim that the people of the present government are maintained in power only by Exotic pressures on Ste. Marie?"

"They are appeasers, plain and simple, Mr. Olyn. The government—no, no! Call them the Green Front, which is all they are! They claim to represent all the people of Ste. Marie. They—You know our political situation, here?"

"I understand," I said, "that your constitution laid out your planet originally into political districts of equal areas, with two representatives to a planetary government from each district. Now I understand your party claims that the growth of city population has allowed the rural districts to control the cities, since a city like Blauvain with half a million inhabitants has no more representation than a district with three or four thousand people in it?"

"Exactly, exactly!" O'Doyne rocked forward and boomed confidentially at me. "The need for reapportionment is acute, as it always has been in such historic situations. But will the Green Front vote themselves out of power? Not likely! Only a bold move—only a grassroots' revolution can get them out of power and our own party, representing the common man, the ignored man, the disenfranchised man of the cities, into government."

"You think such a grass-roots' revolution is possible at the present time?" I adjusted downward the volume control on my recorder.

"Before Coby, I would have said—*no!* Much as I would have hoped for such a thing—*no!* But, since Coby—" He stopped and rocked triumphantly backward, looking at me significantly.

"Since Coby?" I prompted, since significant looks and significant silences were no use to me in doing a job of straight reporting. But O'Doyne had a politician's caution about talking himself into a corner.

"Why, since Coby," he said, "it's become apparent—apparent to any thinking man of this world—that Ste. Marie may have to go it alone. That we may have to do without the parasitic, controlling hand of the Exotics. And where are men to be found who can steer this troubled ship of Ste. Marie through the stormy trials of the future? In the cities, Newsman! In the ranks of those of us who have always fought for the common man. In our own Blue Front party!"

"I understand," I said. "But under your constitution wouldn't a change of representatives require an election? And can't an election only be called for by a majority vote of the current representatives? And don't the Green Front have that majority now, so that they are unlikely to call an election that would put most of them out of office?"

"True!" he boomed. "True!" He rocked back and forth, glaring at me with the same broad hint of significance.

"Then," I said, "I don't see how the grass-roots' revolution you talk about is possible, Mr. O'Doyne."

"Anything is possible!" he answered. "To the common man, nothing is impossible! The straws are in the wind, the wind of change is in the air. Who can deny it?"

I shut off my recorder.

"I see," I said, "we're getting nowhere. Perhaps we could make a little better progress off the record?"

"Off the record! Absolutely! Indeed—absolutely!" he said heartily. "I'm as willing to answer questions off the record as on, Newsman. And you understand why? Because to me, on—on and off—are one and the same. One and the same!"

"Well, then," I said, "how about some of these straws in the wind? Off the record, can you give me an example?"

He rocked toward me and lowered his voice.

"There are—gatherings, even in the rural areas," he muttered. "Stirrings of unrest—this much I can tell you. If you ask me for places—names—why, no. I won't tell you."

"Then you're leaving me with nothing but vague hints. I can't make a story out of that," I said. "And you'd like a story written on this situation, I suppose?"

"Yes, but—" His powerful jaw set. "I won't tell you. I won't risk—I won't tell you!"

"I see," I said. I waited for a long minute. He opened his mouth, closed it, and then fidgeted upon the couch. "Perhaps," I said slowly, "perhaps there's a way out of this."

He flashed a glance almost of suspicion at me, from under white eyebrows.

"Perhaps I could tell you instead," I said quietly. "You wouldn't have to confirm anything. And of course, as I say, even my own remarks would be off the record."

"You—tell me?" He stared hard at me.

"Why not?" I said easily. He was too good a public man to let his bafflement show on his face, but he continued to stare at me. "In the News Services we've got our own avenues of information; and from these we can build up a general picture, even if some parts are missing. Now, speaking hypothetically of course, the general picture on Ste. Marie at this moment seems to be pretty much the way you've described it. Stirrings of unrest, gatherings and rumblings of discontent with the present—you might say, puppet—government."

"Yes," he rumbled. "Yes, the very word. That's what it is, a—*darn* puppet government!"

"At the same time," I went on, "as we've already discussed, this puppet government is well able to subdue any kind of local uprising, and is not about to call an election that will remove it from power; and—barring the calling of such an election—there seems no constitutional way of changing the status quo. The highly able and selfless leaders that Ste. Marie might otherwise—I say *might*, being neutral myself, of course—find among the Blue Front, seem legally committed to remaining private citizens without the power to save their world from foreign influence."

"Yes," he muttered, staring at me. "Yes."

"Consequently, what course remains open to those who would save Ste. Marie from her present government?" I went on. "Since all legal avenues of recourse are stopped up, the only way left, it may seem to brave men, strong men, is to set aside normal procedure in such times of trial. If there are no constitutional ways to remove the men presently holding the reins of government, they may end up being removed otherwise, for the ostensible good of the whole world of Ste. Marie and everyone on it."

He stared at me. His lips moved a little, but he said nothing. Under the white eyebrows, his faded blue eyes seemed to be popping slightly.

"In short—a bloodless coup d'état, a direct and forcible removal from office of these bad leaders seems to be the only solution left for those who believe this planet needs saving. Now, we know—"

"Wait—" broke in O'Doyne, booming. "I must tell you here and now, Newsman, that my silence mustn't be construed as giving consent to any such speculation. You shall not report—"

"Please," I interrupted in my turn, holding up a hand. He subsided rather more easily than one might have expected. "This is all perfectly theoretical supposition on my part. I don't suppose it has anything to do with the real situation." I hesitated. "The only question in this projection of the situation—theoretical situation—is the matter of implementation. We realize that as far as numbers and equipment, forces of the Blue Front outnumbered a hundred to one in the last election is hardly to be compared with the planetary forces of the Ste. Marie Government."

"Our support—our grass-roots' support—"

"Oh, of course," I said. "Still, there's the question of actually taking any physically effective action in the situation. That would take equipment and men—particularly men. By which I mean, of course, military men able either to train raw native troops, or themselves to take powerful action—"

"Mr. Olyn," said O'Doyne, "I must protest such talk. I must reject such talk. I must"—he had gotten up to pace the room, and I saw him going back and forth, with his arms waving—"I must refuse to listen to such talk."

"Forgive me," I said. "As I mentioned, I'm only playing with a hypothetical situation. But the point I'm trying to get at—"

"The point you're trying to get at doesn't concern me, Newsman!" said O'Doyne, halting in front of me with his face stern. "The point doesn't concern us in the Blue Front."

"Of course not," I said soothingly. "I know it doesn't. Of course, the whole matter is impossible."

"Impossible?" O'Doyne stiffened. "What's impossible?"

"Why, the whole matter of a coup d'état," I said. "It's obvious. Any such thing would require outside help—the business of militarily trained men, for example. Such military men would have to be supplied by some other world—and what other world would be willing to lend valuable troops on speculation to an obscure out-of-power political party on Ste. Marie?"

I let my voice dwindle off and sat smiling, gazing at him, as if I expected him to answer my final question. And he sat staring back at me as if he expected me to answer it myself. It must have been a good twenty seconds that we sat in mutually expectant silence before I broke it once more, getting up as I did so.

"Obviously," I said, with a touch of regret in my voice, "none. So I must conclude we'll be seeing no marked change of government or alteration in relations with the Exotics after all on Ste. Marie in the near future. Well"—and I held out my hand—"I must apologize for being the one to cut this interview short, Mr. O'Doyne; but I see I've lost track of the time. I'm due at Government house across the city in fifteen minutes, for an interview with the President, to get the other side of the picture; and then I'll have to rush to get back to the spaceport in time to leave this evening for Earth."

He rose automatically and shook my hand.

"Not at all," he began. His voice rose to a boom momentarily, and then faltered back to ordinary tones. "Not at all—it's been a pleasure acquainting you with the true situation here, Newsman." He let go of my hand, almost regretfully.

"Good-bye, then," I said.

I turned to go and I was halfway to the door when his voice broke out again behind me.

"Newsman Olyn—"

I stopped and turned.

"Yes?" I said.

"I feel"—his voice boomed out suddenly—"I have a duty to ask you—a duty to the Blue Front, a duty to my party to require you to tell me of any rumors you might have heard concerning the identity of any world—any world—ready to come to the aid of good government here on St. Marie. We are your readers here, too, on this world, Newsman. You also owe us information. Have you heard of some world which is—reported, rumored, what have you—to be ready to extend aid to a grass-roots' movement on Ste. Marie, to throw off the Exotic yoke and ensure equal representation among our people?"

I looked back at him. I let him wait for a second or two.

"No," I said. "No, Mr. O'Doyne, I haven't."

He stood, unmoving, as if my words had fixed him in position, legs spread a little wide, chin high, challenging me.

"I'm sorry," I said. "Good-bye."

I went out. I do not think he even answered my farewell.

I went across to Government house and spent a twenty minutes full of reassuring, pleasant platitudes in interview with Charles Perrinni, President of the Ste. Marie government. Then I returned, by way of New San Marcos and Joseph's Town to the spaceport and the spaceliner for Earth.

I paused only to check my mail on Earth and then transshipped immediately for Harmony, and the site on that planet of the United Council of Churches, which together governed both Friendly worlds of Harmony and Association. I spent five days in the city there, cooling my heels in the offices and wardrooms of minor officers of their so-called Public Relations Bureau.

On the sixth day, a note I had sent immediately on arriving to Field Commander Wassel paid its dividend. I was taken to the Council building, itself; and, after being searched for weapons—there were some violent sectarian differences between Church groups on the Friendly worlds themselves, and they made no exceptions, evidently, even for Newsmen—I was admitted to a lofty-ceilinged office with bare walls. There, surrounded by a few straight-backed chairs, in the middle of the black-and-white tile of the floor, sat a heavy desk with the seated man behind it dressed entirely in black.

The only white things about him were his face and hands. All else was covered. But his shoulders were as square and broad as a barn door and above them his white face had eyes as black as the clothing, which seemed to blaze at me. He got up and came around the desk, towering half a head over me, to offer his hand.

"God be with you," he said.

Our hands met. There was the hint of a hard touch of amusement in the thin line of his straight mouth; and the glance of his eyes seemed to probe me like twin doctor's scalpels. He held my hand, not hard, but with the hint of a strength that could crush my fingers as if in a vise, if he chose.

I was face to face, at last, with the Eldest of that Council of Elders who ruled the combined churches of Harmony and Association, him who was called Bright, First among the Friendlies.

Chapter 19

"You come well recommended by Field Commander Wassel," he said after he had shaken my hand. "An unusual thing for a Newsman." It was a statement, not a sneer; and I obeyed his invitation—almost more order than invitation—to sit, as he went back around to sit down behind his desk. He faced me across it.

There was power in the man, the promise of a black flame. Like the promise, it suddenly occurred to me, of the flame latent in the gunpowder, stored in 1687 by the Turks within the Parthenon, when a shell fired by the Venetian army under Morosini exploded the black grains and blew out the center of that white temple. There had always been a special dark corner of hatred in me for that shell and that army—for if the Parthenon had been living refutation of Mathias' darkness to me as a boy, the destruction wrought by that shell had been evidence of how that darkness conquered, even in the heart of light.

So, viewing Eldest Bright, I connected him in my mind with that old hate, though I was careful to shield my feelings from his eyes. Only in Padma had I felt such a penetrating power of gaze, before now—and there was a man here, too, behind the gaze.

For the eyes themselves were the eyes of a Torquemada, that prime mover of the Inquisition in ancient Spain—as others had remarked before me; for the Friendly Churches were not without their own repressors and extinguishers of heresy. But behind those eyes moved the political intelligence of a mind that knew when to leash or when to loose the powers of two planets. For the first time I realized the feeling of someone who, stepping into the lion's cage alone for the first time, hears the steel door click shut behind him.

For the first time, also, since I had stood in the Index Room of the

Final Encyclopedia and loosened the hinges of my knees—for what if this man had *no* weaknesses; and in trying to control him, I only gave my plans away?

But the habits of a thousand interviews were coming to my rescue and even as the doubts struck and clung to me, my tongue was working automatically.

". . . the utmost in cooperation from Field Commander Wassel and his men on New Earth," I said. "I appreciated it highly."

"I, too," said Bright harshly, his eyes burning upon me, "appreciated a Newsman without bias. Otherwise you wouldn't be here in my office interviewing me. The work of the Lord between the stars leaves me little time for providing amusement for the ungodly of seven systems. Now, what's the reason for this interview?"

"I've been thinking of making a project," I said, "of revealing the Friendlies in a better light to people on the other worlds—"

"To prove your loyalty to the Creed of your profession—as Wassel said?" interrupted Bright.

"Why, yes," I said. I stiffened slightly in my chair. "I was orphaned at an early age; and the dream of my growing years was to join the News Services—"

"Don't waste my time, Newsman!" Bright's hard voice chopped like an axe across the unfinished section of my sentence. He got to his feet once more, suddenly, as if the energy in him was too great to be contained, and prowled around his desk to stand looking down at me, thumbs hooked in the belt at his narrow waist, his bony, middle-aged face bent above me. "What's your Creed to me, who move in the light of God's word?"

"We all move in our own lights, in our own way," I said. He was standing so close above me that I could not get to my feet to face him as my instincts urged me. It was as if he held me physically pinned in my chair, beneath him. "If it weren't for my Creed I wouldn't be here now. Perhaps you don't know what happened to me and my brother-in-law at the hands of one of your Groupmen on New Earth—"

"I know." The two words were merciless. "You'll have been apologized to, some time since, for that. Listen to me, Newsman." His thin lips quirked slightly in a sour smile. "You are not Anointed of the Lord."

"No," I said.

"In those who follow God's word, there may be a cause to believe that they act from faith in something more than their own selfish interests. But in those without the Light, how can there be any faith to anything but themselves?" The quirking smile on his own lips mocked his own words, mocked at the canting phrases in which he called me a liar—and dared me to deny the sophistication in him that had permitted him to see through me.

I stiffened this time with a look of outrage.

"You're sneering at my Newsman's Creed only because it isn't your own!" I snapped at him.

My outburst moved neither him nor his quirk of a smile.

"The Lord would not choose a fool to be Eldest over the Council of our Churches," he said—and turning his back on me, walked back around to sit down once more behind his desk. "You should have thought of that before you came to Harmony, Newsman. But at any rate you know it now."

I stared at him, almost blinded by the sudden brilliance of my own understanding. Yes, I knew it now—and in knowing it, suddenly saw how he had delivered himself out of his own mouth into my hands.

I had been afraid that he might turn out to have no weakness of which I could take advantage as I had taken advantage of lesser men and women with my words. And it was true—he had no ordinary weakness. But by the same token he had an extraordinary one. For his weakness was his strength, that same sophistication that had lifted him to be ruler and leader of his people. His weakness was that to have become what he was, he had to be as fanatic as the worst of them were—but with something more, as well. He had to have the extra strength that made him able to lay his fanaticism aside, when it came to interfere in his dealing with the leaders of other worlds—with his equals and opposites between the stars. It was this, *this* he had unknowingly admitted to me just now.

Unlike the furious-eyed, black-clad ones about him, he was not limited to the fanatic's view of the universe that painted everything in colors of either pure black or pure white. He was able to perceive and deal in shades between—in shades of gray, as well. In short, he could be a politician when he chose—and, as a politician, I could deal with him.

As a politician, I could lead him into a politician's error.

I crumpled. I let the stiffness go out of me suddenly as I sat in my chair with his eyes newly upon me. And I heaved a long, shuddering breath.

"You're right," I said in a dead voice. I got to my feet. "Well, it's no use now. I'll be going—"

"Go?" His voice cracked like a rifle shot, stopping me. "Did I say the interview was over? Sit down!"

Hastily I sat down again. I was trying to look pale, and I think I succeeded. For all I had suddenly understood him, I was still in the lion's cage, and he was still the lion.

"Now," he said, staring at me, "what did you really hope to gain from me—and from us who are the Chosen of God on these two worlds?"

I wet my lips.

"Speak up," he said. He did not raise his voice, but the low, carrying tones of it promised retribution on his part if I did not obey.

"The Council—" I muttered.

"Council? The Council of our Elders? What about it?"

"Not that," I said, looking down at the floor. "The Council of the Newsman's Guild. I wanted a seat on it. You Friendlies could be the reason I could get it. After Dave—after what happened to my brother-in-law—my showing with Wassel that I could do my job without bias even to you people—that's been getting me attention, even in the Guild. If I could go on with that—if I could raise public opinion in the other seven systems in your favor—it'd raise me, too, in the public eye. And in the Guild."

I stopped speaking. Slowly I looked up at him. He was staring at me with harsh humor.

"Confession cleanses the soul even of such as you," he said grimly. "Tell me, you've given thought to the improvement of our public image among the cast-aside of the Lord on the other worlds?"

"Why, that depends," I said. "I'd have to look around here for story material. First—"

"Never mind that now!"

He rose once more behind his desk and his eyes commanded me to rise also, so I did.

"We'll go into this in a few days," he said. His Torquemada's smile saluted me. "Good-day for the present, Newsman."

"Good—day," I managed to say. I turned and went out, shakily.

Nor was the shakiness entirely assumed. My legs felt weak, as if from tense balancing on the edge of a precipice, and a dry tongue clung to the roof of my dry mouth.

I puttered around the town the next few days, ostensibly picking up background material. Then, on the fourth day after I had seen Eldest Bright, I was called once more to his office. He was standing when I came in, and he remained standing, halfway between the door and his desk.

"Newsman," he said abruptly, as I came in, "it occurs to me that you can't favor us in your news reports without your fellow Guild members noticing that favoring. If this is so, what good are you to me?"

"I didn't say I'd favor you," I answered indignantly. "But if you show me something favorable on which I can report, I can report on it."

"Yes." He looked hard at me with the black flames of his eyes. "Come and look at our people, then."

He led me out of his office and down an elevator tube to a garage where a staff car was waiting. We got in and its driver took us out of the Council City, through a countryside that was bare and stony, but neatly divided into farms.

"Observe," said Bright dryly as we went through a small town that was hardly more than a village. "We grow only one crop thickly on our poor worlds—and those are the bodies of our young men, to be hired out as soldiers that our people may not starve and our Faith endure. What disfigures these young men and the other people we pass that those on the other worlds should resent them so strongly, even while hiring them to fight and die in their foreign wars?"

I turned and saw his eyes on me with grim amusement, once again.

"Their—attitudes," I said cautiously.

Bright laughed, a short lion's cough of a laugh deep in his chest.

"Attitudes!" he said harshly. "Put a plain word to it, Newsman! Not attitudes—*pride! Pride!* Bone-poor, skilled only in hand toil and weapon-handling, as these people you see are—still they look as if from lofty mountains down on the dust-born slugs who hire them, knowing that those employers may be rich in worldly wealth and furniture, fat in foodstuffs and padded in soft raiment—yet when all peoples pass alike beyond the shadow of the grave, then they, who have wallowed in power and wealth, will not be endured even to stand, cap in hand, below those gates of silver and of gold which we, who have suffered and are Anointed, pass singing through."

He smiled at me, his savage, predator's smile, across the width of the staff car.

"What can you find in all you see here," he said, "to teach a proper humbleness and a welcome to those who hire the Bespoken of the Lord?"

He was mocking me again. But I had seen through him on that first visit in his office, and the subtle path to my own end was becoming clearer as we talked. So his mockery bothered me less and less.

"It isn't pride or humbleness on either side that I can do much about," I said. "Besides, that isn't what you need. You don't care what employers think of your troops, as long as they hire them. And em-

ployers will hire them, if you can make your people merely bearable—
not necessarily lovable, but bearable."

"Stop here, driver!" interrupted Bright; and the car pulled to a halt.
We were in a small village. Sober, black-clad people moved between the buildings of bubble-plastic—temporary structures which
would long since on other worlds have been replaced with more sophisticated and attractive housing.

"Where are we?" I asked.

"A lesser town called Remembered-of-the-Lord," he answered, and
dropped the window on his side of the car. "And here comes someone
you know."

In fact, a slim figure in a Force-Leader's uniform was approaching
the car. It reached us, stooped slightly, and the face of Jamethon Black
looked calmly in on both of us.

"Sir?" he said to Bright.

"This officer," said Bright, to me, "seemed qualified once for high
service in the ranks of us who served God's will. But six years past,
he was attracted by a daughter of a foreign world who would not have
him; and since then he has seemed to lose his will to rise in rank
among us." He turned to Jamethon. "Force-Leader," he said. "You
have seen this man twice. Once in his home on Earth six years ago,
when you sought his sister in marriage; and again last year on New
Earth when he sought from you a pass to protect his assistant between
the battle lines. Tell me, what do you know about him?"

Jamethon's eyes looked across the interior of the car into mine.

"Only that he loved his sister and wanted a better life for her,
perhaps, than I could give her," said Jamethon in a voice as calm as
his face. "And that he wished his brother-in-law well, and sought protection for him." He turned to look directly into the eyes of Bright. "I
believe him to be an honest man and a good one, Eldest."

"I did not ask for your beliefs!" snapped Bright.

"As you wish," said Jamethon, still calmly facing the older man;
and I felt a rage swelling up inside me so that I thought that I would
burst out with it, no matter what the consequences.

Rage against Jamethon, it was. For not only had he the effrontery
to recommend me to Bright as an honest man and a good one, but
because there was something else about him that was like a slap in the
face. For a moment, I could not identify it. And then it came to me.
He was not afraid of Bright. And I had been so, in that first interview.

Yet I was a Newsman, with the immunity of the Guild behind me;
and he was a mere Force-Leader facing his own Commander-in-Chief,
the Warlord of two worlds, of which Jamethon's was only one. How

could he—? And then it came to me, so that I almost ground my teeth in fury and frustration. For it was with Jamethon no different than it had been with the Groupman on New Earth who had denied me a pass to keep Dave safe. That Groupman had been instantly ready to obey that Bright, who was the Eldest, but felt in himself no need to bow before that other Bright, who was merely the man.

In the same way now Bright held the life of Jamethon in his hand, but unlike the way it had been with me, in holding this he held the lesser part of the young man before him, rather than the greater.

"Your leave home here is ended, Force-Leader," Bright said sharply. "Tell your family to send on your effects to Council City and join us now. I'm appointing you aide and assistant to this Newsman from now on. And we'll promote you Commandant to make the post worthwhile."

"Sir," said Jamethon emotionlessly with an inclination of his head. He stepped back into the building from which he had just emerged, before coming back out a few moments later to join us. Bright ordered the staff car turned about and so we returned to the city and his office.

When we got back there, Bright turned me loose with Jamethon to get acquainted with the Friendly situation in and around Council City. Consequently, the two of us, Jamethon and I, did a certain amount of sightseeing, though not much, and I returned early to my hotel.

It required very little in the way of perception to see that Jamethon had been assigned to act as a spy upon me while performing the functions of an aide. However, I said nothing about it, and Jamethon said nothing at all, so that, almost strangely, we two moved around Council City, and its related neighborhood, in the days that followed like a couple of ghosts, or men under a vow not to speak to each other. It was a strange silence of mutual consent that agreed that the only things worth talking about between us—Eileen, and Dave and the rest—would reward any discussion only with a pain that would make the discussion unprofitable.

Meanwhile, I was summoned from time to time to the office of Eldest Bright. He saw me more or less briefly on these occasions and spoke of little that was to the point of my announced reason for being on the Friendlies and in partnership with him. It was as if he were waiting for something to happen. And eventually I understood what that was. He had set Jamethon to check me out, while he himself checked out the interstellar situation which, as Eldest of the Friendly Worlds, he faced alone, searching for the situation and the moment in which he could best make use of this self-seeking Newsman who had offered to improve the public image of his people.

Once I had realized this, I was reassured, seeing how, interview by interview, day by day, he came closer as I wanted to the heart of the matter. That heart was the moment in which he might ask my advice, must ask me to tell him what he should do about me and with me.

Day by day and interview by interview, he became apparently more relaxed and trusting in his words with me—and more questioning.

"What is it they like to read, on those other worlds, Newsman?" he asked one day. "Just what is it they most like to hear about?"

"Heroes, of course," I answered as lightly as he had questioned. "That's why the Dorsai make good copy—and to a certain extent the Exotics."

A shadow which may or may not have been intentional passed across his face at the mention of the Exotics.

"The ungodly," he muttered. But that was all. A day or so later he brought the subject of heroes up again.

"What makes heroes in the public's eyes?" he asked.

"Usually," I said, "the conquering of some older, already established strong man, villain or hero." He was looking at me agreeably, and I took a venture. "For example, if your Friendly troops should face up to an equal number of Dorsai and outfight them—"

The agreeableness was abruptly wiped out by an expression I had never seen on his face before. For a second he all but gaped at me. Then he flashed me a stare as smoking and hot as liquid basalt from a volcano's throat.

"Do you take me for a fool?" he snapped. Then his face changed, and he looked at me curiously. "—Or are you simply one yourself?"

He gazed at me for a long, long moment. Finally he nodded.

"Yes," he said, as if to himself. "That's it—the man's a fool. An Earth-born fool."

He turned on his heel, and that ended our interview for the day.

I did not mind his taking me for a fool. It was that much more insurance against the moment when I would make any move to delude *him*. But, for the life of me, I could not understand what had brought such an unusual reaction from him. And that bothered me. Surely my suggestion about the Dorsai could not have been so farfetched? I was tempted to ask Jamethon, but discretion as the better part of valor held me wisely back.

Meanwhile the day came when Bright finally approached the question I knew he must ask me sooner or later.

"Newsman," he said. He was standing, legs spread, hands locked together behind his back, looking out through the floor-to-ceiling window of his office at the Government Center and Council City, below. His back was to me.

"Yes, Eldest?" I answered. He had called me once more to his office, and I had just walked through the door. He spun around at the sound of my voice to stare flamingly at me.

"You said once that heroes are made by their defeat of some older, established heroes. You mentioned as examples of older heroes in the public gaze the Dorsai—and the Exotics."

"That's right," I said, coming up to him.

"The ungodly on the Exotics," he said, as if he mused to himself. "They use hired troops. What good to defeat hirelings—even if that were possible and easy?"

"Why not rescue someone in distress, then?" I said lightly. "That sort of thing would give you a good, new public image. Your Friendlies haven't been known much for doing that sort of thing."

He flicked a hard glance at me.

"Who should we rescue?" he demanded.

"Why," I said, "there're always small groups of people who, rightly or wrongly, think they're being imposed on by the larger groups around them. Tell me, don't you ever get approached by small dissident groups wanting to hire your soldiers on speculation for revolt against their established government—" I broke off. "Why, of course you do. I was forgetting New Earth and the North Partition of Altland."

"We gained little credit in the eyes of the other worlds by way of our business with the North Partition," said Bright, harshly. "As you well know!"

"Oh, but the sides were about equal there," I said. "What you've got to do is help out some really tiny minority against some selfish giant of a majority—say, something like the miners on Coby against the mine owners."

"Coby? The miners?" He darted me a hard glance, but this was a glance I had been waiting for all these days and I met it blandly. He turned and strode over to stand behind his desk. He reached down and half-lifted a sheet of paper—it looked like a letter—that lay on his desk. "As it happens, I have had an appeal for aid on a purely speculative basis by a group—"

He broke off, laid the paper down and lifted his head to look at me.

"A group like the Coby miners?" I said. "It's not the miners themselves?"

"No," he said. "Not the miners." He stood silent a moment, then he came back around the desk and offered me his hand. "I understand you're about to leave."

"I am?" I said.

"Have I been misinformed?" said Bright. His eyes burned into mine. "I heard that you were leaving for Earth on a spaceliner this evening. I understood passage had already been booked by you."

"Why—yes," I said, reading the message clear in the tone of his voice. "I guess I just forgot. Yes, I'm on my way."

"Have a good trip," said Bright. "I'm glad we could come to a friendly understanding. You can count on us in the future. And we'll take the liberty of counting on you in return."

"Please do," I said. "And the sooner the better."

"It will be soon enough," said Bright.

We said good-bye again and I left for my hotel. There, I found my things had already been packed; and, as Bright had said, passage had already been booked for me on a spaceliner leaving that evening for Earth. Jamethon was nowhere to be seen.

Five hours later, I was once more between the stars, shifting on my way back toward Earth.

Five weeks later, the Blue Front on Ste. Marie, having been secretly supplied with arms and men by the Friendly worlds, erupted in a short but bloody revolt that replaced the legal government with the Blue Front leaders.

Chapter 20

This time I did not ask for an interview with Piers Leaf. He sent to ask for me. As I went through the Guild Hall and up the elevator tube to his office, heads turned among the cloaked members I passed. For in the two years since the Blue Front leaders had seized power on Ste. Marie, much had changed for me.

I had had my hour of torment in that last interview with my sister. And I had had, while returning from that to Earth, the first dream of my revenge. Afterward, I had taken the two steps, one on Ste. Marie, one on Harmony, to set that revenge in motion. But still, even with those things done, I had not yet changed inside me. For change takes time.

It was the last two years that had really changed me—that had brought Piers Leaf to call upon me, that had caused the heads above the capes to turn as I passed. For in those years the power of my understanding had come full upon me, in such measure that it now seemed by contrast to have been a weak, newborn and latent thing, even up through the moment in which I shook hands and said farewell to Eldest Bright, three years before.

I had dreamed my primitive dream of a revenge, sword in hand, going to a meeting in the rain. Then for the first time, I had felt the pull of it, but the reality I felt now was far stronger, stronger than meat or drink or love—or life itself.

They are fools that think that wealth or women or strong drink or even drugs can buy the most in effort out of the soul of a man. These things offer pale pleasures compared to that which is greatest of them all, that task which demands from him more than his utmost strength, that absorbs him, bone and sinew and brain and hope and fear and dreams—and still calls for more.

They are fools who think otherwise. No great effort was ever bought. No painting, no music, no poem, no cathedral in stone, no church, no state was ever raised into being for payment of any kind. No Parthenon, no Thermopylae was ever built or fought for pay or glory; no Bukhara sacked, or China ground beneath Mongol heel, for loot or power alone. The payment for the doing of these things was itself the doing of them.

To wield oneself—to use oneself as a tool in one's own hand—and so to make or break that which no one else can build or ruin—*that* is the greatest pleasure known to man! To one who has felt the chisel in his hand and set free the angel prisoned in the marble block, or to one who has felt the sword in hand and set homeless the soul that a moment before lived in the body of his mortal enemy—to these both come alike the taste of that rare food spread only for demons or for gods.

As it had come to me, these two and more than two years past.

I had dreamed of holding the lightning in my hand over the sixteen worlds and bending them all to my will. Now, I held that lightning, in sober fact, and read it. My abilities had hardened in me; and I *knew* now what failure of a wheat harvest on Freiland must mean in the long run to those who needed but could not pay for professional education on Cassida. I saw the movements of those like William of Ceta, Project Blaine of Venus, and Sayona the Bond, of both Exotic Worlds—all of whom bent and altered the shape of things happening between the stars—and I read their results-to-be clearly. And with this knowledge I moved to where the news would be, and wrote it even as it was only beginning to happen, until my fellow Guild members began to think me half-devil or half-seer.

But I cared nothing for their thoughts. I cared only for the secret taste of my waiting revenge, the feel of the hidden sword in my grasp—the tool of my *Destruct!*

For now I had no doubts left. I did not love him for it, but Mathias had seen me clearly—and from his grave, I worked the will of his anti-faith, but with a power he could never have imagined.

Now, however, I was at Piers Leaf's office. He was standing in the door of it, waiting for me, for from below they would have warned him I was on my way up. He took my hand in a handshake and held it to draw me inside his office and close the door behind us. We sat down not at his desk, but to one side on the floats of a sofa and an overstuffed chair; and he poured drinks for us both with fingers that seemed thinned by sudden age.

"You've heard, Tam?" he said without preamble. "Morgan Chu Thompson is dead."

"I've heard," I said. "And a seat on the Council is now vacant."

"Yes." He drank a little from his glass and set it down again. He rubbed a hand wearily over his face. "Morgan was an old friend of mine."

"I know," I said, though I felt nothing for him at all. "It must be hard on you."

"We were the same age—" He broke off, and smiled at me a little wanly. "I imagine you're expecting me to sponsor you for the empty seat?"

"I think," I said, "the Guild members might think it a little odd if you didn't, the way things have been going for me for some time now."

He nodded but at the same time he hardly seemed to hear me. He picked up his drink and sipped at it again, without interest, and set it down.

"Nearly three years ago," he said, "you came in here to see me with a prediction. You remember that?"

I smiled.

"You could hardly forget it, I suppose," he said. "Well, Tam—" He stopped and sighed heavily. He seemed to be having trouble getting down to what he wished to say. But I was old and experienced in patience nowadays. I waited. "We've had time to see things work out and it seems to me, you were both right—and wrong."

"Wrong?" I repeated.

"Why, yes," he said. "It was your theory that the Exotics were out to destroy the Friendly culture on Harmony and Association. But look at how things have gone since then."

"Oh?" I said. "How?—For example?"

"Why," he said, "it's been plain for nearly a generation now that the fanaticism of the Friendlies—acts of unreasoning violence like that massacre that took your brother-in-law's life on New Earth three years ago—were turning opinion on the fourteen other worlds against the Friendlies. To the point where they were losing the chance to hire out their young men as mercenary soldiers. But anyone with half an eye could see that was something the Friendlies were doing to themselves simply by being the way they are. The Exotics couldn't be to blame for that."

"No," I said. "I suppose not."

"Of course not." He sipped at his drink again, a little more heartily this time. "I think that was why I felt so much doubt when you told me that the Exotics were out to get the Friendlies. It just didn't ring right. But then it turned out to be Friendly troops and equipment backing that Blue Front revolution on Ste. Marie, right in the Exotics' back yard under the Procyon suns. And I had to admit there seemed to be something going on between the Friendlies and the Exotics." He stopped and looked at me.

"Thank you," I said.

"But the Blue Front didn't last," he went on.

"It seemed to have a great deal of popular support at first," I interrupted.

"Yes, yes." Piers brushed my interruption aside.

"But you know how it is in situations like that. There's always a chip on the shoulder where a bigger, richer neighbor's concerned—next door or on the next world, whichever. The point is, the Ste. Marians were bound to see through the Blue Front shortly and toss them out—make them an illegal party as they are now. That was bound to happen. There were only a handful of those Blue Front people, anyway, and they were mostly crackpots. Besides, Ste. Marie isn't set up to go it alone, financially or any other way, in the shadow of two rich worlds like Mara and Kultis. The Blue Front thing was bound to fail—anyone outside the picture had to see that."

"I suppose so," I said.

"You know so!" said Piers. "Don't tell me anyone with the perception you've demonstrated couldn't see that from the start, Tam. I saw it myself. But what I didn't see—and apparently you didn't either—was that, inevitably, once the Blue Front was kicked out, the Friendlies would put in an occupation force on Ste. Marie to back up their claim for payment from the legal government for the help they'd given the Blue Front. And that under the mutual assistance treaty that had always existed between the Exotics and the legal government of Ste. Marie, the Exotics would *have* to reply to the Ste. Marians' call for help to oust the Friendly occupation forces—since Ste. Marie couldn't pay the kind of bill the Friendlies were presenting."

"Yes," I said. "I foresaw that, too."

He darted a sharp glance at me.

"You did?" he said. "Then how could you think that—" He broke off, suddenly thoughtful.

"The point is," I said easily, "that the Exotic expeditionary forces haven't been having too much trouble pushing the Friendly forces back into a corner and cutting them up. They've stopped for the winter season now; but unless Eldest Bright and his council send reinforcements, the soldiers they have on Ste. Marie will probably have to surrender to the Exotic troops this spring. They can't afford to send reinforcements but they have to anyway—"

"No," said Piers, "they don't." He looked at me strangely. "You're about to claim, I suppose, that this whole situation was an Exotic maneuver to bleed the Friendlies twice—both for their help to the Blue Front, and again in the cost of sending reinforcements."

I smiled inside, for he was coming to the very point I had intended to come to three years ago—only I had planned that *he* should tell *me* about it, not I, him.

"Isn't it?" I said, pretending astonishment.

"No," said Piers strongly. "Just opposite. Bright and his council intend to leave their expeditionary force to be either captured or slaughtered—preferably slaughtered. The result will be just what you were about to claim in the eyes of the fourteen worlds. The principle that any world can be held ransom for debts incurred by its inhabitants is a vital—if not legally recognized—part of the interstellar financial structure. But the Exotics, in conquering the Friendlies on Ste. Marie, will be rejecting it. The fact that the Exotics are bound by their treaty to answer Ste. Marie's appeal for help won't alter things. Bright will only need to go hunting for help from Ceta, Newton and all the tight-contract worlds to form a league to bring the Exotics to their knees."

He broke off and stared at me.

"Do you see what I'm driving at now? Do you understand now why I said you were both right—in your notion of an Exotic-Friendly vendetta—and wrong? Do you see," he asked, "*now*, how you were wrong?"

I deliberately stared back at him for a moment before I answered.

"Yes," I said. I nodded. "I see now. It's not the Exotics who are out to get the Friendlies. It's the Friendlies who're out to get the Exotics."

"Exactly!" said Piers. "The wealth and specialized knowledge of the Exotics has been the pivot of the association of the loose-contract worlds that allowed them to balance off against the obvious advantage of trading trained people like sacks of wheat, which gives the tight-contract worlds their strength. If the Exotics are broken, the balance of power between the two groups of worlds is destroyed. And only that balance has let our Old World of Earth stand aloof from both groups. Now, she'll be drawn into one group or another—and whoever gets her will control *our* Guild, and the up until now impartiality of our News Services."

He stopped talking and sat back, as if worn out. Then he straightened up again.

"You know what group'll get Earth if the Friendlies win," he said, "the tight-contract group. So—where do we, we in the Guild, stand now, Tam?"

I stared back at him, giving him time to believe that his words were sinking into me. But, in reality, I was tasting at last the first slight flavor of my revenge. Here he was, at last, at the point to which I had set out to bring him, a point at which it seemed the Guild faced either the destruction of its high principle of impartiality, forcing it to take sides against the Friendly worlds; or its eventual capture by that partisan group of worlds to which the tight-contract Friendlies belonged. I let him wait, and think himself helpless for a little while. Then I answered him slowly.

"If the Friendlies can destroy the Exotics," I said, "then possibly the Exotics can destroy the Friendlies. Any situation like this has to have the possibility of tilting with equal force either way. Now if, without compromising our impartiality, I could go to Ste. Marie for the spring offensive, it might be that this ability of mine to see a little deeper into the situation than others can, might help that tilt."

Piers stared at me, his face a little white.

"What do you mean?" he said at last. "You can't openly side with the Exotics—you don't mean that?"

"Of course not," I answered. "But I might easily see something that they could turn to their advantage to get out of the situation. If so, I could make sure that they see it, too. There's nothing certain of success about this; but, as you said, otherwise, where do we stand now?"

He hesitated. He reached for his glass on the table and, as he picked it up, his hand shook a little. It took little insight to know what he was thinking. What I was suggesting was a violation of the spirit of the law of impartiality in the Guild, if not the letter of it. We would be choosing sides—but Piers was thinking that perhaps for the sake of the Guild we should do just that, while the choice was still in our own hands.

"Do you have any actual evidence that Eldest Bright means to leave his occupation forces cut up as they are?" I asked as he hesitated. "Do we know for sure he won't reinforce them?"

"I've got contacts on Harmony trying to get evidence right now—" he was beginning to answer when his desk phone chimed. He pressed a button and it lit up with the face of Tom Lassiri, his secretary.

"Sir," said Tom. "Call from the Final Encyclopedia. For Newsman

Olyn. From a Miss Lisa Kant. She says it's a matter of the utmost emergency."

"I'll take it," I said, even as Piers nodded. For my heart had lurched in my chest for some reason which I had no time to examine. The screen cleared and Lisa's face formed on it.

"Tam!" she said, without any other greeting. "Tam, come quick. Mark Torre's been shot by an assassin! He's dying, in spite of anything the doctors can do. And he wants to speak to you—to you, Tam, before it's too late! Oh, Tam, hurry! Hurry as fast as you can!"

"Coming," I said.

And I went. There was no time to ask myself why I should answer to her summons. The sound of her voice lifted me out of my chair and headed me out of Piers's office as if some great hand was laid upon my shoulders. I just—went.

Chapter 21

Lisa met me at the lobby entrance to the Final Encyclopedia, where I had first caught sight of her years before. She took me into the quarters of Mark Torre by the strange maze and the moving room by which she had taken me there previously; and on the way she told me what had happened.

It had been the inevitable danger for which the maze and the rest of it had been set up originally—the expected, reasonless, statistically fatal chance that had finally caught up with Mark Torre. The building of the Final Encyclopedia had from its very beginning triggered fears latent in the minds of unstable people on all the sixteen civilized worlds of men. Because the Encyclopedia's purpose was aimed at a mystery that could be neither defined nor easily expressed, it had induced a terror in psychotics both on Earth and elsewhere.

And one of these had finally gotten to Mark Torre—a poor paranoiac who had kept his illness hidden from even his own family while in his mind he fostered and grew the delusion that the Final Encyclopedia was to be a great Brain, taking over the wills of all humanity. We passed his body lying on the floor of the office, when at last Lisa and I reached it, a stick-thin, white-haired, gentle-faced old man with blood on his forehead.

He had, Lisa told me, been admitted by mistake. A new physician was supposed to have been admitted to see Mark Torre that afternoon. By some mistake, this gentle-looking, elderly, well-dressed man had been admitted instead. He had fired twice at Mark and once at himself, killing himself instantly. Mark, with two spring-gun slivers in his lungs, was still alive, but sinking fast.

Lisa brought me at last to him, lying still on his back on the blood-stained coverlet of a large bed in a bedroom just off the office. The clothing had been taken from his upper body and a large white bandage like a bandolier angled across his chest. His eyes were closed and sunken, so that his jutting nose and hard chin seemed to thrust upward almost as if in furious resentment of the death that was slowly and finally dragging his hard-struggling spirit down under its dark waters.

But it was not his face that I remember best. It was the unexpected width of chest and shoulder, and length of naked arm he showed, lying there. I was reminded suddenly, out of the forgotten past of my boyhood history studies, of the witness to the assassinated Abraham Lincoln, lying wounded and dying on the couch, and how that witness had been startled by the power of muscle and bone revealed in the unclothed upper body of the President.

So it was with Mark Torre. In his case, the muscle had largely wasted away through long illness and lack of use, but the width and length of bone showed the physical strength that he must have had as a young man. There were other people in the room, several of them physicians; but they made way for us as Lisa brought me up to the bedside.

She bent and spoke softly to him.

"Mark," she said. "Mark!"

For several seconds I did not think he would answer. I remember even thinking that perhaps he was already dead. But then the sunken eyes opened, wandered, and focused on Lisa.

"Tam's here, Mark," she said. She moved aside to let me get closer to the bed, and looked over her shoulder at me. "Bend down, Tam. Get close to him," she said.

I moved in, and I bent down. His eyes gazed at me. I was not sure whether he recognized me or not; but then his lips moved and I heard the ghost of a whisper, rattling deep in the wasted cavern of his once-broad chest.

"Tam—"

"Yes," I said. I found I had taken hold of one of his hands with one of mine. I did not know why. The long bones were cool and strengthless in my grasp.

"Son . . ." he whispered, so faintly that I could hardly hear him. But at the same time, all in a flash, without moving a muscle, I went rigid and cold, cold as if I had been dipped in ice, with a sudden, terrible fury.

How dare he? How dare he call *me* "son"? I'd given him no leave, or right or encouragement to do that to me—me, whom he hardly knew. Me, who had nothing in common with him, or his work, or anything he stood for. How dare he call me *"son"*?

But he was still whispering. He had two more words to add to that terrible, that unfair, word by which he had addressed me.

". . . take over. . . ."

And then his eyes closed, and his lips stopped moving, though the slow, slow stir of his chest showed that he still lived. I dropped his hand and turned and rushed out of the bedroom. I found myself in the office; and there I stopped in spite of myself, bewildered, for the doorway out, of course, was still camouflaged and hidden.

Lisa caught up with me there.

"Tam?" She put a hand on my arm and made me look at her. Her face told me she had heard him and that she was asking me now what I was going to do. I started to burst out that I was going to do no such thing as the old man had said, that I owed him nothing, and her nothing. Why, it had not even been a question he had put to me! He had not even asked me—he had *told* me to take over.

But no words came out of me. My mouth was open, but I could not seem to speak. I think I must have panted like a cornered wolf. And then the phone chimed on Mark's desk to break the spell that held us.

She was standing beside the desk; automatically her hand went out to the phone and turned it on, though she did not look down at the face which formed in the screen.

"Hello?" said a tiny voice from the instrument. "Hello? Is anyone there? I'd like to speak to Newsman Tam Olyn, if he's there. It's urgent. Hello? Is anyone there?"

It was the voice of Piers Leaf. I tore my gaze away from Lisa and bent down to the set.

"Oh, there you are, Tam," said Piers out of the screen. "Look, I don't want you to waste time covering the Torre assassination. We've got plenty of good men here to do that. I think you ought to get to Ste. Marie right away." He paused, looking at me significantly in the screen. "You understand? That information I was waiting for has just come in. I was right, an order's been issued."

Suddenly it was back again, washing out everything that had laid its hold upon me in the past few minutes—my long-sought plan and hunger for revenge. Like a great wave, it broke over me once more, washing away all the claims of Mark Torre and Lisa that had clung to me just now, threatening to trap me in this place.

"No further shipments?" I said sharply. "That's what the order said? No more coming?"

He nodded.

"And I think you ought to leave now because the forecast calls for a weather break within the week there," he said. "Tam, do you think—"

"I'm on my way," I interrupted. "Have my papers and equipment waiting for me at the spaceport."

I clicked off and turned to face Lisa once more. She gazed at me with eyes that shook me like a blow; but I was too strong for her now, and I thrust off their effect.

"How do I get out of here?" I demanded. "I've got to leave. Now!"

"Tam!" she cried.

"I've got to go, I tell you!" I thrust past her. "Where's that door out of here? Where—"

She slipped past me as I was pawing at the walls of the room and touched something. The door opened to my right; and I turned swiftly into it.

"Tam!"

Her voice stopped me for a final time. I checked and looked back over my shoulder at her.

"You're coming back," she said. It was not a question. She said it the way he, Mark Torre, had said it. She was not asking me; she was telling me; and for a last time it shook me once more to my deepest depths.

But then the dark and mounting power, that wave which was my longing for my revenge, tore me loose again and sent me hurtling on, through the doorway into the farther room.

"I'll be back," I assured her.

It was an easy, simple lie. Then the door I had come through closed behind me and the whole room moved about me, carrying me away.

Chapter 22

As I got off the spaceliner on Ste. Marie, the little breeze from the higher pressure of the ship's atmosphere at my back was like a hand from the darkness behind me, shoving me into the dark day and the rain. My Newsman's cloak covered me. The wet chill of the day wrapped around me but did not enter me. I was like the naked claymore of my dream, wrapped and hidden in the plaid, sharpened on a stone, and carried now at last to the meeting for which it had been guarded over three years of waiting.

A meeting in the cold rain of spring. I felt it cold as old blood on my hands and tasteless on my lips. Above, the sky was low and clouds were flowing to the east. The rain fell steadily.

The sound of it was like a rolling of drums as I went down the outside landing stairs, the multitude of raindrops sounding their own end against the unyielding concrete all around. The concrete stretched far from the ship in every direction, hiding the earth, as bare and clean as the last page of an account book before the final entry. At its far edge, the spaceport terminal stood like a single gravestone. The curtains of falling water between it and me thinned and thickened like the smoke of battle, but could not hide it entirely from my sight.

It was the same rain that falls in all places and on all worlds. It had fallen like this on Athens on the dark, unhappy house of Mathias, and on the ruins of the Parthenon as I saw it from my bedroom vision screen.

I listened to it now as I went down the landing stairs, drumming on the great ship behind me which had shifted me free between the stars—from Old Earth to this second smallest of the worlds, this small terraformed planet under the Procyon suns—and drumming hollowly upon the Credentials case sliding down the conveyor belt beside me. That case now meant nothing to me—neither my papers nor the Credentials of Impartiality I had carried four years now and worked so hard to earn. Now I thought less of these than of the name of the man I should find dispatching groundcars at the edge of the field. If, that is, he was actually the man my Earth informants had named to me. And if they had not lied.

"Your luggage, sir?"

I woke from my thoughts and the rain. I had reached the concrete. The debarking officer smiled at me. He was older than I, though he looked younger. As he smiled, some beads of moisture broke and spilled like tears from the brown visor-edge of his cap onto the tally sheet he held.

"Send it to the Friendly compound," I said. "I'll take the Credentials case."

I took it up from the conveyor belt and turned to walk off. The man standing in a dispatcher's uniform by the first groundcar in line did fit the description.

"Name, sir?" he said. "Business on Ste. Marie?"

If he had been described to me, I must have been described to him. But I was prepared to humor him.

"Newsman Tam Olyn," I said. "Old Earth resident and Interstellar News Services Guild Representative. I'm here to cover the Friendly-Exotic conflict." I opened my case and gave him my papers.

"Fine, Mr. Olyn." He handed them back to me, damp from the rain. He turned away to open the door of the car beside him and set the automatic pilot. "Follow the highway straight to Joseph's Town. Put it on automatic at the city limits and the car'll take you to the Friendly compound."

"All right," I said. "Just a minute."

He turned back. He had a young, good-looking face with a little mustache and he looked at me with a bright blankness. "Sir?"

"Help me get in the car."

"Oh, I'm sorry, sir." He came quickly over to me. "I didn't realize your leg—"

"Damp stiffens it," I said. He adjusted the seat and I got my left leg in behind the steering column. He started to turn away.

"Wait a minute," I said again. I was out of patience. "You're Walter Imera, aren't you?"

"Yes, sir," he said softly.

"Look at me," I said. "You've got some information for me, haven't you?"

He turned slowly back to face me. His face was still blank.

"No, sir."

I waited a long moment, looking at him.

"All right," I said then, reaching for the car door. "I guess you know I'll get the information anyway. And they'll believe you told me."

His little mustache began to look like it was painted on.

"Wait," he said. "You've got to understand. Information like that's not part of your news, is it? I've got a family—"

"And I haven't," I said. I felt nothing for him.

"But you don't understand. They'd kill me. That's the sort of organization the Blue Front is now, here on Ste. Marie. What d'you want to know about them for? I didn't understand you meant—"

"All right," I said. I reached for the car door.

"Wait." He held out a hand to me in the rain. "How do I know you can make them leave me alone if I tell you?"

"They may be back in power here someday," I said. "Not even outlawed political groups want to antagonize the Interstellar News Services." I started to close the door once more.

"All right," he said quickly. "All right. You go to New San Marcos. The Wallace Street Jewelers there. It's just beyond Joseph's Town, where the Friendly compound is you're going to." He licked his lips. "You'll tell them about me?"

"I'll tell them." I looked at him. Above the edge of the blue uniform collar on the right side of his neck I could see an inch or two of fine silver chain, bright against winter-pale skin. The crucifix attached to it would be down under his shirt. "The Friendly soldiers have been here two years now. How do people like them?"

He grinned a little. His color was coming back.

"Oh, like anybody," he said. "You just have to understand them. They've got their own ways."

I felt the ache in my stiff leg where the doctors on New Earth had taken the needle from the spring-rifle out of it three years before.

"Yes, they have," I said. "Shut the door."

He shut it. I drove off.

There was some religious medal on the car's instrument panel. One of the Friendly soldiers would have ripped it off and thrown it away, or refused the car. And so it gave me a particular pleasure to leave it where it was, though it meant no more to me than it would to him. It was not just because of Dave and the other prisoners they had shot down on New Earth. It was simply because there are some duties that have a small element of pleasure. After the illusions of childhood are gone and there is nothing left but duties, such pleasures are welcome. Fanatics, when all is said and done, are no worse than mad dogs.

But mad dogs have to be destroyed; it is simple common sense.

And you return to common sense after a while in life, inevitably. When the wild dreams of justice and progress are all dead and buried, when the painful beatings of feeling inside you are finally stilled, then it becomes best to be still, unliving, and unyielding as—the blade of a sword sharpened on a stone. The rain through which such a blade is carried to its using does not stain it, any more than the blood in which it is bathed at last. Rain and blood are alike to sharpened iron.

I drove for half an hour past wooded hills and plowed meadows. The furrows of the fields were black in the rain. I thought it a kinder black than some other shades I had seen. At last I reached the outskirts of Joseph's Town.

The autopilot of the car threaded me through a small, neat, typical Ste. Marie city of about a hundred thousand people. We came out on the far side into a cleared area, beyond which lifted the massive, sloping concrete walls of a military compound.

A Friendly noncom stopped my car at the gate with his black spring-rifle and opened the car door at my left.

"Thou hast business here?"

His voice was harsh and high in his nose. The cloth tabs of a Groupman edged his collar. Above them his forty-year-old face was lean and graven with lines. Both face and hands, the only uncovered parts of him, looked unnaturally white against the black cloth and rifle.

I opened the case beside me and handed him my papers.

"My Credentials," I said. "I'm here to see your acting Commander of Expeditionary Forces, Commandant Jamethon Black."

"Move over, then," he said nasally. "I must drive thee."

I moved.

He got in and took the stick. We drove through the gate and turned down an approach alley. I could see an interior square at the alley's far end. The close concrete walls on either side of us echoed the sound of our passage as we went. I heard drill commands growing louder as we approached the square. When we rolled out into it, soldiers were drawn up in ranks for their midday service, in the rain.

The Groupman left me and went in the entrance of what seemed to be an office set in the wall on one side of the square. I looked over the soldiers standing in formation. They stood at present-arms, their position of worship under field conditions; and as I watched, the officer facing them, with his back to a wall, led them into the words of their Battle Hymn.

Soldier, ask not—now or ever,
Where to war your banners go.
Anarch's legions all surround us.
Strike! And do not count the blow!

I sat trying not to listen. There was no musical accompaniment, no religious furniture or symbols except the thin shape of the cross whitewashed on the gray wall behind the officer. The massed male voices rose and fell slowly in the dark, sad hymn that promised them only pain, and suffering, and sorrow. At last, the final line mourned its harsh prayer for a battle death, and they ordered arms.

A Groupman dismissed the ranks as the officer walked past my car without looking at me, and passed in through the entrance where my noncommissioned guide had disappeared. As he passed I saw the officer was Jamethon.

A moment later the guide came for me. Limping a little on my stiffened leg, I followed him to an inner room with the lights on above a single desk. Jamethon rose and nodded as the door closed behind me. He wore the faded tabs of a Commandant on his uniform lapels.

As I handed my Credentials across the desk to him, the glare of the light over the desk came full in my eyes, blinding me. I stepped back and blinked at his blurred face. As it came back into focus I saw it for a moment as if it were older, harsher, twisted and engraved with the lines of years of fanaticism, like a face I remembered standing over the murdered prisoners on New Earth.

Then my eyes refocused completely, and I saw him as he actually was. Dark-faced, but thin with the thinness of youth rather than that of starvation. He was not the face burned in my memory. His features were regular to the point of being handsome, his eyes tired and shadowed; and I saw the straight, weary line of his mouth above the still, self-controlled stiffness of his body, smaller and slighter than mine.

He held the Credentials without looking at them. His mouth quirked a little, dryly and wearily, at the corners. "And no doubt, Mr. Olyn," he said, "you've got another pocket filled with authorities from the Exotic worlds to interview the mercenary soldiers and officers they've hired from the Dorsai and a dozen other worlds to oppose God's Chosen in War?"

I smiled. Because it was good to find him as strong as that, to add to my pleasure of breaking him.

Chapter 23

I looked across the ten feet or so of distance that separated us. The Friendly Groupman who had killed the prisoners on New Earth had also spoken of God's Chosen.

"If you'll look under the papers directed at you," I said, "you'll find them. The News Services and its people are impartial. We don't take sides."

"Right," said the dark young face opposing me, "takes sides."

"Yes, Commandant," I said. "That's right. Only sometimes it's a matter of debate where Right is. You and your troops here now are invaders on the world of a planetary system your ancestors never colonized. And opposing you are mercenary troops hired by two worlds that not only belong under the Procyon suns but have a commitment to defend the smaller worlds of their system—of which Ste. Marie is one. I'm not sure Right is on your side."

He shook his head slightly and said, "We expect small understanding from those not Chosen." He transferred his gaze from me to the papers in his hand.

"Mind if I sit down?" I said. "I've got a bad leg."

"By all means." He nodded to a chair beside his desk and as I sat down, seated himself. I looked across the papers on the desk before him and saw, standing to one side, the solidograph of one of the windowless high-peaked churches the Friendlies build. It was a legitimate token for him to own, but there just happened to be three people, an older man and woman and a young girl of about fourteen, in the foreground of the image. All three of them bore a family resemblance to Jamethon. Glancing up from my Credentials he saw me looking at them; and his gaze shifted momentarily to the graph and away again, as if he would protect it.

"I'm required, I see," he said, drawing my eyes back to him, "to provide you with cooperation and facilities. We'll find quarters for you here. Do you need a car and driver?"

"Thanks," I said. "That commercial car outside will do. And I'll manage my own driving."

"As you like." He detached the papers directed to him, passed the rest back to me and leaned toward a grille in his desktop. "Groupman."

"Sir," the grille answered promptly.

"Quarters for a single male civilian. Parking assignment for a civilian vehicle, personnel."

"Sir."

The voice from the grille clicked off. Jamethon Black looked across his desk at me. I got the idea he was waiting for my departure.

"Commandant," I said, putting my Credentials back in their case, "two years ago your Elders of the United Churches on Harmony and Association found the planetary government of Ste. Marie in default of certain disputed balances of credit, so they sent an expedition in here to occupy and enforce payment. Of that expedition, how much in the way of men and equipment do you have left?"

"That, Mr. Olyn," he said, "is restricted military information."

"However"—and I closed the case—"you, with the regular rank of Commandant, are acting Commander of Forces for the remnants of your expedition. That position calls for someone about five ranks higher than you. Do you expect such an officer to arrive and take charge?"

"I'm afraid you'd have to ask that question of Headquarters on Harmony, Mr. Olyn."

"Do you expect reinforcements of personnel and more supplies?"

"If I did"—his voice was level—"I would have to consider that restricted information, too."

"You know that it's been pretty widely mentioned that your General Staff on Harmony has decided that this expedition to Ste. Marie is a lost cause? But that to avoid loss of face they prefer you here to be cut up, instead of withdrawing you and your men."

"I see," he said.

"You wouldn't care to comment?"

His dark, young, expressionless face did not change. "Not in the case of rumors, Mr. Olyn."

"One last question then. Do you plan to retreat westward, or surrender when the spring offensive of the Exotic mercenary forces begins to move against you?"

"The Chosen in War never retreat," he said. "Neither do they abandon, or suffer abandonment by, their Brothers in the Lord." He stood up. "I have work I must get back to, Mr. Olyn."

I stood up, too. I was taller than he was, older, and heavier-boned. It was only his almost unnatural composure that enabled him to maintain his appearance of being my equal or better.

"I'll talk to you later, perhaps, when you've got more time," I said.

"Certainly." I heard the office door open behind me. "Groupman," he said, speaking past me, "take care of Mr. Olyn."

The Groupman he had turned me over to found me a small concrete cubicle with a single high window, a camp bed and a uniform cabinet. He left me for a moment and returned with a signed pass.

"Thanks," I said as I took it. "Where do I find the Headquarters of the Exotic forces?"

"Our latest advice, sir," he said, "is that they're ninety kilometers east of here. New San Marcos." He was my height, but, like most of them, half a dozen years younger than I, with an innocence that contrasted with the strange air of control they all had.

"San Marcos." I looked at him. "I suppose you enlisted men know your General Headquarters on Harmony has decided against wasting replacements for you?"

"No, sir," he said. I might have commented on the rain for all the reaction he showed. Even these boys were still strong and unbroken. "Is there somewhat else?"

"No," I said. "Thanks."

He went out. And I went out, to get in my car and head ninety kilometers east to New San Marcos. I reached it in about three-quarters of an hour. But I did not go directly to find the Exotic Field Headquarters. I had other fish to fry.

These took me to the Wallace Street Jewelers. There, three shallow steps down from street level, an opaqued door let me into a long, dimlighted room filled with glass cases. There was a small elderly man at the back of the store behind the final case and I saw him eyeing my correspondent's cloak and badge as I got closer.

"Sir?" he said as I stopped across the case from him. He raised gray, narrow old eyes in a strangely smooth face to look at me.

"I think you know what I represent," I said. "All worlds know the News Services. We're not concerned with local politics."

"Sir?"

"You'll find out how I learned your address anyway." I kept on smiling at him. "So I'll tell you it was from a spaceport auto-dispatcher named Imera. I promised him protection for telling me. We'd appreciate it if he remains well and whole."

"I'm afraid—" He put his hands on the glass top of the case. They were veined with the years. "You wanted to buy something?"

"I'm willing to pay in good will," I said, "for information."

His hands slid off the countertop.

"Sir." He sighed a little. "I'm afraid you're in the wrong store."

"I'm sure I am," I said. "But your store'll have to do. We'll pretend it's the right store and I'm talking to someone who's a member of the Blue Front."

He shook his head slowly and stepped back from the case.

"The Blue Front is illegal," he said. "Good-bye, sir."

"In a moment. I've got a few things to say first."

"Then I'm sorry." He retreated toward some drapes covering a doorway. "I can't listen. No one will come into this room with you, sir, as long as you talk like that."

He slipped through the drapes and was gone. I looked around the long, empty room.

"Well," I said a little more loudly, "I guess I'll have to speak to the walls. I'm sure the walls can hear me."

I paused. There was no sound.

"All right," I said. "I'm a correspondent. All I'm interested in is information. Our assessment of the military situation here on Ste. Marie"—and here I told the truth—"shows the Friendly Expeditionary Forces abandoned by their home headquarters and certain to be overrun by the Exotic forces as soon as the ground dries enough for heavy equipment to move."

There was still no answer, but the back of my neck knew they were listening and watching me.

"As a result," I went on—and here I lied, though they would have no way of knowing—"we consider it inevitable that the Friendly Command here will have got in contact with the Blue Front. Assassination of enemy commanders is expressly in violation of the Mercenaries' Code and the Articles of Civilized Warfare—but civilians could do what soldiers could not."

Still there was no sound or movement beyond the drapes.

"A news representative," I said, "carries Credentials of Impartiality. You know how highly these are held. I only want to ask a few questions. And the answers will be kept confidential."

For a last time I waited, and there was still no answer. I turned and went up the long room and out. It was not until I was well out on to the street that I let the feeling of triumph within spread out and warm me.

They would take the bait. People of their sort always did. I found my car and drove to Exotic Headquarters.

These were outside the town. There a mercenary Commandant named Janol Marat took me in charge. He conducted me to the bubble structure of their HQ building. There was a feel of purpose, there, a sure and cheerful air of activity. They were well armed, well trained. After the Friendlies it jumped at me. I said so to Janol.

"We've got a Dorsai Commander and we outnumber the opposition." He grinned at me. He had a deeply tanned, long face that went into creases as his lips curved up. "That makes everybody pretty optimistic. Besides, our Commander gets promoted if he wins. Back to the Exotics and staff rank—out of field combat for good. It's good business for us to win."

I laughed and he laughed.

"Tell me more, though," I said. "I want reasons I can use in the stories I send back to News Services."

"Well"—he answered the snappy salute of a passing Groupman, a Cassidan by the look of him—"I guess you might mention the usual—the fact our Exotic employers don't permit themselves to use violence and consequently they're always rather generous than otherwise when it comes to paying for men and equipment. And the OutBond—that's the Exotic Ambassador to Ste. Marie, you know—"

"I know."

"He replaced the former OutBond here three years ago. Anyway, he's something special, even for someone from Mara or Kultis. He's an expert in ontogenetic calculations. If that means much to you. It's all over my head." Janol pointed. "Here's the Field Commander's office. He's Kensie Graeme."

"Graeme?" I said, frowning. I could have admitted to knowing about Kensie Graeme, but I wanted Janol's reactions to him. "Sounds familiar." We approached the office building. "Graeme . . ."

"You're probably thinking of another member of the same family." Janol took the bait. "Donal Graeme. A nephew. Kensie is Donal's uncle. Not as spectacular as the young Graeme, but I'll bet you'll like him better than you would the nephew. Kensie's got two men's likableness." He looked at me, grinning slightly again.

"That supposed to mean something special?" I said.

"That's right," said Janol. "His own likableness and his twin brother's, too. Meet Ian Graeme sometime when you're in Blauvain. That's where the Exotic embassy is, east of here. Ian's a dark man."

We walked into the office.

"I can't get used," I said, "to how so many Dorsai seem related."

"Neither can I. Actually, I guess it's because there really aren't so many of them. The Dorsai's a small world, and those that live more than a few years—" Janol stopped by a Commandant sitting at a desk. "Can we see the Old Man, Hari? This is a Newsman from the Interstellar News Services."

"Why, I guess so." The other looked at his desk signal board. "The OutBond's with him, but he's just leaving now. Go on in."

Janol led me between the desks. A door at the back of the room opened before we reached it and a calm-faced man of middle age wearing an Exotic's blue robe, and close-cropped white hair, came out. His odd, hazel-colored eyes met mine.

It was Padma.

"Sir," said Janol to Padma, "this is—"

"Tam Olyn. I know," said Padma softly. He smiled up at me, and those eyes of his seemed to catch light for a moment and blind me. "I was sorry to learn about your brother-in-law, Tam."

I went quite cool all over. I had been ready to walk on, but now I stood stock still and looked at him.

"My brother-in-law?" I said.

"The young man who died near Dhores on New Earth."

"Oh, yes," I said between stiff lips. "I'm surprised that you'd know."

"I know because of you, Tam." Once more the hazel eyes of Padma seemed to catch light. "Have you forgotten? I told you once that we have a science called ontogenetics, by which we calculate the probabilities of human actions in present and future situations. You've been an important factor in those calculations for some time." He smiled. "That's why I was expecting to meet you here, and now. We've calculated you into our present situation here on Ste. Marie, Tam."

"Have you?" I said. "Have you? That's interesting."

"I thought it would be," said Padma softly. "To you, especially. Someone like a Newsman, like yourself, would find it interesting."

"It is," I said. "It sounds like you know more than I do about what I'm going to be doing here."

"We've got calculations," said Padma in his soft voice, "to that effect. Come see me in Blauvain, Tam, and I'll show you."

"I'll do that," I said.

"You'll be very welcome." Padma inclined his head. His blue robe whispered on the floor as he turned and went out of the room.

"This way," said Janol, touching my elbow. I started as if I had just wakened from a deep sleep. "The Commander's in here."

I followed him automatically into an inner office. Kensie Graeme stood up as we came through the door. For the first time I stood face to face with this great, lean man in field uniform, with a heavy-boned, but open, smiling face under black, slightly curly hair. That peculiar golden warmth of personality—a strange thing in a Dorsai—seemed to flow out from him as he rose to meet me and his long-fingered, powerful hand swallowed mine in a handshake.

"Come on in," he said. "Let me fix you up with a drink. Janol," he added to my mercenary Commandant from New Earth, "no need for you to stick around. Go on to chow. And tell the rest of them in the outer office to knock off."

Janol saluted and went. I sat down as Graeme turned to a small bar cabinet behind his desk. And for the first time in three years, under the magic of the unusual fighting man opposite me, a little peace came into my soul. With someone like this on my side, I could not lose.

Chapter 24

"Credentials?" asked Graeme as soon as we were settled with drinks of Dorsai whisky—which is a fine whisky—in our hands.

I passed my papers over. He glanced through them, picking out the letters from Sayona, the Bond of Kultis, to "Commander—Ste. Marie Field Forces." He looked these over and put them aside. He handed me back the Credentials folder.

"You stopped at Joseph's Town first?" he said.

I nodded. I saw him looking at my face, and his own sobered.

"You don't like the Friendlies," he said.

His words took my breath away. I had come prepared to fence for an opening to tell him. It was too sudden. I looked away.

I did not dare answer right away. I could not. There was either too much or too little to say if I let it come out without thinking. Then I got a grip on myself.

"If I do anything at all with the rest of my life," I said, slowly, "it'll be to do everything in my power to remove the Friendlies and all they stand for from the community of civilized human beings."

I looked back up at him. He was sitting with one massive elbow on his desktop, watching me.

"That's a pretty harsh point of view, isn't it?"

"No harsher than theirs."

"Do you think so?" he said seriously. "I wouldn't say so."

"I thought," I said, "you were the one who was fighting them."

"Why, yes." He smiled a little. "But we're soldiers on both sides."

"I don't think they think that way."

He shook his head a little.

"What makes you say that?" he said.

"I've seen them," I answered. "I got caught up front in the lines near Dhores on New Earth, three years ago. You remember that conflict." I tapped my stiff knee. "I got shot and I couldn't navigate. The Cassidans around me began to retreat—they were mercenaries, and the troops opposing them were Friendlies hired out as mercenaries."

I stopped and took a drink of the whisky. When I took the glass away, Graeme had not moved. He sat as if waiting.

"There was a young Cassidan, a buck soldier," I said. "I was doing a series on the campaign from an individual point of view. I'd picked him for my individual. It was a natural choice. You see"—I drank again, and emptied the glass—"my younger sister went out on contract as an accountant to Cassida five years before that, and she'd married him. He was my brother-in-law."

Graeme took the glass from my hand and silently replenished it.

"He wasn't actually a military man," I said. "He was studying shift mechanics and he had about three years to go. But he stood low on one of the competitive examinations at a time when Cassida owed a contractual balance of troops to New Earth." I took a deep breath. "Well, to make a long story short, he ended up on New Earth in this same campaign I was covering. Because of the series I was writing, I got him assigned to me. We both thought it was a good deal for him, that he'd be safer that way."

I drank some more of the whisky.

"But," I said, "you know, there's always a better story a little deeper in the combat zone. We got caught up front one day when the Cassidan troops were retreating. I picked up a needle through the kneecap. The Friendly armor was moving up and things were getting hot. The soldiers around us took off toward the rear in a hurry, but Dave tried to carry me, because he thought the Friendly armor would fry me before they had time to notice I was a non-combatant. Well"—I took another deep breath—"the Friendly ground troops caught us. They took us to a sort of clearing where they had a lot of prisoners and kept us there for a while. Then a Groupman—one of their fanatic types, a tall, starved-looking soldier about my age—came up with orders they were to reform for a fresh attack."

I stopped and took another drink. But I could not taste it.

"That meant they couldn't spare men to guard the prisoners. They'd have to turn them loose back of the Friendly lines. The Groupman said that wouldn't work. They'd have to make sure the prisoners couldn't endanger them."

Graeme was still watching me.

"I didn't understand. I didn't even catch on when the other Friendlies—none of them were noncoms like the Groupman—objected." I put my glass on the desk beside me and stared at the wall of the office, seeing it all over again, as plainly as if I looked through a window at it. "I remember how the Groupman pulled himself up straight. I saw his eyes. As if he'd been insulted by the others' objecting.

" 'Are they Chosen of God?' he shouted at them. 'Are they of the Chosen?' "

I looked across at Kensie Graeme and saw him still motionless, still watching me, his own glass small in one big hand.

"You understand?" I said to him. "As if because the prisoners weren't Friendlies, they weren't quite human. As if they were some lower order it was all right to kill." I shook suddenly. "And he did it! I sat there against a tree, safe because of my News Correspondent's uniform, and watched him shoot them down. All of them. I sat there and looked at Dave, and he looked at me, sitting there, as the Groupman shot him!"

I quit all at once. I hadn't meant to have it all come out like that. It was just that I'd been able to tell no one who would understand how helpless I had been. But something about Graeme had given me the idea he would understand.

"Yes," he said after a moment, and took and filled my glass again. "That sort of thing's very bad. Was the Groupman found and tried under the Mercenaries' Code?"

"After it was too late, yes."

He nodded and looked past me at the wall. "They aren't all like that, of course."

"There's enough to give them a reputation for it."

"Unfortunately, yes. Well"—he smiled slightly at me—"we'll try and keep that sort of thing out of this campaign."

"Tell me something," I said, putting my glass down. "Does that sort of thing—as you put it—ever happen to the Friendlies themselves?"

Something took place then in the atmosphere of the room. There was a little pause before he answered. I felt my heart beat slowly, three times, as I waited for him to speak.

He said at last, "No, it doesn't."

"Why not?" I said.

The feeling in the room became stronger. And I realized I had gone too fast. I had been sitting talking to him as a man and forgetting what else he was. Now I began to forget that he was a man and became conscious of him as a Dorsai—an individual as human as I was, but trained all his life, and bred down the generations to a difference. He did not move or change the tone of his voice, or any such thing; but somehow he seemed to move off some distance from me, up into a higher, colder, stonier land into which I could venture only at my peril.

I remembered what was said about his people from that small, cold, stony-mountained world: that if the Dorsai chose to withdraw their fighting men from the services of all the other worlds, and challenge those other worlds, not the combined might of the rest of civilization could stand against them. I had never really believed that before. I had never even really thought much about it. But sitting there just then, because of what was happening in the room, suddenly it became real to me. I could feel the knowledge, cold as a wind blowing on me off a glacier, that it was true; and then he answered my question.

"Because," said Kensie Graeme, "anything like that is specifically prohibited by Article Two of the Mercenaries' Code."

Then he broke out abruptly into a smile and what I had just felt in the room withdrew. I breathed again.

"Well," he said, putting his glass down empty on the desk, "how about joining us in the Officers' Mess for something to eat?"

I had dinner with them and the meal was very pleasant. They wanted to put me up for the night, but I could feel myself being pulled back to that cold, joyless compound near Joseph's Town, where all that waited for me was a sort of cold and bitter satisfaction at being among my enemies.

I went back.

It was about eleven P.M. when I drove through the gate of the compound and parked, just as a figure came out of the entrance to Jamethon's headquarters. The square was dim-lighted with only a few spotlights about the walls, their light lost in the rain-wet pavement. For a moment I did not recognize the figure—and then I saw it was Jamethon.

He would have passed by me at some little distance, but I got out of my car and went to meet him. He stopped when I stepped in front of him.

"Mr. Olyn," he said evenly. In the darkness I could not make out the expression of his face.

"I've got a question to ask," I said, smiling in the darkness.

"It's late for questions."

"This won't take long." I strained to catch the look on his face, but it was all in shadow. "I've been visiting the Exotic camp. Their commander's a Dorsai. I suppose you know that?"

"Yes." I could barely see the movement of his lips.

"We got to talking. A question came up and I thought I'd ask you, Commandant. Do you ever order your men to kill prisoners?"

An odd, short silence came between us. Then he answered.

"The killing or abuse of prisoners of war," he said without emotion, "is forbidden by Article Two of the Mercenaries' Code."

"But you aren't mercenaries here, are you? You're native troops in service to your own True Church and Elders."

"Mr. Olyn," he said, while I still strained without success to make out the expression of his shadowed face—and it seemed that the words came slowly, though the tone of the voice that spoke them remained as calm as ever, "My Lord has set me to be His servant and a leader among men of war. In neither of those tasks will I fail Him."

And with that he turned, his face still shadowed and hidden from me, and passed around me and went on.

Alone, I went back inside to my quarters, undressed and lay down on the hard and narrow bed they had given me. The rain outside had stopped at last. Through my open, unglazed window I could see a few stars showing.

I lay there getting ready to sleep and making mental notes on what I would need to do next day. The meeting with Padma had jolted me sharply. Strangely, somehow I had almost managed to forget that his calculations of human actions could apply to me personally. It shook me now to be reminded of that. I would have to find out more about how much his science of ontogenetics knew and could predict. If necessary, from Padma himself. But I would start first with ordinary reference sources.

No one, I thought, would ordinarily entertain the fantastic thought that one man like myself could destroy a culture involving the populations of two worlds. No one, except perhaps a Padma. What I knew, he with his calculations might have discovered. And that was that the Friendly worlds of Harmony and Association were facing a decision that would mean life or death to their way of living. A very small thing could tip the scales they weighed on. I went over my plan, nursing it in my mind.

For there was a new wind blowing between the stars.

Two hundred years before we had all been men of Earth—Old Earth, the mother planet which was my native soil. One people.

Then, with the movement out to new worlds, the human race had "splintered," to use an Exotic term. Every small social fragment and psychological type had drawn apart by itself, and joined others like it and progressed toward specialized types. Until we had half a dozen fragments of human types—the warrior on the Dorsai, the philosopher on the Exotic worlds, the hard scientist on Newton, Cassida and Venus, and so forth.

Isolation had bred specific types. Then a growing intercommunication between the younger worlds, now established, and an ever-increasing rate of technological advance had forced specialization. The trade between the worlds was the trade of skilled minds. Generals from the Dorsai were worth their exchange rate in psychiatrists from the Exotics. Communications men like myself from Old Earth bought spaceship designers from Cassida. And so it had been for the last hundred years.

But now the worlds were drifting together. Economics was fusing the race into one whole again. And the struggle on each world was to gain the advantages of that fusion while holding on to as much as possible of their own ways.

Compromise was necessary—but the harsh, stiff-necked Friendly religion forbade compromise and had made many enemies. Already public opinion moved against the Friendlies on other worlds. Discredit them, smear them, publicly here in this campaign, and they would not be able to hire out their soldiers. They would lose the balance of trade they needed to hire the skilled specialists trained by the special facilities of other worlds, and which they needed to keep their own two poor-in-natural-resources worlds alive. They would die.

As young Dave had died. Slowly. In the dark.

In the darkness now, as I thought of it, it rose up before me once again. It had been only midafternoon when we were taken prisoner, but by the time the Groupman came with his orders for our guards to move up, the sun was almost down.

I remembered how, after they left, after it was all over and I was left alone, I crawled to the bodies in the clearing. And how I had found Dave among them; and he was not quite gone. He was wounded in the body and I could not stop the bleeding.

It would not have helped if I had, they told me afterward. But then it seemed that it would have. So I tried. But finally I gave up and by that time it was quite dark. I only held him and did not know he was dead until he began to grow cold. And that was when I had begun to change into what my uncle had always tried to make me. I felt myself die inside. Dave and my sister were to have been my family, the only family I had ever had hopes of keeping. Instead, I could only sit there in the darkness, holding him and hearing the blood from his red-soaked clothing falling drop by drop, slowly, on the dead variform oak leaves beneath us.

I lay there now in the Friendly compound, unable to sleep and remembering. And after a while I heard the soldiers marching, forming in the square for midnight service.

I lay on my back, listening to them. Their marching feet stopped at last. The single window of my room was over my bed, high in the wall against which the left side of my cot was set. It was unglazed and the night air with its sounds came freely through it along with the dim light from the square which painted a pale rectangle on the opposite wall of my room. I lay watching that rectangle and listening to the service outside; and I heard the duty officer lead them in a prayer for worthiness. After that they sang their battle hymn again, and I lay hearing it this time all the way through.

> *Soldier, ask not—now, or ever,*
> *Where to war your banners go.*
> *Anarch's legions all surround us.*
> *Strike—and do not count the blow.*
>
> *Glory, honor, praise and profit,*
> *Are but toys of tinsel worth.*
> *Render up your work, unasking,*
> *Leave the human clay to earth.*
>
> *Blood and sorrow, pain unending,*
> *Are the portion of us all.*
> *Grasp the naked sword, opposing.*
> *Gladly in the battle fall.*
>
> *So shall we, anointed soldiers,*
> *Stand at last before the Throne.*
> *Baptized in our wounds, red-flowing,*
> *Sealed unto our Lord—alone!*

After that they dispersed to cots no different from mine.

I lay there listening to the silence in the square and the measured dripping of a rainspout outside by my window, its slow drops falling after the rain, one by one, uncounted in the darkness.

Chapter 25

After the day I landed, there was no more rain. Day by day the fields dried. Soon they would be firm underneath the weight of heavy surface-war equipment, and everyone knew that then the Exotic spring offensive would get under way. Meanwhile both Exotic and Friendly troops were in training.

During the next few weeks, I was busy about my newswork—mostly feature and small stories on the soldiers and the native people. I had dispatches to send and I sent them faithfully. A correspondent is only as good as his contacts; I made contacts everywhere but among the Friendly troops. These remained aloof, though I talked to many of them. They refused to show fear or doubt.

I heard these Friendly soldiers were generally undertrained because the suicidal tactics of their officers kept their ranks always filled with green replacements. But the ones here were the remnants of an expeditionary force six times their present numbers. They were all veterans, though most of them were in their teens. Only here and there, among the noncoms and more often among the commissioned officers, I saw the prototype of the noncom who had ordered the prisoners shot on New Earth. Here, the men of this type looked like rabid gray wolves mixed among polite, well-schooled young dogs just out of puppyhood. It was a temptation to think that they alone were what I had set out to destroy.

To fight that temptation I told myself that Alexander the Great had led expeditions against the hill tribes and ruled in Pella, capital of Macedonia, and ordered men put to death when he was sixteen. But still the Friendly soldiers looked young to me. I could not help contrasting them with the adult, experienced mercenaries in Kensie

Graeme's forces. For the Exotics, in obedience to their principles, would hire no drafted troops or soldiers who were not in uniform of their own free will.

Meanwhile I had heard no word from the Blue Front. But by the time two weeks had gone, I had my own connections in New San Marcos, and at the beginning of the third week one of these brought me word that the jeweler's shop in Wallace Street there had closed its door, had pulled its blinds and emptied the long room of stock and fixtures, and moved or gone out of business. That was all I needed to know.

For the next few days, I stayed in the vicinity of Jamethon Black himself, and by the end of the week my watching him paid off.

At ten o'clock that Friday night I was on a catwalk just above my quarters and under the sentry-walk of the walls, watching as three civilians with Blue Front written all over them drove into the square, got out and went into Jamethon's office.

They stayed a little over an hour. When they left, I went back down to bed. That night I slept soundly.

The next morning I got up early, and there was mail for me. A message had come by spaceliner from the director of News Services back on Earth, personally congratulating me on my dispatches. Once, three years before, this would have meant a great deal to me. Now I only worried that they would decide I had made the situation here newsworthy enough to require extra people being sent out to help me. I could not risk having other news personnel here now to see what I was doing.

I got in my car and headed east along the highway to New San Marcos and the Exotic Headquarters. The Friendly troops were already out in the field; eighteen kilometers east of Joseph's Town, I was stopped by a squad of five young soldiers with no noncom over them. They recognized me.

"In God's name, Mr. Olyn," said the first one to reach my car, bending down to speak to me through the open window at my left shoulder. "You cannot go through."

"Mind if I ask why?" I said.

He turned and pointed out and down into a little valley between two wooded hills at our left.

"Tactical survey in progress."

I looked. The little valley or meadow was perhaps a hundred yards wide between the wooded slopes, and it wound away from me and curved to disappear to my right. At the edge of the wooded slopes, where they met open meadow, there were lilac bushes with blossoms several days old. The meadow itself was green and fair with the young chartreuse grass of early summer and the white and purple of the lilacs, and the variform oaks behind the lilacs were fuzzy in outline, with small, new leaves.

In the middle of all this, in the center of the meadow, were black-clad figures moving about with computing devices, measuring and figuring the possibilities of death from every angle. In the very center of the meadow for some reason they had set up marking stakes—a single stake, then a stake in front of that with two stakes on either side of it, and one more stake in line before these. Farther on was another single stake, down, as if fallen on the grass and discarded.

I looked back up into the lean young face of the soldier.

"Getting ready to defeat the Exotics?" I said.

He took it as if it had been a straightforward question, with no irony in my voice at all.

"Yes, sir," he said seriously. I looked at him and at the taut skin and clear eyes of the rest.

"Ever think you might lose?"

"No, Mr. Olyn." He shook his head solemnly. "No man loses who goes to battle for the Lord." He saw that I needed to be convinced, and he went about it earnestly. "He hath set His hand upon His soldiers. And all that is possible to them is victory—or sometimes death. And what is death?"

He looked to his fellow soldiers and they all nodded.

"What is death?" they echoed.

I looked at them. They stood there asking me and each other what was death as if they were talking about some hard but necessary job.

I had an answer for them, but I did not say it. Death was a Group-man, one of their own kind, giving orders to soldiers just like themselves to assassinate prisoners. That was death.

"Call an officer," I said. "My pass lets me through here."

"I regret, sir," said the one who had been talking to me, "we cannot leave our posts to summon an officer. One will come soon."

I had a hunch what "soon" meant, and I was right. It was high noon before a Force-Leader came by to order them to chow and let me through.

As I pulled into Kensie Graeme's Headquarters, the sun was low, patterning the ground with the long shadows of trees. Yet it was as if the camp were just waking up. I did not need experience to see the Exotics were beginning to move at last against Jamethon.

I found Janol Marat, the New Earth Commandant.

"I've got to see Field Commander Graeme," I said.

He shook his head, for all that we now knew each other well.

"Not now, Tam. I'm sorry."

"Janol," I said, "this isn't for an interview. It's a matter of life and death. I mean that. I've got to see Kensie."

He stared at me. I stared back.

"Wait here," he said. We were standing just inside the headquarters office. He went out and was gone for perhaps five minutes. I stood, listening to the wall clock ticking away. Then he came back.

"This way," he said.

He led me outside the back between the bubble roundness of the plastic buildings to a small structure half-hidden in some trees. When we stepped through its front entrance, I realized it was Kensie's personal quarters. We passed through a small sitting room into a combination bedroom and bath. Kensie had just stepped out of the shower and was getting into battle clothes. He looked at me curiously, then turned his gaze back on Janol.

"All right, Commandant," he said, "you can get back to your duties, now."

"Sir," said Janol, without looking at me.

He saluted and left.

"All right, Tam," Kensie said, pulling on a pair of uniform slacks. "What is it?"

"I know you're ready to move out," I said.

He looked at me a little humorously as he locked the waistband of his slacks. He had not yet put on his shirt, and in that relatively small room he loomed like a giant, like some irresistible natural force. His body was tanned like dark wood and the muscles lay in flat bands across his chest and shoulders. His belly was hollow and the cords in his arms came and went as he moved them. Once more I felt the particular, special element of the Dorsai in him. It was not even the fact that he was someone trained from birth to war, someone bred for battle. No, it was something living but untouchable—the same quality of difference to be found in the pure Exotic like Padma the OutBond, or in some Newtonian or Cassidan researchist. Something so much above and beyond the common form of man that it was like a serenity, a sense of conviction where his own type of thing was concerned that was so complete it made him beyond all weaknesses, untouchable, unconquerable.

I saw the slight, dark shadow of Jamethon in my mind's eye, standing opposed to such a man as this; and the thought of any victory for Jamethon was unthinkable, an impossibility.

But there was always danger.

"All right, I'll tell you what I came about," I said to Kensie. "I've just found out Black's been in touch with the Blue Front, a native terrorist political group with its headquarters in Blauvain. Three of them visited him last night. I saw them."

Kensie picked up his shirt and slid a long arm into one sleeve.

"I know," he said.

I stared at him.

"Don't you understand?" I said. "They're assassins. It's their stock in trade. And the one man they and Jamethon both could use out of the way is you."

He put his other arm in a sleeve.

"I know that," he said. "They want the present government here on Ste. Marie out of the way and themselves in power—which isn't possible with Exotic money hiring us to keep the peace here."

"They haven't had Jamethon's help."

"Have they got it now?" he asked, sealing the shirt closure between thumb and forefinger.

"The Friendlies are desperate," I said. "Even if reinforcements arrived tomorrow, Jamethon knows what his chances are with you ready to move. Assassins may be outlawed by the Conventions of War and the Mercenaries' Code, but you and I know the Friendlies."

Kensie looked at me oddly and picked up his jacket.

"Do we?" he said.

I met his eyes. "Don't we?"

"Tam." He put on the jacket and closed it. "I know the men I have to fight. It's my business to know. But what makes you think you know them?"

"They're my business, too," I said. "Maybe you've forgotten. I'm a Newsman. People are my business, first, last and always."

"But you've got no use for the Friendlies."

"Should I?" I said. "I've been on all the worlds. I've seen the Cetan entrepreneur—and he wants his margin, but he's a human being. I've seen the Newtonian and the Venusian with their heads in the clouds, but if you yanked on their sleeves hard enough, you could pull them back to reality. I've seen Exotics like Padma at their mental parlor tricks, and the Freilander up to his ears in his own red tape. I've seen them from my own world of Old Earth, and Coby, and Venus and even from the Dorsai, like you. And I tell you they've all got one thing in common. Underneath it all they're human. Every one of them's human—they've just specialized in some one, valuable way."

"And the Friendlies haven't?"

"Fanaticism," I said. "Is that valuable? It's just the opposite.

What's good, what's even permissible about blind, deaf, dumb, unthinking faith that doesn't let a man reason for himself?"

"How do you know they don't reason?" Kensie asked. He was
standing facing me now.

"Maybe some of them do," I said. "Maybe the young ones, before
the poison's had time to work in. What good does that do, as long as
the culture exists?"

A sudden silence came into the room.

"What are you talking about?" said Kensie.

"I mean you want the assassins," I said. "You don't want the
Friendly troops. Prove that Jamethon Black has broken the Conven-
tions of War by arranging with them to kill you; and you can win Ste.
Marie for the Exotics without firing a shot."

"And how would I do that?"

"Use me," I said. "I've got a pipeline to the political group the
assassins represent. Let me go to them as your representative and out-
bid Jamethon. You can offer them recognition by the present government now. Padma and the present Ste. Marie government heads would
have to back you up if you could clean the planet of Friendlies that
easily."

He looked at me with no expression at all.

"And what would I be supposed to buy with this?" he said.

"Sworn testimony they'd been hired to assassinate you. As many
of them as needed could testify."

"No Court of Interplanetary Inquiry would believe people like
that," Kensie said.

"Ah," I said, and I could not help smiling. "But they'd believe me
as a News Service Representative when I backed up every word that
was said."

There was a new silence. His face had no expression at all.

"I see," he said.

He walked past me into the salon. I followed him. He went to his
phone, put his finger on a stud and spoke into an imageless gray screen.

"Janol," he said.

He turned away from the screen, crossed the room to an arms
cabinet and began putting on his battle harness. He moved deliberately
and neither looked nor spoke in my direction. After a few long minutes,
the building entrance slid aside and Janol stepped in.

"Sir?" said the officer.

"Mr. Olyn stays here until further orders."

"Yes, sir," said Janol.

Graeme went out.

I stood numb, staring at the entrance through which he had left. I could not believe that he would violate the Conventions so far himself as not only to disregard me, but to put me essentially under arrest to keep me from doing anything further about the situation.

I turned to Janol. He was looking at me with a sort of wry sympathy on his long, brown face.

"Is the OutBond here in camp?" I asked him.

"No." He came up to me. "He's back in the Exotic Embassy in Blauvain. Be a good fella now and sit down, why don't you? We might as well kill the next few hours pleasantly."

We were standing face to face; I hit him in the stomach.

I had done a little boxing as an undergraduate on the college level. I mention this not to make myself out a sort of muscular hero, but to explain why I had sense enough not to try for his jaw. Graeme could probably have found the knockout point there without even thinking, but I was no Dorsai. The area below a man's breastbone is relatively large, soft, handy and generally just fine for amateurs. And I did know something about how to punch.

For all that, Janol was not knocked out. He went over on the floor and lay there doubled up with his eyes still open. But he was not ready to get up right away. I turned and went quickly out of the building.

The camp was busy. Nobody stopped me. I got back into my car, and five minutes later I was free on the darkening road for Blauvain.

Chapter 26

From New San Marcos to Blauvain and Padma's Embassy was four-teen hundred kilometers. I should have made it in six hours, but a bridge was washed out and I took fourteen.

It was after eight the following morning when I burst into the half-park, half-building that was the embassy.

"Padma," I said. "Is he still—"

"Yes, Mr. Olyn," said the girl receptionist. "He's expecting you."

She smiled above her blue robe. I did not mind. I was too busy being glad Padma had not already taken off for the fringe areas of the conflict.

She took me down and around a corner and turned me over to a young male Exotic, who introduced himself as one of Padma's secretaries. He took me a short distance and introduced me to another secretary, a middle-aged man this time, who led me through several rooms and then directed me down a long corridor and around a corner, beyond which he said was the entrance to the office area where Padma worked at the moment. Then he left me.

I followed his direction. But when I stepped through that entrance it was not into a room, but into another short corridor. And I stopped dead. For what I suddenly thought I saw coming at me was Kensie Graeme—Kensie with murder on his mind.

But the man who looked like Kensie merely glanced at me and dismissed me, continuing to come on. Then I knew.

Of course, he was not Kensie. He was Kensie's twin brother, Ian, Commander of Garrison Forces for the Exotics here in Blauvain. He strode toward me; and I began once more to walk toward him, but the shock stayed with me until we had passed one another.

I do not think anyone could have come on him like that, in my position, and not been hit the same way. From Janol, at different times, I had gathered how Ian was the converse of Kensie. Not in a military sense—they were both magnificent specimens of Dorsai officers—but in the matter of their individual natures.

Kensie had had a profound effect on me from the first moment, with his cheerful nature and the warmth of being that at times obscured the very fact that he was Dorsai. When the pressure of military affairs was not directly on him he seemed all sunshine; you could warm yourself in his presence as you might in the sun. Ian, his physical duplicate, striding toward me like some two-eyed Odin, was all shadow.

Here at last was the Dorsai legend come to life. Here was the grim man with the iron heart and the dark and solitary soul. In the powerful fortress of his body, what was essentially Ian dwelt as isolated as a hermit on a mountain. He was the fierce and lonely Highlandman of his distant ancestry, come to life again.

Not law, not ethics, but the trust of the given word, clan-loyalty and the duty of the blood feud held sway in Ian. He was a man who would cross hell to pay a debt for good or ill; and in that moment when I saw him coming toward me and recognized him at last, I suddenly thanked whatever gods were left that he had no debt with me.

Then we had passed each other, and he was gone around a corner.

Rumor had it, I remembered, that the blackness around him never lightened except in Kensie's presence, that he was truly his twin brother's other half. And that if he should ever lose the light that Kensie's bright presence shed on him, he would be doomed to his own lightlessness forever.

It was a statement I was to remember at a later time, as I was to remember seeing him come toward me in that moment.

But now I forgot him as I went forward through another entrance into what looked like a small conservatory and saw the gentle face and short-cropped white hair of Padma above his blue robe.

"Come in, Mr. Olyn," he said, getting up, "and come along with me."

He turned and walked out through an archway of purple clematis blooms. I followed him, and found a small courtyard all but filled with the elliptical shape of a sedan air-car. Padma was already climbing into one of the seats facing the controls. He held the door for me.

"Where are we going?" I asked as I got in.

He touched the autopilot panel; the ship rose in the air. He left it to its own navigation and pivoted his chair about to face me.

"To Commander Graeme's headquarters in the field," he answered.

His eyes were the same light hazel color, but they seemed to catch and swim with the sunlight striking through the transparent top of the air-car as we reached altitude and began to move horizontally. I could not read them or the expression on his face.

"I see," I said. "Of course, I know a call from Graeme's HQ could get to you much faster than I could by ground-car from the same spot. But I hope you aren't thinking of having him kidnap me or something like that. I have Credentials of Impartiality protecting me as a Newsman, as well as authorizations from both the Friendly and the Exotic worlds. And I don't intend to be held responsible for any conclusions drawn by Graeme after the conversation the two of us had earlier this morning—alone."

Padma sat still in his air-car seat, facing me. His hands were folded in his lap together, pale against the blue robe, but with strong sinews showing under the skin of their backs.

"You're coming with me now by my decision, not Kensie Graeme's."

"I want to know why," I said tensely.

"Because," he said slowly, "you are very dangerous." And he sat still, looking at me with unwavering eyes.

I waited for him to go on, but he did not. "Dangerous?" I said. "Dangerous to whom?"

"To the future of all of us."

I stared at him, then I laughed. I was angry.

"Cut it out!" I said.

He shook his head slowly, his eyes never leaving my face. I was baffled by those eyes. Innocent and open as a child's, but I could not see through them into the man himself.

"All right," I said. "Tell me, why am I dangerous?"

"Because you want to destroy a vital part of the human race. And you know how."

There was a short silence. The air-car fled on through the skies without a sound.

"Now that's an odd notion," I said slowly and calmly. "I wonder where you got it?"

"From our ontogenetic calculations," said Padma as calmly as I had spoken. "And it's not a notion, Tam. As you know yourself."

"Oh, yes," I said. "Ontogenetics. I was going to look that up."

"You did look it up, didn't you, Tam?"

"Did I?" I said. "I guess I did, at that. It didn't seem very clear to me, though, as I remember. Something about evolution."

"Ontogenetics," said Padma, "is the study of the effect of evolution upon the interacting forces of human society."

"Am I an interacting force?"

"At the moment and for the past several years, yes," said Padma. "And possibly for some years into the future. But possibly not."

"That sounds almost like a threat."

"In a sense it is." Padma's eyes caught the light as I watched them. "You're capable of destroying yourself as well as others."

"I'd hate to do that."

"Then," said Padma, "you'd better listen to me."

"Why, of course," I said. "That's my business, listening. Tell me all about ontogenetics—and myself."

He made an adjustment in the controls, then swung his seat back to face mine once more.

"The human race," said Padma, "broke up in an evolutionary explosion at the moment in history when interstellar colonization became practical." He sat watching me. I kept my face attentive. "This happened for reasons stemming from racial instinct which we haven't completely charted yet, but which was essentially self-protective in nature."

I reached into my jacket pocket.

"Perhaps I'd better take a few notes," I said.

"If you want to," said Padma, unperturbed. "Out of that explosion came cultures individually devoted to single facets of the human personality. The fighting, combative facet became the Dorsai. The facet which surrendered the individual wholly to some faith or other became the Friendly. The philosophical facet created the Exotic culture to which I belong. We call these Splinter Cultures."

"Oh, yes," I said. "I know about Splinter Cultures."

"You know about them, Tam, but you don't know them."

"I don't?"

"No," said Padma, "because you, like all our ancestors, are from Earth. You're old full-spectrum man. The Splinter peoples are evolutionarily advanced over you."

I felt a little twist of bitter anger knot suddenly inside me. His voice woke the echo of Mathias' voice in my memory.

"Oh? I'm afraid I don't see that."

"Because you don't want to," said Padma. "If you did, you'd have to admit that they were different from you and had to be judged by different standards."

"Different? How?"

"Different in a sense that all Splinter people, including myself, understand instinctively, but full-spectrum man has to extrapolate to imagine." Padma shifted a little in his seat. "You'll get some idea, Tam, if you imagine a member of a Splinter Culture to be a man like yourself, only with a monomania that shoves him wholly toward being one type of person. But with this difference: instead of all parts of his mental and physical self outside the limits of that monomania being ignored and atrophied as they would be with you—"

I interrupted, "Why specifically with me?"

"With any full-spectrum man, then," said Padma calmly. "These parts, instead of being atrophied, are altered to agree with and support the monomania, so that we don't have a sick man, but a healthy, different one."

"Healthy?" I said, seeing the Friendly Groupman who had killed Dave on New Earth again in my mind's eye.

"Healthy as a culture. Not as occasional crippled individuals of that culture. But as a culture."

"Sorry," I said. "I don't believe it."

"But you do, Tam," said Padma softly. "Unconsciously you do. Because you're planning to take advantage of the weakness such a culture must have to destroy it."

"And what weakness is that?"

"The obvious weakness that's the converse of any strength," said Padma. "The Splinter Cultures are not viable."

I must have blinked. I was honestly bewildered.

"Not viable? You mean they can't live on their own?"

"Of course not," said Padma. "Faced with an expansion into space, the human race reacted to the challenge of a different environment by trying to adapt to it. It adapted by trying out separately all the elements of its personality, to see which could survive best. Now that all elements—the Splinter Cultures—have survived and adapted, it's time for them to breed back into each other again, to produce a more hardy, universe-oriented human."

The air-car began to descend. We were nearing our destination.

"What's that got to do with me?" I said, at last.

"If you frustrate one of the Splinter Cultures, it can't adapt on its own as full-spectrum man would do. It will die. And when the race breeds back to a whole, that valuable element will be lost to the race."

"Maybe it'll be no loss," I said, softly in my turn.

"A vital loss," said Padma. "And I can prove it. You, a full-spectrum man, have in you an element from every Splinter Culture. If you admit this you can identify even with those you want to destroy. I have evidence to show you. Will you look at it?"

The ship touched ground; the door beside me opened. I got out with Padma and found Kensie waiting.

I looked from Padma to Kensie, who stood with us and a head taller than I, two heads taller than OutBond. Kensie looked back down at me with no particular expression. His eyes were not the eyes of his twin brother—but just then, for some reason, I could not meet them.

"I'm a Newsman," I said. "Of course my mind is open."

Padma turned and began walking toward the headquarters building. Kensie fell in with us and I think Janol and some of the others came along behind, though I didn't look back to make sure. We went to the inner office where I had first met Graeme—just Kensie, Padma and myself. There was a file folder on Graeme's desk. He picked it up, extracted a photocopy of something and handed it to me as I came up to him.

I took it. There was no doubting its authenticity.

It was a memo from Eldest Bright, ranking Elder of the joint government of Harmony and Association, to the Friendly War Chief at the Defense X Center, on Harmony. It was dated two months previously. It was on the single-molecule sheet, where the legend cannot be tampered with or removed once it is on.

Be Informed, in God's Name—

—That since it does seem the Lord's Will that our Brothers on Ste. Marie make no success, it is ordered that henceforth no more replacements or personnel or supplies be sent them. For if our Captain does intend us the victory, surely we shall conquer without further expenditure. And if it be His will that we conquer not, then surely it would be an impiety to throw away the substance of God's Churches in an attempt to frustrate that Will.

Be it further ordered that our Brothers on Ste. Marie be spared the knowledge that no further assistance is forthcoming, that they may bear witness to their faith in battle as ever, and God's Churches be undismayed. Heed this Command, in the Name of the Lord:

By order of him who is called—
Bright
Eldest Among The Chosen

I looked up from the memo. Both Graeme and Padma were watching me.

"How'd you get hold of this?" I said. "No, of course you won't tell me." The palms of my hands were suddenly sweating so that the slick material of the sheet in my fingers was slippery. I held it tightly, and talked fast to keep their eyes on my face. "But what about it? We already knew this, everybody knew Bright had abandoned them. This just proves it. Why even bother showing it to me?"

"I thought," said Padma, "it might move you just a little. Perhaps enough to make you take a different view of things."

I said, "I didn't say that wasn't possible. I tell you a Newsman keeps an open mind at all times. Of course"—I picked my words carefully—"if I could study it—"

"I'd hoped you'd take it with you," said Padma.

"Hoped?"

"If you dig into it and really understand what Bright means there, you might understand all the Friendlies differently. You might change your mind about them."

"I don't think so," I said. "But—"

"Let me ask you to do that much," said Padma. "Take the memo with you."

I stood for a moment, with Padma facing me and Kensie looming behind him, then shrugged and put the memo in my pocket.

"All right," I said. "I'll take it back to my quarters and think about it. I've got a groundcar here somewhere, haven't I?" And I looked at Kensie.

"Ten kilometers back," said Kensie. "You wouldn't get through anyway. We're moving up for the assault and the Friendlies are maneuvering to meet us."

"Take my air-car," said Padma. "The Embassy flags on it will help."

"All right," I said.

We went out together toward the air-car. I passed Janol in the outer office and he met my eyes coldly. I did not blame him. We walked to the air-car and I got in.

"You can send the air-car back whenever you're through with it," said Padma, as I stepped in through the entrance section of its top. "It's an Embassy loan to you, Tam. I won't worry about it."

"No," I said. "You needn't worry."

I closed the section and touched the controls.

It was a dream of an air-car. It went up into the air as lightly as thought, and in a second I was two thousand feet up and well away from the spot. I made myself calm down, though, before I reached into my pocket and took the memo out.

I looked at it. My hand still trembled a little as I held it.

Here it was in my grasp at last. Proof of the evidence Piers Leaf had heard of back on Earth, and what I had been after from the start. And Padma himself had insisted I carry it away with me.

It was the lever, the Archimedes pry-bar which would move not one world but two. And push the Friendly peoples over the edge to extinction.

Chapter 27

They were waiting for me. They converged on the air-car as I landed it in the interior square of the Friendlies' compound, all four of them with black rifles at the ready.

They were apparently the only ones left. Jamethon seemed to have turned out every other man of his remnant of a battle unit. And these were all men I recognized, case-hardened veterans. One was the Groupman who had been in the office that first night when I had come back from the Exotic camp and stepped in to speak to Jamethon, asking him if he ever ordered his men to kill prisoners. Another was a forty-year-old Force-Leader, the lowest commissioned rank, but acting Major—just as Jamethon, a Commandant, was acting as Expeditionary Field Commander, a position equivalent to Kensie Graeme's. The other two soldiers were noncommissioned, but similar. I knew them all. Ultrafanatics. And they knew me.

We understood each other.

"I have to see the Commandant," I said as I got out, before they could begin to question me.

"On what business?" said the Force-Leader. "This air-car hath no business here. Nor thyself."

I said, "I must see Commandant Black immediately. I wouldn't be here in a car flying the flags of the Exotic Embassy if it wasn't necessary."

They could not take the chance that my reason for seeing Black wasn't important, and I knew it. They argued a little, but I kept insisting I had to see the Commandant. Finally, the Force-Leader took me across into the same outer office where I had always waited to see Jamethon.

I faced Jamethon alone in the office.

He was putting on his battle harness, as I had seen Graeme putting on his earlier. On Graeme, the harness and the weapons it carried had looked like toys. On Jamethon's slight frame they looked almost too heavy to bear.

"Mr. Olyn," he said.

I walked across the room toward him, drawing the memo from my pocket as I came. He turned a little to face me, his fingers sealing the locks on his harness, jingling slightly with his weapons and his harness as he turned.

"You're taking the field against the Exotics," I said.

He nodded. I had never been this close to him before. From across the room I would have believed he was holding his usual stony expression, but standing just a few feet from him now I saw the tired wraith of a smile touch the corners of his straight mouth in that dark, young face for a second.

"That is my duty, Mr. Olyn."

"Some duty," I said. "When your superiors back on Harmony have already written you off their books."

"I've already told you," he said calmly. "The Chosen are not betrayed in the Lord, one by another."

"You're sure of that?" I said.

Once more I saw that little ghost of a weary smile.

"It's a subject, Mr. Olyn, on which I am more expert than you."

I looked into his eyes. They were exhausted but calm. I glanced aside at the desk where the picture of the church, the older man and woman and the young girl stood still.

"Your family?" I asked.

"Yes," he said.

"It seems to me you'd think of them in a time like this."

"I think of them quite often."

"But you're going to go out and get yourself killed just the same."

"Just the same," he said.

"Sure!" I said. "You would!" I had come in calm and in control of myself. But now it was as if a cork had been pulled on all that had been inside me since Dave's death. I began to shake. "Because that's the kind of hypocrites you are—all of you Friendlies. You're so lying, so rotten clear through with your own lies, if someone took them away from you there'd be nothing left. Would there? So you'd rather die now than admit committing suicide like this isn't the most glorious thing in the universe. You'd rather die than admit that you're just as full of doubts as anyone else, just as afraid."

I stepped right up to him. He did not move.

"Who're you trying to fool?" I said. "Who? I see through you just like the people on all the other worlds do! I know you know what a mumbo-jumbo your United Churches are. I know you know the way of life you sing of through your nose so much isn't what you claim it is. I know your Eldest Bright and his gang of narrow-minded old men are just a gang of world-hungry tyrants that don't give a damn for religion or anything as long as they get what they want. I know you know it—and I'm going to make you admit it!"

And I shoved the memo under his nose.

"Read it!"

He took it from me. I stepped back from him, shaking badly as I watched him.

He studied it for a long minute, while I held my breath. His face did not change. Then he handed it back to me.

"Can I give you a ride to meet Graeme?" I said. "We can get across the lines in the OutBond's air-car. You can get the surrender over with before any shooting breaks out."

He shook his head. He was looking at me in a particularly level way, with an expression I could not understand.

"What do you mean—no?"

"You'd better stay here," he said. "Even with ambassadorial flags, that air-car may be shot at over the lines." And he turned as if he would walk away from me, out the door.

"Where're you going?" I shouted at him. I got in front of him and pushed the memo before his eyes again. "That's real. You can't close your eyes to that!"

He stopped and looked at me. Then he reached out and took my wrist and put my arm and hand with the memo aside. His fingers were thin, but much stronger than I thought, so that I let the arm go down in front of him when I hadn't intended to do so.

"I know it's real. I'll have to warn you not to interfere with me any more, Mr. Olyn. I've got to go now." He stepped past me and walked toward the door.

"You're a liar!" I shouted after him. He kept on going. I had to stop him. I grabbed the solidograph from his desk and smashed it on the floor.

He turned like a cat and looked at the broken pieces at my feet.

"That's what you're doing!" I shouted, pointing at them.

He came back without a word and squatted down and carefully gathered up the pieces one by one. He put them into his pocket and got back to his feet, and raised his face at last to mine. And when I saw his eyes I stopped breathing.

"If my duty," he said in a low, controlled voice, "were not in this minute to—"

His voice stopped. I saw his eyes staring into me; and slowly I saw them change and the murder that was in them soften into something like wonder.

"Thou," he said softly, "thou hast no faith?"

I had opened my mouth to speak. But what he said stopped me. I stood as if punched in the stomach, without the breath for words. He stared at me.

"What made you think," he said, "that that memo would change my mind?"

"You read it!" I said. "Bright wrote you were a losing proposition here, so you weren't to get any more help. And no one was to tell you for fear you might surrender if you knew."

"Is that how you read it?" he said. "Like that?"

"How else? How else can you read it?"

"As it is written." He stood straight facing me now and his eyes never moved from mine. "You have read it without faith, leaving out the Name and the will of the Lord. Eldest Bright wrote not that we were to be abandoned here, but that since our cause was sore tried, we be put in the hands of our Captain and our God. And further he wrote that we should not be told of this, that none here should be tempted to a vain and special seeking of the martyr's crown. Look, Mr. Olyn. It's down there in black and white."

"But that's not what he meant! That's not what he meant!"

He shook his head. "Mr. Olyn, I can't leave you in such delusion."

I stared at him, for it was sympathy I saw in his face. For me.

"It's your own blindness that deludes you," he said. "You see nothing, and so believe no man can see. Our Lord is not just a name, but all things. That's why we have no ornament in our churches, scorning any painted screen between us and our God. Listen to me, Mr. Olyn. Those churches themselves are but tabernacles of the earth. Our Elders and Leaders, though they are Chosen and Anointed, are still but mortal men. To none of these things or people do we hearken in our faith, but to the very voice of God within us."

He paused. Somehow I could not speak.

"Suppose it was even as you think," he went on, even more gently. "Suppose that all you say was a fact, and that our Elders were but greedy tyrants, ourselves abandoned here by their selfish will and set to fulfill a false and prideful purpose. No." Jamethon's voice rose. "Let me attest as if it were only for myself. Suppose that you could give me proof that all our Elders lied, that our very Covenant was false. Suppose that you could prove to me"—his face lifted to mine and his voice drove at me—"that all was perversion and falsehood, and nowhere among the Chosen, not even in the house of my father, was there faith or hope! If you could prove to me that no miracle could save me, that no soul stood with me, and that opposed were all the legions of the universe, still I, I alone, Mr. Olyn, would go forward as I have been commanded, to the end of the universe, to the culmination of eternity. For without my faith I am but common earth. But with my faith, there is no power can stay me!"

He stopped speaking and turned about. I watched him walk across the room and out the door.

Still I stood there, as if I had been fastened in place—until I heard from outside, in the square of the compound, the sound of a military air-car starting up.

I broke out of my stasis then and ran out of the building.

As I burst into the square, the military air-car was just taking off. I could see Jamethon and his four hard-shell subordinates in it. And I yelled up into the air after them.

"That's all right for you, but what about your men?"

They could not hear me. I knew that. Uncontrollable tears were running down my face, but I screamed up into the air after him anyway.

"You're killing your men to prove your point! Can't you listen? You're murdering helpless men!"

Unheeding, the military air-car dwindled rapidly to the west and south, where the converging battle forces waited. And the heavy concrete walls and buildings about the empty compound threw back my words with a hollow, wild and mocking echo.

Chapter 28

I should have gone to the spaceport. Instead, I got back into the air-car and flew back across the lines looking for Graeme's Battle Command Center.

I was as little concerned about my own life just then as a Friendly. I think I was shot at once or twice, in spite of the ambassadorial flags on the air-car, but I don't remember exactly. Eventually I found the Command Center and descended.

Enlisted men surrounded me as I stepped out of the air-car. I showed my Credentials and went up to the battle screen, which had been set up in open air at the edge of shadow from some tall variform oaks. Graeme, Padma and his whole staff were grouped around it, watching the movements of their own and the Friendly troops reported on it. A continual low-voiced discussion of the movements went on, and a steady stream of information came from the communications center fifteen feet off.

The sun slanted steeply through the trees. It was almost noon and the day was bright and warm. No one looked at me for a long time; and then Janol, turning away from the screen, caught sight of me standing off at one side by the flat-topped shape of a tactics computer. His face went cold. He went on about what he was doing. But I must have been looking pretty bad, because after a while he came by with a canteen cup and set it down on the computer top.

"Drink that," he said shortly, and went off. I picked it up, found it was Dorsai whisky and swallowed it. I could not taste it, but evidently it did me some good, because in a few minutes the world began to sort itself out around me and I began to think again.

I went up to Janol. "Thanks."

"All right." He did not look at me, but went on with the papers on the field desk before him.

"Janol," I said. "Tell me what's going on."

"See for yourself," he said, still bent over his papers.

"I can't see for myself. You know that. Look—I'm sorry about what I did. But this is my job, too. Can't you tell me what's going on now and fight with me afterward?"

"You know I can't brawl with civilians." Then his face relaxed. "All right," he said, straightening up. "Come on."

He led me over to the battle screen, where Padma and Kensie were standing, and pointed to a sort of small triangle of darkness between two snakelike lines of light. Other spots and shapes of light ringed it about.

"These"—he pointed to the two snakelike lines—"are the Macintok and Sarah Rivers, where they come together, just about ten miles this side of Joseph's Town. It's fairly high ground, hills thick with cover, fairly open between them. Good territory for setting up a stubborn defense, bad area to get trapped in."

"Why?"

He pointed to the two river lines.

"Get backed up in here and you find yourself hung up on high bluffs over the river. There is no easy way across, no cover for retreating troops. It's nearly all open farmland the rest of the way, from the other sides of the rivers to Joseph's Town."

His finger moved back out from the point where the river lines came together, past the small area of darkness and into the surrounding shapes and rings of light.

"On the other hand, the approach to this territory from our position is through open country, too—narrow strips of farmland interspersed with a lot of swamp and marsh. It's a tight situation for either commander, if we commit to a battle here. The first one who has to backpedal will find himself in trouble in a hurry."

"Are you going to commit?"

"It depends. Black sent his light armor forward. Now he's pulling back into the high ground between the rivers. We're far superior in strength and equipment. There's no reason for us not to go in after him, as long as he's trapped himself—" Janol broke off.

"No reason?" I asked.

"Not from a tactical standpoint," Janol frowned at the screen. "We couldn't get into trouble unless we suddenly had to retreat. And we wouldn't do that unless he suddenly acquired some great tactical advantage that'd make it impossible for us to stay there."

I looked at his profile.

"Such as losing Graeme?" I said.

He transferred his frown to me. "There's no danger of that."

There was a certain change in the movement and the voices of the people around us. We both turned and looked.

Everybody was clustering around a screen. We moved in with the crowd and, looking between the shoulders of two of the officers of Graeme's staff, I saw on the screen the image of a small grassy meadow enclosed by wooded hills. In the center of the meadow, the Friendly flag floated its thin black cross on white background beside a long table on the grass. There were folding chairs on each side of the table, but only one person—a Friendly officer, standing on the table's far side as if waiting. There were the lilac bushes along the edge of the wooded hills where they came down in variform oak and ash to the meadow's edge; and the lavender blossoms were beginning to brown and darken for their season was almost at an end. So much difference had twenty-four hours made. Off to the left of the screen I could see the gray concrete of a highway.

"I know that place—" I started to say, turning to Janol.

"Quiet!" he said, holding up a finger. Around us, everybody else had fallen still. Up near the front of our group a single voice was talking.

"—it's a truce table."

"Have they called?" said the voice of Kensie.

"No, sir."

"Well, let's go see." There was a stir up front. The group began to break up and I saw Kensie and Padma walking off toward the area where the air-cars were parked. I shoved myself through the thinning crowd like a process server, running after them.

I heard Janol shout behind me, but I paid no attention. Then I was up to Kensie and Padma, who turned.

"I want to go with you," I said.

"It's all right, Janol," Kensie said, looking past me. "You can leave him with us."

"Yes, sir." I could hear Janol turn and leave.

"So you want to come with me, Mr. Olyn?" Kensie said.

"I know that spot," I told him. "I drove by it yesterday. The Friendlies were taking tactical measurements all over that meadow and the hills on both sides. They weren't setting up truce talks."

Kensie looked at me for a long moment, as if he were taking some tactical measurements himself.

"Come on, then," he said. He turned to Padma. "You'll be staying here?"

"It's a combat zone. I'd better not." Padma turned his unwrinkled face to me. "Good luck, Mr. Olyn," he said, and walked away. I watched his blue-robed figure glide over the turf for a second, then turned to see Graeme halfway to the nearest military air-car. I hurried after him.

It was a battle car, not luxurious like the Out-Bond's, and Kensie did not cruise at two thousand feet, but snaked it between the trees just a few feet above ground. The seats were cramped. His big frame overfilled his, crowding me where I sat. I felt the butt-plate of his spring-pistol grinding into my side with every movement he made on the controls.

We came at last to the edge of the wooded and hilly triangle occupied by the Friendlies and mounted a slope under the cover of the new-leaved variform oaks.

They were massive enough to have killed off most ground cover. Between their pillar-like trunks the ground was shaded and padded with the brown shapes of dead leaves. Near the crest of the hill, we came upon a unit of Exotic troops resting and waiting the orders to advance. Kensie got out of the car and returned the Force-Leader's salute.

"You've seen these tables the Friendlies set up?" Kensie asked.

"Yes, Commander. That officer they've got is still standing there. If you go just up over the crest of the slope here, you can see him— and the furniture."

"Good," said Kensie. "Keep your men here, Force-Leader. The Newsman and I'll go take a look."

He led the way up among the oak trees. At the top of the hill we looked down through about fifty yards more of trees and out into the meadow. It was two hundred yards across, the table right in the middle, the unmoving black figure of the Friendly officer standing on its far side.

"What do you think of it, Mr. Olyn?" asked Kensie, looking down through the trees.

"Why hasn't somebody shot him?" I asked.

He glanced sideways at me.

"There's plenty of time to shoot him," he said, "before he can get back to cover on the far side. If we have to shoot him at all. That wasn't what I wanted to know. You've seen the Friendly commander recently. Did he give you the impression he was ready to surrender?"

"No!" I said.

"I see," said Kensie.

"You don't really think he means to surrender? What makes you think something like that?"

"Truce tables are generally set up for the discussion of terms between opposing forces," he said.

"But he hasn't asked you to meet him?"

"No." Kensie watched the figure of the Friendly officer, motionless
in the sunlight. "It might be against his principles to call for a discussion, but not to discuss—if we just happened to find ourselves across
a table from one another."

He turned and signaled with his hand. The Force-Leader, who had
been waiting down the slope behind us, came up.

"Sir?" he said to Kensie.

"Any Friendly strength in those trees across the way?"

"Four men, that's all, sir. Our scopes pick out their body heats
clear and sharp. They aren't attempting to hide."

"I see." He paused. "Force-Leader."

"Sir?"

"Be good enough to go down there in the meadow and ask that
Friendly officer what this is all about."

"Yes, sir."

We stood and watched as the Force-Leader went stiff-legging it
down the steep slope between the trees. He crossed the grass—it
seemed very slowly—and came up to the Friendly officer.

They stood facing each other. They were talking but there was no
way to hear their voices. The flag with its thin black cross whipped in
the little breeze that was blowing there. Then the Force-Leader turned
and climbed back toward us.

He stopped in front of Kensie and saluted. "Commander," he said,
"the Commander of the Chosen Troops of God will meet with you in
the field to discuss a surrender." He stopped to draw a fresh breath.
"If you'll show yourself at the edge of the opposite woods at the same
time; and you can approach the table together."

"Thank you, Force-Leader," said Kensie. He looked past his officer
at the field and the table. "I think I'll go down."

"He doesn't mean it," I said.

"Force-Leader," said Kensie. "Form your men ready, just under
the crown of the slope on the back side, here. If he surrenders, I'm
going to insist he come back with me to this side immediately."

"Yes, sir."

"All this business without a regular call for parley may be because
he wants to surrender first and break the news of it to his troops afterward. So get your men ready. If Black intends to present his officers
with an accomplished fact, we don't want to let him down."

"He's not going to surrender," I said.

"Mr. Olyn," said Kensie, turning to me. "I suggest you go back behind the crest of the hill. The Force-Leader will see you're taken care of."

"No," I said. "I'm going down. If it's a truce parley to discuss surrender terms, there's no combat situation involved and I've got a perfect right to be there. If it isn't, what're you doing going down yourself?"

Kensie looked at me strangely for a moment.

"All right," he said. "Come with me."

Kensie and I turned and went down the sharply pitched slope between the trees. Our boot soles slipped until our heels dug in with every step downward. Coming through the lilacs I smelled the faint, sweet scent—almost gone now—of the decaying blossoms.

Across the meadow, directly in line with the table, four figures in black came forward as we came forward. One of them was Jamethon Black.

Kensie and Jamethon saluted each other.

"Commandant Black," said Kensie.

"Yes, Commander Graeme. I am indebted to you for meeting me here," said Jamethon.

"My duty and a pleasure, Commandant."

"I wished to discuss the terms of a surrender."

"I can offer you," said Kensie, "the customary terms extended to troops in your position under the Mercenaries' Code."

"You misunderstand me, sir," said Jamethon. "It was your surrender I came here to discuss."

The flag snapped.

Suddenly I saw the men in black measuring the field here, as I had seen them the day before. They had been right where we were now.

"I'm afraid the misunderstanding is mutual, Commandant," said Kensie. "I am in a superior tactical position and your defeat is normally certain. I have no need to surrender."

"You will not surrender?"

"No," said Kensie strongly.

All at once I saw the five stakes, in the position the Friendly noncoms, officers and Jamethon were now, and the stake up in front of them fallen down.

"Look out!" I shouted at Kensie—but I was far too late.

Things had already begun to happen. The Force-Leader had jerked back in front of Jamethon and all five of them were drawing their sidearms. I heard the flag snap again, and the sound of its rolling seemed to go on for a long time.

For the first time then I saw a man of the Dorsai in action. So swift was Kensie's reaction that it was eerily as if he had read Jamethon's mind in the instant before the Friendlies began to reach for their weapons. As their hands touched their sidearms, he was already in movement forward over the table and his spring-pistol was in his hand. He seemed to fly directly into the Force-Leader and the two of them went down together, but Kensie kept traveling. He rolled on off the Force-Leader, who now lay still in the grass. He came to his knees, fired, and dived forward, rolling again.

The Groupman on Jamethon's right went down. Jamethon and the remaining two were turned nearly full about now, trying to keep Kensie before them. The two that were left shoved themselves in front of Jamethon, their weapons not yet aimed. Kensie stopped moving as if he had run into a stone wall, came to his feet in a crouch, and fired twice more. The two Friendlies fell apart, one to each side.

Jamethon was facing Kensie now, and Jamethon's pistol was in his hand and aimed. Jamethon fired, and a light blue streak leaped through the air, but Kensie had dropped again. Lying on his side on the grass, propped on one elbow, he pressed the firing button on his spring-pistol twice.

Jamethon's sidearm sagged in his hand. He was backed up against the table now, and he put out his free hand to steady himself against the tabletop. He made another effort to lift his sidearm but he could not. It dropped from his hand. He bore more of his weight on the table, half-turning around, and his face came about to look in my direction. His face was as controlled as it had ever been, but there was something different about his eyes as he looked into mine and recognized me— something oddly like the look a man gives a competitor whom he has just beaten and who was no real threat to begin with. A little smile touched the corners of his thin lips. Like the smile of inner triumph.

"Mr. Olyn," he whispered. And then the life went out of his face and he fell beside the table.

Nearby explosions shook the ground under my feet. From the crest of the hill behind us the Force-Leader whom Kensie had left there was firing smoke bombs between us and the Friendly side of the meadow. A gray wall of smoke was rising between us and the far hillside, to screen us from the enemy. It towered up the blue sky like some impassable barrier, and under the looming height of it, only Kensie and I were standing.

On Jamethon's dead face there was a faint smile.

Chapter 29

In a daze I watched the Friendly troops surrender that same day. It was the one situation in which their officers felt justified in doing so.

Not even their Elders expected subordinates to fight a situation set up by a dead Field Commander for tactical reasons unexplained to his officers. And the live troops remaining were worth more than the indemnity charges for them that the Exotics would make.

I did not wait for the settlements. I had nothing to wait for. One moment the situation on this battlefield had been poised like some great, irresistible wave above all our heads, cresting, curling over and about to break downward with an impact that would reverberate through all the worlds of Man. Now, suddenly, it was no longer above us. There was nothing but a far-flooding silence, already draining away into the records of the past.

There was nothing for me. Nothing.

If Jamethon had succeeded in killing Kensie—even if as a result he had won a practically bloodless surrender of the Exotic troops—I might have done something damaging with the incident of the truce table. But he had only tried, and died, failing. Who could work up emotion against the Friendlies for that?

I took ship back to Earth like a man walking in a dream, asking myself why.

Back on Earth, I told my editors I was not in good shape physically; and they took one look at me and believed me. I took an indefinite leave from my job and sat around the News Services Center Library, at The Hague, searching blindly through piles of writings and reference material on the Friendlies, the Dorsai and the Exotic worlds. For what? I did not know. I also watched the news dispatches from

Ste. Marie concerning the settlement, and drank too much while I watched.

I had the numb feeling of a soldier sentenced to death for a failure on duty. Then in the news dispatches came the information that Jamethon's body would be returned to Harmony for burial; and I realized suddenly it was this I had been waiting for: the unnatural honoring by fanatics of the fanatic who with four henchmen had tried to assassinate the lone enemy commander under a truce flag. Things could still be written.

I shaved, showered, pulled myself together after a fashion and went to see about arrangements for passage to Harmony to cover the burial of Jamethon as a wrap-up.

The congratulations of Piers and word of my appointment to the Guild Council—that had reached me on Ste. Marie earlier—stood me in good stead. It got me a high-priority seat on the first spaceliner out.

Five days later I was on Harmony in that same little town, called Remembered-of-the-Lord, where Eldest Bright had taken me once before. The buildings in the town were still of concrete and bubble-plastic, unchanged by three years. But the stony soil of the farms about the town had been tilled, as the fields on Ste. Marie had been tilled when I got to that other world, for Harmony now was just entering the spring of its northern hemisphere. And it was raining as I drove from the spaceport of the town, as it had on Ste. Marie that first day. But the Friendly fields I saw did not show the rich darkness of the fields of Ste. Marie, only a thin, hard blackness in the wet that was like the color of Friendly uniforms.

I got to the church just as people were beginning to arrive. Under the dark, draining skies, the interior of the church was almost too dim to let me see my way about, for the Friendlies permit themselves no windows and no artificial lighting in their houses of worship. Gray light, cold wind and rain entered the doorless portal at the back of the church. Through the single rectangular opening in the roof watery sunlight filtered over Jamethon's body on a platform set up on trestles. A transparent cover had been set up to protect the body from the rain, which was channeled off the open space and ran down a drain in the back wall. But the elder conducting the Death Service and anyone coming up to view the body was expected to stand exposed to sky and weather.

I got in line with the people moving slowly down the central aisle and past the body. To right and left of me the barriers at which the congregation would stand during the service were lost in gloom. The rafters of the steeply pitched roof were hidden in darkness. There was no music, but the low sound of voices individually praying to either side of me in the ranks of barriers and in the line blended into a sort of rhythmic undertone of sadness. Like Jamethon, the people were all very dark here, being of North African extraction. Dark into dark, they blended and were lost about me in the gloom.

I came up and passed at last by Jamethon. He looked as I remembered him. Death had shown no power to change him. He lay on his back, his hands at his sides, and his lips were as firm and straight as ever. Only his eyes were closed.

I was limping noticeably because of the dampness, and as I turned away from the body, I felt my elbow touched. I turned back sharply. I was not wearing my correspondent's uniform. I was in civilian clothes, so as to be inconspicuous.

I looked down into the face of the young girl in Jamethon's solidograph. In the gray, rainy light her unlined face was like something from the stained-glass window of an ancient cathedral back on Old Earth.

"You've been wounded," she said in a soft voice to me. "You must be one of the mercenaries who knew him on New Earth, before he was ordered to Harmony. His parents, who are mine as well, would find solace in the Lord by meeting you."

The wind blew rain down through the overhead opening all about me, and its icy feel sent a chill suddenly shooting through me, freezing me to my very bones.

"No!" I said. "I'm not. I didn't know him." And I turned sharply away from her and pushed my way into the crowd, back up the aisle.

After about fifteen feet, I realized what I was doing and slowed down. The girl was already lost in the darkness of the bodies behind me. I made my way more slowly toward the back of the church, where there was a little place to stand before the first ranks of the barriers began. I stood watching the people come in. They came and came, walking in their black clothing with their heads down and talking or praying in low voices.

I stood where I was, a little back from the entrance, half-numbed and dull-minded with the chill about me and the exhaustion I had brought with me from Earth. The voices droned about me. I almost dozed, standing there. I could not remember why I had come.

Then a girl's voice emerged from the jumble, bringing me back to full consciousness again.

". . . he did deny it, but I am sure he is one of those mercenaries who was with Jamethon on New Earth. He limps and can only be a soldier who hath been wounded."

It was the voice of Jamethon's sister, speaking with more of the Friendly cant on her tongue than she had used speaking to me, a stranger. I woke fully and saw her standing by the entrance only a few feet from me, half-facing two elder people whom I recognized as the older couple of Jamethon's solidograph. A bolt of pure, freezing horror shot through me.

"No!" I nearly shouted at them. "I don't know him. I never knew him. I don't understand what you're talking about!" And I turned and bolted out through the entrance of the church into the concealing rain.

I all but ran for about thirty or forty feet. Then I heard no footsteps behind me; I stopped.

I was alone in the open. The day was even darker now and the rain suddenly came down harder. It obscured everything around me with a drumming, shimmering curtain. I could not even see the ground-cars in the parking lot toward which I was facing; and for sure they could not see me from the church. I lifted my face up to the downpour and let it beat upon my cheeks and my closed eyelids.

"So," said a voice from behind me. "You did not know him?"

The words seemed to cut me down the middle, and I felt as a cornered wolf must feel. Like a wolf, I turned.

"Yes, I knew him!" I said.

Facing me was Padma, in a blue robe the rain did not seem to dampen. His empty hands that had never held a weapon in their life were clasped together before him. But the wolf part of me knew that as far as I was concerned, he was armed and a hunter.

"You?" I said. "What are you doing here?"

"It was calculated you would be here," said Padma softly. "So I am here, too. But why are *you* here, Tam? Among those people in there, there's sure to be at least a few fanatics who've heard the camp rumors of your responsibility in the matter of Jamethon's death and the Friendlies' surrender."

"Rumors!" I said. "Who started them?"

"You did," Padma said. "By your actions on Ste. Marie." He gazed at me. "Didn't you know you were risking your life, coming here today?"

I opened my mouth to deny it. Then I realized I had known.

"What if someone should call out to them," said Padma, "that Tam Olyn, the Ste. Marie campaign Newsman, is here incognito?"

I looked at him with my wolf-feeling, grimly.

"Can you square it with your Exotic principles if you do?"

"We are misunderstood," answered Padma calmly. "We hire soldiers to fight for us not because of some moral commandment, but because our emotional perspective is lost if we become involved."

There was no fear left in me, only a hard, empty feeling.

"Call them then," I said.

Padma's strange hazel eyes watched me through the rain.

"If that was all that was needed," he said, "I could have sent word to them. I wouldn't have needed to come myself."

"Why did you come here?" My voice tore at my throat. "What do you on the Exotics care about me?"

"We care for every individual," said Padma. "But we care more for the race. And you're still dangerous to it. You're an unadmitted idealist, Tam, warped to destructive purpose. There is a law of conservation of energy in the pattern of cause and effect just as there is in other sciences. Your destructiveness was frustrated on Ste. Marie. Now what if it should turn inward to destroy you, or outward against the whole race of man?"

I laughed, and heard the harshness of my laughter.

"What're you going to do about it?" I said.

"Show you how the knife you hold cuts the hand that holds it as well as what you turn it against. I've got news for you, Tam. Kensie Graeme is dead."

"Dead?" The rain seemed to roar around me suddenly and the parking lot shifted unsubstantially under my feet.

"He was assassinated by three men of the Blue Front in Blauvain five days ago."

"Assassinated," I whispered. "Why?"

"Because the war was over," said Padma. "Because Jamethon's death and the surrender of the Friendly troops without the preliminary of a war that would tear up the countryside left the civilian population favorably disposed toward our troops. Because the Blue Front found themselves farther from power than ever, as a result of this favorable feeling. They hoped by killing Graeme to provoke his troops into retaliation against the civilian population, so that the Ste. Marie government would have to order them home to our Exotics, and stand unprotected to face a Blue Front revolt."

I stared at him.

"All things are interrelated," said Padma. "Kensie was slated for a final promotion to a desk command back on Mara or Kultis. He and his brother Ian would have been out of the wars for the rest of their professional lives. Because of Jamethon's death, which allowed the surrender of his troops without fighting, a situation was set up which led the Blue Front to assassinate Kensie. If you and Jamethon had not come into conflict on Ste. Marie, and Jamethon had not won, Kensie would be alive today. So our calculations show."

"Jamethon and I?" The breath went dry in my throat without warning, and the rain came down harder.

"Yes," said Padma. "You were the factor that helped Jamethon to his solution."

"I helped him?" I said. "*I* did?"

"He saw through you," said Padma. "He saw through the revenge-bitter, destructive surface you thought was yourself, to the creative core that was so deep in the bone of you that even your uncle hadn't been able to eradicate it."

The rain thundered between us. But Padma's every word came clearly through it to me.

"I don't believe you!" I shouted. "I don't believe he did anything like that!"

"I told you," said Padma, "you didn't fully appreciate the evolutionary advances of our Splinter Cultures. Jamethon's faith was not the kind that can be shaken by outer things. If you had been in fact like your uncle Mathias, he would not even have listened to you. He would have dismissed you as a soulless man. As it was, he thought of you instead as a man possessed, a man speaking with what he would have called Satan's voice."

"I don't believe it!" I yelled.

"You do believe it," said Padma. "You've got no choice except to believe it. Only because of it could Jamethon find his solution."

"Solution!"

"He was a man ready to die for his faith. But as a commander he found it hard his men should go out to die for no other reasonable cause." Padma watched me, and the rain thinned for a moment. "But you offered him what he recognized as the Devil's choice—his life in this world, if he would surrender his faith and his men, to avoid the conflict that would end in his death and theirs."

"What crazy thinking was that?" I said. Inside the church, the praying had stopped, and a single strong, deep voice was beginning the burial service.

"Not crazy," said Padma. "The moment he realized this, his answer became simple. All he had to do was begin by denying whatever Satan offered. He must start with the absolute necessity of his own death."

"And that was a solution?" I tried to laugh but my throat hurt.

"It was the only solution?" said Padma. "Once he decided that, he saw immediately that the one situation in which his men would permit themselves to surrender was if he was dead and they were in an untenable battlefield position, for reasons only he had known."

I felt the words go through me with a soundless shock.

"But he didn't mean to die!" I said.

"He left it to his God," said Padma. "He arranged it so only a miracle could save him."

"What're you talking about?" I stared at him. "He set up a truce table with a flag of truce. He took four men—"

"There was no flag. The men were overage martyrdom-seekers."

"He took four!" I shouted. "Four and one made five. The five of them against Kensie—one man. I stood there by that table and saw. Five against—"

"Tam."

The single word stopped me. Suddenly I began to be afraid. I did not want to hear what he was about to say. I was afraid I knew what he was going to tell me, that I had known it for some time. And I did not want to hear it, I did not want to hear him say it. The rain grew even stronger, driving upon us both and mercilessly on the concrete, but I heard every word relentlessly through all its sound and noise.

Padma's voice began to roar in my ears like the rain, and a feeling came over me like the helpless floating sensation that comes in high fever. "Did you think that Jamethon for a minute fooled himself as you deluded yourself? He was a product of a Splinter Culture. He recognized another in Kensie. Did you think that for a minute he thought that, barring a miracle, he and four overage fanatics could kill an armed, alert and ready man of the Dorsai—a man like Kensie Graeme—before they were gunned down and killed themselves?"

Themselves . . . themselves . . . themselves . . .

I rode off a long way on that word from the dark day and the rain. Like the rain and the wind behind the clouds it lifted me and carried me away at last to that high, hard and stony land I had glimpsed when I had asked Kensie Graeme that question about his ever allowing Friendly prisoners to be killed. It was this land I had always avoided, but to it I was come at last.

And I remembered.

From the beginning, I had known inside myself that the fanatic who had killed Dave and the others was not the image of all Friendlies. Jamethon was no casual killer. I had tried to make him into one to shore up my own lie—to keep my eyes averted from the sight of that one man on the sixteen worlds I could not face. And that one man was not the Groupman who had massacred Dave and the others, not even Mathias.

It was myself.

Jamethon was no ordinary fanatic, no more than Kensie was an ordinary soldier, or Padma an ordinary philosopher. They were more than that, as secretly I had known all along, down inside myself where I need not face the knowledge. That was why they had not moved as I planned when I had tried to manipulate them. That was why, that was why.

The high, hard and stony land I had visioned was not only there for the Dorsai. It was there for all of them, a land where the tatters of falseness and illusion were stripped away by the clean cold wind of honest strength and conviction, where pretense drooped and died and all that could live was plain and pure.

It was there for them, for all those who embodied the pure metal of their Splinter Culture. And it was from that pure metal that their real strength came. They were beyond doubt—that was it; and above all skills of mind and body, this was what kept them undefeatable. For a man like Kensie would never be conquered. And Jamethon would never break his faith.

Had Jamethon not told me plainly so himself? Had he not said, "Let me testify for myself alone," and gone on to tell me that, even if his universe should crumble about him, even if all his God and his religion were proved false, what was in himself would not be touched.

No more, if armies about him retreated, leaving him alone, would Kensie abandon a duty or a post. Alone, he would remain to fight, though other armies came against him; for though they could kill him, they could not conquer him.

Nor, should all Padma's Exotic calculations and theories be over-turned in an instant—proved untrue and groundless—would it move him from his belief in the upward-seeking evolution of the human spirit, in which service he labored.

They walked by right in that high and stony land—all of them. Dorsai, and Friendly, and Exotic. And I had been fool enough to enter it, to try to fight one of them there. No wonder I had been defeated, as Mathias always had said I would be. I had never had a hope of winning.

So I came back to the day and the downpour, like a broken straw of a man with my knees sagging under my own weight. The rain was slackening and Padma was holding me upright. As with Jamethon, I was dully amazed at the strength of his hands.

"Let me go," I mumbled.

"Where would you go, Tam?" he said.

"Any place," I muttered. "I'll get out of it. I'll go hole up somewhere and get out of it. I'll give up." I got my knees straightened finally under me.

"It's not that easy," said Padma, letting me go. "An action taken goes on reverberating forever. Cause never ceases its effects. You can't let go now, Tam. You can only change sides."

"Sides?" I said. The rain was dwindling fast about us. "What sides?" I stared at him drunkenly.

"The side of the force in man against his own evolution—which was your uncle's side," said Padma. "And the evolutionary side, which is ours." The rain was falling only lightly now and the day was brightening. A little pale sunlight filtered through the thinning clouds to illuminate more strongly the parking space around us. "Both are strong winds bending the fabric of human affairs even while that fabric is being woven. I told you long ago, Tam, that for someone like you there's no choice but to be effective upon the pattern one way or another. You have choice—not freedom. So, merely decide to turn your effect to the wind of evolution instead of to the force frustrating it."

I shook my head.

"No," I muttered. "It's no use. You know that. You saw. I moved heaven and earth and the politics of sixteen worlds against Jamethon— and he still won. I can't do anything. Just leave me alone."

"Even if I left you alone, events wouldn't," answered Padma. "Tam, open your eyes and look at things as they are. You're already involved. Listen to me." His hazel eyes caught what little light there was for a moment. "A force intruded on the pattern on Ste. Marie, in the shape of a unit warped by personal loss and oriented toward violence. That was you, Tam."

I tried to shake my head again, but I knew he was right.

"You were blocked in the direction of your conscious effort on Ste. Marie," Padma went on, "but the conservations of energies would not be balked. When you were frustrated by Jamethon, the force you had brought to bear on the situation was not destroyed. It was only transmuted and left the pattern in the unit of another individual, now also warped by personal loss and oriented toward violent effect upon the pattern."

I wet my lips.

"What other individual?"

"Ian Graeme."

I stood, staring at him.

"Ian found his brother's three assassins hiding in a hotel room in Blauvain," said Padma. "He killed them with his hands—and by so doing he calmed the mercenaries and frustrated the plans of the Blue Front to salvage something out of the situation. But then Ian resigned and went home to the Dorsai. He's charged now with the same sense of loss and bitterness you were charged with when you came to Ste. Marie." Padma hesitated. "Now he has great causal potential. How it will expend itself within the future pattern remains to be seen."

He paused again, watching me with his inescapable yellow gaze.

"You see, Tam," he went on after a moment, "how no one like you can resign from effect upon the fabric of events? I tell you you can only change." His voice softened. "Do I have to remind you now that you're still charged—only with a different force instead? You received the full impact and effect of Jamethon's self-sacrifice to save his men."

His words were like a fist in the pit of my stomach—a blow as hard as the one I had given Janol Marat when I escaped from Kensie's camp on Ste. Marie. In spite of the new, watery sunlight filtering down to us, I began to shiver.

It was so. I could not deny it. Jamethon, in giving his life up for a belief, where I had scorned all beliefs in my plan to twist things as I wanted them, had melted and changed me as lightning melts and changes the uplifted sword-blade that it strikes. I could not deny what had happened to me.

"It's no use," I said, still shivering. "It makes no difference. I'm not strong enough to do anything. I tell you, I moved everything against Jamethon, and he won."

"But Jamethon was wholehearted; and you were fighting against your true nature at the same time you fought him," said Padma. "Look at me, Tam!"

I looked at him. The hazel magnets of his eyes caught and anchored mine.

"The purpose for which on the Exotics it was calculated I should come to meet you here is still waiting for us," he said. "You remember, Tam, how in Mark Torre's office you accused me of hypnotizing you?"

I nodded.

"It wasn't hypnosis—or not quite hypnosis," he said. "All I did was to help you open a channel between your conscious and unconscious selves. Have you got the courage, after seeing what Jamethon did, to let me help you open it once again?"

His words hung on the air between us; and, balanced on the pinpoint of that moment, I heard the strong, proud-textured voice praying inside the church. I saw the sun trying to pierce through the thinning clouds overhead; and at the same time, in my mind's eye, I saw the dark walls of my valley as Padma had described them that day long ago back at the Encyclopedia. They were there still, high and close about me, shutting out the sunlight. Only, like a narrow doorway, still ahead of me, was there unshadowed light.

I thought of the place of lightning I had seen when Padma held up his finger to me that time before; and—weak, and broken and defeated as I felt now—the thought of entering that area of battle again filled me with a sick hopelessness. I was not strong enough to face lightning anymore. Maybe I never had been.

"For he hath been a soldier of his people, who are the People of the Lord, and a soldier of the Lord," the distant, single voice praying from the church came faintly to my ear, "and in no thing did he fail the Lord, who is our Lord, and the Lord of all strength and righteousness. Therefore, let him be taken up from us into the ranks of those who, having shed the mask of life, are blessed and welcomed unto the Lord."

I heard this, and suddenly the taste of homecoming, the taste of an undeniable return to an eternal home and unshakable certainty in the faith of my forefathers, was strong in my mouth. The ranks of those who would never falter closed comfortingly around me; and I, who also had not faltered, moved into step and went forward with them. In that second, for a second, then, I felt what Jamethon must have felt, faced with me and with the decision of life and death for himself on Ste. Marie. Only for a moment I felt it, but that was enough.

"Go ahead," I heard myself saying to Padma.

I saw his finger lifted toward me.

Into darkness, I went—into darkness and fury; a place of lightning, but not of open lightning any longer, but roiling murk and cloud and storm and thunder. Tossed and whirled, beaten downward by the rage and violence about me, I battled to lift, to fight my way up into the light and open air above the storm clouds. But my own efforts sent me tumbling, sent me whirling wildly, pitching downward instead of up—and, at last, I understood.

For the storm was my own inner storm, the storm of my making. It was the inner fury of violence and revenge and destruction that I had been building in myself all these years; and as I had turned the strengths of others against them, now it turned my own strength against me, pushing me down and down, ever farther into its darkness, until all light should be lost to me.

Down I went, for its power was greater than mine. Down I went, and down; but when I was lost at last in total darkness, and when I would have given up, I found I could not. Something other in me *would not.* It kept fighting back and fighting on. And then, I recognized this as well.

It was that which Mathias had never been able to kill in me as a boy. It was all of Earth and upward-striving man. It was Leonidas and his three hundred at Thermopylae. It was the wandering of the Israelites in the wilderness and their crossing of the Red Sea. It was the Parthenon on the Acropolis, white above Athens, and the windowless darkness of my uncle's house.

It was *this* in me—the unyielding spirit of all men—which would not yield now. Suddenly, in my battered, storm-beaten spirit, drowning in darkness, something leaped for wild joy. Because abruptly I saw that it was there for me, too—that high, stony land where the air was pure and the rags of pretense and trickery were stripped away by the unrelenting wind of faith.

I had attacked Jamethon in the area of his strength—out of my own inner area of weakness. *That* was what Padma had meant by saying I had been fighting myself, even while I was fighting Jamethon. That was why I had lost the conflict, pitting my unbelieving desire against his strong belief. But my defeat did not mean I was without a land of inner strength. It was there, it had been there, hidden in me all along!

Now I saw it clearly. And ringing like bells for a victory, then, I thought I heard once more the hoarse voice of Mark Torre, tolling at me in triumph; and the voice of Lisa, who, I saw now, had understood me better than I understood myself and never abandoned me. Lisa. And as I thought of her again, I began to hear them all.

All the millions, the billions of swarming voices—the voices of all human people since man first stood upright and walked on his hind legs. They were around me once more as they had been that day at the Transit Point of the Index Room of the Final Encyclopedia; and they closed about me like wings, bearing me up, up and unconquerable, through the roiling darkness, with the lift of a courage that was cousin to the courage of Kensie, with a faith that was father to the faith of Jamethon, with a search that was brother to the search of Padma.

With that, then, all my Mathias-induced envy and fear of the people of the Younger worlds was washed away from me, once and for all. I saw it, finally and squarely. If they had only one thing in actuality, I had all things in potential. Root stock, basic stock, Earth human that I was, I was part of all of them on the Younger worlds, and there was no one of them there that could not find an echo of themselves in me.

So I burst up at last through the darkness into the light—into the place of my original lightning, the endless void where the real battle

SOLDIER, ASK NOT   755

lived, the battle of whole-hearted men against the ancient, alien dark
that would keep us forever animals. And, distantly, as if down at the
end of a long tunnel, I saw Padma standing under the strengthening
light and dwindling rain of the parking lot speaking to me.

"Now you see," he said, "why the Encyclopedia has to have you.
Only Mark Torre was able to bring it this far; and only you can finish
the job, because the great mass of Earth's people can't yet see the
vision of the future implicit in its being finished. You, who've bridged
the gap in yourself between the people of the Splinter Cultures and the
Earth-born, can build your vision into the Encyclopedia, so that when
it's done, it can do as much for those who now can't see, and so begin
the remodeling that will come when the Splinter Culture peoples turn
back to recombine with Earth's basic stock into a new, evolved form
of man."

His powerful gaze seemed to soften a little in the strengthening
light. His smile grew a little sad.

"You'll live to see more of it than I will. Good-bye, Tam."

Without warning, then, I did see it. Suddenly it flowed together
and clicked in my mind, the vision and the Encyclopedia as one reality.
And, in the same moment, my coursing mind leaped full-throated onto
the track of the opposition I would face in bringing about that reality.

Already they began to take shape in my head, out of my knowledge
of my own world—the faces and the methods I would encounter. My
mind raced on, caught up with them, and began to run on into plans
ahead of them. Even now, I saw how I would work differently than
had Mark Torre. I would keep his name as our emblem and only
pretend the Encyclopedia continued to build on according to his
forelaid plans for it. I would name myself as only one of a Board of
Governors, who all in theory would have equal powers with me.

But actually I would be directing them, subtly, as I could; and I
would be free, therefore, of the need for Torre's cumbersome protec-
tions against madmen like the one who had killed him. I would be free
to move about Earth, even while I was directing the building, to locate
and frustrate the efforts of those who would be trying to work against
it. Already I could see now how I would begin to go about it.

But Padma was turning to leave me. I could not let him go like
that. With an effort I tore my attention away from the future and came
back to the day, the fading rain and the brightening light.

"Wait," I said. He stopped and turned back. It was hard for me to
say it now that I had come to it. "You . . ." My tongue stumbled. "You
didn't give up. You had faith in me, all this time."

"No," he said. I blinked at him, but he shook his head.

"I had to believe the results of my calculations." He smiled a little, almost ruefully. "And my calculations gave no real hope for you. Even at the locus point of Donal Graeme's party of Freiland, with five years' added information from the Encyclopedia, the possibility of your saving yourself seemed too small to plan for. Even on Mara, when we healed you, the calculations offered no hope for you."

"But—you stayed by me . . ." I stammered; staring at him.

"Not I. None of us. Only Lisa," he said. "She never gave you up from the first moment in Mark Torre's office. She told us she had felt something—something like a spark from you—when you were talking to her during the tour, even before you got to the Transit Room. She believed in you even after you turned her down at the Graeme locus; and when we set up to heal you on Mara, she insisted on being part of the process, so that we could bind her emotionally to you."

"Bind." The words made no sense.

"We sealed her emotional involvement with you, during the same process by which we repaired you. It made no difference to you, but it tied her to you irrevocably. Now, if she should ever lose you, she would suffer as greatly, or more greatly, than Ian Graeme suffered his loss of a mirror-twin at Kensie's death."

He stopped and stood watching me. But I still fumbled.

"I still don't—understand," I said. "You say it didn't affect me, what you did to her. What good, then—"

"None, as far as we could calculate then, or we've been able to interpret since. If she was bound to you, you were of course bound to her, as well. But it was like fastening a song-sparrow by a thread to the finger of a giant, as far as the relative massivity of your effect on the pattern, compared to hers. Only Lisa thought it would do some good."

He turned.

"Good-bye, Tam," he said. Through the still misty, but brightening air I saw him walking alone toward the church, from which came the voice of the single speaker within, now announcing the number of the final hymn.

He left me standing, dumbfounded. But then, suddenly, I laughed out loud, because I suddenly realized I was wiser than he. Not all his Exotic calculations had been able to uncover why Lisa's binding herself to me could save me. But it had.

For it surged up in me now, my own strong love for her; and I recognized that all along my lonely self had returned that love of Lisa's, but would not admit it to myself. And for the sake of that love, I had wanted to live. A giant may carry a songbird without effort against all the beating of little wings. But if he cares for the creature he is tied to, he may be made to turn aside out of love where he could not be turned by force.

So, along that invisible cord binding us together, Lisa's faith had run to join with my faith, and I could not extinguish my own without extinguishing hers as well. Why else had I gone to her when she called me to come at Mark Torre's assassination? Even then I was turning to compromise my path with hers.

Seeing this now, the whole needle of my life's compass abruptly spun right about, a hundred and eighty degrees, and I saw everything suddenly straight and plain and simple in a new light. Nothing was changed for me, nothing of my hunger and my ambition and my drive, except that I was turned right about. I laughed out loud again at the simplicity of it; for I saw now that one aim was merely the converse of the other.

DESTRUCT: CONSTRUCT

CONSTRUCT—the clear and simple answer that I had longed for all those years to refute Mathias in his emptiness. It was this which I was born to do, *this* which was in the Parthenon, and the Encyclopedia, and all the sons of men.

I had been born, as were we all—even Mathias—if we did not go astray, a maker rather than a smasher, a creator, not a destroyer. Now, like one clean piece of metal, hammered free finally of impurities, I chimed clear through every atom and fiber of my being to the deep, unchanging frequency of the one true purpose in living. Dazed and weak, I turned away at last from the church, went to my car and got in. Now the rain was almost over and the sky was brightening faster. The faint mist of moisture fell, it seemed, more kindly; and the air was fresh and new.

I opened the car windows as I pulled out of the lot into the long road back to the spaceport. And through the open window beside me I heard them beginning to sing the final hymn inside the church.

It was the *Battle Hymn of the Friendly Soldiers* that they sang. As I drove away down the road the voices seemed to follow me strongly, not sounding slowly and mournfully as if in sadness and farewell, but strongly and triumphantly as in a marching song on the lips of those taking up a route at the beginning of a new day.

Soldier, ask not—now or ever!
Where to war your banners go! . . .

The singing followed me as I drove away. And as I got farther into the distance, the voices seemed to blend at last until they sounded like one voice alone, powerfully singing. Ahead the clouds were breaking. With the sun shining through, the patches of blue sky were like bright flags waving, like the banners of an army, marching forever forward into lands unknown.

I watched them as I drove forward toward where they blended at last into open sky; and for a long time I heard the singing behind me, as I drove to the spaceport and the ship for Earth and Lisa that waited in the sunlight for me there.